Praise for CHARLES MCCARRY

"McCarry's novels are among the best of our time."
— *The Wall Street Journal*

"McCarry is one of the highly appreciated veterans of the genre, a writer of thoughtful, well-constructed prose whose works have frequently been compared to those of Graham Greene and John le Carré, which is a burden he didn't ask for and doesn't necessarily deserve . . . Does this make him le Carré's equal? No, I think it makes him his superior."
— *Los Angeles Times*

"McCarry is an exceptional novelist who writes about espionage."
— ALAN FURST

"At a moment when the C.I.A.'s travails are evoking nostalgia for a golden age when it supposedly operated effectively, McCarry offers a useful reminder that such an era never existed. That alone is reason enough to welcome the return of his excellent Paul Christopher novels."
— *The New York Times*

"As a storyteller, McCarry surpasses Len Deighton and John le Carré . . . His novels have a multi-dimensional quality, a deep sensitivity, and a verisimilitude that tells you the author knows what he's talking about."
— *The Washington Post*

"McCarry is the best modern writer on the subject of intrigue—by the breadth of Alan Furst, by the fathom of Eric Ambler, by any measure."
— P. J. O'ROURKE

NOVELS BY CHARLES MCCARRY

The Shanghai Factor

Ark

Christopher's Ghosts

Old Boys

Lucky Bastard

Shelley's Heart

Second Sight

The Bride of the Wilderness

The Last Supper

The Better Angels

The Secret Lovers

The Tears of Autumn

The Miernik Dossier

CHARLES McCARRY

SHELLEY'S HEART

OVERLOOK DUCKWORTH
NEW YORK • LONDON

First published in paperback in the United States in 2010 by
Overlook Duckworth, Peter Mayer Publishers, Inc.
New York & London

NEW YORK:
141 Wooster Street
New York, NY 10012
www.overlookpress.com
For bulk and special sales, please contact sales@overlookny.com,
or write us at the above address.

LONDON:
30 Calvin Street
London E1 6NW
info@duckworth-publishers. co.uk
www.ducknet.co.uk
For bulk and special sales, please contact sales@duckworth-publishers.co.uk,
or write us at the above address.

Library of Congress Cataloging-in-Publication Data
McCarry, Charles.
Shelley's heart : a novel / Charles McCarry.
p. cm.
I. Title.
PPS3563.C336S49   1994   813.54—dc20   94-15360

A catalogue record for this book is available from the British Library

Manufactured in the United States of America
ISBN 978-1-59020-475-7 (US)
ISBN 978-0-7156-4506-2 (UK)
3 5 7 9 10 8 6 4 2

For La Famiglia
Lost Angel of a ruined Paradise!
Adonais

After the fire was kindled . . . more wine was poured over
Shelley's dead body than he had consumed
during his life. This with the oil and salt made the
yellow flames glisten and quiver. The corpse fell open
and the heart was laid bare. . . . The brains literally seethed,
bubbled, and boiled as in a cauldron, for a very
long time. . . . But what surprised us all, was that the heart
remained entire. In snatching this relic from the
fiery furnace, my hand was severely burnt;
and had any one seen me do the act
I should have been put into quarantine.

EDWARD JOHN TRELAWNY
Recollections of the Last Days of Shelley and Byron

PRINCIPAL CHARACTERS

BEDFORD FORREST LOCKWOOD, incumbent President of the United States

FRANKLIN MALLORY, his predecessor as President and his opponent for reelection

ZARAH CHRISTOPHER, a young woman befriended by both Lockwood and Mallory

ARCHIMEDES HAMMETT, Chief Justice of the United States

R. TUCKER ATTENBOROUGH, Speaker of the House

SAM CLARK, Majority Leader of the Senate

JULIAN HUBBARD, President Lockwood's chief of staff

HORACE HUBBARD, Julian's half brother, a former U. S. intelligence officer

ROSS MACALASTER, a journalist

JACK PHILINDROS, Director of the Foreign Intelligence Service

NORMAN CARLISLE BLACKSTONE, counsel to President Lockwood

ALFONSO OLMEDO C., a lawyer

JOHN L. S. McGRAW, an investigator

BAXTER "BUZZER" BUSBY, senator from California

AMZI WHIPPLE, Minority Leader of the Senate

ALBERT TYLER, Attenborough's majordomo and confidant

HENRY TYLER, M.D., Albert's son

SUSAN GRANT, Mallory's lover

EMILY HUBBARD, Julian Hubbard's wife

ROSE MACKENZIE, a computer expert, Horace Hubbard's lover and former colleague

SLIM AND STÜRDI EVE, lawyers, disciples of Chief Justice Hammett

O. N. LASTER, friend and adviser to former President Mallory

WIGGINS AND LUCY, bodyguards to Mallory

BOBBY M. POOLE, an Associate Justice of the Supreme Court

PATRICK GRAHAM, a network anchorman

I

1

It had snowed the night before the Chief Justice's funeral, paralyzing the city of Washington and closing down the government. Now, at midmorning, the sun shone brightly, transforming the brilliant white mantle that covered Mount St. Alban into slush. Snowmelt from the roof of the National Cathedral flowed from the mouths of gargoyles, drowning the hushed notes of the organ that played within. Franklin Mallory, a lover of music ("like other Huns before him," as some opposition wit had written when he was President of the United States), recognized the strains of Johann Sebastian Bach's D minor toccata and fugue. Mallory found this famous work untidy and illogical and annoyingly reminiscent of Buxtehude—but then, organ music in general made him impatient. Like the rhetoric of his political enemies, it was overwrought.

He had just alighted from his car and entered the narthex, or western porch, of the great Gothic cathedral. The service was scheduled to begin in five minutes, and everyone else except the incumbent President, who would arrive last, had already been seated. The dean of the cathedral, skeletal and bald, a fiftyish man with an anxious face that bore no marks of life whatsoever, recoiled when he saw Mallory approaching. He had come outside to welcome the President himself, never expecting that he would run into his worst political enemy. The dean's manner was perfunctory—a damp handshake, a muttered "Mr., uh, Mallory," but no smile, no eye contact.

For reasons of ideology, the dean could not bring himself to call Mallory "Mr. President." At the dawn of the twenty-first century, he abided by the same powerful convictions and taboos he had embraced with hormonal fervor as a campus radical more than three decades before, still believing that the planet, the entire solar system, was in imminent danger of being destroyed by the appetites of imperialistic capitalism. He abominated Mallory, regarding him not merely as the leader of the political right, but as a bad man, an imperialist, a deceiver of the people. Mallory, on the other hand, thought that the dean and others who shared his apocalyptic views were victims of a collective dementia that rendered them incapable of seeing the world as it really was. In short, each believed that the other was an enemy of the people. Mallory, who saw some humor in this state of mutual paranoia, gave the dean a droll wink. The dean, to whom matters of religion were no laughing matter, stepped back from Mallory's physical person with visible disgust. To an usher he said, "Geoffrey, will you kindly show this . . . *gentleman* to his place?"

Mallory said, "Not just yet."

"But President Lockwood is expected at any moment." Geoffrey made a gesture indicating men and women in sunglasses who had taken up positions in the narthex. "The Secret Service—"

"That's all right," Mallory said. "They know me."

Eight years before, after a tumultuous election campaign, Mallory had defeated an inept and unpopular but liberal President by tactics that people like the dean regarded as kicking a man when he was down: he had pointedly ignored an appalling personal scandal that swirled round the incumbent and dwelled caustically on the man's virtually unbroken string of disastrous policy mistakes. After one term, Mallory himself was defeated by Lockwood, and when he ran against Lockwood a second time, two months ago, he lost by the smallest margin of popular votes in history. After that, though he continued to loiter in the nightmares of those who deplored him, his image had vanished from the news media, reducing him overnight from the enormous dimensions of world repute to his original puny size and being, as if fame itself were a floppy disk that could be inserted into the collective consciousness or removed from it according to the whim of some Olympian computer operators.

Now, encircled by his own security people, Mallory turned his back and took up a position deeper inside the porch, between the gateway and the inner door. It was January 19, the day before Inauguration Day. Mallory had been trying for days to reach Lockwood—"Frosty" Lockwood to the news media and to the whole nation—but the White House had not returned his calls. Now Mallory intended to waylay him as he entered the cathedral. He knew that there is no better place to have a private word with a President, who is never alone otherwise, than at a public event.

Mallory was under no illusion that Lockwood would be glad to see him. During the campaign, to beat Mallory to the punch, Lockwood had gone on television to admit that his administration had condoned the assassination of an oil sheik to prevent him from providing terrorists with nuclear weapons. The man had been killed by his own son, who had subsequently been executed for the crime. As Lockwood explained the matter to the American people, he had been informed in advance that this murder was being plotted but had done nothing to prevent it from happening. The victim's name was Ibn Awad, and though he was a virulent hater of Jews, he had been regarded as a harmless mystic before U.S. intelligence learned that he was planning to detonate nuclear bombs in Tel Aviv, and perhaps New York City. Mallory had called Ibn Awad's death a clear case of homicide and promised to investigate American involvement in it "as the first order of business of my second presidency."

From his vantage point, Mallory could see into the vast nave of the cathedral. The coffin, covered by a pall, stood several hundred feet away, with the high altar glittering beyond it. Owing to the storm, which had stranded many in the suburbs, not more than half the pews were filled. Minutes passed. A bodyguard, listening to the Secret Service cellular net over an earpiece, informed Mallory that the President's motorcade had just turned north onto Massachusetts Avenue at Twenty-third Street, about two miles away. Lockwood was famous for being late, and today, with the slippery streets as an added excuse, he was a full half hour behind schedule. Inside the cathedral, the organist changed from Bach to Elgar; Mallory, who liked a melody and did not mind the cold, listened happily to the music as the dean shivered in his vestments in the shadow of the cathedral.

Lockwood was an enormously tall, gaunt, homely man who somewhat resembled Abraham Lincoln physically, and he had adopted a humble style to emphasize the similarity. He traveled in a convoy of unmarked cars, without sirens or motorcycle escort, stopping at red lights and obeying all other traffic laws. No flags flew from the fenders of the plain dark-blue Chevrolet that Lockwood used as a presidential limousine. The car wasn't even marked with the presidential seal. It was armored, of course, and crammed with expensive communications equipment and secret defensive devices that would be quite useless against any but the most inept amateur assassin. The front passenger seat had been removed to make room for the President's long legs—he was even taller than Lincoln—and the whole vehicle had probably cost about the same as the bulletproof Cadillac Mallory had used.

Other costs were even higher. In the closing weeks of the last presidential campaign, after Lockwood's broadcast about the assassination of Ibn Awad, a total of six terrorists from a mysterious organization called the Eye of Gaza had blown themselves up in public places. Only once had this happened in Lockwood's presence, when a Secret Service agent was killed during a campaign speech in San Antonio by a hurtling thigh bone that pierced his chest. Lockwood, though soaked with gore, escaped injury, but in this and other incidents several innocent bystanders were killed or maimed. Now the President was protected by an unusually large and well-armed convoy of Secret Service vehicles and plainclothes agents, and a special quick-reaction military antiterrorist unit hovered overhead in helicopters.

At last the motorcade arrived at the cathedral. The dean collected himself and stepped forward, smiling benignly, to greet the President. He halted suddenly as Lockwood, alighting from the car, slipped in the tread-marked slush, lost his balance, and staggered comically before being grabbed and righted by one of the several large agents whose job it was to stop with their own bodies any bullets aimed at him. Lockwood made a joke to the man who had prevented him from falling down. The agent and his fellows, staring at the little neighborhood crowd that had gathered behind a police barrier, smiled but did not relax as they marched him toward the gateway.

The day was now extremely bright as the diagonal rays of the sun reflected from the film of unmelted snow that still stuck to the ground. Coming out of this dazzling eruption of light, Lockwood did not immediately spot Mallory at the back of the shadowy porch. But the Secret Service had forewarned him of Mallory's presence, and pretending that he saw the other man, Lockwood raised his shaggy head in recognition and gave him a broad, friendly wink.

The dean, who thought the wink was for him, grinned in unfeigned delight and held out his hand to Lockwood. "The Lord hath made his face to shine upon thee, sir!" he said, flinging his other hand upward to show that he was making a pleasantry about the sunshine, which was removing the snow that had threatened to interfere with the next day's inaugural parade.

"He hath also made my way slippery and difficult," said Lockwood in his backwoods Kentucky accent, which grew more exaggerated with every year he spent away from his native state. "I damn near fell on my ass out there."

The dean smiled even more broadly at this mild vulgarism. He felt flattered, included among the good people, by Lockwood's earthiness.

The President grasped the other man's limp, slippery hand in his great horny one and squeezed. At the same time he seized his shoulder with his left hand and bore down upon it with all his weight. Lockwood, who stood six foot seven in his socks and weighed two hundred fifty pounds, had been an All-American football player in college. As President he kept in shape not by running or playing tennis but by working for an hour every other day with a pick and shovel or an ax alongside the White House gardeners. Few men could prolong a conversation when the President leaned on them. After a few seconds, the dean's knees buckled slightly inside his chasuble.

Lockwood bore down harder and boomed, "I hope you've got a good send-off planned for the Chief Justice. He's earned it."

"We'll do our best, sir," gasped the dean.

"I know you will, Reverend," said Lockwood, releasing him. No high-falutin' Anglican titles for Frosty, thought Mallory, meeting the President's eyes.

Lockwood stepped around the dean and his retainers and walked straight to Mallory. He said, "Mr. President, my condolences." The two men had known each other for twenty years, but Lockwood, though he prided himself on being down-to-earth, was rank-conscious and a stickler for honorifics. Mallory was not.

"Thanks, Frosty," he said. "Old Max almost outlived you."

"That's right; the old fart always said he would. And by God he might have, except for New York and California."

Lockwood's victory the previous November had come in three last-minute surges of votes in the poorest precincts of major cities in New York, California, and Michigan.

"We're going to have to talk about New York and California," Mallory said. "Soon."

He took Lockwood's arm in the European style and walked him toward the nave. The bodyguards, taking themselves out of earshot, made a wider circle around the two men.

Mallory said, "There seems to be something wrong with the White House phones. I've been trying to reach you for a week."

Lockwood glowered. "Maybe they thought you were phoning to call me a murderer again," he said. "Like you did on the Patrick Graham show last November."

"No." Mallory paused for effect. "Something worse."

Lockwood scowled, then laughed. "Same old sore loser, Franklin."

Inside the cathedral, word of the President's arrival was spreading. Heads turned toward the entrance and a whisper ran through the crowd. Lockwood and Mallory had been walking toward the great inner door, and now they were framed in it—mortal enemies glimpsed in a brief moment of truce.

"Are we going to go in together," Lockwood asked, "when they play 'Here Comes the Bride'?"

He was making jokes to prevent Mallory from saying whatever it was he had been waiting to say to him. Mallory, who knew Lockwood's methods and had never hoped to get a word in edgewise, held out his hand as if to congratulate his opponent on his triumph and wish him well; this was the first time they had met since the election. When Lockwood gripped Mallory's hand, the latter pressed a note into his callused palm. It was folded into a wad.

"Read that," Mallory said. "I'll wait for your call." He turned on his heel and walked into the nave.

Behind him, Lockwood opened the note, an engraved calling card twice folded in half. It read, in Mallory's clear, almost spinsterish script: "I must see you urgently and alone, well before you take the presidential oath tomorrow, to make you aware of documentary evidence of election fraud in California, Michigan, and New York that brings into question your legal right to assume office."

By now Mallory had reached his pew, where three other former Presidents of his own party were already seated; they turned as one and bowed to the newcomer.

"You little prick," Lockwood said aloud as the organist, forgetting protocol, struck up "Hail to the Chief" and the congregation rose to its feet in his honor.

2

As President, Franklin Mallory had regularly escaped from the White House for late suppers with a small circle of old friends. He had done this without detection by passing through the tunnel that led from the cellars of the executive mansion to the Treasury Building next door. A second tunnel took him under Pennsylvania Avenue to the Treasury Annex, and thence into the outside world through a little-used door opening onto an alley. Once through the door, he had been free to roam the city on foot and in the automobile he kept in a nearby garage. Unlike the outsize, nobly ugly Lockwood, he was a man of average height and build, with a run-of-the-mill American face. Because people were not expecting to see him, no one ever recognized him, and he passed among them dressed in casual clothes, wearing a cap to cover his famous silver hair.

At precisely two o'clock in the morning of what was supposed to be Lockwood's Inauguration Day, former President Mallory presented himself at the alley door at the rear of the Treasury Annex. He had walked there, alone, from his house on Kalorama Circle; this had taken about half an hour, and the exercise had made him feel good. The temperature had dropped into the twenties, and he wore a black knitted watch cap and a heavy sailing sweater under a waterproof parka. Inside the nimbus of lamplight that enclosed the city, the streets shone with melted snow, and in the alley, where there had been little traffic, the pavement was icy. Mallory pounded on the door. As it was opened from within, a large rat scrabbled across the toes of his walking shoes—he could feel the grip of the animal's muscular little feet through the soft leather—and darted inside. Lockwood's chief of staff, Julian Hubbard, who had let the rat in, leaped backward with a grunt of surprise, letting go of the heavy door.

Mallory caught it before it swung shut and stepped inside. "Hello, Julian," he said. "One more feeder at the public trough. They're all over this town—always have been. One Sunday I decided to walk over to church at St. John's. A big fat rat followed me all the way across Lafayette Square. It even waited next to me for the WALK sign at H Street. As the rat and I stood there while the light changed, an old bag lady who lived on one of the park benches jumped up and yelled, 'There goes Mr. Nixon!' I figured she was a Democrat, so I wasn't sure which one of us she meant."

Julian—no one in Washington, not even people who had never met him, ever called him by any name but his first one—listened to this story without the slightest flicker of interest. He belonged to a political generation, the one that came of age during the war in Vietnam, that regarded humor as an opiate of the people unless it came from someone who had the right to be funny because he was one of the people, like Lockwood.

Still silent, Julian set off with long, rapid strides through the warren of the Treasury cellars. He was as tall as Lockwood, and even though there seemed to be plenty of clearance, even for a man his size, he ducked his head repeatedly as he passed beneath the larger drains and pipes that hung from the ceiling. Although he knew the way better than his guide, who kept making wrong turns, Mallory followed without demur.

At length—the whole underground walk took at least fifteen minutes, even at a brisk pace—they emerged into a narrow moatlike space formed by the west wall of the Treasury Building and a concrete wall opposite, blank except for a thick steel door equipped with television cameras and a keypad security lock. Normally this area, used in daytime as a parking lot for high officials, was brightly floodlit, but now it was dark, and they groped their way among battered vehicles belonging to the night cleaning staff. The sun had not penetrated here, so there were patches of unmelted snow underfoot. Its sterile odor mingled with the metallic smell of rust from the dented cars.

Julian punched in the code that opened the door in the wall. They walked through it into a well-lighted tunnel that led to the cellars of the East Wing of the White House. It debouched into a bunker, still furnished with obsolete military radios with dead batteries, army cots, crates of rations, and sealed jeroboams of fifty-year-old drinking water, all covered with dust. In this makeshift command post, Presidents of the Cold War era would theoretically have taken shelter in case of nuclear attack. Eisenhower and Kennedy were said to have come down here during air raid drills, knowing that they would have been incinerated along with everyone else in the District of Columbia and its suburbs in a real attack by even the most primitive H-bomb. What would they have done if the Russians had launched their missiles? Mallory knew what *he* would have done: launched the counterstrike, then taken someone he loved by the hand and waited in the Rose Garden, ground zero, to be vaporized.

An elevator brought them to the ground floor, near the kitchens. The East Wing was silent, deserted, dimly lit and barely heated, in conformity with Lockwood's policy of conserving natural resources and protecting the environment. Julian stayed with Mallory until they passed by the library and arrived at another elevator, near the main staircase, that gave access to the family quarters upstairs.

"The President is waiting for you in the Lincoln sitting room," Julian said, speaking for the first time but gazing with the same absence of expression as before into Mallory's face. "I think you know the way." Then, without so much as a nod, he strode down a corridor toward his office in the West Wing.

Mallory was quite alone. He had not been inside the President's house for four years. Now that he was, he felt no tug of sentiment. Even when he lived in it, the White House had always seemed to him impersonal, just another other public building.

The elevator door opened. Mallory got in. The cabin, summoned from above, rose with an electrical whine that was louder than he remembered. When the door opened again he found Lockwood waiting for him in the hallway. He was in shirtsleeves, necktie pulled loose, half-moon reading glasses perched on the tip of his nose. His eyes were tired, bloodshot. His clothes were rumpled; they always were. It was part of the image.

"Hold the door," Lockwood said. Jean McHenry, a brusque woman who had been Lockwood's secretary since the beginning of his career, hurried down the corridor, grasping a sheaf of scribbled-over manuscript pages and a stenographic pad. "Just type that sucker up one last time, Jeannie, then go on home," Lockwood said to her.

Jean got onto the elevator with Mallory, who had remained inside with his finger on the OPEN DOOR button, and though she had known him for many years, she waited with an empty stare for him to get off. Mallory admired her behavior; Julian's, too. Lockwood had good people around him, fiercely loyal people, and each and every one of them hated Franklin Mallory with a passion. Lockwood and Mallory, on the other hand, had always liked and understood each other. Both had grown up in poverty, one in Massachusetts and the other in Kentucky, and each thought that the other had a natural right to his politics that no person of the upper middle class ("That's what you get when you send white trash to college," said Lockwood) could possibly claim.

"Working on your speech for tomorrow?" Mallory asked.

"If you thought it was tough the first time," Lockwood answered, "let me tell you it ain't no easier the second, with the damn speechwriters trying to turn you into Abe Lincoln and Martin Luther King and Ted Sorensen rolled up in one. Come on down the hall."

He led the way between walls hung with sentimental nineteenth-century paintings from the national collections—Mississippi steamboats, the Rocky Mountains, farmers making hay in some New England clearing while a thunderstorm formed in the west and wild-eyed horses hitched to the hayrick got ready to run away. Dear dead days beyond recall: Lockwood's specialty.

The Lincoln sitting room, where Lockwood habitually worked at night, was littered with papers and books. In his day, Mallory had never brought work upstairs. He hated clutter; he had routinely fired untidy people or those who worked late when there was no need to do so. Lockwood cleared off an easy chair for him, dropping the stack of documents and looseleaf briefing books onto the floor with a thump. Mallory, still in his parka, sat down. A fire of sputtering apple logs burned on the hearth, but even so there was a chill in the air. Lockwood didn't seem to feel it.

"You changed the furniture," Mallory said.

"Polly did, right after we moved in. It's two-thirty in the morning, Franklin. What do you want?" Slumped in his chair with his lanky legs stretched out before him, Lockwood was cold-eyed, deathly still, aggravated. At the moment he looked more like Tiberius about to pronounce a death sentence, Mallory thought, than the homely, joke-cracking rail-splitter of his media image. Clearly he had been stewing all day about Mallory's note. "What's this horse manure about election fraud?" he said.

"It's all in here," Mallory said, handing over a thick manila envelope.

"*What's* in here?"

"Hard evidence of vote stealing. The lawyers say they've never seen such an open-and-shut case."

"What lawyers?"

"Mine, and the three former attorneys general of the United States I retained to review the file."

"Only three?" Lockwood said. "What's the matter, are all the other ones dead?"

Mallory nodded without expression, as if no wisecrack had been uttered; this was his way of being witty, and Lockwood recognized it.

Snorting, Lockwood dropped the unopened envelope into his lap. He pressed a button on the telephone beside his chair. "Julian," he said into the instrument, "come on up." To Mallory he said, "I don't want to read your lawyers' homework papers. Just tell me what you think you've got. Spit it out."

Julian must have been nearby, because he appeared in the doorway before Mallory could answer. Lockwood handed him the envelope. "Have this looked at—you and Norman, nobody else—and come back ready to talk about it in fifteen minutes," he said. Julian vanished.

Lockwood turned his hooded eyes on Mallory again. "Shoot."

"All right," Mallory said calmly. "We should have discussed this days ago, but you didn't return my calls. I have incontrovertible evidence, including copies of every computer keystroke, every telephone connection, videotape with audio recordings of the guilty parties working the computers, plus sworn eyewitness testimony, that U.S. government computers belonging to the Foreign Intelligence Service—these are located under that bank in New York City—were used on the night of last November seventh to alter the vote in more than a thousand precincts in California, and in several hundred others in cities in upstate New York and in Detroit. Whoever did this stole the election."

"Stole the election," Lockwood repeated. His voice was toneless.

"That's right," Mallory said. "You weren't elected President of the United States by the voters last fall. I was."

"The lefties are right," Lockwood said. "You're crazy as a loon. No son of a bitch, especially not you, is going to come in here the night before I'm inaugurated and tell me I stole an election. I've earned every vote I ever got."

Mallory remained seated. "I haven't said you stole the election," he said without emotion. "And I never will say that to you or anyone else, because it isn't true. I know you're incapable of such an act. So does everybody else in the world. What I *am* telling you, whether you like it or not, is that your people stole it for you behind your back."

"You mean I'm so damn dumb I wouldn't know. If you're so goddamn smart, Franklin, suppose you tell me why anybody who worked for me would do such a thing."

"Well, you had a lot more than the election to lose. So did they."

"What's that supposed to mean?"

"Ibn Awad."

Lockwood glared. "The fact that you sank low enough to call me a murderer in front of the people doesn't make me one. I haven't got a thing to fear from you or any damn investigation you or your friends on the Hill can put together, and I don't believe a word, not a word, of this crap you're dumping on me."

A moment passed before Mallory said, "You'd better believe it, my friend. Because I want what the voters gave me, and you have no choice but to give me what's mine. None. Ask Julian."

3

As the grandfather clock down the hall whirred and then struck the quarter before the hour, the phone rang. Lockwood picked it up. From a distance of three feet, Mallory could hear Julian's overbred voice coming out of the earpiece—the cocksure tone, not the words.

"Yes, damnit," Lockwood said. "Bring Blackstone with you."

Mallory stood up, as if to leave.

"Stay," Lockwood said. "We've got more talking to do."

The President's bony fists were clenched, his breath rapid; the ruptured veins in his face and in his misshapen nose, many times broken on the football field, were engorged with blood. Mallory knew that Lockwood was really a somewhat less cartoonish version of the good and sympathetic person the news media made him out to be. He also knew that he had the violent temper of a child. In days gone by, he had seen him shatter chairs against a wall when angry, or throw typewriters through closed windows. The physical signs he was exhibiting suggested he was not far from doing something like that now.

Julian Hubbard entered, accompanied by the presidential counsel, a former Wall Street lawyer named Norman Carlisle Blackstone. He too was tall, but unathletic, with thick rimless glasses, stooped shoulders, and a sunken chest above a small paunch spanned by a gold watch chain. In the newspapers, Carlisle Blackstone—he was called by his middle name—had been cast as the Beau Brummell of the Lockwood administration. Tonight he wore a flawlessly tailored pin-striped suit of a pattern—four-button single-breasted jacket, waistcoat with lapels, high-waisted trousers with the suspender buttons sewn to the outside of the waistband—that had last been in fashion during the Wilson administration. Mallory had never before met him, and when no one introduced them, he held out his hand.

"Franklin Mallory," he said, as if Blackstone might not be able to place him. "You have the best name for a lawyer I've ever heard, outside of Dickens."

Mallory flashed the thin, quick humorless smile Blackstone had seen so often on television.

"Let's get on with it," Lockwood said. "Have you read Franklin's billy-doo?"

"We've scanned it," Julian said. "It appears that I'm a member of the cast in this . . . comedy, or at least related to one of the so-called actors, so Carlisle here will do the talking, if that's all right with you, Mr. President."

"How's that?"

"I don't want to spoil the surprise," Julian said. "The twists and turns of the plot will emerge."

He stared at Mallory, who gave him a thin smile. Blackstone glanced at Mallory too, as if wondering how much more to say in his presence.

"Go ahead," Lockwood said. "As you just found out, nobody has any secrets from Franklin—even if he has to hire every living ex–attorney general to make them up."

Blackstone cleared his throat and began to summarize in a dry, emotionless voice. Reading from notes on a yellow legal pad, he confirmed that the file presented by Mallory contained a collection of documents and other exhibits purporting to prove that a senior official of the U.S. intelligence service named Horace Hubbard, aided and abetted by an FIS computer expert named Rose MacKenzie, had used the Foreign Intelligence Service computers in New York to give Lockwood a plurality of the popular vote in all three states.

"This is Julian's brother we're talking about?" Lockwood asked.

"Half brother," Blackstone replied. "Both these people are longtime FIS employees. Horace Hubbard is a senior officer, the chief of Middle East operations."

Lockwood, expressionless for once, avoided all eyes but gestured impatiently for Blackstone to continue.

Blackstone said, "In any case, the number of votes allegedly transferred from other candidates to you, Mr. President, was precisely enough to win the election for you, according to this scenario."

"How many votes would that represent?" Lockwood asked.

Blackstone consulted his notes. "Surprisingly few. About twenty-five thousand out of eleven million or so in California, roughly the same number in New York, and less than five thousand in Michigan." There was a note of excitement in Blackstone's voice; clearly he was intrigued by the numbers and by the audacity of the operation.

Lockwood said, "Is what they charge true? Did this stuff really happen?"

There was a silence. Mallory spoke. "I'd be interested in Julian's opinion."

Julian said nothing. Lockwood did not instruct him to speak up. After another brief hush, Blackstone responded. "Well, sir, that's the sixty-four-thousand-dollar question, isn't it? It's impossible to say without running an investigation of our own that would examine the allegations. Obviously this cannot be done in the secrecy from which Mr. Mallory has so far benefited as a private citizen. Making the contents of this file public would touch off an epidemic of investigations by Congress, by a special prosecutor, by the courts. This file"—he tapped it sharply—"is a blueprint for—well, I don't know what to call it."

Lockwood said, "How about pandemonium?"

"Worse, Mr. President—another Watergate. With all due respect to our distinguished visitor, think who'd be on the other side this time. There'd be no mercy."

"There wasn't a hell of a lot of that the first time around," Lockwood said. "Give me the details. What have they got exactly, besides this theory of fraud? Is this coming out of left field, or will it stand up in court?"

"On the face of it, they have everything they need except confessions— what purport to be television pictures of the culprits in the act of committing their crimes, voice recordings, duplicate files of everything the computer did."

"Purport to be or *are*, damnit?"

"I can't say from my own knowledge. It has the odor of fact. But of course it's cleverly designed to smell that way. However, the bottom line is that it's one hundred percent circumstantial. Obviously it would be a mistake to take at face value evidence submitted by a man who has the presidency to gain if he is believed."

"But the pictures are there, the words are there, all this stuff exists?"

"I hold it in my hand. It's very persuasive, I'm sorry to say."

"Goddamnit, Carlisle, is it genuine or isn't it?"

"I called up Jack Philindros, the director of FIS—"

"I know who Jack Philindros is. Get on with it."

"Yes, sir. There's a memorandum about this episode signed by Philindros in the file, and I asked him if the information we had been given reflected his own knowledge of the case. His answer was yes. Evidently FIS installed fail-safe devices in the computer to record abuses or unauthorized use of the equipment. These devices are connected to an earth satellite whose existence is known only to the director and a very small unit, code name ZIWatchdog, located somewhere in the desert in New Mexico, or maybe Utah or somewhere else; the file doesn't say and Philindros wouldn't tell me. Everything was sucked up by the satellite, even the pictures and sound recordings of the thieves at work—"

" 'ZIWatchdog'?" Lockwood said. "You ever hear of that, Julian?"

"No, sir," Julian replied.

Lockwood said, "An earth satellite only Philindros knows about? Who authorized that?"

Blackstone replied, "President Mallory did, sir. It was launched during the second fiscal year of his administration with secret funds. According to Philindros, you knew about the satellite. Or at least Julian did."

"Jack Philindros told you that?"

"Yes, sir. He wasn't at all surprised by my call. He had all the facts at his fingertips."

"Looks like you appointed the right man director, Franklin," Lockwood said.

Mallory, who had been blessed with almost unbelievable luck in making important appointments, had nominated Philindros to be the first director of FIS. The Senate had confirmed his appointment to a statutory ten-year term. Under a new national security statute, his agency was modeled on the Federal Reserve Board—governed by trustees, independent of the President, and outside the political process. As one of the safeguards of its integrity, the director could neither succeed himself nor be removed except by a unanimous vote of the Foreign Intelligence Board. The FIS had replaced the Central Intelligence Agency after it collapsed under the weight of the failures and scandals resulting from its misuse by twentieth-century Presidents.

Lockwood turned back to Blackstone. "Then these characters were on candid camera the whole time they were allegedly stealing the election?"

"That's the imputation. Philindros says these ZIWatchdog people out in the desert just came upon the material as a matter of routine."

"When?"

"Over Christmas. They were working overtime because they were a couple of months behind. They're outnumbered by the people using the computers and they have a tough time keeping up."

"Who handed this information over to Mallory instead of giving it to the duly constituted authority? Did Mr. Philindros have that fact at his fingertips?"

"No, sir. He couldn't explain how that happened."

"I'll bet he couldn't," Lockwood said.

"It may be relevant that the satellite was built under government contract by Universal Energy," Julian said in a significant tone. The head of Universal Energy, an enormous multinational corporation, was Mallory's close friend and adviser.

"Hell, that was just Franklin helping out his old pal," Lockwood said. "Nothing sinister in that. All right, Carlisle, what's your advice?"

Blackstone glanced at Mallory. Did Lockwood really want him to speak freely in the presence of the enemy?

"Never mind him," Lockwood said. "You're not likely to think of anything Franklin hasn't already figured out with the help of every lawyer in America except you. What do we do about this?"

"That depends on what Mr. Mallory is going to do," Blackstone said. "On the face of it, taking Philindros's corroborating testimony into account, the information in the file could conceivably constitute grounds for a federal judge, even a Supreme Court justice, to issue an injunction against your taking the presidential oath at noon tomorrow. Of course there's no precedent for such an action, but there are plenty of right-wing judges who would love to reverse the results of the election. That includes at least four Mallory appointed to the Supreme Court."

During his single term as President, Mallory had appointed four justices besides the dead Chief Justice who shared his philosophy. This happened in a single year after two members of the Supreme Court retired, one died of natural causes, and two were assassinated by terrorists.

Lockwood said, "Suppose some half-ass judge does issue an injunction. Then what?"

"Then you'd have to fight it out in the courts, for starters," Blackstone answered. "But the presidency would be vacant."

"What happens to the Vice President?"

"If you weren't legally elected, then neither was your running mate. Both offices would be unfilled."

"Then the Speaker of the House succeeds. You can't tell me the Lord God wanted R. Tucker Attenborough to be President of the United States."

"In these circumstances, I'm not sure the Speaker would, in fact, succeed. The Constitution implies he can only replace a duly qualified President. If you weren't legally elected, you're not qualified. I don't want to exaggerate, but this opens constitutional questions that have never before been contemplated. In any other country, the military would have to take over in a situation like this."

"The military?" Lockwood said. "Get a grip on yourself, Carlisle." He turned to Mallory. "Is that what you're going to do, Franklin—go for an injunction?"

"That's one possibility," Mallory replied in a reasonable, friendly tone of voice, as if he were as much on Lockwood's side as his lawyer. "But I hope we can work things out in a way that does less damage to the country. Watergate has been mentioned. Remember what that was like. Truth and decency went up the chimney, everyone went crazy, and a lot of people on both sides have stayed that way up to the present day. If you make the wrong move, it will happen again. You won't be able to govern, and you'll go the way of Nixon. Only worse; this time there'll be no Jerry Ford."

"Are you offering me a pardon?"

"No," Mallory said. "I'm offering you a way out that serves justice and the good of the country. The key is to get this situation behind us quickly, using constitutional means. The Twentieth and Twenty-fifth amendments give you the power to control events yourself, instead of turning your fate over to others."

Lockwood's eyes had narrowed to mere slits; the color had left his face. "Go on," he said.

Mallory said, "Under the Twentieth Amendment, you become President for a second term tomorrow at noon, whether you take the oath or not, and Willy Graves becomes Vice President. Under the Twenty-fifth Amendment, you have the power to appoint a Vice President, with the approval of Congress, in case that office is vacant."

"I'm not sure I agree that anyone can become President without taking the oath," Blackstone said.

Lockwood said, "Shut up, Carlisle. Let him finish."

"It doesn't matter one way or the other," Mallory said. "This is what I propose to you. Take the oath if you want to—Graves, too. Then, on the podium, Graves resigns as Vice President. You immediately appoint *me* Vice President, explaining that you have learned at the eleventh hour that the election was stolen and you refuse to benefit from such a violation of the people's trust. Then you withdraw on the spot and I become acting President until Congress certifies my election on the basis of a recount."

"And if it finds for me?"

"Then I'm out of there and you're President again. But that won't happen."

Lockwood laughed, one single hillbilly whoop. "Breathtaking," he said. "Breathtaking, Franklin, by God."

"You'd go out with honor," Mallory said. "So much honor, in fact, that you could run again four years from now, more of an honest American than ever. I can't run again, so you might win fair and square next time—you've done it before. It's just that you just didn't quite make it this time, Frosty."

"Says you."

"Says the evidence. Frosty, we've known each other a long time. Do you really think I'd invent something like this?"

Lockwood did not answer the question. "And if I don't hand you the presidency," he said. "Then what?"

"Then I'll call a press conference on the grounds of the Capitol while you're getting ready to take the presidential oath under false pretenses and make everything in the file, and maybe a little more besides, public."

" 'Maybe a little bit more'? What's that supposed to mean?"

"You know what it means," Mallory said. "Ibn Awad."

"If I don't step down, you'll throw me out and then try me for the murder of a lunatic who wanted to blow up all the Jews in Israel and New York. Is that what you're threatening me with?"

"I'm not threatening you with anything. Once the process starts, it will be impossible to keep anything off the public record."

"I'm not afraid of the truth. Never have been. Never needed to be."

"I'm glad to hear that, because the truth as I understand it is pretty ugly. That's why I let the Awad business alone last fall until you brought it up. I don't want to go into it now, but if it's the reason why your boys stole the election—and I don't know what other reason there could be, even for a bunch of idealists like them—the truth will come out. Nobody can prevent it. We both know that."

Lockwood made no response. Even more tousled than before and clearly exhausted, he sat for a long moment with his head resting on the back of the chair. Then he got to his feet. His shirttail was out.

"Franklin," he said, "you dirty, rotten son of a bitch, you're one of a kind." There was admiration in his voice.

"So are you," Mallory replied. "And you'll never have a better chance to prove that to the world, and to make sure of your place in history, than the opportunity I'm offering you. I promise you I won't move against you before eleven o'clock in the morning. The whole thing is up to you. You have a chance to be remembered as the greatest of all American patriots. I hope you'll have sense enough to grab it."

"I know you do. But Mrs. Lockwood didn't raise no idiot sons. Now go on home, Franklin. Go on."

Mallory rose to his feet. "If I don't hear from you personally by eleven this morning," he said, "I'll know we've got a fight on our hands."

Lockwood waved a hand. "Mind the steps on the way out," he said.

Julian Hubbard got to his feet, inviting Mallory to go ahead of him through the door.

"That's all right, Julian, I can find my own way out," Mallory said. "I'm sure the President needs you."

. . .

The President's men waited to speak until the whine of the elevator ceased. In the ensuing hush, the grandfather clock, said by the Smithsonian's curator of timepieces to have belonged to Andrew Jackson, ticked loudly. Several seconds passed before Julian Hubbard broke the silence. He said, "You've got to fight the bastard, Mr. President."

"Sure I do," Lockwood said. "But how do I do it?"

"Claim the presidency tomorrow. By the law of the land and every precedent in American history, it's yours. Then preempt his press conference with a statement of your own. Throw the onus on Mallory. Get the whole thing out in the open in your inaugural speech. Remember, half the country hates Mallory, and everybody knows Jack Philindros is his man. When people hear that the FIS is involved in this, they're going to scream bloody murder. From day one, people have got to see this for what it is—an attempt on Mallory's part to steal the presidency. So go on the offensive. Investigate his report, find the holes in it, discredit it. Sue Mallory for libel. Haul him onto the witness stand, under oath. Destroy the son of a bitch once and for all. Go to the country. Go to your friends. Go for the jugular. Have no mercy."

"Suppose what he says turns out to be the truth?"

"When did Mallory ever tell the truth? You can never admit the possibility that this is anything but a conspiracy to overthrow the government. If you give him the slightest benefit of the doubt, he wins."

Lockwood listened carefully. Then he said, "How about you, Julian? We heard Horace's name mentioned tonight. Do *you* admit the possibility?"

"I am not my brother's keeper," Julian said. "But there is a higher duty to democracy than abiding by election returns that would destroy it. We learned that in Germany in 1932."

Andrew Jackson's noisy clock struck five. "Interesting point," Lockwood said. "You two go on home and get some sleep. Big day tomorrow."

4

After leaving the White House, Mallory went directly to a house on Capitol Hill where he had lived with his wife when he was in the Senate. Between his election to the presidency and his inauguration, while she was still a young woman, Marilyn Mallory had died in her sleep of an embolism, in the same bed in which her widower now spent the few hours remaining before sunrise. In the eight years since her death, he had kept the place exactly as she left it. Tucked away in a row of identical Palladian-style houses, it was tall and narrow; the reception rooms were furnished with Hepplewhite and Sheraton furniture (English reproductions, but old enough to qualify as antiques), while the sitting room, library, and bedroom on the fourth floor were decorated as morning rooms, with comfortable chairs covered in chintz and many vases of fresh flowers.

When Mallory came out into the sitting room after his shower at eight in the morning, he found his breakfast, a dozen fresh strawberries with yogurt and a cup of espresso coffee, on the low table between two sofas. Half a dozen morning newspapers, their pages pressed with a hot iron to dry the ink, lay on the table. All the front pages carried the same stories in the same positions under headlines that said the same things; he ignored them. The house was deeply quiet. The servants, a couple from El Salvador whom his wife had hired many years before, stayed discreetly out of sight. Though he usually rose at dawn, Mallory made it a rule to see no one before ten o'clock in the morning; he did not even take telephone calls before that hour, and normally devoted the time to reading, writing, and thought. He lived by a rigid schedule because he believed that routine set him free. Spontaneity was chaos.

He gazed at the Capitol dome through the triptych Serliana windows of the sitting room. The morning was bright and cold. Swarms of police surrounded the Capitol itself. Military units, high school bands from all over the United States, floats, and other elements of the inaugural parade were forming up in the surrounding streets, and the breath of these hundreds of people had condensed into a man-made cirrus cloud that shimmered above their heads in the horizontal light. The soldiers, sailors, and Marines wore overcoats, and some of the teenage musicians were wrapped in blankets, boys and girls bundling up together. Meanwhile the bigwigs arrived on the other side of the Capitol and took their reserved seats. Being wrapped up in a blanket with a drum majorette, Mallory knew, was a hell of a lot more enjoyable than spending the morning making small talk with the sort of people who were able to get tickets to an inauguration.

Mallory's staff had already delivered copies of the file he had given to Lockwood, together with a letter from Mallory announcing his intention of challenging the election, to every member of his own party in Congress, and to reactionary members of Lockwood's party. At precisely 11:20 A.M., the same package, with a slightly different statement in the form of a press release, would be handed to the broadcasting networks and the Washington press corps and faxed to every newspaper and radio and television station in the country. At 11:30, as Lockwood was taking his seat on the podium on the west front of the Capitol, Mallory would hold a press conference on the steps of the east front. He knew that this choice of place and time would enrage Lockwood's people and torment the news media, which would be forced to think about two things at once, a feat normally beyond their capacity.

Mallory had never imagined that Lockwood would call him at eleven o'clock and offer to hand over the presidency. The advice he had given Lockwood the night before was excellent, and following it would certainly be in the best interests of the country and of Lockwood himself. But Lockwood was a politician to the depths of his being, and his office was all he had. Like most political figures of his generation who embraced progressive convictions, Lockwood had never in his adult life been any-thing but a politician. The only life he knew was public life. Unlike his heroes, Jefferson, Jackson, and Lincoln, he had never taken a mistress, fought a duel, or stood up for an unpopular cause. Every idea he had ever espoused was politically correct and brought him praise and approval among the opinion makers. The only money he had ever earned was government money: he had gone through a state college on an athletic scholarship, served for a while in the Army, where he played football and basketball instead of leading a platoon of rifles in Korea like many of his classmates now dead. Back home, after marrying a rich girl from the Bluegrass whose family had influence in rural politics, he started running for office on the basis of his lovable personality, his humble childhood (he came from the hollows of the eastern Kentucky mountains), and his celebrity as an athlete. He had nothing to go back to, no other life to lead.

This was not true of Mallory, to whom the presidency had been a way station. With the help of his wife, he had made a huge fortune in business before he was forty, and then began to run for office. By saying things about the nature of American life that middle-class voters regarded as home truths but the intelligentsia could not bear to hear, he made ene-mies. But as the desperate effort to deprive him of power by stealing the election had shown, a plurality of Americans wanted him to run the country. Having sought election, he had no choice but to do as they wished.

Mallory finished his coffee and went into the library at the back of the house, closing the door behind him; the room, whose windows faced east, was filled with morning sunlight. He selected a book at random from among the thousands on the shelves. The one that came to hand hap-pened to be Lord Macaulay's *History of England*. He had heard that Adolf Hitler, with whom Mallory was often compared by his detractors in academia and the more literary press, used to read only the last chapters of books. Mallory read them all from front to back, then returned them to the shelf, sometimes for years, before taking them down to reread the passages that he remembered.

Now, while he awaited the arrival of his first visitor of the day, he sat down with his Macaulay and read with deep pleasure the stately sentences of the grand old Whig, turning pages rapidly to find the ones he already knew by heart: "He [Oliver Cromwell] felt toward those whom he had deserted that peculiar malignity which has, in all ages, been characteristic of apostates." And "In every age the vilest specimens of human nature are to be found among demagogues."

The radicals, Mallory believed, were a herd of demagogues driven by some primal instinct that had little to do with the mind. They were the Puritans of the present age, oppressing mankind in the name of their own moral superiority. How like they were to the earlier crowd (what, after all, was the difference between an Elite and an Elect?), except that they had not yet found their Cromwell. God forbid that ever they should, he thought, in a sort of prayer to Macaulay's memory.

5

Ross Macalaster, a Washington journalist who believed that he knew where all of Mallory's safe houses were located, had never before been to the house on Capitol Hill. The man was full of secrets. Macalaster had been summoned to appear before the former President at ten o'clock on inaugural morning "to learn," as Mallory's handwritten note put it, "something that will be of interest to you." This communication was delivered at six A.M. to Macalaster's house in a quiet street off Foxhall Road, on the far side of the city's peaceful white enclave, by one of Mallory's boy-and-girl teams. His staff always worked in couples, like the missionaries of some strange long-ago religious community in which the sexes loved and trusted each other.

Mallory and Macalaster were acquaintances in the transient, half-clubby, half-furtive way that big-time politicians and reporters know one another in Washington. They had few things in common apart from the coincidence that both were outsiders to the rest of their profession and both were widowers. When Macalaster's wife was killed in a car crash, having driven her BMW at high speed into a stone wall on the George

Washington Parkway, Mallory wrote him a long, sympathetic note, referring to the memories of his own, happier marriage. He even came to the funeral, one of only a dozen people who bothered to do so.

For reasons Macalaster never fully understood, Mallory seemed to like him. As senator and President, he had given him inside information, never asking anything in return, and never complaining when Macalaster repaid him by writing unfavorably about Mallory in other contexts. Once, after receiving Mallory's letter of condolence, he had been weak enough to mention this balancing of journalistic books. "Don't worry about it," Mallory had replied. "It's only human." Another man might have quoted Harry S Truman: "If you want a friend in Washington, buy a dog."

Like his father and his immigrant grandfather before him—like Mallory, for that matter—Macalaster had been a manual laborer early in life. He would never have gone to college if he had not been inducted into the Army at nineteen and sent to Vietnam in the place of some rich kid who dodged the draft. His social background won him assignment as a rifleman in the First Infantry Division, and he was wounded twice by enemy fire, both times superficially, in battles around the Iron Triangle.

While attending Williams College in the early 1970s as a representative of the deserving poor, he had been bullied in class and undermarked by leftist professors while being regarded as a baby-killer by members of the antiwar movement, who constituted the majority of the student body. At the same time, Movement chicks from Bennington College who imagined themselves to be undercover members of the Viet Cong crawled through his window at night, as if he were a prisoner of war who excited their sexual fantasies. At Williams Macalaster discovered in himself a deep, undiscriminating curiosity and a gift for writing, and after serving an apprenticeship on a Buffalo newspaper, he got a job with a paper in Washington. While he was still new in town, he stumbled onto a story that metastasized into a scandal that resulted in the defeat—by the hated Mallory—of the liberal candidate for re-election. Even in an age of total revelation, this revelation astounded: the incumbent President, known for his appetites, had tested positive for an incurable sexually transmitted disease. He had kept this fact entirely to himself for more than a year. The many politically aware women with whom he had copulated were either infected with the virus already or at risk of finding out that they were at some unknowable future date. So, of course, were their husbands and other lovers, nearly all of whom were ideologically committed to the doomed President and to the Cause.

For the remainder of their lives these people would live in fear of sex, even marital sex. Some of those affected were journalists themselves. Naturally they projected their terror and their anger with the President and what he had done to them and to the Cause onto Macalaster. Full of wine and fury, his wife shrieked, "You've made everyone we know, *all the good people,* look depraved and contagious!" Macalaster had named none of those who had been exposed; he had never even tried to find out who they were. Moreover, he thought his wife had made a strange choice of words (what did being "good" have to do with being immune, or being depraved have to do with being infected, unless you were not considerate enough to mention you were infected before engaging in sex?), but he knew he could never win this particular game of politico-conjugal Scrabble. The bottom line was, he had committed the paramount sin of hurting the Cause, and he could never be forgiven.

Macalaster's information had come from a mysterious anonymous informant whose identity he never revealed, and because of the political damage it wreaked, many believed that Mallory had been his secret source. There was no truth in this. In fact Macalaster had been tipped off by a manipulative radical activist who had never thought that the stricken President was militant enough. The source had personal as well as ideological reasons for what he did: he regarded the Chief Executive's illness as a treacherous threat to his own health and life because he was acquainted with a number of the women who had slept with the President; his own information came from one such infuriated female. Nevertheless the mere existence of gossip that Macalaster had made a bargain with the Devil was enough to get him drummed out of the secular religion to which his diploma from Williams had provisionally admitted him. Eventually he gave up his work at the newspaper and devoted himself to writing books, appearing on talk shows on cable television, and writing a twice-weekly syndicated column. These activities made him modestly famous and prosperous, and this reinforced the idea that he was being paid off for doing dirty work.

Quite soon Macalaster had no friends at all. The shunning to which he had been sentenced affected his wife, too, and this was the underlying reason why she lost her balance. In the sixties she had been a Movement chick who had marched against the war and hurled obscenities and feces at the police. Because she was a female and could not escape from that fate no matter how hard she tried, she regarded herself as a Third World person even though she had gone to the Brearley School and Bennington and her father was a senior partner in a famous brokerage house on Wall Street. While Macalaster covered his beats in Buffalo and Washington, she cut off the magnificent long hair she had worn in college as a badge of belongingness and went to law school on a grant for disadvantaged students. She became a public defender, then counsel to a feminist organization. The last thing she imagined was that she would ever become an outcast. When she became one along with Macalaster, she found that she could not live without the moral support she had always received from her family, her friends, her professors, and her professional colleagues. And so she had died for his sins.

At ten o'clock precisely Macalaster was shown upstairs in the house on Capitol Hill. The noise of the celebration was by now inside the walls. Washington row houses, brick, with no windows at the sides, resemble chimneys, drawing odors, voices, and, in summer, the sodden equatorial heat of the city up the stairwells. As Macalaster entered the library, Mallory put down his book, rose to his feet, and shook hands. The pressure was firm and dry and lasted only as long as was necessary to contract the finger muscles and then relax them again.

"Good of you to come on such short notice," he said.

"I was in the neighborhood anyway," Macalaster replied.

Mallory did not smile at this weak jest; he rarely smiled, even when there was a reason to do so. It did not come naturally to him. In this, as in nearly every other way imaginable, he was a contrast to the perpetually jovial Lockwood. Macalaster was surprised to find Mallory alone. Politicians of his magnitude nearly always had a witness present, and in Mallory's case the third party was invariably his chief of staff and constant companion, a woman named Susan Grant; he applied the rule of couples even to himself. Macalaster, a connoisseur of unattainable women, was sorry that Grant was not present. She was a pleasure to look at, a long-legged blonde with disconcerting light-brown eyes and the aloof, bored countenance of a cheetah.

Mallory indicated a chair; a file folder marked in large computer-generated type with Macalaster's name lay on a low table before it. The manservant, grave, short, and bowlegged in flannels and a made-to-measure blazer, gave Macalaster an excellent cup of coffee and asked if he wanted anything else, then withdrew.

At this point in the proceedings, Lockwood would have devoted five minutes to small talk or a joke before getting down to business. Mallory was brusque. He said, "Ross, at eleven-thirty this morning, I'm going to challenge Lockwood's inauguration on grounds that the November election was stolen by means of vote fraud in California, New York, and Michigan." He picked up the file and handed it to Macalaster. "Why don't you read this while you drink your coffee? Then I have a proposition for you."

The file was a typical Mallory product: terse, logical, complete, and seemingly unanswerable. Macalaster, whose fears regarding the political future of the country were deep, read it with a rising feeling of nausea. The night before, he had drunk twelve ounces of Swedish vodka, a bottle of California cabernet sauvignon, and a couple of snifters of calvados; like many others who lived in desirable Washington neighborhoods, he drank himself to sleep most nights of the week. Though naturally a fast reader, he lingered over the last pages in the hope of gaining control of his facial expression before looking at Mallory again. When at last he did look up, he realized, from the flicker of perception in Mallory's eyes, that he had not succeeded in hiding his reaction.

"Am I the first to read this?" he asked.

"No," Mallory replied. "Lockwood was—or rather, his court readers were—Julian Hubbard and the White House lawyer, Blackstone. But you're the first member of your profession to see it. It will be delivered to the others later this morning."

"What was Lockwood's reaction?"

"I don't know yet." Mallory described his visit to the White House the night before, leaving out nothing essential but speaking so economically that he was through in a short time.

Macalaster took no notes; he prided himself on being able to recall an entire conversation verbatim. He said, "What do you think Lockwood is going to do?"

"Fight, of course," Mallory replied. "His advisers will tell him to deny everything, to go on the attack, to try to make it look like a right-wing plot involving the FIS."

"Do you think he can win?"

"He can confuse the issue. But there's only one way he can win: do as I advised him to do, step aside and rise to fight another day. But it's not in him to do that. His people—please note that I say 'his people,' not Lockwood—would rather see the country go up in smoke than see me back in the White House."

Macalaster raised his voice slightly. "*All* of them? Did each and every one of them take part in stealing the election?"

"No. But how many of them would disapprove of the operation?"

"Some would say that what you're doing is just as likely to send the country up in smoke. And that your real objective is to destroy the political left and all its ideas so that the right can take over on a permanent basis."

Mallory was unruffled. "Of course they'll say that, but even *they* know it isn't true," he said. "I'm in the right, and that makes a happy result possible. For one thing, Lockwood won't have the heart to continue if he becomes convinced that the election really *was* stolen."

"You believe that?"

"Absolutely. He's an honorable man. He knows that the country will go back to normal very quickly if the truth is served. But if the truth is not on his side, and he listens to those radicals who surround him and gets himself acquitted, he'll be a thief and a liar, and one way or another, he'll still be brought down. This involves the most basic of all issues. The popular vote is the American equivalent of the divine right of kings. Lockwood is not one to fly in the face of the Almighty. He knows that usurpers come to no good end."

"Elections have been stolen before."

"Yes, and look what happened afterward. Assassination, war, scandal, cover-up, the wholesale falsification of history. The people behind this kind of thing are always idealists like Julian and his brother, true believers who think that they know better than the people. But it's the Lockwoods who pay with their reputations, even their lives."

Macalaster's tone was sarcastic. "So what you're doing is your attempt to save Lockwood's place in history?"

"No, only Lockwood can do that. My purpose is to preserve the principle that the people, and *only* the people, choose their President, and that the people is always right. Next to that, Lockwood's fate, or my own for that matter, means very little."

" 'The people,' Macalaster repeated, 'is always right'? What famous person said that?"

"I did," Mallory replied. "But there was a time when the idea seemed so obvious that nobody had to say it.

"Now for the proposition." He was studying Macalaster closely. This was a disconcerting experience. Few people of the journalist's anxiety-ridden generation were used to sustained eye contact; it was dangerous in public, compromising in private. "I think we agree that this situation is interesting."

"Interesting?" Macalaster said. "It's going to tear the country apart."

"That depends on what Lockwood does. My own expectation is that Julian Hubbard will win out over Frosty's better instincts and that we'll have a donnybrook."

"Civil war."

"Let's hope it doesn't come to that, though I've always said the people would need all the guns they can get if the Julians of this country ever gained absolute power."

"You weren't joking about that?"

"No. Certainly not. These characters despise the people; every time they're rejected at the polls they think the voters have been duped. If there was no vote, truth—as they call their gibberish—would prevail and they'd damn well see to it that human nature was replaced by a code of conduct devised by themselves. 'The aim of revolution,' said Zhou Enlai, 'is to change man himself.' "

This was vintage Mallory. Macalaster said, "You really do hate those people, don't you?"

"Hate them?" Mallory replied. "No. But I think I understand them." He waited for Macalaster to reply, but the other man had nothing to add. "All right," Mallory said, "back to the point. What usually happens in a situation in which one side is composed of true believers who are in the wrong, and the other is made up of defenders of an older faith, is that everyone tells virtuous lies. There is no authentic account of what really occurred. Look at the Spanish Civil War, the wars of liberation of the last century, the whole Marxist-Leninist epoch. There is no honest history of these events because the people involved, especially the educated classes, habitually lied about events, not only to the world but also to themselves."

"You think the left lies?"

"Yes. About everything. They systematically falsify reality as a matter of keeping faith with their political delusions. They're in their final days—a vanguard elite with a secret agenda who stopped being a popular movement a long time ago and have survived for half a century by lying to the people. Like all liars, they live in a panic because they know they may be discovered at any moment. If it's proved that they stole the election, they could be finished as a political force—out of power in this country for all time to come. They'd do anything to escape that fate."

"Come on, Mr. President," Macalaster said. "This is Frosty Lockwood you're talking about."

"No, it isn't," Mallory replied. "I thought I'd made that clear. Lockwood didn't steal the election. Others did it for him. Why should they consult *him* about it? Frosty's no maximum leader; he's just the Muppet they show the people every fourth November to prove how harmless they are."

"That's harsh."

"No use wasting Christian kisses on a heathen idol's foot," Mallory said.

"That must be Kipling," Macalaster said.

"It is. Now, here is my offer. If you undertake to write a book about the events that are about to unfold and agree to devote yourself primarily to this task, I'll tell you everything I know and everything we're going to do as we go along, and give you complete access to my files."

"In return for what?"

"In return for an honest account based on authoritative sources."

"An honest account of your side of the story, you mean."

"Yes, but you're free to be honest in regard to the other side, too. I have everything to gain by this, which is why no one else in your business will be honest about Lockwood. In fact, that's a condition of the deal. Lockwood has to do the same as I'm doing."

Macalaster snorted. "Why would he do that?"

"Because Julian will try to turn you around as soon as he hears about our deal."

"You don't mind my telling him?"

"Why should I? I haven't said anything to you, nor will I, that I wouldn't be glad to see on page one of *The Washington Post*."

Macalaster knew that what Mallory said about Julian was true. He would do everything he could to undermine Mallory's version of events. "Let me ask a question," he said. "Why me?"

"Because you're clean," Mallory said. "You have no allegiance to me and nothing more to lose from the other side." Amusement flashed in his eyes. "Besides, it tickles me to imagine actually having the truth about this episode written by the modern American equivalent of the omniscient narrator, an investigative journalist."

He rose to his feet and spoke Macalaster's name, his way of saying "dismissed." The Salvadoran manservant had already appeared in the door, poised to usher the visitor out in obedience to some unalterable timetable.

"If you want to go ahead with this project, call Susan," Mallory said. "She'll make the arrangements."

"Right," Macalaster said, knowing, as Mallory did, that he had already taken the bait.

6

As Mallory read his Macaulay, Lockwood had been listening to Julian Hubbard's morning report. Meanwhile he ate his usual breakfast of pancakes and highly seasoned venison sausage, provided by the Kentucky Long Rifle Association, whose members stalked the whitetail deer with flintlock rifles. This was not so romantic as it seemed. Owing to the steady encroachment of the eastern forest on what had previously been farmland and the work of the animal rights lobby, there were now so many deer in America that they were commonly seen by night even in big cities; pet dogs hunted them through wooded neighborhoods in packs. In Washington, they had practically denuded the parks and traffic circles of the grass and flowers that had formerly beautified the city, and were now in the process of killing off the deciduous trees by eating their bark.

Haggard from lack of sleep, Lockwood was seated at a small table in the Lincoln sitting room with the same books and papers strewn around him as on the night before. He wore the Kentucky University sweat suit in which he had slept and heavy sweat socks on his enormous feet. As far as Julian knew, he did not own pajamas or slippers, let alone a dressing gown. Julian finished his report and waited for the President to speak.

Finally Lockwood put his fork down on his plate, looked up, and said, "Who's administering the oath today, seeing that there's no Chief Justice?"

This was an irrelevant question, but Julian was not surprised by it. In moments of stress, Lockwood often focused on things that did not matter.

Julian said, "Bobby Poole, Mr. President."

"That goddamn little fly fisherman?" Lockwood said. "Why not somebody from our side? What about that black girl from Harvard?"

"Poole is first in line of seniority. It's protocol."

"Goddamn right-wingers live too long—they eat better when they're kids. How old was Max Goodrich—ninety-five?"

"Only eighty-nine. It just seemed like he lived longer than that."

Lockwood squinted quizzically at Julian over his glasses (he could not see to eat without them) but made no response. Despite the fact that the timing of the Chief Justice's death, and the opportunity it created to control events, were all-important in Julian's plans for the struggle with Mallory, he did not pursue the subject. This was not the moment to do so; Lockwood was always cranky in the morning, and when he was cranky he disapproved proposals just for the pleasure of doing so. He said, "The hell with the Supreme Court. What am I going to say to these people you've lined up this morning?"

In a series of terse telephone calls beginning at dawn, Julian had arranged two meetings for Lockwood: the first at nine o'clock, in the White House, with the leaders of the party in Congress, the second at eleven, in a small conference room in the Capitol, with a select group of journalists. Julian, who knew all the hideouts in the warren of the much-reconstructed old building, had chosen the smallest available space. He wanted the reporters to be physically close to Lockwood, to feel a sense of intimacy when the President told them that Mallory was attempting, on a legal technicality, to reclaim the presidency that every good person believed he had lost forever.

To both groups Julian had said the same thing: "The President has something of fundamental import to say to you about a threat to the presidency."

Thanks to Mallory, the senators and congressmen already knew what the threat was, so they asked no questions. Every single one of the journalists had replied, "*What* threat to the presidency?"

"Only he can tell you that. In the meantime, don't believe anything you hear from other sources."

To Lockwood Julian said, "The important point is, this way you'll have the first word and the last word. According to the rules he made himself, Mallory can't move until eleven o'clock, when you either call him or don't call him with your answer. We know he's set up a press conference at eleven-thirty on the east steps of the Capitol. You've got to hand it to him—he understands symbolism. At that moment you'll be on the west side of the same building, getting ready to take the oath of office. It's important to get your position implanted in the mind of the front-line press before they listen to Mallory. Otherwise they won't ask him the right questions."

"Thanks for the briefing," Lockwood growled. "My question was, What do I tell these guys?"

"The truth. That Mallory is going to try to steal the presidency on a technicality."

"You call what he's got a technicality?"

"I don't know what else we should call it. Until it's proved under courtroom rules of evidence it's just an allegation like any other—politics as usual. In the minds of these people, it will be whatever you say it is. They want to help you. They want to hear that you're not going to let Mallory get away with this outrage. Hit the FIS angle hard—forces of darkness, secret satellites in the sky, mysterious eavesdroppers hidden in the desert that you didn't know about but Mallory did, even though you're President of the United States. Who are these spooks working for?"

Chewing the last of his food, Lockwood listened with a wary expression in his eyes. Julian handed him half a dozen large blue index cards on which talking points had been typed in letters large enough to be legible without reading glasses. Lockwood read them aloud, in a voice tinged with derision. His patience had been much taxed by his speechwriters in recent days, but there was more to his performance than that. For all his charm, he was an insecure man, sensitive to the slightest criticism, and even when he was in a good mood he ridiculed the people around him. This was his defense against what he perceived as their superior breeding and education; it put them off balance to be taunted by a man who had the looks and manners of a sergeant in the regular army. Like a noncom in charge of the awkward squad, Lockwood gave nearly everyone he knew a sardonic, often obscene or scatological nickname. The overdressed Norman Carlisle Blackstone was "Spats." His name for Richard Nixon, while the indestructible old Red hunter was still alive, had been "Dickless Tracy." In moments of affection he called Julian "Enrico" because his beard was dark and fast-growing; the President pretended that Julian's great-great-grandmother, a patroness of the Metropolitan Opera in the days of the Diamond Horseshoe, had been made pregnant during a dressing-room tryst with Enrico Caruso: "That's where old Julian's five o'clock shadow comes from, an Eyetalian quickie."

"Not bad, Enrico," Lockwood said of the talking points. "I like the part where I call old Franklin 'an enemy of the poor and disadvantaged, a billionaire who has shown that he is a dictator at heart.' Is that your fine Eyetalian hand?"

"Yes, sir," Julian replied. "Everyone else was home in bed."

"You think I should come right out and call him a dictator?"

"It's an important thought to get out into the media stream, and it has the virtue of being something they all want to believe. You can do it on background; don't worry, the press will write it as long as they have a source to blame it on."

"Don't worry," Lockwood said. "I'll lay the onus on the son of a bitch. I've got no choice. You know the old saying: If you've got the facts on your side, hammer hell out of the facts; if you've got the law, hammer hell out of the law. If you've got neither, hammer hell out of the table."

Lockwood was more like himself by the minute. Eating had brought a little color into his cheeks, and the high sugar content of the food was giving him energy.

"You've got more than the table on your side," Julian said. "First of all—"

Lockwood held up his hand. "Not now," he said. "It's too early in the morning to be smart. All I have time to do today is smack Franklin in the mouth as hard as I can. Gotta make the crowd roar. We'll get to the fine points later."

"You're right, of course. But we've got a damn good case."

Lockwood smiled for the first time since rising. "Damn right we do," he said. "You need a shave, Enrico. Get you some breakfast and scrape off some of those whiskers. I'll see you downstairs in half an hour."

Ross Macalaster reached Julian Hubbard on the telephone moments later and told him what Mallory had proposed to him.

"Are you going to do this?" Julian asked.

"Write the book? Sure I am. If I don't, he'll find someone else to do it you may like even less than you like me. It will be a better book if you and Lockwood talk to me too."

"What exactly has Mallory told you?"

"He showed me a file with a lot of circumstantial information in it. It involves computers and the presidential vote last November in California, Michigan, and New York. Shall I go on? I'm on a cellular phone."

"No. Do you think the information is genuine?"

"I found it plausible. He said it was the same material he gave Lockwood last night. Did the two of them meet last night?"

Julian ignored the question. He said, "You understand that he's trying to pull off a coup d'état?"

"Is that so? All I know is what I read in the file. That's why I'm calling."

"Mallory is playing mind games. He's good at that, so watch yourself."

Julian had not invited Macalaster to the press briefing in the Capitol; it was limited to writers and broadcasters he knew he could trust. Julian regarded the news media as a transmission belt for the political word. He wanted no one at Lockwood's briefing who did not owe him favors, no one who would ask the wrong questions. Macalaster did not fall into that category.

Julian said, "Do you know where the Vice President's office is in the Capitol—off the Senate chamber?"

"Yes."

"Meet me there during Lockwood's speech. Just walk in; I'll tell the guards you're coming. We'll watch the speech together. And talk."

7

There are no windows in the Roosevelt Room, where Lockwood met with the leaders of his party, but in any case he had lost the habit of looking out of the windows since his move into the White House. He was surprised, therefore, when the agent in charge of the presidential protection detail of the Secret Service intercepted him in the hall outside the Oval Office and told him that snow was falling again.

"Thanks, son," he said, unable for the moment to remember the man's name. "But what difference does it make?" Lockwood's mind was still in the meeting, and he kept on walking.

The Secret Service man followed him into the Oval Office. He was the archetype of a Secret Service agent: calm, brave, intelligent, strong and agile as a professional boxer, and fanatically dedicated to preserving the President's life. "It's a wet, heavy snow, Mr. President, and it's going to stick," he said. "Visibility could be close to zero by noon, and the forecast is for ten to fifteen inches by late afternoon."

Lockwood reached his desk, made by the great Nisei woodworker George Nakashima from a three-inch slab, bark still attached, of a black walnut felled on the banks of the Big Sandy River by Lockwood himself. He picked up the telephone and dialed Julian's extension. The agent's name, Bud Booker, came back to him. He was still there.

Lockwood put his hand over the mouthpiece of the telephone and said, "You have something to add, Bud?"

"Yes, sir. We think you should move the ceremonies indoors and cancel the parade."

Lockwood hung up the phone, cutting off Julian, who had just come on the line. "Goddamnit, Bud, we've been over this before. The answer is no."

"Mr. President, we think you should reconsider."

"Who is 'we'?"

"The chief, myself, the agents on duty—all of us. We can't function even at minimum efficiency in a whiteout."

"A whiteout? Hell, it's just a little old January snowstorm. Back where I come from, babies get made in the woods in worse weather than this."

Booker was accustomed to Lockwood's hillbilly wit. He smiled dutifully, but stuck to his argument. "I've got a bad feeling about today, sir," he said.

Lockwood glared at the young man, then relaxed. "I know you do, Bud, and I know you're only trying to do what's best. But I'm not going to hide under the back porch like a whipped hound dog just because some crazy Arab wants to blow himself up in the front yard."

Booker, his face controlled, his big wingtip shoes planted on the blue carpet, stood his ground. "With all due respect, Mr. President," he said, "you're not the only one at risk."

Lockwood's expression darkened. "Watch it, son," he said softly. Booker made no apology; he was standing up for his troops. Lockwood understood this. In a different tone of voice, he said, "Every one of us stood up on our hind legs in the open air during the worst of it last fall, and by God I'll stand up in the open air today and take the oath of office. I have my reasons. And that's that." He softened his tone even further. "I'm just not going to hunker down," he said. "Now you and your men just do the best you can, Bud."

Booker made a stiff military about-face—Lockwood did not miss the symbolism—and left. Watching the man go, he murmured sardonically to himself, "Of course we may not draw much of a crowd." Then he put the encounter out of his mind and redialed Julian's number. "Get in here," he said, "and bring that half-wit we've got for a lawyer with you."

Lockwood started talking in a loud voice while his two aides were still in the doorway. "Carlisle, what the hell's wrong with you? You've got to stop saying that Mallory's got the goods on us and the damn army is going to have to take over the country."

"That's not what I said, Mr. President."

"Goddamnit, don't tell me what you said. I heard you say it. All those damn Chicken Littles from the Hill heard you too. It scared the living shit out of them. Did you see those faces? By the time you got through going over the evidence my own party was ready to impeach me by acclamation. Jesus! Where the hell was *our* side of the story? What's our defense going to be? *That's* what they wanted to hear. You made it sound like there was nothing I'd like better than to put on my Sunday clothes and be burned at the stake on national TV."

Blackstone tried to defend himself. "I understood Julian was going to brief them on our political strategy. My job was to lay out the charges Mallory has made."

"What's Julian got to do with it? He's not a lawyer. If this is the way you do things on Wall Street, it's no wonder half the Stock Exchange is in jail. And one more thing, Julian. Stop calling this back-alley fight a coup d'état."

"Whatever you say, Mr. President," Julian said. "But what do you want us to call it?"

"What the hell does that have to do with anything? Stick to the point. What are we going to do to beat this pack of damn lies Franklin's putting out? That's what I want to know. That's what they all wanted to know in the Roosevelt Room, but we sure as hell didn't satisfy their curiosity."

Lockwood had reason to be disturbed. The meeting with the party leaders had gone badly. Most of the senators and congressmen present had already read Mallory's file; copies had been delivered to them shortly after dawn by his messengers. Its contents had shaken them. It was obvious that Mallory was going to go for impeachment unless Lockwood stepped aside, and some of them had seemed to think this wasn't such a bad idea.

Lockwood had ridiculed the possibility. "That's just Franklin feeling up our titties," he had told them. "We're going to win this one. *Got to.* Think of the alternative."

Before Lockwood could say more to Julian and Blackstone, the intercom buzzed. He picked up the handset, listened to his secretary's voice, and said, "Send him on in." He made a gesture of dismissal to Julian and Blackstone. "Carlisle," he said, "I want you to read the Constitution and tell me how to use it to screw Mallory. Read slow and careful. I want a complete rundown by three o'clock. Skip lunch."

Samuel Rees Clark of Massachusetts, the Majority Leader of the Senate, came through the door. Strictly speaking, there was no majority in the Senate because for the first time in history it was divided evenly between Lockwood's party and Mallory's, each side having fifty seats. Clark would keep the title and his party would organize the Senate because Lockwood's Vice President, Williston Graves, always called Willy, would break tie votes in the administration's favor. Lockwood had known Clark for thirty years. Both were men of the political center who had been elected to the House of Representatives in the same year, and three terms afterward they had moved up to the Senate together, not long after Mallory was elected. From earliest days, Clark had believed that his friend Lockwood would be President someday. He had always stuck by him, pushed his programs, rounded up the votes he needed, fighting the reactionaries and flattering and bribing the radicals.

Lockwood said, "You still here? Thought you'd gone."

"I've been using the facilities," Clark replied. "You know what George the Fifth said to George the Sixth—never miss a chance to take a pee."

Lockwood led his friend across the carpet to a spot where they could speak in privacy. Clark looked around him to make sure they were alone, then said, "Frosty, I've got to tell you that was one sorry excuse for a meeting you just held."

"I was just mentioning that to the boys, Sam. We'll do better soon as we figure out the windage."

"I hope so. This is going to cause a commotion. It may last the whole four years of your term."

"I know that, Sam."

· "Franklin's likely to bring up what happened to that sheik who wanted to nuke all the Jews."

"I know that."

"They're going to go for impeachment unless you step aside."

"I know that, too."

"Unless you get a grip on this situation, they may win. Franklin is a sly son of a bitch who's richer than the government and doesn't know when to stop, and the Hill ain't what it used to be when it comes to party loyalty."

"Hell, Sam, we never knew it when it was. What are you saying to me?"

"I'm saying you should think about the whole problem and consider all the alternatives. I'm saying this isn't going to be like old times, Frosty. The rest of 'em are already worrying about their own asses. If the House returns articles of impeachment, the Senate will have to try you. I can't predict how it would come out. Last thing I can do is get out in the open if I'm going to be sitting in judgment on you."

"So what are you advising? You want me to step aside like my worst enemy wants me to and let him be President?"

"No. Just don't let Franklin Mallory be the only man in town who's willing to think the unthinkable."

"I don't plan to."

"Glad to hear it. First thing you should do is get yourself a real lawyer. Today. What you need is an alley fighter. That dummy you've got now is a handful of shit waiting to hit the fan. Make him ambassador to Papua New Guinea and hire a man who'll kill for you—one of us."

Lockwood nodded. "I understand what you're saying to me, Sam."

"I hope so, Mr. President." Clark put a hand on his friend's shoulder. The two men were standing together in front of the bulletproof glass doors that looked out onto the lawn. The ground, which had been bare when the sun rose, was already white with snow, and huge cottony flakes fell in a curtain that seemed to absorb the daylight as it descended.

"Really coming down," Clark said. "The radio says it's only the beginning."

"Yes, sir," Lockwood replied. "It sure does look that way."

8

Franklin Mallory's security apparatus was famous for its efficiency. It was state-of-the-art. His houses, including the one on Capitol Hill, were equipped with sensors, cameras, listening devices, silent alarms—and, according to rumor, wondrous inventions capable of immobilizing an intruder with a cloud of nerve gas or a dart tipped with a tranquilizer that paralyzed the central nervous system in milliseconds.

It was partly because Mallory's security measures were so good—and partly, of course, because there was no precedent of a former President's briefing the news media while his successor was in the act of being inaugurated—that the Secret Service gave its approval for his 11:30 A.M. news conference on the east steps of the Capitol. Each journalist invited to the event was furnished with a plastic name badge imprinted with a hologram of Mallory's political logo, Jupiter and its moons. One of these moons, Ganymede, flew an oversize American flag because Mallory, who believed that the future of the human species lay in space, had landed American astronauts there and established a base for future colonization. Because he also believed that the future of the universe depended on capitalist development, he had also licensed the first private mining operations on the moon, on Ganymede, and in the asteroid belt. As a further precaution, journalists were provided with a password, in this case BALLOT BOX, which they were expected to repeat to any member of the Mallory entourage who asked for it. This requirement was particularly distasteful to media stars whose faces were household images, and some of these celebrities believed—possibly with reason—that the bodyguards singled them out for challenges as a way of humiliating them. Finally, all participants in the news conference were asked to pass through a trailer housing a metal detector and a low-roentgen X-ray machine and chemical sensor. This equipment was sufficiently sensitive to detect implanted explosives such as those used by the Eye of Gaza, as well as the gossamer wires the terrorists had employed to detonate the plastic beneath their skin by means of a weak electrical signal from a battery concealed in a wristwatch or a paging device.

Owing to Lockwood's draconian reductions in the White House budget—he even returned half of his own salary to the Treasury—the Secret Service could not afford such gear. Its agents, stalking ahead of the President or deployed on the flanks of his entourage, were forced to rely on methods that differed little from Stone Age tactics formerly practiced by war parties of American Indians and other primitive peoples. Instead of searching for painted enemies concealed among the trees, the Secret Service was trying to discover psychotic killers concealed in crowds of normal Americans who looked, and in most visible respects behaved, just like them. It was an impossible job. As Mallory pointed out when the Eye of Gaza was stalking Lockwood, these methods had failed to prevent the assassination of several nineteenth- and twentieth-century Presidents.

Macalaster had planned to attend Mallory's press conference, then find his way through the labyrinth of the Capitol to the Vice President's office for his meeting with Julian Hubbard. One of Mallory's security teams had provided him with the necessary badge and watchword as he left the house on Capitol Hill. By then it was 10:33, and the first occasional flakes of snow were beginning to fall as the leading edge of the slow-moving storm, coming from the west, hit Capitol Hill fifteen minutes later than the White House.

The change in the weather drove Macalaster indoors. After making his call to Julian Hubbard over the cellular telephone that he, like nearly every other Washington journalist and official, always carried with him, he wandered down Second Street and entered the Library of Congress through the back door. In the main reading room, which was nearly deserted, he sat down at one of the long tables and transcribed his conversation with Mallory into a miniature computer.

Macalaster was about halfway through this task when he looked up and caught a glimpse of a reporter he knew. The man, whose name was Montague Love, was a relict of a bygone age of journalism. He represented twenty-six independent weekly newspapers and local radio stations across the country. Each of his employers covered a minute portion of his salary, so he received twenty-six paychecks every week. Love wore a Mallory press conference badge pinned to the lapel of his ancient chocolate-brown Kmart raincoat, and it was clear from the direction and speed with which he was moving that he was headed for the men's room. Love walked with a limp on a built-up shoe, and whatever misfortune had crippled him evidently had weakened his bladder and bowels as well; he was well known for hurrying out of press conferences, even presidential ones, and then returning after having relieved himself. Macalaster had often given him a fill, sharing his own notes with him on the parts he had missed.

By now it was eleven o'clock. Macalaster packed up his computer and started for the press conference. He had to pass the door of the men's room on his way to the outdoors, and decided to stop in. He had time. The walk to the Capitol couldn't take more than five minutes; add another ten for the security check and he still had plenty of leeway. There was no need to arrive early. Everything Mallory did began precisely on time.

As Macalaster entered the men's room, another man, young and well-dressed, emerged. He had dark eyes, nut-colored skin that was darker than an Arab's but lighter than an Indian's, and a hook nose. When he saw Macalaster, he quickly put his hands into the pockets of his coat, as if he had something to hide. He was clearly a person of mixed parentage—not an American in whom many bloodlines mingled, but someone who was half one thing and half another, but almost certainly a foreigner. He smelled strongly of Mediterranean cologne. Evidently he had dashed inside out of the storm only moments before: there was a crust of snow on the astrakhan collar of his blue overcoat, and his black hair was damp and freshly combed straight back; the tracks of the comb revealed a scrupulously clean, bluish scalp. He too wore a Mallory news conference badge. Macalaster did not recognize him as he brushed by, nor could he read his name, which was half hidden under the large fleece collar. On Inauguration Day, the fact that he was a stranger meant nothing; he could have flown in from Tiflis or Montevideo to do a stand-up for some local TV station.

Macalaster asked, "Is it snowing harder outside?" The other man, hurrying away, flung back the word "blizzard," elongating the *l*. This enunciation and his somewhat false voice added to the impression that he was a broadcaster and a foreigner. So did the fact that he wore sunglasses to the bathroom on a snowy day in January.

Inside the men's room, the first thing Macalaster saw was Monty Love's feet, the left shoe with a sole three inches thicker than the right, protruding from beneath one of the cubicle doors. He shouted, "Monty!" and pushed the door inward. Love was lying on his back with his head beside the toilet and his trousers down. There was blood on the floor. His thick glasses, wire rims bent out of shape, hung from one ear. Macalaster realized at once that somebody had reached beneath the door, grabbed Love by the ankles, and pulled him violently off the toilet. Possibly he had hit his head on the way down, but his assailant must have slammed his skull against the rim of the bowl again, because his wounded scalp gushed blood.

Macalaster could see that Love was not dead. He breathed in a quick, shallow way, and his fingers toyed reflexively with a hole in his raincoat where his assailant had cut off his press badge with a sharp knife or razor, removing the patch of fabric to which it had been pinned. The blade had sliced through Love's blazer and shirt, incising a bloody circle in his skin. Was this the identifying mark of some terrorist gang? Macalaster dismissed the thought as crazy. The entire assault and robbery could not have lasted more than thirty seconds. Like the mid-twentieth-century ink-stained legman that he was, Love was in the habit of taking notes on a wad of blank newsprint copy paper that he carried in his coat pocket. This was missing. Macalaster knew that he would have written everything he had heard that day into his notes, including the password.

Dialing 911 on his cellular phone as he ran, Macalaster sprinted down the long hall that led to the front entrance. As he burst through the west door of the library, the guard, who recognized him, shouted, "Watch the snow, my man!"

A second later, Macalaster's feet went out from under him as he stepped into two inches of fresh wet snow. As he fell, his telephone spun away into the whiteness and he heard a tinny black female voice saying, "All 911 operators are busy. Please hold. If you are not reporting an emergency, hang up *now* and call—" His head hit the granite pavement with a hollow thump, and as unconsciousness overtook him—very slowly, it seemed to him—the woolly snowflakes that descended toward his upturned eyes transformed themselves into sheep he had seen grazing on a hillside as he swam, many years before, in the surf off the island of St. Barts. He had almost drowned that day. For the first time in months, he saw his wife's face in his mind's eye; she had been swimming beside him that day and saved his life. As the undertow seized him and started to drag him out to sea, she turned easily in the water—she was a wonderful swimmer—and gave him an inscrutable smile.

9

Earlier, on his way out of the house on Capitol Hill, Macalaster had caught a glimpse of Susan Grant. She had neither smiled nor said hello. Uttering necessary words was not Grant's way. She was Mallory's lover. Thanks to the news media, the whole country knew this. For all intents and purposes, she was his wife, and had been even when he was President. The couple had never gone through a wedding ceremony, but neither had they ever denied that they lived together as if married. They had met about a year after Marilyn Mallory died, and within weeks Grant had moved into the White House as chief of staff, right-hand person, and de facto hostess and first lady. This arrangement surprised no one who understood Mallory. While she lived, he and his first wife, childhood sweethearts who had married at twenty, were not only one flesh but one intellect that formed an indivisible unit in business and later in politics. He was an intensely monogamous man who believed that the scheme of creation had endowed the human male and female with different but complementary qualities, and that the one was not complete without the other.

Although Mallory was not religious in the usual sense, the notion that a man and a woman were the right and left hemispheres of an organism that had divided itself by mistake and was intended by nature to recombine exercised a mystical influence on his life. This was the reason why everyone who worked for Mallory did so with a partner of the opposite sex. He hired only young single people and permitted them to select their own workmates as they settled in. Once paired, they did not usually remain uncoupled in other ways for long. Like his business empire, his administration was almost certainly the most connubial since the Moonies of the late twentieth century. As he put it in a motivational equation reproduced on countless posters and lapel pins, $\male \leftrightarrow \female$. Feminists referred to this formula as the Hyena Equation.

Liberated though Grant was, she never slept in the house on Capitol Hill. This was still Marilyn Mallory's territory, and the otherwise unsuperstitious Grant half-believed that she haunted the place. Not only was every item in the household exactly where the departed wife had placed it, but her scent was still in the air. The Salvadoran housekeeper made sure that the sachet of dried flower petals that Marilyn had preferred was regularly renewed in all the closets and dresser drawers.

"You don't think she's a malevolent spirit?" Mallory asked.

"No," Grant replied. "But if I were she, I wouldn't want some other woman in my bed with you, or hanging her clothes in my closets. Or drinking out of my glasses. Or anything else."

Grant had spent the earlier part of the morning making the final arrangements for the news conference and monitoring the media. After Mallory filled her in on his conversation with Macalaster, she briefed him on press reaction.

"The word is out," she said. "Lockwood met with Clark and the others this morning, and they've been leaking ever since. Of course that was the purpose of the enterprise. He's meeting right now with the lapdog press." Grant, the female, was merciless to Mallory's enemies.

"What are they saying on TV?"

"They've been hitting the FIS angle hard. You might think that a bunch of spooks had stolen the election from Lockwood instead of the other way around."

"Do they have details?"

"Not many so far. They've been interviewing each other. But of course they'll have the whole file in their hands in less than an hour. Some of them may have it already, courtesy of some staffer on the Hill. It's embargoed until eleven-thirty, but that won't mean much with a story as big as this one, especially when they can't get to anybody until after lunch because all their usual sources are with Lockwood."

By now it was nearly eleven. Side by side on a sofa, Mallory and Grant waited patiently for the call they knew would never come. As Grant had pointed out, one of Julian Hubbard's purposes in organizing the meetings between Lockwood and the congressional leaders, and later with his loyal friends in the news media, was to leak the fact of Mallory's challenge and to raise questions about it. At 11:10, emerging early from the press meeting with Lockwood, Patrick Graham, dean of Washington media figures, described what was happening as a "putsch."

"Franklin Mallory has called a press conference at eleven-thirty here at the Capitol to explain himself," Graham said. "Even for him, this should be an interesting exercise. Not even Nixon, not even the dark figures we remember from prewar Germany, ever made such an attack on an opponent's honor." He paused dramatically. "I have just seen President Lockwood, who at this hour gives every sign of standing fast."

"Good old Patrick," said Grant. "Always the mot juste. I haven't heard anyone use the word 'putsch' since college. He also managed to announce your press conference on national television."

Knotting his plain blue necktie by sense of touch—he disliked mirrors— Mallory nodded and went on watching. He had expected this. He was not in the least disturbed; on the contrary, he was pleased that Lockwood's shock troops were already on the move. It meant that they were stung.

As soon as Patrick Graham faded out, Mallory and Grant, accompanied by a security team, left the house and walked together down Maryland Avenue past ranks of bandsmen and others waiting to march in Lockwood's parade. These included fifty half-drunken men wearing buckskins and coonskin caps and carrying Kentucky long rifles. Mallory and Grant walked side by side under a large blue-and-white golf umbrella. The umbrella created problems for the cameramen who were walking backward, crab-fashion, in front of them because it gathered and reflected their brilliant lights, washing out facial details. She was an inch or two taller than he, and about thirty years younger. Because Mallory had an ageless face and a body that was sinewy by nature, the difference in height was somewhat more noticeable than the difference in age. This was true even though the milky light was not kind to Mallory, who, with his silvery hair, heavy eyebrows, and burning dark eyes, was naturally telegenic. The snowstorm was doing the work of television directors who, whenever they could, counteracted the camera's love for Mallory by shining too much light on him. In an earlier age, Whistler or Sargent would have made a patrician figure out of him, elongating his body by posing him on a pedestal. Such effects were not the business of the people who processed news into entertainment. They wanted public figures to be as neverchanging, as one-dimensional, as instantaneously recognizable, as actors in situation comedies. This was why they cast politicians in roles as soon as they came to town and made sure they stayed in character—Lockwood as Lincoln, Mallory as Richard III.

The walk to the Capitol took just under five minutes at the regulation 120 steps per minute. Such a pace was impossible in the slippery footing, but after about four minutes, a long time by television standards, the ivory dome of the Capitol became faintly visible in the pointillist mist of snowflakes that surrounded it. Though only Mallory and his party knew this, the Capitol itself was not their immediate destination, and to the surprise of the TV crews, they went into the Hart Senate Office Building. For security reasons, the plan called for them to take the senatorial underground train to the Capitol, then emerge onto the central steps leading down to the plaza. As Mallory stood before the microphones at the bottom of the steps, this would place the columns of the east face, the rotunda, and the huge flag that flew over the building, directly behind him.

A pair of youthful staffers waiting for Mallory and Grant by an open elevator in the lobby of the Hart building briefed them on the weather as the car descended into the subbasement. "The networks are complaining about standing outside in the snow," the female said. "It's bad for their equipment—they have to keep wiping off the lenses—and they're all afraid of catching cold."

"They suspect we're doing it just to make them suffer," the male added. "We confirmed their suspicions, playing straight with the media."

Mallory said, "Recommendation?"

"We can hold the news conference in the Old Supreme Court Chamber," the female said. "That's all cleared with the powers that be. Lockwood is upstairs with the congressional leadership in Sam Clark's office, waiting to watch you on the tube. There's no chance of running into him."

"That chamber is like a crypt," Mallory said. "Voices echo. I don't like the symbolism. Is Lockwood moving his show in out of the snow?"

"Apparently not, Mr. President. The word is that he's determined to hold the ceremony outside. The Secret Service is very upset. They'll be playing blindman's buff in a blizzard with the Eye of Gaza. That's a factor to consider."

"We'll stick to the plan," Mallory said. "I've never done anything to offend the Eye of Gaza." He smiled at his young people. "We don't want the pundits to say we were driven indoors while the old rail-splitter braved the blizzard."

As he spoke, the elevator doors opened onto a phalanx of photographers. He had voiced the word "pundits" with a wry twist that made his staff smile, and it was a grinning bunch of lithe, neatly dressed, supremely confident people that the cameras captured. Mallory's sense of the ridiculous amused Susan deeply. It was the first thing she had liked about him, and despite the cameras she turned to him now and gave him a look of strong sensual affection.

Time was short, and they went outside again immediately. At the stroke of eleven-thirty, Mallory took his place behind the massed microphones, which were being protected from the weather by a network employee holding another golf umbrella. Because Mallory was so punctual, the camera lights went on just before he spoke his first word, and despite the deadening effect of the snow, he heard the faint snicker of several dozen tape recorders being switched on as the reporter's digital watches all displayed the half hour at more or less the same instant.

Speaking as always without visible text or notes, Mallory said, "What I have to say to the American people this morning will not take long. It is my belief, based on detailed and unquestionably authentic evidence that has already been made available to President Lockwood, that the last presidential election was corrupted by fraud, rendering the officially certified result null and void. Through the use of highly advanced computers owned by the United States government, a small group of criminal conspirators falsified the election returns in California, New York, and Michigan, crediting Mr. Lockwood with several thousand votes that were not, in fact, cast in his favor. The total number of votes thus counterfeited was sufficient to change the outcome of the election by giving my opponent a tiny plurality of the popular vote in the states in question, and hence their electoral votes. This means, very simply, that my opponent was not elected President of the United States. I was.

"Last night I informed President Lockwood in person of these facts and presented him with the full file of evidence available to me. I invited him to step aside as President in a constitutional manner while this matter is investigated by the means laid down by the law of the land. He has not responded to this suggestion, or offered any other way out of the dilemma in which this atrocious fraud has placed him and the American people. But the principle involved is simple. If he was not elected by the people, he cannot be President.

"A few minutes from now, Mr. Lockwood is scheduled to take the oath of office. If he goes ahead and does so, under what I am prepared to prove beyond a reasonable doubt are false pretenses, then I will defend the American people and the Constitution of the United States by taking every legal action open to me to evict him from the office he has usurped, to make certain that the truth of this matter is pursued and the underlying motive for this atrocious crime is established, and to ensure that justice is done in regard to all concerned. That is all I have to say. I will take questions for ten minutes exactly."

Most of the reporters gathered below him on the steps had just come from the meeting with Lockwood, and they were still under the influence of the emotion it had generated. Julian had been right to crowd them into a small space; the experience had heightened their normal instinct to run as a pack. It seemed to Mallory that they were breathing in unison, as if they had merged into a single being. He had noticed this phenomenon on other occasions when he had made these people angry. This time he had gone further than ever before, not only by placing in question the legitimacy of an election they had all—or nearly all—hoped Lockwood would win but, what was worse, by revealing a secret they had not even dreamed existed. Like the rest of the Washington Establishment, they lived by the illusion that they were insiders, choosing their friends, their clothes, their manners, their vocabularies, even their children's schools, to sustain the impression that they knew things that ordinary mortals could never know. Now Mallory was adducing evidence that there was an inside of whose existence they had never been told by the people they trusted most. The psychological effect of this revelation, with its undertone of betrayal, threatened everything they believed themselves to be.

The first question came from Patrick Graham. His famous voice shook with emotion. "Are you suggesting that President Lockwood was personally involved in the theft of the presidential election?"

"No," Mallory said.

"Let me follow up. Do you think Frosty Lockwood is capable of such a thing?"

"In my opinion, no," Mallory said. "That's why I suggested to him that he step aside while the issue is being investigated, in order to avoid contamination."

Another reporter, also visibly shaken, demanded, "Then who's supposed to have done this terrible deed?"

"Supposition has nothing to do with it, Mr. Rodaghast. This is an open-and-shut case. You have all been provided with the facts as they are known up to the moment, including the names of conspirators that have so far come to light."

"You mean the *alleged* conspirators?"

"No. I mean what I said—*conspirators*, pure and simple. The evidence is unequivocal."

A wrenlike woman shouted the next question in a surprisingly powerful contralto. "Are you telling the American people everything you know about this?"

"It has always been my policy to confide fully in the people," Mallory said. "I think it's an excellent policy, and I recommend it to everyone who speaks or writes to the people. As time goes on, we may know more. Believe me, Philomena, if new facts come to light, I won't be the one to cover them up."

"Do you expect that your majority on the Supreme Court will be a help to you in this matter?"

"If by that peculiar choice of words, Miles, you mean the five justices I appointed owing to the tragic circumstances of a few years ago, I would say to you that your question is a cynical insult to them and to the highest court in the land. One of those distinguished jurists, Chief Justice Goodrich, was laid to rest only yesterday."

The weather was now so bad that Mallory could barely see his questioners, and except for those with trained voices, like Graham and the little contralto, he had difficulty hearing what they said. However, their collective attitude was unmistakable. They did not want to believe what he was saying to them.

Elbowing aside a gesticulating reporter from his own network, Patrick Graham asked the last question. "Supposing you're right, and these conspirators, as you call them, *did* steal enough votes in California, New York, and Michigan to give Lockwood the election. How do you know they stole those votes from *you*? Why couldn't they have been stolen from Nguyen Van Dinh, who finished third in California, or from the Vegetarian candidate, or a few at a time from half a dozen other candidates on the ballot?"

"That's an ingenious question, Patrick, and I'm sure the President's lawyers will take note of it," Mallory said. "But it will get them nowhere. The fact of the matter, fundamental and inescapable, is that the election was stolen. Therefore Lockwood cannot assume the presidency for a second term without violating the first principle of American democracy—that the people, and only the people, are empowered to choose the President. And if he attempts to continue in office, I will fight him to the last breath in my body. The American voters gave me the presidency. I must claim it or betray them—and that, sir, I will never do. Thank you."

Graham shouted another pugnacious question. Mallory ignored him. Stepping away from the microphones, he walked toward Grant, who had been standing behind him and off to the left, out of the frame. Now the cameras captured the look of loving admiration and approval she gave to him.

Then, as millions afterward saw over and over again in slow motion, she spotted something beyond Mallory. The sight horrified her. Her expression changed instantaneously from wifely affection to one of such ferocious female protectiveness that she looked more than ever like some impossibly smart and beautiful great cat. And like a cat, she sprang with amazing quickness past Mallory, placing her body between his figure and that of a gunman who suddenly materialized out of the storm. This person wore a white hooded caftan, his face covered by a gas mask, and as he rose up out of the snow where he had been lying, he fired a pistol with almost unbelievable rapidity.

The first two shots shattered Grant's skull, killing her instantly. Four more high-velocity 9mm Parabellum rounds passed through her dead but still upright body and struck Mallory's torso with enough force to make him stagger, but because he was wearing a bulletproof liner under his overcoat, he was not wounded.

Even as he looked down at the spreading circle of scarlet that seeped from Grant's body, Mallory could not believe that she was dead, or even injured.

10

Susan Grant's assassin was not captured or, as more often happens in such cases, killed on the spot. There were a number of reasons for this, the most important being the gunman's evasive actions and the effectiveness of his disguise. His face was completely hidden by the gas mask. He dropped two grenades onto the snow before he began shooting. The first to explode released an improved type of CS gas that induced violent nausea and excruciating abdominal pain on inhalation. This prostrated Mallory, his security men, and such police as were present, as well as the journalists attending the news conference. The second was a common smoke grenade that discharged a cloud of dense vapor into which the killer vanished theatrically in his white ethnic costume.

Because of the pointed hood, some eyewitnesses, including a few highly trained observers of the Washington press corps, mistook the assassin's caftan for the regalia of the Ku Klux Klan. However, the garment, commonly worn in North African countries, was found abandoned in the snow a few yards away, along with the killer's gas mask and a semiautomatic pistol manufactured in Vietnam under Austrian license. The weapon and the fourteen cartridges remaining in its extracapacity twenty-round clip were made entirely of nonmetallic materials. The olive-drab gas mask and gas canisters, also made of plastic, were obsolete U.S. military issue with all identifying numbers removed. Such hardware was readily available on the open market.

By the time Macalaster had regained consciousness and extricated himself from the paramedics and the Capitol police who had been summoned by the guards at the Library of Congress, his information about the assassin was of little use to the authorities. He had not made eye contact with the man; this was something most men avoided in public toilets. He did not remember the man's face—only his coat, the badge he had presumably robbed from Monty Love, and his luxuriant Oriental hair. That fact that

Macalaster thought his scalp was blue suggested that the suspect might have been wearing a wig. Macalaster also thought he was well under six feet tall and slender. He looked much taller and huskier on videotape—an effect, Macalaster suggested, of his hooded caftan, which he was probably wearing on top of his blue overcoat with the astrakhan collar.

Macalaster was surprised to learn that the local police, not the FBI, were investigating the assassination. He said so to the homicide detective in charge.

"The Metropolitan Police have jurisdiction over all homicides committed in the District of Columbia," the detective said.

"Even in cases like this?"

"You mean even when white people get offed? Yeah. Amazing, eh? What have you got to tell me?"

The detective listened deadpan to Macalaster's theory. It was obvious that he did not believe that the man Macalaster had seen was the assassin. "It would have been impossible for him to get through Mallory's security with a gun, a gas mask, and two grenades concealed on his person," he explained.

"Why? They were all made of plastic, which doesn't show up on X rays."

"Trust us. It couldn't be done."

"Then how did the weapons get to the scene of the crime?"

"Maybe they were buried on the Capitol grounds a long time before and dug up. Or stashed in some other way. We're looking at a lot of territory with many potential hiding places—trees, flower beds, fountains, statues, underground plumbing and wiring. We'll find the answer to that question."

"Will you just consider the possibility that what I'm telling you has significance?"

"You bet. But so does the fact that Mr. Love was robbed of his solid gold presidential Rolex watch that he got for Christmas, his expensive Mont Blanc pen and pencil, and his wallet, containing two hundred forty-six dollars and plastic. Terrorists don't usually waste their time on stuff like that."

"All that could have happened afterward. Someone could have come in after I left, seen him lying there, and robbed him."

The detective nodded solemnly, holding Macalaster's eyes with a steady gaze of his own opaque brown ones. "True," he said. "The world is full of opportunists. Do you happen to remember if Love usually wore a fifteen-thousand-dollar gold Rolex?"

"No."

In an involuntary reaction that interested the detective, Macalaster smiled faintly as he answered because he thought that the watch was probably a fake made in Russia, and that Monty Love, an incurable player of angles, was hoping to collect from his insurance company for the loss of a genuine Rolex.

Love, who had suffered a depressed fracture of the skull and lower-back injuries whose exact nature had not yet been identified, never saw his assailant's face. Out of long habit, he told the police, he had been sitting there going over his notes. He remembered nothing but being yanked off the seat with incredible force, and the subsequent explosion of white light and pain in his head.

The police hypothesis was that the killer had buried himself in one of the snowbanks created when the Capitol steps were shoveled. He had done this, they speculated, before the news conference began, under cover of the falling snow, and had burst forth, steady as an automaton, after lying doggo for more than an hour under a heap of slush. If this was so, Macalaster thought, he was one cold-resistant fanatic.

According to the time display on the networks' videotape of the crime, the assassin had fired his first shot at precisely 11:48:54 A.M. Macalaster asked the detective a question: "If he attacked Monty Love between eleven and eleven-five in the Library of Congress, how could he have walked across First Street, gone through security, made his way across the plaza to the foot of the Capitol steps, and then burrowed into this snowbank while dozens of TV people were stringing cables and setting up their equipment twenty feet away?"

"Good question, assuming your suspect is the shooter," said the detective. "The only part we can answer is the last part. The snowbank was eight point six meters from the camera stand. Visibility was about five meters."

"Didn't any of the security people check the snowbanks?"

"No assassin has ever concealed himself in one before, so it wouldn't be part of the routine."

"How did the assassin know that?"

"Maybe he just took a chance . . ." The detective paused. "Look, this procedure will take up less of your time if you let us ask the questions."

Macalaster knew that he would get nowhere by arguing. As often happens in Washington, and, he reflected, probably also happened in Ur of the Chaldeans, no one wanted to hear arguments that challenged the collective wisdom of the day.

Lockwood was late for his own inauguration because he had been watching Mallory on television. He had not broken away until 11:38, when the press began to ask Mallory questions. At about that same time, word had been brought to him that the members of Mallory's party in Congress would boycott the inaugural ceremony and the luncheon afterward.

"That would have made great television," Sam Clark said. "All those empty places. But I've got 'em resetting the tables, so every chair will be occupied."

Lockwood listened closely; in politics, appearances were everything. "Good work," he said. "Nobody gives a rat's ass if they don't show up, as long as it's not too noticeable. Let 'em march around outside with signs."

"Eleven forty-seven," Agent Bud Booker said. "We'll just about make it."

Lockwood and his retinue were racing through the stone bowels of the Capitol in an effort to reach the podium on the west face in time to take the oath at noon.

As they proceeded, half-trotting to keep up with Lockwood, Clark monitored Mallory's press conference on a pocket television receiver. Suddenly he seized Lockwood's arm. "Jesus," he said. "There's been a shooting. Mallory's down."

Lockwood stopped in his tracks, and the hurrying procession in his wake accordioned as it tried to halt its forward momentum. "What do you mean he's down?" he demanded. "Give me that thing."

Clark handed Lockwood the miniature TV. He put on his reading glasses, and on the tiny screen, no larger than a business card, he saw Susan Grant lying on the snow with Mallory crouched over her motionless body as if to shield it. The rest of the people had sunk to their knees or lay flat on the ground. All were deathly silent; some writhed in agony. Yet the picture was oddly static, like an image from a sentinel camera left behind on another planet. Lockwood realized that the camera operators were down, too, and the networks were broadcasting images from a fixed camera that was on the equivalent of automatic pilot.

Lockwood, who had trouble operating any apparatus more complicated than a telephone, cried, "There's no damn sound!"

Booker, standing on tiptoe, screwed the sound button into his ear, and he heard the half-tremulous, half-exultant voice of an anchorman describing what had happened. "Franklin Mallory is alive, and apparently unharmed," he reported. "He has escaped."

Suddenly a flying squad of Mallory security men, federal agents, and uniformed policemen flooded the beautifully clear color picture, surrounding Mallory and hiding him from view. There were cameramen in this group, too, and the first close-up of Grant, twisted on the snow as though her long, elegant body had been struck by something much heavier than pistol bullets, made it obvious that she was dead. A medical team surrounded her, inside a ring of armed men. Mallory, resisting at first, was hustled away by another squad of agents. Lockwood knew that they would carry him bodily inside the building. The entrance they would use was just beyond the east wall of the crypt.

As the broadcaster talked, his voice grew steadier, more gossipy, but also more resentful that the story wasn't bigger. "Listen to that son of a bitch," Lockwood cried. "He's *disappointed*!"

Of course, Booker could not hear, and in any case all his senses were elsewhere engaged as he searched the crowd with his eyes and his finely trained instincts for a second assassin.

Lockwood turned around and faced the excited crowd behind him. He towered over most of its members, and when he raised a hand for silence, their babble ceased. "According to the TV, somebody has shot Susan Grant," he said. "It looks like she's dead. President Mallory seems to be all right, and they're bringing him into this building. Now if you'll please make way, I have to go to him."

Booker stepped in front of Lockwood. "I'm sorry, Mr. President," he said. "But you can't go out there."

Lockwood put his hand flat on Booker's chest. "I know that, Bud," he said. "But they're right outside. And by the time we get to the door, they'll be inside. Now get your ass in gear and take me where I want to go. That man used to be President of the United States." He raised his voice. "The rest of you folks disperse. Go somewhere safe. The ceremony is delayed."

Associate Justice Poole was right behind him. Lockwood looked at the cheap black drugstore watch he always wore. "Eleven fifty-seven," he said. "Can you administer the oath right here, Mr. Justice Poole?"

"Yes, Mr. President," said Poole. "I can."

"Then let's do it. Where's Polly?"

Lockwood's wife was already on the podium outside with the family Bible in her lap.

"Does anyone have a Bible?" Poole asked.

"We don't need a Bible," Lockwood said. "Just say the words, Bob, and I'll swear to them in the name of the Lord."

Sam Clark said, "Wait, there are no cameras."

"To hell with the cameras," Lockwood said, again glancing at his watch. "It's twelve o'clock, Mr. Justice Poole. Let's do it."

Poole recited the words of the oath in a mellow up-country North Carolina accent. Lockwood repeated them after him. As Mallory had reminded Grant only an hour or so before, these sepulchral rooms in the bottom of the Capitol were full of echoes, and Lockwood's loud voice reverberated off the stones.

12

Lockwood found Mallory behind an unmarked door, in one of the hideaway offices reserved for leaders of the Senate. Four grim-faced agents armed with shotguns stood outside, but there were no cameras; at Lockwood's request, Sam Clark had penned up the news media in another part of the Capitol. Polly Lockwood had left the podium on hearing the news, catching up to her husband as he rushed along the Brumidi corridors with their sentimental murals depicting America as the new Eden. They walked the rest of the way holding hands. Before they went in, Polly handed Lockwood a Kleenex.

"Better wipe your eyes, love," she said.

Lockwood took the Kleenex and mopped away the copious tears that wet his cheeks. All his life he had wept at significant moments, sad or happy. As an athlete, he had scored most of his winning touchdowns with tears in his eyes, and on their wedding night Polly had discovered to her surprise that he cried with joy when he made love. Each of his elections to office, all of them close, had set tears flowing. In this case his wife wasn't sure whether he was weeping for Mallory in his tragic loss or because he had just taken the presidential oath under such strange circumstances—or because, as was usually the case, he sensed that nothing would ever be the same again.

Even before the murder of Susan Grant, there had been little chance that things would ever be the same again with Mallory, but in Lockwood's mind, everything that had happened between them in their struggle over the presidency was just politics. He was a throwback to the age when American politicians were Christians first and ideologues second. Such men forgave and forgot; to them, politics was a game, not a religion. Lockwood had been Mallory's friend for more than twenty years, and Mallory had been his. In spite of all the fouls on both sides, he was Mallory's friend even now. Nothing could change this, and it was the Mallory he first took a liking to, not the implacable stranger who had taken possession of his friend's body, whom Lockwood had come to comfort and console.

The door opened into an anteroom crowded with Mallory people who were talking in murmurs to each other and into telephones. Those who had been present at Grant's murder were shaken by what they had witnessed and deathly pale as a result of convulsive vomiting. Their eyes were swollen and bloodshot from weeping and the effects of the CS gas. Two of Mallory's young people greeted the Lockwoods; they, too, had been crying.

Polly, a maternal woman even if childless, took each of them by the hand. "How is Franklin?" she asked.

"He's alone right now," the young woman said. "But I know he'll want to see you."

She led them into the inner room, where Mallory stood, all by himself, in the center of the carpet. Like the others, he was drained and red-eyed. His hair was disheveled and the knees of his gray trousers were dark with moisture where he had knelt in the snow beside Grant's body. Polly Lockwood had never before seen this man with a hair out of place. Even such insignificant untidiness as she now observed made Mallory seem lost, grotesquely not himself, as if he were drunk or under arrest.

Polly rushed across the room and put her arms around him and hugged him. Although she had scarcely known Susan Grant, she and Marilyn Mallory had been loving friends, bound together by their childlessness and their husbands' ambitions. In early Senate days, the wives had gotten the two couples together for Scrabble (Lockwood always won), bridge (Mallory always won), and movies and barbecues. Polly knew that the two husbands had become mortal political enemies for all future time, but she too was calling on a past incarnation of Franklin Mallory. The sympathy she felt for him at this moment had as much to do with her own grief over his first wife's death as with the present tragedy. To Polly's astonishment, Mallory hugged her back, breathing spasmodically as if about to break down. He did not seem to be able to let go. Lockwood, who had been waiting his turn to comfort Mallory, saw what was happening and stepped forward, awkwardly throwing his long arms around both of them and resting his hard, heavy skull against Mallory's.

Finally Mallory stepped back. "I'm glad you came," he said. "It means a lot to me."

"We're just so sorry, Franklin," Polly said.

Still close together, they looked into one another's faces for a moment. Of the three, Mallory was the only one whose cheeks were not wet with tears. Unable to trust himself to speak, Lockwood bit his lower lip and nodded.

"It's odd," Mallory said. "But I feel just like I did when Marilyn died. Robbed. Women are not supposed to go first. And not this way."

Polly shook her head. "We never imagine that we will. What will you do now, Franklin?"

"Go on," he said. "Just like Frosty would."

Lockwood said, "I hope I never have to." He drew Polly against his side; new tears coursed down his cheeks. "Couldn't go on," he said with a catch in his voice. "*Could not do it.*"

Mallory looked him in the eyes. "Oh, yes, you could," he said.

13

Lockwood canceled the inaugural parade and the luncheon that Congress had planned to give him under the dome of the Capitol, and although Grant was not entitled to any such honor, he ordered the flags on government installations to be lowered to half-staff. In Statuary Hall, where microphones and cameras had been set up for his inaugural address, Julian Hubbard had a word with him.

"This is a terrible thing that's happened, Mr. President," he said. "But it has its up side."

"Its '*up*' side'?" Lockwood said. "What exactly would that be, boy?"

There was disgust in his voice. In all their years together, he had never before called Julian "boy," his ultimate term of condescension. He had treated him like a favorite child, continually teaching, encouraging, and confiding. But something had changed since the night before. He had lost patience with Julian, and in every case involving other people that Julian could remember, this had always meant that he had first lost trust.

Julian said, "All I mean was, it gives us some breathing room. You don't have to respond to Mallory's charges today. You can go on the air and extend your personal sympathy, give thanks that Mallory was delivered from harm, and then give your original speech. The text will be on the TelePrompTer. We can deal with the mischief Mallory has made another day."

"Mischief?" Lockwood said. "Is that your word for it? I'm just glad that son of a bitch in the white nightshirt didn't kill *him*. Then you'd know what mischief is. You hear me?"

Julian nodded. Lockwood waited, eyes burning, as if expecting Julian to defend himself against some accusation that he, Lockwood, could not bear to make. But the younger man remained silent.

After the usual prayers and Sam Clark's subdued introduction, Lockwood went to the bank of microphones. "I have seldom agreed with Franklin Mallory on questions of public policy, but I have always believed that he is a patriot and an honest man," he said. "Today he has been the victim of a terrible tragedy, and my heart goes out to him and to the family of the fine young American, Susan Grant, who died today at the hand of a brutal and cowardly assassin. In light of what has happened, and because of the inclement weather, I have ordered that the celebrations planned for today will not take place."

He paused and gazed into the cameras. "My fellow Americans, as you all know, my defeated opponent has made a statement charging that there were irregularities in the counting of ballots in three of our states in last November's elections. As we all realize, this is a matter of the highest import, and I will respond to his statement in detail before long. But this is not the time to do so, except to say that I believe myself to be the people's rightful choice as President of the United States, whose Constitution I have just sworn in the name of the Lord to preserve, protect, and defend. And so now I will speak to you of more enduring things."

Then, as Julian Hubbard had counseled, Lockwood read his prepared speech, which shimmered on the translucent panels of the TelePrompTer as if written on air.

14

The day after the shooting, the authorities were directed by an anonymous phone call to a tiny apartment located in a violent neighborhood about a mile southeast of the Capitol. Although murder, rape, robbery, and drug traffic were hourly occurrences here, the police seldom ventured into these streets except to protect firemen when a major fire threatened to spread to more highly valued parts of town. This rarely happened because the prevailing winds blew toward the east, and everything the city government wished to preserve lay to the west. The apartment—a small, windowless furnished room equipped with a hot plate and a refrigerator—had been rented only six days before by a young person who gave his name as Abdul Ahmed Jackson.

According to the landlady, her tenant had paid the security deposit and one month's rent, a total of six hundred dollars, with clean, new twenty-dollar bills. He had kept to himself. He was "a light-skinned, good-looking individual, not black exactly, but not a white man either, maybe an Arab, had that kind of a nose." In any case he was dark enough to fit into the neighborhood. As she had talked to him only once, and he had said almost nothing on that occasion, she could not say whether he was an American or a foreigner. He had been suspicious of strangers. Everybody in that part of town was, but Jackson had seemed especially paranoid where women were concerned. "Girl smile at him or knock on his door, he be *gone*," the landlady told Channel 7 News.

Abdul Ahmed Jackson's apartment contained Near Eastern groceries, a well-thumbed copy of the Koran, books and pamphlets in Arabic by Near Eastern revolutionaries, fundamentalist Islamic religious tapes, also in Arabic, and a Baluchi prayer rug oriented toward Mecca by means of an arrow inked onto the floor. Although the arrow was pointed so precisely that it could not have been drawn without the aid of a compass, no compass was found, leading investigators to deduce that Jackson had not intended to return; they were proud of this bit of reasoning and made sure the news media reported it.

The authorities did find the familiar paraphernalia of the demented assassin: newspaper clippings about Mallory, pictures of him with targets drawn over his heart or with his face obliterated, a diary, written in a skewed, barely legible hand that listed his "crimes against humanity." Among these offenses, the one that seemed to have bothered the alleged assassin most was Mallory's campaign against abortion.

Before Mallory was elected President, his mechanism for good works, the Mallory Foundation, had financed research that made it possible, by pumping about a pint of saline solution mixed with antibiotics and blood protein into the uterus of a pregnant woman, to flush out a fertilized ovum eight days after conception. This technique, developed by animal scientists, had routinely been used since the mid-twentieth century by breeders of livestock, especially cattle. The Mallory Foundation opened a string of free clinics in which the method was adapted for use by human subjects.

A woman who had engaged in unprotected coitus and was nervous about the consequences had only to call the clinic on the morning after and make an appointment for an immediate pregnancy test and, if the results were positive, recovery of the fertilized ovum a week later. Inevitably, these clinics came to be called MACs, short for Morning After Clinics.

Mallory's aim was to provide a safe, convenient, and painless alternative to the destruction of about two million fetuses a year by surgical or pharmaceutical methods. MAC clinics made it possible to reimplant a healthy embryo in the original mother at a future date, in case she changed her mind about bearing the child, or alternatively, to grow it to term in the womb of a different woman. In a few instances, when the natural or surrogate parents requested the procedure, embryos had been surgically divided under a microscope before reimplantation, a procedure that resulted in the gestation and birth of normal identical twins.

All embryos that were not transplanted within a few days were enclosed in a protective ampule and frozen in an amniotic atmosphere of liquid nitrogen at a constant temperature of minus 325 degrees Fahrenheit. There was no scientific reason why an embryo thus preserved could not be implanted and successfully gestated in the womb of a female born thousands of years after its original mother. As Mallory could not resist putting the matter in announcing the program, "This would be something like King Solomon, an unwanted baby adulterously conceived around the middle of the tenth century B.C. by King David and his paramour, Bathsheba, being born during the Kennedy administration to a surrogate mother."

A transplanted embryo could, of course, be carried to term by a woman of another race and emerge, genetically speaking, as the same child it would have been if it had remained in the womb in which it was conceived. Many affluent women spared themselves the discomforts of pregnancy by hiring surrogates, usually from the Third World, to gestate their children under medical supervision in commercial maternity homes, unrelated to Mallory's operation, that sprang up all over the world.

All embryos were genetically coded and tagged on recovery, and experts at the huge multinational corporation Universal Energy had developed a computer program capable of retrieving any given specimen from storage almost instantaneously. This was an important breakthrough: an eight-day embryo contains all the genetic information needed to produce a child unique in its characteristics, but it cannot be seen by the naked eye unless magnified at least ten times.

Tens of thousands of implantations had been performed in the MAC clinics with normal results. But because many recovered embryos were not reimplanted, more than one hundred thousand remained in the legal custody of the Mallory Foundation. According to statistics published in the newspapers, nearly ninety percent of such unclaimed frozen embryos were classified by the computer as "other than Caucasian or East Asian."

If his writings and the crude cartoons with which he illustrated them were to be believed, Abdul Ahmed Jackson had become obsessed by the idea that Mallory intended to transport the many thousands of frozen nonwhite embryos in his custody into outer space, split them all into identical twins "under weightless conditions," gestate them in artificial wombs, and employ the human beings thus produced as slave labor in mines owned by Universal Energy on the moons of Jupiter and other extraterrestrial locations. According to his diary he believed that "jezebels and harlots" had been assigned by Mallory and his close friend O. N. Laster, head of Universal Energy, to entrap him, the assassin, into impregnating them. On the evidence contained in his diary ("O my sons! O my daughters! I weep for thee in thy chains and bondage!"), he was convinced that he was the biological father of some of the embryos that were marked for lives of slavery on Ganymede.

15

Susan Grant's murder was pushed out of the news by the two huge stories that broke on the day on which it happened: Lockwood's inauguration and Mallory's challenge to the authenticity of his presidency. Something more subtle was also going on. Owing to her choice of Mallory as a life partner, Grant was not the sort of person whose death aroused a sense of loss among people who entertained progressive political opinions, as most Washington journalists did. Even the reporters who witnessed the shooting did not treat it as an interesting crime, except in terms of the dining-out value of their personal exposure to danger and discomfort.

Lockwood had been right: the media were disappointed in the story. If Mallory himself had been killed immediately after charging that the election had been stolen from him, *that* would have had potential. His assassination under such circumstances would have activated the entire political apparatus of the United States of America and, with it, its doppelgänger, the news industry. But the Susan Grants of this world arrive in Washington out of nowhere with every new administration, have their hour of reflected glory, and then go back to nowhere. From the Establishment's point of view, Grant had, for all practical purposes, committed suicide, earning her fate by flaunting the reprehensible sexual and political life she had led as Mallory's lover and adviser.

Most reporters and other members of the intelligentsia accepted without question the explanation provided by the all-too-familiar clues discovered in the suspect's ghetto hideout. Plainly Jackson, like so many American loser-assassins before him, was a textbook psychopath who had been plotting to kill Mallory for months, possibly even years. This explanation had many weaknesses. One in particular bothered Macalaster. How had the assassin known that Mallory was going to give a press conference in time to make an attempt on his life? The first announcement of the event was broadcast at 11:10 A.M., at about the time Abdul Ahmed Jackson was supposed to have buried himself in the snowbank, and about five minutes *after* Macalaster had bumped into him coming out of the men's room in the Library of Congress. Because a cordon sanitaire had been thrown up by the police and federal troops to keep people like Jackson's neighbors away from the inaugural ceremonies, there was no vehicular traffic for fifteen blocks east of the Capitol on Inauguration morning. Macalaster knew, because he had timed it, that it took more than forty minutes for a man walking fast to cover the distance between Jackson's room and the Capitol.

After watching the tapes of the killing over and over, Macalaster was sure that the man he had seen was the assassin; the sleeves and the hem of his blue overcoat could be seen as he raised the pistol with both arms, hitching up the loosely fitting caftan. Besides, gas mask or no gas mask, caftan or not, Macalaster *knew* that this was the person he had encountered. His every instinct told him so.

All this he explained to the detective in charge of the case. They met for the second time in a cubicle in the First District station house on North Capitol Street. The detective listened politely while Macalaster talked.

"Did you walk the route yourself?" he asked.

"Yes, I did," Macalaster replied.

"That was a good piece of detective work. But I gotta tell you . . ." He shook his head ruefully. "The mind plays tricks."

"Why do you discount everything I say?" Macalaster asked him.

"We don't discount anything any citizen tells us. We value your input. But at the same time, many hands don't necessarily make light work. We have a certain amount of experience in these matters. Let's go over what happened to you. You saw someone in a blue overcoat with a Persian lamb collar come out of the men's room. You went inside and there, to your shock and horror, you found your poor handicapped friend Montague Love lying in a pool of blood in a toilet stall. With his pants down—significant detail. Then, instead of doing what you knew was the right thing, which was to call the cops and an ambulance and wait for them at the scene of the crime, you panicked, ran, and fell down and hit your head on a stone floor, knocking yourself cold. When you woke up you learned that someone you knew personally had been shot dead while you were unconscious. Naturally your unconscious mind, the part of us that old-timers used to call the conscience, got right to work, trying to make a pattern out of these random events. That's what's going on with you, Mac. Your conscience is trying to make sense of the inexplicable. We see this all the time in all kinds of people. The more decent they are, the more responsible citizens, the more likely the syndrome."

"The 'syndrome'?"

A nod of the head, a gentle smile, a look of sincere sympathy—the sequence recommended by the manual for handling difficult witnesses. This was an educated cop. Diplomas from two universities hung on the wall of the cubicle. "As a rule," the detective said, "we recommend talking to a professional in cases like yours. I've got a list right here of some of the best."

"You think I'm imagining things?"

"Of course not; we know a lot about you, and we respect your reputation for truthfulness and honesty, which is a pretty fine one, by the way. But maybe you're misinterpreting things. That's nothing to be ashamed of. It's only human. Farther than that it would be wrong for a nonprofessional to go. We're getting into deep waters here, Mac. Obviously, you feel terrible—and not only emotionally. You've had a nasty concussion. You saw the victim, who was someone you knew personally and admired, just a few minutes before she died. No normal man wants an attractive, educated young woman to die; it's against nature. You also suffered a sudden personal loss yourself not so very long ago. Sometimes it takes someone who understands the mysteries of the human mind to make all these factors add up. Because to be brutally honest, your theory doesn't add up for purposes of this investigation. We wish it did. But it doesn't."

Macalaster said, "Neither does yours, pal."

The detective smiled compassionately but raised both pink, unwrinkled palms in a gesture that said, "Please—no more."

In a matter of days, the horrifying images of Grant's murder would disappear into the national unconscious along with the footage of thousands of other pointless killings.

16

On his way home, Macalaster rang Mallory's number from his car and, after punching in a private code for confidential messages that Mallory had given him, told the computer that answered that he had unique information relating to the events at the news conference. Five minutes after he walked into his house, a pair of Mallory security operatives named Wiggins and Lucy knocked on the door. They were thirtyish, and like most Mallory people, they were prime examples of the healthy mind in the healthy body. Macalaster had the impression that either one of them could easily run five miles, bike ten miles, swim two miles, and then, in less than two seconds, while still standing chest-deep in the water, fire eighteen vinyl-tipped explosive/expansive rounds from a 6mm pistol into a three-inch bull's-eye from a distance of fifty yards. According to tabloid folklore, this was a fitness test every Mallory security agent had to pass once a month.

Wiggins and Lucy debriefed him by asking him to tell his story into the microphone of a tiny computer that transformed speech into printed English. With Wiggins doing most of the talking and Lucy most of the thinking, they questioned him much more efficiently than the detective had done. They knew the ground so well, and were so impervious to surprise, that Macalaster found himself wondering whether they did not already know everything he had said to the detective only an hour or two before, but their discretion was so ostentatious that there was no point in asking them. Neither commented in any way on Macalaster's story.

"President Mallory will have immediate access to your input," Lucy told him. "However, he regrets that he won't be able to see you for a few days. Susan's funeral will be held tomorrow in Kansas City—"

Macalaster said, "Is that where she's from?"

Lucy ignored the question. "The service will be private, for security reasons, and also because her parents do not wish to have the media present," she said. "Unfortunately that includes you. We are instructed to tell you that nothing has changed in regard to the arrangements President Mallory made with you personally, and that he will be in touch as soon as possible."

Macalaster asked them to wait while he wrote a letter of condolence to Mallory. While he scrawled his dozen awkward lines in repayment for Mallory's earlier letter of sympathy to him, Lucy went out to the car and transmitted his statement from the computer to Mallory Industries' mainframe. The whole exercise lasted no more than five minutes, but as Macalaster handed over the letter, Wiggins said, "President Mallory thanks you for the information you've provided. He read it raw on his screen as it came up from the scanner."

"What does he think of it?"

"He didn't say. Goodbye, sir."

17

On the morning after Grant's funeral, in pitch darkness and the muffled suburban silence of six A.M., Lucy called Macalaster.

"Wiggins and I will pick you up in a car at seven o'clock exactly, if that's convenient," she said. "You're scheduled for a working breakfast at seven-thirty."

"I'll be waiting outside," Macalaster said.

"No, please don't do that. We'll call as we turn into your street, then ring the bell."

By now the snow had melted, and even before dawn the thermometer was in the forties. As the car, with Wiggins at the wheel, rolled smoothly alongside the Potomac, then crossed the Chain Bridge into Virginia, the stereo played country music. Lucy turned around in the front seat and said, "Is the music all right?"

"I like it," Macalaster said. In twisting her body to face him, she had revealed the butt of a pistol in a shoulder holster next to her left breast, which was the only plump thing about her. He smiled. "Nice big gun."

Lucy smiled in return—no teeth or eyes, just a fleeting compression of unpainted lips. "You should see Wiggins's," she said. This was reflex, and he could see she regretted the wisecrack immediately—not because she cared about Macalaster's feelings, but because it was a breach of discipline. He did not mind. He already knew that Malloryites did not like the press, no matter what their auspices.

Because of the shooting, Mallory was staying—or at least receiving visitors—in the deep isolation of a Norman manor house set in a woods near Great Falls. The long front drive passed between two rows of stumpy plane trees, whose whippy branches had been trimmed back for winter. Acres of muddy vineyards lay to either side. "These are all New World grapes, collected in the wild from all over the Western Hemisphere," said Lucy, though Macalaster had asked no questions. "The idea is to cross different varieties for desirable genetic characteristics, such as sugar and water content, and make American wines that owe nothing to Europe. The people involved think that genetic engineering will produce a better wine in two or three generations than the Old World managed to develop in thousands."

She imparted this information with an air of condescension, as if Macalaster might not have the money or the inside knowledge needed to understand the mysteries of winemaking. Witticisms occurred to him, but he suppressed them. Creating an all-American viticulture seemed an odd ambition in the twenty-first century, when even famous Burgundies and Bordeaux grands crus consisted mostly of mass-produced wines with traces of Pommard or Médoc added by the bottler to satisfy the labeling laws.

Mallory's Norman manor house had tiny diamond windowpanes glazed with thick imitation crown glass that admitted little light (and, Macalaster guessed, was designed to stop a bazooka round). In the gloomy morning room where Mallory greeted him, food was laid out in chafing dishes on a sideboard. Mallory, who ate solid food only at dinner, drank a cup of tea while Macalaster, taught by his working-class mother that breakfast was the most important meal of the day, helped himself to sausages, scrambled eggs, fried potatoes, and toast.

"Thank you for your letter," Mallory said. "It was a comfort to me." Macalaster started to reply, but Mallory changed the subject before he could speak. "I understand you've been beating your head against the bureaucracy," he said.

"I've tried to get them to pay attention to the information I gave them, yes."

"You really think the fellow you saw in the library is the assassin?"

"There's no question in my mind that he was."

Macalaster repeated the reasons for this, including the clues in the television footage and his inner certainty.

Mallory listened patiently to the end. "I see why you feel as you do," he said. "But you do understand, don't you, that all questions of who and how are irrelevant?"

Macalaster was taken aback. What was Mallory talking about? "If the objective is to identify the person responsible and bring him to justice," he said, "then how can any information be irrelevant?"

"Because the question is not who did it, or the methods and tools he used," Mallory said. "The question is *why* it was done, and we are in the process of asking why."

"Are you?" Macalaster replied. "Whom are you asking?"

"So far, the computers, to establish the probabilities, based on the known facts. The candidates for questioning almost certainly will not include the gunman. We already know everything about him that we need to know."

"Really? What do you know?"

"That all he knows is what he did, not why he did it."

"You don't believe that stuff about your sending his frozen children to the moons of Jupiter?"

"I think the evidence found in his room may answer too many obvious questions in too obvious a way. Do you remember what Orwell's hero perceived in *1984*? 'The best books are the ones that tell you what you know already.' That includes textbooks on assassins; according to the psychologists, they're all alike. But that's not the only reason Abdul Ahmed Jackson doesn't count. If he wasn't a homicidal delusionary, as his diary and all other clues found in his hideout so plainly suggest, then the next possibility is that he was an agent acting for others. In which case he would never be told whom he was working for or the true reason for the murder he was commissioned to commit."

"In either case, he tried to kill you once, so it's possible he might try again."

Mallory's eyes changed expression. "What makes you think," he asked, "that he was trying to kill *me?*"

Macalaster was stunned. He said, "Why else would he come at you with a gun?"

"He didn't come at me with a gun," Mallory said. "He came at Susan, and he killed her. She was the target. Do you really think a man who behaved as efficiently as he did—like an automaton, as you put it—would shoot the wrong person? He killed Susan with a brain shot and put five more bullets into her body before she could fall down. While this happened, I was standing less than two feet away from her. He had all the time in the world to blow out my brains with one of the fourteen live rounds of ammunition remaining in the magazine of his pistol. Nobody could have stopped him."

"But he tried to kill you by firing through her body when she jumped between you."

"What evidence is there for that assumption? He had a clear shot at me one second after he killed Susan. There was no need to be artistic about it. There was no one to stop him. But he disappeared into a cloud of smoke instead. Why?"

" 'Artistic about it'?" Macalaster said. He was shocked that Mallory could use such a phrase—even think of it—in connection with the experience of seeing the woman he loved shot to death in front of his eyes.

Mallory read Macalaster's reaction and waited a moment for it to pass. Then he repeated his question. "Why didn't he shoot me? He had time, he had ammunition, and God knows he had the nerve."

"How would I know?" Macalaster said. "Maybe he just lost his head. Maybe he killed the wrong person, then froze."

"Automatons don't lose their heads," Mallory replied. "Assassinations take a long time to plan; the killer may miss, but there is no such thing as a target of opportunity. His job is to hit the primary target; nothing else matters. Study the tapes again. What happened was not an attempt on my life. It was a warning from people who know that they aren't strong enough to kill me and still get what they want."

"Nameless people?"

"So far."

"Like the Eye of Gaza?"

"That makes no sense whatsoever. The Eye of Gaza wants Lockwood punished for the murder of Ibn Awad. I'm the fellow who promised that justice would be done. Why would they come after me, especially moments after I announced I was going to throw Lockwood out of the presidency and investigate the Ibn Awad case? You're not asking the right questions."

"All right, what is the right question, besides 'Why?' "

"Try 'Who profits?' "

"You actually think this has something to do with your promise to prosecute the Ibn Awad case?"

"I think it's a respectable hypothesis," Mallory said.

"You're asking me to think the unthinkable," Macalaster said. His instincts and experience told him that he was listening to nonsense, but everything Mallory had ever told him in the past had turned out to be true, and some of those things had also sounded strange on first hearing. He believed in hidden truths; exposing them had been his life's work.

Mallory said, "What's so unthinkable about it?"

"Correct me if I'm wrong, but aren't you asking me to believe that Lockwood is behind what happened?"

"No, of course not," Mallory said. "But politics makes strange bedfellows."

"All right, I'll accept the hypothesis if you can give me just one fact to support it."

Mallory's stare was unwavering. "All I can do is indicate a direction in which you might go," he said. "One of the people we haven't been able to talk to is Horace Hubbard. Do you know him?"

"No. I've seen him around town, that's all."

"He seems to have vanished. So has his friend Rose MacKenzie. Even Jack Philindros doesn't know where Horace has gone—or so he says. According to Jack, Horace retired from the FIS last November—on the day before the election, oddly enough. Some say he's on a special mission for the White House."

"How can he be on a special mission if he retired?"

"Good question," Mallory said. "But don't ask me; ask someone who's in a position to know."

"Fine, I'll do that," Macalaster said.

"Good. You might do better than we have."

Macalaster said, "Mr. President, I have to be frank with you. I'm having trouble getting my mind around what you've been telling me."

"I'm not surprised to hear that," Mallory replied. "Nothing makes a man sound crazier than to describe what crazy people are trying to do to him."

Macalaster became aware that his time was up. Someone came into the room behind him and caught Mallory's eye. He nodded, his first physical movement of the interview, and rose from his chair. To Macalaster he said, "I'll have to say goodbye for now."

"All right. I'll follow up on all this."

"Good. But beware of false scents. They'll be creating diversions." He picked up a book that had been lying on the table beside his chair. "Do you ever read Goethe?"

"Not lately," Macalaster replied.

"This morning I ran across something in *Elective Affinities* that seemed to apply to things to come," Mallory said. "I've marked the place; bear the words in mind as events go along."

He handed the book to Macalaster. It was a nineteenth-century volume, bound in limp leather, printed on the thinnest rag paper, with a red ribbon sewn into the binding as a bookmark, a pleasure to hold and smell. Macalaster opened it at the bookmark as if to read the passage.

"No, take it with you; leave it in the car," Mallory said. "I'd make you a present of it, but I know you wouldn't accept." He seemed tired; it was the first time Macalaster had ever noticed any sign of this in him.

Wiggins and Lucy were waiting for him just outside the front door. In the car, Macalaster read the passage Mallory had marked with neat penciled chevrons: "Everything seems to be following its usual course because even in terrible moments, when everything is at stake, people go on living as if nothing were happening."

Just like Mallory, Macalaster thought.

18

That night Lockwood went on television. By this time Congress was in an uproar and the news media had had time to create an atmosphere of almost hysterical expectation inside the Beltway. According to a public opinion sample of the remainder of the United States, only eight percent of the respondents were "very interested" in the issue of the stolen election. Sixty-two percent were "somewhat interested." The rest "didn't know." Fifty-eight percent thought that vote-stealing was a common practice of all political parties, with only eleven percent doubting that this was so, and the rest having no opinion.

On camera in the Oval Office, Lockwood was his usual self, rumpled and honest. As one commentator said fondly, he looked as though he had placed the suit he was going to wear on television under the mattress the night before to make sure it was properly wrinkled. This Lincolnian touch, devised by himself long before he fell into the hands of image makers, was intended to create a contrast to his eloquence. Unlike Lincoln's nearly inaudible twang, Lockwood's voice was deep and strong, almost barking, and even on television he let it loose, having learned that any attempt to tone it down made him sound, as he said, "like Lyndon caught in the chicken coop."

"As every American must know by now," Lockwood said with only a terse "Good evening, my fellow Americans" as preamble, "Mr. Franklin Mallory called on me here in the White House in the early morning hours of January twentieth and told me that he believes that last November's election was stolen from him and consequently he is the rightful President of the United States.

"I think he is wrong on both counts. Otherwise I would never have taken the oath as President. Nevertheless, there is not the slightest doubt in my mind that this is former President Mallory's sincere conviction. Clearly it would be wrong for me to believe these shocking charges on the basis of his word alone, but it would be just as wrong to reject them simply because I think he is mistaken. He has produced evidence which is persuasive to him, but he is an interested party. I am also an interested party. In the end, the only party whose interest counts is the American people. Even if my opponent is wrong and I have been duly elected President, as I believe to be the case, I do not have the authority to decide this question. Still less do I possess any such authority if, as former President Mallory charges, I was not elected by a true plurality.

"Under the Constitution, only Congress has the power to decide questions of presidential tenure, and believing as I do that Congress embodies the collective wisdom of the American people, I am content that it should investigate this matter down to the last particle of evidence and decide whether the people elected Franklin Mallory or myself. If the answer is Mallory, I will relinquish the presidency. If it is Lockwood, I will remain where the people have put me. I ask that the Congress act on this supremely urgent and important matter with the least possible delay consistent with a just outcome. God preserve the United States of America."

After the cameras were turned off, White House staffers standing along the walls broke into applause. Some of the network crew joined in. A strong-voiced floor man called out, "That was damn near as good as the Gettysburg Address, Mr. President. Hang in there!"

All this drew no smile or rejoinder from a brooding Lockwood. Standing quietly with the others, Julian Hubbard offered neither comment nor advice, although while his chief was speaking he had had a brilliant idea—one so brilliant, in fact, that he believed it might save the presidency.

II

1

By the time Lockwood became President, advances in computer technology had made it possible to communicate with any point on earth, and with many places elsewhere in the solar system, with such rapidity that it became necessary to divide the second, formerly the smallest measurement of time that had any meaning in human thought, into ever-smaller fragments—the microsecond, the millisecond, and then the nanosecond, which is to a second what a second is to thirty years. At the same time, the bottomless but unpredictable appetite of the news media for data created a situation in which the government, like a mother with a finicky child or a lonely person with a difficult cat, gave up its own life in order to devote itself to tempting the creature to eat the treats that it set before it. Among other benefits to mankind, this combination of developments rendered obsolete the secrecy in which governments had always operated. Sharing a secret with anyone, even a close associate, became an act of folly because no matter how much you trusted your confidant, he was almost certain to leak it to a journalist. If he did not betray you, your enemies, foreign or domestic, would find a way to do so.

Speaking of confidential matters over the telephone or by means of fax or computer became unthinkable. Every telephone, every power outlet, every visitor's tie clip was a potential listening device. The virtual certainty of being found out and misunderstood, no matter what precautions rulers and their chamberlains took, slowed the inner business of politics to a pace not much faster than the one that applied in the time of Charlemagne. People like Julian committed no vital communication to writing, even in code. They spoke to each other in whispers, face to face, in the open air, in the most remote locations possible.

This was the reason why Julian invited a friend of his from Yale days, Archimedes Hammett, to go cross-country skiing with him on the weekend after Lockwood's inauguration, at the Harbor, as the Hubbards called their country place in the Berkshire Hills of western Massachusetts. This isolated eighteenth-century farmhouse, surrounded by hundreds of acres of thick forest, was the last place in North America where Julian could be fairly certain of privacy. Not even Mallory or the Japanese could bug every tree.

Privacy was essential because Hammett was even more of a media figure than Julian. The role assigned to him by network bureau chiefs was Man of Conscience. Since his graduation from Yale Law School, he had won fame as a defender of terrorists and others who had been swept over the brink of conscience by the excesses of capitalism. The fact that his courtroom strategy was usually designed with propaganda rather than acquittal in mind had only improved his reputation. The target of his argument was not the jury; it was the news industry. Most of his clients, having claimed responsibility for premeditated murder, expected to be sentenced to death or life imprisonment, and wanted nothing more than to be recognized as martyrs.

Hammett argued that whatever the crimes his oppressed clients had committed, including the wanton murder of other innocents like themselves, they had a moral warrant to act as they did. "Only the victims of society have a right to take life, or give it, in the cause of social justice," he had said. Although he never accepted money for defending a criminal case, he had earned large amounts as a public speaker and benefited from a steady flow of contributions to The Fund for Justice, a charitable foundation he had established to pay the costs of defending his penniless clients.

Never married, Hammett lived alone in apparent celibacy in the style of the last surviving monk of some unimaginably virtuous but now vanished religious order. He did good in the world, studying continually, eating nothing but organic vegetables and whole-grain bread and dressing in the same jeans and workshirts he had worn as an undergraduate. His Yale salary easily covered the expenses of the extremely simple life he led. He dwelled in an apartment on a back street in New Haven that was antiseptically clean but otherwise not much more luxurious than the hideout of Abdul Ahmed Jackson, whom he would almost certainly defend if he was ever arrested.

Hammett and Julian had met in the 1960s at Yale; Hammett was a class ahead of Julian, who admired him above all other human beings, including Lockwood. This was not because they came from similar backgrounds. Hammett's seemingly patrician name and Old Blue credentials were deceptive. He had gone through Yale and its law school on full financial aid. His grandfather, a descendant of Spartans from the Mesa Mani, a wild and impoverished region of mountains on the extreme southern tip of the Peloponnesus, had emigrated to the United States after the Balkan Wars of 1912–13. His Greek name, an ancient one, was Gika Mavromikháli, but he had been renamed George Hammett by a U.S.

immigration official because he had arrived without papers and, being illiterate, could not write out Mavromikháli, even in Greek letters. When the immigration officer bullied him, Gika hawked out the Greek word for "fuck": *"Gamoto!"* The stupid fellow heard this as "Hammett" and wrote it down as the newcomer's American surname. Gika was willing to accept this gift of a new official identity because he was on the run from the Turkish secret service as a result of his patriotic activities during the war in Serbia and Macedonia, in which, as a sniper working behind the line of the enemy's retreat, he had killed a large number of Turks of all sexes and ages. Destroying one's enemy from long range while lying in a place of concealment was the traditional Maniáte way of fighting.

Setting up the meeting with Hammett required ingenuity. Julian could not, especially now, make sensitive calls from the White House or even from his home telephones. Nor could he risk using a pay phone; he was too recognizable.

Fortunately, Julian's wife, Emily, a free-lance writer, picked him up from work that evening, and he was able to use the phone in her rattletrap car while she dashed in to a Safeway to buy groceries for their supper; he was home for a meal so infrequently that she did not keep solid food in the refrigerator.

Because there was need for secrecy, Julian did not call Hammett directly, but instead dialed a number in Stamford, Connecticut. It was answered on the second ring by another Yale man, who sometimes, when it was wiser for the two men not to talk to each other over an open line, acted as a cutout between Julian and Hammett. Julian had never made a more sensitive call to Hammett than this one.

To let the go-between know that this was the case, he did not identify himself by name but used a code phrase known only to a very small circle of men. "What," asked Julian without preamble, "did Trelawny snatch from the funeral pyre at Viareggio?"

The go-between replied, "Shelley's heart."

These words referred to the famous romantic gesture of Percy Bysshe Shelley's friend, Edward John Trelawny (1792–1881), who burned the drowned poet's body as Shelley had wished, with the rites accorded to a hero of ancient Greece, and, by his own account, reached into the raging fire to recover the heart. The phrases were the secret greeting and response of the Shelley Society, the most obscure of Yale's many private clubs. Although two of its members had served as president of Yale, and at least one as President of the United States, neither the university nor the U.S. government had any inkling that the Shelley Society existed. Its motto and purpose were taken from Percy Bysshe Shelley's fiery pamphlet *A Defence of Poetry:*

> A man, to be greatly good, must imagine intensely and comprehensively; he must put himself in the place of another and of many others; the pains and pleasures of his species must become his own.

To this was added the key passage from another of Shelley's political works, *A Philosophical View of Reform:*

> Equality of possessions must be the last result of the utmost refinements of civilization . . . toward which it is our duty to tend.

The first passage was known within the society as the Shelley Definition, or more often simply the Definition, the second as the Duty. Living by these two plain but noble precepts was regarded as every member's first purpose in life. The purpose of the Shelley Society was, and always had been, to force what Shelley had called "the moral progress of politics"— American politics above all, but the world political order as well. *A Defence of Poetry* was written in 1821. The Shelley Society was established ninety-eight years later by Yale men who had come back from the First World War disillusioned by the slaughter in the trenches, alienated from the privileged class to which they belonged, and determined to make the world a better place, no matter by what methods. On being inducted into the society they swore to work toward the time when justice for all finally became a reality. In Shelleyan parlance, this moment in the future was called the Year Zed. All Shelleyan meetings began and ended with the toast "To the Year Zed!" The British pronunciation of the letter Z had become part of the ritual because one of the society's founders had served in the Royal Flying Corps.

To outsiders, if an outsider could have known anything about it, such ritual might have seemed silly. There was nothing silly about it in the mind of any Shelleyan; to the last man they believed that the Year Z would come, and that they would will it into being by doing good by stealth. Shelleyans, like the Poet himself, had always been renegade sons of the Establishment; to leaven the society's patrician character and keep it in touch with the real world, a proletarian like Archimedes Hammett was chosen every fifth year. That was the theory; in practice the poor boys tended to be greater snobs than the rich ones. Nevertheless, the Shelley Society was profoundly subversive in terms of family, class, church, and country, not to mention the ideas then underlying a Yale education.

Paradoxically, it was certainly the most exclusive club to which an Old Blue could belong.

The paradox did not end there. Only one member was taken in, as a junior, from each class, and again in theory, a member knew the identities of just two other Shelleyans: the man who tapped him and the man he himself tapped the following year, with the advice and approval of his sponsor. In reality, everyone knew everyone, but members never communicated with each other directly. Instead, they always went through another member of their own cell, even with the simplest messages and requests. This cumbersome way of doing things preserved the illusion of impenetrable secrecy while giving every Shelleyan access to every other member.

There were no dues or meetings or regular communications; no written register of Shelleyans existed. The only spoken rule of membership was that every Shelleyan must grant any favor or service asked of him by any other Shelleyan "in the name of the Poet." If a man could not do the favor or perform the service himself, then he must find another Shelleyan who could. This rule was absolute. Once requested, no such favor or service could ever be left undone.

Shelleyans, even when known to one another by their real names, were addressed by the last two digits of their class year. Julian was Seven-Oh, Hammett Six-Nine, the man in Stamford whom Julian had called on the telephone, Seven-One.

"How can I help you?" asked Seven-One.

Julian said, "I want to get hold of Six-Nine to invite him to a party this weekend."

"I'll be glad to do that for you," said Seven-One. "Where's the party?"

"In the hills."

This was the Shelleyan term for the Harbor, which many members of the Society had visited. Julian's father had been Two-Six; his half brother, Horace, was Five-Five.

Julian continued, "My plan is to pick him up around eleven tonight at his local airport."

"I'll get word to him," said Seven-One.

"Thank you," said Julian, and disconnected.

Then he smiled at his wife, who had appeared with her arms full of groceries just as he was in the act of hanging up.

Emily got into the car and took the wheel. As she backed out of the parking space, tires spinning in the thawed and refrozen remains of the snow, Julian placed a hand on her slim thigh and said, "How would you like to go up to the Harbor this weekend? We can do some cross-country skiing."

She was surprised. "Leave town with all that's happening?" she asked. "Who'll manage the crisis?"

"It can manage itself for a couple of days. Lockwood has already gone to Kentucky to get away from it all."

"Are you talking about just the two of us?" she asked.

"Would you rather not go?"

They were sitting close together, especially because he was so large and the car, a Fiat, was so small. Emily's braid—she wore her hair long to please him—was caught beneath the collar of her coat. Gently he pulled it free and lifted it to his nostrils. It had a lovely, sweet weight to it, like one of her breasts, and smelled of health-store shampoo and fresh air.

"Well?"

"I'd love to go," Emily said. "It should be beautiful in the woods with all this snow."

"Then we'll fly up tonight," Julian said.

Emily maneuvered the car into traffic. Looking at him in the rearview mirror, she said, "You haven't answered my question."

"Ah, so I haven't," Julian said. "Actually, I *have* asked someone to join us. Archimedes Hammett."

"*Hammett?*"

Emily put on the brakes. The car slid into the curbstone with a thump that activated the air bag. Horns blew; taxis scattered. Emily's oversize horn-rim glasses, one bow mended with Scotch tape, were knocked askew by the inflated balloon.

"Whoopsie!" she said. Her hands dropped limply from the steering wheel; she smiled in goofy embarrassment.

Julian decided to regard the smile as a gesture of forgiveness. He said, "How I love you, Mouse."

A large tear, magnified by the lens of her glasses, appeared in Emily's eye, then rolled down her cheek. Julian wiped it away with a knuckle, realizing, with an intensity that flooded his entire being with all the emotion he had repressed over the days just past, that he did love this woman who was too young for him, and too beautiful and too innocent. And though he fought against it, he thought about Mallory, too, and about what had happened to Susan Grant. How could any man bear such a loss?

Emily glared at him. "*Hammett*," she said. "How could you?"

2

That night about ten, Julian and Emily took off from National Airport in Julian's airplane, an aged two-engine, six-passenger Beechcraft. He had learned to fly as a Navy pilot during the Vietnam War, and the plane was one of his greatest pleasures. Emily was afraid of flying and hated the noise of the engines and the smelly, overheated atmosphere in the cabin, but she understood that he expected her to find it romantic, so she did her best to hide her terror. When they were courting, he had flown her in this plane to a fishing cabin in Labrador, to a party in France, to beaches in the Caribbean.

A few moments after takeoff, they broke through the cloud cover above Chesapeake Bay. A lopsided icy moon shone brightly off to the right. On the other side of the plane, Venus glowed.

"Wonderful sky," Julian said.

"What was the sky like in Vietnam?" Emily asked.

He laughed in surprise. "Why?"

"I always think about you in Vietnam when we're flying."

"Do you, Mouse? Actually, I didn't see much of it. We flew by instruments."

"There's something else I wonder," Emily said. "What made you go to war? Nobody else went."

"They didn't?"

"Not people we knew. How many Yale men were killed in Vietnam?"

"I have no idea."

"The exact number is fourteen," Emily said. "And twelve from Harvard. I read that in a book by a Republican."

Julian said, "That was the reason I went."

The real reason, of course, was the Shelley Definition. How could he possibly have put himself in the place of another and of many others and let the pains and pleasures of his species become his own if he did not see the war through his own eyes and understand its evil through his own deeds? But he could not tell Emily this; no wife, no woman of any kind, had ever been told about the Shelley Society, and in his heart he did not believe that any woman could understand war.

The plane was now on automatic pilot, headed for the suffused glow of a city. Baltimore? Emily had no sense of direction even when she was on the ground. Julian put his seat back and turned to face her. "What made you think about Vietnam all of a sudden?" he asked.

"I told you, it's not so all of a sudden," she replied. "Every time I wake up before you do I look at your scars and wonder how you got them."

His Phantom fighter-bomber had been shot down by enemy ground fire and he had nearly died; the marks of this experience, wounds and burns, were all over his body.

"You don't like the scars?"

"I hate them. You don't deserve them."

"I wouldn't be too sure about that," Julian replied.

At the time, most people he knew thought that he deserved whatever he got in Vietnam. His decision to join the Navy had lost him the revolutionary (Vassar '70) who loved him, though not forever. After he came home from the war she became his first wife and the mother of his two children.

"What do you mean, I shouldn't be too sure?" Emily said. "Sure of what?"

"I killed a lot of people."

"Weren't they trying to kill you, too?"

"Yes. With spears. Let me tell you something I've never told anyone before. . . ."

His words trailed off. She took his hand; it remained inert. She kissed it; it smelled of the machine he had been flying.

Julian said, "On the day I crashed into the sea, I was glad to be shot down. I was sure I was going to die, and all I could think was 'Good for you!'"

"Good for who?"

"The people who shot me down."

"You *wanted* to die? That's why you went?"

"It seemed appropriate." In the eerie green glow of the instrument panel, immobilized by old emotions, he looked like the dead man he had wanted to be.

For a moment, Emily could think of nothing to say in return. She understood what Julian meant, but the idea made no sense to her. Because of the difference in their ages, neither had ever really understood the way the other thought or felt.

She said, "You thought that the enemy was virtuous?"

"Compared to us? Yes. What else would I think?"

"But the Viet Cong did horrible things," she said. "The people who shot you down could have been the ones who massacred children, raped women, disemboweled village elders, couldn't they? Such things happened in Vietnam."

"How do you know that? From more Republican books?"

"Don't condescend to me, Julian. You know it's true."

Julian said, "I'm not sure I do know that. But if such things were done by the V.C., there was always a political rationale. Always."

His features were once again in repose. "There was a *political rationale*?" Emily said. "That explains everything?"

Julian had no chance to answer before the radio emitted some incomprehensible message from air traffic control that required him to respond. But for Julian, Emily realized, it *did* explain everything.

3

After Julian parked the Beechcraft near the passenger terminal in New Haven, Emily looked out the window and saw Archimedes Hammett walking across the tarmac with a knapsack on his back and a picnic cooler in his hand. Under a 1960s-style duffel coat with ropes for buttonholes, he wore his trademark chambray shirt and dungarees.

Emily said, "Shit."

Julian switched off one of the engines. As the propeller vibrated to a stop, he said, "Come on, Mouse."

Emily turned her face away. "Don't call me Mouse," she said.

She climbed into the backseat and feigned sleep for the remainder of the flight. After landing in Pittsfield and driving over snowy roads in a rented car, they arrived at the Harbor around midnight. The caretaker had turned up the heat and lit a fire of maple logs in the library fireplace. Emily put Hammett in a room at the opposite end of the house from the one where she and Julian would sleep. Then she returned to the library, where Julian was sitting in front of the fire, drinking the fifteen-year-old single-malt Scotch whisky she had given him for Christmas.

Holding up the glass, he said, "Want some? It's whisky."

"I can smell," Emily said. "No. I'm going to bed."

He looked at her. "You *are* mad at me."

She made no reply, but when he came to bed, she attacked. When he tried to slow her down she straddled him and said, "No, now."

They had not made love for weeks. Now, more quickly than either of them could ever remember its happening, she uttered a long female cry, half groan, half howl, then collapsed, gasping, on his chest. In the ensuing silence, Julian could hear the wind moaning in the eaves and the nearly human noises of the shifting timbers. His father, the seventh generation of Hubbards born in this house, had said that the Harbor "creaked its bones" when the winter wind blew. All the rooms were called after ancestors; they had slept in "Fanny," named for Fanny Harding de Saint-Christophe, a name later Englished as Christopher, who had married a Hubbard as her second husband sometime around the French and Indian Wars.

Julian cupped Emily's cheek in his hand, thinking to tell her this, but he realized she was weeping, so instead of speaking, he turned her over and made love to her again. Her slight body, always new to him, surprised him into a shout of pleasure and love. Or, as he thought when he was able to think again, the two made one.

They were awakened just after first light by bursts of static and loud music as Archimedes Hammett, a news addict, fiddled with the eight-band radio that he carried with him wherever he went. Finally he found the all-news station he was looking for and adjusted the volume downward.

Julian said, "Archimedes must be paying us back for last night. I hope he wasn't too shocked."

Julian humorously pretended to believe that the reclusive Hammett was a virgin. Emily's womanly instincts told her that this joke might well be the reality. Hammett suffered from a pathological fear of germs and infection. He would not shake hands, even with an old friend like Julian. He never touched money or mail but did all his banking and correspondence by computer. He carried an atomizer of disinfectant in his pocket and sprayed it on telephones and toilet seats when he had to make a call or relieve himself while away from home. A whiff of tobacco smoke in the street or the dust from a construction site sent him into a near-panic. For his weekend with the Hubbards he had brought his own sheets, his own towels and hospital soap, and, in the picnic cooler, even his own food. Everything he ate or drank, including water, came from a farm in the Connecticut Valley that was operated on strict organic principles by two female ecolawyers, former students of his who had a practice in Hartford. When he was on the road lecturing or defending a client for longer than a day or two, this couple sent him his daily rations, cooled by blue ice, via overnight mail.

Up close, Hammett looked to Emily like a Richard Avedon photograph of Muammar Qaddafi. He was a short, scrawny person with a large Old World nose and burning dark eyes. For breakfast he ate an orange and a bowl of homemade granola and drank a cup of herbal tea made with bottled water from the organic farm. He used dishes he had brought with him—plastic, because paper plates contained microscopic pits and fissures in which bacteria might lurk. All this Emily knew from earlier encounters. "Hammett," she said, without preamble, "how old were your grandparents when they died?"

Warily, for these were almost the first words she had spoken to him and he knew how she felt about him, he replied, "They were in their nineties."

Emily said, "Funny they lasted so long when you think of the stuff they must have eaten as kids. No refrigerators in Macedonia."

"The Peloponnesus," Hammett said firmly.

"Sorry. But the fact remains."

"Actually, the diet was very healthy. Low fat all the way. Olives, bread, wild herbs, vinegar, a little wine. Meat only at Easter. They fasted the rest of the year. Because the Turks had cut down all the trees, they had to bring wood up into the mountains on donkeys, hundreds of donkeys loaded with twigs to roast the lamb. Sometimes the Turks would attack the donkey train. Break their legs, shove them over the cliff."

"Oh. Well, that certainly explains the longevity. They always had something to look forward to."

"What?"

"The paschal lamb."

"You can make a joke of it," said Hammett, "but that egg you're eating will kill you."

"I know—lots of cholesterol."

"That's just the tip of the iceberg. They put chemicals and hormones in the hen's food—in the water, in the grit, in everything it touches—so the chicken can't escape having its body converted into a mechanism for profit."

"Wow," Emily said, mopping up the yolk with a piece of toast. "Doesn't sound like the hen is going to live forever. Did you speak Greek at home?"

Hammett was reluctant to answer; he hated trivia and personal questions. Finally he said, "Yes, always."

"Can you still speak it?"

"Yes, but only the Maniátes can understand me."

"The who?"

"My grandfather's people."

Hammett told her no more. Idle conversation annoyed him, and of course he realized that Emily was teasing him. He looked around the kitchen, as if fixing the location of the exits in his mind.

Before Emily could ask another question, Julian interrupted. "Emily, my dear," he said, "why don't you wax the skis? I'll take Archimedes for a ride on the snowmobile and make a trail."

This made sense. Skiing through the woods was easier on a trail that had been packed down by the treads of a snowmobile.

"Okay," Emily said, "but please don't be the whole morning about it. It's too nice to stay in."

Sunlight, reflecting off the enormous snowdrifts that lay around the house, burst through the kitchen windows. Emily brought the skis and wax kit out of the cellar while Julian got out the snowmobile, checked the gas and oil in his methodical way, and started it up. Wearing a red knitted cap that made her scalp itch, she waited inside until he put it in motion. She hated this machine, which smelled even worse than Julian's airplane and made a noise so deafening that it blotted out not just hearing but all other senses as well. You couldn't see or feel your own flesh as it roared through the woods, generating a freezing wind in the face, bucking like a mechanical bull, and threatening to plunge over a hidden cliff at any moment. She was amazed that Hammett, who lived in fear of breaking his skin, let alone his bones, got on behind Julian and let himself be driven through the trees at thirty miles an hour.

As soon as the men were out of sight, she took the temperature of the snow with the wax-smeared thermometer from the kit, chose the right wax for the temperature and snow condition, and began to apply it to the narrow skis. Julian's, of course, were immensely long; they had to be made to order and were so expensive that he and Horace, who was exactly the same height as his younger brother, frugally shared the single pair. Despite the sun, it was bitter cold, so that when Emily breathed deeply, the air seemed to contain invisible shards of ice that produced a slight pain under the breastbone, as if she had swallowed a bite of sherbet too rapidly. This weather and the beautiful snowbound wilderness all around her made her happy.

She finished waxing Julian's skis and started working on her own. Somewhere on the mountain, miles away probably, the snowmobile stopped whining as Julian throttled down and parked. After a few moments, the engine started again, but she could tell that the machine was not moving. Because the wind blew in her direction and the mountain itself acted like an amphitheater, causing sound to rebound into the valley, she could distinctly hear the irritating *pop-pop* of the idling engine.

She shivered—not from the cold, from a sudden chill of jealousy. Julian and Archimedes Hammett must be having the conversation that was the real reason for this weekend at the Harbor. She pictured them standing close together in the snow, with the frosted hemlocks and the skeletal maples all around them, talking politics. Even in the woods, in the middle of nowhere, Julian had left the damn thing running in case anyone tried to overhear. Who would the eavesdroppers *be* out here in the middle of nowhere—the ghosts of the Mahicans from whom the Hubbards had bought these woods almost exactly four centuries ago for a barrel of ale, a keg of nails, five hatchets, and £15? What could he and Archimedes have to say to each other that made them so conspiratorial? Or was it just male behavior that meant nothing at all, like most of the things men did?

Speaking to herself again, she said, "I'm tired of waiting." Although there was a strict rule, laid down by the Hubbard males, against skiing alone, she put on her skis and started off, following the track of the snowmobile with a rhythmic sliding stride that became easy as soon as she broke a sweat and the exercise loosened the muscles that had been drawn tight by a life without lovemaking.

4

After switching off the snowmobile's engine, Julian said, "Listen."

"To what?" Hammett asked.

"Just listen."

Wind soughed among the treetops, a haunting, premusical sound. A narrow brook, rising from a spring a little higher up the rocky mountainside, rushed downhill beneath the brittle crust of ice that covered its surface. In the remote distance a dog barked; the mountain caught the sound and threw it back to the animal. The dog barked back at itself. The wind-billowed snow was marked by the tracks of rabbits and birds and the dimples made by snow blown from the trees, and Julian knew that they would not have to go far from this path before finding the imprint of wing feathers in the snow where an owl had made a kill. Above all, it was clean and virginal.

"This should be antiseptic enough even for you," Julian said.

"Antiseptic? I don't get it." Hammett was pretending not to understand what Julian meant, as he usually did when reference was made to his eccentricities.

Throwing back his head, Julian read the Lucite thermometer that dangled from the zipper of his parka. "It's four below zero without the windchill factor," he said. "Germs can't live in cold like this."

Hammett pounced on this boast. "That's what you think. Four below zero means nothing to a virus. They live on asteroids at absolute zero."

"There goes another family story," Julian said. "Way before the American Revolution, the Mahicans caught smallpox. One of my female ancestors set up a quarantine camp for them right near where we're standing. They died like flies until the ground froze, then the disease went away."

"The weather had nothing to do with it."

"Thanks to you, I know that now, Archimedes. My cousin and I found the smallpox burial ground when I was a kid, in a sort of rock chamber under the roots of a maple. Skulls and bones. We're standing on it right now."

"What cousin was that?"

"Paul Christopher," said Julian, naming a first cousin once removed who had been an American intelligence agent during the Cold War. He had spent years in prison after turning up in Communist China under mysterious circumstances.

"Ah, yes," Hammett said in instantaneous recognition; he kept a mental directory of all enemies of the Cause, past, present, and potential, and Christopher's name had been in the newspapers. "The poet-spy, the prisoner of Mao. Someone told me he had a daughter who's just like him."

Coming from anyone else, this observation might have been nothing more than small talk. Hammett, however, had no small talk; if he asked this question, it was because he had some political reason to be interested in Christopher's daughter. Julian, who fiercely protected his family from all outsiders, even other Shelleyans, did not wish to supply information about the Christophers.

"*Is* there a daughter?" Hammett insisted. "What's her name?"

"Zarah, with a Z."

It was clear even to Hammett that there was no point in asking further questions about Zarah Christopher; besides, the subject did not really interest him. After a brief pause he asked a question whose answer did interest him. "So, Julian," he said. "How much of Mallory's case against you people is factual?"

Julian said, "All of it, essentially."

There was no need to swear Hammett to secrecy; everything they had ever said to each other had been said in secrecy.

"How did this happen?"

"Five-Five and his girlfriend used the FIS computers to steal the election."

Hammett pursed his lips, then nodded. He said, "Under whose orders was this operation carried out?"

"There were no orders. They acted on my suggestion after Five-Five told me it was possible."

"Lockwood wasn't aware of what was going on?"

"I told him nothing. Nobody else involved had the access to tell him anything. My assumption is that he knows nothing for certain even now. Believe it or not, he sincerely believed he'd won a squeaker until Mallory showed up with his evidence last week."

"That's in character," Hammett said. "Anyone else involved?"

"Philindros may have acquiesced, but I'm not sure of that."

"Philindros? He is Mallory's man. Why would *he* acquiesce?"

"We didn't do what we did just to win the election," Julian said. "More was at stake. It was the Ibn Awad matter that triggered everything."

Hammett blinked. This was something he had not known. He said, "Explain that, please."

"Lockwood ordered Philindros to assassinate Ibn Awad."

"You mean he winked at Philindros and Philindros pulled the trigger."

"No, that's not the way it's done anymore. Lockwood uttered an unequivocal verbal order in my presence. Philindros insisted on it."

"You were the only witness?"

"Yes. But Philindros has the conversation on tape."

"You let that happen?"

"We didn't frisk him to see if he was wired. Let me finish. According to our intelligence, which we have no reason to question, Mallory has a copy of the tape in his possession."

"Philindros gave it to him?"

"Maybe, but I doubt it. Mallory has a lot of sympathizers in the FIS."

"And you figured Mallory would use this tape to send all of you to prison if he was elected."

Julian said, "That's what he promised to do on the Patrick Graham show three days before Election Day. But it was more than that. If he had that tape, Mallory had the means to destroy the Cause in this country. Forever. Do you disagree?"

Hammett said, "No, I don't disagree. You did the right thing. Getting caught was the mistake. So what do you want me to do? Defend Lockwood?"

"I thought of that," Julian said. "But no; he has to be acquitted, and that's not your specialty. I want the President to appoint you Chief Justice of the United States."

Hammett stepped back a pace and gazed for a long moment at the track the snowmobile had left behind it through the woods. This time his surprise was genuine. Julian started to speak again, but Hammett held up a mittened hand to cut him off. "Don't tell me why," he said. "I understand the reason, but I don't want to hear it from you."

"All right," Julian said. "But will you do it?"

"On what basis are you asking that question?"

"In the name of the Poet."

Hammett said, "Then I'm in no position to refuse." He looked down the trail again. "Here comes your wife," he said.

Hammett had keen eyesight. Even on so crystalline a morning, Julian had to squint to see Emily, who was far down the trail among the trees. He waved. Emily saw the movement, paused, took off her bright red hat, and waved back. He heard her laugh.

To Hammett he said, "I'll speak to the President on Monday."

Hammett nodded, then cleared his throat several times before deciding not to speak. Julian realized that his friend was in the grip of an emotion. He smiled down on him benevolently, then waved again at Emily, who was coming up the trail like a champion.

5

On Monday morning, in the Oval Office, Lockwood said, "Archimedes *Hammett*? For Chief Justice of the United States? What the hell's the matter with you, Julian?"

"Nothing as far as I know, Mr. President."

"Forget it. Next subject."

Julian held Lockwood's eyes. "Whatever you wish," he said. "But can I explain my reasoning first? It won't take long."

With a wave of the hand, Lockwood gave him permission to continue.

Julian said, "In the paragraph on impeachment trials, the Constitution says—these are the exact words—'When the President of the United States is tried, the Chief Justice shall preside.' It says nothing about a substitute. Ergo, if there is no Chief Justice, there can be no trial."

Lockwood was suddenly alert. "Where does that 'ergo' come from?"

"From the Constitution."

"Right. I heard that the first time. But who says no Chief Justice, no trial? What legal authority are you quoting on that?"

"Hammett believes it's a defensible legal position."

"Hammett's a propagandist. He's never won a case in court in his life."

"Blackstone agrees we could make a case."

"Blackstone! Jesus, boy, Carlisle wants to hand the country over to the Joint Chiefs of Staff. Those twelfth-century minds Mallory put on the Supreme Court will knock this idea in the head without blinking a goddamn eye."

"I don't see how. They're supposed to interpret the Constitution literally. This is as literal as you can get."

"They won't give a hoot about that when the presidency is in the balance," Lockwood said. "They're not serious about that crap. We'll have Bobby Poole presiding over the impeachment trial. Son of a bitch will sit up there tying himself a royal coachman or a gray hackle while the rest of the fishing expedition fries me up in bacon grease."

"Not while the nomination process is going on."

Lockwood's intercom buzzed. He ignored it. It sounded again, insistently. In his irritation with Julian, he turned on the speakerphone and shouted, "Damnit, Jeannie, stop buzzing me!"

Jean McHenry's calm voice replied, "It's Senator Clark, Mr. President. He says it's urgent. On line one."

Lockwood said, "I just spent the weekend on the phone with him."

Jean repeated, "He says it's urgent."

Lockwood uttered a wordless roar of exasperation, closed his eyes for a moment, then pressed another button. "Sam," he said in a normal tone. "What can I do for you?"

Clark's rasping voice came through the speaker. "The Speaker of the House just called," he said. "According to him, Mallory's whips have got somewhere around a hundred and fifty members of the House to agree to sign a letter asking you to invoke the Twenty-fifth Amendment and step aside until the question of who was elected is decided."

"That ain't exactly a majority of the House."

"You're right. But it's a serious number. And as you know, nobody's got a majority in the Senate."

"We have, as long as the Vice President presides."

"And as long as we can get our fifty people together the way Franklin Mallory will hold his together. And he will, because if they win this one they'll have *their* Vice President in the chair. Mr. President, this is pretty serious."

"It's chicken scratch for the goddamn media."

"They're talking about delivering the letter to the White House en masse. All two hundred and fifty of them."

"Let 'em come," Lockwood said. "There's courage in numbers. How come that yellow son of a bitch Attenborough doesn't call me himself about something like this instead of going through you? Is he the Speaker or isn't he?"

"He's the Speaker, all right," Clark said. "But he may be the President pretty soon. If you go, Willy Graves will have to go, and under the law he's next in line."

"Is that what the little back-stabber says? If he wasn't sniffing the ass end of blind ambition, there wouldn't be any damn maneuvers. Tell him I said that. Is he in the same party as me or not?"

Clark said, "You know he is, Mr. President."

"I hope you're right, but I'm keeping an open mind. Are *you* with me, Sam?"

"Always have been, my friend, always will be. But you'd better find a way to slow this juggernaut down."

"I'm trying, goddamnit."

Lockwood switched off the phone and returned his attention to Julian. "Enrico, you were saying?"

Julian took up where he had left off. "I was saying, Mr. President, that announcing the appointment of Archimedes Hammett as Chief Justice of the United States would slow down the impeachment process."

"How?"

"It would divert the attention of the Congress and the whole lobbying apparatus. It would stop the media dead in their tracks."

"True," Lockwood said. "But there are just a few little problems. Hammett isn't qualified, half the country thinks he's the reincarnation of Judas Iscariot, and he's got about as much chance of being confirmed as my dog Rover."

"I'm not so sure about that, sir. He's regarded as one of the most brilliant and innovative legal minds in the country. He's a professor of law at Yale. The other half of the country, the one that counts in Washington, thinks he's the reincarnation of Plato."

"Those people aren't half the country."

Julian said, "They've got more than half the brains and ninety percent of the media. Every lawyer in America who isn't on Mallory's payroll thinks Hammett walks on water. He's got a network of disciples and admirers in the media, in the law, in the universities, in the pressure groups, that will put heat on the Senate to do the right thing and confirm him. His ex-students and their friends control the Bar Association, and he's the only figure in American law who has no traditional party affiliation. He may be a little odd by some standards, but the universal perception is that he's an honest and independent man. He's as clean as a whistle. I don't think he's ever kissed a girl or taken a drink."

"That's some recommendation," Lockwood said. "Ought to make him compassionate as hell. Besides, he has no judicial experience."

"Neither did Felix Frankfurter or Earl Warren."

"They didn't have his enemies."

"Hammett's enemies may be his biggest asset. They'll be so pissed off at the idea of him on the Court that they're bound to make a mistake. If they go too far, he's in. You'd have to make a deal with the Senate on future appointments, but you'll have to do that no matter whose name you send to the Hill. After all, everybody will know you're appointing your own judge in case of impeachment."

Lockwood uttered an explosive laugh. " 'In case of' doesn't come into it; it's going to happen," he said. "Julian, I'm not even sure if this guy is an American in his heart. He's totally unpredictable."

Julian said, "Unpredictable? Who do you think Archimedes Hammett, whatever is in his heart, would rather have sitting where you're sitting—you or Mallory?"

Lockwood did not reply.

"The unpredictability is the most important part of the equation," Julian said. "Hammett is perceived as being incorruptible, committed to principle, the enemy of power and privilege. Not a bad guy to have in your corner."

"You're sure that's where he'd be—in my corner?"

"He'd have nowhere else to go. I've known him as well as I've ever known anyone, for more than thirty years. We roomed together for a semester in college."

"Oh," Lockwood said. "How come I didn't know that before now?"

Julian said, "It was never relevant before now."

Lockwood fell into a silence. Julian watched impassively as the President considered the advantages and disadvantages of appointing a man he believed to be an enemy of democracy as Chief Justice of the United States.

With a grimace of distaste, Lockwood made his decision. "All right," he said. "Ask around. Test the waters."

"Yes, sir," Julian said. "But we'll have to be quick. This isn't something that will keep, Mr. President. Surprise is our best friend."

"I know that, damnit. If it looks like it'll go, we can announce it tomorrow, before I put the fire hoses to Attenborough's crowd. I assume you've already talked to Hammett."

"Yes, sir. He'll accept the nomination if it's offered."

"I'll bet he will," Lockwood said. "But I want you to know, Enrico, that if I do nominate this guy, it'll be because I don't think he can be confirmed. It'll just be a way to gain time."

"Good plan," Julian said. He nodded, as if yielding to superior wisdom, gathered up his papers, and went down the hall to start lining up support for a nomination that was designed to fail.

6

When Ross Macalaster's doorbell rang at 6:05 on Tuesday morning, he assumed that Wiggins and Lucy had come to call. Instead he found Julian Hubbard standing on the steps. A pair of Zeiss binoculars dangled from his neck. Like everything else Julian owned, the glasses were near-antiques, so much used that four fingerprints of shiny steel were worn through the black paint on the barrels.

"I was birding along the canal," Julian said. "Thought I'd drop by."

" 'Birding'?" Macalaster said. "Spot any owls?"

Julian, smiling genially, shook his head. The C&O Canal ran through a wood, the haunt of violent criminals, about a quarter of a mile below Macalaster's house. Macalaster looked through the open door and saw only impenetrable darkness; there had been no visible moon the night before and the sun would not rise for another hour and a half.

"Come on in."

Wordlessly Macalaster led the way to the kitchen. He got a jug of orange juice out of the refrigerator and held it aloft.

Once again Julian shook his head. "Are we alone?" he asked.

"Manal is upstairs, but my guess is she's asleep."

"Ah, the medium. She made a very strong impression on Emily."

Swallowing orange juice, Macalaster nodded. Long before she knew Julian, when she was an intern at the *Post*, Emily had baby-sat with Manal. From an early age, the little girl had claimed to be able to communicate with the spirits of the dead through a Ouija board, and one night while the Macalasters were dining out, she had put Emily in touch with her dead grandmother, who had spoken from beyond the grave in pig Latin, the language she and Emily had used together when Emily was a child, and said things that only she could know. Julian thought this was nonsense—charming nonsense, but nonsense just the same.

"Beautiful name, Manal," he said. "Where did you find it?"

"Brook named her for an Egyptian poet," Macalaster said.

"One of Brook's friends?"

"A kindred spirit."

"Poor Brook," said Julian.

Julian had known Macalaster's wife since Movement days as a fervent worker for the Cause. He sighed, remembering her. Her life had been a series of failed self-portraits: civil rights worker, member of a commune, campus agitator, sexual revolutionary, feminist, adopter of a Romanian orphan, lawyer, suicide. After a silent moment, he looked at the kitchen clock and came to the point. "Look, Ross," he said, "I have something to tell you, and a favor to ask." Then he confided that President Lockwood, probably the next day, was going to announce the appointment of Archimedes Hammett as Chief Justice.

Macalaster said, "You're joking."

Julian looked puzzled. "Why do you say that?"

"You'll never get away with it. If one of those human bombs had gone off close enough to Lockwood to kill him, he would have defended the people responsible."

"That's what lawyers do. Nobody does it better than Hammett. The President just thinks that it's time to make a courageous appointment to the Court, someone who will stand up to the Mallory faction."

"Hammett will do that, all right."

"The President thinks so," Julian replied. "No—no coffee, thank you."

Then he laughed. He had responded not to any offer made by Macalaster, but to the recorded sound of a saccharine female voice that fluted, "Coffee is ready!" when the coffeemaker, a Christmas gift from Manal, finished its cycle. Macalaster poured himself a cup.

"Besides," Julian said, as if he had never been interrupted, "one man's terrorism is another man's noble cause."

Macalaster lifted his eyebrows. "I didn't know an old fighter pilot like yourself thought in such theopolitical terms," he said.

"'Theopolitical'? Is that a word?"

"It is now."

"You invented it? Then I'll start using it," Julian replied. "These are mind-stretching days. Everything I just told you is yours exclusively until the end of the day. Strictly on deep background, of course."

This meant that Macalaster could print everything Julian had told him but could not identify his source. Macalaster said, "Fine."

Glancing at the clock again, Julian continued, "That's one reason I came by so early. I know your column comes out on Wednesdays."

"I'm grateful for the leak," Macalaster said. "What's the favor?"

Julian looked puzzled. "The favor?"

"You mentioned a favor."

"Oh, yes. Almost forgot. It's very hard for the President to meet privately with anyone. I wonder if you'd mind his getting together with Hammett here, in your house."

"When?"

"Tonight."

"Sure. What time?"

"It's a little more complicated than a simple meeting. We'd like you to have a small dinner party, including Hammett. Lockwood would come by for coffee afterward, and the two of them would just sort of run into each other."

"Fine. Just tell me who you want invited and what they want to eat."

"All that will be taken care of," Julian said. "The caterer will be in touch this morning." He produced a file card on which a list of names had been typed. "This is the guest list; we'll make the calls. See you at eight tonight."

Julian left by the back door. Macalaster read the names on the card. The Hubbards, Sam Clark and his wife, and Hammett. The last entry, scribbled in a hurried, half-legible hand that Macalaster recognized as Emily's, was Zarah Christopher.

7

Instead of coming to Macalaster's dinner for dessert, Polly and Frosty Lockwood arrived midway through the cocktail hour. They had ridden across town incognito, behind the smoked windows of Sam Clark's Lincoln, inside a protective formation of unmarked Secret Service cars. Whatever degree of anonymity this subterfuge afforded was quickly dispelled. As soon as the President was inside the house, the street was blocked at both ends, agents armed with automatic rifles patrolled the neighborhood, and helicopters equipped with blinding searchlights clattered overhead.

Lockwood entered. Hammett came almost imperceptibly to something resembling attention. Instead of his emblematic workshirt and jeans, he wore a dark chalk-striped Savile Row suit with a white shirt and an expensive maroon silk polka-dot tie.

"Hello there, Archimedes," Lockwood said, waving off Macalaster's attempt at an introduction even though he had never met this man. "They told me you never wore a suit of clothes, but you look like a regular member of the bar tonight."

"Well, this is a special occasion, Mr. President."

"Is that the only suit you've got?"

"The only good one, sir."

In his broadest eastern Kentucky accent, Lockwood said, "Is it tailor-made? Looks like one of those bespoke English suits that cost two thousand dollars apiece."

"That's what it is."

"Then they've got your measurements on file over there in London in case you need to have 'em whip you up a few more?"

Hammett nodded.

"Glad to hear that," Lockwood said. He turned to Macalaster. "Ross, how's it going? Who's this glorious young lady I see before me?"

Mock flirtatiousness was part of Lockwood's stock-in-trade, although he was, like Mallory, famously chaste and strictly monogamous—"Lyndon without the hound-dog lust," as the Southern contingent had called him when he was Senate Majority Leader. Macalaster introduced Zarah.

"Paul Christopher's daughter?" Lockwood said. Zarah nodded. Lockwood said, "You look like him. Mighty fine American, your dad. The country's in his debt."

"That's a kind thing to say, Mr. President."

"Just truthful. I *know* what he did—some of it, anyway, I guess nobody knows all of it—from my days on the Senate Intelligence Committee. I didn't know your mother, but I think Polly did. Honey?"

Polly Lockwood turned away from Hammett, whom she had begun to interrogate in her gentle way. "Yes, dear?"

"Wasn't this young lady's mother a Bluegrass girl?"

Zarah said, "My mother was Catherine Kirkpatrick."

"Cathy was your mother?" Polly said. "My goodness, yes. We lived just a couple of farms away. Your grandmother and grandfather were Lee and Lee Kirkpatrick, wonderful folks but you never knew who was talking to whom because they had the same first name. Your mama was the most beautiful girl anyone has ever seen, and just as nice as she could be. Rode like an angel. Played the piano like one, too. Are you the girl she raised out there in the Sahara Desert, so far away from everyone else?"

"I'm the only one she had."

"My goodness. I'd like to hear all about that. Emily, you bring her over for tea next week; we'll never get it all talked out tonight." She put a hand on Zarah's arm. "Sarah? Have I got it right?"

"Zarah, with a zed," Zarah replied.

Hammett had been listening. This expression out of Shelleyan ritual startled him. "With a '*zed*'?" he said. "Why do you pronounce it that way?"

"Sorry, I forgot myself."

"Forgot yourself?"

"I had British teachers as a child." Zarah addressed herself to Polly. "It's a boy's name, really. It means 'sunrise' in Hebrew."

"Hebrew?" Hammett said, startled. Zarah was blond and gray-eyed, with a face out of a Dürer drawing. "Are you Jewish?"

"No, are you?"

Hammett, defender of Jewry's most implacable foes, uttered a strangled guffaw. "Good God, no, but it's a novelty to be asked. In fact, it's a novelty to meet someone who doesn't read the papers. Does that come from growing up in the Sahara Desert?" Staring at her with intense concentration, he waited for her answer, which did not come. Zarah simply absorbed his question into some pool of silence at the center of her personality.

Lockwood's eyes flicked in open amusement from Hammett to Zarah. He said, "No offense to old Ross here, but if you can get away from the newspapers in the Sahara Desert, that's where I want to be. Can you actually do that, Zarah?"

With all the easy charm she had been withholding from Hammett she said, "You sure can if you go to the right place, Mr. President. I never saw one, even in Arabic, until I was grown up."

Hammett said, "What did you do for news?"

"There wasn't any."

"Then what was there?"

She paused for a beat. "Life," she said without expression.

"Zarah grew up on a diet of locusts," Emily said. "The nomads boil them, Mr. President, then dry them in the sun. They taste like shrimp."

"That's poor folks' talk," Lockwood said. "Back home we always said mushrat tasted like fried chicken."

"My grandfather and grandmother were from the poorest part of Greece," Hammett said, speaking directly to Zarah. "For a hundred generations their people ate meat only once a year, at Easter."

"Sounds like the klephts of the Mesa Mani," Zarah said.

Thunderstruck, Hammett said, "What do you know about the Maniátes?"

"Not much. That they were murderous brigands, romanticized as patriots by people like Shelley."

" 'Romanticized'?" Hammett was outraged. "Shelley had nothing to do with it. The Maniátes were heroes who fought for their freedom for two thousand years. Sacrificing everything." Zarah shrugged. Hammett said, "It's pretty obvious you don't know an idealist when you see one."

"Whatever you say," Zarah said with a level look.

Hammett spun on his heel and plunged across the room, stopping midway across the carpet when he realized there was no one else to talk to except Lockwood and Clark, whom he did not wish to approach, or Julian Hubbard, who was responsible for luring him into this den of unpredictable strangers.

"I think you touched a nerve there," Macalaster said to Zarah.

"Or something," Zarah replied.

She did not smile; her voice was toneless. Yet Macalaster had the impression that Zarah knew exactly who Archimedes Hammett was, was aware of his whole résumé, and thought him a dangerous fool. From across the room, Hammett scowled; with wonderful economy, as if she had fired a pellet of sanity into his brain, she had made him know this too. But how? And why?

As soon as Lockwood finished his ounce of lukewarm Maker's Mark bourbon, his favorite drink, the caterer's butler announced dinner. Lockwood took Zarah's arm. "I'll escort you, little lady," he said. "I don't care what the place cards say, you're going to sit next to me."

Macalaster took Polly Lockwood in. At his back, he could hear Hammett talking to Julian Hubbard. "What's with that Christopher female?" he asked. "She was just trashing Shelley. What does she know about Shelley?"

Julian responded with a quizzical grin. "Well, she grew up in a place where there wasn't much to do but read."

"Where was that?"

"The Maghreb, among the Berbers. It's quite a story."

"Tell me. I'm dying to know. What is she, a trained killer raised on a secret CIA base, like the rest of her family?"

Into the pocket of silence this remark produced, Polly Lockwood said to Macalaster, "Why, Zarah's even lovelier than her poor mother, though I would never in this world have thought such a thing was possible."

The First Lady looked up into Macalaster's face and smiled encouragingly. Her own features were still a little pink from the anger Hammett's remark had provoked. Macalaster wondered if she knew about the honor her husband was about to bestow on this strange, angry man. At dinner, all his doubts on this score were erased by the velvety way in which Polly examined Hammett on his past, his beliefs, his purposes in life. He answered gruffly in monosyllables, as if he were being interrogated by an agent of a hostile intelligence service under deep cover. Lockwood, busy telling stories to Zarah and Emily and swapping guffaws with Clark, ignored him completely. The menu was Washington-caterer short-notice weeknight fare: lobster bisque, Dover sole with asparagus and miniature boiled potatoes, salad, and fruit compote.

"What exactly is a bisque?" Lockwood said. "You grew up in a foreign country, Zarah. Can you tell me?"

"Soup made from shellfish, Mr. President."

"Is that right? That's a relief. I thought it was French for some part of the lobster they didn't want to describe in plain English."

Hammett ate nothing. He left each dish untouched, waving it away when the waiter came around to collect the china at the end of the course. Neither did he taste his wine or even his water.

"This sole is delicious, Archimedes," Polly said at last. "You haven't eaten a bite. Don't you like seafood?"

"Oh, I'm just fine," Hammett said. As a gesture to her motherly concern he broke a fillet of Dover sole in half with his fork before pushing it aside.

"Archimedes doesn't trust American food," said Emily from across the table. "He thinks it's poisoned by capitalist agents."

All heads turned in Hammett's direction, expecting him to reply to what those who did not know him took to be a straight line. Instead, he gazed at the ceiling.

Finally Lockwood said, "You've got nothing to worry about, Archimedes. That's why I brought Sam along—he's my taster. Just watch him for the first few bites. If he doesn't die, you can go right ahead and eat."

Clark laughed; everyone except Hammett did. When the merriment died down, the party rose from the table. While the others went into the sitting room for coffee, Julian, who had been shown the way earlier, led Lockwood and Hammett down the hall to the library.

While the dinner party was in progress, Secret Service technicians in evening clothes had "sanitized" Macalaster's library—that is to say, they had searched it visually and electronically for listening devices and installed counterbugs designed to deafen any transmitters or microphones or deflect any beams of electrons that had escaped detection or might be activated after Lockwood and Hammett entered the room. The windows were masked. The phone was removed and the whole phone system for the house disconnected, and because the electrical wiring of any house constitutes a ready-made antenna into which eavesdroppers can tap with simple equipment, all outlets in the room were fitted with jamming devices. Julian listed all these precautions on the way down the hall.

"There's no such thing as an effective counterbug," said Hammett. "To open each door there's a key."

Julian smiled tightly. "How well we know that."

"It makes no difference one way or the other," Lockwood said as soon as the door closed behind them. "I'm not going to say anything to you, Mr. Hammett, that I wouldn't say on national TV, and you'd be wise to follow the same procedure."

Now that they were in private, the "Archimedes" of first meeting became "Mr. Hammett"; the President's etiquette was the reverse of the usual practice. He was jovially familiar with strangers in public encounters, coldly formal behind closed doors. Picking up on this change in mannerisms, Hammett started to say something that would demonstrate his own seriousness, but Lockwood held up one of his hands to stop him; it was a paw, huge and freckled with liver spots. "Now as I understand it," he said, "Julian has told you what we have in mind for you."

"Yes, Mr. President, he has," said Hammett, who carried an undetected, and indeed undetectable, voice-activated tape recorder in the inside pocket of his jacket so as to capture everything on tape. "Julian Hubbard has told me"—Lockwood again held up his hand for silence, but Hammett raised his voice slightly and talked right through the gesture—"that you intend to nominate me to fill the vacancy of Chief Justice of the Supreme Court of the United States."

Lockwood gave him a searching look; he knew what it usually meant when visitors spoke so specifically for the record. "That's right," he said. "Now I want to ask you a question. Bearing in mind that the confirmation process is going to be very heated and searching, do you know of any reason having to do with the private part of your life that might, if discovered, disqualify you or embarrass me?"

Hammett lifted his eyebrows. "I think that's what's called the Harding Question," he said.

Lockwood said, "Boy, I already know you're clever as a whole damn barrel of monkeys; you don't have to prove it to me. But what you're about to go through has nothing to do with life as you've known it up to now. Nobody is going to give you the benefit of the doubt because you've got all the right ideas and a silver tongue. Courtroom rules of evidence aren't going to mean a damn thing. You're going to have to prove your innocence of every crime on the books, including original sin, to a bunch of people who'll be out to screw and tattoo both of us. So please answer the damn question."

Hammett's dark eyes glittered with resentment. He replied, "The answer is no."

"You're sure about that?"

"I've answered your question, Mr. President. Do you think I'd be crazy enough to expose myself to this process if I had anything to hide?"

"Crazy doesn't come into it. Ambition and hoping for the best have been known to play a part in these situations. All I'm saying to you is, you'd better be sure you're clean, because tomorrow morning will be too late to change your story."

"Noted," Hammett said.

Lockwood relaxed. He said, "Well, I can see you don't like to take any crap, and that's a pretty good qualification for Chief Justice. You're going to have to stand your ground up there."

"You needn't worry about that, Mr. President."

"Maybe not. But I'm not too sure what your ground is." Hammett opened his mouth to speak. "No," Lockwood said. He dug a horny forefinger into Hammett's breastbone to make sure he had his attention. "Don't tell me. I've got enough to worry about as it is."

They were standing up, face to face. Hammett's chest throbbed as if he had been punched; he was sure the gouging fingertip had left a mark on his skin. Lockwood's breath smelled of fish and whiskey. By genetic endowment the Maniátes were an undersize people, and though he was much taller than his grandfather, Hammett was at least a foot shorter than Lockwood. Nevertheless he raised his own forefinger to the level of the President's nose, which was full of wiry gray bristles. "If you're not comfortable with me, Mr. President, we can call the whole thing off right now," he said. "I have a life already. I don't need what you're offering."

Lockwood's deeply lined face relaxed into its customary good-natured expression. "Nothing personal, Archimedes," he said. "All I know about you is what I read in the newspapers and what Julian tells me about your sterling personal qualities. I'm not nominating you as the person I'd like to be marooned on a desert island with, and history suggests you'll turn out to be the man nobody knew as soon as you climb up on that bench. So all I want to know is, have you kept your pecker in your pants? You say you have. I have to believe you; I've got no choice. But if you're hiding anything, I'm telling you, you're going to be one sorry Greek."

Hammett glared at the President. Although he had made a career of denouncing others, he could not bear to be criticized in even the mildest way, or to have his own moral rectitude brought into question. Lockwood's words had outraged him, and his manner, which suggested that he believed that Hammett, like an ordinary mortal, had something to hide and might not be able to conceal it under pressure, had been even worse. Most injurious of all, because it was true, was the scornful message in Lockwood's exhausted eyes: This jasper wants what I'm offering him, so he's mine.

In an abrupt change of mood, a tactic that had always served him well, the President threw an arm around Hammett's shoulders and hugged him hard. He was enormously strong. Because he had avoided embraces all his life, Hammett had not realized that a human being could be so strong. Lockwood was grinning down at him, breathing on him. Hammett realized that this alien, bearlike creature somehow understood his phobias and was taunting him.

"Say hello to Sam Clark," Lockwood said, turning Hammett around, physically moving him 180 degrees, to face the Majority Leader, who had just come into the room. "Sam's going to introduce you to the fellows on the Judiciary Committee, and if you need any advice in any shape, form, or substance about the U.S. Senate, he's the man to talk to. Starting tomorrow morning. We're all too tired to go into it tonight."

Clark said, "Is breakfast at eight all right for you, Archimedes? I've invited the chairman and some of the others."

Hammett hesitated, envisaging ham and eggs and other poisonous animal products being chewed and swallowed by a tableful of fat people.

Lockwood said, "Say yes, Archimedes. You can eat some locusts before you go."

"I'll be there."

"Good," Clark said. In his loud speech and broad gestures, he evoked Lockwood's manner so strongly, Hammett thought, that he might have been a stand-up comic doing an impersonation. "Just come to my office in the Capitol at seven forty-five. Just you, no staff."

"I travel alone, Senator."

"So they say," Clark said, unsmiling. "Come in the Senate door on the east face. A pretty young lady will meet you there and show you the way."

In Sam Clark's Lincoln on the way back to the White House, Clark said, "I don't like that son of a bitch, Frosty."

Polly said, "I wouldn't trust him."

Lockwood let a moment pass; the tires hummed on the pavement beneath them. Finally he said, "Sounds like we've got us the right man."

8

Manal Macalaster, who had been playing in a school basketball game, came home soon after the President's clamorous departure. She asked no questions about the dinner party. Famous people did not interest her. From the cradle onward, her mother had instilled in her Lord Acton's dictum that great men were almost always bad men, even though her father was always talking to them on the telephone.

Hammett, who disliked hotels, had sometimes stayed with the Macalasters when she was small, and though he had ignored her—he was not interested in children—she remembered him kindly because his being in the house had pleased her mother so. She shook hands with him and all the others and said "How do you do?" in a perfectly composed way.

Manal was a natural gentlewoman who had one single, benevolent manner for everyone she met. One of her many Third World nursemaids, a Maya Indian from Guatemala, believed that she had been a queen in an earlier life; this notion had infuriated Brook, who wanted the child's ancestry to be as wretched as possible. Who wanted to preserve the gene pool of royalty, especially Romanian royalty? Brook preferred to believe that Manal, who was dark in complexion and merry in nature, had Gypsy blood—or, even better, was descended from a mysterious group of Africans who, as she had been assured by a former U.S. ambassador to Bucharest, had somehow found their way to Romania in centuries past. She had adopted Manal on political impulse after the fall of Ceauşescu (a dictator doomed, in Brook's view, not because he was a Stalinist in his methods, but because he had been a CIA collaborator), when many other enlightened women were also adopting orphans from Eastern Europe. Manal (emphasis on the second syllable) was named after a female Egyptian poet with whom Brook had fallen in love during her militant feminist phase. In infancy, the child had been ill almost continually, owing to the aftereffects of the six or seven diseases with which she had been found to be infected on arrival from Bucharest. When she was old enough to go to school, it was discovered that she was dyslexic. Ten years later this was regarded as an advantage by the college counselor at the expensive school for the learning-impaired that she attended: many highly selective universities were enhancing their student bodies by admitting a certain number of disadvantaged persons with intellectual disabilities, and Manal was regarded as a sure bet for one of the Seven Sisters, and might even get into Princeton or Brown. This development would have delighted Brook, but the fact of the matter was that she had lost interest in Manal as soon as a new political fashion came along.

Now, embracing Emily Hubbard, Manal smiled in a way that made her seem quite beautiful. Soon the three females were seated together in a tight circle, talking and laughing.

Manal touched her father on the hand. "Emily would like to have a séance," she said. "Is it all right, Daddy?"

"Yes, sure," Macalaster said, looking at his watch. "But not a very long one; it's almost ten o'clock."

Hammett stared incredulously at Macalaster and the girl. "A *séance?*" he said.

Manal looked at him without expression, and without answering. "We'll do it in the den," she said. "The visitors like that room."

Hammett gave her a questioning look. " 'The visitors'?"

"The spirits of the dead," Manal explained. "They like the den because it's small and everyone is close together."

"Ah-*ha.*"

Hammett looked trapped and started to turn away, but Emily took his arm and drew him along with the others. "Come on, Hammett," she said. "Be a sport."

As a Ouija board Manal used a brown-paper supermarket bag on which she had scrawled, in Magic Marker, the letters of the alphabet and the numbers 1 through 0. Owing to her dyslexia, some of the letters were backward or upside down. The planchette that moved over the surface of the board was an inverted two-ounce shot glass that slid easily over the waxy brown paper. Everyone except Hammett placed a forefinger on the shot glass.

After a short wait, while Manal appeared to concentrate on some absent force or entity, and to grow less alert as she did so, the shot glass began to move in a jerky, random way over the alphabet. At first it spelled out nonsense, and in one case, obscenities.

Manal, who could not read the words, evidently could somehow hear them, because she responded to this and all subsequent spirit messages by speaking aloud. When the shot glass, sliding over the paper at a furious rate, spelled out a string of four-letter words, she said, "Please don't speak to us like that." The same obscenities were repeated, spelled backward. "I'm sorry," Manal said, "but we just can't talk to you anymore."

Manal took her finger off the glass. "Some of the visitors are crazy," she explained. "And a lot of them are really unhappy, especially if they died before their time. If they've been murdered, they can't get out of darkness until their murderer dies."

" 'Darkness'?" Hammett said. "What's that mean?"

"It's where the dead go right after they die, to wait."

"I always heard you saw a brilliant white light."

"That's not what the visitors say," Manal replied.

"Shush," Emily said. "I want to talk to Grammy."

The glass spelled out another obscenity.

Zarah said, "I don't think we should go on with this."

With a twist of the lips, Hammett said, "You mean you believe in ghosts? This is very interesting."

Zarah ignored him and made as if to get up. She was seated on the floor, with her wide skirt spread around her. The glass moved again, very rapidly.

"Come on, Zarah, don't give up now," Emily said. "I-ay ant-way oo-tay alk-tay oo-tay y-may randma-gay."

Zarah hesitated, then placed her forefinger with the others' on the shot glass.

Macalaster fought sleep. He had never been able to bring himself to play this game, if that was the word for it. This was not because he was a skeptic. He had no doubt that Manal was a genuine medium, and he harbored the notion that Brook would someday be among the visitors.

Manal said, "Stay awake, Daddy. This one wants *you.*"

Steeling himself—he knew it was foolish to feel as he did, but it made him queasy nevertheless—Macalaster touched the shot glass.

To the spirit, Manal said, "Who are you?"

SUSAN. The letters were spelled slowly and hesitantly.

"Do you recognize the name, Daddy?"

Macalaster shook his head and yawned. He was relieved; whoever this was, it wasn't his dead wife. Wrong name, wrong vibrations. He felt anger and accusation in the air. But not enough of either for Brook to be present, dead or alive.

Manal said, "Do you have something to tell Ross?"

YES.

"We're listening," Manal said.

I WAS MURDERED.

"We're so sorry. Do you know who did it?"

YOUR FRIEND SHELLEY KNOWS.

"We have no friend named Shelley," Manal said.

WRONG. MANY SHELLEYS. TWO ARE WITH YOU NOW.

The shot glass flew off the table as if flung by an invisible hand.

"Susan?" Manal said. There was no reply. "She's gone away," Manal said. "I think we should stop now."

Julian and Hammett were looking at each other with great intensity and solemnity. Macalaster noticed that Zarah was watching the two men closely. Hammett felt her eyes on him and gave her a sharp look.

"Susan is still very angry," Manal said matter-of-factly. "She hasn't been dead very long. Did you notice how slowly she spelled until she got used to it? That's always a sign. The murdered are always confused at first and filled with bitterness. Some never get over it, never get out of darkness."

Zarah was quite pale, and even quieter than before. She said, "Manal, that was very interesting. How often do you do this?"

"Not often. It's tiring. I don't really like it."

"Why not?"

"They're so unhappy."

Zarah nodded as if she understood perfectly. "You remind me of someone I used to know very well. You should be careful with this."

Manal said, "I know. But that last one will be back no matter what we do."

"I know she will be," Zarah said.

"You *know*?" Hammett said. "That's very interesting."

She looked Hammett full in the face with her steady gray eyes. Her eyes, shimmering with intelligence, seemed to project an accusation or a message he couldn't quite read. He could not hold her gaze and looked away, only to discover the same eyes looking down on him from the mirror above the fireplace. He did not know whether he read the message this time, or whether, as he afterward came to believe, he realized in his own mind which Susan it was who had awakened him.

"I need fresh air," he said. "Julian, walk with me. We have things to talk about."

He left at once, without thanking his host or saying goodbye to anyone.

9

Julian and Hammett walked toward the Potomac down woodsy residential streets. Emily had caught a ride home with Zarah. Two gleaming Secret Service cars, one half a block behind the men and the other the same distance ahead, kept pace with them, radios crackling. Otherwise the posh neighborhood was silent. Then, suddenly, off on the flank, there was the clangor of falling garbage cans. Four deer emerged from behind a house and were immediately transfixed in the cars' powerful spotlights. Hammett froze in panic. Seeing this, Julian identified the threat: *"Deer, Archimedes!"*

The animals bounded away into a cemetery. As they disappeared among the ornate headstones, Hammett relaxed, but not for long. He had been deeply upset by the last part of the séance, especially by its reference to Shelley.

"That whole séance thing was a setup if I ever saw one," Hammett said.

Julian did not immediately respond to this statement, though he knew it was an appeal for confirmation. He looked upward into the overcast sky. There was little hope of reasoning with Hammett when he was in the state he was in now. After a moment, suppressing a sigh, he said, "What exactly do you mean by 'a setup,' Archimedes?"

"I would have thought it was pretty obvious. Unless, of course, you think it really was some creature from the next world who was spelling out 'Shelley' on the Ouija board just now."

"To be honest," Julian said, "I thought the whole thing was a coincidence."

"Of course you did," Hammett said. "You're so afraid of looking paranoid that you can't admit the obvious."

"Maybe," Julian said. "But the obvious isn't always so obvious. Archimedes, we're talking about an adolescent girl."

Hammett snorted derisively. "I'm talking about another female whose name begins with zed. Does that way of saying a certain letter of the alphabet ring a bell?"

Slowly and carefully Julian said, "You think Zarah knows about the Shelley Society?"

Annoyed by his neutral tone of voice, Hammett said, "Somebody had to do the spelling, and know what words and names to spell for maximum shock effect. Why shouldn't she know about it? Your whole family belongs to it."

"Meaning?"

"You live with Zarah's best friend, who just happens to be as curious as a cat. Do you and Horace always watch what you say in front of dear little Emily?"

From long experience Julian knew that Hammett had no sense of what not to say. He found this suggestion outrageous, but he controlled himself in this as in every other situation. In the same calm voice as before, he said, "You think my wife is spying on me?"

"No offense," Hammett replied, "but she's a female. They're born into an eternal CIA that's been keeping files on the other half of the human race ever since Eve was recruited by the serpent."

Coming from anyone else, this statement would have merited an appreciative chuckle. In this case, Julian remained silent because as usual Hammett was perfectly serious. By now they had almost reached the riverbank, where the streetlights were more powerful. Like some great swollen firefly hovering overhead, a buzzing sodium lamp shone down on them, banishing all shadows, giving Hammett's skin a corpselike hue. Because Hammett was Hammett, this was a comical effect, and Julian could not help but smile.

Hammett was offended by this levity. "What's so funny?"

"The light," Julian responded. "I was wondering if I look as dead as you do. At least we're not in darkness."

Hammett, who did not like any kind of joke, liked jests about death least of all. "Maybe you *think* you're not in the dark," he said. "But there's something going on, some kind of mind game, and I'm going to find out what it is and what it means."

As they moved out of the light Julian rolled his eyes; Hammett was off to the races. There was no such word as "coincidence" in his vocabulary; all unexplained events were the result of conspiracy. Julian knew all the signs.

In a half-whispered monologue that lasted the length of a long city block, Hammett went on about the séance, and Zarah's part in it.

At last Julian said, "Archimedes, calm down."

" 'Calm down'?" Hammett said. "That's your response to what happened?"

"Archimedes, nothing happened. Zarah just sat there like the rest of us. The séance was a parlor game."

"Like hell it was. It was a provocation. You don't want to admit that anything is going on, that's all."

Julian took two or three deep breaths before answering. "Archimedes," he said at last. "Anything is possible. But this is no time to get into a tizzy about the sanctity of the Shelley Society. You have more important things to think about."

"Nothing is more important."

"Not many men in your position would say that."

Hammett said, "Then maybe I should withdraw my name. I'm telling you for the last time, there's a connection between what happened tonight and what will happen to my nomination."

Julian stopped walking and turned to face his friend. He said, "Archimedes, get serious. Come *on*."

Hammett stopped in his tracks. "*You* come on," he said. "You're the guy who got me into this . . . in the name of the Poet, no less."

They were standing in ordinary street light now, and the play of emotion on Hammett's face was easier to read. He was afraid; he wanted reassurance. Fuck him, Julian thought, forming in his exhausted mind a word he would never have spoken aloud. He was too tired to continue the conversation; had he been talking to almost anyone else, he would have ended it minutes ago. He signaled the trailing Secret Service car, and its driver pulled forward to the spot where they stood. "Get in the car," he said.

His voice rising, Hammett said, "Why?"

"Because it's bedtime."

"But it isn't even midnight yet."

"Get in the car," Julian repeated. "They'll take you to your hotel."

Julian had invited Hammett to stay with them—the children were on a cruise to Antarctica with their mother and her new husband—but Emily had refused to have him in the house. Julian thought, God bless Emily. They lived in a Georgetown row house, low and dark, originally built as quarters for slaves. Already too small for the Empire furniture and other heirlooms that filled it, the house offered no escape from guests, even those who behaved rationally. Holding open the car door, he said, "Don't forget breakfast with Senator Clark. These same agents will pick you up in the morning and drive you to the Capitol."

With one last sour look of accusation, Hammett said, "Something's going on. Mark my words." Then, with exaggerated huffiness, he turned away and got into the backseat.

10

Julian found Emily in bed, reading. He lay down beside her and put a hand on her stomach.

"How's the book?" he asked.

Emily turned a page and held up a finger for patience. She lay between him and the lamp, and while she read, concentrating deeply, he studied her profile, so lovely and young and unguarded. Now she slid down between the sheets and fitted her small soft body to the curve of his long, bony one.

"So tomorrow is Archimedes' big day," she said. "You must be looking forward to it."

"On the whole, I'd rather be in Philadelphia."

Emily drew back, propping herself on one elbow in the dim light coming in from the street. "My father was always saying that," she said. "What does it mean?"

Julian was often surprised at what his wife did not know, but of course she was not old enough to remember W. C. Fields. He said, "Those are the words W. C. Fields said he wanted on his gravestone. Where he is, it's even deader than it is in Philadelphia. Get it?"

"Oh. Is Philadelphia dead?" Emily's family came from there.

"There are lots of jokes that say so."

"Tell me another."

"All right, but just one. When Edward the Seventh was Prince of Wales, he visited there and was wined and dined by the local upper crust. Afterward he said, 'Philadelphia is full of Scrapples, and they all eat Biddle for breakfast.' "

Emily received this story with exaggerated solemnity. "Gee," she said, "do you know any more?"

She was in an excellent mood after the party. She loved company; she had talked to her dead grandmother in pig Latin; Hammett had been discomfited by Zarah; and seeing Zarah always made her happy. Now that she had finished her chapter, she wanted to talk for a while—put the party to bed, too—before she slept. "Anyway," she said, "Manal made a believer of him tonight."

Longing for sleep and knowing that he would have none if he started thinking about Hammett, Julian patted her warm bare bottom. "Nobody has to make a believer out of Archimedes," he said. "He's the original of the type. Now go to sleep."

11

Hammett, who lived by night because he preferred to be alone, spent the hours between midnight and dawn on the telephone. Those who knew him were accustomed to being awakened in the small hours of the morning by a collect call from "Professor Good," his telephone name. Because most such people were former students of his, they were flattered to hear from him and glad to pay the reversed charges, even though he sometimes talked for hours if the issue was important to him.

On this night, all his calls were brief. He told everyone the same thing, in the same words: "Hello, ———? Please listen to what I'm going to say, then just hang up. I can't chat or answer any questions tonight. I'm calling to tell you something you ought to know before the rest of the world finds out about it. Tomorrow morning the President is going to announce my appointment to replace Maxson Goodrich on the Supreme Court. I've agreed to drink this spongeful of vinegar even though I know it means going through hell. The other side is going to go crazy when they hear this. They'll come after me like they've never come after anyone before. I'm not worried because I have nothing to worry about, but I just wanted to call before I jump into the fishbowl with the sharks. Your friendship means a lot to me. I just wanted you to know that. So do the things we both believe in. Otherwise I wouldn't be doing this—and neither would Frosty. He's taking a fantastic risk for the Cause on this one, not to mention his own fate and the future of the whole Cause."

Beginning with the preeminent Patrick Graham, whom he had known at Yale as a fellow undergraduate, Hammett rang journalists first, then a long list of lawyers who worked for federal agencies and congressional committees, and finally the large network of Yale Law School graduates who labored as lobbyists or legal advisers for law firms and the dozens of Washington-based pressure groups that were devoted to promoting progressive causes. These were Hammett's shock troops, a network of fighters bound to him by his teachings and by a carefully designed system of irresistible rewards.

Hammett was a believer in B. F. Skinner's theory of operant conditioning, which holds that any organism will naturally repeat behavior when it is reinforced by properly designed rewards. By "organism" Skinner meant any sentient being, from pigeons to members of the I.Q. Elite. Pigeons, for example, were conditioned by his methods to guide nuclear missiles to a target by inducing them to peck an electronic switch in response to a certain radar picture. The bird was instantaneously rewarded with something to eat every time its beak struck the right button in response to the correct image. The objective of operant conditioning is not to "cure" or "correct" negative behavior or to instill unnatural behavior, nor does punishment play any part in the system. Its objective, rather, is to reinforce an already existing tendency or instinct to behave in a certain way by rewarding the organism in such a way that it associates the reward with the behavior. Soon the organism develops such a craving for the reward that it will invariably behave in the way that produces it.

Men and women, though capable of far more complex behavior than pigeons in response to much more subtle stimuli, will nevertheless behave in the same predictable fashion in response to a well-designed program of stimulus and reward. Hammett was interested in reinforcing a certain kind of political behavior, based on a system of beliefs that had already been instilled in his subjects by earlier teachers. His predecessors had created a tribe of young believers by bestowing such irresistible rewards as personal encouragement and praise, higher grades than were strictly deserved, honors, prizes, scholarships, recommendations for graduate school, and so on. Hammett built on this foundation by offering a higher order of rewards. These included knowledge of secrets and the trust this implies, praise, recognition, power, and the psychic support of a like-minded tribe—and, of course, side benefits in which Hammett himself was not interested, chiefly sex and money. By his teaching he gave his pupils a purpose in life: the reinvention of society, and, by exercising his influence to get them jobs in the right places, he made it possible for them to fulfill that life purpose—or at least to have the illusion that they were doing so. In short, he taught them to want a certain reward, self-esteem, and then gave it to them in return for Shelleyan good works. This was the ultimate Skinnerian result.

From an early age Hammett had wanted to change the world, and he had always realized that it could only be changed piecemeal, according to a systematic plan. A frontal assault on the Establishment could never succeed. It must be conquered camp by camp—first academia, where minds were formed; then the news media, the churches, and the arts, which transmitted the orthodoxy to lesser minds; then a whole new apparatus of special interest groups to bring irresistible pressure on the government in concert with all of the above; then, in the Year Z, the whole world.

Above all, this required endurance. From his grandfather Hammett had learned to think like a man surrounded by enemies, and to believe in the treachery of all who ruled over others with money and laws. These were infinitely stimulating habits of the mind. Gika Mavromikháli had told him how Romans, Franks, Venetians, Turks, and their slaves the Albanians had all tried to subdue the Maniátes in their mountain fastness and had all failed in their turn, the Turks after nearly five hundred years of occupation. He told the boy how Christian hated Muslim, how family hated family, how brother hated brother and cousin cousin; how *compáre*, as people who had the same godfather were called, hated *compáre*, and how families and parts of families would declare war on one another by proclaiming it in the streets, and would then kill one another from ambush, or in clashes in the streets, or kill women by gunfire or torture and be killed by them by the same means, and when they won the war, how the victors would pull down the houses of the vanquished enemy, scattering the stones, burning the roof beams, and turning those who survived the massacre into the hills to plot revenge, for the balance of death was never perfect. Any means of killing an enemy for revenge was acceptable. A man waiting to avenge the death of a relative would not eat meat or shave until he had killed his man; by the time Hammett knew Gika, the patriarch's magnificent white *mustakia* hung down to his breastbone.

"They tried for two thousand years to starve us out, so we learned to live without eating, they tried to turn families into spies and traitors, so we learned to live without trust, they corrupted the priests, so we learned to live without prayer," said Gika. Archimedes was Gika's only hope for the continuation of the struggle of the Maniátes to overcome the outsiders who had been trying to wipe them out for so many centuries. "Remember, three things make a Maniáte strong: hatred, fasting, and revenge," the old man told Archimedes. "When I die, you will be alone. Trust no one. Make the world safe for yourself, just one Maniáte among all the thousands who have been oppressed. Rise above our enemies, who are everyone and everywhere, and I will be with you at the head of an army of ghosts."

Later on, as an undergraduate at Yale, Archimedes had come into contact with the driving political idea of the twentieth century, that everything is personal and that nothing in the visible world is what it seems to be. He understood that the world's greatest minds—Pasteur in medicine, Einstein in physics, Freud in psychology, Marx in economics, Mao in warfare and politics—had validated his grandfather's teachings, though the old man had known nothing of books. It was because of his grandfather that Hammett was sympathetic to terrorists even though most of them were Muslims and therefore the ancient enemies of the Maniátes. He understood their impatience—which was in reality an inchoate rage produced by centuries of being lied to, starved, and punished for nothing—as no one but the child of many generations of the oppressed, conquered, and humiliated can understand it. "Every fighter must find his own replacement or else the war will end when he dies," Gika told the boy on his deathbed. "You are the me that I was when I was young, and you must someday be the me they would not let me be."

To achieve this forbidden personhood, to pay back his grandfather's oppressors, was Hammett's purpose in life, and though he concealed it from the world, there was nothing subconscious about his ambition. Never a day went by that he did not remember the lessons his grandfather had taught him. After the old man died, he had studied under some of the finest teachers in America, but in Hammett's mind the wisest man he had ever known was Gika Mavromikháli, who could neither read nor write nor count to any number above twelve, the largest sum that could be reckoned by touching the joints of the fingers of one hand with the tip of the thumb.

The first prophetic proof of the soundness of what Hammett called "the theory of nakedness," which was the key to all his grandfather's teachings, was his own election to the Shelley Society. Six-Eight, the senior who tapped him, had made friends with him the year before, and Hammett had poured out his heart to him. The other man, born to wealth, was greatly impressed by Hammett's hatred of injustice, by his disillusion with the established order, and by his apparent intelligence. Actually his I.Q. as recorded in his admissions file was only 115, barely higher than normal, but his verbal brilliance, his passion, and a peculiar mental gift that enabled him to store and recall verbatim great swatches of everything that he read or heard made him seem much smarter than was indicated by the usual standards of measurement. Of course, there are many different kinds of intelligence, and Hammett's, formed and perfected by centuries of interbreeding among the Maniátes, who depended on memory for everything, probably could not be measured by any test developed by oppressors. .

Six-Eight made it plain to Hammett that he had been chosen for what he was, because the Shelleyans thought it was essential to have people like him inside the perimeter of the privileged classes. "You must be our conscience," Six-Eight had said. "Never be tempted to be like us; we're the ones who should try to be like you."

Listening to this unmanly speech by a rich man's spoiled son, Hammett had thought, Grandfather, they are so weak! But he knew that Gika Mavromikháli, killer of Turks, would have replied, "No, they are just washing your feet for the sake of their own souls. Beware the enemy when he pretends to be humble."

And of course the old man would have been quite right. The Shelleyans might treat him like a *compáre*—after all, they were motivated by some romantic high-minded idea of being the godsons of Shelley. But Hammett knew that in the eyes of Six-Eight and the others, he was in reality a talking animal, an exotic pet, a trophy, no more. But he was inside the tent of the enemy, and he knew himself to be better loved, in a way, by all who lived inside those walls than they loved their own kind.

12

By morning, as he arrived on the dot of seven forty-five for his breakfast with Sam Clark and the progressive members of the Senate Judiciary Committee, Hammett was once again in good spirits.

"Ready to go into the lion's den?" Clark asked him.

Beneath a miasma of shaving lotion and toothpaste, the Majority Leader's breath smelled of last night's bourbon and cigar smoke. As a vegetarian and teetotaler, Hammett was sensitive to such aromas. He knew from his reading that Baluba tribesmen had thought that the first American missionaries to arrive in Katanga were the awakened dead because they bathed every day with soap and did not smell of sweat and the other pungent odors given off by people living in a natural state. In his own time and place, Hammett had the opposite problem; most people smelled too strongly of life for his comfort.

"You haven't got a hell of a lot to worry about from this crowd," Clark was saying. "They all know and love you."

Hammett was not amused. What Clark said was true up to a point. Hammett had often testified before the Judiciary Committee on questions of terrorism and the legal rights of people who committed atrocities as an expression of political or religious faith—or, as was often the case, a combination of both. But, as was true of everything that involved televised proceedings, there was a strong element of playacting in all this. Neither Hammett nor the senators could behave before the American public in an entirely natural way.

"Just the same, I'm a little nervous," Hammett said. "The President made me that way last night."

"Forget Frosty; he's just an old jock who likes to see people squirm," Clark said. "You've always been a good witness."

"Any advice on how to be a better one?"

Clark looked at him tiredly. "Just do what you've always done, Archimedes. Take the Constitution as your text and make like Portia about how mercy is a gentle rain from heaven. We like that kind of bullshit up here, especially the part about it falling on the just and the unjust."

Hammett detected a note of ridicule. "You suspect me of hypocrisy?"

"Of course not," Clark said. "Everyone knows you mean every word you say."

Again Hammett recognized that Clark did not like him or trust him, but he also knew that there was truth in what he said. Despite Lockwood's dire warnings, he had little to fear from the confirmation process. Fair-minded members, and especially the committee chairman, Baxter T. "Buzzer" Busby, an Old Blue windmill guard who was so called because his last-second set shot from the centerline had beaten Harvard in the long-ago 1950s, had always treated him gently. There were reasons for this that only Hammett knew. Five of the calls he had made the night before had been to lawyers on the committee staff who were former students of his. These included the chief counsel, a brilliant graduate of Yale Law School whom Hammett had recommended for his job through the good offices of the Shelley Society. He did not know the details of how the appointment had been engineered; he had simply made a call in the name of the Poet and it had happened.

Just then Senator Busby arrived, carrying what Hammett recognized as a thermos bag designed to keep food hot or cold. Waiters were already rolling steam trolleys into the room, where a gleaming conference table had been laid with china and silver for a dozen people.

"Where's Archimedes sitting?" Busby asked.

"Next to me, across from you," Clark said.

Giving Hammett a broad wink, Busby opened the zipper on his thermos bag. "I brought our breakfast, Archimedes," he said. "Yogurt," he said, thumping a plastic container onto the tabletop. "Fruit salad. Whole-grain muffins. Tea. Every item organically grown back home in California on our own family farm, flown in special, and prepared this very morning by my own hands."

He stepped back with a flourish and gave Hammett a triumphant look. Hammett was not reassured. What Busby called the "family farm" was, in reality, a huge industrialized agricultural operation in the Central Valley that collected millions from the federal government in crop subsidies and had sales of vegetables and fruits amounting to more than $1 billion a year. Imagining clouds of pesticides blown onto the Busby kitchen garden from the acreage surrounding it, Hammett managed a feeble smile. He was saved from the necessity of saying something nice about Busby's "health food" by the arrival of the rest of Busby's bunch—the left flank of the Judiciary Committee. Half a dozen of them traveled in a pack, all talking at once, all saying the same things, all wearing tailor-made suits and shirts and hundred-dollar neckties that they could not possibly have afforded on their salaries. And these, Hammett thought, are the good guys.

The breakfast went well, twenty minutes of pleasantries while the senators and the staff lawyers wolfed their fried food and sugary breads, followed by forty minutes of chitchat. At Clark's invitation, the senators asked questions in order of reverse seniority, so that the chairman could speak last. The questions were not questions; they were statements of support, couched in such a way that Hammett could reply with a precisely calibrated compliment to the senator who had just praised him. He was good at this game. The competition was stimulating; to exchange flattery with a tableful of U.S. senators is something like working out with the U.S. Olympic track team if you yourself are a world-class athlete: you understand how training and practice have enhanced the gifts of God.

One freshman senator strayed into forbidden territory by asking what Hammett proposed to do to frustrate the reactionary judges who had long controlled the Court, but Busby immediately intervened. "That's not really an issue," he said. "Our task is to confirm that the nominee is qualified." He smiled. "Beyond that be dragons."

The younger member replied testily, "How he's going to slay the right dragons is a question that speaks to his qualifications."

"Not really," said Busby firmly. "Let's move along."

But the other man persisted. "Are we allowed to ask how Mr. Hammett feels about the prospect of presiding over an impeachment trial in the Senate, since that will probably be the first job he has to do as Chief Justice?"

Busby said, "Nope."

One of the senior members grunted as though Busby's word had been a body punch. Hammett was protected from such inquiries by the long Senate tradition that considers the innermost thoughts, political opinions, and guiding moral convictions of an appointee to the Court out of bounds. Hammett himself thought that this tradition was insane, but he was perfectly willing to benefit from it.

Senator Marjorie Rynas, the only female present, spoke up. "Mr. Hammett," she said, "you've been quoted as saying that unsuccessful nominees for the Supreme Court are usually destroyed for ideological reasons by extremists in the opposition party."

Hammett nodded cautiously. This woman was an ally of Clark's and therefore no friend of his.

"Will you tell us why do you think that's so?" She arched her eyebrows. "I ask this question because it's sure to be asked by extremists on the other side."

His face pleasant yet unsmiling as it always was, Hammett nodded understandingly. "What I have told students and audiences is that extremists at both ends of the political spectrum are fundamentally antidemocratic," he replied. "They have always regarded control of the Supreme Court, and of the federal court system in general, as the key to political action because the rulings of the Court are not subject to democratic restraints. If you control the Court, you control policy without having to answer to the people, who sometimes may not know what's best for them. The Court's words are final, and in many respects an American judge can do whatever he wants to do. He has the power to restrain the President from carrying out certain actions, he has the power to overrule laws passed by Congress, he has the power to put anyone who misbehaves in his presence in jail without trial for contempt of court and to keep him there indefinitely."

"These are dictatorial powers. Isn't that what you've said in the past?"

"Yes, Senator. But always for the purpose of provoking thought and discussion. Clearly the judicial system, if perverted from its constitutional purposes, can be a prescription for absolute power. I've said many times that if we ever have a dictator in this country, it's entirely possible that he'll wear the robes of the Chief Justice."

Busby had not liked Senator Rynas's question, and he did not like the trend of Hammett's answer; it was a bad thing to have on the record. He said, "You don't really think this will ever happen, do you?"

"Not unless some great, unprecedented crisis destroys the power of the executive and legislative branches to govern," Hammett replied. "If that ever happened—and so far we've never even come close—only the Supreme Court could step in. The American military would never do it."

"So we could have a dictatorship of judges?"

"Of course we could, in theory," Hammett said. "Anything is possible. But we're just playing what-if, Senator. This isn't the apocalypse. Such a development would require terminal chaos and a Chief Justice who was a totalitarian personality. I say again: We've never even come close to having such a combination."

Silence fell. After a moment Sam Clark ended it, saying, "Not yet, anyhow."

Busby gave Hammett a long, thoughtful look while the other senators studied the tabletop. Everyone present knew that Hammett himself was a totalitarian personality. And notwithstanding the fact that his admirers vehemently rejected the description, this quality was the basis of his appeal on the radical left, just as the extreme right perceived Mallory as a leader who was capable of imposing their ideas on the country before it was too late.

Perceiving the mood, Hammett adroitly turned it to his advantage. "In my opinion, we don't have much to worry about," he said. "If Mallory couldn't find a way to appoint a dictator to the Court, nobody else is going to do it."

All heads nodded except Sam Clark's. He said, "I guess even Franklin never thought of destroying the country in order to save it." He balled up his napkin and threw it on the table. "And let that be our thought for the day."

The breakfast came to an end. Clark summed up. "I think we can all agree that the Senate has seldom, if ever, considered a candidate for Chief Justice who is quite like Mr. Archimedes Hammett," he said. "We can't know what kind of a Chief Justice he'll make. Even he doesn't know that. God knows we've had all kinds in the past, and the republic has always survived. The President of the United States wants him on that bench. Nobody in this room has any reason to say him nay. Others do, but they're outnumbered, and since we're dealing with Mr. Hammett here, maybe they'll even be outsmarted. In any case, the Senate will do its duty, Mr. Chief Justice-designate. The rest will be up to you."

With a curt nod to Hammett, but no handshake, Clark got up from his place and walked out of the room. One by one, the other senators filed by, shaking Hammett's hand as they left. Finally there was no one left in the room except Buzzer Busby. He was a tall, florid man with beautifully barbered white hair who wore a Yale class ring, a piece of jewelry seldom seen on the finger of a man of his social class, and large solid-gold cuff links that caught the light. He gazed benignly at Hammett, plainly wanting to speak some important last word, but the waiters lingered. Finally he said, "Mr. Hammett, come on into the next room for a minute, where we can be alone."

Hammett was immediately apprehensive. Things had gone well, but not perfectly. Why did Busby want to be alone with him? What was he going to say? Did he have some message from Clark, some warning about Clark's intentions? What doubt, what mental reservation, had Clark's skeptical behavior created? He followed Busby through a door into a small, unoccupied office.

Busby closed the door behind them. He said, "There's a question I couldn't ask you with the others present."

Hammett nodded. "Okay."

"I'm only asking it now because you seem a little worried and I want you to understand there's no reason for that." Busby moved closer. Then, looking Hammett straight in the eyes, he said, "What did Trelawny snatch from the funeral pyre at Viareggio?"

13

The White House announced Hammett's appointment at midmorning. In a matter of hours, as if some signal had been sent from a previously dormant lobe of its brain to every nerve in its body, the vanguard elite of his constituency went into action. In Skinnerian terms, the nomination was the greatest single stimulus ever administered to this particular tribe of believers, and the response was immediate and powerful. Before noon every United States senator who was not a sworn enemy of the Cause had received telephone calls from every single interest group backing the nomination, and from numerous journalists in Washington and back home. This added up to a great many calls, none of which a senator could afford to ignore. All knew that these calls from the priesthood were merely the first wave of the onslaught to come. Still before them were the calls, faxes, and letters from the faithful, hundreds of thousands of people all over the country whose first and sometimes only interest in life was the issue supported by a particular interest group.

At breakfast the next morning, Macalaster mentioned this process to Franklin Mallory.

Mallory nodded. "These people are having a religious experience," he said. "In the Dark Ages, monks preserved the knowledge of writing by copying out the Scriptures and making them more pleasing to the eye by illumination. What Hammett's folks want to do is take the country apart like a Rolex watch they got from Santa Claus, shake up the parts in a bucket according to methods perfected in the old USSR, and thereby produce a good proletarian alarm clock."

Though he was amused, Macalaster grunted noncommittally. He agreed with Mallory's point, but it would have been inelegant to say so. Too much harmony between writer and subject violated the unspoken protocol that governed relationships between politician and journalist.

It was still early. Wiggins and Lucy had called Macalaster at their accustomed hour of seven and driven him to another of Mallory's houses, this one a fortresslike granite mansion that overlooked Rock Creek Park. While breakfasting, he and Mallory watched a montage of television news coverage recorded earlier that morning and the night before—image after image of garrulous politicians and journalists forecasting quick and easy confirmation of Hammett by the Senate Judiciary Committee. Most of those interviewed also commented solemnly on the probability of Lockwood's impeachment, followed by conviction or exoneration, depending on the party affiliation of the man being interviewed. The Malloryites interviewed tended to be the most outrageous right-wing figures in his party; by no coincidence, they were usually also the least telegenic.

Mallory's video system, like all his other gadgets, was somewhat beyond state-of-the-art. To summon any particular interview onto the screen, he had only to speak the name of the person he wanted to see and hear; there were no visible controls. As Macalaster spread a spoonful of honey on his toast, Mallory said, "Busby." Instantaneously the chairman of the Senate Judiciary Committee appeared in a clip from the Patrick Graham show, saying, "That's an interesting question, Patrick. But I think it's accurate and fair to say that the committee isn't supporting this nomination as a matter of party loyalty, but because Archimedes Hammett is perceived as perhaps the only person in American life who has the credibility to preside over an impeachment trial, if it comes to that." Worriedly, Graham said, "*Will* it come to that, Senator?" Even more worriedly, as if personally feeling the weight of history (which of course he was), Buzzer Busby replied, "Patrick, as an American and a loyal member of my party, I'm sad to say I think it's inevitable. In our democracy, painful questions simply must be answered." The camera cut back to Graham, who said, "Even questions that perhaps should never have been asked." Busby looked thoughtful but said nothing as the camera lingered on his grave, handsome, dignified face.

Mallory switched off the set with a sharp monosyllable, and said to Macalaster, "We now come to what I wanted to talk to you about."

"Which is?"

"What it all means," Mallory said. "What you are observing is an example of the law of unintended results. Lockwood—or more likely Julian Hubbard—thought that the White House could tie up the system and delay the impeachment process by nominating a Chief Justice who could never be confirmed. But they miscalculated. The loonies will not be denied on this one. Hammett is going to sail through. We're going to have a psychopath as Chief Justice of the United States."

"You think Hammett's a psychopath?"

"What else would you call him?"

Macalaster blinked. There was a rare note of dislike in Mallory's voice. Clearly, beneath the urbanity, he was enough of a reactionary—and enough like Hammett—to think that the next Chief Justice was part of a conspiracy.

"I'm not sure I follow you," Macalaster said. "What exactly *does* all this mean for Lockwood?"

"It means the end of him," Mallory replied.

"But you yourself have told me that others stole the election, not Lockwood."

"What difference does that make? No matter who stole the election, the bottom line is that Lockwood wasn't elected President of the United States. So he'll have to go."

"Granted, assuming that your charges stand up in court. But why should he be finished?"

"If he resigns like a man, he won't be finished."

"Even if he's innocent of any crime?"

"Ah, innocence," Mallory said. " 'The more innocent they are, the more they deserve to die.' "

Macalaster said, "Another quote?"

"Bertolt Brecht, speaking of the defendants at the Moscow trial," Mallory replied. "And in less than a week every Hammett admirer in the country will be saying the same about Frosty Lockwood. He's wounded, he's old, he's a danger to the tribe. Get rid of him."

In a louder voice, directed to the television set, Mallory said, "Graham." The screen, enormous and perfectly tuned, sprang to life, revealing a tight shot of Patrick Graham.

"Archimedes Hammett's nomination," Graham was saying to his vast audience, "is an appeal to the conscience of every decent American. Nothing in our lifetime has been more important to the future of justice in America than this nomination."

Mallory turned off the set. "Pop goes the weasel," he said.

14

Lockwood himself quickly realized that Julian Hubbard had underestimated Hammett's power to appeal to and unite the radicals.

"This son of a bitch has laid a big kiss on Snow White," he said to Julian. "She's wide-awake and hot to trot."

Julian grinned at this Lockwoodian imagery.

"It's not funny, boy," Lockwood said. "I spent half the night on the phone with Sam Clark. He says the phones are ringing off the hook up on the Hill and the media are coming through the windows. They all want to line up and take a loyalty oath to Archimedes just as quick as they can."

"What about confirmation?"

"One week maximum. Pro forma hearings. Sam says the Senate is seized by the urgency of the situation. That wasn't the game plan you sold me. This guy was supposed to be unconfirmable."

"I know that, Mr. President. I'm as surprised as anyone."

"You'd better get used to surprises," Lockwood said. "Sam says that Attenborough is pushing the House Judiciary Committee to start its hearings on Mallory's charges next week. Hear that? *Next week.*"

This shocked Julian—not the statement itself, but the fact that he'd had no warning that these things were happening, and therefore had been unable to warn the President what was coming. In his world, where information was power, the worst possible fate was to be the last to know. He said, "They can't possibly move that fast."

"Like hell they can't. Attenborough wants to be President. His philosophy is, Why wait? They'll have articles of impeachment on the floor in ten days, and that fucking Pontius Pilate you went to Yale with will be presiding at my trial before the Senate by the end of March."

"What about Mallory's people?"

Lockwood threw up his arms in exasperation. "Franklin wants my ass out of the White House," he said.

"Yes, sir. But does he want Attenborough to be President?"

"One thing at a time. If you're thinking of advising me to put my faith in Franklin Mallory, forget it."

Julian started to reply, but Lockwood held up a hand. "No more bright ideas," he said. "It's getting away from us, boy!"

15

Late at night, after transcribing the notes of his meeting with Mallory, Macalaster worked on his column, a meditation on the subliminal aspects of the Hammett appointment. This caused him to think with great concentration about the radical he had known best, his late wife, and at one point, while composing a sentence about her that he later erased, he found himself weeping. Whether the tears were for Brook, or for Susan Grant, or for the waste of time and love and expectation in his own life, he did not know. Somehow the murder of Grant had given him the courage to think about his wife's violent end. Brook, he knew, would have used the word "sick" to describe the way in which the assassination of a woman she regarded as a Nazi bitch had released his emotions about her own death.

Macalaster wrote all this out in green luminescent letters. The computer screen, so like another consciousness in its eager response to every thought and word, had an almost hypnotic effect on him. It permitted him to talk about himself in perfect freedom and privacy. As he typed, he realized that he thought about Brook more lovingly now, and with less anger, than he ever had when she was alive. He was a man, after all, and it was her body that he remembered. He remembered it always as the body of a girl: long legs and long hair, a certain backward glance as she departed on the morning after the first night they went to bed together, a face animalized by sudden desire or wet with tears of sexual relief.

Such memories would have infuriated the living woman by confirming all her worst suspicions about Macalaster's real feelings toward her. He had never, as she had demanded, been able to love her mind as he loved her flesh; she had been right to accuse him on this score. One night, under the influence of gin, he had told her that he might have loved the mind she was born with had he ever known it, but by the time he met her she had joined the counterculture and swapped it for the model all the other girls were wearing that year. "You're a bunch of Barbie dolls, changing ideas like you used to change her outfits, and you don't even know it," he had blurted. "You bastard! You pig!" she had cried. "But I'll say this much," Macalaster had continued in drunken tones. "If the mind God gave you was anything like your ass, I would have been crazy about it." She came after him with the gin bottle and would have brained him if he had not defended himself. But moments later their death struggle turned into something else. For both of them, the physical aspect of their marriage had provided its only moments of happiness from their first night together right up to the end, twenty years later. Only in the unthinking moments of foreplay, coitus, and orgasm was Brook able to be what she really was, an American girl made for love, instead of the make-believe militant, half mad with anger because she did not really have anything to be angry about, into whom she tried to remake herself.

Macalaster was startled out of this line of memory by the ringing of his doorbell and a loud pounding on his front door. Because he was slightly deaf as the result of explosions he had heard at close range in Vietnam, and because the room where he worked behind a closed door was at the top of the house, Manal had to come upstairs in her pajamas to tell him what was happening. Like every other gently reared young female in America, she had been warned since earliest childhood never to answer the door unless she knew who was outside it. It was two o'clock in the morning, and the noise had alarmed her. As Brook had trained her to do, she carried a portable telephone in her hand in case she needed to call the police.

After running downstairs, Macalaster peered through the fisheye lens of the peephole in the front door and saw a fun-house version of Archimedes Hammett's face. He opened the door.

"I'm here to collect a favor," Hammett said.

Macalaster felt a rush of apprehension. Like so many others, he was bound to Hammett by a secret connection that placed him deeply in his debt. Neither of them had spoken about the matter for years, but Macalaster did not imagine that Hammett had come to his door in the small hours of the morning to ask for a trivial favor in return for having made him rich and famous.

"Ask away," Macalaster said.

"I need somewhere safe to stay for the next few days," Hammett said. "If I don't have a place to disappear to during the hearings, I won't have a moment's peace. Will you put me up?"

Macalaster was in no position to refuse. But he said, "Why here?"

"Because you're such a leper, Ross. No one would ever think of looking for me at your house."

During all this, the door stood open. Even though he wore a scarf and overcoat, Hammett was shivering. A weather front seemed to be moving through Washington. Trees bent in a brisk westerly wind; gusts of arctic air blew what remained of the inaugural snow.

"When do you want to move in?"

"Now. I've checked out of the hotel."

"All right."

"Super," Hammett said.

Macalaster blinked; he had before never heard the man use a word like "super." Hammett made a gesture to someone inside a Volvo station wagon that was parked at the curb with its motor idling. Two women dressed in ankle-length calico dresses and hiking boots got out of the car and started unloading picnic coolers and the cardboard boxes of files, notes, and books without which Hammett never traveled. One was blond, thin and willowy, with enormous blue eyes, like a *Vogue* model. She wore no coat and her thin skirt blew around her long and unusually beautiful legs. Despite the weather, they were bare.

Macalaster said, "The skinny one is going to catch pneumonia."

"Not her," Hammett said. "She's absolutely impervious to cold."

The other one, who was almost as dark as Manal, was rawboned and as tall and broad-shouldered as a good-sized man, but she was bundled up in a puffy down parka. She caught Macalaster staring at her friend's legs and sneered in feminist disgust.

Macalaster waved to her cheerily. To Hammett he said, "Are the Bulimia sisters staying too?"

"No. Slim and Sturdi just drove my stuff down from Connecticut."

" 'Slim and Sturdy'? They let you get away with calling them those sexist names?"

"I didn't make them up. Slim is the real name of the one with blond hair. Sturdi likewise—it's short for Sturdevant, her chattel name. She was a great athlete in college. Almost made the Olympics."

"As what? A weight lifter?"

"As a matter of fact, she does work out. But her event was the heptathlon. Do they put the shot?"

"She goes by her, uh, chattel name?"

"She did until she changed it to Eve a couple of years ago. Slim is also surnamed Eve."

"I see," said Macalaster with a tight-lipped smile. If his wife were still alive, no doubt she would now be legally known as Brook Eve. Among militant feminists the surname Eve had lately come into fashion as an alternative to what they termed the "chattel names" that had been imposed on them by the males who had impregnated their female ancestors. In emulation of Malcolm X, who had exhorted blacks to rid themselves of slave names half a century before, the originators of this fashion argued that every surname was a reminder of bondage because every daughter was named for and by her mother's rapist. "She" had been considered as an alternative appellation, but it was rejected because it contained the name of the enemy—"he"—hidden within it. Finally they settled on the simple and beautiful alternative "Eve," which was a sign of female infinity because it was spelled the same forward and backward. Equally important, it was the name assigned by genetic researchers to the single primal female from whom, as the scientific examination of the DNA of the placenta had established, all women, but no men, were descended. Every woman now alive, every woman who had ever lived, carried the genetic code of this single first female who was, in effect, the mother of humanity. In the beginning and ever after, Life was Woman—or as Slim and Sturdi spelled the word, Womon. But no man's body could ever possibly contain the code of Eve, because no man could produce a placenta.

Macalaster said, "What do Eve and Eve do when they're not handling baggage?"

"They're lawyers specializing in environmental issues, animal rights, and so on—from a feminist orientation, of course."

"Of course."

Hammett made it clear by a change of expression that this subject was exhausted. His eyes and mind were already elsewhere. His attention had been captured by a movement behind Macalaster inside the house, and he smiled and gazed upward at someone on the staircase. Macalaster followed his glance. Manal stood on the landing with the phone in her hand.

Macalaster said, "Archimedes is going to stay with us for a few days, Manal. Until the hearings are over."

"We'll have to keep my being here a secret," Hammett said, "or you'll have a media circus on the front lawn, so don't tell anyone I'm here, okay?"

Manal nodded in her silent way. Hammett nodded in return and kept on smiling as if he had many fond memories of their earlier times together. Calling up the stairway to the child, he said gaily, "I hope we can have one of those sessions of yours quite soon."

Manal looked puzzled by his choice of words.

"Like we had the other night, with the words spelled out," Hammett said.

"Oh. A séance."

Manal smiled noncommittally, then walked away in the direction of her bedroom. Macalaster looked at Hammett with curiosity. For the first time in all the years he had known him, the other man seemed to feel that he had to explain himself. "I thought it was great fun, talking to the departed," Hammett said.

Then he winked. *Winked.* Long afterward, this was what Macalaster would remember.

III

1

Norman Carlisle Blackstone, Esq., was a detail man, a slow worker, a careful thinker, a painstaking briefer. These qualities had won him respect and large fees on Wall Street, where he had spent many years managing the estates and trusts of the old rich and preserving the new rich from indictment.

However, ponderous deliberation was not a quality that President Bedford Forrest Lockwood greatly admired. He himself lacked it almost entirely. He had completed forward passes, shot baskets, won the presidency, on pure instinct. As long as he was himself and delivered the goods, positive things happened. On the morning after his encounter with Hammett, Lockwood could not bear the thought of hearing Blackstone's report on the legal aspects of the impeachment process. "Just get the essentials and boil 'em down for me," he said to Julian.

"I think that would be a mistake," Julian said. "Carlisle may be a pain in the neck sometimes, but he has a fine legal mind."

"Goddamnit, Julian, I haven't got the time, I haven't got the patience."

"Mr. President, you're a lawyer; I'm not. I think you should be the one to listen to the details."

Lockwood had gone to law school for the credential but had never practiced and had no great interest in the subtleties of the law.

Julian said, "He's on his way down the hall right now."

"Damn!" Lockwood said. But he wasn't truly displeased; if Blackstone bored him nearly to tears, he also amused him to the same result because he was such a wonderful example of his type. Lockwood liked his people eccentric but pigeonholed.

"Old Spats reminds me of the story about the Boston hotel clerk and Daniel Webster," he said. "Every morning around five, the clerk would be sweeping up the lobby and Daniel Webster would roll in after a night of revelry. After about a week of this, the clerk can stand it no more. He says, 'Senator, can I ask you a question?' Webster says, 'Fire when ready.' Clerk says, 'We're both freeborn one hundred percent Americans. Every morning of my life I get up at four, fix breakfast for my dear old sickly mama, get to work fifteen minutes early and stay fifteen minutes late, then go home and cook the supper. I make two dollars a week sweeping floors and taking guff from anyone who feels like giving it to me. I've never once laid a lascivious hand on a woman, never taken a drop of liquor, never smoked, never cussed. The only enjoyment I have is getting up at five-thirty on Sundays to pump the organ down at the Congregational Church, coffee and doughnuts afterward.' In his booming voice, Webster says, 'A worthy life! But what's the question?' Clerk says, 'I'm ready to ask it. You stay out all night, come in at dawn every blessed morning reekin' of cigar smoke, whiskey, and perfume, then you sleep all day and go out again when the sun goes down.' Webster says, 'All correct. What's the question?' Clerk says, 'Here's the question. Given the way we both serve the Lord and our fellow man, how come you're a United States senator, rich and famous, and I'm just a two-dollar-a-week hotel clerk that's never even had a piece of tail?' And old Daniel Webster replies, 'The trouble with you, young fella, is you're no damn good when you *do* get up.' "

When Blackstone came into the Oval Office gripping his briefing book, he found Lockwood and Julian guffawing and wiping their eyes. He had overheard the last line, and there was little doubt in his mind that the joke was on him. Nevertheless, he admired the President's astonishing aplomb. Nothing, not even the prospect of impeachment and disgrace, could prevent this noble savage from making jokes. Some might have thought Lockwood's behavior common, even vulgar, but Blackstone saw it as a sign of unconquerable vitality. He had worked it out in his mind that the secret of Lockwood's greatness—and in Blackstone's opinion he had to be considered a great man—was that he *was* ordinary, but ordinary in a magnified, peculiarly American way, like Andrew Jackson and Abraham Lincoln and Harry Truman, so that people saw themselves in him.

"Come on in, Carlisle," said Lockwood, as if surprised but delighted to see Blackstone. "Join the group. We've been talking about American history."

Stooped and intense, peering through his pince-nez, wearing one of his Edwardian costumes with watch fob and stickpin, Blackstone tried to enter into what seemed to be the manly spirit of the occasion. "I guess some parts of it have been pretty funny," he said.

"It's a laugh a minute," Lockwood said.

Many things about working in the White House had surprised Blackstone, but nothing more than the condition of ignorance in which high policy was made and executed. He soon realized that the President and his aides lived out their fifteen-hour days in fifteen-minute segments, getting through one appointment after another just for the sake of doing so, and forgetting what had happened as soon as one encounter ended and another began. There was no time to think, much less reflect on the lessons of history. Decisions were made on the spur of the moment, with no regard for causes or consequences. Since boyhood Blackstone had believed that the world would be saved when at last it was ruled by wisdom. How, then, in the highest councils of the greatest nation on earth, could there be no philosophical basis for policy, no inventory of national interests, no *scholarship*? Had this always been so in America? He suspected that the answer was yes.

Amiably, but hoping to set a serious tone, Blackstone said, "You've been very busy, sir—"

"Yep, sure have been," said Lockwood, cutting off the rest of a pleasantry for which he had no use. "But the best is yet to come. Now, Counselor, sit ye down and tell me everything you know about impeachment. Or"— he winked—"haven't you done your homework?"

Smiling stiffly, Blackstone abstained from mentioning that he had not been home for a week and had the worst case of eyestrain of his lifetime. He knew better than anyone that he bored the President; he did not want to do so now, at least not unduly.

Lockwood saw that he had given offense. "Hell, Carlisle," he said in a more kindly tone, "I only ask because I've had complaints about your leaving the lights on all night. That's a violation of my national energy policy."

Blackstone relaxed a little. Lockwood said, "What have you got for me?"

"I have the constitutional briefing you requested," Blackstone said. He cleared his throat. "But I also have some substantive information."

"About what?"

"About the likely authenticity of Mallory's data on the election."

"Don't tell me," Lockwood said. "Let me guess. You've proved his case for him."

"Perhaps you'd rather just read my report," Blackstone said, offering a sheaf of documents.

Lockwood waved them away. "No. I'm all ears, Spats. Go."

Blackstone said, "I asked our pollster to check a scientifically selected sample of the polling records in the suspect precincts in Michigan, New York, and California, matching these against the result of exit polls taken among voters who had just cast their ballots." He paused, as if reluctant to go on without permission.

"And?" Lockwood said.

"And the exit polls do not match the actual results in any case. In all but a few instances, a majority of people in those precincts told the poll takers they had voted for one of your opponents. But according to the final results you won the actual vote."

" '*One* of my opponents'?" Lockwood pounced on the phrase. "What are you trying to tell me, Carlisle?"

"There were more than two candidates for President on the ballot in all three states," Blackstone replied. "If votes were, indeed, stolen, it does not follow that all were stolen from Mallory."

"They could have been stolen from any of the three."

"Or from all three."

"Does that mean what I think it means?"

"It means that Mallory may be able to demonstrate that you were not elected. But unless he can trace every stolen vote, he will find it difficult to prove in a court of law that he, himself, *was* elected."

"And you think that's to our advantage?"

"It is always advantageous to be able to raise doubts about the legitimacy of your adversary's case."

"Not if everybody loses," Lockwood said. "What I want to do is win. Remember that. Next subject."

Blackstone put one set of papers away and produced another. He was sitting with his knees together, documents on his lap. He said, "Shall I assume that you know the constitutional basics, Mr. President?"

"You dastn't assume a damn thing where I'm concerned, Carlisle. Nobody in my job has been impeached for a hundred and fifty years, so start from scratch."

The actual number of years since the Andrew Johnson case was 133. Blackstone did not point this out. He handed Lockwood the briefing book and proceeded on memory. "First, briefly, some history," he said. "Essentially, impeachment is a device to charge and try persons, noblemen and others, who are traditionally above the law. In Britain, where it has been in use since the seventeenth century, this never meant the sovereign, who derived his rights from God."

"Fascinating." Lockwood leaned forward, planting his elbows on his knees and his chin in his hands. As Blackstone knew, this was always a sign that the President was losing his concentration. A polka-dot handkerchief flowed from the lawyer's breast pocket. Lockwood stared at it fixedly, apparently to focus his mind. This was disconcerting to Blackstone, who felt that he was talking to a cross-eyed man.

Blackstone continued, "However, as is the case with so much that the Founding Fathers handed down to us, the American form of impeachment is in some ways the same as the British, but in other particulars profoundly different. The chief dissimilarity is that the House of Representatives can impeach the head of state. A second difference is that the British monarch may pardon a person convicted of an impeachable offense, but the President of the United States may not do so."

Lockwood interrupted with a lifted forefinger. "What about Nixon?"

"He was not impeached. He resigned before his case came to a vote," said Blackstone. "Shall I expand on that?"

"No. Move on. Tell me how the whole thing works, from day one."

"For reasons it deems sufficient—there is no other test—the House of Representatives passes a resolution. The wording in the Andrew Johnson case was simple: 'Resolved, that Andrew Johnson, President of the United States, be impeached for high crimes and misdemeanors.' Essentially the same form was followed in the case of Richard Nixon."

"Then it goes to the Judiciary Committee."

"In Nixon's case, yes. However, Johnson's impeachment was handled by the House Committee on Reconstruction. The House can designate any one of its committees to handle this phase of the process, or it can create an entirely new one for the purpose. And if that committee finds grounds to believe an offense has taken place, it prepares articles of impeachment for transmittal to the House. The House then votes on the articles of impeachment. A simple majority of all members present is required for adoption."

"What exactly constitutes 'high crimes and misdemeanors'?"

"There is no definition of these terms in law. Richard Nixon seems to have been condemned not for what he did, for which there was no documentary evidence until the Supreme Court, in effect, ordered him to incriminate himself by releasing the famous tapes, but for what a majority of the House of Representatives and the news media perceived him to be—a bad man. Andrew Johnson was impeached for firing his Secretary of War, Edwin M. Stanton, after Congress passed the Tenure of Office Act requiring the consent of the Senate to any such dismissal and providing that a violation of its terms should be 'a high misdemeanor.' From this, a reasonable man might conclude that the act was designed to entrap the President, a political maneuver pure and simple. And as you yourself have suggested, sir, so, in a more complicated way, was the Nixon case. Alexander Hamilton, who opposed the inclusion of impeachment provisions in the Constitution, warned that the process would always be driven by politics, not legal principles."

"Forewarned is forearmed," Lockwood said. "How is the trial conducted?"

"Like any other trial, except that it takes place in the Senate chamber,"

Blackstone said. "The articles of impeachment adopted by the House are read, evidence is introduced, witnesses are examined, the Chief Justice presides and makes rulings as required, and the lawyers present arguments. When the case is completed, the Senate, with each member under oath or affirmation, convicts or acquits, with the question of guilt or innocence being put to each senator in alphabetical order by roll call. The votes of two thirds of the members present are required for conviction."

Lockwood shifted his gaze from Blackstone's pocket handkerchief to his long, troubled face. "Who prosecutes?"

"The House appoints the prosecutors, called 'managers,' from among its members," Blackstone said.

"How long did Johnson's trial last?"

"Two months."

"Too long," Lockwood said. "And after all that, the Senate acquitted him by one vote. Is that right?"

"That's one way of putting it," Blackstone said. "In more accurate terms, the Senate vote in favor of conviction fell short of a two-thirds majority by a single vote. The exact count was thirty-five yes to nineteen no, with seven Republicans joining twelve Democrats for acquittal. Johnson remained in office, but it cannot be said that he was vindicated."

"So if I say to hell with vindication, all I need is thirty-four votes to survive?"

"Exactly," Blackstone said. "But I must tell you, sir, that you have a much more difficult case to defend than Andrew Johnson did. Or even Nixon."

Lockwood glared. "Worse than Nixon?" he cried. "Jesus! How's that, Counselor?"

"The charge, stealing a presidential election, is the most serious that can possibly be brought. It strikes at the heart of the Constitution. This is no defiance of Congress or camouflaged struggle on the part of Congress to wrest control of policy from a duly elected President, as with Johnson and Nixon. The controlling question is, Who is the rightful President? The main objective of all concerned, including yourself, will be to reestablish the fundamental sovereignty of the people by arriving at the truth. No sensible prosecutor will even suggest that political advantage is a consideration. He'll hammer hell out of the facts *and* the law. And barring a miracle, assuming the evidence stands up, he will surely win."

Lockwood bared his teeth. He snarled, "Your long experience as a political expert and a trial lawyer tells you this?"

Unblinking, Blackstone said, "Mr. President, we both know I'm not a trial attorney. But I went to law school at night in a tough neighborhood—not Harvard or Yale, but a school that prepares you to work in the world as it really is—with several fellows who are pretty darn good courtroom lawyers. I consulted them. It's their opinion—their unanimous opinion—that I am passing on to you."

"And what did your legal eagles say the defense would do while the prosecution is eating us alive?" Lockwood's tone was contemptuous. He was hearing things he did not want to be told, and he was suddenly irritated by Blackstone's New York accent, which had grown steadily stronger as he spoke.

Blackstone wearily removed his pince-nez and looked Lockwood straight in the eyes. "The defense would hope to save the President by throwing some lesser figure to the wolves," he said. "I think Julian had better tell his brother that it's time to come home."

2

No one was more interested in the whereabouts of Horace Hubbard than the Speaker of the House of Representatives, R. Tucker Attenborough, Jr., of Dead Horse Mountain, Texas. Before entering Congress forty years earlier, at the age of twenty-five, the Speaker had been nicknamed "One-Question Attenborough" for winning the acquittal of the owner of an isolated gas station who had caused the untimely death of a bearded stranger from Cambridge, Massachusetts. The victim had sealed his own fate by passing a remark about the beautiful young woman who happened to be the Texan's bride of three weeks.

The state of Texas alleged that the defendant had committed murder in the second degree, or at the very least first-degree manslaughter, by knocking the bearded stranger unconscious with a blow of his fist, binding him hand and foot with electrical wire, and then lowering him into an abandoned quicksilver mine shaft in nearby Terlingua by means of a rope tied beneath his armpits. When the accused went back a couple of days later to haul the bearded stranger to the surface (he didn't return sooner because his bride pleaded with him not to do so, on grounds that he was still mad enough to kill him), he found him dead of suffocation.

Attenborough called just one witness for the defense, the insulted wife, and in the incredibly loud bass voice for which he was later to achieve nationwide fame, asked her a single question: What were the exact words uttered in her hearing by the bearded stranger on that fateful day? And though she was a Christian girl in whose presence, as she testified, no male had ever before uttered a word stronger than "golly" or "gosh," Attenborough gently urged her to bring herself to repeat the words the man had spoken because the life of her young husband was at stake. She did so, in a tremulous whisper that could barely be heard in the hushed courtroom, only after lifting her lovely face to heaven and uttering a silent prayer for forgiveness. The words were, "Wow, man! That's eatin' pussy!" Whereupon Attenborough thundered, "The defense rests."

The Attenborough family was long on brains but short in physical stature; Attenborough's father, the Reverend Dick T. Attenborough, had been known as "the shortest Dick west of the Pecos," which was why the Speaker went by the name R. Tucker. While making his closing argument to the jury, he had had his client stand beside him; the accused was six foot three, the lawyer five foot two. Attenborough said, "Now, my client may have been a little bit naughty, and he may have been a little bit hotheaded, but if he'da wanted to kill that bearded stranger, he sure coulda done so. Look at the size of him, ladies and gentlemen of the jury. No hippie from Cambridge, Massachusetts, site of that justly celebrated institution Harvard University, could have survived this young giant's wrath if he had vented it. But this recent bridegroom, so deeply in love with his pure young bride, did not want or intend to do murder or manslaughter or commit any other crime. No, he merely wanted to teach the man who had offended her some manners. It wasn't this richly deserved lesson in gentlemanly comportment that killed that foulmouthed stranger, for the Book of Isaiah, chapter the first, verse the seventeenth, tells us to 'take wrongdoing out of my sight, learn to be good, discipline the violent.' All this boy was trying to do, friends, was what the Good Book advises us all to do, and why a greater punishment was imposed in the dark and mysterious depths of that old mine shaft, only the all-seeing Almighty knows." The jury reached its verdict for acquittal on all charges after just seven minutes of deliberation.

Now, three decades later, Attenborough bellowed, "I've got just one question, Mr. President. Where the hell is Horace Hubbard?"

"Tucker, how the hell would I know?"

They were drinking Maker's Mark at the end of the day in the windowless room in the Executive Office Building that Lockwood used for discreet meetings.

"If I were you, I'd find out," Attenborough said, holding out his glass for a refill.

The two men were in shirtsleeves, seated on opposite sides of a conference table, with the bottle and a bucket of ice between them.

Lockwood said, "What do you think I'm trying to do? But it ain't easy. Old Horace is a master spy. Even the goddamn FIS can't find him."

"The FIS couldn't find its own pecker if Miss America held the mirror for 'em," Attenborough replied. "Have you tried asking Horace's brother where he is?"

"Half brother. What for? If Julian knew, he'd tell me."

"You think so? You don't know a hell of a lot about brothers, Brother."

Lockwood said, "Don't call me brother. All you want out of Horace Hubbard is a witness you can ask one question: 'How soon can I be President of the United States, even though I could never in a million years get my sorry Texas ass elected because it's too close to the ground.' "

Attenborough let silence gather before replying in dignified tones to this insult. "There's no need for that kind of talk, Frosty," he said at last. "Neither one of us wrote the Constitution. You're the President, you're the head of our party, and you're my friend, and you know damn well I'd rather farm rattlesnakes than have the job that you've got—no matter how Franklin Mallory says you got it."

"Right," Lockwood said. "It took 'em two, three months to impeach and try old Andrew Johnson. What's your schedule?"

Attenborough shifted in his chair seat. He said, "Well, frankly, Frosty, I was hoping you'd control the schedule." He opened the battered old leather briefcase with his initials on it, given to him for graduating first in his class from the law school at El Paso, extracted a letter, and laid it between them.

"What's this?" Lockwood said.

"It's a letter."

"I thought you and your boys were going to deliver it in a body—have a pep rally out front."

"That's not the way we do business, Mr. President."

About two thirds of Attenborough's bourbon had vanished. Lockwood topped him up again with a steady hand, then took the letter out of the unsealed envelope and looked at it without his glasses. The three or four typed lines at the top were a blur, and so were the several pages of signatures that followed.

"My arm's not long enough to make this out," he said. "What's it say?"

"It asks you and the Vice President to stand aside under the Twenty-fifth Amendment until the issue of the outcome of the last presidential election is resolved by the Congress."

Lockwood waved the letter. "How many signatures is this?"

Attenborough replied, "A hundred and thirty-seven."

"Is yours one of them, Tuck?"

"No, sir."

"I thought it might be missing, just in case I said yes and you reluctantly had to step into my job," Lockwood said.

"Goddamnit, Frosty, for the last time, I don't *want* your job. I'm just trying to find a way to resolve this unholy mess them rich boys have got you into without impeaching you. If you're not in the presidency, nobody can throw you out of it. Use your head, boy!"

"In other words, this is a trick."

"You can call it that. It's a way out for you and the party."

"That's what I figured," Lockwood said. "You can save me the trouble of saying this a hundred and thirty-seven more times. Go on back and tell the boys I said, 'Shove it.' "

3

At two o'clock the following morning, Julian stopped in to see Carlisle Blackstone. The lawyer sat with his back to the door, absorbed in his work, and was not aware that he had a visitor until Julian spoke.

"Still at it, Carlisle?"

Blackstone turned around to face him. "As you see." He made no effort to smile.

Julian leaned against the doorjamb and crossed one ankle elegantly over the other, the burnished toe of an English oxford resting on the carpet. To all appearances he was wholly at ease despite his desperate circumstances. Only a man of his breeding could have struck such a pose when his own brother's chances for disgrace, even prison, were so great— or so Blackstone believed as the result of a lifetime of opposing nonchalant WASP lawyers whose clients were as guilty as sin.

"I've just put the Boss to bed," Julian said. "He's a little sheepish about having raised his voice to you this morning."

"No need. I didn't expect him to like what I told him."

"He understands that you were just doing your duty. He's a lawyer himself, in a manner of speaking. But he feels he was a little sharp."

Blackstone waited, wondering if Julian would say something about the suggestion that his brother—*half* brother; the correction was becoming automatic—be thrown to the wolves.

But of course Julian did not mention the matter. He unwound his legs, looked at his watch, and flinched in mock surprise at what it told him. "I'd better go home. Doesn't your wife complain about your hours?"

"She wouldn't come down here with me—too hot, too slow, too far from everything; it makes her nervous to ride in taxis that don't have meters. We spend weekends together in New York."

"*Really?*" Julian said, genuinely interested and surprised. "I had no idea."

"Well," Blackstone said, "those are the facts of the case."

It was Blackstone's turn to smile; although he and Julian had worked together every day for four years, neither man had met the other's wife except at state dinners. Even then the encounter consisted of a vague smile, a compliment, an introduction as a means of escape. When Caroline was replaced in Julian's bed by Emily, he had introduced his second wife by title alone ("Mr. and Mrs. Blackstone, my wife"), as though presenting a new special assistant to the President; it was the office, not the occupant, that counted. Emily, a fresh-faced friendly girl who looked (as Blackstone realized the next time he went to the National Gallery of Art) like Renoir's portrait of Mme. Henriot, had supplied her own first name, along with a firm handshake.

An hour after Julian went home, Blackstone's telephone rang. Lockwood's voice resounded in the earpiece. "Come on upstairs."

In the Lincoln sitting room, Lockwood offered five kinds of Kentucky bourbon, Scotch, gin, vodka. Blackstone shook his head no to each.

Finally Lockwood said, "Coffee? Tea? Glass of milk?"

"Thank you, Mr. President. Nothing."

"Do you take any kind of stimulants, Carlisle?"

"Wine with dinner, martinis on weekends in the privacy of my own home. Gin has an unpredictable effect on me."

"You too? Makes me mean or horny, usually at the same time. Polly made me give it up years ago. That's probably why I'm where I am today, which goes to show you there are worse things than a martini fit."

Blackstone smiled appreciatively, understanding that Lockwood was making up for his earlier lack of graciousness. Clearly the President was perfectly sober now, his liver having metabolized the half-pint of Maker's Mark he had consumed a few hours earlier in the company of Attenborough. From the litter of papers surrounding him, he produced a sheet of stiff White House bond on which the names and capsule biographies of half a dozen famous trial lawyers had been typed.

"Give this a gander."

Blackstone read it. He had not seen the document before, but he immediately recognized it for what it was: Julian Hubbard's short list of candidates to defend Lockwood before the Senate. He knew every lawyer on the list; he had bested some of them, and been bested by others, in past legal encounters.

"Opinion?" Lockwood said.

"All good men."

"I *know* that, Spats. Every one of them is a Harvard or a Yale. What's your opinion of that?"

"The first part of my opinion is that it's only natural, since Julian drew up the list with the advice of the people he's known all his life."

"What's the second part?"

"That any one of these fine lawyers, or any combination thereof, will cost the U.S. government many millions of dollars in fees and expenses in return for losing the case."

Lockwood was slumped and tousled; he beckoned for more words.

Blackstone said, "After President Nixon fired the special prosecutor who did him in, Professor Archibald Cox of Harvard, and after the Harvard-educated attorney general who had hired Cox, Elliot Richardson, had also resigned, a local lawyer sent Nixon a message through confidential channels. It read: 'Tell the President never again to put himself in the hands of the Harvards.' " Blackstone tapped Julian's list. "Mr. President, men like these don't give a tinker's dam what happens to you. The way they look at the world, you were nothing to begin with, so you've got nothing to lose if you lose the presidency."

Lockwood grunted. "Those are hard words."

"I know that, sir. I chose them with care. Appoint any of these people and it'll look good in the newspapers. The whole Ivy League will clap hands in unison—old Winthrop got the case. And when it's over, they'll all get together in the clubs and say, 'Old Winthrop did his best, but the peasant—what was that fellow's name?—did steal the sheep, so naturally they had to hang him.' "

"On what do you base this opinion, Counselor?"

"On a lifetime of watching these types operate."

"I think I understand your general proposition. Anything in particular bothering you about the individuals on the list?"

"No, sir. They're all alike; the whole point of the system that produces them is to turn out a type. There's not a one of them who would pick you if it came to a choice between you and somebody like Horace Hubbard."

Lockwood feigned a broad smile of amusement. "You've sure got it in for poor old Horace," he said.

"Mr. President, I don't know Horace Hubbard from Job's off ox," Blackstone said. "But it was poor old Horace, acting on the very instincts I've just described, who got you into this situation in the first place. Do you think he stole those votes to save *your* skin?"

"I think he may have thought so at the time."

Blackstone laughed aloud, a single derisive un-Blackstone-like honk. "He may say just that when we lay hands on him. I'll be surprised if he says anything else. He may even believe it. But noblesse oblige is no defense before the law."

Lockwood sighed, closed his eyes, sighed again. A lengthy silence ensued. When he reopened his eyelids, Blackstone said, "Think of yourself, Mr. President. Think of the country. Think of the future. You can't harm the Hubbards of this world."

Lockwood stared at him, eyes cold, mouth stubborn, color creeping into his cheeks. Finally, holding out his hand for the return of Julian's list, he said, "You do agree I need a lawyer? Besides you, I mean."

"Yes, sir."

"And you've got a candidate in mind."

"Yes, sir. I have."

"Can he save my ass?"

"I don't know," Blackstone said. "But if anybody can, he can."

Lockwood did not ask the man's name. He said, "Then whoever he is, have him here, in this room, at midnight tomorrow. Just the three of us." He put on his reading glasses and peered over the rims. "Good night."

Blackstone left him. Walking down the hall, he heard Lockwood's voice calling his name. He turned around. The President was out of sight, evidently still in his chair. "Spats!" he called after him. "Keep up the good work."

4

That day's editions of *The Washington Post* printed the full text of the letter to Lockwood with the signatures of all one hundred thirty-seven members of Congress appended. The unnamed member of the House who had leaked the letter expressed shock and dismay that the President had angrily refused to accept delivery of this epistle from the Speaker of the House. "Our intention," said the source, "was to let the President know our thinking without making it public. He let us know he didn't want to listen." Meanwhile, *The New York Times* reported that a second anonymous but "highly placed and knowledgeable source"—reporters' shorthand for R. Tucker Attenborough, Jr., thought Lockwood—had told a different journalist that a resolution for impeachment was imminent.

"That little son of a bitch is trying to steal the presidency!" Lockwood said to Sam Clark over the telephone.

"You're free to suspect anything you like but in this case you're way off base," Clark replied. "However, I agree that there's more to this than meets the eye."

"There is? What?"

"You know as well as I do."

Lockwood exploded. "Jesus H. Christ, Sam, how the hell would *I* know? I haven't had an original idea, or heard one, since they locked me up in this place four years ago. Just tell me what you're talking about."

"All right. It's too quiet out there, friend. Everybody's falling all over themselves to say Archimedes Hammett is the finest Supreme Court nominee since Felix Frankfurter came down from Harvard lugging the stone tablets of the New Deal. Where's all the hooraw that was supposed to be stirred up by nominating a man from Mars for Chief Justice?"

"Mallory's people just haven't got their act together yet. I took 'em by surprise."

"They're over the surprise, but they're still not saying a word," Clark said. "It's not natural."

In a tone of mockery, Lockwood said, "You think there's a plot?"

Clark was not amused. He replied, "I think you'd have to be crazy not to take that possibility into account. But if there is one, Tucker Attenborough isn't in on it."

Lockwood respected Sam Clark's opinion on the way things work in Washington above that of anyone else in the world, but he was not in a mood to listen to kind words about Attenborough. He remained silent for a long moment. Then he said, " 'Bye, Sam," and hung up the phone.

Julian was not privy to this conversation, nor did Lockwood mention it to him. Julian was working the telephones, calling in chips, counting heads. The coin and currency of Washington commerce were gossip and rumor. As Julian came in and out of the Oval Office that day, Lockwood listened to everything he had to report, even though he already knew or had guessed most of it as a result of experience and instinct. Little happened that had not happened before or would not happen again in this inbred community, where nearly every newcomer reminded an old hand like Lockwood of someone he used to know. Being President in his present circumstances, he thought, was like being the terminally ill patriarch of a vast clan of white trash. Every single member was engaged in a family fight over his estate. Everybody was out to screw everybody else. They all kept secrets from him. But he knew exactly what was going on out back: the cousins were just doing what they'd always done, counting their chickens before they hatched and lying on top of each other making more half-wit cousins who thought every idea they had was completely original. If you knew this you knew it all. "To hell with all of 'em!" he said aloud to the walls of his grand but lonesome office.

At eight o'clock, Lockwood drove Julian out of the White House. "Go home!" he said in a voice of command. "Take Emily out to dinner, watch a movie. Gather ye rosebuds while ye may, for tomorrow . . . well, you know the rest."

"I should stand by."

"Goddamnit, boy, I don't *want* you here. I've had enough for one day. I want my supper, I want my mommy, I want some peace and quiet. Go."

Resentfully, though he did not betray this or any other feeling, Julian went.

5

Norman Carlisle Blackstone ushered Alfonso Olmedo C. into the Lincoln sitting room on the stroke of midnight. The C. stood for Crespo, his mother's maiden name; although he had been born in the United States, he retained the Spanish style of nomenclature prevalent in Bolivia, whence his family came. Having a final initial instead of a middle one set him off from the crowd, and, as he invariably said to pretty women and journalists, it had the added advantage of sowing confusion in the telephone company.

Lockwood was surprised by Olmedo's costume. He was dressed in a tuxedo and ruffled shirt with a wide black tie. He wore a large diamond ring on the little finger of his right hand and a diamond-studded solid-gold Cartier watch on his left wrist. As he drew closer to shake hands, Lockwood detected cologne. Crushing his hand, the President said, "Adolphe Menjou, by God!"

Olmedo, a former Golden Gloves welterweight from the South Bronx who was still quite strong, returned the pressure on his metacarpal bones ounce for ounce and arched a quizzical eyebrow. "My appearance surprises you, Mr. President?"

"I expected a rabbi," Lockwood said.

"Carlisle raises everyone's expectations," Olmedo replied with an almost undetectable Hispanic intonation in his resonant voice.

Lockwood could not quite place this man; he frowned. "Olmedo!" he said after a second or two of concentration. "Now I remember. You're the fellow that beat Franklin Mallory in his own Supreme Court."

"Hardly that, Mr. President. What I did was argue the case that established a woman's future property rights in regard to an embryo fertilized in her womb and subsequently removed therefrom."

"That's right. He lost, you won."

"Possibly." Olmedo lowered his eyebrows and changed the subject. "But please forgive the way I'm dressed, Mr. President. I was the speaker at a dinner in New York, and I had no time to change before flying down."

"No problem, Adolphe."

Olmedo was a wiry man of average height, but he held himself in such a way that Lockwood had the impression he was looking at someone his own size. Olmedo's skin was bronze, the eyes dark and piercing, the abundant black hair brushed straight back from a high sloping forehead. Lockwood thought, Jesus, he looks like the king of the Incas. He said, "Have we ever met before?"

"Once, at one of Carlisle's functions, but it was only a handshake."

"You and he are old friends?"

"We went to college and law school together."

"Fordham. The Seven Blocks of Granite, Frankie Frisch, the Fordham Flash, player-manager of the Gashouse Gang. You're a Catholic?"

Olmedo looked at Lockwood with curiosity. No American had asked him such a question in years. "Of that tradition. But I don't practice a religion."

"That's good; neither do I," Lockwood said. "You think your buddy here is a pretty good lawyer?"

"I know of none better."

"Why's that, exactly?"

With a smile Olmedo said, "Make yourself deaf, Carlisle. The reason is a simple one, Mr. President. He has a scholarly mind that is both brilliant and perfectly honest. The former qualities are rare in a member of our profession. The last is almost unheard-of."

"Take a chair," Lockwood said, as if Olmedo had just passed some arcane initiation rite and earned the privilege of sitting in his presence. "I appreciate your coming down on short notice."

Olmedo nodded, acknowledging the aptness of this remark. His time *was* valuable. Every American half century has its preeminent courtroom performer, its Clarence Darrow or its Melvin Belli. By common consent Olmedo now held custody of this honor. In his way he was as famous as the President of the United States, and consequently just as busy.

Lockwood continued, "If you've been reading the newspapers, you know I'm going to need a lawyer. I've never needed one before, so I don't know exactly where this conversation is supposed to go from here."

"Very few honest men ever need a lawyer more than once in their lives," Olmedo said.

"Thanks for the compliment, Adolphe."

Olmedo flinched at the nickname, but let it pass without response. He said, "Carlisle has briefed me on your case. It is a difficult one."

"Carlisle is not my most optimistic adviser."

"Then you would be wise to embrace him very tightly, Mr. President."

"You agree with his assessment of the facts and prospects?"

"I agree that it is a difficult case. Most cases are. Like most other intense experiences in life, being charged with a crime out of a clear blue sky is something that cannot be understood until it is over, and sometimes not even then. The important thing is to keep your peace of mind."

"Is that what you sell, Counselor?"

Without moving a muscle, Olmedo recoiled. "No, sir. I am not a swami. Peace of mind comes only from within. I presume your innocence . . ."

Lockwood started to speak; Olmedo, appropriating the gesture the President himself made so frequently, held up an imperious hand for silence. "Please! Do not disturb *my* peace of mind by telling me whether I am right or wrong on that score; I have a certain idea of you that is necessary to my method."

"You don't want to know one way or the other?"

"Why should I want to know? The jury—in this case, presumably, the United States Senate—will not take my word for it. Only the evidence will convict or acquit."

"Do you have an opinion on which way it would go if tried today?"

"The case will not be tried today, so I cannot play that game. I have read the evidence presented by Mr. Mallory. It makes a strong case that the election was corrupted. But it's only an argument for his own interests. It's not the final word."

"In the context of a trial, that's true," Lockwood said. "But there's reason to wonder if I could survive even if I was acquitted. As you know, a lot of people think I should stand aside under the Twenty-fifth Amendment. What do you say to that?"

"Never. That's what I say."

Lockwood leaned forward. "All right. Why?"

"Because you are not disabled. There is no question of your competence, only of your legitimacy. A question, even an earthshaking question, is only a question. It's not a judgment."

"Yeah, but I've got a country to run, and all this makes it pretty damn hard to get anything done. That's one reason why Nixon resigned."

"Yes, and he made a grievous mistake that is now coming back to haunt you," Olmedo said.

"True," Lockwood said. "But the fact is, he resigned the presidency because he knew he didn't have the votes in the Senate to be acquitted. He thought of the country, of what would happen if the government was paralyzed by a trial he knew he couldn't win."

"A noble gesture perhaps, but nobility is not the point."

"I understand that."

"It is important that you do. Otherwise no lawyer can help you."

Lockwood made a gesture that meant All right, goddamnit! but said, "Will you help me?"

For a long moment, Olmedo stared at the toes of his gleaming black evening pumps. Then he said, "Yes. I will represent you, Mr. President. But there are conditions."

"Shoot."

"You must see me without delay when I deem it necessary. You must have no other lawyers besides Carlisle and me."

"Just the two of you? The House and Senate will have hundreds opposing you."

"Let them. I will provide my own investigator, and you must instruct the government, including the intelligence service, to provide him, and me, with any information I request."

"Investigator? Is that singular?"

Blackstone and Olmedo exchanged a smile. "That is certainly the word for my associate, Mr. John L. S. McGraw. He and Attorney Blackstone and I have worked together many times before. Three is the right number."

"It can't be done with three."

"Then I can't serve you, sir. By nature I am a barrister. I argue cases. My brother in the law Mr. Blackstone is a solicitor, also by nature, and he prepares the cases. Our associate Mr. McGraw gets the goods. That's the way we work. The objective is to concentrate on essentials. Let the other side run around in circles and build a castle of paper."

Lockwood pondered these words. But only for a moment. "All right. You've got the case. What's your fee?"

"No fee, sir."

"No fee? Jesus Christ, Adolphe, you *are* a subversive."

Olmedo smiled. "I admit it. In regard to the embryos, for example, I thought I was representing *them*, not their mothers. If the Supreme Court put a money value on these microscopic human beings, I reasoned, they would perhaps be safer."

Lockwood, who loved conundrums, laughed in delight when he realized what had been said to him. Olmedo rose to his feet, smiling genially, and held out his hand. "There is one more condition, Mr. President," he said. "I do expect a fee after all. It is this: you must not call me Adolphe, or by any other name except my own."

6

By happenstance the whereabouts of Horace Hubbard was a topic of discussion at the dinner party at which Franklin Mallory took the first steps toward replacing Susan Grant with Zarah Christopher as the other half of his being. Early that day, Mallory had called in person to invite Ross Macalaster to dine at his Kalorama house. "Will you bring someone?" he asked.

"All right."

For no reason that Macalaster could explain to himself, Zarah popped into his mind. He rang her number immediately—years of calling up people who did not really know him and might not want to talk to him had cured him of any vestige of telephone shyness—and to his surprise she accepted without hesitation. He supposed this was because she wanted to meet Mallory; most people, even those who believed that he was another Hitler, were consumed by curiosity about him. He said, "If you'll give me your address, I'll come by for you a little before seven." Zarah replied, "No need; I can meet you at his door. I live in the neighborhood."

Although it was dark and a wind swirling out of the Rock Creek ravine whipped her skirt, she was waiting for him on the sidewalk when he got out of his car. This gave Macalaster, who might otherwise have been struck dumb by her beauty, something uninventive to say as an ice-breaker: "Which one is your house?"

"That one," Zarah replied, pointing.

Dark-blond hair blew across her face. Macalaster, who had known any number of psychotic beauties, had ceased romanticizing women on the basis of appearances a long time before, but he was charmed by the way she looked. He said, "That used to be the O.G.'s place."

"That's right," Zarah said. "Did you know him?"

Macalaster said, "I knew the figure of mystery. Not the real man. Did you?"

Zarah laughed, another delight because it was so unstudied. "They were one and the same, I think."

The O.G.—the initials stood for "Old Gentleman"; he'd had a proper name, but no one ever called him by it—had been the head of U.S. intelligence under half a dozen Presidents. Nearly everyone in the world who had a claim to any kind of fame, from heads of state to the humblest journalists, had been welcomed to his house at one time or another.

Another gust of wind came out of the ravine. Zarah said, "I think we'd better go in."

Inside the high-security entrance, a butler took their coats and showed them down a corridor. Walking ahead, Zarah vigorously shook her disheveled hair, and every strand fell back into place. They arrived in a reception room at the back of the house. Because it was intended as a place to have one drink before dinner, it had no chairs. The other guests, Jack Philindros of the FIS and Senator Amzi J. Whipple of Oklahoma, the Minority Leader of the Senate, and their spouses, already held glasses in their hands. As they joined the group, Bitsy Whipple was whispering, "It seems so *funny* not to see Susan in this room!"

Eleanor Philindros kissed Zarah. After looking Zarah up and down, Bitsy, a still-voluptuous former first runner-up for the title of Miss Oklahoma who was many years younger than her white-maned, corpulent husband, smiled a dazzling contestant's smile and moved protectively closer to the senator. Zarah took a glass of California chardonnay from a tray offered by a servant. Macalaster accepted the Swedish vodka with lemon peel and freshly ground green peppercorns that was known in this house to be his drink of choice.

Meanwhile Mallory was deep in conversation with Philindros on the other side of the room. Alerted by the stir of an arrival, Mallory looked up, saw Zarah, and gave a visible start—the only involuntary physical response Macalaster had ever detected in him. Still talking to Philindros, he fastened his eyes upon her. His gaze was so intense, his attention so obviously distracted, that Philindros, who had his back to the room, turned around to see what was going on. Mallory put a hand on Philindros's arm and walked him across the room.

Macalaster, pleased at the impression his companion had made, said, "Mr. President, this is Zarah Christopher, a neighbor of yours."

Mallory shook hands with her. In the five steps it had taken him to reach them he had regained his composure. He said, "A neighbor? How near?"

Zarah gave the house number. Mallory, who of course had been a friend of the O.G.'s, knew all about the house. With a smile he said, "Have you kept the bric-a-brac?" The O.G. had been a famous collector of exotic junk.

Zarah shook her head. "No. He left all the furnishings, except the books and the wine, to his Boston club."

"They must have been delighted. Who got the books and wine?"

"My father got the books; he left the wine to me."

"Lucky woman," Mallory said. "I hope you'll tell me more about that at dinner."

They sat at a round table. Mallory did not believe in rectangular ones, and said so when Zarah remarked on it. "Long tables establish a hierarchy and encourage plots," he said. "Put any three human beings in isolation, as at the head of a table, and two of them immediately form a cabal against the third. Two people in the same situation will usually form an attachment, especially if one is male and the other female."

"The famous *Pax Sexualis Malloryana*, isn't that right, Mr. President?" said Senator Whipple. "How's my Latin?"

"Naughty," Bitsy said.

Whipple was old enough and eminent enough to tease former Presidents, though he scrupulously called them by their titles. He was, as well, the grand old man of the reactionary movement. As its first outright candidate for President many years before, he had paved the way for Mallory's own candidacy and election. Mallory grinned at Whipple with transparent affection. Macalaster, who had never before observed him in private among his own kind, was surprised by the pleasure he took in the company.

Zarah said, "Is this theory of threes the reason why you do everything in twos?"

Mallory was seated across from her, no doubt on his own orders. He nodded approvingly. "Exactly. Even numbers are the building blocks of harmony. You've heard the expression 'odd man out'? It's basic to human nature."

Senator Whipple laughed. "Mallory's Second Law. Bitsy agrees with that one, don't you, honey?"

Whipple was famously indulgent of his alcoholic wife. During his presidential campaign the tabloids, followed by the mainstream press, had published nude photographs for which she had posed while attempting to become a movie actress. The pictures had little effect on the outcome of the election—Whipple had known from the start that he had almost no chance of winning. But Bitsy believed that their publication had cost him the presidency, and he believed that guilt had driven her to drink.

He winked at Zarah. "My dear wife *hates* threesomes."

"I do; I readily admit it," said Bitsy, directing her words to Zarah with another incandescent smile. "Odd woman out is my motto."

Zarah looked back at her in the same way she had looked at Hammett a few nights earlier, steadily but without expression of any kind. A silence fell. Looking around the table, Mallory waited for someone to change the subject so that he himself would not have to slight a guest, even a tipsy one, by doing so. Trained to cope with awkward moments, Eleanor Philindros said, "I have something funny to tell you all. The rug man came to pick up one of our carpets for cleaning right after Jack came home from the office yesterday. He took one look at Jack and said, in this really heavy Middle Eastern accent, 'You're not an American.' Jack said, 'Yes, I am.' The man said, 'No, you're not. I've lived all over this country for forty years, and I know every American face by heart because I've seen them all. And yours is not one of them.'"

Philindros, a dark man who dressed in dark clothes, was so unassertive that he was often overlooked by flight attendants when they handed out drinks and snacks. Now he found all eyes upon him.

"Well, I can see what he meant," said Bitsy Whipple flirtatiously. "You *are* exotic, Jack. I've always said so."

"It made us laugh," Eleanor Philindros said quickly, "because wherever we've been posted all these years, even in places like Japan and India, the locals always thought Jack was one of *them*. They'd argue with him about it when he denied it—which wasn't always. The O.G. always said he could pass for anything but an American, and I guess he was right."

Mallory said, "The O.G. usually was, about things like that. Speaking of appearances, Zarah, you remind me of somebody I used to know. You're not Paul Christopher's daughter?"

"Yes. You're the second President in a week to notice the resemblance."

"The other was Lockwood?"

"Yes."

"How was he?"

"Likable."

"Himself, in other words," Mallory said.

Forgetting Bitsy, Amzi Whipple winked at Zarah; by now every man at the table was directing nearly everything he said to her. He said, "Your host has a weakness for Frosty Lockwood."

Zarah said, "I can understand that."

"Well, I can't," Bitsy Whipple said. "I'm sorry, Mr. President, but I just can't. First he had that poor harmless old holy man Ibn Awad assassinated, and then he stole the election—"

Whipple said, "Now, Bitsy."

"Well, he did, Amzi, he killed that poor old Arab and then he stole votes to get back into the White House. You know he did. And it was those horrible Hubbards who put him up to it." Bitsy turned to Zarah. "Did the charming Lockwood happen to say where he's hidden Horace Hubbard? Because the whole world would like to know."

Macalaster said, "The subject didn't come up, Bitsy."

Bitsy turned her head in his direction. He saw that her eyes were wasted by drink. "How would *you* know?" she asked.

"The party was at my house, and I don't allow my guests to ask visiting Presidents rude questions."

"You don't?" Bitsy let go a peal of laughter. "It was at your house? My, Ross, you do flit from blossom to blossom, don't you?"

Everyone smiled appreciatively, as if at a genuine witticism. The conversation died; servants cleared the plates. As soon as the entrée was served, Bitsy said to Philindros, "Jack, is it true what they say about Horace Hubbard?"

Philindros, who had uttered not a single word during dinner, said nothing in reply to this unanswerable question.

Mallory said, "If they say that Horace and Julian Hubbard are Zarah's cousins then, yes, Bitsy, what they say is true."

"Cousins? Oh, my!" Bitsy smiled her great big smile, turning to look at everyone—Zarah last. "Oh, I *knew* that," she said. "My, Franklin, but this chicken is delicious. It's so tender."

"I'm glad you like it," Mallory said. "We must remember to have it again next time you come."

"What I want is the recipe."

"Then you shall have it," Mallory said.

The sound of string instruments being tuned drifted in from another part of the house. Mallory said, "After dinner we're going to have some music in the parlor. That's the string quartet tuning up—young people, spirited but serious. I hope you like Beethoven's C-sharp minor quartet."

Whipple said, "Will I like it, Miss Zarah?"

"If you like deaf old men in despair."

"Well, I like the Senate."

Zarah smiled cautiously at the nice old man, whose eyes were fastened on his wife's flushed face.

"Mmmm, this chicken," said Bitsy.

Without comment, the rest of the guests ate the entrée, grilled swordfish in a sauce that tasted of mustard and fresh herbs.

7

For obvious reasons, Mallory's security people routinely checked the background of every new person who came to see him. This involved no fuss or bother. On hearing the visitor's name, the team on duty merely asked the computer for all available information. Normally this produced in a matter of seconds the entire life history of the subject: date and exact time of birth (useful in predicting the behavior of Orientals and others who rely on horoscopes), order of birth and number of siblings; education, including Scholastic Aptitude Test (SAT) and I.Q. scores; physical appearance, including photograph, fingerprints, and voiceprint; records of military service if any; political and sexual orientation; pattern of drug and alcohol consumption; marital status and/or details of other cohabitations; personal friendships and associations since childhood; medical records, including prescription drugs used and any psychotherapeutic treatment received; job history, including earnings and performance evaluations; police, immigration, tax, and credit records and financial assets; an inventory of real estate and other property and possessions. A second data bank provided an indexed summary of all unevaluated gossip collected over the years by investigative agencies engaged by creditors and potential employers—and, for the period since background checks for sensitive government appointments were taken away from the FBI and privatized under the Mallory administration, all personal information gathered by investigative contractors on behalf of the U.S. government. Though it did not constitute a truly comprehensive picture of the individual checked, this computer profile provided a silhouette from which basic characteristics and probable behavior could be deduced.

The check conducted by Wiggins and Lucy on Zarah during the twenty-minute cocktail period came up blank except for a United States passport issued under her birth name, Zarah Meryem Kirkpatrick, and the date and country ("Morocco or Algeria") of her birth to Catherine Eugenie Kirkpatrick. There was no entry under paternity. The passport had been renewed punctually every ten years as it expired. Beyond this, there was only a routine U.S. Customs list of less than a dozen entries and exits at American ports. The discovery of such a barren file was a rare, indeed almost unheard-of, event, and to Wiggins and Lucy it was very disturbing. Usually, the system drew a blank only in the case of impostors, who were by definition highly dangerous. The armed and highly trained security operatives who were on duty as servants for the dinner party were placed on full alert. Mallory was aware that this had happened because the tiny blue lapel pins they had been wearing earlier were replaced between cocktails and dinner with white ones. Lucy activated the listening devices in the dining room long enough to record a sample of Zarah's voice, but the computer found no match. She dusted Zarah's chardonnay glass, recovering a perfect thumbprint and three good fingerprints from the right hand, and transmitted these for identification to the data bank that contained every fingerprint from every source in the world. Zarah's were not on file.

In theory this result could not occur because it was impossible to obtain an American passport without being fingerprinted. Lucy accessed the State Department records again and discovered that Zarah's passport had been issued to her at birth by the American consul at Casablanca, who had waived the footprint then required by State Department regulations for infants born abroad of American mothers. His authorization for this highly unusual omission was a cable with an identifying number that Lucy traced to the U.S. intelligence service; this number contained a string of digits that identified it as the personal code of the man known as the O.G., who was then head of American intelligence. The name of the consul who had issued the passport did not appear on the register of Foreign Service officers for the period, which almost certainly meant that he had been an intelligence officer who was using the post as official cover. The nature of these data told Lucy that the computer would be able to tell her no more than it already had, because the computer itself had never been told what Lucy described to Mallory, immediately after dinner, as "the rest of the story."

"All we know for certain about this woman," Lucy said, "is that she appears to be left-handed."

"Appears to be," said Wiggins. "We'd better alert the boss." As dessert was served, he passed Mallory a note.

Mallory asked Jack Philindros to stay behind after the other guests departed. While Eleanor Philindros chatted with Lucy, whom she had known since childhood because Lucy's father was an Outfit officer who had served with Philindros in a number of foreign assignments, Mallory and Philindros discussed Zarah.

"There should be more than that in the files," Philindros said. His voice was nearly inaudible.

Mallory moved closer and cupped a hand behind his ear. "Really? Tell me what isn't there."

Philindros cleared his throat and tried to speak louder, but he could not, so his answer emerged as a murmur. "That no one can do, Mr. President," he said. "However, I can tell you what I know. Zarah's mother, born Catherine Kirkpatrick, and Paul Christopher, whom you know about, separated a few days after Zarah was conceived. After divorcing him in Paris and reassuming her maiden name, Catherine disappeared and never again communicated with her husband or any other member of either of their families, not even her parents. Paul Christopher didn't know of Zarah's existence until she turned up on his doorstep a few years ago. It turned out she had spent her life in the Atlas mountains of North Africa with an isolated tribe of Berbers."

"Zarah spent her whole life among these people?"

"Until her mother was killed a few years ago, yes."

"Her mother was killed? How?"

"She stumbled onto a terrorist training operation in the Sahara Desert and was murdered. The Christophers are an unlucky family."

Mallory was frowning, not because he was displeased with what he was hearing but because he was having so much difficulty hearing it. He said, "But this woman is highly educated."

"Yes, more so than most," Philindros whispered. "Cathy's idea was to make her self-sufficient so that she would never be beholden to a man. Four or five languages and their literature, art, history, mythology, music, even a course in medicine. She can set bones and deliver babies. She plays the piano. She's an expert on primitive Judaism."

"You mean to say she had no contact with a university or with people of her own kind until she was over twenty?"

"Her mother brought in tutors—Brits and Australians mostly, never Americans—who also taught the Berber kids. That whole age group of the tribe are whiz kids. Cathy and Zarah lived well, in a big house. Cathy had money of her own."

"Sounds like she was also well ahead of her time."

"Something like that."

"Zarah must have traveled abroad," Mallory said.

"Evidently not. She had no contact with anybody except the tutors and the tribespeople. That was her mother's whole idea. She didn't want her to be like her own kind, especially the Christophers, and even more especially, not like her father."

"But she seems to be just like him."

"Yes, she does," Philindros said. "So much for planned parenthood."

His nearly inaudible voice was failing him; he cleared his throat in discomfort. Mallory made a gesture. As Philindros understood it would be, it was picked up by a hidden camera, and within seconds a servant appeared with a glass of mineral water on a tray. Gratefully, Philindros took it and drank.

"I'll let you go home soon," Mallory said. "But I don't understand why none of this is in the data bank. If you know this much, how can the computer draw a blank?"

Philindros took a sip of his water as he considered how to answer this question. "It's possible Patchen had the data wiped," he said at last. "She was with him when he died."

"Zarah was with Patchen?"

Philindros nodded. David Patchen, the last director of the Outfit, the familiar name by which the operational secret intelligence service had formerly been called, had been captured, tortured, and murdered by terrorists five years before. This event had led to the dissolution of the Outfit, on grounds that its secrets had been irreparably compromised by what Patchen had presumably told his torturers. Thereupon the FIS had been created to replace it.

Although Mallory, as President of the United States, had made the decisions and signed the executive orders and the legislation that made these changes possible, he had never been told what Philindros was now telling him. "Why don't I know this?" he asked.

"Because the Outfit itself didn't know all the details," Philindros answered. "Patchen ran the whole operation himself, for his own reasons, telling no one inside what he was up to."

"What operation? I thought Patchen was kidnapped."

"He was. But some people think it was a sting. He set up his own capture."

"What for?"

"To replace the Outfit, which was a worn-out relic of the Cold War, with a new intelligence service, the FIS."

"That's an established fact?"

"No, but that's the way things turned out, and it's the fixed opinion of everyone who knew the way Patchen's mind worked that he designed it that way."

"You mean he and this girl were the only ones in on the operation?"

"No. We think, though we do not know, that there were others, all Outfit old boys and their buddies."

"Who?"

"The O.G., Paul Christopher. Yeho Stern, formerly head of the Israeli intelligence service, a money manager in New York—Patchen sold a painting to finance the operation. Some paramilitary friends of Zarah's from the Maghreb who conducted the rescue. I really can't tell you more, Mr. President, because it's all speculation."

"Was *she* tortured?"

Philindros said, "Something like that showed up in the debriefing." His voice failed altogether; he paused to drink again. "Or so I heard. There's nothing in the files. It wasn't an official debriefing."

"Not an official debriefing?"

"Technically there was nothing to debrief her about; she just happened to be in the wrong place at the wrong time with the wrong man, Patchen. She was never an agent or an asset of ours. Or anyone else's."

"Then why did she do whatever it was she did for Patchen at the risk of her life?"

Philindros shrugged; he did not like to be pressed for answers he could not support with hard data. He said, "Genes?"

"That can't have been the only factor."

"Probably not, but as I said before, it was an old boy thing. The O.G. was always close to the Christophers. Paul Christopher was his godson. He obviously regarded Paul's daughter as more than a great-goddaughter; he left her his whole estate."

"Why doesn't *that* show up on the computer? An inheritance is a routine transaction. Why conceal it?"

"The O.G.'s ways were not a computer's ways," Philindros said with a trace of hero worship. "If he designed something to remain undiscovered, it won't be discovered."

"But what was the point of all this?"

Philindros stood mute. If he knew, as Mallory was sure he must, he was bound by some spy's oath never to tell. Mallory said, "*De mortuis nil nisi bonum.* Is that your reply?"

"I don't know what that means."

" 'Speak only good of the dead.' "

Philindros smiled, a flash of white in a dark face. "That's one way of putting it."

8

Mallory was excited by the knowledge that there were no known facts about Zarah. Her blank file might mean that she was actually free of the baneful influences that in his opinion had produced in the children of the American intelligentsia a strange compulsion to hate everything young people might normally be expected to love: their species, their families, their country, their culture, their very language. And, of course, themselves. Even while Philindros talked, he decided that he must know this woman better.

As was his way, Mallory acted immediately on his decision. Thirty minutes after Zarah got home from his dinner party, he rang her doorbell. At first, examining a television image of her caller on the screen of the surveillance system that came with the O.G.'s house, she did not recognize him because he wore a black knitted cap that covered his hair and altered the entire aspect of his face. It was a simple but amazingly effective disguise. As far as she could tell, he was alone, without protection; at least no bodyguards were picked up by the camera over her door.

"I hope this isn't inconvenient," he said when she opened the door. She understood that this was a plain statement of fact; he was being courteous, not trying to make himself charming.

Zarah stood aside. "Come in."

As she led him back through the house, Mallory examined it with a practiced eye. The furniture was good, probably inherited—mostly French and English antiques with a few American pieces. A bronze head with mud-pie features that could only have been done by Daumier stood on a pedestal, and in rooms that opened off the corridor he saw several good paintings, including, again unmistakably, a Monet of the Giverny phase.

Zarah guided him past two or three unlit rooms to a small sitting room with a bar. Abstract paintings: a Braque—newspaper glued to the canvas and a lopsided cat clawing a violin—that was entirely new to him, two pieces by a painter unknown to Mallory, and an arrangement of cascading terra-cotta cubes like a hillside village in Spain that was probably by Juan Gris. Hanging over the cold fireplace was a portrait in oils and tempera of two women, one fair and the other dark, seated side by side on a bench in a lush garden. Their stiff mirror pose suggested that they might be dolls or manikins instead of living persons. They wore identical white dresses and red shoes. The painter had exaggerated the size of their eyes, making these the focus of the composition. Mallory was strongly drawn to this picture. He read the signature aloud: "S. Zaentz, 1932. Who was that?"

Zarah said, "A friend of my grandparents' in Berlin." She indicated the pictures Mallory had not recognized. "Those are some of his later works."

But Mallory was interested only in the double portrait. "This one is wonderful. Why isn't he better known?"

"He suffered interruptions."

"Why?"

"He was a Jew in Nazi Germany."

Mallory did not ask for further clarification of this statement but returned his attention to the painting; the computer would tell him whatever he wanted to know about Zaentz later on.

"I don't like pointing out a family resemblance twice in one evening," he said. "But the figure on the left—"

"My grandmother, Lori Christopher. The other woman was her best friend. Meryem. My godmother."

"Your godmother was not a German?"

"She was a Ja'wab—Berber from the Maghreb."

"A Muslim in Berlin in the thirties?"

"Not exactly. She was an unusual person."

Mallory leaned closer to the canvas. "There's something strange about the women."

"Look again," Zarah said. "The painter gave them each other's eyes."

Mallory leaned closer. The fair woman had dark eyes, the brown woman blue ones.

"I see it now," he said. "Why did the painter do that?"

"Because they saw things in the same way. At least Zaentz thought so. But there were other reasons. It was painted as the frontispiece for one of my grandfather's novels, which was about Lori and Meryem and him. The book was an example of what he called 'reality as fiction.' It was done as an experiment. Everything in it actually happened to the three of them, but by design. They were following an outline written by Grandfather, who then wrote down what happened."

"What was the result of the experiment?"

"It destroyed their lives. But that's not in the book."

"Then I must read it."

"You have time for such things?"

He turned away from the picture. "In an organized life there's time for everything important."

Zarah suppressed a smile.

Mallory said, "Philindros told me a little about you after you left—your life with your mother, the connection to the O.G. But he knew only a little."

Ah, thought Zarah, now comes the cross-examination. He would be disconcerted by the exercise. Americans of the scholastically successful class always were, because they could not locate points of reference in her answers to their questions. They themselves were mostly the children or grandchildren of men who had broken out of the working class after World War II by attending college on the G.I. Bill. Consequently they equated social status with academic credentials. On meeting her they wanted to discover where she came from in the States—What did her father do? Where had she gone to school? What was her career? Whom did she know?—and found out that she was from another planet. Living as they did in such a vast and artificial society, they had no way of knowing one another except by chance meeting; they married strangers and lived in places where everyone was a stranger. Consequently they were always demanding to examine credentials and asking, on first meeting, the brusque questions that other nationalities put to foreigners at the frontier to make sure they had no criminal purpose. This lust for the personal, for the familiar, for passwords and countersigns, was a national affliction. No one in this strange and constantly changing caste of arrivistes who depended on diplomas instead of ancestry could ever be quite sure that he, or especially she, was not conversing with a liar.

However, Mallory surprised her by letting her ask the first question.

She said, "What do you want to know that Jack Philindros didn't tell you?"

"Nothing," Mallory said. "What I already know is enough; as far as that goes, what I knew before I talked to him was enough."

"You're satisfied with very little."

"The rest will emerge with time."

" 'With time'? Am I about to become part of your organized life?"

"That's my hope," Mallory said. "That's why I'm here."

"It is?" She was amused. "Is this a draft notice? Will there a physical examination?"

Mallory changed the subject. "You've done the house up very nicely," he said. "It doesn't seem as gloomy as before. Or as cluttered. Do you spend much time here?"

"No," Zarah replied. "I'm in Washington for my half sister's birthday. She'll be fourteen on Friday."

"Another half sibling, like Horace and Julian."

"It runs in the family. All the Christophers are half Hubbards and vice versa. They—we—have been marrying each other for a long time."

"There are no single Hubbards your age?"

"None."

"That's a relief."

This remark was some sort of declaration. Of what, Zarah did not know, but she received it with neutral good manners. It was clear that he hoped for more than good manners. Examining Mallory's earnest face, she became aware that he had extraordinary eyes. His dark-blue—nearly black—gaze was surprisingly benevolent. Her father had the same sort of eyes and so had Lori, judging by the ones Zaentz had given to Meryem in the painting. A strange idea came into her head: If she reminded Mallory of Paul Christopher, Mallory reminded her of the same person—not in looks, not in voice, not in his way of thinking, but in the calm intelligence that emanated from him as an almost visible aura, and in his deep sadness. When at last she had met her father after a lifetime of imagining what he was like, she felt that she had suddenly been granted the full use of the other hemisphere of her brain, which had hitherto been inaccessible to her. Knowing her father at last, she knew twice as much about herself.

Nor was that all. On very first sight she had discerned in her father something that she could only call an absence. She had thought that this must be the psychic space that had formerly been occupied by his mother, now empty forever. When the Gestapo had arrested Lori before her son's eyes when he was fifteen years old, the brutal parting, followed almost certainly by her murder, had created within him a void that could not be filled. She now perceived the same emptiness in Mallory, who had recently seen Susan Grant murdered before his eyes. A tear ran down her cheek.

Mallory said, "Have I said something to upset you?"

Zarah shook her head, her hair moving in the silken fashion that Macalaster had noted, as if bound together by light or electricity. "No," she said. "I was thinking about my father."

9

"You think you're dying but everyone else thinks it's funny." That was what somebody from Hollywood, Macalaster could not remember who, had said about jealousy. In his neurotic profession and marriage he had observed jealousy in nearly all its guises, and had always regarded it as a particularly maddening form of stupidity. Yet while driving home from the dinner party at Mallory's, he felt the stab of dread, the rush of suspicion, the panicky fear of ignominious discovery that are the symptoms of the emotion. This was not, he told himself, a wholly irrational response to the situation into which he had blundered by inviting Zarah to accompany him.

Macalaster was a trained observer. He had understood the effect Zarah Christopher had on Franklin Mallory. In making his goodbyes, Mallory had been more cordial to him than ever before, shaking his hand, making an adroitly flattering joke, suggesting an early meeting. A less practiced student of the behavior of the rich and famous might have thought Mallory was trying to make him look good in front of his date. But Macalaster knew better. The son of a bitch was *thanking* him for what he took to be a vassal's gift of a golden woman on whom he could exercise droit du seigneur at his leisure.

Macalaster cursed his own stupidity as he drove down Foxhall Road at forty-five miles an hour in his ten-day-old Jaguar convertible. As he came around a curve he collided with a two-hundred-pound whitetail buck that leaped out of nowhere straight into his headlights. The impact of the inflating air bag twisted his wire-rim glasses out of shape and gave him a bloody nose. The deer, a ten-point buck, sustained two broken legs and thrashed piteously in the roadway as it was savaged by the pack of pedigreed Rottweilers, Labradors, and spaniels that had been pursuing it. The environmental police arrived after half an hour and fired a lethal dart into the neck of the half-devoured creature. The Jaguar, with 134 miles on the odometer, looked as though it had hit a tree. It was after midnight by the time Macalaster finished dealing with the consequences of this episode, which included a Breathalyzer test, a two-hundred-dollar charge for towing his wrecked car to the body shop, and a summons for "depriving a wild animal of a safe habitat."

Yet when he arrived home in a taxi, all the windows of his house glowed with electric light. Owing to Brook's apocalyptic worries about the environment and his own tendency to lurk in his third-floor study or read in bed by the light of a single lamp, he had never before seen the place fully illuminated. Perhaps it never had been, he thought, as the taxi pulled up to the curb. Then he felt another stab of anxiety, this time for Manal. Had something happened to her? He rushed to the front door. It was triple-locked. This, too, was unprecedented. Did he have all three keys?

Struggling with the locks, Macalaster looked through the window into the bright interior. Nothing moved. Finally the door opened. Monophonic Indian music—sitars and percussion instruments repeating a single melodic line—played on the stereo system. Incense burned. The smell of jasmine tea mingled with the wafting incense. Nothing unusual about all this: these were among Manal's favorite things. Two Himalayan cats, also Manal's, patrolled the dining-room table, sniffing the remains of dinner— four soiled plates, four glasses, a half-empty bottle of water, the uneaten end of a flat loaf of unleavened bread. Four for dinner? Had Manal had a party without asking his permission? Macalaster called out her name. She did not answer. He went into the living room to switch off the music. Every table, chair, and sofa was littered with law books and other volumes lying open on their faces, tattered newspapers with their pages full of holes where articles had been clipped, and long streamers of computer print-outs.

This was not Manal's sort of mess, but perhaps she could explain it. Macalaster inhaled, intending to shout her name. Then he remembered that Archimedes Hammett was his houseguest. This was *his* kind of mess. He switched off the stereo and went from room to room, calling not Manal's name—he supposed she was long since in bed—but Hammett's. No one answered, and he was about to go upstairs to make sure Manal was all right when he heard the murmur of voices in the den. He opened the door and found Manal, Hammett, and Slim and Sturdi Eve, the insepa-rable ecolawyers who looked after Hammett's food, seated in a circle around the brown-paper Ouija board.

As Macalaster appeared—in the circumstances, he thought, "materialized" was a better word—Hammett, wearing a stricken look, rose to his feet. "Good God," he said in an unsteady voice. "You're covered in blood."

Macalaster said, "Covered with blood? I am?"

He had forgotten his bloody nose. Looking into the mirror in which he had watched Zarah's troubled face a few nights before, he saw that his upper lip and chin were crusted with dried blood, and that his shirt and tie were stained with it. "So I am," he said. "I had an accident on the way home."

Manal said, "Daddy!"

Macalaster knew she was remembering the highway crash that had killed her mother. He said, "It's okay. I hit a deer."

Sturdi said, "*You killed a deer?* With a *Jaguar?*"

"No, crippled it," Macalaster said. "The police finished it off."

Sturdi turned to Slim, who was sitting beside her on the floor. "This is disgusting," she said. Slim gave her a look of sympathy and held out her hand. Sturdi enfolded Slim's pale and fragile hand in her large swarthy one. Like Hammett, she was obviously the product of an unmixed gene pool. She had jet-black hair like Manal's, though it was cut short and concealed beneath a blue bandanna.

Macalaster stepped over the Ouija board in order to look at himself in the mirror.

Scrambling out of the way, Hammett said, "Don't come any nearer!"

Macalaster said, "Why not?"

Slim said, "Archimedes already told you. You're bleeding."

"Not anymore," Macalaster said. "But what if I were?"

Sturdi got to her feet and backed away. Slim, rising also, put an arm around her. Hammett, keeping as far away from Macalaster as possible, was in the process of leaving the room. Suddenly Macalaster understood. All the anger he had been feeling toward Mallory, all the dumb rage he had suppressed about the hypnotized deer for being in the wrong habitat in the wrong era, broke through the dam. "Do you think I'm going to give you AIDS?"

Slim and Sturdi did not answer the question.

"Jesus Christ," Macalaster said. "You do!"

The women stood their ground, as if providing a diversion so that Hammett, whose life was more valuable than their own, could escape. Seconds later, Hammett did slip through the door; he could be heard running up the stairs to his room.

Finally Slim said, "You spoke the word, we didn't. Which proves it's not such an outrageous thought."

"It's not? After a fucking deer has wrecked a brand-new hundred-thousand-dollar automobile? After *this?*" Macalaster pointed to his swollen nose as if he were a hypochondriac, too. "You come into my house and tell me not to bleed on you because I might be HIV positive? What the fuck is this?"

Slim and Sturdi clung to each other, two stringy bodies dressed in the sort of Grant Wood clothes that real farmers had not worn since the invention of the milking machine. Their eyes were wary, hostile, defiant. Macalaster knew this had little, if anything, to do with him or his nose-bleed; they would be defiant as a matter of self-discipline toward anyone who lived in a house like his, toward any male except Hammett or a dumb animal.

"Look," Macalaster said. "This is my house. I didn't invite you here. I don't like your keeping my daughter up until one o'clock in the morning on a school night. I don't like the disgusting mess you and your leader have made. I don't like your phony clothes, I don't like your zero-fat body image, I don't like the looks on your faces. So get out of here. Now."

Manal said, "Daddy, it was only a séance. Mr. Hammett asked me—"

Macalaster turned on the child. "And you," he shouted. "You get your little brown bottom up the stairs and into bed right this minute, and don't let me catch you having another of these ridiculous damn horror shows ever again."

Manal bowed her head submissively, pressed her palms together in front of her downcast eyes, and bowed out of the room. She meant this as a snippy joke. Sturdi did not know this. She spoke at last, in a voice filled with the bottomless contempt that comes from having your worst suspicions confirmed. "You're not fit to have power over another human being," she said. "Manal will remember this behavior."

"Good," Macalaster said. "I hope you will, too."

"Oh, you needn't worry about that," said Sturdi. "We won't forget a single detail."

10

When he looked back on this incident the thing that surprised Macalaster was that he had done what he had done while almost perfectly sober. He knew this to be the case because he had passed the Breathalyzer test, thanks to Franklin Mallory's policy of serving only one before-dinner drink and very little dinner wine to his guests. Consequently he felt no shame or remorse for having treated Hammett's friends with such brutal candor, as he certainly would have if he had behaved in the same way while drunk. In fact, the aftereffect was quite pleasing. He had got rid of the anger and resentment he had been feeling toward himself, and he had been absolutely, unquestionably in the right. He felt refreshed and vindicated.

Manal was another matter. To give her time to settle down, he cleared the table, rinsed the dishes, and stacked them in the dishwasher. Then he filled a bowl with butter pecan ice cream, Manal's favorite, and carried it up to her room. She was in bed, with her back to the door. Her night lamp, Kermit the Frog, radiated a dim greenish light that made her dark skin glow.

He said, "Are you asleep?"

Unmoving, Manal said, "Yes."

"Then wake up and eat your ice cream."

Perhaps because she had spent her childhood observing the havoc wreaked by Brook, who had not known the meaning of the word "forgiveness," Manal had always been quick to pardon affronts. Macalaster closed the door and handed her the bowl of ice cream. She sat up in bed, threw back the magnificent blue-black hair that Brook had considered her daughter's only good feature, and began to eat.

"I'm sorry I yelled at you," Macalaster said. "None of what happened downstairs was your fault. I know that and I apologize."

"It's all right, Daddy."

"No, it's not all right."

Manal paused, a spoonful of ice cream halfway to her mouth. "Okay. It's not all right with you. But it's all right with me."

"Then everything must be all right."

They grinned at each other. Macalaster had never loved this girl as he believed he could have loved any of the several natural children Brook had aborted. He had never even kissed Manal, and he doubted that Brook had ever done so, either. But he had always liked her and approved of her. She wished the world well and accepted life as it came. She always had. Even as an infant, being delivered by the adoption agency's courier into the bewildering culture that would never understand her, she had seemed to be a fatalist. Looking up at the Macalasters for the first time moments after her arrival at Dulles International Airport, this small brown baby had shuddered briefly, as if submitting to the weird reality that she had been reincarnated as the child of political criminals (now political martyrs) and then sent halfway around the world to be claimed by a marijuana- and wine-besotted American woman who wanted to feel good about herself. Or was Macalaster romanticizing the girl, as Brook had done, because she was to all outward appearances so ordinary? "Whoever marries you will be a lucky man," he said, meaning it.

"That will be nice," Manal said.

Macalaster sat quietly on her bed while she finished her ice cream. Finally she licked the spoon, smiling. Her tongue was purplish, like the scalp of Susan Grant's murderer; this mark of ethnicity had astonished and delighted Brook, who did not notice it for years because nannies had always taken care of feeding the child.

Manal said, "It really is all right, Daddy. I was glad you came in when you did and sent everybody to bed."

"Oh? Why's that?"

"Mr. Hammett was very upset. The same visitor as before came back."

"Which one was that?"

"Susan—the one that wanted to talk to you. She asked for you again. She's still in darkness. She's very, very angry."

"Why?"

"Because she was murdered. They're always angry when that happens because everything is unfinished."

"What did she say this time?"

"The same thing." Manal said. " 'Shelley.' "

"Do you know anyone named Shelley?"

"No. Maybe it's someone Mr. Hammett was involved with. Romantically."

"That I doubt."

"Or knew in another life. It really shook him up."

Macalaster took the bowl and tapped Manal gently on the knee with the spoon. "Good," he said. "Forget what I said. You can have all the séances you want."

Manal turned over. "I already have," she said, and wiggled her long slender fingers in farewell.

11

Julian Hubbard uttered a shout of surprise when he read about the appointment of Alfonso Olmedo C. in the daily White House press summary. He sprang to his feet and hurried down the corridor toward Norman Carlisle Blackstone's office. It was seven o'clock in the morning, forty-five minutes before his routine morning meeting with the President in the Lincoln sitting room.

He expected to find Blackstone alone as usual. However, he had a visitor. Both men faced away from the door. They were deep in conversation. Julian paused on the threshold and stared at the back of the stranger's head, which was covered with a mass of carrot-red curls.

"Carlisle," he said. "Excuse me."

"Ah, Julian," said Blackstone, swiveling in his chair to face him. "Good day to you. Come in. We were just talking about you."

"Were you now?"

"Indeed we were. I'd like you to meet Mr. John L. S. McGraw, an associate of Alfonso Olmedo, about whom I think you know."

Julian said nothing in reply to this. The stranger stood up and turned around. His lantern-jawed Celtic face was freckled and battered—skewed broken nose, thick eyebrows interrupted by thicker white scars, more scars around the bright-green eyes. Red hair grew on the back of his bony, large-knuckled hands. He wore a powder-blue glen-plaid suit with a pair of cheap brown bucks and figured socks, a semitransparent polyester shirt that revealed the curly red hair on his chest, and a yellow necktie with brown and green stripes. As Julian stepped closer in order to shake hands, he saw that the stripes were actually made up of a printed motto that read—he squinted to make it out—"*Non carborundum bastardum est*," which Julian remembered was beer-joint Latin for "Don't let the bastards grind you down."

Gripping McGraw's hand, Julian said, "How do you do."

"Okay. How about you?" McGraw replied in a staccato New York voice. He spelled out his surname. "And before you ask, no, I'm no relation to Iron John McGraw of the Giants, and yes, the L. S. stands for John L. Sullivan."

"Ah," said Julian. "The boxer."

McGraw said, "Carlisle here was just going to bring me down to your office. I've got a few questions for you about your half brother."

Julian said nothing, but lifted his eyebrows in polite inquiry.

McGraw said, "It won't take long. I know you're busy."

Julian looked down at him. The splotched face was full of shrewd intelligence. "You're a lawyer on Olmedo's staff?" he asked.

McGraw shook his head. "Mr. Olmedo doesn't have a staff. There's just him and his secretary."

"My goodness," Julian said. "Then how do you fit in?"

Blackstone said, "Mr. McGraw is an independent investigator."

"That's right," McGraw said. "Sometimes I help Mr. Olmedo and Mr. Blackstone out. Like now." He cocked his head, displayed a tight-lipped smile, and rocked on his toes. He gave the impression that he was chewing gum as he spoke, though he wasn't. These ticks seemed to be natural mannerisms rather than the involuntary impersonation of Jimmy Cagney that Julian at first took them to be.

"Fascinating," Julian said.

McGraw gave him a look of keen interest, as if this patronizing remark contained an important clue to Julian's character—which, Julian realized, it did.

"Anyway," McGraw said. "Can we do it now?"

"Do what now?"

"Like I said, talk about your half brother."

"Mr. McGraw, it's seven o'clock in the morning. I have a meeting with the President in half an hour and I must prepare for it."

"I understand your situation. That's why I got up early. Because the case can't wait."

Julian shot a puzzled look in Blackstone's direction. Nodding his agreement with McGraw, Blackstone said, "The President did assure Alfonso Olmedo of complete cooperation from everybody."

"He did? When was that?"

"Last night, when he engaged Olmedo as his sole counsel in connection with the Mallory allegations. The situation is moving fast, Julian."

"So it seems." Julian paused, as if to lift an invisible curtain and give them a glimpse of the impossibly busy day, week, and lifetime that lay before him. "All right," he said at last. "Follow me, sir." He gestured McGraw through the door before him, then, sotto voce, said, "Carlisle, I want you in my office at eight-fifteen."

Blackstone smiled perfunctorily in response to these words. As chief of staff, Julian was nominally his superior, but he had never before reminded Blackstone of this fact by giving him an order. Of course Blackstone had never before gone around Julian, the man who stood between the President and everybody else, to accomplish a purpose. He bowed in assent, then swiveled back to face his desk.

Julian and Blackstone, as the two highest-ranking members of the presidential staff, occupied corner offices on the westernmost face of the West Wing. The journey between them was less than fifty of Julian's steps.

McGraw had to hurry to keep up. He said, "I've never been in here before. I thought it would be more impressive."

"Really? In what way?"

"Higher ceilings, nicer furniture, cuter secretaries."

"You must visit the public rooms in the mansion itself. They have high ceilings. And impressive furniture. Carlisle can arrange a tour for you."

Inside Julian's office, McGraw sat down in the single chair in front of the desk and looked around him. It was the only chair in the room besides Julian's worn leather desk chair.

"How come only one chair?" he asked.

"I like to see people one at a time. Now, sir, what can I do for you?"

"My name is John," McGraw said. "This part won't take long. Later on we'll talk again about other stuff."

"Fine . . . John," Julian said, looking at his watch. "Shoot."

McGraw took a small drugstore notebook from his shirt pocket and flipped through it until he found a blank page. He looked at his own watch and wrote something down in a slow painstaking hand, underlining it twice.

"Okay," he said. "Here we go. Horace Elliott Christopher Hubbard is ten years older than you, the only issue of your father's first marriage to the former Alice Earle Parsons Jessup of Manhattan and Chipmunk Island, Maine. This union ended in divorce in nineteen hundred and forty-eight, the year you were born. Both parents are deceased. He's your only sibling."

Julian said nothing. Looking up from his notebook, McGraw said, "Question mark."

"What?"

"Have I got everything straight?"

"All correct."

"Where is he?"

Julian put his fingertips together precisely, whorl to whorl. "I have no idea."

"Any educated guesses?"

"No. My brother makes a habit of disappearing, sometimes for years at a time. He always has. I'm used to it."

"Why does he disappear?"

"For professional reasons."

"You mean he's a CIA man."

"The CIA was abolished years ago."

"Then an FIS man."

"He's a retired banker."

"Which bank?"

"D. & D. Laux & Company, New York."

"That's the one with all the FIS computers in the cellar, right?"

"Our time is limited, John," Julian said. "It might be better to find out what I know rather than impressing me with what you think *you* know."

"You're right."

"No offense."

"Forget it. Let me ask you this. Where are your kids?"

Julian put pressure on his fingertips. Stress: McGraw noted the way the nails changed from pink to white as the blood was forced out of the capillaries beneath them, and Julian could see him watching this happen. He said, "Elliott and Jenny are with their mother and her husband aboard his boat."

McGraw said, "The husband is Leo Dwyer, famous writer, little short guy—correct?" Julian nodded. McGraw continued, "Where are they right now exactly?"

"I'm not sure. On the high seas. It's an oceangoing yacht. They planned to sail down the east coast of South America to Antarctica, then up the west coast to California. I have no exact itinerary."

"What about school?"

"They carry tutors on board."

"You don't worry about not hearing from the kids?"

"They're with their mother."

"On a boat that maintains radio silence?"

"As a matter of fact, yes," Julian said. "Leo writes on the boat. He requires complete isolation."

"So he always maintains radio silence on all his voyages?"

"That's right. It's a ritual connected to his writing."

"Okay, that clears that up," said McGraw. "Your ex-wife, Caroline, now Mrs. Leo Dwyer. She's on good terms with your brother?"

"Yes, certainly."

"So they're friends, her and Horace? And Leo?"

"Yes, good friends—for years in Caroline's case. Horace and her father were classmates in college."

"Yale class of fifty-five?"

"That's right. Leo is a friend by happenstance, of course."

" 'Happenstance.' I like that word." McGraw wrote it down. Then he said, "Caroline's a Lockwood voter?"

Julian blinked at what seemed to be a non sequitur. "I've always assumed so."

"Leo, too?"

"Very likely."

"They're both avid, uh, liberals?"

"How do you define 'avid'?"

"Want their man to win at all costs, want to save the world, and especially the trees and the wild animals, give money to their candidates and causes till it hurts, hate Mallory and all he stands for."

"By that definition 'avid' is the word."

"Back in the sixties, while you were flying F-4s in Vietnam, before you married her, your ex-wife spent some time in a commune on East End Avenue in Manhattan with a bunch of other Ivy League Maoists who thought they were urban guerrillas, like the Montañeros in Argentina, M-14 in Colombia, that kind of people?"

Julian said, "Caroline sometimes made those comparisons, but as far as I know she and her friends never did anyone harm."

"But she did undergo this sixties experience? Passwords, plots, mumbo jumbo, bomb-making lessons?"

"I guess you could describe it that way. The truth of the matter is, it was just a game for kids with well-to-do parents."

McGraw threw up a hand. "Jeez, funny you should say that. That was my neighborhood where they were holed up, and that's what we always said. I had an uncle who rented slum apartments to hippies. He'd put in extra rats and cockroaches, he'd sabotage the toilets. They'd pay whatever rent he asked for because their fathers were paying the bills. They liked it squalid, he said."

"Interesting man, your uncle."

"Not half as interesting as your family, Julian," McGraw said. He closed his notebook. "That's all I need. Thanks."

"It is?" Julian was surprised that the interview was over so soon, and that so little of real interest had been discussed. But he said in cordial tones, "Glad to be of help. Be in touch if you need anything more."

"Thanks, I will be," McGraw replied.

12

The word most often applied by op-ed page pundits to the relationship between Lockwood and Julian Hubbard was "symbiotic," because they were two dissimilar types living together for mutually beneficial purposes. In the unwritten dictionary of the Cause, this meant that Julian, the patrician, the intellectual, the disinterested ideologue, had politicized Lockwood, the primitive from Appalachia, in the same way that his missionary ancestors had christianized the heathen Chinese: by learning the rudiments of their language and simplifying the message of salvation into a version of the Scriptures that could not possibly be misunderstood because it left out every contradiction that might confuse the issue. Though he would never have put it so baldly, in his innermost mind Julian himself believed that there was some truth in this analogy.

Lockwood knew this, and understood what malarkey it was. He also understood how useful the illusion was to himself. Vanity was a powerful motivator of missionaries and clerks, and Julian was the product of a system—the prosperous family, the Church Genteel, St. Grottlesex and the Ivy League, the creed of good works, the seal of secret societies—that was designed, like its model, the British public school system, to produce a class of competent, hardworking, unshakably self-satisfied clerks.

History was overrun with underlings who believed they had empowered the monarch. But as all human beings except the clerks knew, a ruler's right to rule actually came from magic. Lockwood, who sometimes spoke in terms so simple that Julian, trained to deal with complexities, could scarcely comprehend them, actually called this right "the Magic." Julian had always assumed that this term was one of the President's homely, self-deprecating jokes. But it was not.

"Smoke from the volcano, divine right of kings, democratic elections all come down to the same thing," Lockwood had said to Julian one night, out on the campaign trail. "One man gets anointed and everybody else says, 'Right! He's got the Magic.' "

"Do you really think it's as primitive as all that?"

"Hell, yes. Think about it. What do all rulers have that nobody else has? The right to offer human sacrifice. The Caesars crucified folks. Montezuma did it by having priests cut out people's hearts. The kings of England chopped off heads. Lincoln and Wilson and FDR and JFK and LBJ and the rest of 'em sent American boys off by the carload to get blown up in wars. It's all the same damn thing. Nobody questioned their right to do it, then or now. Public slaughter makes everybody feel better."

"Not everybody."

"Yeah, well, a bleeding heart's a pretty good sign that nothing else is leaking."

Whatever others might think, both men knew that Lockwood was the one who had the power, and therefore the last word. Julian's first wife had left him for another man when she realized that Lockwood was the host and Julian the parasite. She had imagined that it was the other way around, that the purpose of life for people like Julian and herself was to do the thinking and the finer feeling for the Lockwoods of this world. They might reign, but they could not be permitted actually to rule. The chief lesson of modern times was clear: When the common people were allowed to act for themselves, they listened to their brute nature instead of their teachers and elected someone like Hitler or Mallory, never their true friends. Lockwood understood this, too. However, he loved Julian like a son or a younger brother. He thought his chief of staff was a silly kid who thought too much and was never satisfied to let well enough alone, but he had brains, he meant well, and of course he was willing to do most of the work. In Lockwood's opinion, any damn fool could run the U.S. government. He made decisions and let Julian make sure that the cabinet and the rest of the hierarchy took care of the details. What was important in the presidency were the very things Julian dismissed as superfluous: ceremony, symbolism, tone, ritual appearances—in short, the Magic.

All these memories and perceptions were jumbled up in Julian's mind as he made his arguments to Lockwood against entrusting the entire defense of himself, his presidency, and the Cause to one man neither of them knew, Alfonso Olmedo C. Expressionless, his stocking feet propped on an antique table, a cup of cold coffee balanced on his stomach, Lockwood heard him out.

"Of course Olmedo is a brilliant courtroom advocate," Julian said. "No one denies that. But I've had several calls already from people who wonder where he stands politically. Is he really with us?"

Lockwood said, "Let me guess who made the first call. Patrick Graham." Julian nodded, just as expressionless as Lockwood. The President continued, "What did you tell him?"

"You don't *tell* Patrick anything. You listen to his list of multiple-choice questions and try to check the right answer."

"Which was, in this case?"

"The President has his reasons, which only the President knows. But these will become apparent. Be patient. Trust us. This is only the first step in a journey of a thousand miles."

"That's the stuff," Lockwood said. "But I've got to tell you, for your ears only, so you won't waste your time worrying about it and trying to catch old Spats's dingus in the wringer, that there ain't going to be no more steps. Olmedo is it."

Julian was stunned. "But he knows nothing about this town or how it works."

"Who the hell does?"

"You do. Your enemies do. The other side will have dozens of lawyers, hundreds of staffers working day and night and inundating us with requests for information. How can one man cope with that? Olmedo doesn't even have a staff."

"He's got Spats."

"He's also got one investigator. One, Mr. President."

"I know Olmedo's outnumbered. So was Horatio at the bridge."

"Yes, sir, and I imagine there were moments when Horatius wished he had some help. I hope you'll reconsider. Olmedo is a fine advocate, but he needs backup."

"Well, as I just got through saying, he's got Norman Carlisle Blackstone. Plus this investigator, Macilaguddy."

"McGraw."

"Lookahere, Julian," Lockwood said. "I don't give a rat's ass what this gumshoe's real name is. Or Horatio's either. If they need backup, they've got the whole damn Justice Department and two thousand useless lawyers across the alley in EOB. Let them idle minds and hands shuffle the papers. All it is is a bunch of goddamn useless bullshit."

"Yes, sir. But we can drown in it."

"No, we can't. What you've got inside the Beltway is the Dead Sea. Ain't worth a damn except to let you imagine what it used to be like. No fish can live in it. A little fresh water trickles in from outside, but none ever gets out. All it produces is evaporation, day in and day out. But the one thing you cannot do in the Dead Sea is sink in it, because it's turning into concrete. The shore is crowded with people who *want* to see you drown. Pricks like Tucker Attenborough and Patrick Graham come out in boats and hit you over the head with the oars to make you sink. But it won't work. The best the sons of bitches can do is drive you crazy so's you'll do away with yourself."

Julian said, "Is that what you're trying to do to yourself, Mr. President?"

He had gone too far. "That's enough," Lockwood said, glaring. "There's only one question: Was I elected or was Franklin? That's what we stand or fall on."

"Mr. President, I'm sorry, but it's more complicated than that."

Lockwood uttered a roar of frustration. "Julian, don't say 'more complicated than that' in my presence! That's what the goddamn intellectuals always say, so you'll think they're the only ones smart enough to run the world. But it's a bunch of hogwash."

The briefing book on impeachment history and procedure that Blackstone had given him lay on the floor at Lockwood's feet. He picked it up, and using both hands as if shovel-passing a football, threw it at Julian, who caught it.

"It's all in there," Lockwood said. "I've been up all night reading that sucker. And what this case is going to come down to, just like with the other two raggedy-ass poor boys they tried to throw out of the presidency in 1868 and 1973, is five or six articles of impeachment. Four of 'em will just be the statutory-rape and cruelty-to-dumb-animals charges, in there for the sake of pure meanness. The Senate will never even vote on 'em. The two articles that count will, number one, charge me with stealing the election, and number two, charge me with ordering the murder of Ibn Awad. Number two is the get-the-bastard-anyway article. Now any damn fool could get me off on the first charge, because I did not steal the election or tell your half brother Horace and his girlfriend or anybody else to do so in any way, shape, or form, and no son of a bitch on this planet can prove I did. Where I'm going to need Alfonso Olmedo is on charge number two, because I'm guilty as hell. And hell is probably exactly where I'm going to go when I die if there's a God in heaven. But I'm not going to jail first if I can help it."

As he finished speaking, Lockwood was breathing audibly. For the first time, Julian noticed all the signs that the President really had been up all night. He was unshaven, haggard, red-eyed, still dressed in the shirt he had worn the day before. His hands trembled and his face was flushed, familiar indications that he had drunk too much coffee and driven up his blood pressure.

In a gentler tone, Lockwood said, "One more thing, Julian. If you were my own son I couldn't love you more. I want you to know that. But I'm in this mess, on all counts, because I listened to you. And I've learned my lesson."

To his own amazement, Julian gasped. He heard his breath rushing out of his lungs, filling his larynx, producing a sound that was hardly human. No such involuntary reaction had ever occurred before. But then no one had ever hit him quite so squarely with the battle-ax of the truth before.

He said, "Are you asking for my resignation?" His voice broke on the question.

"No," Lockwood said. "This isn't the moment, and we both know it. It would look bad, it would make things worse."

"Then what do you want from me?"

"I want you to do your regular job, keep things running while I take care of the problem. Keep out of the legal process. I mean *out*—completely. Get yourself a lawyer to tell you how to do it."

"I understand."

"I hope you do," Lockwood said. "You're a good man, Julian. You have my interests at heart. I know that. I don't know what I'd do without you. But I just want you to understand why I'm not hiring any lawyer you recommend."

13

When Sam Clark and R. Tucker Attenborough, Jr., met for their regular biweekly working breakfast, called the Odd Wednesday breakfast, Attenborough told a story about Lockwood.

"Frosty thought up the name Odd Wednesday when he was Majority

Leader," Attenborough said. "His idea was, the Leader and the Speaker would meet and commiserate every Wednesday that fell on an odd day of the month. Sounded ingenious as hell. I whipped out my pocket calendar and said, 'Shoot, Frosty, there's twenty-six odd-numbered Wednesdays, and there's fourteen days between 'em, so we'll just be meeting every other week like we always do.' And old Lockwood, he cackled like he does sometimes and said, "Yeah, but it *sounds* bad in case we get caught praying in secret by Patrick Graham. Should be worth two thousand Baptist votes in your district alone."

Though he had heard this story many times before, Sam Clark nodded appreciatively. He knew that the Speaker merely wanted to remind him that he was just as old a friend of Lockwood's as he was. He said, "That was the time Graham ripped the lid off prayer breakfasts?"

"That was it. Old Patrick uncovered the link between saying grace and receiving campaign contributions from the evangelicals. Everybody had to learn to pray without moving their lips."

That, too, was a Lockwood line, though Attenborough gave him no credit for it. After 1992, when the Republican Party was captured from within by the religious right, just as the Democratic Party had earlier been captured by its own left wing, no politician who was not dependent on the evangelicals for votes and money wanted to be accused of mingling piety and politics.

"Who knows?" Clark said, "maybe prayer will make a comeback. Most things do in this town if you hang around and wait."

"Not in our lifetime, Sam." Attenborough sighed heavily; extremists were a sore burden to him in the House, as they were to Clark in the Senate. "One side's as big a pain in the ass as the other."

They had been discussing the probable effect the two groups of extremists, left and right, would have on the two chief pieces of future business before the Senate and House, the confirmation of Archimedes Hammett as Chief Justice and the impeachment and trial of Lockwood.

"Both bunches want him out," Attenborough said. "The evangelicals because they think he's a tool of the atheistic left, the radicals because they think he's wounded so bad he can't govern."

"Have they got the votes?"

"Not at the moment, but one thing's for sure. Frosty doesn't have to go out of his way to make things look bad anymore."

When Clark, watchful and taciturn, made no reply, Attenborough said, "I wonder if Frosty realizes that."

Clark said, "What do you mean by that?"

To show how delicate this subject was, Attenborough put down his coffee cup with great care so as not to make so much as a symbolic noise. Then, in grating tones, he said, "Damn it all to hell, Sam, you know as well as I do he's going around saying I want to steal the presidency from him. If that gets out, everything hits the fan."

"You think he's serious?"

"Damn right he is. That's what he told me right to my face just the other day."

"Was that after you handed him that letter with the hundred and thirty-seven signatures?"

Attenborough scowled. Lockwood *had* been talking; that's what he had wanted to find out. He said, "Then you do know he's got this paranoid idea in his head."

"He's mentioned his concern."

"I hope you told him he had nothing to worry about."

"I did," Clark said. "But I'm not sure he was listening."

He changed the subject. "What's going to happen in the House on impeachment, and when?"

"Nothing's going to happen until we have a Chief Justice. When is *that* going to occur?"

"Pretty soon, I imagine."

"Then that joker will make it?"

"I don't see what's to prevent it," Clark said. "There's nothing against Archimedes Hammett but the suspicion of the right wing that he's either crazy or the brain behind international terrorism, and he's probably got more on them than they've got on him."

"So he's got no scruples and no sense. But can he be confirmed?"

"If he can't it won't be the fault of the loonies that love him. They've put on a full-court press. Busby's got the votes on the Judiciary Committee because he packed it with the politically correct. It took the Bar Association, which is also politically correct, two whole days to announce that Hammett is highly qualified. The new president of it called me up. He said, 'In Hammett's case what we mean by "highly qualified" is *ideal.*' As far as the media goes, Patrick Graham and the rest of 'em have certified that this fellow's either Tom Paine or the Lord Jesus come back to save us all. Hammett's a slick son of a bitch when the cameras are on him, and I don't think there's going to be any unflattering pictures or stories in the papers about how he sneaks out at night and fucks chickens. When it comes to a vote on the floor, Amzi Whipple's folks will sound alarms and all fifty of them will vote no. If all fifty of us vote yes, Willy Graves will break the tie and he'll be confirmed. All Hammett needs to do is act sane for a couple of weeks and he's home free.".

"You sound like *you* think he's crazy."

"Do I? I sure don't mean to. But I guess we'll find out."

Attenborough gave a tight-lipped smile. "Sounds like we can get this whole mess cleaned up in no time."

"You're going the impeachment route?"

"That's not up to me," Attenborough said, "but nothing less than impeachment will clear up the question Mallory has raised. Frosty may have had some idea we could have a committee hearing—the son of a bitch never looks, much less talks to anybody, before he jumps, so who knows what was going on in his mind? But bear in mind, Sam, we're talking about the sanctity of a presidential election."

"Just remember the situation. The Senate is a tie vote on everything."

"You need two-thirds to convict. That's Franklin's fifty plus seventeen of ours. You think that can happen?"

"It's happened before." For a moment Clark was silent. Then he said, "Tucker, what's the objective of the House in this situation?"

"To find the truth," Attenborough said, "just like the President of the United States, if that's what he is, has asked us to do."

"What if the truth is that Mallory was elected?"

"We'll cross that bridge when we come to it. Or rather the Senate will."

"And if somebody blows up the bridge?"

"Then we don't have a President."

"I see."

Attenborough's face flushed when he was agitated. It was now a bright shade of pink. "*What* do you see, Sam? Tell me. I'd like to know."

Clark said, "The abyss, Tucker. That's what I see."

14

The fundamentals of Archimedes Hammett's public persona—his insistence on standing alone, his ideological purity, his prodigious memory, and his unerring instinct for the jugular—carried him through his confirmation hearings with flying colors. Three weeks to the day after Lockwood had nominated him, he was sworn in to testify on his own behalf before the Senate Judiciary Committee.

The hearing room was packed with Hammett enthusiasts. The advocacy groups that had formed themselves into a pro-Hammett front had obtained nearly every ticket in the hands of sympathetic senators, and then assigned volunteers to line up for the public seats at midnight the night before. As Hammett pointed out to the organizers in phone calls, the gallery played a pivotal role in the history of rituals of approval and disapproval.

His supporters, whose political movement had been made real by cameras, did not really need to be reminded of this truth. They arranged several coups de théâtre as symbols of solidarity. A number of well-known representatives of minorities and genders, together with some movie stars and authors, a delegation of academic celebrities, and a few venerable veterans of the Kennedy administration, took seats that had been held for them in the front rows.

Hammett arrived alone, without ceremony, through the public entrance. He had declined the usual courtesy of being escorted into the hearing room through a private door by the chairman of the committee and other senators, and in fact he had not been seen in the flesh by any senator or member of the staff since the breakfast with Busby and the other sympathetic members. This did not mean that he had not been active in his own cause. On the contrary, he had been on the telephone all night, every night, feeding his advocates facts and phrases, suggesting sources of support and information, organizing telephone and mail campaigns, and above all guiding and nurturing journalists by reminding them, by tone of voice and vocabulary—though never in so many words—that he was the enemy of their enemies.

Seated alone at the large baize-covered witness table, Hammett appeared to be completely relaxed. He had reason to be. When Hammett called Baxter T. Busby at three o'clock that morning, just as he had called him every morning at the same hour since the confirmation process began, Busby had assured him that a diligent search by the committee staff had failed to turn up a single negative fact about his personal life. "Amzi Whipple and the evangelicals will come after you on general principles," Busby said. "Amzi likes to live up to his biblical name. It means 'strong,' as he'll probably tell you if he ever gets you alone."

Hammett had avoided being alone with Whipple or any other senator in the opposition by omitting the time-honored ritual of paying courtesy calls on the members of the Judiciary Committee. This calculated snub had offended Whipple and other minority members, but it had generated think pieces in the press that reinforced Hammett's image as an uncompromising idealist, and therefore made the support of his own constituency even stronger. In their minds, at least, he had made his right to privacy the issue and provided himself with an unspoken reason for not answering questions about his beliefs, opinions, and associations. His reason was simple: Almost nothing was known about his private life or his true opinions, and he wanted to keep it that way. It would have been self-defeating to give his questioners the opportunity of sounding him out in advance on sensitive issues. Let them deal with his answers on the same basis with which he had to deal with their questions: without preparation. This gave Hammett the advantage. Senators—in fact the whole government apparatus—had long been out of the habit of living by their wits. Some had entirely lost the knack of expressing a complete thought. The prime function of the news media was to fill in the blanks, so that all a public figure usually had to do to win a front-page story with half a column of runover or a full minute on the evening news was to utter a burst of language on the issue of the day that contained a strong noun and a colorful adjective. Hardworking journalists to whom words came easily did the rest. Spontaneity was Hammett's best friend precisely because it was so rare among politicians.

Senator Amzi Whipple sensed Hammett's contempt for the institution of the Senate, and tried to take advantage of it by turning the tables on him at the outset. "Mr. Hammett, the news media have taken note of the fact that you did not call upon a single one of the minority members of this committee to pay your respects," he said as preamble to his first question to the nominee. "According to this clipping from *The Wall Street Journal*, this was because you disdain—and I quote—'disdain the empty courtesies of the Washington establishment.' Is that a fact, sir?"

MR. HAMMETT: Very little that comes out of Wall Street is a fact, Senator. *(Laughter)*
SENATOR WHIPPLE: Are you so contemptuous of this committee that you will not traffic with it even to respond to a question?
MR. HAMMETT: Senator Whipple, the answer is no. But let *me* quote some words back to *you*, sir. The day President Lockwood paid me the honor of sending my name to the Senate for confirmation as Chief Justice of the United States, you were quoted by the Associated Press as saying, "Archimedes Hammett is the most dangerous man in the United States. Making him Chief Justice would be tantamount to making Karl Marx the Pope." Those words, which held me up to ridicule and contempt, were broadcast and rebroadcast in every city and hamlet in the United States of America and in many places abroad. Senator, I knew even before you made this extraordinary public statement that you did not like me or respect my lifework. There seemed little point in giving you the opportunity of telling me in private what you had already told the world, or in my trying to persuade you that you're wrong.

SENATOR WHIPPLE: Is it your testimony that I am wrong about you, sir?

MR. HAMMETT: My testimony is that you said what you said, and I found your words an outrageous confession of your belief in a double standard. Would you have said the same thing about any of the justices nominated by your own party's President?

SENATOR WHIPPLE: It's a simple question I have asked you, sir. Answer it, if you please.

MR. HAMMETT: Perhaps you should repeat the question, sir, so I will be absolutely sure I am responding to your need.

SENATOR WHIPPLE: The question is, Am I wrong about you, sir?

MR. HAMMETT: Of course not, Senator. *(Laughter)*

The laughter was prolonged.

Hammett's easy triumph over Whipple made the other Republican senators wary. It was not the nominee who frightened them, but the television cameras. They knew that they could win a long exchange with the witness and still lose the encounter if he made them look foolish or unfair with so much as a single clever answer. Whipple's humiliation would play on the evening news in every living room in North America; they did not want to join him in being outwitted on camera. They also wanted to strike while the iron was hot in the matter of impeaching Lockwood and knew that they could not try him and install Mallory in the White House unless they had a Chief Justice. Even Hammett would do for this purpose.

One after another, the other reactionaries delivered homilies instead of asking questions. The radicals, having been assured by Busby that all the tough questions had been asked at the working breakfast, and being anxious to install a Chief Justice friendly to the Cause, were even less vocal.

The hearings continued for another day for the examination of other witnesses. A day after that, by a vote of eleven to ten, the Judiciary Committee recommended to the Senate that Hammett be confirmed as Chief Justice. Two days later he was confirmed by the full Senate on a tie vote on strict party lines, broken by Vice President Graves.

After the floor vote, Amzi Whipple caught up with Baxter Busby in the cloakroom. "You got your puff of white smoke, Buzzer," he said. "What now?"

Busby laughed and clapped his old friend on the back. "The odor of burning paranoia, Amzi. You'll recognize it when you smell it."

"I know what I smell, my friend. A rat."

15

On the day of Hammett's confirmation by the Senate, Slim and Sturdi Eve returned to Macalaster's house to gather up Hammett's belongings. They had rented an apartment for him in one of the new high-security buildings just west of Capitol Hill on Pennsylvania Avenue. A place in the suburbs, though more private and secure, was out of the question because Hammett, fearing a highway crash with all its incalculable consequences to his body and peace of mind, refused to commute.

In the aftermath of the confirmation process, Hammett felt dreamy, removed from reality. His whole life, after all, had just changed. He had never been one to live in the present moment; his mind was always bounding ahead to the future or lingering over the lessons of the past. But on this day, the greatest so far in his eventful life because it represented not only the reward for all he had done but also the beginning of all he hoped to do, his grandfather was much in his thoughts. During his testimony before the Judiciary Committee, he had felt the mystical presence of the old fighter so strongly that he would not have been surprised to look over his shoulder from his place at the witness table and see his grandfather—brooding, watchful—perched on one of the empty chairs behind him. This fierce hawk-faced apparition would have whispered, "Overcome them, Archimedes, my son! Aim for the heart!"

It may have been some inexplicable impulse to be alone with the memory of his grandfather that caused Hammett to leave Slim and Sturdi to their packing and wander up the stairs to the attic of Macalaster's house. It was a Saturday. Macalaster had gone somewhere early that morning and had not yet returned, and Manal was attending a birthday party. Hammett knew her schedule because, hoping to persuade her to have another séance, he had made a point of joining her at breakfast every morning and talking to her about the trivial events in her life.

Manal responded by telling him a lot about her life, but not everything. He was sure of that. Someone, he sensed, was using her, feeding her dangerous information. The name Shelley, the angry nonsense spewed by the so-called trapped spirit called Susan, who was clearly supposed to be

Susan Grant, and all the rest of the mumbo jumbo were designed to tantalize him into some damaging self-revelation. There was no other plausible explanation for the words spelled out on the Ouija board. But who was doing this? What was the purpose? These were the questions to which he wanted answers.

Hammett walked down the windowless attic corridor. The door of Macalaster's office was ajar. Looking around to make sure he was not being observed, he laid a ballpoint pen on the floor to mark the door's exact position, so that he could leave it precisely as he had found it when he left. Then he pushed the door open and went inside. In the half-darkness of the winter afternoon, he saw what he might have expected— filing cabinets, shelves of books, heaps of newspapers and magazines, a television monitor, a desk piled high with what appeared to be a lifetime accumulation of junk mail.

The computer, an ancient made-in-Korea IBM clone, was on, cursor blinking. Hammett sat down in front of the coffee-stained keyboard and typed DIR. The directory of Macalaster's files scrolled. All the titles were in plain English, a surprising sign of the owner's naïveté. But when Hammett tried to access the data under "Hammett" and "Mallory", he discovered that they were protected by passwords. Hoping to hit on it by chance, he tried "Manal," "Brook," "Ross," the telephone number and house address, Macalaster's date of birth (which he had once had a reason to commit to memory), and several variations on these typed forward and backward, but was unable to unlock the files. It did not occur to him that this was a strange thing for the Chief Justice of the United States to be doing on the day after his confirmation by the United States Senate.

Hammett, whose genetic heritage included exceptional hearing as well as excellent eyesight, heard a car pull up outside. He switched the computer off and on to clear the screen and remove the evidence of his snooping, then went to the round window that overlooked the street. Manal was getting out of a car. Although a light rain was falling, she remained at the curb, smiling and waving goodbye, as the car pulled slowly away. Suddenly she remembered something and ran frantically after the vehicle, waving her arms to attract the driver's attention.

The car stopped. It was a small, plain machine of American manufacture. Catching up, Manal bent over and said something through the window. The driver, wearing a hooded rainjacket that hid her hair, got out, keys in hand, and opened the trunk. As Manal removed her school-bag, still chattering away, Hammett saw that the woman was Zarah Christopher. He thought, Breakthrough!

Now was the moment to talk to Manal. He knew that it might, in fact, be his last opportunity to identify the person who was tormenting him by planting names and ideas in the girl's head. After positioning the door of Macalaster's office at its original angle and retrieving his ballpoint pen from the floor, Hammett dashed down to the second floor and waited in the hallway for Manal to come upstairs. He knew she would do so immediately when she saw Slim and Sturdi working in the living room; she did not like them. To cover his intentions, he took a piece of paper from his inner pocket and made a pretense of reading it. An instant later, Manal's head with its great swinging mop of black hair appeared at the head of the stairs.

"Manal," he said in a tone of surprise. "You're home. How was the party?"

"Fun."

"Good. Whose birthday was it? I forgot to ask."

"Lori Christopher's."

"Who's Lori Christopher—a schoolfriend?"

"Different school." Manal was not a chatterer.

Hammett said, "Christopher. Is that lady who was here the other night her mother?"

"Who? Oh, you mean Zarah. No, that's her sister. She brought me home."

Manal pointed to the bustling figures of Slim and Sturdi. "What's going on?"

"I'm packing to leave," Hammett replied. "I have to start my new job."

"Oh. It went through?"

"Yep. I aced them."

Manal smiled at him. Hammett responded with a pained grimace that she knew was meant to be a friendly smile. He seemed small and nervous and somehow out of place, not like a Chief Justice—but then, practically nobody her father brought home ever looked like what they really were up close. "Well, good luck," she said.

Hammett nodded his thanks and turned away, resuming the reading of the slip of paper he carried in his hand. Then, as if on impulse, he whirled on his heel and said, "Manal? Would you do me a favor before I leave this house?"

"If I can."

"Get back in touch with that spirit you were talking to the other night, that Susan."

Manal gave Hammett a level look. "Sure, why not?" she said. "But you can never be sure they'll be there when you call."

However, the visitor called Susan came on line immediately, and what she spelled out on the Ouija board made Hammett go serious and pale.

"That was funny," said Manal when the visitor had withdrawn back into darkness. "I've never known one of them to talk in numbers before."

16

All his adult life, and even before, Julian Hubbard's father had kept a diary. No matter how tired he was, or what joy or tragedy had occurred that day, or who was waiting for him in bed, he made a ritual of setting down the events of every day before he retired for the night. He wrote two pages every night, never more, never less. As Elliott Hubbard explained this habit to his sons, it helped him to remember what he wished to remember with accuracy, and to expurgate the rest so that he could sleep with an easy mind. He called it the writing cure and believed that any bad memory, any misfortune, any fixation, even the most enslaving sexual fantasy, could be banished from a man's life by recalling its details exactly and putting them down in English sentences on good rag paper with a gold-nibbed fountain pen. By the old man's own account, he had cured himself of both his divorced wives by this method, and of many other troublesome memories. What these were, exactly, would never be known because in his will he had commissioned his older son, Horace, to burn unread the sixty-two leatherbound volumes, one for each year, that he had filled up in his adult lifetime.

Horace had never kept a journal, presumably because it was impossible to do so in his line of work. But Julian, as in many other matters, emulated his father by becoming a compulsive diarist. Lately his conscience had troubled him because he had been neglecting his entries. The press of work created by Mallory's accusations, the stress of the resulting constitutional crisis, Lockwood's anguish and his own, everything had got in the way. However, on the night of Hammett's confirmation, unable to sleep, he rose at two in the morning and went down to his basement study, where his own diaries were locked up in the same large green gilt-lettered safe that Elliott Hubbard had used for the same purpose.

Julian wrote steadily, losing track of time, putting down all that he could remember about the events since the inauguration. As he wrote, the burden of Lockwood's change of heart lifted. Line by line, he understood the reasons for it and accepted its consequences. He was not a natural writer. He had to struggle to put into words what he remembered as a kaleidoscope of images, a jumble of impressions, a cacophony of voices. But he was proud of his results. He avoided flourishes, he made no excuses for himself, he resisted interpretation even though he believed that he knew and understood the reasons behind the actions of the powerful better than almost anyone else of his generation. He let the facts speak for themselves.

This process induced in Julian an almost hypnotic state, in which he saw and heard nothing outside the little pool of light cast by the green-shaded lamp on the writing table. Consequently he was startled enough to leap when he heard someone speak his name. This involuntary jump of the nerves occurred even though he recognized the visitor's voice at once.

"Good grief, Archimedes! How did you get in here?"

Hammett said, "Your wife let me in."

"You woke her up?"

Hammett ignored the question. What difference did it make if Emily's sleep had been disturbed? "Julian," he said, "something very strange is going on."

Julian capped his pen, blotted and closed his diary and slipped it under a newspaper lying on the desk. He had no wish to discuss the existence of his journal with Hammett, whose curiosity was as bottomless as his suspiciousness. He tried to smile, but he was too tired, and he knew that he would have to write down whatever Hammett was going to tell him before he could sleep with an easy mind. "Really?" he said. "What?"

"Macalaster's daughter had another séance tonight, and—"

"A *séance?* For heaven's sake, Archimedes. You became Chief Justice of the United States today. Congratulations, by the—"

"She told me things she could not possibly know, things that no one knows. She told me—" Hammett was flinging himself from one side of the small room to the other, flapping his arms in agitation.

Julian said, "Sit down before you crash into something, Archimedes. You're flying around like a bat in a bridal chamber."

"No. You have to hear this. She knows all about the Shelley Society. That ghost, Susan, called me Six-Nine. She said, 'Five-Five will know the secrets of Six-Nine.' Five-Five is Horace."

"So it is." Julian shook his head. "Archimedes, why are you so paranoid? What if Manal does know something about the Shelley Society? What can this child possibly know that could harm you or anyone else? We're just a bunch of little old ladies doing good works in the world."

"If that's what you believe, *you* should be a little more paranoid. The ghost says Five-Five will tell the world about Six-Nine. Horace is going to betray me. That was the message."

For a long moment Julian stared at Hammett in disbelieving silence. Finally he said, "Archimedes, go home. You're making no sense whatsoever."

"You don't want to hear the rest?"

"No. I've heard enough. Go home."

"All right, but one thing you're going to hear whether you want to or not. The source of all this nonsense is somebody you know."

"Oh? And who might that be?"

In spite of himself, Julian was interested in what might come next. Hammett usually had a reason for his suspicions. In the past, when in the grip of a delirium like this one, he had often sounded like a madman, only to be proved right in the end.

"I'll tell you who," Hammett said. "In fact, I told you once before. Or at least mentioned a feeling I had about a certain person."

A certain person. Where did Hammett get his outlandish vocabulary? Now he was waiting with glaring eyes for Julian to speak. Julian knew that he wanted him to ask him to go on—it was his way of wringing an apology from him—but he refused to be the first to break the silence.

At last Hammett said, "I know you'll be surprised. The name begins with Z."

Julian was exasperated and exhausted and still half in his writing trance. "Z?" he said. "I don't think I know anyone at that end of the alphabet."

"Oh, yes you do."

"Archimedes—"

"All right, call it Zed. Remember the party for Lockwood at Macalaster's house."

Julian realized whom he meant. "Zarah?" he cried. "Be serious."

Hammett replied, "I have never been more serious in my life."

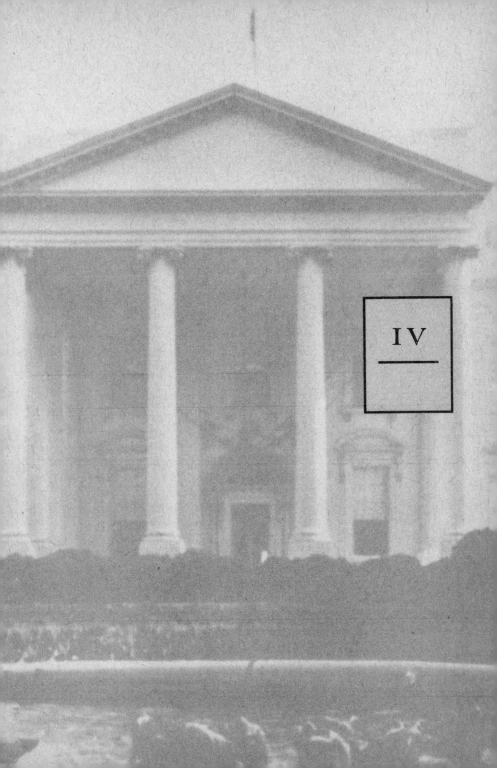

IV

1

Owing to his short stature, R. Tucker Attenborough had a nervous habit of speaking even louder than usual on first meeting with a person of consequence. To Alfonso Olmedo C., he bellowed, "Rainbows!"

Olmedo caught a whiff of the hundred-proof vodka the Speaker had drunk to fortify himself for this meeting. It was seven o'clock in the morning. Attenborough was pasty-faced and his eyes were concealed behind dark-green sunglasses. He pointed upward with his thumb. Olmedo tilted back his head in order to gaze at the frosted glass roof of Washington's Botanic Garden. The sprinkler system was operating in another part of the greenhouse, and diagonal rays of sunlight shone through a mist of chlorinated water, revealing the colors of the spectrum.

"How lovely," said Olmedo.

"Imagine seeing something like that indoors," Attenborough said. "They used to water with hoses, but I got 'em this sprinkling system. Creates a fog, runs on a timer, saves water."

"What happened to the people who ran the hoses?"

"I guess they went on to something else. I keep telling them they should pipe birdsong, American birdsong, into this place to make it even more restful, but they won't do it."

"Then perhaps you should surprise them with birdsong funds."

Attenborough peered into Olmedo's face to see if he was making fun of him, but the latter's expression was friendly and plainly lacking in irony. "Not a bad idea," Attenborough replied. He breathed deeply, taking in and expelling several lungsful of the damp, ferny air. His influence had got them admitted to the building a couple of hours before the doors opened to the public, and the two men were the only visitors.

"I love this place in the morning," Attenborough said. "Lots of times I come on down here before I start the day to think or talk to people. Makes you feel better to breathe the same air as all these trees."

"There may be a reason for that," Olmedo replied. "In Bolivia, whose cities and towns are mostly high up in the Andes, people are subject to sudden fits of violence. A man will go into a restaurant with a woman and somebody who doesn't have a woman of his own, a perfect stranger, will pull out a gun and shoot him dead in a fit of jealous rage that the killer cannot afterward explain. My father always said this strange behavior was induced by a shortage of oxygen to the brain because of the altitude. So maybe there's a surplus of oxygen in here, with all this vegetation at work."

"You figure I need extra oxygen?"

What a suspicious man, Olmedo thought; these politicians were as sensitive as mafiosi. He smiled reassuringly and said, "Don't we all, living in the city?"

"Could be," Attenborough said, only half mollified. "Maybe that's why I get so sleepy all the time. Nod right off when someone's talking to me—do it all the time. I thought it was boredom."

They arrived at the desert plants, growing in a room by themselves, and Attenborough stopped. "You asked for this meeting, Counselor," he said. "Shoot."

"Very well," Olmedo said. "I had hoped, Mr. Speaker, that you might be able to tell me what to expect from the House of Representatives in regard to my client."

Attenborough snorted. "Jesus," he said, "is *that* all?"

Olmedo smiled, as if baffled by Attenborough's sarcasm. "I mean in terms of procedure. Also timing."

Stepping back and gazing upward, Attenborough conducted a lengthy survey of Olmedo's face and elegantly tailored form. Then he said, "Does Lockwood still think I'm trying to steal his job?"

Olmedo had not realized how tiny the Speaker was before meeting him in person. He registered astonishment at his words. "The President hasn't mentioned any such idea to me. Nor would I be interested. My only concern is in the legal aspects of the situation."

"Then you're in for an education, my friend. The law won't have a whole hell of a lot to do with the way things turn out. This is a political can of worms, and every slimy son of a bitch in town is squirming around in there with the rest of 'em. Plus a whole bunch of daughters of bitches— don't want to be sexist. Everybody wants to get in on the hanging, regardless of gender, race, or religion."

"You regard impeachment as a foregone conclusion?"

"Yep. But not necessarily the hanging. What you should be worrying about, Counselor, is getting your client through the ordeal with both nuts still in his scrotum." Attenborough looked at his watch. "I've got an eight forty-five on my calendar, so we're going to have to speed this up. Ask questions, Alfonso."

/ 192

"Gladly. When will the House act on this matter?"

"It could happen next week, maybe the week after that, if it goes the way I'm trying to make it go."

"So soon? You're in a hurry?"

"Damn right I am, my friend, because I'm a Lockwood man, whatever he may think, and I sure as hell don't want to have to take over the presidency. What we're going to do is cut the foreplay to the minimum. No hearings in front of the Judiciary Committee. I'm not handing this thing over to forty-one lawyers so's they can have peacock fights in the media. The House will suspend the rules and resolve itself into a committee of the whole. Then the chair will entertain motions for three articles of impeachment for stealing votes in Michigan, New York, and California. Said motions will be debated under a rule limiting speeches by members to fifteen minutes. Then the articles will be voted on and no doubt adopted." Uttering the next four words, Attenborough spoke more loudly: "In the order stated."

Olmedo replied, "Michigan first, California last? Is that order significant?"

"It's significant. The evidence of vote fraud is weakest in Michigan, middling in New York, and strongest in California. The history of impeachment trials has been that if you fail to get two thirds of the Senate in favor of impeachment on the first one or two articles, they forget the rest and go on home. That's history. What will happen this time, nobody knows."

Olmedo nodded gravely. "One last question," he said. "What makes you think you can control the number of articles of impeachment?"

"Did I say I could do that?"

"No, Mr. Speaker, you did not. I apologize and rephrase. *Can* you control the number of articles?"

"Let me put it to you this way, Alfonso. I'll be leaning heavily on the Book of Isaiah, chapter the fifty-third, verse the first: 'Who hath believed our report? and to whom is the arm of the Lord revealed?' "

"What report is that, Mr. Speaker?"

"The report in every newspaper and TV set in the land to the effect that your client is as clean as a hound's tooth in every thought and deed. That he is the certified second coming of Honest Abe. That his trusted underlings stabbed him in the back in Michigan, New York, and California. That line of media horseshit is the best thing you've got going for you."

"Horseshit? Is there any reason for anyone *not* to believe that this perception is wrong?"

Attenborough looked to left and right and behind him, then beckoned

Olmedo closer. The latter bent at the waist. In an earsplitting whisper, Attenborough said, "Ibn Awad."

Olmedo said, "The Arab sheik who was assassinated by his son to keep him from giving nuclear weapons to the Eye of Gaza?"

"With the secret blessing of the Lockwood administration in its fourth month in office. That's the man."

"I was under the impression that the whole story had come out during the campaign. Didn't Lockwood himself make it public?"

"Franklin Mallory didn't think so. He said murder had been done by the President of the United States and by God he was going to investigate it as the first order of business of his new presidency."

"I don't remember that."

"Hardly anybody does. He said it the day before the election on the Patrick Graham show. The rest of the media ignored it, what with the election being so close, and those kids from the Eye of Gaza blowing themselves up all over Frosty and him going on TV and saying he'd saved the world from nuclear holocaust, just don't ask him for the details on how he did it. So the media didn't ask."

"Did Mallory mean what he said?"

"He usually does, Counselor."

"Does that mean he has proof of some kind, in your opinion?"

"I don't know beans about what old Franklin's got and I sure hope I never do. But why the hell else would he call the President of the United States a murderer on network television?"

"Then why didn't he include that in the bill of particulars about election fraud?"

"Maybe he's saving the best for last."

"Are you suggesting that this issue may come up as an article of impeachment?"

"I'm suggesting it's mighty funny nobody's brought it up so far."

"Why?"

The question tried Attenborough's patience. "Because, Counselor, some people might say it looks like the damn election was stolen a day after Mallory said the first thing he was going to do as President was to investigate the man he defeated as an accessory to premeditated homicide."

Olmedo said, "Are you suggesting a connection between the Ibn Awad affair and the theft of the election?"

"Not me. But if somebody else decides to do so by making it an article of impeachment, you're going to find yourself with the trial of the century on your hands."

"But why didn't Mallory make this charge at the outset?"

Attenborough looked anxiously at his wristwatch. "Who knows?" he said in what was for him a normal voice. "But one thing I've learned in the twenty-five years I've known Franklin Mallory is that he is one smart son of a bitch. All this fuss about shifting votes around, which has always been the American way, may just be old Franklin's way of getting the impeachment process started so that his people can bring up Ibn Awad. And by so doing, nail Frosty and everything the world thinks he stands for to the cross. It would finish progressive reform in this country. We'd be out for*ever*."

Attenborough had put a hand on Olmedo's arm as he uttered these last four words. Olmedo waited for him to remove it before he replied. Then he asked, "Is that a worst-case scenario, Mr. Speaker, or do you think it might really happen?"

Attenborough shrugged. "One thing's for sure. Frosty don't *want* it to happen."

"Meaning what, Mr. Speaker?"

"Meaning it may all come down to what Frosty's got to trade and what Franklin's price is," Attenborough said. "And your client knows that. Good morning to you, sir."

Without another gesture or glance, the little man hurried away among the potted trees.

Following him out at a slower pace, Olmedo learned one of the reasons for his haste as he was drenched by what seemed to be a small cloudburst. Through some freak of greenhouse atmospherics, water was being condensed beneath the glass sky and then released as warm, sticky rain that smelled of swimming pool chemicals and rotting vegetation.

2

John L. S. McGraw, the investigator, awaited Olmedo outside the Botanic Garden at the wheel of a rented Ford. As they crossed the Potomac and drove down the jammed parkway to the airport, Olmedo told him every detail of his conversation with Attenborough.

When he was finished, McGraw said, "The random element has been introduced."

"As you say, Watson," said Olmedo. "Obviously time is important. It would be best to go to the prime source."

McGraw said, "You mean the client, or the little man who wasn't there?"

"The latter. I doubt if the client knows much of value beyond the question of his guilt or innocence. He might even be shaky on that. Presidents are not burdened with details by the sort of men who carry out disagreeable duties on their behalf. How are you coming with your inquiries?"

"Okay, I think," said McGraw. "Just a few more details; I'm almost there. If things work out like they should, I may be able to go get him today. But if I have to travel, I'm going to need some bona fides."

"What did you have in mind, John?"

"A handwritten letter from the client saying it's okay to tell me the whole truth and nothing but, plus something from Julian that says the same."

"I'll call Blackstone before I get on the plane. Do you need anything else?" McGraw responded with a sidewise New York smile. They had arrived at National's shuttle terminal. With his hand on the door handle, Olmedo said, "You understand that we must produce the witness. Mere information won't be enough."

"Yeah, I understand," said McGraw. "Have a nice flight."

A couple of miles down the parkway, McGraw found a roadside turnoff that was sufficiently far away from the airport to provide reasonably good microwave reception. He parked, locked himself inside the car, got out the miniature computer he always carried in the zipper gym bag that served as his briefcase, and began punching out commands. Before entering into his association with Olmedo, McGraw had been a New York City detective assigned to antiterrorist duty. He retired on a disability pension—artificial left hip, artificial left knee, no left kidney, no left lung, no spleen—after a terrorist whom he surprised in the act of planting a bomb fired fourteen 9mm Parabellum rounds into his torso. While recovering from his wounds and the million dollars' worth of surgery required to replace or repair his shattered body parts, McGraw had become a dedicated computer hacker, not because he was fascinated by technology—he hated machines—but because he could not resist a situation in which the very air was saturated with information of every conceivable kind. All you had to do to find it was figure out what you needed to know, and then ask the computer to provide the facts. McGraw, who knew many cops in many countries, supplemented this with personal inquiries, also conducted by computer through the confidential electronic bulletin boards that policemen used to help each other out in a world in which the criminals had most of the advantages.

In seconds, McGraw was connected to one such bulletin board. He entered a password, then asked the Chilean customs outpost in Punta Arenas, Tierra del Fuego, for certain information from the navigational satellite that served the Southern Hemisphere. Then he switched to several other sources and bulletin boards to put together the picture he was painting. This process took about an hour. Lastly, using the computer again, he called up the available flights to Santiago de Chile, booked the cheapest seat on the first available plane to that city, and telephoned Norman Carlisle Blackstone at the White House.

"Has Alfonso been in touch?"

"Yes," Blackstone answered. "I have the item from the client, and the other man is with me now."

"Is he cooperating?"

"Yes, of course."

"Glad to hear it. Can you messenger the stuff out to me at Dulles? I'm leaving on a flight at four-twenty."

"Quick work."

"No time like the present."

"I agree," Blackstone said. "A man will meet you at the gate exactly one hour before flight time."

"Thanks. If you're talking to Alfonso again, just tell him I should be back the day after tomorrow."

After hanging up, McGraw consulted his map of the Washington area and drove to a shopping center off Interstate 66. In a Giant supermarket he bought a three-day supply of dehydrated meals-in-a-cup, bottled water, dried fruit, and granola bars—he had no time for a bout of diarrhea induced by foreign food—and, on sale in the Eddie Bauer store elsewhere in the mall, a waterproof Gore-Tex parka with a zip-in woolen lining. Then he drove on to Dulles International Airport, where he turned in the rental car. In the airport bookstore he bought diskettes of Lottman's *Truly Exhaustive Guide to South America* and a novel about the Troubles in Ireland that he had already read twice. Settling down to wait for Blackstone's messenger, he inserted the novel into his computer and began to read. At three-twenty sharp, a young lawyer from the White House delivered the package. McGraw identified himself with his private investigator's badge and license and signed the receipt.

"The originals are in sealed envelopes inside here," the messenger said. "Your own copies are separate."

"Great," McGraw said. He put the envelope, unopened, into his gym bag. He could look inside after he got to Santiago. Between now and then he wanted to rest his mind, so after passing through security and checking in at the gate, he went back to the novel. Some of the contents he remembered, other parts seemed new, and he noticed details this time that he had missed in earlier readings. This was why he read the books he liked over and over again. They reminded him that you seldom understood everything the first time you looked at something, no matter how systematic you thought you were being. It was impossible to see every detail unless you kept going back for another look, and then another and another.

3

McGraw, who lived by making comparisons, had expected everyone in Chile to be Incan, pensive, and aloof, like Alfonso Olmedo C. Instead, they looked Mediterranean, hurried, and preoccupied by the petty details of life, like the clientele of Katz's delicatessen ("SEND A SALAMI TO YOUR BOY IN THE ARMY") in his old Lower East Side neighborhood.

The boatman he hired to ferry him out to the yacht *Caroline*, which was anchored in the roadstead off the remote southern port of Ancud, wore an especially worried expression. In keeping with McGraw's often-tested belief that waking people up out of a sound sleep was a good way to begin an investigative relationship, they set sail before dawn. Ancud is located near the forty-second parallel, even in midsummer one of the stormiest of the southern latitudes. The continental shelf is precipitous along the Chilean coast, so the water, which in the murky half-light seemed as gray and heavy as molten lead, is hundreds of feet deep. And because the waves had encountered no significant obstacle on their six-thousand-mile progress across the empty South Pacific Ocean, the surf was mountainous.

The boat, an antique diesel-powered lighter with a wooden hull, rose and fell dramatically. As the rim of the sun appeared over the Andes, McGraw noted with interest that the difference between the trough of one wave and the crest of the next literally became the difference between night and day. When the boat went up, it ascended into hesitant sunlight; when it went down, it descended into a starless night that smelled of icebergs. McGraw had never before smelled anything so unpolluted, so primeval.

The engine thumped loudly as the rolling, pitching boat skidded down a steep wave and the whirring propeller came out of the water. "Very difficult!" the helmsman shouted in Spanish. Nevertheless they porpoised steadily closer to the *Caroline*. It was an odd process. One moment the big

/ 198

white yacht was hidden from sight; the next they were looking down on its masthead lamp from the vantage point of a gull. "Maybe impossible!" cried the helmsman. McGraw used his hands and his bushy red eyebrows to mime two vessels rising and falling in frenzied opposition to each other, then, after adjustment, in happy coordination. In the pidgin Spanish he had picked up as a young cop in East Harlem he shouted, "¡Como bailar, no como follar!"—like dancing, not like screwing. The helmsman grinned.

But when the moment came, the helmsman mated his shabby vessel to the elegant yacht with practiced seamanship. While clambering from one boat to the other, however, McGraw lost his footing and nearly fell into the heaving sea. As he was saved by a sailor on the yacht, who seized his arm and hauled him aboard, he felt a small detonation of anger within himself. Each time he was placed in a situation like this one, in which he had to call on his cobbled body to do something it could no longer do, he remembered every detail of the shooting. The terrorist had had a shaved head and a beautiful face with large frightened eyes, set wide apart. Because of the shaved head, McGraw had never been sure whether this person was a woman or a pretty boy. The doelike eyes had remained wide open and unblinking as she or he fired off the entire magazine. The weapon had been equipped with a silencer. It was a weird sensation to see the red-yellow-and-blue sparkle of the muzzle blast, and to feel—actually consciously feel—the needle-sharp rounds stinging your flesh, but to have this happen in absolute silence, hearing no noise of gunfire even though you knew you were in the act of being killed by a lunatic.

"*Forget* that shit," McGraw said to himself, staggering on his artificial hip and knee as he gained the pitching deck of the *Caroline*. To the deckhand who had grabbed him before he fell into the sea he said, "Thanks for giving me a hand there, pal."

The sailor said, "No problem. What do you want?"

"I saw this boat from shore and wondered if it's for sale."

"You've got the wrong boat, pal."

"I have? Then I guess I'm stuck."

The workboat from which McGraw had debarked had already cast off and was thumping back toward the wave-lashed shore. McGraw shivered, as he had been doing all the way from shore, in his drenched Eddie Bauer parka; Gore-Tex provided little protection against the frigid seawater. Two more crewmen, big North Americans who kept their right hands in the pockets of their yellow slickers, had joined the first one. Naturally they took it for granted that he was a terrorist or a cop.

McGraw said, "I'm going to go into my inside pocket for a piece of paper, okay?"

They nodded. He produced a calling card and handed it to the largest sailor, who glanced at it indifferently. Then, raising puzzled eyes, he said, "This is Julian Hubbard's card. But what's this written on it?"

Scribbled across the face of the engraved card, in Greek letters, was the following message: "Ναμε οφ τηε ποετ." By referring to the international character sets in the memory of his pocket computer, McGraw had transliterated these Greek letters into the English words "Name of the poet." What the phrase meant in Julian's circle, he did not yet know. Shrugging, he replied to the crewman's question. "It's Greek to me. But maybe somebody on board will know. Give it to the tallest grown-up you can find."

"The *tallest* one?"

McGraw nodded. The man stared at him for a moment, then disappeared through the door into the yacht's interior.

Thirty seconds later a lanky bareheaded man with a long Anglo-Saxon face emerged. He had the milky English gaze that McGraw's Dublin-born great-grandmother, who remembered the Troubles of 1916, had called "hangman's eyes." Smiling amiably, he held out his hand to McGraw. "Welcome aboard, sir," he said. "I'm Horace Hubbard."

McGraw said, "Glad to meet you. My name's John McGraw, and I've got a letter for you." McGraw handed the tall man the letter from Lockwood, still sealed in its blank envelope.

Horace Hubbard tore it open, read it at a glance, and then, instead of returning his gaze to McGraw, looked beyond him for a long moment toward the disk of the sun as it broke free of the mountaintops. Then he turned his gaze on McGraw again, this time with no trace of a smile, no hint of friendliness. In the brief moment consumed by these actions, dawn turned into daylight, rendering the color of Horace's eyes an even icier blue. "Do come below, Mr. McGraw," he said in a *basso cantate* boarding-school voice that sounded a lot like his half brother's. "You're just in time for breakfast."

4

Although Franklin Mallory did not hunt—in moments of tender irony, Susan Grant had sometimes called him the lama because he would sooner open a window to let a fly escape than swat it—he owned a big game reserve in the Uinta Mountains near the Utah-Wyoming border. Horned and antlered species from every continent except Antarctica grazed or munched on air-dropped fodder inside electrified fences. These barriers, disguised as natural features of the land, were designed to protect the animals from the formerly endangered grizzly bears, wolves, and coyotes that overran the high country as the result of two decades of corrective wildlife management. Some of the reestablished carnivores had been genetically enhanced by animal scientists to give them a better chance of survival against their cruelest enemy, man, and of course this endowed them with more than natural advantages in attacking their prey. These now consisted primarily of Mallory's exotic deer and antelope because the predators had already killed and eaten most of the range cattle, sheep, mule deer, and other creatures on which they ordinarily fed.

Mallory regarded his nearly complete collection of beautiful ruminants as a work of art and permitted no one to harm the animals, but visitors were free to shoot any carnivore detected in the act of stalking them. Over the years, O. N. Laster, an enthusiastic sportsman, had slain many such predators. Laster hunted only in the dark—even the more intelligent and dangerous beasts produced by genetic engineering were too easy by day—and his private jet had landed on Mallory's airstrip in the early hours of the morning so as to give him some relaxation before the two men met for a working breakfast at six-thirty. Two hours before dawn he bagged three gray wolves, a huge male and two younger animals—he let the mature females escape—that were about to attack a rare Siberian sable antelope. The wolves were dead before they knew they were being hunted. Correcting his aim for a brisk crosswind, Laster brought them down in an elapsed time of 1.97 seconds with three perfect head shots from a range of 535 meters. He was certain of the arithmetic because the night-vision electronic telescope on his noiseless, nonmetallic 6mm antiterrorist sniper's rifle, manufactured by his own company, Universal Energy, measured time and distance with the same laser beam that guided the tiny mercury-filled vinyl bullet to the target at a muzzle velocity that only just escaped breaking the laws of ballistics.

Because he was operating in a different time zone, Laster made his kills at about the same hour that John McGraw went aboard the *Caroline*, so by the time he returned to the lodge to have breakfast with Mallory, the personal assistant traveling with him was able to tell him that McGraw had made contact with Horace Hubbard. Laster's man knew this because the *Caroline* had at last broken radio silence for a phone call from Horace to Julian Hubbard, and Universal Energy's computers had been programmed to intercept any transmission from the yacht that passed through the southern communications satellite—which had, of course, been manufactured and placed in synchronous orbit by Universal Energy.

(It was by no means unusual for the name of this supremely efficient and profitable multinational corporation, or consortium, as Laster preferred to call it, to occur three times in any single sentence describing the inner workings of the purified technological society in which mankind was just beginning to live. Universal Energy was the prime creator of this new society because Laster, nearly alone among American entrepreneurs, had understood that the future lay in investing in the next stage of technology at a time when most people in U.S. industry and government were fixated on the twentieth-century technology that Japan had brought to a state of perfection at the precise historical moment when it was ceasing to be relevant. Now Japan was irrelevant, and would remain so until it was time for it to be late for another technological revolution.)

At breakfast with Mallory, Laster played a recording of this conversation. There wasn't much to it—just Julian confirming McGraw's bona fides and the Hubbards keeping stiff upper lips after, as Laster put it, Yale had lost the big game to John Jay College of Criminal Justice. "What a joke that this one little ex-cop from New York did what the entire investigative apparatus of the U.S. government could not do," said Laster to Mallory.

"I don't suppose," Mallory replied, "that you're surprised by the outcome."

"Ha!"

O. N. Laster believed as strongly in the comical incompetence and impotence of the federal government as the leftists whom he hated, and who hated him, believed in its sinister and all-encompassing power and knowledge. As for Mallory, he had long ago learned that there was no more point in arguing with either opinion than in trying to convince an evangelical that the Bible was allegorical or an evolutionist that the Book of Genesis provided a not-altogether-implausible explanation for the existence of life on earth. Mallory himself was capable of holding both ideas in his mind at the same time, and routinely did so— together with a couple of additional theories about the origin of species that made much more sense to him in terms of scientific and political probabilities.

The two men were seated at a rustic table before a roaring fire of aspen logs. Wind whistled down the chimney, scattering sparks over the stone hearth. There was the hint of a blizzard in the air, and Laster, though happy with himself and with the good news from Chile, was impatient to get down to the business that had brought him here from London. It was he who had requested the meeting, and Mallory had flown out from Washington in his own identical Gulfstream.

Because he was slightly deaf and could not hear other people speak while he chewed, Laster ate his high-protein, low-fat breakfast before getting down to business. In the relentless protection of his body from all alimentary dangers Laster resembled his arch-enemy, Archimedes Hammett. Although they were alike in other ways because both were single-minded political extremists, there was no physical similarity between the two. Unlike the stooped, furtive Hammett, Laster was a large, outdoorsy man who believed that appetite was the great driving force of creation. Few people outside his intimate circle of supercapitalists and oil sheiks knew what he looked like, or even exactly how rich and powerful he was. He avoided being photographed or interviewed.

"Tell me something, Franklin," he said. "Are you going to use the Ibn Awad thing on Lockwood or not?"

"As I've told you before, Oz, I hope not."

"You *hope* not. What does that mean, exactly?"

"It means that I hope proving the theft of the election—or the certainty of proving it—will be enough to remove him from office without having to provide a casus belli for a resumption of the holy war between Islam and Christendom."

With a precise click of cup into saucer, Laster put down his herbal tea. "There won't be a holy war if justice is done and the Arabs see it done by you, the best friend they ever had in the White House," he said. "This man ordered the assassination of a foreign head of state who was also considered to be an authentic saint by half the world. You've got it all on tape."

Laster did not add "*thanks to me*," but he had, in fact, arranged for the delivery to Mallory of a copy of the taped conversation between the President and Jack Philindros in which Lockwood seemed to issue specific verbal orders for the murder of the Arab patriarch.

Mallory, who had never acknowledged receipt of this gift, said, "No argument. Lockwood did what he did. But he thought he had good reason to act."

Laster replied, "You mean he wanted a reason and the Hubbard boys invented one for him."

"Terrorists blowing up New York and Tel Aviv with suitcase fission bombs is a pretty persuasive reason to do what he did."

"Would you have done what Lockwood did in the same circumstances?"

"No."

"All right!" Laster snapped his fingers in triumph. "See, Franklin? You don't even hesitate. Your answer in good old American English is 'No'—just plain 'No.' Why?" Mallory gave him a faint smile. Laster said, "Don't smirk, Franklin. I want to know your thinking."

Mallory knew he would have to answer if he wished to be left in peace; Laster had not become chairman and chief executive officer of the most powerful cartel in the world, and extended its operations into the solar system, by taking no for an answer. He was here because he had something to say to Mallory, and his questions were a device to maneuver Mallory into giving him the opportunity of saying it.

"All right," Mallory said. "I wouldn't have done it for three reasons. Number one, killing people is wrong. Number two, it's a good way to get yourself killed in revenge. Number three, killing Ibn Awad was a wasted effort because, assuming these famous suitcase nukes actually existed, *he* wasn't going to plant them. All he did, according to the FIS reports, was pay for them. The Eye of Gaza was going to plant them."

"So what *would* you have done?"

Mallory, sighing, replied, "Oz, really. What's the point of playing these games of what-if?"

Laster pressed on. "I have my reasons; bear with me," he said. "It's a simple question: If you had been Lockwood, what would you have done?"

"I would have found the bombs and destroyed them, or tried to. Meanwhile I would have let Ibn Awad know that if they *were* used, the United States would strike every strategic target in his own country with neutron weapons that would kill every living thing but leave all its wealth intact and in our possession."

"That's all?"

"What more would have been necessary?"

"You wouldn't even have cleaned out the Eye of Gaza—is that what you're saying?"

"Only as a side effect of finding the bombs. What would be the point? Without the bombs they're just another bunch of armed psychotics plotting mayhem in some Middle Eastern slum."

As Mallory spoke, Laster vigorously nodded his head—not in agreement, though he certainly held the same opinion as Mallory in this matter, but in encouragement. As soon as the last word was out of Mallory's mouth, he said, "Good thinking, Franklin. Now you've stated the case and removed any personal reason you may have had for not going after this guy with everything you've got."

Amused, Mallory said, "I have?"

"You bet you have. You believe in his fundamental human decency. Fine; I agree. Lockwood isn't evil. He's stupid. And that's why he has to go."

"He's going, Oz."

"Maybe he is, maybe he isn't. My information is that Tucker Attenborough and the rest of the boys are trying to rig the process so that the most damning evidence, the frauds in California, will never even come to a vote in the Senate. The strategy of the defense is to throw the Hubbard boys to the wolves on grounds that they done wrong, but that Lockwood never told 'em to—"

"That's true enough, but it doesn't alter the fact that Lockwood wasn't elected."

"Think again, buddy. Olmedo is the smartest lawyer in this country. He'll play the Senate like a Stradivarius and raise enough reasonable doubts to get a verdict of guilty but innocent. He knows all those gutless wonders want is a way out, and he'll give it to them. Congress will then solemnly certify that Lockwood lost but unfortunately it can't be proved that you won, at least not beyond the shadow of a doubt. Lockwood will go home to Kentucky to raise racehorses, and Attenborough, a falling-down drunk with a brain like a pickled cactus, will be President of the United States while the Hubbard boys count mouse turds in a jail cell on Sitka. Franklin, I'm telling you the facts."

Mallory smiled yet again. He liked Laster—admired his single-minded passion, his gift for conviction—but in political matters he did not value his opinion any more than that of any other zealot.

In a softer tone, Laster repeated, "I'm telling you."

Mallory said, "Just like Horace and Julian told Frosty."

The comparison hit home. Laster shook his big skull in resentment. Before he could retaliate, his assistant, a willowy young man called Hugo Fugger-Weisskopf, entered the room, pausing just inside the door for permission to speak. Like all of O. N. Laster's personal staff, Hugo was a German from the eastern provinces; Laster believed that these people, natural followers who had lived under totalitarian systems for almost sixty years, were the only ethnic group that remained capable of blind loyalty.

Harshly, as a means of signaling his indignation to Mallory, Laster said, "What?"

With stout deference, Hugo replied, "The pilot says we should leave, sir. It's beginning to snow."

"Tell him to start engines. I'll be outside in one minute."

Laster meant one minute. Hugo departed, not bothering to report that Laster's bags were packed, his rifle cleaned and stowed, his wolves skinned and the pelts packed in refrigerated containers for shipment to the taxidermist. Of course all this had been done. This was what Hugo was paid for—to make life easier for his employer.

To Mallory, with a forgiving smile that was half quizzical, half exasperated, Laster said, "One last question. Will you do what's necessary?"

Mallory replied, "Oz, one last request. Let me handle this."

Laster smiled.

Mallory said, "I mean it. I have a plan."

Laster said, "I know you do. But then, so do Lockwood and the rest of the pinkos."

He made no assurances. Mallory knew that this man sincerely believed that he, Mallory, and Mallory alone, could save America from the people who hated her and wanted to destroy all that she stood for. But who would save Mallory from his better instincts? This was a question Laster had often asked himself, and asked Mallory.

As they walked toward the door, Laster threw an arm across Mallory's shoulder and gave him a manly half-hug. "Greater love hath no man," he said. "I admire you, Franklin. I wish I could be like you. You're a goddamn Christian."

5

Lockwood's letter to Horace Hubbard, written on White House stationery in the big block draftsman's capitals favored by the President, wasted no words:

> YOU WILL ACCOMPANY THE BEARER, MR. J. L. S. MCGRAW, FORTHWITH TO
> A DESTINATION IN THE UNITED STATES, AND THERE AWAIT FURTHER IN-
> STRUCTIONS FROM DULY CONSTITUTED AUTHORITY.
>
> B. F. Lockwood

To eliminate any question about its authenticity, the letter was impressed with the presidential seal. McGraw recognized this for what it was, a fussbudget Blackstone touch. He knew as well as Blackstone—or, for that matter, Horace—that Lockwood's peremptory order had no legal force. Horace was outside U.S. territory and, having quit the FIS, was not subject to the President's authority. But McGraw was not relying on law; he was relying on the code of conduct by which Horace had always lived.

Once they were inside the *Caroline*'s cabin, Horace did not argue or even ask a question. "Let me just leave a note for my hosts," he said. "Then we'll go ashore." On the other hand—and this, too, was consistent with the honor system—he did not volunteer any information about his accomplice, the FIS computer expert Rose MacKenzie. However, McGraw had determined, through the professional courtesy of the Ancud customs post, that this individual was also aboard the *Caroline.*

McGraw said, "I also have a letter for a Rose Elizabeth MacKenzie. Ph.D."

Horace received this information in the same steady way in which he had read Lockwood's letter, as something unpleasant but inevitable. "She's terribly seasick," he said. "They all are, even some of the crew."

"Then she should be glad to get off the boat," McGraw said.

"I suppose you're right; I'll call her," Horace replied after the briefest of hesitations. He looked quizzical—another mannerism, like his haughty way of talking, which McGraw supposed he had been born with, just as he himself came equipped with a standard-issue Hell's Kitchen Irish accent and set of gestures. These characteristics, designed to make you fit in, became oddities only when you got separated from the herd.

On the trip between ship and shore, Rose MacKenzie, a good-looking but disheveled woman who was no longer young, and in her present physical and mental misery looked even older than she was, hung over the side of the *Caroline*'s dinghy, retching convulsively into the offshore swell. She did not speak to McGraw or even look at him, and in return, as a matter of kindness, he ignored her. He knew that not many hours remained of the privacy she had taken for granted all her life; let her enjoy what little was left.

On the northward flight from Santiago to Washington (due north: McGraw had been surprised to relearn from the guidebook that the west coast of South America lay to the east of New York) Rose MacKenzie slept, or pretended to, and he continued to leave her alone. He was not even interested in pumping Horace Hubbard. The economy-class cabin of an airliner was no place to conduct an interrogation, even if McGraw had wanted to do so. He did not; his job was to deliver these witnesses to Olmedo, who would examine them. Nor did Horace ask McGraw any questions. He had spent his life in a profession in which credentials counted for nothing because they were assumed to be forged. Auspices were everything, and McGraw had certainly demonstrated that he had these. Even if Julian had not vouched for him over the telephone, Horace would have accepted him as the genuine article. It was obvious that he could not be anything else.

Nevertheless a certain camaraderie developed between the two men, as often happens between policeman and suspect once an arrest is made. As the plane sped them homeward, they chatted about Antarctic icebergs. Horace had long been interested in them as a possible source of wealth and political influence, and seeing them up close from the deck of the *Caroline* in the Bellingshausen Sea had reawakened the idea. Or so he said.

"Sheik Ibn Awad, who had banned foreigners from his part of Arabia, let drilling teams into his country twenty years ago because he was told they might find water under the desert," he told McGraw. "Water is what he prayed for, but *ma shā'a-Llāh*, thanks be to God, they found half a trillion barrels of oil instead."

With this abrupt mention of Ibn Awad's name, Horace peered alertly into McGraw's eyes for some sign of unrevealed knowledge. This was a murderer's trick. McGraw knew that Horace's intention was to check out his reaction to hearing the name spoken aloud; he wanted to know what McGraw knew or suspected about the circumstances of the victim's death. Therefore McGraw registered no response whatsoever. In a normal, next-guy-at-the-bar tone, he said, "Did that piss this sheik off—finding oil instead of water?"

"At first it did somewhat," Horace replied just as casually. "Then he was put in touch with a man who believed that icebergs could be floated to Near East ports from Antarctica and melted down for irrigation of the desert."

"The ice wouldn't melt en route?"

"Some, but not all. Even if you lost half to meltage, there'd be millions of barrels of water left. These bergs are enormous, you know. Some are the size of Manhattan Island, but upside down, so that skyscrapers of ice are submerged. They're big enough to create their own weather systems; theoretically, you could cause local rainstorms if you anchored enough of them in the Persian Gulf. The beauty of the idea is, they're composed of the purest water on earth. Icebergs may be the only unpolluted objects left on the planet, in fact. Up close, they smell incredibly clean—like spring water on the morning of creation."

This poetic turn of phrase surprised McGraw; he had never before met a WASP who talked like an Irishman. But he saw what Horace meant. "That's what I always thought," he said.

Now Horace was surprised—not disbelieving, but surprised, and for similar reasons. How could a man like this entertain such an aesthetic thought? "Really?" he said. "You've actually thought about how icebergs smell?"

"Yeah, I have—just this morning, in fact, smelling the ocean. . . . Raspberry or date almond?" McGraw, who had refused the airline food, was offering Horace a choice of granola bars from his zipper bag.

"Raspberry, thank you," Horace said.

Chewing, McGraw said, "So why didn't they tow the icebergs to the Persian Gulf?"

"There were a lot of technical problems. It takes a big ship and a lot of power to tow something that large and unwieldy—and of course it would be dangerous in a storm. They thought of making the iceberg self-propelling—installing a nuclear engine, rudder, and screws right in the ice and steering it by satellite. Or towing it with a nuclear submarine. But there was a certain reluctance to sell an Arab with a ninth-century mind nuclear devices, even if he did have billions to spend."

McGraw nodded and locked eyes with Horace. "And of course," he said, "the old guy died very suddenly."

"Yes," said Horace. He flashed a brief smile, then took a bite of his granola bar. "That certainly was a setback as far as the iceberg project was concerned."

6

After passing through customs, a speedy affair since none of them had to wait for luggage, McGraw and his witnesses were met at JFK by a hired limousine, which took them directly to Alfonso Olmedo C.'s offices in a Wall Street tower. As they stepped out of the car into the deserted street, the Sunday hush of the financial district was punctuated by the tolling of a steeple bell farther uptown.

"Church bells," Horace remarked nostalgically. "This really is the most private part of town on weekends. Like a necropolis. Rose lives—lived—just around the corner, you know."

"Is that so?" said McGraw, who had persuaded Dick Condon, the foot-sore, liverish ex-cop who was head of security in her building, to admit him to her apartment. Condon, who was even more Irish than McGraw—as a younger man he'd been a Reagan Democrat out of ethnic considerations—had a key because he took care of MacKenzie's cats. These purring animals, half a dozen lonely, overfriendly Burmese, had rubbed up against McGraw's shins as he worked his way, sneezing, through the nearly unbelievable clutter of computer printouts, books, recordings, newspapers, magazines, scholarly journals, sheet music, and other printed matter that filled the flat. He discovered little of value, though he had come across Rose's Ph.D. diploma from MIT marking her place in a coffee-table book about cats, and this had put him onto something useful. But of course the FBI, the FIS, and probably others had been there before him, disturbing the scene.

In the elevator, as before, Rose MacKenzie said nothing. She had recovered from her bout of seasickness, and her creamy complexion, slightly sunburnt after her ocean voyage, now glowed with health. Despite the shadow of worry within them, her bright blue eyes shone with intelligence and its usual companion, a sense of humor. Although MacKenzie was Protestant and McGraw was Catholic, and though each could tell that this was so by a hundred small signs, both were pure-blooded Celts, and McGraw had to admit to himself that he liked the look of this female. Too bad she had got mixed up with Horace, who was so obviously descended from Englishmen. But then, the Scots had always let themselves be used by the bastards, from the time of Cromwell and William of Orange. Suddenly she lifted her eyes and stared at him, as if detecting this thought by means of some dormant tribal instinct. She smiled at him, but she still did not utter a word.

In his modestly furnished corner office, Olmedo shook hands and offered them. lunch. It was almost impossible to get anything to eat in this neighborhood on weekends. A tray of delicatessen sandwiches and a bowl of fruit stood on the coffee table, along with bottles of seltzer water, crystal tumblers, and a thermos of coffee.

Rose eyed the sandwiches hungrily. "How romantic," she said to Horace, who smiled fondly in return; she loved delicatessen food, and he had brought her hot pastrami sandwiches on the night they locked themselves into the FIS computer room beneath D. & D. Laux & Co., only a block or two away, and stole the election. Rose, whose digestive track was entirely empty after days of vomiting, seized half of an enormous corned beef on rye and bolted it. Then, more daintily, she ate an apple. Horace, upper lip twitching in affectionate amusement, ate a plain bagel with cream cheese and drank a cup of coffee.

Olmedo waited for them to finish their food. It was evident without an exchange of words that both Horace and Rose knew exactly who he was; no doubt Rose had called up all the computerized data about him after he was appointed. Olmedo must have made this assumption, because he offered no précis of the situation or description of his own role.

"I thought it would be better for us to meet here rather than in Washington, at least in the first instance," Olmedo said. "Mr. McGraw assures me that you are here voluntarily. Is that the fact?" Horace replied, "Yes, certainly." Rose said nothing. A little more emphatically, Olmedo said, "Dr. MacKenzie?" Rose put her apple core on the plate and replied, "You could say that." This was the first time McGraw had heard her voice; the intonation was, or originally had been, midwestern, and the timbre was surprisingly deep; over the phone, you wouldn't be sure of her gender.

Olmedo said, "As I assume you know, I represent President Lockwood in his current legal situation. I represent him only as any lawyer would represent any other client. I have no official position, no authority as an officer of the government, and I am not here to collect information for the benefit of anyone except my client. Under the law, I will be obliged to share anything you may tell me that is material to the defense with the lawyers on the other side. Indeed, it will be my purpose to make every relevant fact in this case public, insofar as any such fact might help my client. I hope you will talk to me on the record about what you know about this matter. If you want a lawyer of your own present, that will be fine."

"That won't be necessary in my case," Horace said.

"Nor in mine," Rose said. "In for a penny, in for a pound."

Olmedo gave her a slow, solemn look. "The price may be somewhat higher than that, Dr. MacKenzie," he said.

Rose, who had been wolfing the other half of the huge corned beef sandwich, ignored the warning; perhaps she did not even hear it over the noise of her own chewing. She stood up and peeled off a sweater, further tousling her heavy hair. She and Horace were still in their sailing clothes, layers of wool beneath thick turtleneck sweaters, and even though the heat was turned low because the building was closed, her forehead shone with perspiration.

"The best way to begin may be for you to read this," Olmedo said. "It's a copy of the material given to Lockwood by Franklin Mallory."

Horace let Rose do the reading. She accomplished this with amazing speed, licking her forefinger and flicking the pages as she scanned them. Finally she said, "We're familiar with these data."

"Then I must ask you this," Olmedo said. "To the best of your knowledge, is any of this inaccurate in any particular?"

Rose said, "No, of course not. It came from the memory of the FIS computer."

"So the two of you actually did all the things you are described as doing?"

"Yes, absolutely."

Horace smiled indulgently. "Wait a minute, Rose. You weren't in on *absolutely* everything."

"No. I ran the computer. I can speak to that. And what you have here is accurate in that respect, as far as it goes."

"You remember every detail? There's a great deal of data in that file."

"No, I don't remember every detail. All I did was keyboard commands, and I can't possibly remember all of them because I was improvising. This particular task had never been done before. There was no need to remember what I was doing; all that mattered was the result. The computer does the remembering. That's what it's made to do, in the simplest possible terms—remember everything."

"And it's never mistaken in its memory of events?"

"By definition, no. It can't be."

"It cannot be corrupted? Data cannot be changed?"

"The computer can't be corrupted. Data can be. But as this file demonstrates, the computer remembers everything it is told to do. What we did was substitute invented data for what you might call 'real' data, quote unquote."

"*False* data."

"A human being might use that term. To a computer, data are data. It has no capacity for value judgments, no way of differentiating between the qualities you call true and false. I told it something. I told it what to do with what I told it. It did it. That's what it remembers. In human terms, what has happened here is that the computer has been induced by a hypnotist to recall from dormant memory—from its subconscious, so to speak—what it knows about this particular sequence of events."

Olmedo said, "Would you say it has told the truth, the whole truth, and nothing but the truth?"

Rose smiled the same knowing smile she had given McGraw in the elevator. To her, computers were what Samoans had been to Margaret Mead, a happier breed about whom she knew more secrets than she was prepared to betray. "Well," she said, "nothing but the truth, certainly. As for the rest . . ."

She looked sidelong at Horace. Something passed between them—a flicker of conjugal conspiracy, a warning, a signal. McGraw saw this happen, and so did Olmedo. With a sudden look of alarm, Rose leaped to her feet and said, "Oh-oh. Ladies' room."

McGraw took her arm; prisoners who suddenly had to go to the bathroom made him apprehensive, especially if they were ex-FIS employees. "Come with me."

"All right," said Rose, her bright eyes filled with urgency. "But walk fast." She clapped her free hand over her mouth and accompanied him out of the room at a brisk walk.

Horace smiled after her, and though he was too much the gentleman to mention Rose's distress, a husbandly look of amused concern lingered on his windburned face.

Olmedo said, "Dr. MacKenzie seemed on the point of telling me something significant."

Horace looked interested but slightly baffled by this observation. "Did you think so?" he asked.

"Yes, I thought so. Why did you stop her, sir?"

Before answering, Horace looked for a long moment at the carpet, a moderately good Heriz. "I thought it was the corned beef sandwich that stopped her," he said. "But it is true—perhaps you've found this out in your own work—it *is* true that people who've been in the business of keeping secrets, as Rose has been, often don't know how to stop themselves once they start telling what they know."

Olmedo nodded. "That's so."

Horace nodded in eager agreement; he and Olmedo understood each other on this important consideration. "Now, Mr. Olmedo," he said, leaning forward confidingly, as if doing something he had done many, many times before, "let's you and me get to the crux of this matter."

He took a tape recorder out of his pocket and handed it to Olmedo.

"You may want to sample this before you hear my offer," he said. "Use the earpiece, please."

7

Lockwood said, "He wants *what?*"

"Immunity from prosecution for Julian and Rose MacKenzie," Olmedo replied. They were alone in the Lincoln sitting room; the lawyer had things to discuss with his client that could not be said in the presence of a witness, not even Norman Carlisle Blackstone.

"He thinks Julian's got something to worry about?"

"Apparently the whole thing was Julian's idea. He asked Horace to do it."

"In my name?"

"No." Olmedo paused. "But for your sake."

"For my sake? In what way?"

"To preserve you from a charge of murder in the Ibn Awad case."

Lockwood gave Olmedo a long look of black and silent resentment. Finally he said, "That's what Julian said?"

Olmedo nodded. "According to his half brother, yes."

"Those were his *words?*"

"Yes, sir. I took them down in writing."

"You took them down in writing."

Lockwood's voice was flat, as if he wished to hear these scarcely believable words in his own voice before accepting that they had actually been spoken aloud. His mobile face was expressionless for the first time in

Olmedo's experience. He fell into a lengthy silence. Olmedo waited patiently for the President to break it. Finally Lockwood said, "So now that you've got Horace, what do you think you've got?"

"We have an eyewitness who can testify as to your complete innocence in regard to the theft of the election, Mr. President."

"Oh. I thought maybe you still thought you had that sacrificial lamb you were talking about just now. Is Horace willing to be led to the slaughter?"

"He is willing to testify that you knew nothing about the theft of the election, and that all knowledge of it was kept from you as a matter of deliberate choice."

"Whose choice?"

"Julian's. Horace told him you wouldn't agree. Julian replied . . ." Olmedo took an index card from his pocket and read from it: " 'He won't have the opportunity. Philindros told him about Ibn Awad. Was that a good idea?' "

"Where'd you get those words?" Lockwood held out his hand for the index card, but Olmedo put it back into his pocket.

He said, "Horace recorded the conversation."

"He taped his own brother?"

Olmedo made no response. Lockwood's eyes narrowed. His breathing was audible. His unshod feet were propped on an ottoman between them, and Olmedo noted a small hole about the size of a fingernail in the heel of the President's right sock.

Lockwood said, "Are you sure Horace will keep his side of the bargain?"

"Within the bounds of predictability, yes, I think he will. I need hardly tell you, of all people, Mr. President, that one can never be sure what any human being will do when it comes right down to it."

Lockwood nodded curtly. "This guy may be playing some other game altogether," he said.

Olmedo indicated more interest in this obvious thought than in fact he felt; he was discovering that dealing with a President fostered sycophancy. He said, "In what way might that be true, sir?"

"Those goddamn spies lie for a *living*. Horace is an international grand master of false witness. You do realize that?"

Olmedo nodded soberly. "I'll bear that in mind," he said. "But he's not the first grand master of that particular craft that I've ever met."

"Old Horace also thinks he's the original invisible man," Lockwood said. "Maybe he's got an idea he can make what he did look like something it wasn't. A noble deed. Outwit everybody. Get out of it."

"How could any sane person, even a spy, think such a thing under the present circumstances, Mr. President?"

"You think stealing a presidential election is the act of a sane man?"

"I hear what you're saying to me," Olmedo said. "But if he does not say why he did it, if he cannot be induced to say why for reasons of honor—"

"*Honor?*"

"He has his own definition of the word. Most people do. But if he keeps the bargain, then his motive is irrelevant to the case."

"To hell with his motive," Lockwood said. "I didn't kill Ibn Awad or anybody else."

Did Lockwood believe this? It was possible. "As you wish, Mr. President," Olmedo said. "But you should know that Horace Hubbard has your voice on tape, giving Philindros the order to kill this man."

"How the hell could he? I didn't know a thing about it till they told me what they'd done three years after the fact."

They locked eyes. Once again Olmedo nodded, touching his ear. Did this mean he had actually heard the tape played? Lockwood wondered—his curiosity might as well have been spoken aloud, he took such pains to conceal it—but he did not ask. His gaze was steady, controlled, opaque. It admitted nothing and betrayed no emotion. In other words, the President of the United States looked like any other guilty man at the moment when his alibi breaks down; Olmedo had observed such men in such moments by the score.

Olmedo shrugged. Lockwood said, "Did you hear it?"

"Yes, sir. Not by choice, but there was no way to avoid it. He just switched it on."

"I see. So what do we do about this?"

"We play the game or forfeit it," Olmedo said. "The decision, of course, is yours."

"And if we play, what happens?"

"Who can predict? I think Horace stole the election not for his brother's reasons but for his own—to protect the FIS. Perhaps he was afraid that the truth about Ibn Awad would come out if Mallory was elected, and that if it did, it would be the end for American intelligence."

"Small fucking loss."

"You know infinitely more about that than I ever could, Mr. President. What Horace hopes to do by coming forward is to create such a diversion by telling all about the election, and thereby demonstrating beyond a shadow of a doubt that you are innocent of all wrongdoing, that the crime of which he, at least, believes you *are* guilty—the premeditated murder of Ibn Awad—will never be revealed, much less tried in any American court. Unless, of course, there really was reason to fear what Mallory might know, what evidence he might have—"

"Such as what?"

"The obvious possibility is that there is more than one copy of the tape."

Lockwood grunted. "Anything's possible," he said, "including this: What if the tape is a fake? Those spooks can fake anything."

"If a reasonable doubt could be raised on that point, the jury might consider you innocent."

"Do you?"

Before replying, Olmedo stared fixedly at the fleck of skin that showed through the hole in Lockwood's sock. He was strangely worried by this little sign of self-neglect. More than any of the many indications of Lockwood's mortality that he had observed this evening, it seemed to confirm that he was in the presence of a man who was near the end of his resources.

Olmedo answered Lockwood's question like a lawyer, from the head, not the heart. "I've told you, sir, that when in court I argue from the known facts and from the law," he said, "never from conviction."

"Whatever that means," Lockwood said. "Well, I can't do anything for Horace Hubbard, much less for myself. You'd better talk to Clark and Attenborough about immunizing the other two. But don't be surprised if you don't hear no cries of eager delight."

Olmedo nodded soberly. Like Blackstone, he was not entirely sure whether he was supposed to be amused by Lockwood's deliberate use of bad language, including bad grammar.

8

To Zarah Christopher, Polly Lockwood said, "You were an only child, dear, just like your mother was?"

"Yes," said Zarah, "but I wasn't lonely. There were lots of other children to play with in the village."

"You must have stood out, being the only American."

Zarah was used to questions of this kind. "I suppose so," she said pleasantly, "but no one ever mentioned it."

"Sounds like you grew up with angels, dear."

"Among friends, anyway."

"That was nice, being so hidden away from all your own kind. Your mother was a solitary child, born in the Great Depression, when there were hardly any children at all coming into the world, and she was all alone in that great big old house with hardly even a colored child her age around the place because your grandparents had her so late in life. She was always doing solitary things—playing the piano, riding, talking to the dogs. She used to sit up in a big old hickory tree in the home pasture and read poetry. She was such a romantic sight, like a wood nymph, with that long yellow hair down her back and those pretty legs dangling down."

Like Zarah's mother, Polly dropped her final *g*s and talked with a Southern belle's dazed amusement when she was being polite to company or talking about life in the Bluegrass country. The two women were seated on a sofa before a low table, drinking oolong tea and eating cucumber sandwiches. The invitation to tea at the White House, mentioned in passing at Macalaster's dinner party, had been tendered that morning by a member of the First Lady's staff. Zarah had been about to refuse because she had planned to meet Franklin Mallory at five that afternoon to look at some pictures he had given anonymously to the National Gallery. But the woman on the telephone had said, "Ms. Christopher, it is not customary to *hesitate* when you are invited to the family quarters."

"There really should be cake and cookies," Polly said, offering a cucumber sandwich, "but nobody wants to be pleasingly plump anymore. You certainly don't seem to have that tendency. The Kirkpatricks were always lean, of course. Did your mother ever put on an extra ounce?"

"I don't think so. But she hardly ate and never touched alcohol, and she rode in the morning and played the piano for two or three hours every afternoon, so she got plenty of exercise."

"She rode in the Sahara Desert? In all that heat?"

"We were in the mountains, and in winter it's cool even on the desert floor. She loved to race ostriches."

"Ostriches?"

"They run faster than a horse and a whole lot farther, always in an absolutely straight line. No horse can possibly stay with them, so there was no possibility of ever catching them, let alone harming them. It was better than fox hunting, Mother said."

"My goodness."

Behind them, suddenly, Lockwood's resounding voice said, "Honey?"

"Here he is," Polly said. "Frosty, you remember Cathy Kirkpatrick's girl Zarah."

"Sure do; that's why I came upstairs," Lockwood replied. "How do, Miss Zarah. Polly, are those poor limp little things with the crust cut off *sandwiches?*" He picked up three of them and ate them in rapid succession, then grinned at Polly. "May I have another, Mother?" He ate four more, chewing and swallowing vigorously as he dragged a fragile Louis XV chair across the rug and dropped his weight into it, facing the women. "Miss

Zarah, if compliments to ladies were not strictly forbidden under the treaty between my administration and the Feminists' Republic of America, I'd tell you that you're looking mighty pretty. How've you been?"

Smiling, as she knew she was expected to do, Zarah said, "I've been well, Mr. President. I hope you have been, too."

Lockwood reached for another handful of sandwiches, the last on the plate. "Me?" he said. "I'm keeping one nostril above the Dismal Swamp. Just barely. Is there anything to drink besides that tea, Polly? Can you order me up a Coc'-Cola? I'd appreciate it."

A servant appeared, apparently in answer to a hidden bell; Polly ordered the drink and it was brought on a silver tray, in the can, the way Lockwood liked it. He popped it open and took a long swig.

"We were talking about Zarah's family down in the Bluegrass," Polly said.

"I didn't know them," Lockwood said. "Didn't know there was such a thing as a sandwich made out of cucumbers, either, until I met Polly. Tell me all about the Kirkpatricks, Zarah."

"I didn't know them, either," Zarah said.

As soon as these words were spoken, Lockwood's face took on a look of intense interest. "Is that a fact?" he said. "Your own grandfolks?" But there was no glimmer of true curiosity in his eyes, and Zarah realized that his reaction was a politician's reflex; over the years he had learned to feign interest in others. Without changing expressions, he suddenly gave up the pretense and wiped a drop of mayonnaise from his lower lip with a knuckle.

"I'm tired out, damnit," he said, and closed his eyes.

He remained so for several moments, his head thrown back, his legs sprawled before him. Watching maternally, Polly kept complete silence, and took Zarah's hand in a tight grip as if to hold her in place in case she mistook Lockwood's behavior for a signal to leave. The ticking of a clock could be heard, a most unusual sound in America; when, after a while, it whirred and struck the quarter hour, Lockwood opened his eyes. For a long moment he gazed intently at Zarah, as if trying to remember whether he had ever seen her before. She submitted calmly to this scrutiny. It did not make her in the least uncomfortable. There was no male interest in the examination, not even any personal interest—nor, as far as she could judge, emotion of any kind. He seemed blank, spent, indifferent. Was this the same man who five minutes before had been gobbling sandwiches and making flirtatious jokes? The change was mystifying.

Abruptly, in the same loud tone as before, Lockwood said, "They tell me you're keeping company with Franklin Mallory. Is that so?"

"We see each other," Zarah said.

"How often?"

"Quite often, Mr. President."

"When will you see him again?"

Zarah let a moment pass before answering. "As soon as I leave here, Mr. President. It's a long-standing appointment."

"Good," Lockwood said, "because I want you to tell him something for me. Do you mind carrying a message to Garcia?"

Zarah laughed, understanding why she had been invited to tea. "Is it customary to mind when the President asks you to do something?"

"Not if it's a patriotic deed," Lockwood said. "And this is. What I want is for you to ask Franklin a question and bring me back the answer tomorrow. Will you do that?"

"If that's what you want me to do. But why me?"

"Because there's no other way I can talk to him or he can talk to me in this damn goldfish bowl full of piranhas. And I've got to be able to talk to him and know it'll stay confidential. It's vital—vital."

"Mr. President, aren't you assuming a lot? You hardly know me."

Lockwood glowered again. "Bloodlines is all I need to know," he said. "Besides, there's no one else that knows us both and that nobody else knows."

"All right," Zarah said, "I'll be glad to help."

"Atta girl," Lockwood said. "This is the question: Is he going to leave things as they are, or is he going to take the next step? Got that?"

Zarah nodded. For a moment, Lockwood gazed mournfully into her eyes. Then with a grimace of pain he closed his own eyes tightly and pinched the bridge of his nose. "Headache," he said. "Must have been the cold Coc'-Cola, it always does it to me."

Polly released Zarah's hand and gave her a look that unmistakably meant *go*. Zarah got to her feet as Polly rose too. Lockwood remained seated. Lifting a hand, he said, "Sure appreciate it."

"How shall I give you Mallory's answer, assuming there is an answer?"

"If I know Franklin, there'll be an answer," Lockwood said. "Come on back here at nine o'clock tomorrow morning. Right here, to this same room. Polly'll have 'em let you in."

9

At five-thirty, late for her appointment with Mallory, Zarah left the White House by the northeast gate and hailed an eastbound taxi on Pennsylvania Avenue. Sturdi Sturdevant, who had followed Zarah to the White House two hours before and had been waiting for her in Lafayette Park behind a screen of homeless people—excellent cover because they attracted no more notice than the ginkgo trees that had themselves long ago ceased to be curiosities—set off in pursuit. Rush-hour traffic was at its height, so she had no trouble keeping pace with the cab as it inched its way eastward. In fact, Sturdi sometimes had to jog in place in order to stay in the driver's blind spot. It wasn't likely that the cabby, a dusky Third Worlder who was talking animatedly to his passenger, was in the pay of Mallory or some other hostile element. However, Sturdi gave him no benefit of the doubt; she operated on the sound assumption that everyone was an enemy until proven to be otherwise. She herself looked like any of a hundred runners of indeterminate gender who were taking their evening laps. Her costume drew admiring glances. The trendiest athletic gear was Sturdi's only concession to fashion. Today she was dressed entirely in black—baggy sweats that cloaked her muscular body, the latest helium-filled running shoes, a sweat-wick cap with ventilated crown drawn down onto her thick dark eyebrows, goggles, and a highly advanced, feather-weight antipollution mask that reduced inhalation of exhaust emissions and other airborne poisons by seventy-three percent.

Hammett wore this same kind of mask when outdoors during the hours of peak atmospheric danger. Not that he had instructed Sturdi, in so many words, to follow Zarah, but she knew he wanted to know everything—*everything*—about this woman, and twenty-four-hour close-up observation was the quickest, surest way to compile the necessary data base. They were starting from scratch. Like Wiggins and Lucy before them, Sturdi and Slim had found no trace of Zarah in the usual files; she seemed not even to have gone to college anywhere in the world, a freak of biography that was completely off the graph of twenty-first-century reality. How could a person be said to exist, much less to matter, when lacking the most basic credentials? Even the fertilized ova in Mallory's deep freeze were better documented than this creature whose gleaming blond hair and classic profile showed in the rear window of the taxi. Physical beauty in another person affected Sturdi deeply and the sight of Zarah filled her chest with longing, but in this case she fought against the reaction, knowing that it was mere autonomic stimulation and could lead to nothing. This was a woman made for men, a relic of the old femininity; Sturdi could see this by the way Zarah moved, and by the way she was attuned to the male admiration in which she was continually bathed. She even smelled like a sex object; Sturdi knew, because she had a real gift for this sort of work and more than once had been close enough to apprehend the natural scent of Zarah's body.

The fact that Zarah had been to the White House, entering and leaving by an entrance reserved for invited visitors, was interesting but not surprising: at Macalaster's dinner party Hammett had overheard Polly Lockwood inviting her to tea. He had also noted Lockwood's strong response to her physical appearance. Judging by the time of day and the amount of time spent inside and a number of other small signs, including the fact that she had entered and left the President's house through the East Wing, which was First Lady's territory, it was reasonable to suppose that she had in fact been invited to tea. Sturdi could not be sure that this was so because Zarah's phone was regarded as too sensitive to tap—not because Zarah herself was likely to detect a surreptitious listener, but because some of the other people who could be assumed to have tapped her line might already have done so. These included Mallory, the FIS, and certain terrorist elements who had reason to suspect or even hate this woman because of her family connections.

Sturdi loved the investigative aspect of her work. Each possibility, each weakness, each folly, each seemingly mundane detail, was part of the process of rediscovering that every reality worth knowing was concealed beneath a seemingly innocent surface. With her carefree beauty and inexplicable knowledge of people and things and her secret connections, Zarah Christopher was a perfect example of this central truth. Sturdi's world was a mare's nest of such snarled threads; this was what made it so inexhaustibly interesting and also made it worth the labor and sacrifice required to live within it as a fully committed person.

Zarah's cab dropped her at the entrance of the East Building of the National Gallery. Sturdi dropped back behind a belching metropolitan bus and looked at her watch. She was baffled by this destination. It was after six; the gallery was closed. Why was Zarah getting out of the cab here? She was talking to the driver as she paid him. Sturdi accelerated so as to get within earshot. Although she did not speak or understand Arabic, she recognized it when she heard it as a result of her many encounters with Hammett's Near Eastern clients. Zarah was speaking to the driver in that language, spinning out sentences as easily as she spoke English. This was a new detail; switching on the miniature tape recorder clipped to the waist of her sweatpants, Sturdi recorded as much of the exchange as she could. It might be useful. Sometimes even the cleverest operatives talked more freely when they were speaking a language that they imagined was incomprehensible to eavesdroppers. Sturdi jogged in place at the end of the crosswalk as if waiting for the light to change. With a camera disguised to look like a pedometer, she took several photographs of Zarah and the cabdriver, of whom she was now truly suspicious, and also snapped the license plate and logo of his taxi, although she had committed these items to memory during the thirty-minute run from the White House.

With an empathetic smile and a final burst of glottal Arabic, Zarah turned away from the clearly smitten cabby and strode swiftly over the cobblestones toward the glass doors of the East Building, skirt swinging round her legs, pale hair lifting and falling in an iridescent cascade. She had the air of someone who is late—not anxious, not hurried, but determined not to waste a moment. The interior of the building was dim; Sturdi, who had superb eyesight, could only just make out the paddles of the huge Calder mobile turning airily in the currents generated by the ventilation system. Surely Zarah realized that the place was closed and that she would encounter a locked door, or did she think the sesame of her beauty would cause the gates to swing open?

As Zarah approached the glass wall in which the locked and bolted revolving doors were set, three indistinct figures appeared on the other side. Sturdi, who knew she was staying too long in one position but had no choice if she wanted to see what happened next, grasped her left shoe and pretended to stretch. At the last possible moment, the door was opened by a young woman whom Sturdi, an expert on Mallory's security operations, recognized as Lucy. Wiggins, whose face was also known to Sturdi, stepped outside and took up a station between the door and the world, blocking the view. Sturdi dropped her foot and moved a few steps to the left, improving her angle of vision, and in so doing attracted Wiggins's attention by her movement, which meant that she would never be able to wear these black running togs again. She felt a pang—the outfit was almost new and she had little money to spend on another one—but the feeling passed when she saw Franklin Mallory, unmistakably himself with his shock of white hair, his suit and tie whose cost would have fed an African village for a month, and his master-of-all-he-surveyed body language, greeting Zarah just inside the door. At the sight of her his face exploded—there was no other word—into a grimace of delight, an expression absent from the millions of photographs of him published in the news media. He gazed happily into Zarah's eyes while rapidly speaking words that Sturdi could neither hear with her own ears nor hope to pick up with her recorder through the thick plate glass. But one thing was plain: This man, so recently bereaved of the love of his life, adored this woman who had just been drinking tea with the wife of the greatest enemy he had in the world. What a discovery!

10

Had he been aware of Sturdi's analysis of his feelings toward Zarah Christopher, Mallory would have agreed that her intuition was sound. He had loved two other women and been happy with them sexually, but he had taken each into his life not out of any overwhelming desire but as a matter of conscious choice. Both Marilyn and Susan, coming to him at different stages of his career, had been right for him in terms of his needs at the time, and this was why he had made his decisions to love and cherish them and had abided by them faithfully. Romance had had nothing to do with the matter.

With Zarah, however, he was now experiencing, on the verge of old age, something that he had always been sure did not exist: love at first sight. As in Sturdi's case (and of course that of many other people of both sexes; Zarah had looked this way for several years), this woman's physical being acted in some inexplicable way upon the involuntary functions of his own body. Mallory being Mallory, he had attempted to analyze this phenomenon. The impression Zarah made on his senses when he saw her across the room on that first night in Kalorama had been something like the effect of a sudden burst of interstellar static on a shortwave receiver; he lost, without hope of recovery, the emotional signal to which he had been listening all his life. Thereafter he breathed differently, thought and spoke differently; he even fancied that his heart was functioning in a different way, that his blood was a different temperature, that the amount of oxygen being furnished to his brain was different. All these things began to happen to him before he even spoke to Zarah, much less began to discover the subtleties of her mind and to sense that stillness at the center of her being which was so mysterious that it suggested reincarnation: it seemed possible to him that she had lived many times in the past. Mallory amazed himself with this bizarre idea. He was not given to high-flown thought or language—famously not given to it—but these were the terms in which he found himself explaining his feelings about Zarah to himself; that same morning, he had written all of the foregoing conceptions down on a tablet while flying home to Washington from his hunting lodge in Utah. This torn-off sheet of notepaper was now folded up in his coat pocket.

"I want to tell you something quite strange," he said to her now. "With everything that's been going on in this country, and in my own life, over the past week, with who knows what hanging in the balance, the thing I've thought about most is showing you these pictures. And talking to you about them."

Mallory stepped aside and made a gesture for Zarah to precede him into the gallery. The room was dark when they entered, and then all the lights went on at once, illuminating the paintings on the wall.

Looking into his happy face in this sudden glow, Zarah felt a twinge of guilt. Normally she was not a victim of this emotion, thanks to the systematic way in which her mother had insulated her from the politics, secrets, and other romantic fantasies that had, as Cathy believed, ruined her own life and Paul Christopher's, as well as the lives of most of the rest of their generation. But Zarah had just come from the White House, where she had been entrusted by Lockwood with a secret message for Mallory. Clearly it was wrong to let this man tell her anecdotes and show her paintings as if nothing had happened. The burden of the mission Lockwood had forced on her had seemed slightly comical at first because it had been done so dramatically, but now it seemed heavy. She resented knowing what she knew; she did not want to know it.

All this showed in her face. In open puzzlement—what had so suddenly gone wrong?—Mallory asked, "You don't like the pictures?"

Zarah shook herself. "Sorry," she said. "It has nothing to do with the paintings. I haven't even looked at them yet. It's something else."

"What?"

"Later. Let's look at the pictures."

Later, after a dinner of salad and cold chicken in Zarah's kitchen, she delivered Lockwood's message.

Mallory stared at her in disbelief. Color drained from his face and every vestige of good feeling vanished. "That man actually asked you to speak those words to me?" he said. "He had Polly invite you to the White House for tea, and then came upstairs and said this?"

Zarah did not answer; she had already told him the details of her visit.

"The fool!" Mallory said. "The bastard!"

Zarah started; she had never known Mallory to use profanity, had never heard emotion in his voice, had never seen him as he was now. "Why do you say that?"

"Because he's put you in the middle. And that puts you out of my reach."

She gazed at him in puzzlement.

"Meaning what?"

"Remember who your cousins are."

"I've never for a moment forgotten."

"Let me ask you this," Mallory said, calmer now. "Did you feel sorry for this man?"

She said, "Yes, of course. He looked like a man who thought he was going to lose everything."

"That's right. So to equalize matters he wants me to lose you." Mallory actually blushed as these words escaped him. "Forgive me," he said. "That was presumptuous."

"Never mind," Zarah said. "Why don't we just forget this ever happened?"

"Impossible," Mallory replied. "Frosty has seen to that. But I think we'd better sleep on it. Don't you want Lockwood's message decoded? Or did he explain what he was talking about?"

Zarah did not even have to consider the matter. "No," she said, "he didn't explain."

"Thank goodness for small favors."

Zarah found herself thinking about Cathy yet again. She said, "I think I'm beginning to understand what my mother meant when she used to say that somebody ought to burn this town and sow the fields with salt."

Cathy had been perfectly serious about this because she believed that Washington, or what it had symbolized during the Cold War, had robbed her first of innocence and then of the possibility of love.

"Look," Zarah said. "I don't mind doing this if there's something you'd like to say to him."

Mallory looked away for a moment, then back at her. "You understand that this isn't something you can do once and never do again?"

"I think so. But what does it matter?"

"It might matter a great deal, Zarah. Think carefully."

She said, "Do you want to send Lockwood a message or not?"

Mallory sensed what was in her mind—or so it seemed—and with a small but visible effort, once again became the man Zarah knew. "All right," he said, "tell him this: I will not take the next step, but he's crazy if he doesn't think that someone else won't. The means exist. It could happen any time. The best thing for everyone is to end it now by using the mechanism I suggested to him on the night before the inauguration. Between us we have the votes in Congress to save the situation. But once the other thing gets out, neither one of us will be able to control events."

"The other thing?" Zarah said.

Mallory shook his head; he was not going to be the one to tell her this particular secret.

She said, "Franklin, why are you so upset about this?"

"Because this is not what I had in mind for you."

He left her. Wiggins and Lucy awaited him just outside the front door. Sturdi, walking five quarrelsome small dogs down Zarah's street, noted the time of his departure, and observed with professional admiration how very effective his understated disguise was—a watch cap covering his hair, a parka that concealed the shape of his body. She herself wore jeans, a comically oversize sweater, and a curly pepper-and-salt wig. Her own disguise made her look, even to Wiggins and Lucy, like the penniless dog walker—possibly a refugee from a bad marriage or a late-blooming graduate student—that she appeared to be. And in fact was: using an invented name, Sturdi had signed up at a dog-walking service that served this neighborhood.

11

"See how she paints herself for him!" said Archimedes Hammett with a puritanical grimace. In his hand he held an enlarged photograph of Zarah Christopher, applying lipstick as she sat in the backseat of the taxicab. Sturdi had snapped this picture, among several others, with her pedometer camera. She was an excellent photographer—in fact she was good with every sort of technology, despite her deep-seated hatred of it as a symbol of imperialism—and the print was clear but grainy. Zarah was staring into a hand mirror with the self-absorbed rictus of a woman touching up her makeup.

"Did she see you?" Hammett demanded anxiously.

"Certainly not—at least not what I was really doing," said Sturdi. "That look in her eyes is a trick of the light, a reflection from her compact."

Hammett's suspicions were not allayed by this explanation. "You'd better be sure about that," he said. "This is a bad person; it's in her blood."

"Archimedes, if she had spotted me I'd know it."

Hammett paid no attention. He was absorbed in examining the shots of Mallory and Zarah as they greeted each other. They appeared in the eight-by-ten-inch glossies as mere silhouettes behind the shimmering screen of the plate-glass wall. "Yes, yes," he said happily. "There's definitely something going on between those two. But look at this guy in the foreground. He's *identifying* you. Sturdi, you got too close."

At this, Sturdi's face pinkened. "There's no such thing as getting too close if you get the job done," she said. "I think I've proved that."

"Oh, yeah?" Still staring at the photographs, Hammett grunted. "Somebody must have taught Lady Zed the same rule, from the look of this rendezvous with the Führer," he said. "You're sure she came to this assignation straight from the White House? She talked to no one else en route?"

"She talked to no one but the driver. They were awfully friendly."

"They were? What did they say to each other?"

"I don't know. They spoke Arabic."

"Then we'll never know."

Sturdi smiled triumphantly. "Oh, no?" she said. "What if I was close enough to get it on a chip?"

She held up her tiny recorder, an advanced solid-state device that captured sound on a microchip instead of tape, making it possible to play it back into a computer's memory at speeds many thousands of times faster than human speech. Or at its natural speed, as you chose.

"Okay," Hammett said. "Play it back. At least we'll get the flavor."

Sturdi held up her recorder and switched it on. Slim, who had been preparing dinner, came into the room carrying a tray. On the tape Zarah's voice said, "*Shahāda: lā ilāha illā Llāh.*"

Hammett said, "What does that mean, I wonder?"

Slim said, "It means 'There is no God but God.' "

Hammett said, "How do you know?"

Slim put down the tray. "I learned a little Arabic from a friend after college."

Hammett said, "Oh, where exactly was that?"

As though she had not heard the question, Slim continued, "This woman really speaks the language, but with a Maghrebi accent. Play it again." Sturdi did so. Slim said, "Listen to her pronounce the open long *a* before the *L* in 'Llāh.' The name of God is the only word in all of Arabic in which the *l* is hard-palate like that. Not one foreigner in a million can say it correctly."

"Very impressive," Hammett said. "Why didn't you ever tell me you speak Arabic?"

Slim smiled a surreptitious female smile. "A girl has to have some secrets," she said.

"A *girl?*" parroted Sturdi, enforcing terminological discipline.

"I was still a girl then."

"Well, we're all grown-ups now," Hammett said. "You could have saved me, not to mention the Cause, a fortune in translators' fees. I do have a few Arabic-speaking clients, you know."

"I'm not that good," Slim said. "All I really know is bed Arabic."

Sturdi flushed; she did not like to be reminded that Slim had had other lovers before her—even men, before she gave up heterosexual sex after the outbreak of the AIDS epidemic so she could go on handling Hammett's food.

"So what does the fact that this woman can pronounce her *l*s in Arabic tell us about her?" Hammett asked.

Slim said, "It tells us that she may *really* be dangerous." She listened intently to the recorded exchange between Zarah and the taxi driver. "They're talking commonplaces in this recording, but professionals always do, in case a hostile agent overhears them. Who knows what these clichés in Arabic might mean? She already knows things she ought not to know. And look at the way she's shuttling between Lockwood and Mallory."

Hammett said, "This is a real baddy. Keep on her."

"You mean, like *close?*"

Sturdi's tone was teasing. She was asking for positive reinforcement, and Hammett gave it to her. "As close as you think necessary and wise, but remember what you're up against," he said with concern in his voice. "Sturdevant, this is wonderful work. Only you could have done it. But remember, this female is no sorority sister; she comes from the Dark Side for generations and generations. The Christophers are worse, much worse, than Mallory and his torpedoes, so don't make me worry. Be careful."

"Don't worry," Sturdi replied. "I always have been."

"Then scoot," Hammett said indulgently. "I have miles to go before I sleep."

Sturdi asked him no questions; she had too much discipline for that. Actually, she was glad enough to be sent away early. She had to drive home to the farm in Connecticut that night to prepare Hammett's food for the following week and then bring it back to Washington in the Volvo. She would be traveling alone; Slim was staying in Washington for the weekend, doing a job for Hammett. Gathering up the photographs of Zarah, Sturdi was just as glad; the flat images recalled the flesh-and-blood woman, and she did not want to fantasize while in bed with Slim, the person to whom she had made a commitment. But Slim's remark about learning Arabic in bed with a man still stung. Sturdi knew all too well that she herself was only human, and she was not sure she could control the sexual truant that had been let loose in her mind today.

12

After Sturdi left, Hammett telephoned Ross Macalaster. As was his habit, he did not identify himself or even say hello. His first words were "How well do you know the Speaker of the House?"

Macalaster's voice was thick with sleep. "I know him. Why?"

Hammett said, "For years I've heard really bizarre stuff about Attenborough—that he's a racist and a drunk, that he's a compulsive assgrabber. Now I hear he's in deep with the religious right. Is there any truth to any of that?"

"All true. He's even memorized the Bible." Macalaster paused; Hammett could hear him drinking water; he must keep a glass beside the bed in case he awoke dehydrated by alcohol. In a more normal voice Macalaster replied, "Why do you ask?"

"Because I'd like to meet him."

"Would that be proper, Mr. Chief Justice, given the impending impeachment trial and your role in it?"

Hammett permitted a tiny silence to gather before replying, to let Macalaster know that he had noted this indiscreet use of his title over the telephone and disapproved of it. Then he said, "At a social occasion, what would be improper about it? I thought maybe you could have us over to your place together."

"Like before, as an agent of history? I'm not really in that business, you know."

"I never would have guessed from the stuff you've been writing in the newspapers lately. But that was a wonderful party. That was the night I met that lovely Valkyrie."

"Who?"

"That Christopher woman. Can't get her out of my mind. Only this time I'd like to bring my own date."

Macalaster guffawed. "A date? You?"

Hammett ignored this. "I mean our mutual friend Slim, if she's forgiven for the séance. Is she?"

"If she doesn't entrap my kid into another one."

"That won't happen. She can drive me over and bring my food. I was hungry last time."

"All right, but just her. Two vestal virgins are one too many."

Hammett put a note of pleasure into his reply. "Then you'll do it. When?"

"That depends on Attenborough; he may turn down the invitation. But I'll let you know. Is that all you wanted?"

"That's it for now. But I may have something for you by the time we meet."

"Oh? What?"

"Something to your advantage. I may be locked up in this marble sarcophagus now, but sometimes I get a message from the outside world."

"What kind of message?"

Curiosity again. Hammett smiled. "By the way," he said, "did you ever identify the mysterious stranger you ran into in the men's room on Inauguration Day?"

"No. Is that what you have for me—a clue?"

Hammett chuckled. "Just asking. I never go into public toilets."

Macalaster was silent. "Good night," he said at last.

"Oh, by the way," Hammett said.

"Archimedes, good night. It's three in the morning."

Hammett said, "Then go back to sleep. And Ross?" Macalaster grunted. Hammett said, "If you want to invite the Valkyrie, go ahead. Don't mind me."

"I'll call Attenborough in the morning," Macalaster said in a tone of finality, "and the girl of your dreams."

13

In the den of his house in Alexandria, R. Tucker Attenborough, Jr., decided to have a drink of vodka while waiting for Sam Clark to arrive with Lockwood's lawyers. He thought he knew what the lawyers wanted, and he wasn't at all sure that it lay in his power—or in Clark's either—to give it to them. The Congress of the United States wasn't what it used to be when Attenborough, Clark, and Lockwood were young and the two great political parties wanted to do the same things in slightly different ways and always found a way to make things happen. Now everybody behaved like a bunch of damn Frenchmen, each and every one of them wanting to have his own way and to hell with the Constitution, the country, the party, and most of all the idea of civilized behavior.

Attenborough finished his drink, went into the downstairs bathroom, where he kept his vodka in a plastic spring water bottle submerged in the toilet tank, and carefully washed the glass in soap and water to remove the odor of spirits. The face he saw in the mirror looked strange to him and somehow not his own, but alcohol often had that effect. He winked sardonically at the little fellow in the mirror, whom he recognized as the little fellow inside himself; the reflection winked right back. "You look a little green, my friend," Attenborough said. His image shrugged as if to say, You're right, but what the hell. As a matter of fact, his skin *did* look slightly green. He leaned closer. The actual color was more of a yellow; his eyeballs were yellow too, but that had been so for a long time; he chalked it up to malaria, contracted many years before on a fact-finding mission to the Philippines.

When Attenborough emerged into the living room, the doorbell was ringing. When he opened the door, his heart sank. There, side by side with Olmedo, stood Norman Carlisle Blackstone. The son of a bitch was wearing a derby hat. Attenborough was not sure that he could get through a briefing by this fellow, and made reckless by eight ounces of hundred-proof vodka drunk at room temperature, he might have said so—or at least commented on the derby—if at that exact moment Sam Clark had not appeared on the doorstep. So instead of hurting Blackstone's feelings with a wisecrack, as he had on other occasions, he said, "Howdy, folks. Come right in and grab a chair." His tone was hearty, but Blackstone, no fool, smiled uncomfortably. He knew well enough that he annoyed the Speaker as much as he bored the President.

"Sorry to be late," Blackstone said. "My fault entirely."

They were ten minutes behind schedule. To avoid being observed, the two lawyers had driven across the river in Blackstone's small, uncomfortable car. He was a tyro driver and an inattentive one; he had spent his life up to now riding in taxicabs and the New York subway, in which the trick of survival was to absent the mind until it was time to get off at your destination. Half-lost for the entire journey through the unfamiliar city with its bewildering traffic circles and illogical diagonal avenues, he had taken several wrong turns before finally finding Attenborough's house, a modest ranch house, located in a cul-de-sac among others exactly like it.

Attenborough waved off Blackstone's apologies. "Every Yankee except U. S. Grant has always got lost as soon as they cross the bridges into Virginia," he said. "How's the President?"

Blackstone said, "Bearing up, Mr. Speaker. He's asked us to fill you and the Majority Leader in on certain developments."

"Shoot." Attenborough did not offer them a drink; except for his vodka, replenished daily, he kept no liquor in the house, believing that the omission created the impression that he was abstemious, if not a teetotaler.

Blackstone began; as Attenborough had feared and expected, it was slow going. The briefing covered every last detail of Horace Hubbard's statement to Olmedo, with one omission—the Ibn Awad affair. Olmedo, who had been intently studying the reactions of Clark and Attenborough to Blackstone's words, had the impression that the two men were fearful that they would be told something they did not want to hear. When at last Blackstone stopped talking, they both relaxed in what Olmedo took to be relief.

Clark said, "What exactly does Horace Hubbard mean by 'immunity'?"

Blackstone consulted his yellow tablet. "Total immunity from prosecution for any criminal offense that either Julian Hubbard or Rose MacKenzie may have committed as a result of any action connected in any way to any articles of impeachment that may be brought against President Lockwood."

"*Any* article of impeachment?"

"Yes, sir. He made that quite clear."

Attenborough said, "In other words, he and his brother and his mistress have destroyed Lockwood and his party and maybe the institution of the presidency, but they don't want to be inconvenienced in any way as a consequence?"

Olmedo looked from one grim face to another. "That's a fair assessment," he said, "but the truth of the matter is that it's an interesting offer. The way Hubbard looks at it, it should be irresistible. He'll clear up the doubts surrounding the outcome of the presidential election, exonerate the President, and give your party a chance to redeem itself before the world. He will also let himself be disgraced in the most public possible way and go to jail for the rest of his life, if necessary. All he asks in return is immunity for the two people he says he led into temptation."

"That's what he's asking," Clark said. "Will he take less?"

"Where his brother and the woman are concerned," Olmedo said, "I think not."

"We're supposed to just let the pair of them go?"

"Whatever you do, both will be ruined, their professional lives over."

"Julian has money."

Olmedo wagged his head. "No, sir, he does not."

"You know that for a fact, Counselor?"

"We've looked into the matter. His father spent the last of the Hubbard fortune before he died a couple of years ago. He has what he earns, his house, and a few heirlooms, a valuable painting or two, that's all. The MacKenzie woman has literally nothing; the government would have to pay for her defense. Sparing them prison, which is what Horace is asking, seems a reasonable price to pay for testimony that will help the President in such a unique and vital way."

Clark pointed a forefinger. "Getting Lockwood off the hook is not the only question here, Counselor."

"How right you are, Senator," Olmedo said. "The President is innocent of any corruption of the electoral process. My objective—my only objective—is to establish that fact before the world."

"And you're willing to buy testimony to accomplish this?"

Olmedo smiled coldly. " '*Buy* testimony'? No. Bargain for it in the interests of the truth, with all that means to justice in this case and to the future of our country, yes. What does the punishment of two foolish people mean in comparison with that? Julian and Rose are not going to get away with anything, Senator; they may escape jail, but they cannot escape retribution. Horace Hubbard can testify to the facts. Without him, the truth may never be established, and if that happens, history will be corrupted."

Clark stared for a while into the middle distance. Then he said, "That would certainly be a terrible outcome. But I've got news for you, and for Horace Hubbard. He should have presented his demands to the Lord God, because He's the only one who has the power to grant his prayer."

Olmedo glanced in Attenborough's direction. The Speaker, sitting bolt upright, was sound asleep. This did not seem to surprise Clark in the least. "Then it's unanimous," he said. "I mean, you'd better get rid of the idea that either one of us, or anyone else in this day and age, can appeal to the general interest, to patriotism or common sense, and achieve a result that's in the best interests of the country."

Olmedo listened without expression. He was not surprised to hear these words spoken; even Lockwood seemed to hold the same sour opinion of the government. He wondered why these men wanted to occupy offices for which they seemed to feel such contempt.

Clark looked at his watch. "If that's all, I'll excuse myself," he said. "I've heard enough about the Hubbards for one day."

"Bear with me for one moment longer, please," Olmedo said. "There is one more element."

Clark turned expressionless eyes on Olmedo.

"I'll be brief, and unless you wish me to be otherwise, unspecific," Olmedo said. "There may be grounds for an article of impeachment that has no bearing on the theft of the election."

"Stop right there," Clark said.

Attenborough woke up as abruptly as he had gone to sleep.

"Oh-oh," he said. "Here comes the raghead. 'Thou hast done things unto me that ought not to be done.' Book of Genesis, chapter the twentieth, verse the ninth."

"Please, Tucker," Clark said. "Leave the Bible out of it just this once. Mr. Olmedo, I haven't heard a word of this. Your allusions are Greek to me. Do you understand me?"

"As you wish," Olmedo said, his mild brown eyes fixed on Clark's cold, accusative face, "but permit me to say that Horace Hubbard is the key to containing a situation that no one wants to see develop."

"None of *us*, maybe, but we're not alone in this world."

Olmedo said, "Let me ask one final question. Are you really so reluctant to help? Is the President of the United States, your old friend, on his own?"

"That's not what I said," Clark replied. "I can't speak for the Speaker, but I'll do the best I can to see that due process is observed and justice is done. In fact I'll work hard to make that happen, and if immunizing Julian Hubbard and this female spy is the only way to do so, I'll try to help you out. *Try.*"

Attenborough had relapsed into a trancelike silence. Only one dim lamp burned on a table on the other side of the room. Olmedo leaned closer to the Speaker, noting the unhealthy hue of his skin; he too explained this to himself as a trick of the light. "Mr. Speaker?"

"Me, too," said Attenborough. "But like Sam says, all we can do is try."

"Then you will be doing all we have asked or could wish," Olmedo said. "I'll tell your friend what you've said."

"You can tell Lockwood anything you want to," Clark said, "but we haven't been talking about my friend, Counselor. We've been talking about a President accused of high crimes and misdemeanors."

"I'll tell him that, too, sir."

Clark's face was as blank now as Lockwood's had been earlier. "You do what you have to do," he said. "But don't expect miracles."

14

Arriving at Macalaster's dinner party on Hammett's arm, Slim Eve wore a dark dress that showed a discreet two inches of cleavage and flattered her fair skin and her plum-blue eyes; her hair was curled; she was all smiles and silken calves.

"Who's the *Cosmopolitan* girl?" Macalaster asked.

"It's Slim, I told you," Hammett replied.

"The transformation from ecofreak to starlet is a little disorienting."

"That's the trouble with you journalists," Hammett replied. "You're waterbugs living on the surface of experience."

Across the room, Attenborough was asking Zarah Christopher how she spelled her name. "Ah, the twin that stuck his arm out and the midwife tied a red string on it!" he said.

Slim approached. "A red string?" she asked "Why?"

"To mark the firstborn twin. Good thing, too, because the other one shoved past him and was born first. Genesis, chapter the thirty-eighth, verse the thirtieth: 'And afterward came out the brother that had the scarlet thread upon his hand: and his name was called Zerah.' Judah begat the twins—other one's name was Pharez—upon his lonesome daughter-in-law, Tamar. Not knowing it was her, of course, Judah being a righteous man. She snuck up on him, kind of."

Slim gazed at him in wide-eyed admiration. "That's amazing!" she said.

"That's more or less what Judah said," Attenborough replied. "But thank you. Nothing I enjoy more than amazing a lovely young lady."

At table, Slim looked at the place cards. Zarah's was next to Attenborough, at the end of the table. Slim said, "Can we swap? I'm left-handed." Even though this meant sitting next to Hammett, Zarah, who was left-handed herself, agreed.

Because the Speaker's voice was so loud, other conversation was impossible while he explained to Slim how he happened to know the Holy Bible by heart. "My daddy thought that the Lord gave me this loud voice I've got because it was His will for me to grow up to be a preacher," he said.

"And did you agree with that idea?" Slim asked.

Her rapt tone of voice reminded Macalaster, who sat on her other side, of the dating advice in Eisenhower-era magazines for unmarried females: Get the boy talking about himself.

Attenborough had not answered Slim's question. His eyes were closed. He had nodded off. She touched the back of his hand with her long, polished fingernails. She said, "Well?"

The Speaker woke up and gave her an admiring look. "No, lovely lady, I didn't share my daddy's conviction in this matter," he said. "They dragged me to tent meetings all over West Texas. Everybody else was shedding tears of joy and speaking in tongues. I'd be the only one in the congregation who never could get the spirit."

"Did that bother your father?"

"You bet it did. On the way home from worship he'd tie me up to the tailgate of the pickup truck and try to beat the spirit of the Lord into me with a harness strap."

"How awful!" Slim cried.

Attenborough gave her a pat on the arm, as if she had been the one whupped with a one-inch trace. Then, deftly, he laid a child-size hand on her thigh under the table. She reached down and captured it in her own larger hand, which was surprisingly rough as a result of her work on the farm. "But how did learning the Bible come into it?" she asked.

"Well," said Attenborough, "I figured I needed to find a way around the situation and the only means I had was a good memory, so I began memorizing the Good Book, a chapter a day. After that, when my daddy would haul out that harness strap, I'd sing out something like, 'And he said, I will make all my goodness pass before thee, and I will proclaim the name of the Lord before thee; and will be gracious to whom I will be gracious, and will show mercy on whom I will show mercy.' Book of Exodus, chapter the thirty-third, verse the nineteenth. It worked; Daddy figured the Lord must be whispering the words in my ear because I was too dumb to learn them on my own, so he laid down his rod—or his harness strap, to be more accurate."

The rest of the company, all but Slim and Hammett, laughed in appreciation of the Speaker's anecdote. Slim's large mascaraed eyes swam with sympathy. She squeezed his hand, which had been lying inert in hers. He squeezed back and held on.

"Were you gentle with your own children, Mr. Speaker?"

"*Tucker,* call me Tucker," Attenborough said, stroking the backs of her ringless fingers with his thumb. "Never had any, never was married." He gave Slim's hand a meaningful squeeze.

She said, "Didn't you ever *want* children?"

"Wanting 'em is a whole different thing from knowing what to do with 'em after you've got 'em," Attenborough said. "In my psychology course in college, I read where sons make the same mistakes as their fathers."

"Oh? Where'd you go to college?"

"Saul Ross State College in Alpine, Texas; majored in yelling at football games, minored in panty raids. El Paso for law school. Anyhow, I thought I might do the little critters like my daddy done me, so I didn't have any."

Slim said, "I can't believe you would have done that, Tucker."

"Then somebody else would have, pretty lady. Any kid coming into this world is like somebody from another planet parachuting into the gulag. The guards grab 'em as soon as they land and start slapping 'em around and yelling stupid orders at 'em, saying no to every simple request, making 'em eat when they don't want to and starving 'em when they're hungry. The kid thinks, What's my crime? What am I guilty of that I'm locked up in this damn concentration camp with crazy people four times as big as I am yellin' at me and beatin' on me all day long? And there's no escape, by God; you can't go back where you came from, where nobody bothered you and all you did was snooze and listen to the pipes gurgle. It's a life sentence with no parole."

A waiter in a tuxedo was clearing the plates. He said, "Are you finished with your salmon, Mr. Speaker?"

Attenborough knew this young man from many previous dinner parties, and he had looked him up soon after arrival and given him a twenty-dollar bill to keep his water glass filled with Absolut vodka. "I'm gonna pass on the salmon," he said. "But I could use a little more of that ice water when you have a chance." With an indulgent smile the waiter whisked the empty glass away and after a moment returned with a full one. Attenborough drank deeply.

Macalaster continued to watch with interest as Slim worked her feminine wiles on Attenborough. He was aware that Hammett was also observing the process. Macalaster understood that she was the bait in a trap that Hammett had set for the Speaker. But to what end? What was going on?

Between courses, Slim revealed that she too was a lawyer. She even knew about Attenborough's famous one-question victory in the case of the insulted bride. "With your photographic memory," she said, "you must have been a whiz in law school."

"Did okay." Attenborough, beginning to tire of doing all the talking, said, "You work for the Chief Justice?"

"No, I just admire him tremendously."

"You do? Why's that, honey?"

Attenborough's eyes were no longer smiling. Slim kept up her cheery manner. "Chief Justice Hammett was my professor and academic adviser at Yale Law School," she said.

"Taught you how to think, did he?"

"In a way, yes, I guess you could say he did."

Attenborough's eyes narrowed. This woman must be a goddamn Hammettite. He freed his hand from Slim's in order to help himself to the most well-done slice of beef from the silver platter offered by the waiter. In his other hand the servant held a silver bowl filled with some kind of vegetable casserole. Attenborough sniffed this dish, then waved it away.

"No veggies?" Slim said. "I made that ratatouille myself, out of organically grown ingredients. It's the Chief Justice's favorite. No salt or chemicals of any kind."

"Ratatootie?" Attenborough had slipped deeper into a parody of good-old-boy speech and behavior as the level of the vodka in his water tumbler dropped inch by inch. "Is that some kind of Arab dish?" he asked, pronouncing the word *AY-rab.*

The waiter reached Slim. She picked up the serving spoon in her right hand the serving fork in her left. Attenborough's small, moist, feverishly hot hand pressed her leg, just above the knee. The monkey's paw, Slim thought with a shudder. His fingers walked upward, as in a child's game of mousie-mousie. She was unable to defend herself and lift food from the platter at the same time. With amazing swiftness and dexterity Attenborough's hand lifted her short skirt, folded it back over her napkin, and scurried up the inside of her thigh. Startled, yet not surprised, she twitched slightly, relaxing her legs; through a rip in the crotch of her panty hose, two scurrying fingers found her labia. A third searched for her clitoris; she was back in high school, the pre-enlightened Slim. She clamped her legs shut. Attenborough's fingers, though entrapped, continued working; she felt the scratch of a fingernail as he enlarged the gap in the nylon.

Slim finished taking her food, ratatouille only. "What, no meat?" Attenborough said with a look of perfect innocence. Slim returned it, innocence for innocence.

A testy conversation about Shelley was going on between Hammett and Zarah Christopher. To her surprise, Slim realized that she was approaching orgasm. It wasn't Attenborough who was producing this pleasure, it was the situation, it was the memory of other men. But she could not let it go on. Feigning interest in what was being said across the table and continuing to eat with her left hand, she reached down and grasped Attenborough's hand with her free right hand and dug her thumbnail into the tender wrist joint. Nothing happened, so she twisted his little finger until she thought it might break. Attenborough might as well have been anesthetized—which of course he was—for all the effect these karate holds produced. He resisted her effort to drag his hand from her crotch; he was incredibly strong. Moreover, his fingernail seemed to be razor-sharp. Did he keep it long for just this purpose? She felt the fabric tearing between her legs. She grasped his wrist with her other, stronger hand and tried to stop him, glaring angrily into his face. This struggle enlarged the hole in her panty hose. Stroking her exposed skin, he smiled beatifically; then, groping all the while, he turned his head to listen to something Zarah Christopher was saying to Hammett across the table.

"What do you know about Shelley?" Hammett was asking.

"Very little," Zarah said. "Except that he was a totalitarian."

Hammett's sulky face darkened. "Explain that," he said.

Zarah liked this rude and dogmatic man even less on second meeting. There was something sly, even unnatural here, as if he behaved as he did on the advice of a psychoanalyst or a case officer. "All right," Zarah said. "*Prometheus Unbound* reads like a dream Stalin had in an opium den. Shelley describes heaven on earth as a place where people fall asleep and when they wake up they're not human any longer. They've taken off their human nature and condition like a disguise; therefore they're happy because now they're all alike, thinking beautiful thoughts. Utopia always turns out to be an eternal prison camp with people like Shelley in the commandant's office."

"What absolute sick nonsense!" Hammett cried, recoiling.

With a look of deep interest, Attenborough leaned toward Zarah and said, "Is this the Shelley that wrote 'To a Sky-Lark'?" She nodded. "Never realized he was an early pinko," the Speaker said. Then, with a broad smile breaking over his puffy face, he lifted his goblet and declaimed, " 'Hail to thee, blithe Spirit! / Bird thou never wert—' "

Slim shrieked, "Help!"

Underneath the table, Attenborough's middle finger had broken through. His victim leaped to her feet, overturning her chair. Beneath her skirt, she was still holding his wrist in both her hands. It was an extremely short skirt. Slim had truly wonderful legs, and there was no mistaking what had been happening.

"You filthy swine!" Slim shouted, showering saliva. Her face was crimson and her staring eyes burned with rage and disgust.

Her sudden movement had dragged Attenborough off his chair, and he staggered after her, attempting to free his captured hand. He held his goblet of vodka in his other hand, trying in vain to keep it from spilling. Suddenly, with a single violent movement, Slim lifted his hand above her head. Then, turning her own superbly conditioned body on her spike heels, she yanked it downward in an expert martial-arts maneuver that slammed him to the floor.

Attenborough struck the carpet face-first, shattering the tumbler and slashing his hand. Breathing hoarsely, Slim stared down with glittering eyes at his prone body with an expression of triumph and hatred, then lifted her skirt. "Look!" she cried. "I want you all to see this!"

Hammett stared in horror at the shredded fabric in Slim's panty hose: pink skin and curly hair showed through a large and spreading hole. "Please!" he cried in genuine revulsion. Obediently Slim dropped her skirt.

At her feet, Attenborough stirred, groaned, and raised himself on an elbow. His hand was bleeding onto the pale-blue Persian carpet. Macalaster rushed to the Speaker's side and bandaged the hand in a napkin snatched from the table.

"Look at that little creep. *Smell* him!" Slim said. "He's drunk! But it's still aggravated sexual battery. You are my witnesses."

A pretty impressive list of witnesses, Macalaster thought, gazing upward from his kneeling position at the impassive face of the Chief Justice of the United States.

"Nineveh," Attenborough muttered confidentially.

Macalaster was trying to stanch the alarming flow from Attenborough's wound. He said, "What?"

"Capital of old-time Assyria, Sin City," Attenborough replied in the same conspiratorial tone. Raising his voice to its normal power, he said, " 'Harlotries of the harlot. . . . I will lift up your skirt over your face. I will show the nations your nakedness and the kingdoms your shame.' " Then, murmuring again and winking at Macalaster, "The Lord of Hosts speaking, book of Nahum, chapter the third."

Macalaster said, "Can you get up? We've got to get you to the emergency room."

"No damn emergency room!" Attenborough said.

"It's that or bleed to death, from the look of things. Somebody give me another napkin."

Zarah gave him hers. Attenborough looked at the blood dripping from the saturated table linen in which his hand was wrapped. "Jesus!" he said. His clouded eyes rolled back in his head until only the bloodshot canary-yellow whites showed, and then he fainted.

15

The emergency room doctor, a stern young female wearing gloves, gown, and a transparent plastic shield over her face to protect her from the AIDS virus, examined Attenborough's wound. It was still bleeding profusely, spattering droplets of gore on her white coat as she turned it this way and that under the strong overhead light, mopping with a swab. Her name tag said ANNA M. CHIN, M.D. She looked intently at his eyes and skin, palpated his right side, lifted his trouser leg, and pressed his calf with a gloved fingertip, noting that the dimple this created in the flesh did not go away. If she recognized her famous patient, she said nothing about it. The Speaker had checked in as Richard T. Attenborough. His health plan card, his driver's license, in fact all of his documentation, had always read that way, a routine precaution against unfortunate publicity.

"How did this happen, Richard?" the doctor asked in an Oklahoma accent that went strangely with her aloof Chinese face, or what little Attenborough could see of it inside the shield.

"Tripped and fell with a glass of ice water in my hand," he said.

"Ice water. Uh-huh."

As she turned her head the shield flashed in the bluish fluorescent light. Attenborough was lying flat on his back, trying to be as pleasant as possible, hoping to put this self-conscious minority person at her ease. He received no smile in return, no nod, no sweetening of voice.

"How long ago did this injury occur?" asked Dr. Chin.

She was spraying something onto his wound. It felt like frozen ammonia and he jumped in nervous reaction. Still no flicker of sympathy in her frozen face, much less recognition.

"Didn't look at my watch," Attenborough said.

"Half an hour ago, Richard? Longer ago than that? Sooner?"

"Like I just got through telling you, honey, I don't know for sure. What'd I do, hit an artery?" He was still bleeding; he had bled all over Macalaster's car on the way to the nearby private hospital, blood soaking right through the several napkins in which his hands had been wrapped while he was unconscious.

"No, your arteries are fine," Dr. Chin replied. "The blood just isn't clotting the way we'd like to see it do."

Another young female in a shield swabbed the inside of his elbow with alcohol and tied a rubber tourniquet around his biceps. "Make a tight fist for me, Richard," she said. "Now release it."

Attenborough looked down and saw blood draining out of his arm into the barrel of a big syringe. "You figure I haven't lost enough of that stuff, sweetheart?" he said. She pulled out the needle. "This is for tests Dr. Chin wants to run," she replied.

"What kind of tests?"

Dr. Chin answered the question. "Just routine. I'm going to leave you for a few minutes. A surgeon is going to sew you up." She gave his name, but Attenborough didn't bother to listen.

The surgeon was a white male in a short-sleeved tunic. "Howdy, Doc," Attenborough said. "You don't hardly see a white arm hanging out of a coat like yours anymore."

No smile from this one, either. He was young, like Dr. Chin, and also wore a plastic shield over his face. His-and-hers space suits, Attenborough thought; maybe they're married and that's how he beat the ethnic odds and got into medical school.

"You won't feel anything except a needle and a slight burning sensation," the surgeon said. "That will be a shot of local anesthetic to make your hand numb." He sutured the cut while a nurse stood by, sopping up blood with one gauze pad after another and dropping them into a transparent plastic bag.

"Why the hell does it keep on bleeding like that?" Attenborough asked.

"That happens sometimes to fellows like you, Richard," the doctor said. "I'll bet you notice the same thing when you cut yourself shaving."

"I don't cut myself shaving."

"You don't?" said the doctor. "That's lucky, Richard. All finished; sixteen stitches."

"No wonder it bled."

"Right. The nurse is going to bandage your hand. What I want you to do after that is keep it elevated. That means hold it up high, like this."

He lifted an inert hand to demonstrate what he meant in case Attenborough had trouble understanding four-syllable words, but the patient didn't hear him; he had fallen asleep again.

An hour later, Dr. Chin had some trouble awakening the Speaker. This did not surprise her in the least because the laboratory tests she had ordered confirmed the diagnosis she had made on the basis of the obvious visible signs. This patient was an advanced case of cirrhosis. He bled so copiously from a trivial wound because his atrophied liver had all but ceased manufacturing the enzymes that cause blood to clot in a healthy person. The jaundiced skin, the saffron eyeballs, the edema the doctor had noted when she depressed the flesh in his calf, and now this deep sleep from which she awakened him by breaking a capsule of spirits of ammonia under his nose, all indicated the nature of his illness.

"Jesus Christ!" Attenborough said, awakening with a gasp. "What the hell was *that?*"

Dr. Chin said, "Do you often fall asleep like that?" She had removed her shield now that Attenborough had stopped bleeding: good-looking girl, but chilly.

Attenborough said, "Do you always wake people up with goddamn smelling salts?"

"Not always. Do you fall asleep a lot without knowing that you're doing it?"

"I nod off sometimes."

"Have you noticed in the mirror how yellow your eyes and skin are?"

Attenborough did not answer this question, or any of the others that she put to him in rapid succession, because the answer to them all was yes and he had the feeling that this girl was leading him toward some incriminating admission that he'd be better off to avoid.

Finally Dr. Chin said, "Your blood alcohol level is four point two, Richard; under the law, one point zero means a person is intoxicated. If you weren't an alcoholic, that level would be high enough to be life-threatening."

"Life-threatening?" Attenborough said. "Hell, honey, you must have got my tests mixed up with some brother you pulled out of a wrecked car."

"No, that's not a possibility. Richard, I want you to listen to me very carefully. You have cirrhosis of the liver. It is in a very advanced stage. That's why you bled so badly. That's why you're turning yellow. That's why you fall asleep all the time. If you don't stop drinking immediately, you will die."

"I will? When?"

"Assuming you continue to consume alcohol at your present rate, it could be a matter of weeks. Even days. Richard, your liver is on the point of complete failure. When it stops working, your kidneys will fail. Then your brain will die. Your heart may keep on beating for a while, but eventually—soon after these events, if you're lucky—it will stop too, and that will be the end."

"Jesus, Doc. All I did was trip over a rug and cut my hand, and I'm going to die from it? Where'd you get your license?" He sat up on the bed or the operating table or whatever it was. It was so high off the floor that Dr. Chin, who was short like himself, had to stand on a footstool to examine him. He swayed; she steadied him. He said, "Gotta go."

They were inside a little cubicle, closed off by curtains, that was designed to give the illusion of privacy. Attenborough wanted to get out of there before somebody overheard this crazy talk and called *The Washington Post.* Christ almighty, Ross Macalaster might be right outside! " 'Scuse me," he said.

With her hand still gripping his arm, Dr. Chin said, "Richard, my medical advice to you is, don't go. Let us help you. Your case is not hopeless—at least not yet. The liver is the one organ in the body that can regenerate itself. If you stop drinking now, it may repair itself over time. You still have a chance to recover and lead a normal life. It's your decision."

"All right," Attenborough said, "I'll give it up. Now I've really got to go."

"It's not as simple as that. You can't do this alone."

"Like hell I can't."

"Richard, nobody can; you need help. We have a detoxification facility right here in the hospital. Let me check you in so that you can get the help you need."

"I told you, I don't need help. I don't have *time* for help. Jesus Jumping Christ, girl, they're going to impeach the President and you want to lock me up in a drunk tank?"

"Impeach the President? Can't they do that without you, Richard?"

Obviously she thought he was crazy, some kind of derelict raving about an imaginary world. He didn't bother to contradict her; it would be even worse, he knew, if she realized who he was. "Where're my clothes?"

"Richard, I can't force you to stay. Who's your personal physician?"

"Don't have one. Never been sick a day in my life, except for malaria, which is what makes my eyes look funny."

"I advise you to see a doctor. Get a second opinion. But do it soon."

"I've already said I'll give up the drinking. Gimme my clothes."

"You're already dressed, Richard, except for your suit coat. Your friend, the one who brought you in, has that."

"Oh. Well, hell, I was so busy listening to the prognosis I didn't notice I already had my pants on. But you got me all wrong, Anna."

"Richard, if you try to give up alcohol on your own, your body won't let you do it. You'll have delirium tremens. DT's. You know what they are?"

"Only by reputation. Doctor, I thank you for keeping me from bleeding to death. You're as pretty as a picture, but you're too damn serious. Now

I'm going to walk out of here and forget you ever made the mistake you just made. No lawsuit, no repercussions of any kind. That's a promise."

Dr. Chin regarded him with Confucian inscrutability. He knew that she was absolutely right about everything she had told him, but he couldn't help that. He had to go. "Got promises to keep, Anna, honey," he said.

Dr. Chin nodded. It was plain to see that she was dismissing him from her mind; she had done her duty. He was just another loser. "Good luck, Mr. Speaker," she said.

16

That night Zarah Christopher was unable to sleep. She had ridden to the hospital in the backseat of Macalaster's car, holding Attenborough's swathed hand in her lap, and when she got home she saw the brown circular bloodstain, big as a dinner plate, that his leaking wound had left on her skirt. Inside the overheated house, the stench of putrefying blood was overpowering, and even though she put the ruined dress into a plastic bag, threw it into the trash, and then took a shower, this particular odor triggered memories. Some were from her own life, some from what she had guessed and dreamed about her family's life, some from both. These amounted to a history of the Christopher family: disappearances, lost loves, death at the hands of fools, betrayal by friends, hopeless desire— every kind of psychic imprisonment provided by the twentieth century.

By now it was five in the morning. Half-nauseated by memory and lack of sleep, she called Mallory, and by five-thirty the two of them were walking together along the tarred bike path in lower Rock Creek Park, a choice of time and meeting place that both knew was safe because it was so manifestly *un*safe: no mugger or rapist would look for victims here for another hour and a half, when the early-morning runners and bicyclists began to come out.

Nevertheless, two ♂ ↔ ♀ security teams covered Mallory, stalking before and behind, murmuring to each other by radio. As soon as the bodyguards drifted out of earshot, Zarah began to speak, very softly. In order to hear, Mallory had to move so close to her that their bodies were only just not touching. He felt the magnetism of her body. She went on talking at the same nearly inaudible volume, seemingly unaware of him physically.

"You say you knew my father," she said. "What do you know?"

"The reputation," Mallory replied, "not the man. The O.G. briefed the

Senate Intelligence Committee when he was captured by the Chinese Communists, Patchen did the same when he was released. It was obvious that he was greatly admired."

"You were a member of the Intelligence Committee at that time?"

"Yes. But I didn't know until recently that you were abducted with Patchen by the Eye of Gaza. Or that your father got you out."

"I see." Her voice was unemotional and unsurprised.

Mallory said, "You saw Patchen die, I understand."

"*Felt* him die. He had his arms around me, shielding me from gunfire with what was left of his body."

"Then he was tortured."

"Yes, but that's not what I meant. He had serious war wounds. They had stripped him, so I saw them. Felt them on his skin."

"And you?"

Though she knew he was asking, because it had happened before, she did not answer the unspoken question: Were you tortured, too? She made a gesture. "Here I am."

"Thanks to Patchen and your father."

"Among others, yes."

"And of course you were where you were because of them, too."

"Was I?"

He put a hand on her forearm, the first time he had touched her since they had shaken hands on meeting. "Zarah, there's no need for you to explain yourself to me."

He spoke with such youthful earnestness that she laughed. She said, "Are you offering me absolution for the sins of my family? I've learned since coming to Washington that people usually offer that when they discover that I come from a line of spies."

"That's not what *I* meant."

"And that's not what I wanted to explain."

"Let *me* explain, then. Your background means nothing to me. What I see is what I want."

"I know that, but what you want is impossible."

Mallory stopped walking and turned to face her. "What is it, exactly, that you think I want?"

In her cool, almost-American voice, Zarah said, "I think you want me to be the missing half of yourself."

"Am I that transparent?"

"Not transparent. Consistent."

They smiled at each other. "And if that is what I want, why would that be impossible?"

"Because, as you just suggested, I am who I am and nothing will change it."

"Explain that, please."

She smiled. "No, not now. The moment has passed."

"Then I'll have to reschedule it," Mallory said. "Consistency, you know."

Without comment or gesture, Zarah walked on. They passed under a streetlamp; in its feeble light they could see a misty rain falling before they felt it on their skin.

"Why were you so upset about Lockwood?" she asked.

One of the security people stepped between them and handed Mallory an umbrella, already open, then fell back out of earshot again. Mallory lifted the umbrella, inviting Zarah to join him underneath.

"Do you really want to know?" he asked.

Rain drummed on the umbrella.

She nodded. He told her about Ibn Awad.

She said, "I already know about that; everyone does. But he was assassinated by his own son. Lockwood said so on television."

"That's true as far as it goes," Mallory replied. "But the assassin was an American agent. Your cousin Horace ran the operation, with Lockwood's authorization, on Julian's initiative."

Zarah said, "That's why they stole the election? To save themselves from the consequences of killing Ibn Awad?"

Zarah walked out from under the umbrella and stood alone in the downpour. They were under another light, beside a park bench on which a derelict was stretched out under a thick layer of newspapers. Even in her distraction, she thought it strange that Mallory's guards seemed to be untroubled by the presence of this unknown person.

Mallory said, "They may have called it something else—a higher duty, perhaps, but yes, I'm sure that was the reason."

Zarah closed her eyes.

An hour had passed since they had met; behind the overcast, the sun was rising. The light and the rain intensified. Now they could see each other's face more clearly, but the noise of the rain obliged them to speak louder than before.

"I'm sorry," Mallory said.

Zarah said nothing in reply. After a moment, she opened her eyes again. The first runner of the day, a lean young person, obviously an athlete, loped by, peering at them through oversize yellow goggles even though there was barely enough light to see the path. But though her mind was still elsewhere, in other lives and places, Zarah recognized the runner.

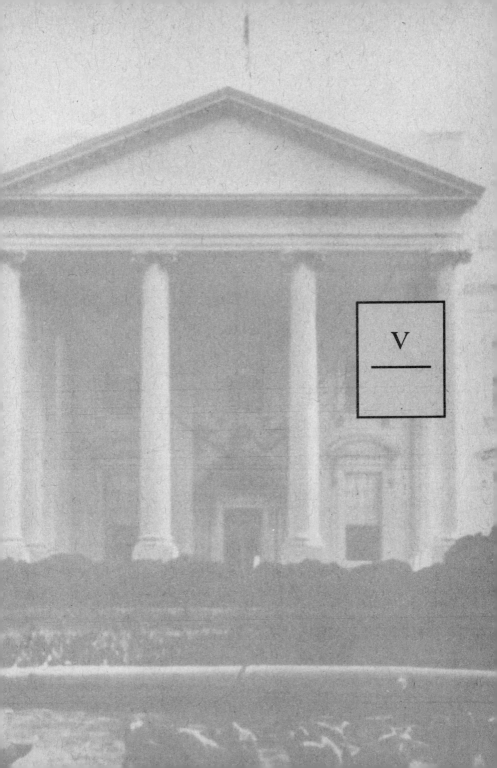

V

1

Later in the day on which Zarah recognized the runner in Rock Creek Park, Hammett and Julian Hubbard met in one of the rooms off the atrium of the Corcoran Gallery of Art. The location, just across Seventeenth Street from the Executive Office Building, was convenient for Julian and involved minimal risk of observation or even recognition. No one who knew them was likely to be here, and they arrived a few minutes before closing time and rendezvoused in front of Samuel F. B. Morse's *The Old House of Representatives*, a painting that does not ordinarily attract crowds of art lovers. In light of his recent encounter with the incumbent Speaker of the House, Hammett thought that the choice of meeting point showed a certain insouciance. Of course Julian had no way of knowing this, and Hammett did not let him in on the joke: He did not want to call attention to his interest in Attenborough, for whom he had certain plans.

Though they now lived and worked in the same city, the secretive Hammett had summoned Julian to this meeting through their fellow Shelleyan, Seven-One of Stamford, Connecticut. The two men had not seen each other since Hammett had burst into Julian's basement office after Manal Macalaster's last séance. Since then, because of his estrangement from Lockwood and his consequent disappearance from the news media, a good deal of life had gone out of Julian. He was faintly stooped, faintly haggard, faintly distracted. His voice was a shade less authoritative. Hammett felt little sympathy for this diminished Julian. Although he was aware that his fellow Shelleyan might have a different opinion of the relationship, he himself had never thought that the two of them were personal friends or ever had been. They were *compáres*, bound together by the godfatherhood of the Shelley Society. They were useful to each other, and in Hammett's scheme of things this was a sounder basis for a relationship than any amount of good old democratic mutual esteem and affection. Besides, it was inconceivable to him that friendship could exist in the absence of a seamless identity of ideological conviction, and while it was true that Julian professed the correct politics and worked for the right outcomes, his beliefs rose from shame and not, as in Hammett's case, from ancient grievances transmitted by blood and the memory of suffering.

In one way Julian had not changed at all. Despite his fall from grace and favor, he regarded everyone else with equestrian condescension, as if nothing whatever had changed in their situations. Old pretensions die hard, thought Hammett. Julian was so used to being the ranking human being in any encounter with another American, let alone a foreigner, that he still behaved like a man who had the power to change the lives of others with a word, a favor, a mere suggestion.

Reminding Hammett that he had recently done exactly this in his own case, Julian said, "How do you like being Chief Justice?"

Hammett replied lightly, "How do you like being the invisible man?"

Julian's smile intensified slightly. "I find it restful. Answer the question."

Hammett shrugged. "Frankly, it's even more boring than I imagined. But that's not what I wanted to talk to you about."

"No?"

"No. I have a question for you. How much do you know about the private life of Lady Zed?"

Julian sighed. This obsession of Hammett's, one among so many, had slipped his mind. What sort of mythical being was he now turning Zarah into? Hammett's tenacity when trying to prove the reality of one of his paranoid hunches was truly unlimited. With another of his patronizing smiles (Hammett read his thoughts as follows: What could this toad possibly know about a cousin of the Hubbards'?), Julian drawled, "Does Zarah *have* a private life?"

"She's dating Franklin Mallory—midnight visits back and forth between their houses, intimate tête-à-têtes over hummingbird tongues, served with exactly the right rare wine, private showings of great works of art, et cetera, et cetera. Is that what you'd call a private life?"

Julian was so surprised by this that he let it show in a gratifying way. "Zarah is seeing Franklin Mallory?" he said. "But he's too old for her."

"He's fifty-five, she's about thirty," Hammett replied. "These June-September matches are quite common." These were also the approximate ages of Julian and Emily Hubbard. Hammett shook his head in mock solemnity. "It's the Montagues and the Capulets all over again," he said. "The kids are just a little older now."

Julian interrupted. "How do you know this?"

"I have my sources, and what they tell me is this," Hammett replied. "Lady Zed is leading a double life. Or maybe a triple or quadruple one. She also romances Ross Macalaster, thus playing off the Lone Ranger of the media against the Prince of Darkness."

"Romances?" Julian said. "*Romances?*" He knew Hammett too well to question the accuracy of his information, as far as it went. He almost always got the surface details right; it was the interpretation of facts that led him into error because he believed so strongly that nothing was what it seemed to be.

Hammett said, "I *thought* you'd be surprised."

"Well, I'm not really," Julian replied. "Zarah has always had admirers. Even you can't seem to forget her." He smiled his lofty smile again.

"Not surprised?" Hammett said. "Why is that?"

"Because nothing the Christophers do ever surprises me."

"Even joining up with the enemies of mankind?"

"Nonsense. All she's done so far, according to what you've told me, is have dinner with Mallory and look at some pictures." He smiled again, eyes intent. "Now if she'd been lying on a tiger skin with him, I'd be worried. Wouldn't want any little Mallory cousins at the Thanksgiving dinner table."

"What amazing genes you must have in common with these Christophers, Julian," Hammett said.

"You don't know the half of it when it comes to consanguinity," Julian said. "The saying in the family is, The Christophers screwed the Hubbards smart."

"Then maybe their genes will help you answer a question: What was Lady Zed up to yesterday afternoon when she went straight from a social call at the White House to a meeting with Franklin Mallory? Or at five o'clock this morning, when she met him, just the two of them, in Rock Creek Park?"

Abruptly Julian stopped smiling. In a voice devoid of humor, he said, "Tell me more."

Hammett shrugged. "That's all I know."

He studied Julian's long, suddenly anxious and puzzled face. Curiosity, as he knew, was one of the greatest of all reinforcements to behavior, and he had just infected Julian with an acute—and, he hoped, incurable—case of it.

The bell rang for closing time. A museum guard, indifferent to their identities, made a gesture for them to depart. Julian seemed relieved. With a nod in Hammett's direction that was so decisive that it ought to have made a noise, he turned on his heel and left.

Hammett sauntered after him, pausing to glance for a moment at John Singer Sargent's painting of Madame Édouard Pailleron. He doubted that the woman had really been as patrician or as interesting as Sargent made her seem. She wore an expression that was a lot like Julian's. No doubt the Hubbards and the Christophers of that era had had themselves painted by Sargent or someone similar, and this must be one of the reasons why they had cultivated that perpetual smile: they were trying to look more like their portraits than like themselves.

"We're closing," said the guard in an insistent tone.

Hammett ignored the man. He walked briskly out the door and down the wide marble staircase, the trace of a smile lingering on his lips as he remembered his insight about Julian and his tribe. Although even he had to admit it would be difficult, in Zarah's case, to improve on nature.

2

Julian's relationship with Lockwood, formerly so interwoven that the world, and even Lockwood and Julian themselves, had scarcely known where one personality ended and the other began, had now changed so profoundly that the President no longer even laughed in the presence of his chief of staff. Where in the past Julian had walked in and out of the Oval Office or the Lincoln sitting room at will a dozen times a day, he now saw the President just twice: at 7:30 A.M. to deliver his morning report and receive his instructions, and again at 7:30 P.M. after the network news, to summarize the routine business of the day.

These were short, formal encounters, with none of the ribald jokes, raucous gossip, and deep confidences of times gone by. Political questions were never discussed, least of all the impeachment process that would decide the fate of both men. The intricate tactics and strategy, the politics of maneuver, which had been Julian's special province and Lockwood's joy, were no longer subjects for discussion. Offers of advice by Julian met with a cold stare and a wall of silent reproach from the President. After the first few rebuffs, Julian stopped offering counsel of any kind. Without ceremony or notice, he had been reduced from the informal but real rank of second most powerful man in the administration, and therefore in the world, to that of glorified clerk.

The demotion had even been gazetted. Patrick Graham, citing "the highest source," which could only mean Lockwood now that the words "unimpeachable source" had been dropped as an identifier, had broadcast a piece revealing that Julian no longer spoke for the President because he was no longer privy to Lockwood's innermost thoughts. After Graham dropped this boulder into the water, causing ripples of withdrawal to spread across the news media, Julian ceased being courted by journalists.

He had not received a call at home from an important reporter for weeks. Hammett's caustic wisecrack about invisibility had been all too apt: though he continued to enjoy his title and perquisites and go to work every day in the second-largest office in the West Wing of the White House, in Washington terms Julian really had sunk from sight. Insiders no longer mentioned him; outsiders who had always before referred to him when dropping names as "Julian" now spoke of him curtly as "Hubbard."

However, the Secret Service's presidential protection detail was still responsive to the chief of staff because he continued to stand between them and the President in the chain of command and communication. Therefore as soon as he returned to his desk after his encounter with Hammett, Julian called Bud Booker into his office. "Give me the details of Zarah Christopher's last three visits to the White House," he said.

Impassively Booker removed his miniature computer terminal (ironically, a Universal Energy product developed for Mallory's security detail on a pro bono basis) from its holster in the small of his back and punched in a code that accessed the central computer's memory bank. Booker listened impassively through his earpiece. "Just one visit shows under that name," he said. "Day before yesterday, sixteen hundred hours to sixteen forty-two hours, tea with the First Lady in the family quarters."

"Where was the President in that time period?" Booker did not reply. After an awkward moment, Julian said, "I *know* where he was, Bud. What I need is the exact time frame. When did he go upstairs and when did he come back down?"

This was family business: Booker seemed reluctant to answer. As if calling a dog, Julian beckoned the information from the agent's lips with a low whistle and a crooked forefinger.

Out of his perfectly blank face, Booker said, "The President was with the visitor and the First Lady from sixteen twenty-one hours to end of visit, when subject was escorted to the East Wing exit by Lieutenant E. Zwingle, the military aide on detail to the family quarters at that time. The President returned downstairs, to his small office, at seventeen oh eight."

"Thank you, Bud."

"No problem."

Booker left. Julian waited five minutes before rising to his feet and striding down the hall to the Oval Office.

"He's *busy*," Jean McHenry called out as he passed her desk, giving the second word a coloratura lilt, but Julian plunged onward. Lockwood, standing by the french doors that looked out onto the portico and the muddy lawn beyond, was deep in conversation with Bud Booker. The look on Lockwood's face told Julian what they were talking about.

Guesswork was not necessary, however. Lockwood turned on Julian with fury in his voice. "What the hell's the idea of checking up on Polly's tea parties?"

"I had a family interest," Julian said.

"Well, by God, so have I!" Lockwood bellowed.

Booker looked from one angry man to the other—Julian, deeply flushed, had stopped in his tracks midway into the room and Lockwood was advancing on him with his huge fists clenched at his trouser seams—then ducked out the french doors and on down the portico.

"I had to hear about Zarah's visit from an outsider," Julian said. "I couldn't believe it."

"Couldn't believe what? What the hell's the matter with you, Julian, going to the Secret Service to spy on my wife?"

"I couldn't imagine that I'd be deceived in this way."

"*Deceived?*" Lockwood said. "Jesus Christ, *you* can speak that word to *me?*"

All the pent-up anger and rejection and frustration of the past weeks ruptured within Julian's bosom. Blood pounded through his heart at a dangerously high pressure—195 over 135 the last time the White House doctor had checked it—that even his medication could not control. A pulse beat painfully—and, he was sure, visibly—in his forehead. Lockwood, very close now, stabbed him on the breastbone with a rigid forefinger.

Julian slapped the President's hand away. "What the hell's the matter with *you*, using my cousin to traffic with the enemy?" he cried. "Don't you know who she is, what she's done for this country, what this can mean?" Lockwood looked studiously at his hand, then back into Julian's contorted face, saying nothing. "You *are* using her to carry messages to Mallory, aren't you?" Julian said. "That *is* what this is all about, isn't it?"

Lockwood said, "Get your ass out of here."

Julian stood his ground. "Isn't that what you're doing?"

Lockwood looked him up and down as though he had walked into the Oval Office naked. Then, without another word or gesture, he turned his back and walked toward the door that led to his small private office.

"What you're doing is demented—worse, it's stupid," Julian said. "Mallory wants to destroy you. He wants to destroy everything you stand for. He'll destroy Zarah."

Lockwood opened the door, which was plastered like the wall and set flush into it, and walked through it, slamming the bolt home behind him. Julian stood where he was, breathing heavily and staring at the locked door, until Jean McHenry said with unwonted gentleness, "Julian, you should go now."

3

It was twilight. Back in his own office, Julian stood by the window gazing southward across the spillway of blinking taillights between the White House and the Potomac bridges. His heart still pounded; he had trouble breathing; the skin burned on his face. Not even when he had crashed his burning Phantom into the South China Sea almost thirty years before had his body taken control of his mind in this way. To himself he silently repeated the words his father had spoken to him once upon a time: "I require you to think quietly, systematically, unemotionally."

Julian's well-worn Zeiss binoculars, the ones his father had taken from the corpse of an SS officer whom he had strangled by night with a wire noose in occupied France, hung by their worn leather strap from a hook in the window sash. He took them down and swept the trees and bushes on the south lawn. In the gathering dusk he saw a movement in the sky above the Ellipse. He refocused the glasses and to his amazement and delight identified a red-shouldered hawk. The unmistakable rufous shoulder patch, rusty body, and ruby underwing all showed up distinctly. The hawk was hunting field mice, its winter prey, or more probably smaller specimens of the Norway rats that teemed among the stately monuments. Suddenly it dove straight downward, then rose again with powerful strokes of its two-foot wings, grasping a writhing animal in its talons. Julian watched the bird out of sight as it pinioned toward the river, a creature with form and instincts out of prehistory.

As he was entering this fortunate sighting in his book (*Buteo lineatus*, time, date, place, and particulars, with the notation, "red in beak and claw as nature itself!"), it occurred to him that the hawk appearing over the heart of the city during rush-hour traffic had been an omen of some kind. This errant thought, so incorrect in terms of the enmity to all forms of superstition by which he had always tried to live, took him by surprise.

Julian was a little calmer now. As if drafting a diary entry, he tried to describe his present situation as a way of understanding it. But he failed to understand it, as he had failed many times before in recent days, because he had nothing to compare it with. Even the end of his first marriage had been affectionate and civilized in comparison with this.

Caroline, his first wife, was a changeful woman who had simply fallen out of love with him and into love with another man, Leo Dwyer. Her second husband, who worked at home, was in a position to be with her all the time, and, as she said outright to Julian—Caroline was not a woman to leave her reasons for doing something unspoken—Leo had enormous sexual energy. Julian had never been home when she needed him, and most of the time he was too tired, too distracted, or rendered impotent by the pills he took for his high blood pressure to be much use to her in bed. He understood why Caroline wanted a change; he let her have it. After a period of chaste cohabitation in the little Georgetown house while the necessary legal arrangements were made, she left. When they parted in the hall on the last morning of their marriage, she might as well have been a daughter kissing her father goodbye before going off to Vassar. It was a turning point; their lives changed irrevocably, but they themselves did not. She would still be Caroline and he would still be Julian. The event was dramatic, but the effects were mild and civilized. They thought no less of each other after the divorce than before; they liked each other's new spouse; each was glad of the other's second chance at happiness—if that's what the limbo of after-youth was called.

What had happened today was not like that at all. There was no residue of affection between Julian and Lockwood, no consciousness, even, of the past. In a flash of insight, Julian understood why. He and Caroline had abandoned their marriage, but they were still alike by birth, education, sensibility, and above all politics, and they were bound together permanently by their son and daughter, who would grow up to be a great deal like them, and by a vast network of relations and friends who were also semblances of themselves.

But when Julian and Lockwood abandoned the thing that had bound them together—the pretense that the pauper could be hero to the prince—nothing remained. It had always been a pretense. The man who had pretended to be Julian's father and the one who had pretended to be Lockwood's son had ceased to exist. The charade was over, and all the sentiment and enjoyment it had engendered, all the sympathy it had inspired for its characters, all the suspension of disbelief that had been necessary to its enjoyment, were left behind.

It was time to go home. Julian closed his birding log and from his desk drawer withdrew a sheet of the stiff White House writing paper whose vulgar ostentation had always repelled him. His ancient Mont Blanc fountain pen, which, like the Zeiss binoculars, had once belonged to his father, was already uncapped. In a fluent hand, he wrote:

Dear Mr. President,

I hereby resign as Chief of Staff to the President of the United States.

Yours truly,

He signed his name and dated the document. There, Pa, he thought—
the ultimate writing cure. Then, with deliberate movements and a lighter
heart, he put his pen and his birding log into his pockets, slung Elliott
Hubbard's captured binoculars over his shoulder, and, standing at his
desk, made one last telephone call at taxpayer expense before going out
the door forever.

Ordinarily Julian would not have used this phone to make this particular call, but circumstances had rendered him reckless. The number he
reached was the one in Stamford, Connecticut, and when Seven-One
answered in slightly drunken tones, for it was late enough in the far
suburbs for the third martini to have been poured, Julian said with a lift
in his voice, "What did Trelawny snatch from the funeral pyre at Viareggio?"

4

When he received word of Julian Hubbard's resignation several hours
before the story broke on television, Mallory was reading Macaulay's
essay on Boswell's *Life of Johnson*. He had just come to the passage about
a philosopher who remarks that life and death are the same to him.
" 'Why then,' said an objector, 'do you not kill yourself?' The philosopher
answered, 'Because it is just the same.' " On reading these words, Mallory,
remembering the sight of Susan Grant's skull being shattered by her
assassin's bullets, slapped the book shut with a shudder of revulsion. His
loss, his loneliness, suddenly seemed unbearable. He tried to remember
Grant's face; he could not do so. He tried again, concentrating hard; he
felt that he owed this to Susan. He failed again; Susan's murderer had
obliterated her.

Just before dawn, Mallory tried to call Zarah. There was no answer. He
went out into the hall, intending to walk over to her house, but Wiggins
and Lucy, who had just arrived at the front door, advised against this.
They had confirmed Sturdi's surveillance of Zarah Christopher at the
same moment that Zarah herself recognized Sturdi in Rock Creek Park.

The derelict in the sleeping bag had been Lucy; Wiggins, wearing running shoes and a Heidelberg (Pennsylvania) College sweat suit, was a pistol shot behind Sturdi when she loped by. Earlier, just as Hammett had feared, Wiggins had spotted her stretching and running in place and watching Zarah outside the National Gallery. Where Zarah went, this person appeared. Why? Only one answer to this question worked in terms of Wiggins and Lucy's mission: because Zarah was close to Mallory, and the stranger wanted to do harm to Mallory. They did not summarize these findings to Mallory or mention their working hypothesis, because this would have meant worrying him needlessly over Zarah's safety. Lucy merely said, "There's an unexplained stranger in the neighborhood. We've had three or four sightings of the same person in various guises."

Mallory looked up in interest. " 'Guises'?"

"As a runner, as a dog walker, as a bicyclist."

"This neighborhood is full of people like that."

"Yes, but we know them all except this one. Plus the computer doesn't like this person's body language."

"What?"

Wiggins said, "We videotaped the subject and the computer analyzed movements against a profile of natural, spontaneous behavior. The unnaturals were abnormally high."

"What does that mean in plain English?"

"The subject walks the dogs, runs, and goes for bicycle rides at odd hours. Is seen in too many places where you are. Behaves *too* naturally. This is a trained operative."

Mallory said, "What do you want me to do?"

"We think you should go to Great Falls until this is cleared up. By helicopter. It's waiting on the pad at National."

Mallory paused, then nodded. "All right. Let's go."

For all his night wanderings Mallory never argued with security precautions. His incognito comings and goings were based on the principle that he controlled the element of surprise because the strangers he encountered did not expect to see him. If this situation was reversed, if someone *he* did not expect to see was lurking about with the idea of taking him unawares, then the risk became foolish.

"One thing," he said. "I still want to talk to Zarah Christopher. Will you please have someone bring her to Great Falls?"

Lucy spoke up. "She isn't home at the moment, Mr. President."

Mallory looked puzzled. It was five o'clock in the morning. "She's not? How do you know that?"

"She was sighted leaving her house forty minutes ago."

"At this hour? Alone?"

Lucy said, "She'll be all right, Mr. President. Wiggins and I stayed with her, then another team took over. She just seems to be walking. Thinking."

Mallory frowned. Zarah was certainly capable of detecting surveillance, even of recognizing the people who were following her as members of his security staff. Then what? With a brisk nod, he dropped the subject.

On arrival at Great Falls, Mallory found O. N. Laster's confidential aide, Hugo Fugger-Weisskopf, awaiting him in the foyer. Like many other citizens of countries that had been sealed off from the rest of the world by Communism for most of the twentieth century, Hugo had the manners and attitudes of an aristocracy long since vanished from the West. With Teutonic clicks of his leather heels, he bowed stiffly to Mallory and kissed Lucy's right hand—surely a breach of intergender etiquette and probably of security, since her shooting hand was the one that he kissed. With another flourish he handed Mallory an envelope. It was ostentatiously brown and plain, and perfectly blank, yet subtly unlike any other envelope in the world. Mallory would have recognized it as coming from Laster if he had found it on the street. He went into the library and opened it in privacy.

The language of the report was just as economical as the format: no date, no greeting, no signature. It was a description of the meeting between Hammett and Julian Hubbard in the Corcoran Gallery of Art—not just the actual words spoken, but the atmospherics, the demeanor of the two men, Julian's obvious agitation at the end, and his sudden resignation. Mallory did not doubt the accuracy of the report. Laster was never wrong about such matters. Through its dozens of subsidiaries, foundations, and international agencies, Universal Energy had many, many relationships of trust, mutual interest, and confidentiality inside the government and throughout the Washington Establishment.

Following the report of the meeting was a detailed history of the long relationship between Hammett and Julian. Though rigorously condensed, it was astonishingly complete, beginning at Yale and progressing through the next quarter of a century. None of it was speculation. Every fact was confirmed, every conversation documented. Every man and woman quoted in the text was a primary source of proven reliability with firsthand knowledge of the confidential information they supplied.

The second page was headed THE APPARATUS, and it listed in chart form the names of many men and women in Congress, both members and staffers, together with scores of others in key positions within the executive departments and regulatory agencies; dozens more in the loose confederation of pressure groups that called itself the Advocacy Constituency; in the legal and other learned professions; in the universities and the national educational bureaucracy; in the national headquarters of the churches; in the news media, and in other centers of political activism and opinion-making.

All of these people had one characteristic in common: they owed something valuable to Archimedes Hammett or Julian Hubbard, or in many cases to both. The precise nature of the debt—usually their admission to graduate school, their government jobs, the funding of their organizations, or all three—was noted in parentheses after each name.

Mallory put down the report, laid his head on the back of the easy chair in which he sat, and closed his eyes. What was he supposed to make of this information? Before a rational answer to this question could form in his mind, a phone rang on his direct, scrambled line, as if activated by a timer set to go off when he finished reading. Even before he picked it up, he knew that he would hear Laster's voice on the line. No doubt Hugo had sent his chief a signal stating the exact time of delivery of the message, and Laster, working from a computerized estimate, had given Mallory the precise amount of time required to read the text.

Laster's voice, broken down by the scrambling equipment into digitalized gibberish and then reconstituted as a slightly slurred version of the original, said, "Have you read it?"

"Just this moment finished," Mallory said.

"Glad I didn't interrupt. Have you talked to Lockwood?"

"Not yet."

"Well, you'll have something new to tell him."

"I'm not so sure about that."

Laster made an astonished noise. "How can you possibly believe that, after what you've just read? Julian's defected. Hammett's mixed up with him in this. The left is going to stab Lockwood in the back."

Mallory replied, "To what purpose?"

"What purpose do you think? To steal the presidency again, and this time do it right, under color of law."

"That's one possibility. It's also possible Julian is leaving to save his own skin or to try to save Lockwood's."

"Right, true Americans like Julian and Hammett deserve a presumption of innocence," Laster said. "All that crowd has done in our lifetime is take over the federal budget, the universities, the schools, the do-good movement, the civil and foreign service, the news media, world literature, the movies, the theater, the ballet and the opera, plus the Democratic Party and organized religion minus the evangelicals. Why would they try for the big hit?"

Listening wearily to words he had often heard before, Mallory did not open his eyes. He said, "Oz, I appreciate your keeping me informed. I know your concerns. But all this is just speculation."

"The enemy's plan is self-evident, my friend."

"That's what my enemies have been saying about my operation, not to mention your own, for a long time."

"They're a bunch of paranoids, for God's sake. What you've just read is a keen perception of reality. Of course the radicals will say black is white and up is down; that's the way they do it. But something's in the wind, Franklin. You've got to make a preemptive strike or lose it all."

"I thought I'd done that. Lockwood is going to be impeached and removed from office."

"Maybe. But what happens then? I'm telling you: If you don't get busy, and damn quick, you'll see things happen that you really won't be able to believe."

"Maybe."

" 'Maybe' is a word for losers."

Mallory let a moment pass before replying. Finally he said, "Oz, forgive me for saying so, but the fact that this scenario seems plausible to you doesn't mean that it won't be laughed out of court by the media."

"The radicals will try to do that. They always do. But the American people won't be laughing."

"Or listening. They'll think it's just politics as usual."

"It is. Life-and-death politics."

Wearily Mallory said, "Oz, forgive me again, but you've spent your life behind the scenes, giving orders to people who were eager to carry them out because they're paid to do just that. You've never had to convince the electorate of anything."

"The only one you have to convince is yourself."

"And then what? Do I tell Lockwood that I'm the devil he knows and that the man he just appointed Chief Justice of the United States is the devil he doesn't?"

"Exactly. And then tell him to get his ass out of the White House like an honest man while he still has the chance to save the country and his own soul."

"I told him that the night before he took the oath of office. He didn't listen to me then. Why should he listen now?"

"Because everything has changed."

"In his eyes all that's changed so far is that he's gotten rid of a chief of staff who had outlived his usefulness."

"A chief of staff who has already stabbed him in the back twice. You've got to move Lockwood out *now*," Laster said, spacing his words for emphasis. "You've got the means. Just think of America and do it. Remember your Machiavelli: 'When you strike at a prince, strike for the heart.' "

"A sound principle," Mallory said. "But Washington is not sixteenth-century Florence."

"Only because nobody's got the guts to act like a Medici, in his own interests."

Mallory said, "Oz, in everybody's interests let me do this my way."

"To what end?"

"To save what's left of the people's trust in the government. The presidency isn't worth much without it, and once it's gone, it's gone."

" 'The people.' " Laster's sigh of heavy disappointment seemed even louder than it was in the metallic echo chamber of the scrambler phone. He said, "This conversation reminds me of what someone said to Marshal Pétain when he was selling another trainload of Jews to the Nazis to save the French people from additional suffering: 'You think too much about the French and not enough about France.' "

"Goodbye, Oz."

Mallory looked at the clock again: 6:57 A.M. He went to the window and looked out on the formal garden and the vineyards beyond, harshly floodlit as a precaution against assassins. Was Zarah home now, was she safe? His mind returned to Macaulay. Life and death were not the same. Marilyn was gone, Susan was gone, Zarah was leaving before he knew her. He had never felt so lonely in his life. Looking out on the shadowless no-man's-land that surrounded his house, he fell back into a state that was part memory, part thought, part dream. But the impressions that formed in his brain were not about Laster, not about the Apparatus—if such a thing even existed—not about Lockwood or the knot of history in which he and all the others were the tightening strands, but about Zarah Christopher. About love, which was to him the difference between life and death.

5

On the morning after Julian's resignation, Emily Hubbard awoke to see blurry images of her husband flickering on the four small muted television screens that stood in a rank along the far wall of their bedroom. Still only half awake, she saw him depicted in a montage of stock footage as a skinny youth whispering into Lockwood's ear at a long-ago Senate committee hearing while Franklin Mallory, off to one side, browbeat a defiant witness; then as a somewhat less melancholy version of the man he was now, walking with Lockwood and some forgotten foreigner through a ruined and smoking city, which one she could not make out; and finally dripping with gore a split second after a suicidal terrorist from the Eye of Gaza blew up himself and some innocent bystanders with a bomb during a campaign rally in front of the Alamo.

Emily reached for her glasses. Between the bed and the television sets, Julian's long-shanked hairy body bounced up and down, arms flailing, knees pumping energetically. He was running in place on a small collapsible trampoline while listening to the commentary over wireless earphones and switching from network to network with a hand-held remote control. Trapped in a sedentary way of life, Julian hungered for exertion. Here and in the office, where he kept dumbbells and a stationary bicycle, he exercised in solitude, as he did practically everything else, because his time belonged to Lockwood and no one else could be permitted to have a claim on it, even as a tennis partner. Usually his predawn exercises, a daily ritual, did not wake Emily; she had got used to his calisthentics in the same way she had got used to the early-morning traffic when she lived on Connecticut Avenue before her marriage. Looking at the television images—they were essentially the same shots, arranged in the same sequences, filling the same time slot, on all four networks—she thought that it must have been his thoughts or his emotions that had pulled her up out of slumber.

But why were they showing pictures of Julian on network television? He hadn't been mentioned by the news media in weeks. She felt a stab of fear: if she had not seen him in the flesh bouncing on his trampoline, she would have assumed he had been murdered by the Eye of Gaza or some other pack of maniacs and this was his obituary. She knew nothing of Julian's resignation. The night before, she had gone to the opera alone, an empty seat beside her; Julian had neither shown up at the Kennedy Center as they had arranged nor called. She had stuck the atonal opera out to the end, though it had turned out to be a depressing tale of a loveless marriage and a passionless adultery sung in Cantonese. When she came home quite early, just after eleven, she found her husband already asleep in their bed. Because he had slept so little since the presidential campaign—actually since that terrorist bomb had gone off in Texas—she had not had the heart to wake him up, despite her astonishment at finding him home from the White House and already asleep hours before he usually arrived.

On screen, talking heads grimaced and moved their lips but issued no sound. There was no point now in asking Julian to turn on the speakers;

he could not hear her through his earphones. She got out of bed, hair tousled, and ran down the length of the long room to the control panel. She wore an old gray sweatshirt as a nightgown. Fixated on the screens, Julian did not notice. Out of the stereo speakers that surrounded them, Patrick Graham's rich baritone intoned, "And so the amoeba of this remarkable identity of minds and purposes has split in two. What consequences this development will have for the evolution of the drama surrounding the presidency no one yet knows. Julian Hubbard, right-hand man extraordinary, has given up the only job he ever had or wanted, and the isolation of Bedford Forrest Lockwood intensifies. Hubbard's letter of resignation, a single terse sentence after a lifetime of devoted service to a President he revered—and some would say *invented*—has the ring of mystery. The reasons why he left so abruptly and without explanation remain an enigma because Julian Hubbard, a chamberlain of the old, silent school, will not comment. But this is surely not the end of the story, for as another pragmatic idealist, Benjamin Disraeli, put it, 'Finality is not the language of politics.' "

Emily said, " '*Amoeba*'? 'One terse sentence'? 'Finality is not the language of politics'? What is this?"

She turned to Julian, waving her arms frantically to get his attention, but he made no sign that he saw her. He was hypnotized by the kaleidoscopic images of himself that seemed to be spilling out of the past and back into his life. That life, a peculiarly American one because nearly every significant moment of it had been reduced to an electronic image for public consumption, was passing before his eyes. Emily realized that he had not even noticed that she had moved into his field of vision. He was sprinting in place now, as he always did during the final segment of the news; the half hour he had been running was, he reckoned, a fair approximation of a ten-thousand-meter run, which had been his best distance in college, and he ran it like a real race, pacing himself against imaginary Harvards and Princetons over the first twenty-five minutes, then going all-out for the finish line, sweating and gasping for breath, for the last five. This room, which ran the length of the house and went up to the roof, was the only one large enough to contain him when he was in such violent motion; still, because he was six feet five inches tall, his head barely missed striking the slope of the ceiling as he bounced furiously up and down, lost in whatever sensation this strange exercise produced. Suddenly Emily slapped him hard on his bare thigh. He looked downward, puzzled and annoyed, and saw her at last, a small, sleepy-faced woman with wild hair and electrified eyes behind big horn-rimmed glasses.

He ripped off his earphones. "Mouse!" he gasped without slowing down.

Emily said, "Don't call me Mouse. You don't have a telephone in your office?"

"I don't even have an office anymore."

"So I just found out, totally by accident. You *resigned*?"

He nodded, smiling down on her, continuing with his pantomime of a long-distance runner's finishing kick.

"Stop that!" she shouted. "Talk to me!"

"Almost finished."

"Goddamnit, Julian! Stop!"

He nodded in meek husbandly submission, but stopping was no simple matter. His body had been generating a lot of energy. The vibrations of the trampoline were such that he could slow down only gradually unless he wanted to be thrown off his feet. Trampolines, even small ones, were tricky. But little by little, making reassuring gestures and sympathetic faces for Emily's benefit, he brought himself to rest. He was gasping and dripping with sweat. "I need a towel," he said, looking toward the bathroom.

"The hell with a towel," Emily said. "Is this true?"

His eyes rested on her at last. "Perfectly true," he said. "I'm a free man. How would you like to fly up to the Harbor for a few days? We could take off from National at first light. Go into seclusion." His grin was too jaunty to be genuine.

Emily ignored the question. She said, "You resigned your job, now of all moments, and I find out about it on television? From Patrick Graham?"

"Sorry. It was quite sudden. And you weren't home when I got here last night."

"You knew where I was, but you went to sleep without me. Why?"

"It wasn't exactly voluntary."

"What wasn't? Resigning or going to sleep?"

"Either one. I saw a hawk—"

"You saw a hawk?"

He told her about sighting the red-shouldered hawk above the Ellipse. He described the meeting with Hammett, the fight with Lockwood, every nuance and detail, and about writing his letter of resignation without recapping his pen after recording the hawk in his log. "I know it seems strange, but for some reason the hawk triggered everything," he said. "It was an irresistible impulse. I hardly knew what I was doing until after it was done. Right after that I came home—or almost right after that, I had something I had to put in motion—and when I found myself alone in the house I had a couple of drinks, and then I just couldn't stay awake." He shrugged apologetically. "Sorry."

"Don't be sorry," Emily said. "I can't believe my luck. You won't change your mind, you won't go back?"

"After all that?" He gestured in the direction of the television sets, whose screens were now filled with commercials for laxatives, sleeping pills, breakfast cereals that preserved those who ate them from cancer, or pills that deadened trivial pains the human race had regarded as perfectly bearable for thousands of years. Hammett was right: the system was a vast scheme to defeat nature, to turn natural resources and human labor into waste, then dispose of it, recycle it, and start all over again. Now it had disposed of Julian. Into what would he be recycled? Dimly, he became aware that his wife was speaking to him.

"You bastard," she was saying, "you don't give a shit about me, do you? I don't exist for you, nothing exists for you but that booby you work for and all the rest of the people in the booby hatch."

He made as if to encircle Emily with his long arms. She darted out of reach. "Well, Mouse," he said, "I don't work for that booby anymore, and to be honest this isn't the best moment to demand emotional support from me. It should be the other way around. I'm the one who just gave up everything."

"Everything? You gave up *everything*? What does that make me?"

"Emily . . ." He wore a look of baffled affection now, wagging his head, again reaching out for her. She didn't believe a single word or gesture and said so. Julian sighed. "Emily, I'd do anything for you. Anything. How can you not know that?"

"You would? Assassinate an Arab? Steal an election? Throw your life away and fling your family's name to the wolves? Would you do those things for *me*?"

Her words and the furious look on her face stunned him. He actually staggered backward, something she had never seen a man do before, and had never imagined that anyone as large and as invulnerable as Julian could, in fact, do. The jerky movement of his arms and shoulders released a burst of sweaty male body odor, as if from an atomizer. His eyes lost expression. He said, "I really need a towel."

In her wrath, Emily realized that she was breathing hard. So was Julian. She felt her temperature rising, as if she might be about to break into a sweat too. Quarreling made her want to fuck—not make love, fuck.

She said, "Come here."

Julian said, "I'm sorry, I have to get a towel."

"Is that all you have to say to me?"

"No, I guess not. There's more. I love you."

"You have a funny way of showing it."

"Sorry. In recent days our romance hasn't exactly been the only thing on my mind." He was angry at last, a sign of life. He said, "Now I'm going to go get a towel."

"Oh, no you're not." Emily stripped off her sweatshirt and threw it in his face. "Here," she said. "Use this."

He looked at her naked body, so pretty and sweet, the neat breasts and bottom still a little whiter than the rest of her even all these months after the end of summer.

"My God, I *do* love you," he said, in a tone of real surprise. Then, like the giant he was, he plucked her from the floor and bore her, kissing and groaning, toward the bed. And as his great ursine weight fell upon her with a brutality that made her gasp with pleasure, Julian had but a single thought in his head: Lockwood *wanted* to get rid of me. He has thrown me to the wolves to save himself.

6

Although she had said nothing about it to Julian—after all, he hadn't given her much chance to do so—Emily had a lunch date that day with Zarah. It required all of her willpower to rise from the warm and pungent bed. Julian had never before made love to her with total concentration, had never, not even before they were married, let his body go entirely. Now that this had happened, the experience had been so intense, so much like a pornographic fantasy about coupling with a stranger at a party on top of the coats in somebody's else's bedroom, that there was something adulterous about it. Even after it was over and Julian had fallen into a deep, boyish sleep, she shuddered as if from delicious guilt at the memory of what had happened.

At lunch with Zarah Christopher in a downtown restaurant called Orlando, a home away from home for independent females, Emily displayed a hearty appetite, and as she consumed a plate of assorted smoked fish, followed by rare lamb chops with exotic vegetables, she talked and talked, as if she had been released by the change in Julian's life from some terrible oath of secrecy and could now say whatever came into her head.

"Imagine waking up and finding out on television that your husband has told the President of the United States to go fuck himself," she said.

"It came as a surprise?" Zarah asked.

"Complete, though God knows it's what I always hoped for. Julian says he acted on an irresistible impulse."

"That doesn't sound like Julian."

"You might even say he did it for you," said Emily, smearing horse-radish sauce on a morsel of smoked trout. "He'd just found out you were carrying messages between Lockwood and Mallory."

"I see. And how did he find that out?"

Emily supplied the answer as casually as if Zarah had asked her what kind of fish she was eating. "Archimedes Hammett told him," she said.

Zarah put down her fork and composed herself. Emily's words awakened some mechanism in the primitive brain, so that she had the feeling that somebody was standing behind her, watching.

"And how," she said, "did Archimedes Hammett happen to know this?"

"His spies are everywhere."

"Seriously."

"I'm perfectly serious," Emily said. "He has this incredible fifth column of malcontents inside the government and other vital nerve centers like the media, who keep a twenty-four-hour watch on the bad guys and report back to him. Phone calls in the night, Morse code tapped out on the water pipes, microfilm in swallowed condoms. He's like the king in the counting house, only he counts all his secrets because he cares nothing about money."

"Hammett actually knew this? And Julian didn't?"

Suddenly the reporter she always had been, Emily pounced. "Then it's the truth?"

Zarah answered without hesitation. "Yes."

"Good, I hoped it might be. Because maybe you know what Mallory's going to do next." She smiled, hatred visible behind the smile. "We have to plan for the future, Julian and I."

"Lockwood would like to know that too. That's what he wanted me to find out from Mallory."

"And did you find out?"

"No. It made Mallory angry that Lockwood had used me as a go-between."

"He was mad, too? Seems to be an epidemic. If he does tell you his plans, give me a call. You might as well be a double agent. It's a family specialty."

Emily giggled, as if she had proposed a harmless girlish prank against the men in their lives. Zarah could think of nothing to say. It never occurred to her to take offense at Emily's words or to explain her own role as a courier, much less apologize for it. What was the use, with Emily in this mood? Zarah looked down at the untouched food on her own plate, a tepid *magret de canard* with bitter greens in a strange vinaigrette similar to the one she had eaten at Macalaster's dinner party. She remembered in minute detail what Mallory had told her in the park about Julian, Horace, and Lockwood.

She said, "Do you think Julian has something to fear from Mallory?"

"According to Julian, everybody has something to fear from Mallory," Emily replied, then changed the subject. "One thing's for sure: now that Lockwood's out of our life I'm going to have to find new ways to be jealous."

Her tone was merry. To Zarah, who had grown up in the perpetual winter of her mother's obsessive jealousy, there was nothing amusing about this emotion. "Jealous?" she said. "You?"

"You have no idea," Emily said. "I've been practically insane with it since the day I met Julian. Other women don't worry me. Julian doesn't seem to notice them. I think they all look alike to him—he told me so once. It's the other men you have to worry about in this town."

"Julian?"

"No, no, you don't understand. Sex has nothing to do with it. What men like Julian get in the Oval Office that they can't get at home. *They get to touch the king.* And they'll do anything to keep on doing it. But now at last it's over."

Zarah said, "You aren't worried about the future?"

Emily looked her in the eyes. "Not worried, terrified. They're guilty, you know, Julian and Horace both."

"I didn't know. I don't think I want to know."

"Take my word for it. They were kind enough to tell me everything, or what I thought was everything, almost as soon as they did it. I even carried messages for Horace like a good little spy and condoned the offense—after all, what's a homicide or a stolen election among the righteous—by sleeping with Julian whenever I could trap him into it because I wanted to be pregnant. That's why I'm so calm and healthy-minded now. I've had my guilt, thank you."

Zarah said, "Emily, I don't think you should be telling me these things."

"Why not? You're carrying messages, too. Welcome to the sisterhood."

Zarah, discomfited, averted her eyes. The waitress came. Emily went right on talking. In her merry social voice, she said, "I think the Hubbards have always been a little jealous of your father because he got to go to prison for committing virtuous crimes. Now they're going to be locked up like the heroes they are for saving the people from themselves. But not for long. It won't be solitary confinement in Manchuria, mind you, but it will be enough to make them feel good about themselves."

"Emily—"

Emily overrode the interruption with a dazzling smile. "It'll probably be quite comfortable—officers' quarters. And after Julian's done his time, he'll be mine, because no one else will want him ever again. *All* mine, maimed and blinded and helpless, like Rochester in the last chapter of *Jane Eyre*. Or was it Heathcliff in *Wuthering Heights*? I can never tell them apart."

Zarah said, "No one can."

Emily had been cutting into the medallion of a lamb chop; she paused, thought, frowned, smiled. "In books *or* life. Because they're all crazy." She finished cutting her meat, lifted a bright pink morsel on her fork and paused with it halfway to her mouth. "Like your friend Mallory."

Zarah, whose eyes were still averted, looked up, meaning to say, "If you want to ask me about Mallory, it's all right." But she had no chance to say it because Emily suddenly began to weep. She did so soundlessly, in a ladylike manner. Tears flowed down her cheeks, her nose ran, and she made no effort to hide these signs of heartbreak. "A word of advice," she said. "Don't get pregnant. I did, right in the middle of everything last fall, but the baby decided not to live. They say they lie in the womb and listen to every word the grown-ups say, so my child must have been the first to know. I think that was the basis of his decision not to be born."

7

The fact was that Julian's resignation was not quite the impulsive action he imagined it to be. All his life he had done nearly everything by calculation, little by impulse, and by the time he got up in the dark of morning and saw his fate being wrested from him on the network news, he realized that his real purpose had been to give Lockwood an opportunity to refuse his resignation and restore him to favor. As he lay beside Emily's sleeping form, he had even imagined the scene: the light flashing on his bedside phone, Lockwood's voice summoning him to the cluttered Lincoln sitting room, the reconciliation, the President's clumsy half-ashamed half-embrace, Polly's motherly smile of contentment that all was right between Frosty and Julian again, the looks on faces along the West Wing corridors as he resumed control of events and won the day as he had done so often in the past. Then he had turned on television and was confronted by reality.

As soon as he woke from the deep slumber into which he had fallen after making love to his wife, Julian made some calls. Not to the White

House—he knew they would not be returned—but to a member of the Apparatus whose lover was Jean McHenry's assistant. This young woman's duties included the keeping of the presidential log, a record of everyone the President saw or spoke to on the telephone. Julian might be out of power and, for all he or anyone else knew, out forever, but he still knew exactly whom to call, precisely what he wanted to know, and exactly what he wanted to do with the information.

He asked a question. Within an hour, a longer delay than should have been necessary, he had his answer. Julian's letter, which had been put into his safe unread by the night security detail, had been discovered by his secretary when she came in at six in the morning. She walked it down to Jean McHenry, who took it upstairs to Lockwood, who immediately summoned Blackstone into his presence. Using the President's own telephone, Blackstone had called Alfonso Olmedo C. in New York. The three-way conversation had been conducted over the speakerphone, with McHenry listening in over earphones and taking shorthand notes that her assistant later transcribed. The typist delivered a Xerox copy of this transcript to her lover over lunch in a cafeteria on Seventeenth Street, which accounted for the hour's delay, even though Julian's informant had read it to him over the restaurant pay phone while still eating his falafel with alfalfa sprouts in pita bread.

LOCKWOOD: He doesn't really mean this. We had words.

OLMEDO: No doubt you're right. But he has done what you would have had to do sooner or later—separated himself from you, the man he wronged, and from the presidency, the office he betrayed.

LOCKWOOD: So what's your advice?

OLMEDO: Accept this unsolicited gift. Announce it immediately to the press before he can call and change his mind.

LOCKWOOD: Should I call him?

OLMEDO: In my opinion that would be unwise, Mr. President.

LOCKWOOD: Remember, that boy and I spent a lot of years together.

OLMEDO: Exactly. Do not call, do not take his calls. Do not praise him or blame him to anyone except your wife. In the presence of others, say nothing about him whatsoever. Think of him as a suicide who took his secret to the grave with him.

LOCKWOOD: Jesus Christ, Alfonso! He could *be* one! All we need is a suicide.

OLMEDO: Mr. President, please listen to what I'm saying to you. You owe this man nothing except the trouble he has brought on you. Silence will be far more eloquent than any words you could speak.

LOCKWOOD: All right, goddamnit.

As soon as the telephone connection was broken, Blackstone had called in the press secretary and given him a photocopy of Julian's letter of resignation for immediate release to the press. "The President has no comment about this event," Blackstone had said. "And neither do you." If Lockwood interfered with these instructions in any way, McHenry's notes did not reveal it.

All this Julian confided later in the same day to Horace Hubbard and Senator Baxter T. Busby, known within the Shelley Society as Five-Four, a class number that made him the man who had tapped Horace, Five-Five, in the autumn of the latter's junior year at Yale. Actually Horace was the older by a couple of years, but he had left Yale as a sophomore in 1951 to fight in Korea as a Marine, and returned two years later after being discharged early because of wounds. The three Shelleyans were seated on facing stone benches in the Hubbard burial ground at the Harbor. Julian had flown up to this meeting in the Berkshires from Washington in his airplane, and Busby had driven up alone from New York City after lunch with a constituent. Horace was already there because he had been living in seclusion at the Hubbard country house with Rose MacKenzie ever since John L. S. McGraw had brought them back from aboard the *Caroline*. The benches on which they huddled were at the exact center of the burial ground, with headstones all around in concentric circles, one circle for each generation of Hubbards and Christophers. The same Christian names were carved into the various ranks of stones. In every generation born before the Second World War, when the two families had stopped intermarrying because they produced only boys—Zarah had been the first girl born into either branch in three generations—there was a Hubbard whose given name was Christopher and a Christopher whose first name was Hubbard.

Buzzer Busby listened intently to Julian's story. He was here first of all, of course, because he was a Shelleyan, but he was also, as chairman of the Judiciary Committee, going to be a key figure in Lockwood's trial before the Senate. In this sense he was the most relevant member of the Shelley Society now alive.

"Did you expect Lockwood to reject your resignation?" Busby asked.

The answer was yes, but Julian could not confess the inmost truth of this matter even to a fellow Shelleyan, so he replied, "Not really, though it wouldn't have surprised me. What I wanted to do was to force the issue—force him into making his choice."

"What choice was that, exactly?"

"Well, he's always had the choice between standing up for what was done in his name and in the name of what was right and necessary, and thereby keeping what he gained from it, or putting his fate and the fate of the Cause into the hands of his enemies."

"May I ask what that has to do with choosing to let you go?"

"I gave the orders to do what was necessary so he wouldn't have to give them, knowing it was what he wanted. If he repudiates me, he acknowledges that a wrong was done. He saves himself, and to hell with everything else."

" 'Everything else' being you and Horace?"

"We're not things. By everything else I mean the Definition and the Duty. If Lockwood goes down—and I now think he *will* go down hard—the things we believe in go with him."

"Ideas are not that easy to kill. Shelley had been dead for a hundred years when the Society was formed."

"Granted. But this could set the Cause back another hundred years."

Knowing this was true, Busby bit his lower lip with his perfect teeth and looked thoughtful. Horace had been silent throughout Julian's speech. In the vale below—the burial ground was situated on a knoll that looked down on the many roofs of the Harbor—Rose MacKenzie and Emily were walking back and forth on the long western porch of the main house, hand in hand and deep in conversation. Horace supposed the women had much to talk about that only the two of them could understand, attached as they were to him and his half brother.

Julian said, "Speak up, Horace. What do you make of this?"

Horace shrugged. "I thought I had a deal in prospect with Olmedo, but it's beginning to look like things aren't going to work out after all."

"What deal was that?" Busby asked.

Horace said, "I would confess all, take all the blame, sanitize the President over the election business, take my medicine, and everyone lives happily ever after."

"And what would you have got in return?"

As amiable as ever, Horace said, "Do you really want to know?"

"Yes."

"Very well. Immunity for Julian and Rose. No retaliation against FIS or its heirs or assigns."

"Olmedo agreed to that?"

"He said he'd try to work it out."

"With whom?"

"Lockwood, who said it was beyond his power. The Speaker of the House thought it was a fine idea. But Sam Clark put his hands over his ears like the Chinese monkey in the middle and looked horrified."

"Olmedo told you all this?"

"Yes. He's an honest broker."

Busby said, "But not a realist if he went to Clark with this. The Sam Clark I know will never agree to anything like that, not in a million years."

"You're sure about Clark?"

Busby waved a hand at the circles of headstones. "Did these people hump each other on cold nights for three hundred years in order to produce you and Julian?" They all smiled at the joke. Busby said, "Or is there a kicker you haven't mentioned, Horace?"

"Well, sort of," Horace said. He told Busby in clinical detail about what he called the last days of Ibn Awad. This took a long while, and by the time Horace had finished the story, Busby's open face was white with shock. In the moral order to which he subscribed, doing violence to a victim of imperialism was the worst of crimes, even if this particular one happened to be the richest oil sheik in the world. He stood up, walked among the sunken graves to the stone wall surrounding them, and looked off at the hemlock-blue hills in the near distance. The afternoon sun, which only a few minutes earlier had been unseasonably warm for Massachusetts in March, was now a heatless moonlike crescent going down through a bank of purple clouds.

Busby shivered. "Is what you've just told me true?" he asked. "Literally true?"

"What a question," Horace said.

"But to suborn a son to kill his own father."

" 'Suborn' is hardly the word," Julian said. There was a defensive tone in his voice; his brother's ethics were being questioned. "All Horace did was make it possible for Prince Talil to do what he wanted to do. He thought his father was an incurable psychopath who was a danger to humanity, and that he himself might go crazy later on, as a matter of inheritance. To my way of thinking he was a selfless hero. Suppose someone like Horace had persuaded Raul Castro to do away with Fidel after the Bay of Pigs? No Vietnam, no LBJ, no Nixon, no Watergate, no Reagan. All Horace did was make his operation work."

"With slightly different historical consequences," Busby said. "Lockwood *ordered* this to be done—have I got that right?"

"Yes," Julian said. "I was there. He said the word—reluctantly. Jack Philindros insisted on it. For once it wasn't a case of sparing a President's tender sensibilities."

Busby took a deep breath, releasing it into the suddenly chilly air as a stream of vapor. "Well," he said, "I guess we'd better start thinking in terms of alternatives."

Julian nodded. Though his mind was busy, Horace said nothing. He was watching the women down below; they were now enfolded in each other's arms. He heard Busby say, "Should someone be asked to get in touch with Six-Nine?" and then heard Julian reply, "No. Archimedes is going to need his credibility. He should be left out of this completely."

Busby said, "Completely?"

"Well," said Julian, "until the last ticktock."

8

From hints and rumors and the law of Washington probabilities, and because Attenborough's encounter with Slim had caused him to think in new ways about the Speaker's habits and methods, Ross Macalaster had cobbled together a column for the Wednesday editions predicting that Attenborough would attempt to bring the question of impeachment before the full House of Representatives, bypassing the Judiciary Committee and circumventing the news media in a scheme designed to contain the damage to his party that would otherwise result from weeks of saturation coverage of committee hearings. Macalaster's editors scoffed at this idea. How could any such maneuver be possible if they had not heard about it? But they published the article anyway.

Attenborough—who was, like most Washington figures, as keenly attuned to the op-ed pages of the *Post*, *Times*, and *Wall Street Journal* as were the wildebeest to ominous movements in the grasses of the African savannah—called him about his piece as soon as the first editions were delivered, just after dawn. Macalaster had not heard from him since he took him home from the emergency room three days before.

"I'm not confirming or denying a damn thing, Ross," Attenborough said. "But did I mention something about this at your house or maybe in the car the other night?"

In the background of Attenborough's call Macalaster could hear what sounded like running water, and he wondered if the Speaker was calling from his bathroom. He replied, "No, Mr. Speaker, not a word. It's just a think piece, all guesswork and rumors."

"Always said you were a smart son of a gun. No point in asking you which rumors, I suppose?"

Macalaster replied, "All I can tell you is that you yourself are completely innocent."

"Glad to know that. But there's got to be a guilty son of a bitch somewhere." High officials of the government, from the President on down, were always trying to catch the leakers in their entourage, for the loose tongues of underlings were the curse of power. Few succeeded in unmasking the guilty, who were assiduously protected by journalists for the sake of the treacheries they might commit in the future. "Well, the hell with it, it's all in a day's work," Attenborough said. He coughed spasmodically, then continued: "That was one hell of a party you gave the other night. Interesting bunch. Is our new Chief Justice an old friend of yours?"

The question interested Macalaster. "I've known him for a long time," he said cautiously.

"Fellow Yalies?"

"I didn't go to Yale. Why?"

"Just wondered. He's a walking Old Blue alumni reunion and storefront lawyer to the world terrorist movement rolled up in one. I don't think we've ever had a Chief Justice who was a whole hell of a lot like Mr. Hammett."

"I don't think so, either, Mr. Speaker."

"You don't? That's mighty interesting . . . and Ross?"

"Yes, sir?"

"Thanks for being a good Samaritan when I hurt my hand the other night. You and that good-looking girl of yours went way above and beyond the call of duty to get me patched up like you did, and I won't forget it."

"She's not my girl."

"She's not? Sorry to hear that for your sake. Must have ruined her dress, bleeding like I was. Not to mention your fine oriental rug. Send me the bills."

"Forget it."

Attenborough chuckled. "Easier said than done. There's a fair amount of talk around town about me and that crazy female Hammett brought to the party. Any idea where the talk's coming from?"

Though it had not yet broken into print or broadcast, the story of Attenborough's brutish grope of a feminist ecolawyer, so far unidentified, had spread through Washington.

"No, not for sure," Macalaster replied.

"You had any calls?"

"Half a dozen maybe. All from reporters."

"What'd you tell 'em?"

"That it was a social occasion, and therefore off the record. But they all had the details already. They were just looking for confirmation."

"*All* the details?"

"Not the name of the hospital."

"Anybody know that detail except the three of us?"

"Not from me. Or Zarah."

Attenborough said, "I didn't think so. The ones calling me up are mostly the kind of folks who admire the hell out of Hammett."

"He's your suspect?"

"Nobody else was there."

"Except Slim."

"Except who?"

"Your dinner partner."

"Well, yeah, she was there, but she said she was from Massachusetts." Attenborough pronounced the name of this commonwealth "Mas-sa*too*setts."

"Connecticut," Macalaster said.

"Well, one of those states up there in New England." To Attenborough's mind, this eliminated Slim as the culprit. She knew no one in town, therefore she did not exist for the media. Though he was not prepared to reinforce Attenborough's suspicions, Macalaster knew that no one except Archimedes Hammett was likely to be the source of the stories. All the reporters who had called Macalaster were people who covered the Cause and identified with it in their minds and hearts. No one else at the dinner party had any motive to talk, and certainly none had Hammett's credibility, his ready and willing network of gossips, or the ruthlessness to merchandise the story in the first place. What Hammett's purposes might be in setting up this foolish old drunk, Macalaster could not guess, apart from his compulsive need to expose members of the Establishment as being just as vile and corrupt as the system that produced them.

Clearly Attenborough had figured out who his nemesis was, and this was the real reason for his phone call. "Well, the hell with it," he said. "You thank Miss Christopher for me, Ross. *She's* got Hammett's number—wish that girl from Massatoosetts hadn't interrupted her with all that racket before she really got his goat about Percy Bysshe Shelley."

"You don't trust Hammett?"

"Never said that. For all I know he's a fine American you could trust with your wallet and your daughter—especially your daughter, from all I hear. But then, what does anybody really know about the son of a bitch except that he's a friend of any poor suffering underdog that knows how to make a bomb out of fertilizer and diesel oil?"

Macalaster said, "Mr. Speaker, are you trying to tell me something?"

"Just passing the time of day, Ross. Well, keep on hound-doggin'. The

Lord loves a hound dog—Book of Matthew, chapter the seventh, verse the seventh."

"I don't quite recall that one off the top of my head, Mr. Speaker."

"Look it up," said Attenborough.

After they said goodbye, Macalaster got down the Bible and looked up the verse. It was one of the most famous passages in the New Testament: " 'Ask, and it will be given you; seek, and you will find; knock, and it will be opened to you.' "

What was Attenborough up to? Macalaster decided to go see him before the business day began. After dressing himself in the clothes he had worn the day before, skipping a shower and breakfast, leaving a note and a twenty-dollar bill for Manal on the refrigerator door, he shaved with an electric razor while driving through still-deserted downtown streets to Capitol Hill.

9

At their regular Odd Wednesday breakfast in the Speaker's office, Sam Clark remarked on Attenborough's sickly appearance. "Tucker, you're looking a little peaked."

"My malaria's come back on me again," Attenborough said.

The Speaker's voice was hollow. Because of Dr. Chin's lecture about cirrhosis of the liver, he had consumed no alcohol for five full days. His last drink had been the pint or so of vodka he had sneaked at Macalaster's house before the disaster on Saturday night. He been unable to eat anything since then except for a little milk—drunk through a straw, out of the carton, so that he couldn't see the milk. When he looked at food since he stopped drinking, it moved: a fried egg would slither across the china like a disembodied eye in a Terrytoon, or if it was something brown, like a steak, it steamed like feces. He didn't know what was the matter with his mind, but he decided he'd better lay off eating until this problem passed. His one visible hand—he hid the injured one on his lap—shook so badly that he could not lift his coffee cup without causing it to rattle and spill.

Clark noted these signs of acute alcoholism without surprise. He had seen Attenborough's malaria recur many times before. "Looks to me like it's worse, and coming back more often," he said. "Maybe you ought to see a doctor."

"No point in it," Attenborough said. "When you get bit by a bad mosquito, you stay bit. Anyway, I got no time to spare for doctoring. We're going to impeachment proceedings as soon as I can get it done."

"How soon?"

"Next Monday. I'll announce it Thursday."

"Tomorrow? That's quick."

"Quick is the whole idea. Ross Macalaster has already figured out the plan. The rest of the media will copy him. Got to limit this damn thing and get it over with."

"How are you going to do that, Tucker?"

Attenborough was feeling shaky, but he answered in his usual confident way. "By going back to the Andrew Johnson precedent. A resolution to impeach was introduced on Washington's Birthday in 1868. The House took one day to think about it, then adopted the resolution two days later, and eleven articles of impeachment within a week or so."

"What about the Judiciary Committee? They took months with Nixon."

"And came up empty. I'm cutting 'em out this time. In the Johnson case the Committee on Reconstruction did the work. This time it'll be a Committee of Managers, with Bob Laval as chairman and six other lawyers tried and true."

Laval was chairman of the House Judiciary Committee, a flamboyant Louisianan famous for his vanity and changeable opinions. (As Lockwood had put it years before, "Bob Laval spelled backwards is Bob Laval.") Clark said, "Laval accepts this?"

"Haven't told him yet, but he'll see the advantages," Attenborough said. "Gives him the limelight and leaves the other forty lawyers on his committee in outer darkness. If we stick to the point and keep the issue simple, we can do it in two sessions, just like they did in 1868."

"How long after that did it go to the Senate in the Johnson case?"

Attenborough had every pertinent fact memorized, but it took him a moment to find the date in his memory. Something was wrong here. "The Senate trial began March thirtieth," he said after a short hesitation. "I hope you can do it quicker this time. You'll have the whole package by the middle of next week."

Clark whistled. "I don't know if the Senate can move that fast."

"The Senate's not my problem, but it'll move fast if you do the same as I'm doing: simplify. What we've both got to do is seize the initiative, cut down on the bullshit, and get this damn thing over with before the jackasses on both sides of the aisle run away with it. We've got to get the country back to normal, Sam. *Got* to. Can't go on much longer with things the way they are."

"Even if that means making Franklin Mallory President?"

"That doesn't necessarily have to happen, but even if it does, it's better than burning down the barn to get the rattlesnake out of the haymow."

Attenborough coughed, a deep phlegmy sound, and automatically covered his mouth with his bandaged hand. Clark had not seen the bandages before; when he had arrived on the stroke of seven, Attenborough was already seated at the table with his hand in his lap.

Clark said, "What happened to your hand?"

"Cut it on a piece of broken glass," Attenborough replied. "How're your ham and eggs? That's genuine Virginia ham, not that damn gummy store-bought crap, given to me by the mountain farmer down on the Tennessee line that cured it, a good Democrat."

"You can tell the difference," Clark said. "What about Ibn Awad?"

Attenborough coughed again, then trembled violently, as if having a racking malarial chill. In his new, strangled voice, he said, "Did you say 'Ibn Awad'?" Clark nodded. Attenborough said, "That's funny. The other day, over at my house with those two lawyers Frosty sent over, I got the impression you didn't want to talk about him."

"That was then, and we weren't all by ourselves. This is now and it's just you and me. Tucker, I won't be party to what I think you're talking about."

"Then you don't know what I'm talking about, Sam. I'm talking about the destruction of our party. I'm talking about the *end*. If the Lockwood liberals go down in flames, the rest of us go with them. We can lose it—I mean *all* of it. We'll go the way of the Whigs and the Wobblies. We're damn near there already, thanks to the Hubbards and Hammetts and Busbys of this world."

"That, and screwing the law."

"Sam, I've never laid a finger on the law, and I ain't going to start now. But that Olmedo fellow told us what we both already knew: Lockwood is innocent of the charge of stealing the election."

"That doesn't mean it wasn't stolen."

"That's a whole different question, and we can argue about it after the impeachment trial is over. This is a one-question case, just like every other case: Did one Bedford Forrest Lockwood, President of the United States and reincarnation of the original rail-splitter, personally have anything to do with stealing the election that put him back in the White House? The answer is no. Establish that and we're all right."

"Maybe."

"No maybe about it."

"What about the succession?"

"That's in the hands of the Lord."

"And you're first in line."

Attenborough laughed loudly. "That's pretty damn funny." He opened his mouth to quote a verse from the Bible, but once again could not remember the words immediately. "Damn!" he said. "What the hell *is* this?"

Clark was staring at him; Attenborough realized that his mouth had been ajar for some time. For the blinking of an eye, Clark's face had turned into Lockwood's; Attenborough ignored this transformation, though he found it peculiar. He said, "That's what Lockwood keeps saying, that I'm setting myself up to take his job, but what he knows about that particular subject begins with Z." His laugh turned into another coughing fit. When it subsided, he said, "Sam, you see what I'm trying to do."

"Tucker, to be honest, I'm not sure I do."

"Jesus Christ, Sam, open your eyes! I'm railroading this like I am because I don't want Lockwood charged with a crime he's *guilty* of, like killing an Ay-rab."

"There's no proof that he's guilty of any crime."

"Not yet."

"But he went on television last fall and told the country the whole story."

"That's not what Lockwood's slick big-time New York lawyer thinks. He thinks Frosty left something out. And we know that's sure as hell not what Franklin Mallory thinks. He probably *knows* what Frosty left out. And you can be damn sure that's not what Lockwood thinks, or he wouldn't be skulking inside the White House like he is, *worrying* about what he left out. So we've got to get this damn thing wrapped up. And like I said, quick."

Clark started to reply, but stopped when he saw a look of horror and fear come over Attenborough's saffron face. Suddenly, shouting a wordless warning, the Speaker leaped to his feet, overturning the folding table on which their breakfast had been laid. Coffee flew from the cups, crockery crashed to the floor.

"Watch out, Sam!" Attenborough cried. "It's the same son of a bitch that killed Mallory's girl!"

Clark turned around. Albert Tyler (Lockwood had always called him Ablert), an aged black waiter and boyhood friend of Attenborough's from West Texas who had worked in the House for thirty years, had come into the room on the stroke of 8:57 A.M., just as he always did, to let the Majority Leader and the Speaker know by his presence that the breakfast was three minutes from being over in case they had lost track of time.

Ross Macalaster was standing right behind Albert in the doorway. "That's him, the one behind Albert!" Attenborough cried, pointing at Macalaster, who held a cellular phone in his hand.

"He's got a gun!" Attenborough shouted, staggering backward with bandaged hand upraised.

Albert, advancing into the room, said, "Now, now, Mr. Speaker." To Macalaster he said, "Put the phone away. Go on out now. Everything going to be all right."

Clark, his suit spattered with the remains of the breakfast, stood where he was, jaw dropping. Albert shot him a look of warning.

"That was a good one, Mr. Speaker," Albert said. "But look what you done to the Majority Leader's brand-new pin-striped suit."

Attenborough was fumbling with the telephone. Somehow he struck his injured hand and howled in pain.

Albert put his body between the Speaker and his visitors. He said, "Mr. Macalaster, Mr. Majority Leader, I think you both ought to withdraw now. Shall I send over and get you a different suit, Senator?"

Clark's eyes were fixed on Attenborough. Without moving them he shook his head. Albert handed him a clean napkin. Whispering, he said, "Go on now; I'll look after him."

Attenborough, eyes wide with alarm, was still fumbling with the telephone. Clark said, "What's the matter with him?"

"It's his malaria, Senator."

"It's the D.T.'s. You'd better get him to a hospital."

"He'd never go," Albert said. "This'll pass. You go on. And Mr. Macalaster, I'm asking you nicely for the last time. You've got no call to be here. This is a private moment."

Macalaster nodded. He and Clark left. After locking the door behind them Albert said, "The man is gone now, Mr. Speaker. They took him away."

Attenborough had subsided into the tall-backed chair behind his imposing mahogany desk, but he was still breathing heavily and sweating, and his eyes were wild.

"What you need, Mr. Speaker, is a nice glass of spring water," Albert said. "You just sit there and I'll get you some out of the place where we keep it."

Attenborough nodded dully. "Appreciate it, Albert."

Albert disappeared into the private bathroom. Attenborough heard the distinctive hollow clunk of the porcelain cover being removed from the toilet tank, then the rattle of an ice cube tray being emptied into the sink. Homely noises. He relaxed a little as he waited. And when the tall clinking glass of hundred-proof vodka was put into his hand, he suddenly remembered the Bible verse that had escaped him earlier and knew he was going to be all right. He always was when his brain was working right. He drank deeply, using both hands to lift the glass. Then he said in the powerful voice that the alcohol had miraculously restored to him, " 'Ye defiled my land, and made mine heritage an abomination.' Book of Jeremiah, Albert, chapter the second, verse the seventh."

"Yes, sir, Mr. Speaker," said Albert, righting the overturned table and surveying the broken dishes, the cold fried eggs, and the half-eaten slices of buttered toast scattered over the Great Seal of the United States that was woven into the bright blue carpet. "Mighty fine passage."

10

Apart from calling Albert later in the day to inquire about Attenborough's condition ("He's just fine now; the fever takes him real sudden like that, but then it goes away just as quick"), Macalaster did nothing with what he had observed in Attenborough's office. He had lived with a drunk for twenty years and he understood that what he had observed was an episode of delirium tremens. Like other reporters in town, he had known for a long time that Attenborough was drinking himself to death, but he had never mentioned this in print and neither had any other journalist. The fact was irrelevant, not worth publishing. Besides, Attenborough was a unique and incorruptible source, and who knew what his successor might be? He had left a message with Albert, the most reliable back-channel of communication with Attenborough, asking for an appointment at the earliest possible moment. Attenborough had not yet called back, but Macalaster knew that he would, sooner or later.

On Manal's advice—the fathers of her schoolfriends were beginning to have heart attacks and she worried continually about his health—and because his attraction to Zarah Christopher had made him conscious of his own physical appearance for the first time in years, Macalaster had begun a regimen of twice-weekly exercise. He chose weight lifting because he could not bear the thought of running through the streets or bicycling along the C&O Canal dressed in a thousand dollars' worth of costuming. To join that crowd would be a betrayal of his father, his grandfather, and every other Macalaster before them who had broken a sweat every day of their lives not for the sake of fashion but in order to put bread on the table.

Hard labor in the open air had shortened their lives. Maybe, Macalaster thought, those asshole runners will die young too.

On the morning after Attenborough's outbreak of paranoia, Macalaster watched *Newsdown with Patrick Graham* on a snowy television screen suspended from the ceiling of ye gods, a weight-lifting establishment on upper Wisconsin Avenue. A blond interviewer named Morgan Pike was putting hostile questions to Attenborough. Pike had been hired twenty-five years before for her looks, and even at fifty, though she hid her corrugated neck from the remorseless eye of the camera with a designer scarf, she retained the flowing hair, long coltish legs, and gamine style of a pre-Movement coed. She was, however, a committed person, solemn in thought and manner.

On-screen, Attenborough was enjoying himself. Earlier that morning, at a sunrise news conference, an innovation unappreciated by sleepy-eyed Capitol Hill reporters used to getting to work at ten, he had announced, as he had informed Sam Clark he would, that the House would begin hearings on the impeachment of President Lockwood the following day.

Frowning suspiciously, Morgan Pike said, "Mr. Speaker, why are you making such a drama out of this process?"

"Well, it's a pretty dramatic situation when the results of a presidential election are challenged," Attenborough said.

He moved closer to the lissome Pike, or tried to, but radiating unreceptivity, she shifted positions, extending her arm at full length to hold the microphone to his lips in order to keep him at a safe distance. Pumping iron, Macalaster smiled sardonically. Clearly, perky Morgan Pike, like most of the rest of the Washington press corps, had heard about Attenborough's encounter with Slim and was wigwagging her knowledge to others in the know.

Morgan frowned slightly as her anchorman, Patrick Graham, fed her a new question through her earpiece. "But why are you acting with so little warning?" she demanded. "Why have you bypassed the Judiciary Committee? Why are you moving so fast?"

Attenborough, who not only knew where these hard questions were really coming from but also seemed to understand what her skittishness signified, and to be amused by it, replied, "That's a whole lot of questions, but there's just one answer. The American people want to know for absolute certain who they really elected President, and we can't go on until we have the right answer to that fundamental question."

Pike did not hear the Speaker's words because she was busy listening to the next question, which Patrick Graham, back in the studio, was booming into her ear. Now she repeated it: "Some say you're ramming this thing through the House without proper notice or debate because the President has something to hide and you know it."

Why was Patrick Graham sending this signal? What was in the wind? Attenborough shook his head in disbelief. "Morgan, Morgan. I'm surprised at you. That dog won't hunt." He lifted a hand as if to lay it on the interviewer's shoulder as a way of reassuring her that he did not hold the question against her personally. Pike flinched, taking a brisk backward step, and compressed her lips into a parody of a smile.

"There you have it, Patrick—open deliberations, openly arrived at, and as they say down Texas way, a dog that won't hunt. This is Morgan Pike on Capitol Hill."

Macalaster finished his workout, mentally composing sentences for his next column as he did so. At this time of day most of the customers at ye gods were women. He wondered if any of them had chosen this establishment on the basis of its name. If so, they would be disappointed in the figure he cut in his shorts and T-shirt. Some were lifting heavier weights than he was. Most were extremely lean, but none seemed to be in the least muscular. A trainer was going from customer to customer with a pair of calipers and a clipboard, measuring body-fat percentages in a pinch of skin: in bodybuilding theory, the more you worked out, the more muscular, and therefore the less fatty, you became. He measured Macalaster's body fat and marked it down in sober professional silence.

"How am I doing?" Macalaster asked.

"We'll begin to see more progress soon." The trainer, nearly all muscle himself, smiled encouragingly. "Anybody can do it," he said.

"Except the women," Macalaster said. "They don't seem to get muscles. Any reason for that? Do they lift in a different way, or what?"

"Women don't get muscles unless they take steroids," the trainer said.

"And if they *do* take steroids?"

"Then they get biceps, just like us." He lowered his voice, imparting secrets. "They also get bitchy. Even men get aggressive when they take steroids, so women usually stay away from them. Besides, their hair can fall out."

"Does it last in women?"

"The bitchiness?" The trainer rolled his eyes.

"The muscles."

"Not if they go off steroids. A woman can get a hell of a set of muscles in just a few months if she works at it, taking anabolics and working out with the right program. But when she stops, she goes back to normal real quick."

"How quick?"

"A month or two."

"That fast?" Macalaster was surprised.

The trainer snapped his fingers. "Nature calls and they're all girl again."

More interested in the political metaphors suggested by what the trainer had told him than in real muscular women, Macalaster was still thinking about the conversation as he walked across the parking lot after finishing his workout. As he got out his car keys, a scrawny, balding, middle-aged male in brand-new Harvard sweats bumped into him at jogging speed. It was a hard collision, sharp knees and elbows, and it knocked off his glasses and caused him to stagger. The runner, panting breathlessly as if unable to speak, steadied Macalaster, shaking his head and slapping him on the shoulder in mute apology and grinning with deliberate foolishness. Then he ran off, taking long, fluid strides on his corded legs. The whole encounter had lasted no more than five seconds.

It wasn't until Macalaster unlocked the door of his Jaguar and saw himself reflected in the smoked glass of the window that he realized that a small plastic bag was dangling from the lapel of the tweed jacket he was wearing. It was tied to a plastic fishing line. He removed it with difficulty, tearing a hole in his jacket. Cursing—the jacket was almost new—he saw that the bag had been attached to his clothing with the tiny barbed hook of a yellow-and-red trout fly. He looked inside. The bag contained a Radio Shack sixty-minute minitape resting inside its tiny transparent box.

Obviously the runner had been waiting for him and had stalked him for the purpose of hooking this package to the fabric of his jacket. It was crazy. Macalaster knew that no one who communicated with him in this demented way could be trusted. Nevertheless, he got into the car, and after fumbling one of the several miniature tape recorders he owned out of the glove compartment, listened to the tape.

It was a recording of a conversation, taped four years before, in the first months of the Lockwood administration, between Jack Philindros and Lockwood, in which the President, in his own unmistakable voice, ordered Philindros, as head of the Foreign Intelligence Service, to assassinate Ibn Awad.

Macalaster's heart pounded. He locked the doors of his car and listened to the tape a second time. Although he knew that technology could produce forgeries, knew that men who specialized in such forgeries were involved in this case, and knew that he lived in a place and time in which it was unwise to trust anything or anybody, he had little doubt that the tape was genuine. He knew the voices and he knew all the other things that he knew. He was in possession of facts that could bring down another

President who was loved by the left. He would never be forgiven. He had no choice but to pursue this matter, to question the owners of the voices, to try to confirm what was on the tape or disprove it. Yet he also knew with complete certainty that in the end it would be impossible to do either. He had not been present at the event in question, and those who had been there would remember the details in different ways. Or they would lie. When all was said and done, he would have to rely, as he always had, as all outsiders like himself must always do, on what people told him, and on how willing he was to believe what they said. He was not in the business of establishing truth, or even of seeking it. It was his job to report what others said, what others thought had happened, what others were prepared to admit. All he had to do was satisfy the world that they had said what they had said, not that they had spoken the truth. In his business attribution was reality, even if the witnesses were anonymous.

Macalaster stopped thinking and turned the ignition key. He had parked the car in front of Julian Hubbard's house before he realized in any conscious way that he had chosen it as his destination.

11

Julian was delighted to see him. "Ross!" he cried on opening the door. He held a rumpled copy of *The Washington Post* in his hand, half-moon reading glasses dangling from a shoestring around his neck. "What a surprise! Come in, sit ye down. Do you have to go to the bathroom?"

Julian was famous for this earthy question. He asked it of everyone who walked through his door, male and female, young and old, mighty or humble.

Macalaster said, "No. Can we talk?"

Julian sensed his troubled mood immediately and acknowledged it with one of his smiles. "Let's go downstairs," he said. "Emily's still asleep."

In his basement office, Julian gave Macalaster his desk chair, the only one in the room, and sat down on his writing table. Macalaster handed him the tape recorder, earplug dangling. Julian lifted his heavy eyebrows in inquiry: Was he supposed to listen? Macalaster nodded; Julian fitted the plug into his ear, put on his reading glasses so he could see which button to push, and started the tape. He listened to the end, his face a complete blank, then removed the earplug and handed the machine back. He did not ask how Macalaster had acquired the tape, nor did Macalaster volunteer an explanation. Under Washington rules, both the question and the revelation were forbidden.

As a young reporter Macalaster had learned to ask the most important question first, because it often eliminated the need to ask any others. You either shocked the truth out of the source or got thrown out. In either case you knew you had a story. Knowing this, Julian waited for what he knew would come next. At last Macalaster said, "Is that conversation genuine?" He did not specify that they were on deep background. Julian was always on deep background with everybody; in his ascendancy, everyone had talked about him, but no one had ever quoted him by name. He had been the "informed source" of hundreds of news stories, always behind the scenes, never out in front of the President.

Julian never made the mistake of lying to a reporter. He nodded. Nodding again at the tape recorder in Macalaster's hand, he asked, "Is that thing on?"

"No, of course not."

"Good. Fire when ready."

Macalaster said, "You were present?"

"As you heard. Yes."

"Lockwood meant what he seems to mean? Nothing is missing, there's been no editing that leaves out words or understandings that might give his instructions a different meaning or interpretation?"

"The essentials are there."

"Can you be a little more forthcoming, Julian?"

"There's not much to be forthcoming about. It had all been discussed beforehand. The President called Philindros to Live Oaks for the express purpose of deciding what to do about Ibn Awad. Philindros told him what the FIS knew or suspected. Lockwood made his decision. As you heard, he had trouble putting it into words, but Philindros insisted."

"He had trouble because he didn't really want to do it and Philindros did, or what?"

"Oh, no, it was the other way around. Jack hated the idea. Lockwood saw it as a necessity of state."

"How did you feel about it?"

"My feelings were, and are, irrelevant. The President had weighed the intelligence and listened to the arguments. He had been presented with options. He had made a finding and issued an instruction. It was the first agonizing decision of his administration, and new as we were, I think we were all aware at the time of what it meant."

"In what terms?"

"In terms of the fate of the world and Lockwood's hope of Heaven. Also our own hopes thereof, Jack's and mine."

"And it was your job to support this decision, no matter what?"

Julian smiled for the first time, charmingly. "I could have resigned. That's what you do if you can't support the policy. But I didn't, did I?"

"At least not right away."

"Whenever, that wasn't the reason."

Silence returned. Although rush-hour traffic moaned on Wisconsin Avenue only a block or two away, no sound penetrated the basement; it was as quiet as a broadcasting studio, and the voices of the two men were flat and unnaturally clear.

Macalaster said, "Julian, you realize what this means?"

"You mean do I realize how it will appear? Oh, yes. But I've been through the whole thing before."

"What do you mean, you've been through it before?"

"Patrick Graham had a copy of this same tape last fall, when he broke the Ibn Awad story. He decided in the end that making it public wasn't a good thing to do."

"Why was that?"

Julian said, "Oh, I think it had something to do with being able to live with himself afterward."

"Patrick's an expert on that, all right."

Julian smiled again. "Aren't we all?" He slid off the writing table, on which he had been balanced on one haunch, and crouched in front of a large old-fashioned green safe. While he twisted the combination dial, Macalaster, a professional collector of details, read the maker's name, *Monroe T. Grossnickel, Dalton, Massachusetts, Est. 1894*, written on the door in gilt script.

The bolt clicked loudly and Julian swung open the door. The safe was filled with books bound in graduated shades of tan goatskin, darker hues at the top, lighter ones at the bottom. He said, "Do you know the exact date of the event in question?"

"You mean what's on the tape?"

"Yes, what's on the tape."

"Yes, I do."

Julian raised a hand before Macalaster could say it aloud. He stood up with a volume in his hand, and dropped it on the writing table in front of him. "Then you'll have no trouble finding the place in this." He closed the door of the safe, turned the handle that shot the bolt, spun the dial, and switched on the green-shaded desk lamp. "I'm going birding along the canal," he said. "When you're finished, just leave things as they are, if you don't mind, and find your own way out."

When the door at the top of the stairs clicked shut behind Julian, Macalaster opened the leatherbound book. The date was stamped in gold on the spine. It was Julian's diary for the first year of the Lockwood administration and contained, in minute detail, in Julian's clear, almost calligraphic handwriting, the entire story of the assassination of Ibn Awad. No dossier of top secret documents from the innermost archives of the White House could have been half so revealing because this was a confession, beautifully expressed, of a man who knew everything. As he read it, Macalaster felt that he was looking into another life through a one-way glass. He did not understand why Julian was letting him do this, but he copied the whole story, which was scattered throughout the volume, into the notebooks he always carried in his pockets. He read none of the passages in between; he understood just how far the limits of Julian's permission ran. When he had finished, he closed the diary and tried unsuccessfully to wipe off the salt stains left on the binding by his sweaty hands.

12

Macalaster was unable to get through to Lockwood—now that Julian had resigned, he did not know whom to go through—so he called Jack Philindros. He had no hope that Philindros would tell him anything of his own knowledge or volition. Philindros did not talk to members of the press; neither did anyone else at FIS who wanted to go on working there. Philindros's first official act as director had been to abolish the public affairs office established after the previous American intelligence service had been deconstructed by publicity. A secret intelligence service, he declared, had no public affairs; therefore it had no reason to traffic with journalists.

Philindros was now in the final months of his ten-year term as the first director of the Foreign Intelligence Service, and as far as anyone knew, he had never in all that time talked to a member of the news media on or off the record. When he encountered such people in social situations he either kept silent, as he had in Macalaster's presence at Mallory's dinner party, or talked about fly fishing; he and Associate Justice Bobby M. Poole went to a mosquito-infested backwoods fishing camp in Labrador every spring to catch trout and salmon, which they released immediately after netting. The FIS switchboard and Philindros's secretaries automatically hung up on journalists. Paradoxically, this inaccessibility had made Philindros popular with the press. Macalaster got through to him because he had found the number of his secure telephone in Julian's diary. It had been entered in block letters at the top of a page, evidently as a reminder, but perhaps, Macalaster thought, as a convenience to himself. In any case, he dialed the number.

It took Philindros a moment to recover from the surprise of picking up the receiver and hearing Macalaster's voice on his ultraprivate line.

"Ah, Ross Macalaster," he said in a faint but civil murmur, "we met not long ago."

Macalaster could barely make out the words. As in person and on the fatal tape recording, Philindros was virtually inaudible.

Macalaster said, "I'd like to meet again. I think we should talk."

"Meet?" Philindros said. "Talk? For what purpose?"

"To discuss a certain conversation between you and the President."

"Goodbye."

The dial tone replaced Philindros's whisper. Macalaster rang back at once. He said, "Let me tell you which conversation."

"They're all the same. Privileged."

"This one's different. Don't hang up until you hear this."

Macalaster played the first two or three sentences of the tape recorder into the mouthpiece. The line remained open. He said, "Mr. Director, will you talk to me about this?"

"No," Philindros said. "And please don't call this number again."

"Then I'm going to have to go ahead without you."

"That's up to you."

"You'll be able to read what I write in tomorrow's paper. In the meantime you should understand that I've been unable to get through to the President to tell him what I know and what I have in my possession and to give him the opportunity of commenting. If you want to mention this to him, you're free to do so."

This time Philindros hung up for good.

13

Macalaster was in his attic office, writing, when the front doorbell rang insistently. He ignored it. A moment later his telephone rang. When he picked it up he heard Lucy's cheery midwestern voice.

"Wiggins and I are out front," she said. "President Mallory would like you to come to him."

Stooping, Macalaster peered through the round window and saw one of Mallory's blue-black automobiles idling at the curb. Lucy stood beside it, holding a cellular phone to her ear. He was surprised by this visit. In spite of all that had been happening, he had not heard from Mallory for a long time, and his calls to him that morning had not been returned.

Macalaster said, "Now?"

"If that's in any way possible, he'd appreciate it."

"It's not possible, really. I'm on deadline."

"He realizes that this is short notice. He apologizes. But he said to tell you that Jack Philindros called him about your call, just in case you wondered what this was about."

"I see. Let me ask you this: Does he want to tell *me* something in relation to the information Jack presumably gave him, or does he want me to tell *him* something?"

"I don't know the answer to that question," Lucy said.

On the way to Great Falls, Macalaster worked on his column on a miniature word processor, and by the time they arrived at the Norman manor house—Wiggins had taken the parkway today, so the trip lasted about forty minutes—Macalaster had finished a rough draft.

Mallory wasted no time on pleasantries. "I've been told you have a story."

"I've just been writing it. You're welcome to read what I have and make comments."

Mallory's voice was cold. "No, thank you. Are you actually going to publish these allegations?"

"I'll publish what I believe to be fact."

"When will it appear?"

"Tomorrow."

"You realize the House begins impeachment hearings tomorrow."

"What a coincidence."

Mallory's eyes turned colder. "What do you mean by that, exactly?"

"Well, it occurred to me that I might be indebted to you for the delivery of this information."

"Then you're making a foolish mistake."

"If that's so, what is this meeting for? Do you want to listen to the tape?"

"I already have a copy, thank you."

"You do?" Macalaster, in whose presence secrets had been blurted out many times before by persons who knew better, was startled nevertheless at this revelation. He said, "What are you telling me?"

"This," Mallory said. "And I want you to understand it clearly. I had absolutely nothing to do with that tape's coming into your possession. And I have nothing to gain from its publication. What makes you so confident that it's completely genuine?"

Macalaster said, "You know I can't tell you that. If you have the tape, why haven't you released it?"

"I told you I have nothing to gain from that."

"Really? It's going to mean the end of Lockwood."

"I'm glad you understand what you're doing. But it may not stop with Lockwood. You might consider that before you leap into this."

Macalaster did not know what to make of Mallory's behavior. "Are you asking me to cover this up?"

"Don't be foolish. But I don't think you realize what the real consequences of publishing this story will be."

"I have an idea. It will cause a donnybrook. But whatever happens or doesn't happen has nothing to do with me. I wasn't in on the plot. So I don't have to search my soul."

"No, I guess not. But maybe you should ask yourself the obvious question about all this."

" 'The obvious question'?" There was an edge of contempt in Macalaster's voice over Mallory's choice of words; for his own reasons he was as scornful of patriotic cant as Julian Hubbard. "What obvious question?"

"Who profits?" Mallory replied.

14

During the design stage of Universal Energy's hyperfrequency communications satellites, O. N. Laster had instructed the engineers to leave a few electronic deaf spots on the face of the earth so that he could escape every now and then from telephones and computers. One of these hushed and unpeopled places was the Kunlun Plateau of northern Tibet, where he had gone to stalk a snow leopard the weekend before the Ibn Awad tape was delivered to Ross Macalaster in Washington. The snow leopard was one of the rarest animals on earth, and possibly the most difficult of all trophy animals to sight because of its nocturnal nature and acute senses. Laster wasn't interested in actually killing this rare beast. He conducted a sporting stalk, approaching within rifle range of the animal, fixing its image in the ectoplasmic field of the night scope, placing the luminous dot of the laser beam sighting device on a vital organ, and snapping the firing pin on an empty chamber. So acute was the cat's hearing that even this tiny sound, carrying eight hundred meters across a craggy abyss, was enough to cause it to vaporize, as it seemed to the supremely happy hunter, into the thin, frigid mountain air.

Even though a Tibetan guide on retainer had spotted the leopard in advance, and Laster had landed within a few miles of its lair in a short-takeoff-and-landing aircraft that had been prepositioned in Lhasa, the sporting stalk had required three full nights, so Mallory was unable to reach him until well into the evening of the day he talked to Macalaster. He finally got Laster on the phone in his Gulfstream somewhere over western China.

Mallory's digitalized voice said, "I'm calling because I have a question for you. Did you have anything to do with the delivery of a certain tape recording to Ross Macalaster?"

"He has the tape—*the* tape?"

"He does. And he's going to print it in two hundred newspapers tomorrow morning."

"Amazing. All I have to say is God bless freedom of the press."

"That's not an answer to my question."

"Have you asked him the same question?"

"Of course not. But he doesn't have a clue."

"Are you telling me he really doesn't know where he got the thing?"

"I imagine he knows *where*. But not who gave it to him."

"It wasn't you?"

"In spite of much well-meant advice to the contrary," Mallory said, "no, it wasn't."

"Amazing." Laster laughed. "The answer is no, it wasn't me or anyone I know. If it had been me, trust me, he'd be in no doubt about the matter because he'd be absolutely sure it came from somebody else."

15

As soon as Mallory broke the connection with Laster, he dialed Zarah Christopher's number. Again there was no answer. No recorded voice inviting him to leave a message. How could this be? He buzzed for Wiggins and Lucy, who had been watching him on television in the adjoining security station and were able to join him in less than a second by means of a hidden door in the wall. The folklore about Mallory's protective technology wasn't completely unfounded.

"She's out walking again," Lucy said.

"Has she been home since the last time we discussed this?"

"No, sir, she has not. She's been wandering all over town, alone, for hours. She went to a movie in Union Station during the afternoon, then ate in one of the junk-food restaurants in the station, then went to the Library of Congress."

"To do what?"

"Nothing. She sat at a computer screen in the reading room for a couple of hours calling up news files on Ibn Awad, then walked down to the National Gallery and looked at pictures for another two hours, then walked the whole length of the Mall."

"Does she seem distraught?"

"No. Thoughtful."

"Why is she doing this?"

"She may be trying to draw surveillance into the open. Her behavior is consistent with this."

"Surveillance? You mean yourselves?"

"We think she knows we're there, Mr. President. But so is somebody else."

Mallory's face grew stern. "Somebody else?"

"We're not quite sure," Wiggins replied. "We just know someone is there."

"You're not *sure?* Have you warned her?"

"No, sir. We haven't interfered."

"Why the hell not? Have you no memory?"

This was a nearly unbearable question. Wiggins flinched. He and Lucy remembered, the entire security staff remembered in dreams and in every waking moment, what had happened to Susan Grant under their eyes on Inauguration Day. Corrective measures had been taken to ensure that the method used by Grant's assassin could not succeed a second time, but of course the attack on her had not been anticipated, and an unanticipated event meant that something even worse could happen in the future. Wiggins replied, "That's why we haven't intervened, Mr. President. We want her to flush the subject for us. Because of the danger to you."

"*Flush the subject?*" Mallory got to his feet, trembling with rage. "You mean you're using her as bait? Why haven't I been told about this?"

Lucy and Wiggins stood mute. Although they still had not been able to establish Sturdi's identity, they had confirmed her surveillance of Zarah Christopher even before Zarah herself recognized the goggled runner in Rock Creek Park. Just as Hammett had feared, Wiggins had in fact spotted Sturdi watching Zarah and himself outside the National Gallery. Then they had spotted her again and again. They had taken advantage of her interest in Zarah because Zarah was often close to Mallory, and protecting him meant protecting and suspecting anyone who had access to him.

Mallory said, "Who is this subject?"

"A female," Lucy said. "We have a good physical profile, even videotape. But so far, no positive I.D." She said no more; neither did Wiggins, though Mallory gave him an opportunity to do so with a glance. The mere fact that Sturdi masqueraded one day as a runner, another as a cyclist, another as a dog walker—what next?—suggested that she was either a psychotic amateur or a highly trained and disciplined professional terrorist who wanted to give the impression of amateurism. Either possibility (Which had Lee Harvey Oswald been? Or Sirhan Sirhan?) made the blood run cold. It was entirely possible that Sturdi's actual purpose was to draw them off, leaving Mallory exposed.

There was no need to voice these possibilities to Mallory. He saw them for himself. He said, "Do you have people with Zarah now?"

"Yes, sir. Every minute."

"I want you to call the team following her and instruct them to walk up to her, identify themselves, and hand her a telephone. Then I want you to put me on the line with her."

Lucy's eyes widened. This meant blowing the entire operation, not only to Zarah, but also to whoever was watching her. It meant that their best chance of learning something fundamental about Zarah herself would be lost, possibly forever. Wiggins and Lucy knew, as well as they knew anything, that Mallory was on the point of choosing this woman as Susan Grant's replacement in his life and work. The moment she accepted his proposal—it never occurred to them that she might refuse—she would be above suspicion, let alone investigation. They had always been uneasy about her; it simply wasn't plausible for a person of her high physical noticeability and intellectual attainments to have come out of nowhere, knowing no one; in the age of computers it wasn't even theoretically possible.

Mallory said, "*Now.*"

"Yes, sir," said Lucy, with a sinking heart. Wiggins, who was already on the phone to the surveillance team, said, "They're almost home, walking north on the east side of Massachusetts between S Street and Belmont. Do you want to wait until she's in her own house, sir? It would preserve the team's integrity."

"No. She may not answer her phone. I want her on the line this minute."

Seconds later Mallory heard Zarah's voice. He said, "The person who just handed you the telephone works for me."

"So he said."

"I didn't know until just now what they were doing. They have some idea of protecting you."

"So I supposed." Her voice was faint, distant, uninterested.

"I've been trying to reach you all day," he said.

"Well, you seem to have called the right number at last."

Mallory paused, then said, "Can you come and see me, please? The people you just met can give you a ride."

Zarah did not answer immediately. He could hear the hoarse respiration of the traffic on Massachusetts Avenue and other low-pitched sounds of the city at dusk. Then she said, "Does this mean you've changed your mind about my role as a messenger?"

"Yes. Something has happened. Or is about to happen. I must see Lockwood. I promise you, if there were any other way to arrange matters, I would."

"What do you want me to do?"

"I want you to call his wife and say I will come in person tonight, at the same hour as before, by the same entrance."

"All right."

She hung up. Mallory repeated her name into the broken connection. On their computer displays Lucy and Wiggins could see the number that Zarah was punching out on the cellular telephone the surveillance team had handed to her. It was Polly Lockwood's private number at the White House. It was not a secure phone. They scanned frantically for an intercept in case someone else was monitoring the call, and though they identified a sudden decrease in radio energy indicating a possible tap, they were unable to confirm it.

They heard Polly answer. Without identifying herself Zarah said, "Please tell your husband that Franklin will come tonight at the same time, by the same entrance."

Polly said, "Zarah, honey, is that you?"

In a voice that contained echoes of her mother's Bluegrass intonations, Zarah said, "Yes, ma'am, it's me. Did you understand the message?"

"I believe so—same hour, same entrance, same visitor. But I'm honestly not sure they'll let him in, dear. Everything has changed."

Zarah said, "For the worse?"

"That's a mild way of putting it," said Polly. "However, dear, I'll see that the message is delivered."

16

This time Mallory was met at the back door of the Treasury Annex at two o'clock in the morning by Norman Carlisle Blackstone and a tall, intensely alert Secret Service agent. Mallory recognized Bud Booker and shook hands with him. "Pleasure to see you, Bud."

"Same here, Mr. President," Booker replied, his eyes probing the shadows of the Treasury cellar. He stepped out ahead of Mallory and Blackstone, just beyond earshot, where he belonged. Another agent trailed behind them. They walked on in silence through the cellars, the parking lot, the underground passage, and finally the mansion itself.

To Mallory's surprise, Lockwood received him in the Oval Office. He had expected to be greeted by a rumpled Lockwood surrounded by the usual litter of documents and coffee cups. But the President was shaved, combed, and dressed in a dark suit and tie with a starched white shirt he had obviously put on for this encounter. Mallory himself was dressed as before, in an old corduroy jacket and a turtleneck sweater. It was evident that Lockwood was in no mood for pleasantries. He neither spoke nor rose to his feet when Mallory entered, nor did he invite him to join him in an easy chair. Instead, he sat his predecessor down like an aide in the hard chair beside his rough-hewn slab desk. Blackstone sat in the other chair. The fact that he did so without his usual deferential hesitancy told Mallory that he had been instructed to remain as a witness.

Evidently Lockwood was waiting for someone else to join them. Pointedly ignoring Mallory, he said, "Where is he?"

Forefinger pressing his earphone tighter, Bud Booker replied, "Inside the gates." He listened again. "Coming down the corridor now, Mr. President."

Time passed—less than a minute, during which Lockwood, still wordless, stared straight at the opposite wall, seemingly absorbed in a Bierstadt landscape that rendered the Rocky Mountains as the Alps, with bison, deer, elk, wolves, and grizzly bears communing like a convention of vegetarians beside a crystalline lake. Mallory himself was in no mood to smile, but he felt a certain rueful amusement, as he always did when confronted by an example of Lockwood's taste in art. The paintings the

President liked had the same sentimental vocabulary as his political rheto-ric: both promised escape into lands where all appetites and temptations had been overcome, the lion lay down with the lamb, and the human heart was as pure as the water in Ibn Awad's icebergs.

Another man came in, late and hurried, even slightly resentful, but in no way apologetic. Recognizing him from his television image and photo-graphs, Mallory found this lack of deference interesting; he himself had received more apologies and more flattery in this room than in all the others he had ever entered combined. Lockwood greeted the newcomer with a stare of displeasure before turning his chilly gaze on Mallory and speaking to him for the first time.

"Mr. President," he said in formal tones, "this is my personal attorney, Alfonso Olmedo. He just flew down from New York. Alfonso, the Honor-able Franklin Mallory."

Mallory and Olmedo nodded wordlessly to each other. There was no chair for Olmedo and Lockwood did not offer him one.

To Lockwood, Mallory said, "I gather this is going to be an on-the-record meeting."

"No, Franklin, just a one-on-three knifefight. Since you're the one and us ordinary folks are the three, I figure that evens things up a little bit. Ears only—no notes, no tapes, everything stays in this room."

"We'd better get down to it," Mallory said. "Mr. President, I assume you know what's coming out in tomorrow's newspapers under Ross Macalaster's byline."

"I've heard rumors. Macalaster's a tight buddy of yours, isn't he?"

"He's a newspaperman. He's got the tape."

"From you?"

"No. But he will print it, and that will change everything. We both know that."

Lockwood leaned forward, his head shooting toward Mallory at the end of his long neck. "Do we?"

Composed as always, Mallory replied, "Yes, we do. I've come to ask you again if you're now prepared to discuss the transfer of the presidency to me under the Twenty-fifth Amendment."

Lockwood smiled, as though these were exactly the words he had been expecting. Then he said, "Franklin, I don't give a damn what's going to be in the newspapers, the answer is still no. Not now, not ever. *No.* I thought I told you that in the first place."

"We are no longer *in* the first place, Frosty."

"What's changed?" Lockwood said. "My election was certified by Con-gress; I took the oath of office; I'm sitting in this chair."

Mallory said, "Congress certified your election on the basis of fraudulent returns. You took the oath under false pretenses. Pretty soon the Senate is going to confirm those undeniable facts, and at that point you'll become nonqualified and so will your Vice President. Both offices will be constitutionally vacant. That will effectively render you powerless to influence the outcome of this situation or any other having to do with the presidency."

"You know what the Senate's going to do for a certainty, do you, Franklin?"

"Unless we're both living in a dreamworld, yes, I'm sure. And so are you." Mallory turned in his chair and spoke to Olmedo. "Mr. Olmedo, having reviewed the documentary evidence and having interviewed the witnesses, have you the slightest hope that the Senate will confirm Mr. Lockwood in the presidency?"

Olmedo looked at Lockwood, who made a gesture giving him permission to answer Mallory's question. Still he did not answer.

"Answer the man, Alfonso," Lockwood said impatiently.

"Very well," Olmedo said. "I can't predict the outcome, but the President's innocence in this matter has never been in doubt—even in your mind, President Mallory."

"That is no longer the issue," Mallory said. "The theft of the election is going to be linked to the murder of Ibn Awad. It will be shown that your client lied to the American people about the facts while professing to confess all. He can't survive that—not the murder, the unnecessary lie. No one could."

Lockwood stared fixedly at Mallory, then once again transferred his gaze to the idyllic scene in the painting over his shoulder.

"Frosty, listen," Mallory said. "It's over. You don't belong here; you can't stay. The people didn't put you here."

Lockwood reddened. "What the hell do you know about the people?"

"The same thing you know, Mr. President. They're sovereign. Not the Hubbard boys, not Congress. The people."

The two Presidents leaned toward each other, gripping opposite edges of the desk, glaring furiously at each other. Olmedo watched, spellbound by the sheer human perversity of what was happening. The fate of the United States, therefore the fate of the world, was at stake, and the two men who held the future in their hands were behaving like taxi drivers after a fender bender. God's masterpiece, Olmedo thought; what hope can there ever be for this harebrained species?

"Whether you like it or not, this time you've got to make a choice," Mallory said.

"Like hell I do," Lockwood said. "Why should I? I'm in. You're out. That's all there is to it."

"Not anymore it isn't. Before, it was just you and me and the truth. Now it's more than that. As soon as Macalaster's story hits the papers you won't have a friend in the world. The radicals will desert you, the media will turn on you, your party will turn and run. You'll be eaten alive, like Lyndon, like Nixon, by the people you've done the most for. You can't win, Frosty. You won't have the votes in either house of Congress."

Shaking his head in mock wonderment, Lockwood said, "Franklin, I'll tell you what I think. There's no way what you say is going to happen can happen. I did the right thing about that maniac."

"Maybe. But you got caught. And then you lied."

"When the whole story comes out, I'll be all right."

"When the whole story comes out, you'll be finished," Mallory said. "For the last time, Frosty: Will you resolve this crisis under the Twenty-fifth Amendment before it's too late?"

Lockwood stopped smiling. "Lemme see if I remember the plan," he said. "Willy Graves resigns as Vice President. He'd be only too glad to do that, of course; all I have to do is ask. Then I appoint you Vice President. Congress will be only too glad to rubber-stamp *that*, seeing as how half of them would like to see you ground up for dog food. Then I resign and you become President. And all because I saved the world from a religious fanatic who was going to blow up Tel Aviv, and maybe New York City, with nuclear bombs and kill all the Jews plus a few million Protestants, Catholics, and Hare Krishnas. Have I got it about right?"

Mallory said nothing in return because he understood at last that Lockwood had decided to go down fighting, that he really thought he could win it in the last minute of play, and that there was no hope of persuading him otherwise. What Lockwood had given him was not a response. It was a performance.

Shaking his head, rising to his feet in dismissal, Lockwood said, "Franklin, you may be President of the United States again someday. Stranger things have happened in this great country. But you're never going to sit in this chair again if I have to put you there."

"You'd better start reading the Constitution. There are other ways this can turn out."

"I don't need to read the Constitution to know what's going to happen in the end. Do you know what that's going to be, boy? Nothing. It was all over on the first Tuesday after the first Monday of November last. You lost, and you're the only guy in the world who doesn't know that."

Mallory said, "You're wrong."

"So you say. But I'm in and you're out."

There was no more friendship in Mallory's eyes. He nodded his head several times, as if agreeing with his own thoughts. At last he said, "As a formality, I ask you this: Mr. President, do I now have your final answer?"

Lockwood said, "As a formality I reply: Yes, sir, Mr. President, you sure do."

Mallory stood up. Bud Booker appeared behind him in the doorway. Mallory said, "Good luck."

"Same to you," Lockwood said. "And don't forget to eat your Wheaties."

Lockwood waited until Mallory and his escort were out of earshot. Then, speaking to Olmedo and Blackstone, he said, "He thinks he's going to lose in the Senate. And by God, he's right. That's what *that* was all about." He looked directly at Olmedo. "Do you agree, Alfonso?"

"Yes," Olmedo said, "I agree that's what he fears."

Norman Carlisle Blackstone cleared his throat. "He has a point, a very interesting one, about the Constitution."

Lockwood glared. "Franklin always has a point. That's why he's such a pain in the ass."

"But there *is* a second constitutional solution."

"Spats," Lockwood said. "Not now."

Blackstone flushed red; Olmedo avoided both Presidents' eyes. He felt something awaken and move within himself. He did not mistake it for anything but what it was: fear, primal, instinctive fear, because all that he had learned in a lifetime of defending human beings in extremis told him that the situation had just gone out of control.

VI

1

Although few would ever realize it, R. Tucker Attenborough, Jr., had chosen to give his life for his country. That was what his decision to resume drinking meant, and he knew it. Though he came from people who believed it was a good and noble thing to die a patriotic death, there was nothing sentimental about his decision. No other option was open to him. He could not go into a hospital in the middle of the greatest constitutional crisis in American history and leave the leadership of the House of Representatives and the fate of his party in other hands. And as his hallucinations had proved, he could not quit drinking on his own and still do what he had to do. After weeks of pondering, he knew exactly what he had to do and exactly how to do it; the whole scenario was mapped out in his mind—every word, every step, every legal precedent. But he had kept the thing to himself, and it was too late now to hand it over to anyone else.

On the day he mistook Ross Macalaster for an assassin, Attenborough sought a second medical opinion. He needed a doctor he could trust, so he called in Albert Tyler's youngest son, Henry, who was an internist on the staff of the small hospital where he had been treated by Dr. Chin. In the privacy of the Speaker's office, Henry looked into Attenborough's eyes, felt his liver, read the results of the tests, and asked a few questions. Then he confirmed Dr. Chin's diagnosis in every respect. Attenborough had three choices: he could check into a treatment program immediately and live, he could try giving up alcohol on his own and lose his sanity, or he could go back to drinking and stay on his feet for maybe two or three weeks before he collapsed and began to die, organ by organ.

Attenborough said, "How about I wait a month, just drinking enough to keep from seeing things, and then check into the hospital? Got a lot to do right now, Henry, and I'm the only one can do it."

Henry said, "Mr. Speaker, you won't live a month if you keep on pumping vodka through your body at the rate of two liters a day."

"How much *can* I pump through it and stay alive and stay awake? What I want to do is work like I normally do and not have any more of thos_ visions."

"I can't advise you on that."

"Sure you can."

Henry wagged his head in stern admonishment. "No, sir," he said. "Even if it was right to tell you that, which it isn't, I'd be guessing, based on what I know now. I'd have to monitor your blood-alcohol level over a period of days and compute a dose to keep it at a certain level. But in order to do that I'd have to aid and abet your suicide. And I won't do that."

Attenborough nodded sympathetically: Henry was the one who had the problem. He wanted to help him solve it. "How often would a fellow take the dose you're talking about and how big would it be?" he asked. Henry gave him a suspicious look. Attenborough said, "Just curious."

Henry hesitated; a half-smile came and went. But he answered the question. "Small doses at frequent intervals would be best, based on habitual intake."

"Call two liters eighty ounces," Attenborough said. "Divided by twenty-four, that's just about three ounces an hour. Right?"

"Mr. Speaker," Henry said, "that's an alcoholic talking and I'm not listening."

"There's more to it than that," Attenborough said. "What you're saying is I got to quit drinking to live, and the only way I can quit is cut myself off from the outside world. Problem is, I need two weeks, maybe three, to get this impeachment business settled. I can't run away from that, and I sure can't get it done from a hospital room."

"Consider the alternative."

"That's what I'm trying to do here, Henry. Worst thing about what's wrong with me is I keep falling asleep in the middle of things. Can you give me something for that?"

Henry was no longer amused. He was a serious young fellow by nature—melancholy, even. He had reason to be. His two older brothers had been shot to death in the children's wars of the nineties and his mother had died young. Trying to preserve Albert from another loss, the Speaker had gotten Henry a job as a House page to keep him off the streets, then had fixed him up with government grants to pay for a New England prep school and college and finally for medical school—Harvard, no less. All along, he had helped him any way he could. Naturally Henry resented this. He said, "I don't see how I could do that either, Mr. Speaker."

Attenborough nodded understandingly; he *did* understand, better than Henry knew. "Henry, I understand what you're saying to me, but I've got to see this thing through. I'm the only one can do what's got to be done. With you or without you, I'm going to do it. Got no choice. I'm making a choice and asking for your help. You'd be doing a good thing, you'd be doing something for this country that we love."

Henry flinched at this final sentence, as Attenborough had known he would; the young man didn't think he had much reason to be patriotic.

"I can't do it," Henry said. "The kind of pills you're talking about don't mix with alcohol. They can kill you."

Attenborough put a hand on his forearm and said, "What difference does that make if I'm going to die anyway?" Henry looked down at the old mottled hand on his sleeve, avoiding Attenborough's eyes. The Speaker said, "Henry, my body's done for anyway—you say so yourself. It's my body, my choice. I don't like to put it to you this way, son, but you owe me."

At these words, Henry's face lost all expression. But he took out a pen and pad and started to write a prescription. "I'll give you enough for two weeks, one every four hours," he said. "Don't exceed the dose."

"Appreciate it," Attenborough said. "Put that in your daddy's name, if you don't mind; might save trouble at the drugstore."

Now, only a day later, Attenborough was pretty much his old self again. Wide awake at six in the morning, he gazed at the desert plants in the National Botanic Garden and thought about his encounter with Henry, thought about death, thought about how strange it was that the most important conversation of his life should have been with a young black man who thought there was a world between them—a world that an old white man like Attenborough could never comprehend. That was bullshit, but how could Henry know?

Despite the improvement in his mental and physical functions, Attenborough's mood was somber. All this introspection about Henry was just a way to avoid thinking about what was happening in the world around him. Before walking down the hill to the greenhouse, he had read Macalaster's column ("the first of a series") about Lockwood and Ibn Awad in the morning newspaper. That's why he was here: to think, to plan, to figure a way out of the mess this was going to cause. Macalaster was saying that Lockwood had put out a contract on Ibn Awad and then lied about it to the country. The paper had not picked up the tale of the tape as a page-one news story—at least not yet—but had printed it under a playful headline ("Dark Doings in the Desert?") in Macalaster's customary spot below the fold on the op-ed page. The New York papers, which did not use Macalaster's column, did not even mention it. This could not last. It was not in the nature of the news media to ignore something like this; it would break out, breed on its own body and multiply; it would gambol among the monuments, it would chew up everything in sight and process it into . . . news.

Although Macalaster had told him nothing in cold print that he had not always known in his bones, Attenborough did not want to be part of this process. He had come down to the greenhouse, letting himself in the back door with his own personal key, not just to think the situation over, but also in the hope of avoiding any reporters who might have been rousted out of bed by their editors and sent down to Capitol Hill to ask him questions. By the time he had left his office, every phone was ringing off the hook. He let them ring. His idea was to avoid being quoted on the morning news, which went off the air at eight-thirty, and to dodge his early-rising colleagues in the House, who would want to talk about what it all meant as soon as they read the papers. He felt safe here, isolated; this was his refuge. The greenhouse staff had not yet come to work and the night guards were out back, drinking coffee. Attenborough was alone with the desert plants; he had the whole building to himself, with four hours to think and drink before he banged the gavel to bring the House to order at ten o'clock, launching the process that would decide the fate of a President and maybe the future of democracy in America. Not to mention the question of whether or not he, Attenborough, was going to die in vain.

The automatic sprinkling system was operating in the next room, cutting off the approach of intruders. The Speaker's wristwatch alarm chimed; he had set it to go off every hour on the hour as an aid to his new system of drinking. He drank exactly three ounces of vodka out of one of the eight-ounce plastic cough-medicine bottles, ounces marked on the side, that he had slipped into the inside pockets of his suit coat.

No man could be sure what would happen once the hounds of politics and press were set loose. But Attenborough knew what he had wanted to *prevent* from happening before this tape fell into Ross Macalaster's hands, and now he was no longer sure he was going to be able to do it. Until he had read the morning papers, his neat and tidy plan had been to get all the procedures adopted by two o'clock, by which time everybody would be so hungry and so anxious to go to the toilet that no objection was likely. He would then adjourn the House until two o'clock the following day, with the expectation of getting the three articles of impeachment adopted in one session if he had to keep it going all night long. After that, he'd appoint the managers for the Senate trial and stay with them until Lockwood's fate was decided or until, as that mean little Chinese girl doctor had admonished, every part of his body stopped working except his heart, whichever came sooner. Not much chance of sticking to that schedule now, thanks to that dumb hillbilly in the White House and whoever was out to get him.

Yet, Attenborough thought, we might just save the country after all. Thanks to the pills, he felt smarter this morning than he had felt since the day, thirty years before, when he came in first in the Texas law examination with a mark of 100 percent—a sawed-off, ugly-faced poor boy out of the Chihuahua Desert who had memorized every word and punctuation mark of every statute and case in the Texas law books. That flawless performance had been the turning point of his life. Good thing or bad? He'd know by the end of the day, and so would the rest of the country. He raised the medicine bottle again, looked at it longingly with the light shining through it, then resolutely put it away.

The sun was shining through the roof. Attenborough sauntered on, looking with never-diminishing pleasure at the rainbows created by the nozzles overhead. He thought, *The R. Tucker Attenborough Memorial Sprinkler System.* He laughed out loud at this idea, but it wasn't such a bad one—better than having an office building named after you, or a statue. Best way to lose your name was to carve it in stone.

Alfonso Olmedo stood at the turning in the path, wearing one of his beautiful New York suits. He was solemn and deliberate in his approach.

"Damn!" In his surprise and resentment at this intrusion, Attenborough spoke loud enough to rattle the greenhouse glass.

Olmedo was unruffled. "I'm sorry to drop in unannounced this way," he said in his courtly manner, "but no one answered your telephone."

"That's because I shut the sucker off for a reason," Attenborough said.

His tone was fierce, but Olmedo, used to dealing with the theatrics of judges, feigned not to notice. "Mr. Speaker," he said, "there has been an unfortunate development and I wanted to be sure you are aware of it."

"What development's that? Macalaster's column?"

"Then you've seen the paper."

"Read the sucker first thing every morning. How much trouble are we in?"

"I don't know," Olmedo said. "Macalaster played a portion of the tape to Philindros over the phone."

"Does Philindros say it's the real thing?"

"I didn't ask that question."

"I don't plan to ask it myself. Others will. What's Lockwood's answer going to be?"

"I can tell you what his answer to Mallory was."

"They've been talking?"

Olmedo described Mallory's visit to the Oval Office.

Attenborough said, "Franklin thinks there's some kind of plot going on, but Frosty made a joke of it?"

"That's one way of describing his reaction."

Attenborough said, "That means they *both* think there's some kind of a plot going on. Does the President still think I'm after his job?"

Olmedo did not know the answer to this question. "Whatever he thinks," he said, "he has decided to fight it out to his last breath and drop of blood."

"That's not a surprise, knowing Frosty—win it in the last second of play by sheer dumb luck and marry the cheerleader. Have you got a game plan to save his ass in light of what's happening, or are you just going to make it up as you go along and throw a few Hail Marys at the end?"

Olmedo bowed perfunctorily to Attenborough's sarcasm. He said, "Our position is twofold—"

"Hold it right there," Attenborough said. "Take my advice and make it onefold, Alfonso. This town is like a horse. It can only think about one thing at a time, so what you want to do if you're planning to stick your arm up its rectum is put a twist on its lip so its mind will not be on the end where the action is."

Olmedo said, "I am always grateful for an expert's opinion. Perhaps you can help me to choose between two thoughts: one, the tape is inadmissible—"

"No chance. Remember Nixon."

"Or, two, it is a politically inspired attempt to distort the truth."

"That's better, because Macalaster can't be called as a witness. Journalists are above the law in this town, and even if they weren't, old Ross has got his principles. He'd go to jail for the rest of his life rather than betray a source, and to hell with the United States of America. So the idea that the tape's a fake is your twist on the horse's lip—unless you still think there are credible witnesses to the conversation."

"I don't think we can count on any help from witnesses," said Olmedo. "The question is, what constitutes credibility on Capitol Hill?"

Through the fine wool of his dark-blue made-for-television suit, Attenborough touched his medicine bottle. "Credibility?" he replied. "It's the same on the Hill as anyplace else in the world: Tell 'em what they already think they know."

"And in this case, Lockwood's case, what do they think they know?"

"Yesterday or today?" Attenborough said. "Yesterday he was the reincarnation of Abe Lincoln. Today the seed of doubt is germinating. What you've got to worry about is tomorrow, because that's when it's going to sprout."

2

Penned in by ropes, the news media awaited Attenborough in Statuary Hall, near the door of his everyday office. As he appeared among the columns and sculptures the reporters surged forward, making a collective noise, as though their many bodies were controlled by a single overloaded brain. He walked straight toward the creature, smiling and winking into its numerous faces; each wore the same expression of vexed suspicion. Microphones bristled, tape recorders waved, notepads fluttered; the Speaker's name was uttered like a mating call by two dozen identically pitched voices. He smiled more broadly, completely at ease. The creature was dangerous but predictable. It was always hungry; to keep it at bay, to prevent it from having bad memories of you, you had to feed it each time you saw it. As long as you did that, it seldom surprised you.

But sometimes it did. Morgan Pike, out front as always, asked the first question. Thrusting the trademark pink bulb of her microphone into his face, she said, "Mr. Speaker, we've just learned that Vice President Williston Graves has died in the night of an apparent heart attack. How will this affect your handling of the impeachment proceedings in the House, especially since you are now next in line for the presidency?"

Willy Graves dead? Attenborough stared in mute disbelief. As the camera searched his face, Morgan Pike concentrated on her next question, which was being fed to her over the earpiece hidden beneath her swinging hair.

Morgan Pike was keen-eyed and succinct. "I'm sorry to be the bearer of bad tidings, Mr. Speaker," she said. "I know he was an old friend of yours. Personal sorrow aside, does this create a conflict of interest for you?"

"Conflict of interest? What do you mean by that?"

"If Lockwood goes, you could be our next President."

"What makes you think President Lockwood is going anywhere?"

"He's about to be impeached by the House."

"As far as I know, Morgan, the House has not yet voted on that."

"I'll rephrase the question. He may be impeached by the House and deprived of his office by the Senate. Are you comfortable with the prospect of presiding over a process that might make you President?"

"Right now, Morgan, my thoughts are with Vice President Graves and his family."

Morgan Pike did not react to his words because she was listening to another incoming question. Her vividly painted face wore the stunned expression of a schizophrenic hearing inner voices. As the camera switched to her, the look disappeared and she was sprightly again. "Will you step aside, Mr. Speaker," she asked, "and let someone else preside over the House during the impeachment hearings?"

"Morgan," he said, "you can tell old Patrick back in the studio that's the dumbest damn question he ever whispered in your pretty little ear."

He had gone too far. It was the pills and liquor. He realized this and reached out a reassuring hand. Meaning to chuckle, he coughed explosively and this raucous sound bounced back and forth across Statuary Hall. Other reporters were shouting questions about Lockwood and Ibn Awad, but Attenborough, bent double, and fighting for breath, waved a hand in apology as he walked rapidly away toward his office at the end of the corridor.

3

When her doorbell rang, Zarah Christopher, dressed for the day in jeans and a blazer, was watching an admiring profile of Chief Justice Archimedes Hammett on *Newsdawn with Patrick Graham:* panoramic shots of his bleak birthplace and of the gothic Yale campus, interviews with his fond teachers, footage of his impassioned defense of wretched outcasts, filmed passages from a seminar with law students.

Zarah pressed a button on the remote control and the broadcast was replaced by the closed-circuit video signal transmitted by the security system. On-screen, replacing Hammett's somber and statesmanlike image, she saw the black-and-white likeness of a blond young woman in a tailored suit, briefcase in hand, face tilted helpfully upward toward the hidden camera above the door. Supposing that this person must be a messenger from Mallory—no one else in Washington had a reason to arrive on her doorstep unannounced—she went downstairs and opened the door. It was then, seeing her in the flesh and close up, that she recognized Sturdi.

Sturdi smiled. The great nose, the furry unplucked eyebrows that suggested equally furry armpits, the faint shadow on the depilated upper lip, contrasted strangely with the bright Teutonic hair of her wig. "Ms. Christopher," she said, "we haven't met, but I believe you know my client, Ms. Slim Eve."

Puzzled, Zarah said, "I do?"

"You met at a dinner party at Ross Macalaster's house on the seventeenth of this month. The Chief Justice and the Speaker of the House were also present."

"Your client," Zarah said. "Is she suing somebody?"

Sturdi gave Zarah another smile—or, rather, a slight intensification of the already intensely pleasant expression she was wearing. She handed Zarah a business card. "S. R. Eve, spelled the same way."

There was something odd about the expression in this woman's eyes; she was gazing at Zarah with what could only be called hunger. Zarah noted this without expression. She said, "What can I do for you?"

"You can talk to me about the dinner party—what you remember."

"For what purpose?"

"My client is exploring her legal options. There could be a lawsuit, even criminal charges. I'm gathering information so that she can make her decision on the basis of the facts."

Zarah wanted to say, "Is that why you've been following me around town wearing all those ridiculous disguises?" Instead she said, "I see."

On tiptoes, Sturdi was peering into Zarah's front hall through the open door. "May I come in?"

Zarah had been studying the androgynous torso, the large chapped hands, the burning eyes surrounded by purposeful smile lines, the almost visible aura of concealed thoughts and disguised purposes. An expensive glove-leather envelope that could contain anything was clasped tightly under Sturdi's left arm, and she wore a heavy silver bracelet that could conceivably be used as a weapon. Zarah did not doubt that Sturdi would use it as a weapon if necessary. She behaved like a lunatic or a terrorist, if there was a difference between the two, someone who was fighting against some deep and irresistible impulse, but only until it was safe to give in to it. Zarah's curiosity was deeply engaged by this combination of signs and by the fact that this woman was showing herself to her in this way. Plainly Sturdi had no idea that Zarah knew who she was or even guessed that she was the runner, the bicyclist, the dog walker who had been following her so relentlessly for two weeks. This meant she must be stupid, and this was the most disturbing of all the signs.

Zarah said, "Actually, you rang the bell just as I was going out. We can walk together if you like."

Sturdi stopped smiling; a stricken look came into her eyes. Obviously she had not foreseen this response. "I'm a little pressed," she said. "Can we possibly make an appointment to meet later in the day? Evening would be best for me, actually. I'd be glad to come back."

"That wouldn't be possible."

"Why not?"

Zarah smiled at the question but did not answer it. She closed the door and pressed the electronic control in the pocket of her jacket; locks snickered shut all over the house and the full security system came on; Sturdi noted this, eyes flickering as though she had just learned something of vital importance. Keeping her visitor squarely in front of her, Zarah looked casually up and down the street. She had not been outdoors since her sidewalk telephone conversation with Mallory, but she assumed that his $\male \leftrightarrow \female$ teams still had her under surveillance. Even if Mallory had called them off, she knew that they continually watched the whole street on video, and that at this moment they must be watching, if not listening to, this encounter. They too would soon identify this primly dressed professional person as yet another version of the person who had been following Zarah—or their equipment would do so. No matter what Mallory's orders were, duty and curiosity would leave them no other choice than to shadow the two of them. As long as she remained in the open—assuming that Sturdi did not pull out a gun and shoot her dead, a possibility she did not dismiss—Mallory's boys and girls would be nearby.

"All right, let's go," Sturdi said with a sudden hoarse giggle. "But I wish I had on different shoes." Her legs—the legs of the runner and bicyclist she was, with loaves of muscle for thighs and calves—were defined even more noticeably by the spike heels and split skirt she was wearing.

Zarah set off at a rapid pace toward Massachusetts Avenue, keeping close to the curb and adjusting her pace so that Sturdi remained well within her peripheral vision. Of course Sturdi kept up easily, heels ringing on the pavement; she smelled of a strong, familiar perfume that Zarah, searching her memory as though for a misplaced name, recognized as a fragrance she had smelled before, in a foreign country, but could not quite identify.

At the corner of Massachusetts Avenue and Belmont Road, they walked through crowds of Muslims who had come to pray at the mosque. Sturdi weaved among them, smiling with strange cordiality, as if she thought they would doubt her goodwill unless she let them know she was a friend.

Zarah said, "What exactly did you want to talk to me about, Ms. Eve?"

Exuding her pungent but elusive scent, Sturdi replied, "About the attempted rape of my client by Attenborough."

" 'Attempted rape'?" Zarah replied. "When did that occur?"

"According to the others at the dinner table, as well as three waiters who were eyewitnesses, at about nine twenty-five on the evening in question. You *were* present?"

"I was present when she jumped up from the table, displayed a rip in her undergarments, and called Mr. Attenborough a name."

"Do you recall her exact words?"

"Yes. She said, 'Oh, you filthy swine!' I was surprised by her vocabulary."

"Why?"

"I had never before heard an American use the word 'swine.' "

Sturdi got out a small tape recorder and switched it on. "What was her emotional state?"

Zarah said, "I don't know."

"But you say you saw her jump up and heard her make an accusation."

"It was more in the nature of an exclamation. But I had no way of knowing what she was feeling."

"You didn't observe her state of mind?"

"I observed her behavior. She seemed to be angry and disturbed. Maybe she actually was."

Once again Sturdi was offended. Zarah had the wrong vocabulary, the wrong sensibilities. "You don't think she really *was* angry and disturbed?"

"She certainly indicated that she was in every possible way." Zarah shrugged. "But if she really was feeling those emotions, it was very sudden. A few seconds earlier she had been happily eating her dinner, drinking wine and listening to Attenborough and Hammett argue, smiling as if she hadn't a care in the world."

"They were arguing? About what?"

"Shelley."

Sturdi looked puzzled.

"The poet," Zarah said. "Shelley seemed to be on Hammett's mind that night. Attenborough was leaning across the table, quoting lines from 'To a Sky-Lark.' He had his back to . . . your client. If he was attempting to rape her, he was doing it in a way that isn't in the *Kama Sutra*."

Sturdi flushed. "You're using a very narrow definition of rape," she said. "Let me tell you what rape is."

Zarah knew what it was, having been drugged and raped by an entire cell of Eye of Gaza terrorists on the night David Patchen was tortured and murdered. Suddenly she realized where she had smelled this pungent cologne before: on one of the terrorists. She said, "That won't be necessary."

"Whatever you say," Sturdi said. "But this is no joking matter."

"I'm not joking. Why do you use the term 'rape'?"

"My client was penetrated."

Zarah looked at Sturdi in puzzlement and surprise; she had to slow down to do so because the other woman kept falling back and disappearing from the corner of her eye like a laggard child. As she glanced to her right, Zarah saw the female member of a ♂ ↔ ♀ team cross Kalorama Road. Other members of the team also took up new positions. Their technique was so perfect that its execution was unmissable.

Zarah realized that Sturdi had observed these maneuvers also, or at least sensed them. In a tense voice, she said, "I said my client was penetrated."

"I heard you," Zarah said. "I'm afraid I didn't observe that part of it."

"The instrument of penetration was a finger with a sharpened nail, the same sharpened nail that shredded the victim's panty hose."

"The victim." Zarah's tone was flat.

"The vaginal tissue was lacerated," Sturdi said, in a louder voice. "We have the medical report." Her face was stern, angry, accusative. "My client was in great psychological and physical distress. How could you not have observed that?"

They had reached Sheridan Circle. Zarah stopped walking. It was time to break off this contact; by now the ♂ ↔ ♀ teams must have obtained all the video images and audio tracks they required, and she herself knew more than she needed to know about Sturdi, who was clearly on the point of giving way to her psychosis.

"As a woman, you *must* have seen how distressed she was," Sturdi said, moving closer.

Zarah stepped back. "No, that's not what I saw," she said. "Your client provoked and flirted with Attenborough from the first moment of the evening. She was wearing a very short dress for a lawyer escorted by the Chief Justice of the United States. She was in a state of almost feverish excitement; at first I thought she might be on drugs. And when suddenly, very suddenly, she leaped to her feet and lifted her skirt to display the damage to her clothing—damage that could not possibly have been done in one single grope by the sharpest fingernail in the world—she was obviously in a state of sexual arousal."

" '*A state of sexual arousal*'?" Sturdi could scarcely bring herself to repeat the words. "How could such a thing be obvious?"

Zarah was calm, watchful. She replied, "Sense of smell, Ms. Eve."

Sturdi's lip twisted in disbelief. "You must have one hell of a sense of smell." The sun was warm, and the strong perfume she was wearing was noticeable over the stench of exhaust fumes.

"Do you think so?" Zarah said. "Then you won't mind my asking you why in the world you're wearing Roger et Gallet after-shave cologne."

Sturdi gasped, blanched, and fumbled with her briefcase. The nearest ♂ ↔ ♀ team swiftly moved even closer. Another team leaped out of a car that had pulled up to the curb just ahead of them.

Sturdi, whose eyes had been fixed on Zarah's face, detected these movements at the edges of her field of vision. Her head swiveled to left and right, spotting the surveillance. She turned away, whirling so energetically that her skirt billowed above her knees, and broke into a run, spike heels beating a tattoo on the sun-splashed pavement as she gestured frantically for a taxi.

For a long moment Zarah stared after this fleeing figure. Then, approaching the nearest ♂ ↔ ♀ team, she handed the male partner Sturdi's card. "You saw who that was?" she said.

The agent nodded. Across the avenue, Sturdi stared at them with wild eyes through the rolled-down window of a Red Sea Cab.

4

Attenborough knew that the sensation created by Vice President Graves's sudden death could not last more than a day. Thereafter the Ibn Awad tape would take over the news, and therefore would take over the impeachment process. Graves, a likable and harmless Californian who reminded friend and foe alike of Ronald Reagan, was a conservative who had been added to the ticket to reassure the right wing of the party. Owing to his position on the political spectrum he had never been a favorite of the media. Even though his was the deciding vote in the evenly divided Senate, the progressive wing of the party was unhappy that Graves had been removed by the hand of fate from the presidential picture. That was the trouble: they realized that one of the best reasons they'd had for defending Lockwood was to make sure that a crypto-Republican like Graves did not succeed to the presidency. That reason had now disappeared. This realization that they had been blessed by an accident of fate was guaranteed to send the radicals off on a chain of thought that could lead anywhere.

There was little that Attenborough could do about this. The radicals were not really members of the party; they were a party within the party, with their own philosophy and their own agenda. There was no telling what effect the revelations about Ibn Awad might have on them, but he knew it was an issue that could drive them, as defenders of the wretched, into a frenzy of righteous anger.

Attenborough loved his party and had always believed that it was the hope of the poor and defender of the people. But he knew that it had a dark side, and he had lived in fear for thirty years that what had happened to Andrew Johnson and Richard Nixon could someday happen to one of his own; in fact he had believed that it was bound to happen, not only because of the revenge factor, but also because he knew, as only a man of his political experience could know, that every President, without exception, is impeachable. All the impeachment process did was give political zealots a way to overthrow the government under cover of the Constitution, and in Attenborough's opinion (though he never ever uttered it aloud), insinuating this Trojan Horse into the scripture of the republic was the biggest damn fool mistake the Founding Fathers ever made.

"This is a simple issue," he told the party leadership at the seven-thirty meeting, "and what we've got to do is keep it that way. Our job in the House is to ask the right question so that the Senate can come up with the right answer and get the country back to normal again."

Now, at last, Attenborough revealed how he planned to do this. "Today we've got three things to accomplish," he said. "First, resolve the House into a Committee of the Whole and elect the Speaker chairman. Second, adopt a resolution to impeach Bedford Forrest Lockwood. Third, elect a Committee of Managers to recommend articles of impeachment for adoption by the full House. Tomorrow we'll adopt three articles of impeachment relating to the allegations of election fraud in Michigan, New York, and California, in that order."

"We're going to do all that in two days?"

"That's all it took in 1868 when the House impeached Andrew Johnson, with a day off in between sessions."

"There was no television in 1868."

"That's one hundred percent correct," Attenborough said. "That's why we've got to get this thing over with, stick to the point and keep it down to one simple question."

"As of this morning," Bob Laval said, "we've got another question. Ibn Awad."

"No, sir, we do not," Attenborough said. "What we have is a mischievous leak to the media designed to divert the House from the main issue."

"That won't wash," Laval said. "Lockwood told the country he just kind of let the Ibn Awad thing happen because it was the only way to save the world. Didn't have a thing to do with it himself."

"Is that what he said?"

"It's what he implied," Laval said. "And the whole world knows it. Now there's this tape where he puts out a contract on the guy. You don't think that has a bearing on the case?"

Laval's tone was pugnacious. He was a big, florid, excitable man with a smashed nose who had worked his way through night law school as a roughneck in the Louisiana oil fields. Of all the people around the table, he was the one who worried Attenborough the most because he was unpredictable, a Southern conservative who had never liked Lockwood or his progressive social programs, and who had often voted against them on the floor of the House.

"What has a real bearing on the case are the lessons of history," Attenborough said. "Andrew Johnson won acquittal in the Senate by one vote because his supporters stuck by him. A hundred and five years later Nixon resigned because his deserted him and he knew he couldn't win. It's votes, not appearances, that count. The people who leaked that tape are trying to confuse the issue and split this party."

"Nixon taught us another lesson," Laval said. "If we ignore this or go easy on it, it's going to look like a cover-up."

"I'm not saying we ignore it or go easy on it. All I'm saying is, keep it separate. Take it up some other time, in some other forum, like the Judiciary Committee."

"How the hell can we do that?"

"We can do it by sticking to the issue Congress was asked to decide," Attenborough said. "There's only one question before the House: Is Lockwood the legally elected President of the United States? That's the question. It is the *only* question, and it is the question the House is going to ask the Senate to answer, as provided in the Constitution. Everything else is beside the point."

"One-Question Attenborough," said Laval. He was smiling, but Attenborough saw rebellion in his face, and in some of the other less ruddy faces around the table, too. The key to success was getting Laval under control and making him part of the team effort by giving him more to lose than anyone else. He said, "I'm going to recommend that Bob Laval, as chairman of the Judiciary Committee, be nominated as chairman of the Committee of Managers. It's a big job with no thanks at the end of it. They're the prosecutors in the Senate trial. Is that all right with you, Bob?"

"What happens to the Judiciary Committee?"

"It's too big and unwieldy to get this done in the time allotted."

"It's the Judiciary Committee's right to get it done."

"The House decides that. In the Andrew Johnson case, the Committee on Reconstruction handled the details because what he was really being impeached for was his policy of mercy toward the South. If you want a committee that's got seventeen of Mallory's smartest lawyers on it deciding the fate of the presidency, that's fine. But I hope you'll not refuse this cup you're being offered."

The historical reference to what the Republicans had done to the South struck home; Laval was from Louisiana, after all. "They're going to feel stepped on, Mr. Speaker," he said.

"I know that," Attenborough said. "But their chairman will be in charge of the process from start to finish, so they won't be left out. Will you do it, Bob?"

Laval understood exactly what he was being offered: center stage in the biggest political drama of the new century. He thought it over, then nodded. "Fine. If I have independence."

"As long as you stick to the point like I just said and get it over with by tomorrow night, you're on your own," Attenborough said. "All you've got to do is get yourself elected to the Committee of Managers by the full House."

Laval knew what this meant: He could not possibly be elected to anything by the House without Attenborough's approval and support, so he had to accept the Speaker's terms or bow out.

"All right," he said. "But I'm telling you we're not going to be able to ignore this other thing."

"That's settled, then," Attenborough said. "You fellows can decide who else should be managers, but you'd better keep it small—say eight members besides Laval, five from our side, three from the other party, good political mix, sensible citizens in the majority. You may want to get most of 'em or all of 'em from Judiciary; that's where the lawyers are."

"Any suggestions?"

"I've made my suggestions," Attenborough said.

He left them to their work and, to avoid further contact with the world, went outside and walked through the landscaped grounds of the Capitol. He was alone except for a few early-rising tourists and a Capitol policeman or two. Though it was still winter in the Northern Hemisphere, Washington's annual false spring had begun, and premature tulips and jonquils sparkling with dew bloomed at his feet. Behind the Capitol, hanging above the eastern horizon, the early sun filled the enormous billowing flag on the roof with flaxen light. Its colors and the other colors of the morning were so intense that they seemed almost otherworldly to the Speaker. He felt the pills and liquor again: they had produced a kind of anti-D.T.'s which made reality seem more vivid than it possibly could be, but he loved what he saw all the same. From within the shadow of the backlit dome, etched on

the lawn in perfect detail right down to the feathers on Freedom's head-
dress, he paused and gazed westward over the emerald Mall to the Washington Monument and the Lincoln Memorial beyond. In between, against
the azure sky, Old Glory, endlessly repeating its translucent rippling
image, flew over Greek temples and Roman rotundas, as though an army
of American boys had invaded classical antiquity and captured it for the
folks back home. Attenborough loved this city, and he was overcome with
a loverlike sorrow at its wanton yet unattainable beauty. Standing in the
shade without a topcoat, he shivered and said aloud, "Sweetheart, life is
too damn short."

5

At 9:55 A.M. Attenborough entered the House, ascended the podium, and
sat down in the Speaker's chair. A number of notes awaited him, including one from Bob Laval; he did not read them because he did not want to
be diverted from his plan of action by the second thoughts of others. Ram
it through, get it done, stick to the game plan—that was what he was
going to do. Down below, on the floor, Laval was gesturing to him with
a cellular phone. He pointed at the phone, then pointed at Attenborough,
telling him to pick up his own instrument. Whatever it was he had to say,
the Speaker did not want to hear it. New opinions at this late hour could
only complicate matters. He shook his head and pointed at his watch.
Laval shook his head in exasperation and turned his back.

At ten o'clock precisely, Attenborough gaveled the House to order.
Laval rose as agreed and offered a resolution to constitute the House as a
Committee of the Whole—"a grand and solemn grand jury of the people's
representatives, empowered by the Constitution"—to consider whether
the President of the United States should be impeached for high crimes
and misdemeanors. The resolution was adopted with only fifty dissenting
votes, nearly all from the far-left wing of the party, which did not want
to consider anything that had originated with Franklin Mallory.

There was little to debate. The rest of the four-hour session went exactly
as Attenborough had planned. The House formally confirmed the
Speaker's powers as chairman of the Committee of the Whole into which
it had resolved itself, a formality but a necessary precaution in case of a
later revolt on the floor. Finally Laval and six others, including the ranking minority member of the Judiciary Committee, were elected as a Com-

mittee of Managers and instructed to draft articles of impeachment for consideration by the House at two o'clock the following afternoon.

At precisely two o'clock Attenborough adjourned the House. As he descended from the podium, Laval tried to intercept him, but the Speaker pretended not to see him and scurried off in the other direction as if on an errand of state. After all that time in the Speaker's chair, his blood alcohol level had dropped below the comfort level and his amphetamine was wearing off, and if he wasn't exactly seeing things yet or falling asleep on-camera, he knew he would soon be doing so unless he had a drink and another pill. He headed for his formal office, whose door opened directly from the floor of the House. After washing down a pill with nine ounces of vodka—he was three hours behind in his dosage—he refilled his medicine bottles and slipped them back into his inside breast pockets. Then he washed his face. He was in no way surprised when he looked up, dripping, from the sink and found his sardonic image in the mirror giving him a knowing wink. Attenborough winked back. "My friend, you got eyes like a couple of dead canaries," he said. The image grinned in agreement.

Attenborough waved goodbye to his doppelgänger and went out to face the press. At the moment it resembled an undulating phosphorescent marine polyp that had attached itself tenaciously to Bob Laval, on whom were concentrated its glowing lights and its bubbling collective voice. The Speaker quickened his pace, hoping to draw near in time to overhear whatever Laval was saying; he was beginning to regret that he hadn't talked to him before he went on television.

Protected by the velvet rope that kept back the lobbyists and the tourists as well as the media, Attenborough walked past the carved figures of King Kamehameha I of Hawaii, Father Junípero Serra, and Frances Willard, forgotten personages who proved his point about statuary. A woman with a big head of wild blond hair called out to him from across the velvet rope. He ignored her, but she ran along beside him, still talking. Mistaking her for Morgan Pike and therefore not looking at her closely, he said, "No exclusives, Morgan." He kept on walking, picking up the pace a little and looking straight ahead. At his side he heard her high heels banging on the marble floor, and because he had always thought that Morgan's gangling legs were her best feature, and because he realized in some part of his mind that he wouldn't be looking at legs much longer, he stole a look. What he saw instead of Pike's showgirl limbs was a pair of calves that belonged in the NFL, and when he lifted his eyes to identify their owner he found himself looking into the face of a black-eyed woman who was a total stranger to him.

She gave him a horrible Junior League grin and said, in a husky, unmistakably Texan voice, "Are you Richard Tucker Attenborough, Jr.?"

Attenborough looked grim and hurried and said, "That's me." She said, "In that case, I have something for you." She thrust a blue-backed legal document into his hands. As she did so the two of them were bathed in camera lights.

Without thinking, the Speaker took the document, looked at it, and immediately realized that he had seen sued. But by whom and for what? Forgetting the cameras, he said, "What the hell is this supposed to be?"

"I think you know what it is—retribution," Sturdi replied.

The light came from a smaller cell of the media, split off from the main organism, that now bounded forward, dragging tentacles of cables and wires behind it. In the distance, Laval broke away from his questioners. They too started to run toward Attenborough, as if the polyp that had been sundered by some action of the sea into two gelatinous parts was now swimming frantically back together again.

Before they could get to him, the real Morgan Pike thrust her pink microphone in his face. "What are your feelings at this moment, Mr. Speaker?"

"About what?" Attenborough said.

"About being sued by a certain Slim Eve for twenty million dollars for the physical injury and mental anguish she suffered when you allegedly raped her."

Attenborough frowned into the cameras, then glanced down at the blue-backed legal document in his hand. Slim Eve? Who the hell was that? He said, "Did what to *who?*"

"Ms. Slim Eve. Over there."

Cameramen scampered to capture the image of Slim, who stood with her attorney, surrounded by a support group of forty or fifty people, nearly all of them women. It took Attenborough a moment to recognize his dinner companion without her miniskirt and cleavage; today she was dressed like a nun, her legs and all the rest of her swathed in black except for her wan, unpainted, tormented face. Her hair, which had been so curly and sexy the last time he saw her, was now skinned back into a knot at the back of her head. It looked dull—gray, even—which heightened the impression that she had undergone a life-altering experience. Certainly she didn't look much like the siren dressed for date rape who'd parted her knees so sweetly under that dinner table. All the other females clustered around her were also costumed as drabs. Like the journalists, they seemed to have merged into a single but much more dangerous organism, all with identical frozen expressions, all wearing somber dark suits with trousers or skirts that descended nearly to the ankles. Among these forbidding beings he recognized seven members of the House, three senators, and two members of Lockwood's cabinet, in addition to the usual actresses, writers, professors, lawyers, advocacy specialists, and other do-gooders whose faces were familiar to him from earlier public appearances in support of various causes within the Cause.

The rest of the media had arrived, lights shining. Attenborough faced them, expecting to be battered by questions about Slim Eve. Politic answers formed in his mind, but for the second time that day, he was surprised by the questions.

"Chairman Laval has just announced he's going to hold a secret session of the Committee of Managers tonight to discuss the Ibn Awad case," one journalist said. "What's your comment on that, Mr. Speaker?"

All of a sudden Attenborough felt the tumbler of vodka he had just drunk very strongly, felt the pill he had just swallowed doing its work, and saw everything with such surpassing clarity that he could not believe that he hadn't seen this coming. With deep solemnity he said, "I am sure the truth will be established. Meanwhile, let there be no rush to judgment."

With triumphant anger, Morgan Pike said, "Is that also your advice concerning the rape charge, Mr. Speaker?"

The many lights of the media shone upon him. Across the crowd, Slim Eve regarded him with the contemptuous plum-blue eyes into which he had fallen like Lucifer.

"You bet it is," he said. "As the Good Book says, 'A foolish woman is clamorous; whoso is simple, let him turn in hither.' Book of Proverbs, chapter the ninth, verse the thirteenth."

6

Attenborough turned on his heel and left Morgan Pike and the rest of them to get on with the job of making Slim famous. Beyond the rope, the media polyp divided momentarily, one part following him, pulsing and glowing, until he reached the sanctuary of his formal office, where Alfonso Olmedo was waiting for him.

Olmedo was angry, and for once he did not conceal his emotion. "What is the meaning of calling a closed meeting of the Committee of Managers on Ibn Awad without notice to the President?"

"I didn't," Attenborough said.

"Well, your man Bob Laval just did on national television," Olmedo said. "How could you permit this?"

"Hold on, there, Counselor," Attenborough said, "do you think *I* knew it was going to happen? Laval just went out there and announced that the lynching was about to begin."

"Lynching? What are you talking about?"

"What do you *think* I'm talking about?"

"I demand a postponement of this hearing. My client has rights, Mr. Speaker."

"He does?" Attenborough laughed aloud. "If you believe that, Counselor, I've got a nice bridge, just slightly used, between Manhattan and Brooklyn that I can let you have real cheap."

Olmedo said, "You can joke—*joke* about a matter of this kind?"

Where was Olmedo's famous superhuman coolness? He was sputtering. Amazed, Attenborough held up a tiny hand. "Don't know what else I can do about it, Counselor," he said.

Olmedo stood silent for a moment. At length, with a rueful shrug, he said, "I apologize, Mr. Speaker."

"No need," Attenborough said. "You've got a right to be pissed off. I've got a bigger right. I should have seen this coming—a blind man would have seen it."

"Can there be a postponement?"

"Of the committee hearing? That's not in my power. And it's not what I was talking about anyway. I was talking about this."

He handed Olmedo the legal document Sturdi had served on him. Olmedo scanned it. When he handed it back, his face was somber. "This could be serious," he said.

"It's serious for your client," Attenborough said. "It takes away every bit of respect and moral authority I ever had, right on the eve of the one session I know I've absolutely got to control."

"You've been sued, but you're still the Speaker of the House."

"Correct. But this is not one of your New York lawsuits. It's not the twenty million dollars they want. All I've got in the world is a mortgaged town house and next month's paycheck, and every lawyer in town knows that. What these people want is something else altogether. I've just been charged with rape in the highest court in the land, the news media. On the evening news and tomorrow morning's TV shows, the witnesses will be heard. Then the newspapers will take a day to ponder the evidence and hand down the conviction. After that I'll be on Death Row, politically speaking, and leaving prayer out of it, I won't be able to do a hell of a lot for myself, let alone for your client."

Olmedo struggled to say something that would show he understood what Attenborough was telling him, even if he was from out of town and a stranger to politics. "The timing *is* suspicious," he said.

"Truer words were never spoken," said Attenborough. "Funny coincidence, ain't it?"

"I hope it won't be as bad as you think."

"Hope springs eternal but it don't swat no flies," Attenborough said. "As far as Ibn Awad goes, I can't stop what's going to happen. Bob Laval even tried to tell me, but I put him off, so it's my own fault I was taken by surprise."

"He tried to tell you? I don't understand."

"I didn't think he'd go ahead and do it *without* telling me. The way things are supposed to work around here, if he didn't tell the Speaker, it couldn't happen. But then I was charged with rape, so it didn't matter whether he told me or not."

"I see," Olmedo said. Attenborough wondered if he really did. The lawyer said, "You can't get him to postpone?"

"Forget it. We don't have a Vice President, and we've got a charge of homicide and conspiracy in the papers against the President. Old Bob decided it was his duty to have hearings and have 'em now, tonight, and there's no way he's going to back away from what he just said on television."

"His duty? To aid and abet slander?"

"Slander? Bob Laval's an honest man, Counselor."

"And a member of Lockwood's party. What *is* his purpose?"

"To find out whether your client, who may or may not be the legal President of the United States, is really so dumb that he actually did what the newspaper says he did." Attenborough paused, surprised to note that his hand was suspended nervelessly in the air, like the yellowed marble hand on his own future statue. He must have been gesturing with it and have frozen without knowing it. Why was his mind on statues? Intimations of mortality?

"You have a pungent way of expressing things, Mr. Speaker," Olmedo said. "Will I have the right to appear before the committee on behalf of my client?"

"Sure you will," Attenborough replied, "if that's what you want to do. But take my advice, don't yell at old Bob like you just yelled at me. And don't start talking about Lockwood's rights."

"Why not? They're being trampled."

"I'll tell you why not. Because a President *has* no rights when he becomes a defendant in a case of impeachment, Counselor. You'd better get yourself used to that idea."

Before Olmedo could reply, Albert Tyler came in with a rattling trolley and started to set up a buffet of canapés and drinks.

Attenborough said, "Hungry?"

Olmedo shook his head impatiently. "I'm intrigued," he said. "Go on."

"Glad to; I'm in the mood for it," Attenborough said. "Read your history. A President is accused, tried, and judged according to rules that the House and Senate make up as they go along, and they can make any rule they want. They can *say* anything they want: it says right in the Constitution that they can't be held accountable anywhere else for what they say in Congress. The President can't talk back; nobody can, including his lawyers. So if you show up tonight before the Committee of Managers *in loco presidentis,* you'll have to sit there and take it with a smile like any other witness."

With a final clatter of crockery, Albert withdrew. Attenborough selected a finger sandwich from the buffet. "Sure you're not hungry?"

Again Olmedo shook his head. He said, "Is this revelation about Ibn Awad likely to become a cause of impeachment?"

"Could be," Attenborough said. "Anything can be. When the Nixon case was going on, Jerry Ford said that an impeachable offense is whatever a majority of the House of Representatives considers it to be at a given moment in history. That's the best definition we have. The alpha and omega of it is, as a committee chairman, Bob Laval can do just about anything he wants to do."

Olmedo smiled fleetingly. "Then I guess it's lucky for everybody he's an honest man."

"Not necessarily," Attenborough said.

Olmedo looked down at this wise, ugly little man whom he found so outrageous, so strange, so pathetic, so intelligent, so symbolic. "Mr. Speaker," he said. "Am I right to suspect that you're telling me that there is no hope?"

Attenborough, who was not really hungry, who hadn't been truly hungry in years, put the sandwich dented by his fingertips back onto the tray with the others. "Damn little, Mr. Olmedo," he replied.

7

Laval kept the hearing simple: closed doors, one material witness, minimum audience. No copy of the Ibn Awad tape was introduced into evidence; the committee didn't even ask for it. As Attenborough had foreseen, Macalaster's copy, the only one known to exist, was sacrosanct because custom protected him as a journalist from revealing his sources, even to a committee operating under the direct authority of the Constitution. Jack Philindros, the single witness called, was not asked if either the Foreign Intelligence Service or he personally possessed the original or knew who, if anyone, did possess it or where it was.

The first hours of the hearing, which lasted from seven o'clock in the evening until two the following morning, were devoted to statements by each of the seven members of the Committee of Managers. Olmedo and Norman Carlisle Blackstone were asked by Laval if they wished to make a statement on the President's behalf.

"Not at this time, Mr. Chairman," answered Blackstone.

"Does that mean you may have something to say later on?"

"We would reserve that privilege, Mr. Chairman."

"Fine," said Laval. "Swear the witness."

To Philindros, seated alone at the witness table, Laval said, "Mr. Director, I just want the record to show that you are here voluntarily in your capacity as Director of Foreign Intelligence, that you have neither sought nor received permission from the President of the United States to appear before this committee, and that you are testifying without restriction or reservation of any kind. Am I right about all that?"

"Yes, Mr. Chairman," said Philindros in his habitual half-whisper, half-murmur. The members of the committee exchanged knowing glances; the audience stirred. He was barely audible.

"Jack," Laval said, "we've turned up the microphones as loud as they'll go for you, but you're going to have to holler at us. Lots of folks on this committee are getting a little hard of hearing, like me. All right?"

Philindros raised his voice to a louder, but still faint, volume. "I'll do my best, Mr. Chairman."

"Good. I also want to state for the record that this Committee of Managers, in fact the entire Congress, as established by the precedents of earlier presidential impeachment proceedings, is operating under the unlimited—I say *unlimited*—authority of the Constitution, which is the supreme authority in American law, and therefore may demand the production of any information whatsoever in the possession or custody of any officer of the United States government, and that it may also compel the testimony of any witness. Other precedents in law and procedure do not apply to this process."

Olmedo rose to his feet. "Mr. Chairman, if that is so, may I inquire why Mr. Julian Hubbard, who was present at the alleged conversation between Director Philindros and President Lockwood, and Mr. Ross Macalaster, whose writings are the issue here, have not been called as witnesses?"

Laval looked over his glasses at Blackstone, not at Olmedo. "Mr. Blackstone, I thought you just got through saying you and your colleague here had nothing to say right now."

"I was referring to a formal statement, Mr. Chairman," Blackstone said. "At the moment Mr. Olmedo seems to be addressing a point of information."

"Well, he can't do that, Mr. Blackstone. This is not a courtroom. Counsel can't stand up and make objections that delay this committee's urgent search for the truth. The clock of history is ticking, Mr. Blackstone."

Olmedo looked from one grim face to another in the frieze of judges who gazed down at him from the committee table and sat down.

"Now I guess we can go ahead and examine the witness," said Laval. "Mr. Philindros, once again I remind you and all others who enter here: There are no secrets before the Constitution. This process *defines* the national security. No other definition thereof applies here. No other oath, no other duty or obligation, limits the oath you have just freely taken. It is your constitutional duty, overriding all others, to tell the truth, the whole truth, and nothing but the truth to this committee. Do you understand and accept that?"

"I do, Mr. Chairman."

"Thank you, Mr. Director." Laval, usually so unceremonial, took on an air of solemn formality. "Now let me say just one more thing. The committee, meeting this afternoon in executive session, voted to grant you immunity from prosecution in respect of any matter about which you may testify before it in your capacity as Director of Foreign Intelligence. Let the record show that Director Philindros neither requested such immunity nor was such immunity ever discussed with him or his counsel. The committee took this action spontaneously and unilaterally in consideration of the director's long and sometimes extremely hazardous service to the United States. Because time is so short, the committee has graciously and unanimously agreed that the chairman will conduct the entire examination."

Laval asked Philindros a few pro forma questions to establish that he had, in fact, flown to Lockwood's farm in Kentucky on the night in question nearly four years before. "What was your purpose in going down to Live Oaks that particular night, Mr. Director?"

"To brief the President on a report that Ibn Awad had financed the construction of two ten-kiloton fission bombs and was on the point of delivering them to the terrorist organization known as the Eye of Gaza."

"And did you brief the President to that effect?"

"I briefed him on all the facts at our disposal."

"What did you tell him about Ibn Awad?"

"That he was an unbalanced individual whose psychosis took the form of religious mania. Ibn Awad believed that an angel had appeared to him while he was praying in the desert and told him to destroy Israel by fire."

"And what did Ibn Awad do in response to that vision?"

"He hired nuclear experts from Iraq to construct the two devices in question, using plutonium, detonators, and other materials smuggled out of Russia."

"To what purpose?"

"The devices were easily transportable; they fit into a large suitcase. It was his hope that suicide squads from the Eye of Gaza would detonate the nuclear devices inside Israel, or failing that, in an American city with a large Jewish population, specifically, New York or Miami."

"Was the Eye of Gaza capable of such an act?"

"Based on all the information and expertise available to us, our judgment was that the Eye of Gaza was capable of anything. We knew that their leader, Hassan Abdallah, had visited Ibn Awad in the desert and had agreed to explode the bombs as planned."

"You regarded your information as reliable?"

"Absolutely."

"Why?"

"We had a reliable source in place in close proximity to Ibn Awad, and every room in his palace, as well as the tent in which he prayed when in the desert, was under continual electronic surveillance."

"In other words, you had him bugged and you heard every word he said."

"That is correct, sir."

"And on the night in question you told President Lockwood everything that you've just told this committee?"

"Yes, sir."

"Thank you, Mr. Director. Now I am going to read aloud from a column by Mr. Ross Macalaster in today's newspapers. The passage is quite short." Laval cleared his throat and began reading:

> PHILINDROS: I'm sorry, sir, but I don't think I understand whether you've just given me an instruction.
> LOCKWOOD: I think you understand, Jack.
> PHILINDROS: No, Mr. President, I do not. Do you, as we have just discussed at your request, desire the FIS to take measures to assassinate Ibn Awad and make it appear to be suicide?

Laval interrupted himself: " 'Here,' Mr. Macalaster writes, 'there is a nine-second silence on the tape, during which the sounds of nature—wind, bird calls, etc.—can be heard, together with the crackle of what seem to be Secret Service radios in the distance. Lockwood does not reply. Then Philindros speaks again.' Quote:

> PHILINDROS: I must have a clear, spoken order. Do you instruct me, Mr. President, to use the assets of the Foreign Intelligence Service to bring about the violent death of Ibn Awad, and to gain possession of the two nuclear devices now in his possession?
> LOCKWOOD (*after another five-second pause, and after taking two clearly audible breaths*): Yes.

"Close quote." Laval took a drink of water. "Now, Mr. Director," he said, "I will ask you if the passage I have just read aloud coincides with your memory of your conversation with President Lockwood."

"Yes, Mr. Chairman," Philindros replied. "It does."

"Is it a verbatim account of what was actually said?"

"Yes."

"Word for word? No doubt in your mind about that?"

"None."

"You were insistent, on that night, that the President give 'a clear, spoken order' to carry out the proposed operation against Ibn Awad. Why was that?"

"Because only the President has the authority to give such an order."

"You have no such authority as director of the Foreign Intelligence Service?"

"The Director of Foreign Intelligence is denied such authority by statute. The President must find that an action is warranted and then authorize the action."

"In writing?"

"Not under current procedures. It may be verbal if a witness is present. Mr. Julian Hubbard was also present."

"So assassinating Ibn Awad was not your idea?"

"Ideas are not the business of an intelligence service."

"No? What was it, then?"

"It was an option presented for the President's consideration."

Laval paused and looked through his papers; the mouselike rustle they made could be heard over his microphone. "And did you cause the President's order to assassinate Ibn Awad and gain possession of the two nuclear devices to be carried out?"

"Yes."

"Was Ibn Awad in fact assassinated by an agent of the Foreign Intelligence Service?"

"Using the term 'agent' in the sense of one person acting on behalf of another person or entity, the answer is yes. The assassin was not under discipline."

Laval said, "You're fading out on us, Mr. Director. Please explain that term."

"Sorry." Philindros raised his voice from a whisper to a murmur. "He was not in our pay or under our orders or control."

"Then what was your role?"

"We made it possible for him to do something that he already wanted to do."

"That's an interesting way to put it. Can you elaborate?"

"He did not carry out the operation in the interests of the United States but in what he conceived to be the interests of his own country," Philindros said. "His interests and ours coincided. That is the basis of covert action. As a general rule, you cannot coerce or compel human beings to carry out actions of this kind. In extreme circumstances people do only what they want to do."

"Could he have done this thing he wanted to do—kill his own father—without us?"

"That's impossible to say."

"You pushed him into it?"

"That would be an overstatement. It would be more accurate to say that we did not discourage him or point out flaws in his reasoning."

"In other words, you made sure he didn't change his mind? You made it happen."

"We intended to make it happen, sir. We encouraged it to happen. It happened. We thought that what happened was a case of cause and effect."

"And did you report the result to President Lockwood in those terms?"

Every neck craned to capture the Director's whispered answer. "In those exact words, Mr. Chairman," Philindros said.

The room, in which there was no audience apart from Olmedo, Blackstone, and seven staff lawyers, one for each member of the committee, was perfectly silent. The soft incandescent light falling from the ceiling was adequate for the human eye, but no more; in the absence of the media's kliegs and strobes, the faces of the politicians were softened by natural shadows, so that they looked sadder and less actorish than usual, as if in this unaccustomed isolation from the media they were alone with their thoughts for the first time in ages.

/ 334

"Thank you, Mr. Director." Laval put down the yellow tablet on which he had written his questions and Philindros's answers. "Members of the committee," he said. "I have no further questions."

Olmedo and Blackstone rose to their feet and left the hearing room. As Attenborough had foretold, there was nothing for them to do there.

8

It happened to be one of those rare moments in history when there were no Shelleyans in the House of Representatives, but this was no inconvenience to Archimedes Hammett, who had his own friends inside the House. As luck would have it, his contact within the Judiciary Committee, a young woman named Lois Graf, was beautifully placed because she was the deputy minority counsel—meaning that she worked for the other side and therefore had access to secrets within secrets. She was, of course, a former student of Hammett's, and he had advised her to take this job against her political instincts; it was offered, irony of ironies, because her father and the ranking minority member of the committee had been fraternity brothers. Hammett's reasoning was simple: The job, he argued, provided a matchless opportunity to study the mind and methods of the enemy. Graf's motivation, however, went beyond dedication to the Cause: soon after coming to work, she had been fondled in an elevator by Attenborough. It was a famous incident in Capitol Hill folklore. Standing behind her in the crowded lift in the Rayburn Building, the Speaker had sneaked a hand under her arm and grasped her left breast. Graf had seized his wrist, lifted it high in the air, and cried out in a loud voice, "And whose naughty little hand is *this*?" Even Attenborough had joined in the ribald laughter that filled the cabin: good old Tucker, copping another feel! His victim's good-natured reaction, however, was a front for darker feelings: if her position had not been so valuable to the Cause, she would have dragged the little lecher before the Ethics Committee for sexual harassment. But Graf knew she could not do that and stay where she was, in the very bosom of the Establishment, so she had behaved on the elevator like what she was supposed to be, a sensible conservative "girl," instead of the politically aware, goals-oriented person she really was.

The first thing Graf did after the Judiciary Committee hearings ended was to call up Hammett with a succinct but detailed report on Philindros's testimony.

Hammett, so difficult to surprise, was thunderstruck by what she told him. "Philindros confirmed the story? Lockwood lied to everybody? He actually *lied?*"

"That was the testimony."

"Lockwood *ordered* this homicide? Made it happen from day one?"

"That's what the man said. They covered it up for, quote-unquote, national security reasons."

"I can't believe this."

"The committee believed it. It's sad when you think what this means for Lockwood."

"Lockwood is history," Hammett said grimly.

"Maybe not. The committee's session was secret. The testimony won't be released."

"Won't be released? It will be *leaked.*"

"I don't think so. Bob Laval doesn't want to do Lockwood any more harm than necessary, and the conservatives don't want to be accused of playing politics with a terrorist threat involving a nuclear bomb."

"You must be joking," Hammett said. "This changes everything. We put Lockwood where he is and he betrayed us."

"Maybe it isn't as simple as that. There *were* those bombs. And he hasn't testified. Shouldn't we at least hear his side of the story?"

"Forget his side of the story," Hammett said. "He just stopped being the President who could not tell a lie. Besides, how is he ever going to tell his side if the story doesn't come out? Can you lay hands on a transcript of the testimony?"

"A diskette."

"Leave it in the usual place. Now."

"They'll know who did it; access is very tight. It could cost me my job."

"Nonsense. The reactionaries will love you for it," Hammett said. "And if they don't, you'll get a better job, one where you can be yourself. Everybody will know you've earned it. Believe me."

Without waiting for her acquiescence, Hammett disconnected and immediately punched out the number of a borrowed house in Southeast Washington where Sturdi was working late with Slim on their schedule for the next day, when they were being interviewed by the newsmagazines and the long-format weekly television shows. The prospect of all this exposure made Slim nervous—Sturdi was amazed at just how nervous, and she had spent the evening calming and reassuring her friend. Sturdi was not glad to hear the phone ring, but she answered circumspectly by reciting the phone number.

Hammett's voice said, "I'd like to order a medium pizza with mushrooms and peppers *under the sauce,* sugar- and sodium-free." Sturdi said,

"Right away, sir. Name and address?" Hammett said, "The name is Charley, spelled with a *y*. Rayburn House Office Building. Just leave it at the desk between one and two. Make it fast."

This gibberish told Sturdi that she was to pick up a package on C Street, between First and Second Streets, from beneath a parked car with the letter *y* soaped on the rear window. She had done this before when Graf had had something for Hammett and the Cause. Sturdi did not welcome the assignment. Slim needed her, and that was not an everyday event. All the same she put on her biking clothes, clipped a tube of red-pepper anti-mugger spray to her wrist because she would be riding through destabilized neighborhoods, and left immediately.

While he waited for Sturdi to carry out her assignment, Hammett began making calls, putting out the bitter, all-but-unbelievable word that Lockwood had betrayed them all, that the President they had trusted was not what they had thought he was—that is, a man from the underclass whom they had raised up to power so that he could act on the basis of their wisdom—but instead was a pawn of the Establishment. On one point, however, he was careful to add a word of caution: "Lockwood is one thing, and to our sorrow we now know what that thing is," he said in his reasonable, collegial, we-all-talk-the-same-language way, to each of the three dozen political activists and public officials he called. "Nothing can atone for what this man did and how he deceived us. But don't make the mistake of blaming Julian. He's with us and always has been. I know for a fact that he deserves no part of the blame. Why do you think he resigned? I can't say more. Just remember all he's done for the Cause and try to imagine what he must be going through because he trusted Lockwood just as we did."

Hammett knew they would all be on the phone themselves as soon as the sun rose, networking, organizing congressmen and key congressional staffers, briefing the second echelon of the media.

Sturdi arrived at Hammett's place just before dawn with the diskette she had retrieved from beneath the parked car on C Street. He read the documents with a reassuring sense of growing calm: knowing the inmost truth—knowing the worst—about anything had always tranquilized him. He understood perfectly what he held in his hands. This bombshell, bursting in the media just hours after the sensation Slim had created with her exposure of Attenborough, would be one of the great one-two punches in the annals of guerrilla journalism.

9

The full story of Attenborough's assault on Slim had already broken on the evening news. Because the accused refused to discuss the matter even on background, the coverage was based on the allegations in Slim's lawsuit, with additional details provided by the knowledgeable sources who had already been talking to journalists about the episode for several days. The words "rape" and "penetration" occurred often, and because it was impossible in a family newspaper to provide full anatomical details, many readers, perhaps even a majority, did not understand which part of Attenborough's body had been the instrument of penetration. "The question is irrelevant," said Sturdi, refusing to be specific but willing to be clinical when it was put by a sympathetic but curious reporter. "My client was violated; she was penetrated; that is rape no matter what instrument the rapist used."

The stories included interviews with anonymous sources among the emergency room staff at a large downtown hospital where Slim had been interviewed and examined immediately after she left Macalaster's house. They described her hysteria, her disorientation, her injuries, which appeared to have been inflicted by a sharp object. Unnamed clerical and technical personnel at the smaller hospital where Attenborough had been treated for a cut suffered in a drunken fall added their recollections. It was reported that Attenborough had called the young Chinese-American resident who treated him "that little Chink doctor with the nice ass." Other women who had been pinched, fondled, or otherwise harassed by the Speaker were quoted at length, also anonymously.

The network morning shows were thronged by agitated women, joined by an enlightened male or two, from the phalanx of feminists who had clustered so protectively around Slim in Statuary Hall. Slim herself appeared on *Newsdawn with Patrick Graham.* Her great, almost irrational fear, she had told Sturdi, was that she would be recognized and accosted by strangers who had seen her on television. Sturdi, who had a way with makeovers, had calmed her friend's fears, though she had not banished them, by inventing a new schoolmarm look for Slim, concealing her most memorable features by covering her legs with a long skirt, skinning back her luxuriant shampoo-model's hair into a bun, and shielding her lavender eyes with tinted granny glasses. The result was a Slim as new and unexpected as the one who appeared at Macalaster's dinner party, a Slim who was the picture of a politically wholesome woman: a trained mind in a mortified body.

Slim did not discuss the specifics of the attack on herself. She did not have to: Graham was already in possession of every detail, and in his introductory remarks he omitted none of them. In her live interview, conducted by Graham personally, she stuck to the larger question of the political implications of male sexuality, despite his pointed demands for a more personal approach: How had she felt then? How did she feel now? How should other women feel if this happened to them?

In reply, Slim made a number of abstract comments that were, feminists agreed, more devastating than any mere clinical report of her humiliation could have been. A sexually ruthless white male member of the governing elite in a position of great power, Slim said, could be compared to the commandant of a concentration camp who selects and uses a female prisoner as a sexual toy. All women know, are born knowing, that something like this can happen to them at any moment.

Patrick Graham heard Slim out with a mixture of sympathy and impatience that sent its own signal to the audience. "Should a man who can be compared to the commandant of Auschwitz be President of the United States, or even Speaker of the House?" he asked.

"That has always been the question," Slim replied. "And now, after centuries of silence, victims are demanding an answer."

If Graham perceived any incongruity in comparing life in a concentration camp to attending a dinner party in the wealthiest zip code in America, he did not let it show. "Ms. Slim Eve, ladies and gentlemen," he said with transparent admiration. "Victim and advocate, woman and citizen, talking about a deeply troubled man who is a heartbeat away from an even more deeply troubled presidency. After these messages, Morgan Pike on Capitol Hill."

10

Attenborough, who was part of Patrick Graham's audience, fell into a deep slumber as soon as Slim went off the air. He had skipped his morning pep pill. Under the circumstances, he didn't really expect to be awakened by callers, and after many sleepless hours he needed rest. He was dreaming about a West Texas sandstorm—grit blowing in through the cracks in the House chamber, burying the members' desks—when Albert woke him just before noon.

"Here's your pill," Albert said. Pouring coffee into a cup that already contained three fingers of Absolut vodka, he added, "Don't take another one till four o'clock. Henry says too many are bad for you."

"Hadn't noticed," Attenborough said. He swallowed the pill, draining the coffee cup to wash it down, and closed his eyes as if to go back to sleep. A minute later he opened them again with a now-familiar snap as he felt the amphetamine take effect. Amazing stuff.

Taking the cleaner's plastic bag off a fresh blue suit and pinning Attenborough's Phi Beta Kappa key to the lapel, Albert said, "Majority Leader wants you to call him soon as you've got a minute."

"Soon as I shave and get dressed. Leave the suit. We got plenty of spring water, Albert?"

"Just put a new bottle in the cooler. Remember what Henry said about that, too."

In the bathroom, Attenborough took a shower and shaved, an exercise in self-denial, before getting out the spring water bottle and having his second three ounces of the day just a few minutes early. The image in the glass winked and said, "Don't do that again, Tucker." Attenborough replied, "Don't worry, you know me."

When he emerged into his office, his scrawny body wrapped in a big Turkish towel that the Turkish ambassador had given him, the Speaker found Sam Clark standing in front of his desk. Clark looked a little apprehensive, as if he thought Attenborough might not be glad to see him. However, his host gave him a wave of welcome, remembering with a rueful twinge how the breakfast flew the last time Sam had been here on an Odd Wednesday. He said, "Howdy, Sam. I was going to call you as soon as I got my pants on." He dropped the towel and began to put on the underwear, socks, shirt, polka-dot necktie, tailor-made suit, and shoes that Albert had laid out for him.

Clark went right on looking worried. "I'll make this short and to the point," he said. "Is this story in the papers true?"

Attenborough looked up a little dizzily from the difficult job of tying his shoes. "You mean the one about my brutally ravishing a spotless, struggling virgin on the dinner table while the Chief Justice and all the ladies present cried 'Stop, stop, in the name of all that's decent and holy'?"

Clark did not crack a smile. He said, "Tucker, just answer the question."

Deftly knotting his tie without a mirror, Attenborough replied, "Okay. The answer is, I felt her up under the table. Got all the way home, in fact. She acted like she was enjoying it. Then, all of a sudden, she jumped up and hollered 'Rape.' What does that sound like to you?"

Staring hard, Clark compressed his lips. Attenborough had never lied to him. As far as Clark knew he had never lied to anybody; when he wanted to avoid telling the truth he made a joke. The Majority Leader said, "It sounds to me like somebody's out to get you."

Attenborough buttoned up his vest, put on his suit coat and buttoned that, too. "Don't it, though?" he said. "Makes you wonder who's next. For all I know they already got poor old Willy Graves."

"You're not serious."

"The hell I'm not. Willy liked the girls. Common knowledge. Maybe that same dolly with the hole in her stockings worked old Willy up till he had a heart attack."

"What are you trying to tell me, Tucker?"

"Sam, I'm not *trying* to tell you anything. It's as plain as the nose on Lockwood's face. Somebody's playing Ten Little Indians with the presidency of the United States. I was trashed in time for the evening news, and after Bob Laval got mouse-trapped into calling that damned hearing, Lockwood's turn is next—unless this town has changed all of a sudden."

"You think Franklin is doing this?"

"No," Attenborough said. "Hell, no. Franklin may be a hardhearted son of a bitch who'd have the Little Match Girl arrested for loitering, but God knows he works right out in the open. That's why we've been put to all this damn inconvenience. Besides, why would he? He thinks he was elected President—and he's probably right, not that it's going to do him much good."

"Then who?"

"Why ask me? Nobody's going to believe a word I say for the rest of my life." Attenborough coughed, a long spasm that brought color to his deadened skin and made him hear his pulse beating in his skull. Looking up at the end of it with tears in his eyes, he winked broadly and said, "I'm talking two weeks. Maybe three."

11

As Patrick Graham walked from the front door of his fine Federal house on O Street to the limousine that would transport him to the studio at 4:30 A.M. on the day after the Laval committee hearings, a bicycle messenger delivered a transcript of Philindros's testimony to him. The messenger, an androgynous being who wore yellow goggles even in the darkness of the morning, sped away into the warren of Georgetown streets before Graham could react.

He read the transcript in the limousine. Included as a bonus were photocopies of supporting documents—memorandums of Philindros's conversations with Lockwood and Julian Hubbard, reports from the FIS officer in the field who handled the assassin (unidentified in the document but known for a fact by Graham to be Horace Hubbard), and transcripts of intercepted conversations between Ibn Awad and the terrorists—that Philindros had submitted to the committee. The whole bundle, neatly bound in red loose-leaf covers, weighed not less than four pounds. The documents were stamped TOP SECRET SENSITIVE EYES ONLY CODE WORD NO FORN in red ink.

Because he knew a history-making story when he saw one, and even more because he was still smarting from the humiliation of having Ross Macalaster print a story that he, Graham, had uncovered months earlier but had been too decent to broadcast, he put it on the air raw before the credits rolled on *Newsdawn*. Then, after the most cursory mention of the other news, he devoted the entire two hours of the show to in-depth interviews with congressmen, leaders of every political grouping that had any conceivable interest in the event, ex-spies, and ordinary people accosted on their way to work by roving reporters. Naturally the story was picked up by all the other morning shows while *Newsdawn* was still in progress, and a brief last-minute story under a 72-point headline (FIS CHIEF SAYS LOCKWOOD LIED) was splashed on the made-over front page of the final edition of the newspaper. Ross Macalaster was given no credit by Graham, or even by his own newspaper, for breaking the story.

By the time the House convened at two in the afternoon, the White House and the Capitol were encircled by chanting pickets. Tens of thousands of phone calls, faxes, and E-mail messages had been delivered to every member of the House, and were still coming in as fast as the phone lines could handle them. Lockwood was denounced on the floor by member after member for "lying to the American people."

At four o'clock, in good time for the evening news, the President was impeached for high crimes and misdemeanors. Two articles of impeachment were adopted, the first for ordering the assassination of Ibn Awad, "contrary to the laws and moral standards of the United States of America," and a second, omnibus article charging him with taking the presidential oath of office "under false pretenses and with mental reservations," in that persons acting in his interest had falsified the outcome of the voting in Michigan, New York, and California. What the false pretenses might be Attenborough could not imagine, but he smelled trouble in the phrase.

Lockwood's own party deserted him in massive numbers. Only twelve votes, including Attenborough's, were cast against the Ibn Awad article. The opposition voted unanimously for impeachment, as they had planned to do all along for political reasons that had nothing to do with the evidence. Fifty members, a tiny minority, voted against the article concerning the presidential oath, a formulation that differed in what Attenborough knew was almost certainly a fatal way from his original formula for impeaching Lockwood on charges of which he was clearly innocent— namely personal involvement in the theft of the election. Attenborough did not think the Ibn Awad article would ever stick, or was meant to; what it *was* designed to do was to turn Lockwood's reputation upside down and make it look as if he were capable of anything, for the purpose of setting him up for conviction on the rest of the articles. The provision on mental reservation was the sleeper: It was the oath that made you President through God's blessing and anointment by the Constitution. Therefore if the oath wasn't valid, Lockwood had never been President. Attenborough did not even want to think about the Pandora's box that this would open, let alone what would pop out of it.

The Speaker did his best not to think about it while the riot in the House lasted. After what had been said about him in the media, he knew he could do little to control the debate and even less to influence the outcome. During the roll call he laid his head against the tall leather back of the Speaker's chair and closed his eyes, opening them only to vote against both articles of impeachment. As he dozed, or seemed to, the network commentators remarked, one after the other, on his fall from grace and power. "When he has finished his nap," said Patrick Graham sonorously, "the Speaker will wake up to find that he has, in a single moment of lust and folly, lost any claim to power and prestige."

After it was over, Attenborough walked past the press, which had again attached itself to Laval. This time the Speaker was close enough to hear the chairman's words. He was saying, "Arguing this case against my old friend Frosty Lockwood is the saddest duty and the heaviest burden of my life, but I will do the best I can. All that matters now is the truth."

Damn right, Attenborough thought, but where have you gone, Joe DiMaggio? No one asked him to put his thoughts into words. He passed in ghostly fashion among the media people and they shrank away from him as if he gave off a sepulchral chill.

Macalaster fell into step beside him. "Mr. Speaker, can we talk?" His tone was embarrassed.

"Sure," Attenborough said, clapping him on the back. "What else would the two most popular boys in school do when they run into each other in the hall?"

Macalaster snorted. It was true that he too was being shunned, though for different reasons. Attenborough was quarantined out of fear that his disgrace might be infectious, Macalaster because he had made the mistake of causing his colleagues to envy him again. He had broken the biggest story of the constitutional crisis and then, in the next news period, been identified as the host of the most infamous dinner party of the year. Both he and Attenborough knew that this wretched excess of insiderism was too much for his more ideologically orthodox competitors to forgive.

Macalaster said, "I just want to tell you I'm sorry about all this grief you're going through."

"Why?"

"Because I feel responsible."

"Well, you're not," Attenborough replied. "Although it has occurred to me, Ross, that I might've been better off sitting next to somebody else at your dinner table that night. Or ordering up a pizza and watching the Spice channel. But how were you to know?"

"That's just it. I *should* have known."

"Should've known what?" Attenborough said.

"That Slim was crazy. I *did* know it."

"Then why did you invite her?"

"I didn't," Macalaster said. "She came with Hammett. He wanted to meet you and asked me to invite you."

All of a sudden, having spotted these two outcasts together, the polyp floated toward them as if it smelled the possibility of Macalaster's sneaking another scoop. Attenborough waved to the advancing organism, which was gesticulating and calling out his name in its many-tongued voice. To Macalaster he said, "You mean Hammett set the whole thing up?"

Macalaster nodded. Something dawned in his eyes.

"Interesting sidelight on history," Attenborough said. "I hope you're not planning to save it for your memoirs." Then he turned to confront the clamoring reporters.

12

"Did you see that little runt up there, pretending to be asleep while the riot went on?" Lockwood said to Sam Clark over the speakerphone. "He thinks he's going to sneak in the back door of the White House and sit in this chair. I knew it all along. The minute Willy Graves's heart stopped beating, my everlasting friend Tucker Attenborough grabbed for the brass ring."

If this was nonsense, Lockwood did not necessarily know it. Despite all his political experience, the disaster in the House of Representatives had knocked Lockwood off balance. Up to the morning of the session he had half-expected, on the basis of his own head counts of the House, not to be impeached. He had never seen so many votes change so fast and with so little notice. Now he was looking for someone to blame. Or so it seemed to Blackstone, who walked into the Oval Office with Olmedo in tow just as Lockwood began to speak. When he realized that Lockwood was on the phone, he made as if to leave, but the President motioned the two of them to sit down and listen.

Clark's voice said, "I just don't buy that theory, Mr. President."

"No?" Lockwood said, "Yesterday the little son of a bitch was telling me it was all under control, everything running smooth as clockwork, all ducks in a row, every Indian on the reservation, nothing to worry about, Mr. President, no sirree, everybody gonna vote the straight Lockwood ticket, you'll have this shit behind you in two weeks because you're innocent and we gonna prove that."

"Until yesterday Tucker believed that, Mr. President. He was trying to save the situation, and if that story hadn't been in the papers he might have."

"Well, everybody's got his own way of being a good Samaritan. That part's over. Now, Sam—"

"Mr. President, let's not leave this subject just yet. Attenborough's down. I'm not going to join any kicking party."

"You mean like the one he just had on national TV in the House of Representatives with me as the football? Don't tell me about Tucker. He was probably too drunk to know what was going on, or maybe he thought he'd just get crocked, take a little nap, and when he woke up Albert would be calling him Mr. President."

The phone hummed emptily for a moment. "Frosty," Sam Clark said, "I'm not going to argue with you about Tucker's motives, but I think you'd better wake up to the fact that he's just about the last real friend you've got on that side of the Capitol. You're going to need all the friends you have. Tucker just had some bad luck at a bad time."

"It was his own doing."

"Spoken like an expert."

Huge hands curled into a stranglehold, Lockwood stared at the instrument from which Clark's dry voice had issued. "Thanks a lot, Sam," he said.

"Sorry if that stung," Clark's voice replied, "but it's the truth. You've let the country down, Mr. President. You've let the party down."

"And miserable son of a bitch that I am, I've let you down worst of all. Isn't that what you really mean, Sam?"

"I mean what I say, and that's all that I mean."

With an effort Lockwood collected himself. He said, "You think I did what they said I did?"

"Didn't you?"

"All I did was happen to be President when a bunch of damn fools did what they did."

"That's not the issue anymore, and we both know it."

Lockwood's knuckles whitened. "So you're going over the side on me like everybody else I ever befriended. Is that the message?"

"No. That's your bad side talking, and you can't afford it. You know damn well I'm with you to the end."

Lockwood's deep blue eyes, an instant before so darkened by anger, suddenly glistened; he was so moved by this expression of loyalty and affection from Clark that Blackstone thought he might actually weep.

"Thanks, Sam," he said. "That means a hell of a lot to me."

"A lot of things mean a lot, Frosty. Somebody in this town is doing you wrong, my friend, but it isn't Tucker Attenborough. Do you hear me?"

"I hear you. Then who the hell is behind all this crap?"

"I wish I knew. But you'd better find out, Mr. President. You've got to stop believing your own misconceptions and start using your head. I'll go down the line with you whether anybody comes with me or not. There's just one condition, and that's why I'm calling."

"Name it, Sam."

"When that last minute comes," Clark said, "just don't make me choose between you and the country."

13

Lockwood switched off the speakerphone and looked at his lawyers. In the space of a single breath, he had put the conversation with Clark and all the events of this terrible week behind him. He had not even mentioned the death of Vice President Graves. Blackstone marveled at his ability to take these staggering blows, pick himself up, and go on to the next thing.

"All right," Lockwood said. "What now?"

"A holding action," Olmedo said.

"After the worst has happened?"

"All that happened today was that you were charged with crimes you did not commit. The worst possible outcome would be conviction of an innocent President. That's why we need time to investigate, time to prepare the defense. And Senator Clark is right—time to think."

"Forget it," Lockwood said. "The juggernaut is rolling. You can't think and play catch-up at the same time. What we've got to do, Alfonso, is run like hell toward the nearest cliff, then step aside at the last minute and let the lynch mob go over the edge."

"A wonderful image," Olmedo said. "But this situation is not a game with certain rules, it is life—"

"Which is chaotic and unpredictable," Lockwood said. "I know about life. Get to the point."

"The point," Olmedo said, "the point is that if Philindros's testimony stands up under cross-examination, if it is corroborated, we've got a serious problem."

"If Jack told the truth, we do."

"Are you suggesting he didn't, Mr. President? Because if he didn't, then you did."

Lockwood mimicked astonishment. "Good thinking," he said. "You mean you're ready to hear my plea? By golly, things *are* desperate."

Grimly Olmedo said, "Did Philindros tell the truth?"

"Some of it," Lockwood said. "Not enough of it."

"What did he leave out? This is important, Mr. President."

"He left out the reality, that's all," Lockwood said. "What happened was, he and Julian cooked the whole thing up and came down to the farm in the middle of the night. Never in a million years did I think I'd ever have to sign a death warrant, especially not in the first springtime of my presidency. But that was the deal they handed me. Philindros said that this nutcase was going to blow up millions of people the next day—*at midnight.* Those were his own words. Old Jack had it timed right down to the minute; that's how sure he was of his facts. The bombs would be delivered at midnight to the Eye of Gaza, a bunch of maniacs I'd never even heard of at the time, though I got to know 'em pretty well later on. They could set them off at any moment after that. It was like that old play where the guy stands up on the stage and tells the audience what everything means—one lantern for a gale, two for a hurricane, three for the end of the world. This was a three-lantern situation."

"So you felt justified in assassinating Ibn Awad."

Lockwood grunted, an angry sound. "Don't put words in my mouth. *I* didn't assassinate the son of a bitch! Horace Hubbard got Ibn Awad's own kid to do it."

Olmedo said, "Semantics, Mr. President. You gave the order."

Lockwood slammed his fist down on his desk. "Do you want to hear the truth or not?"

"Sorry. Go on, Mr. President."

Lockwood said, "They proposed the operation. That's how they talk, changing words on you. I said, 'You're offering me a cup of poison.' Exact words. Why weren't *those* words in the newspaper? I said, 'Get me to this Ibn Awad; let me talk to him.' Exact words. Jack said, 'You can't do that in secret, Mr. President.' I said, 'Secret, hell! I'll go on television and tell the world what's going on and say what I'm trying to prevent.' Exact words. Why weren't they on the tape? Jack said, 'You mean *tell the truth to the world?*' He was shocked by the idea—his eyes rolled back in his head. I said, 'What's wrong with the truth?' Exact words."

Olmedo said, "What was Julian Hubbard saying all this time?"

"Keeping his mouth shut. He chimed in later, but not then. For the first half hour, Jack Philindros was doing all the talking, Julian was just standing there, nodding his head."

"Nodding his head? Why?"

"Because he knew what Jack was going to say and agreed with it before he said a word to me."

"You know that to be true?"

"It was always true. Julian never let anybody in to see me unless he knew in advance what was going to be said."

Olmedo was startled—not by the practice but by what it meant. It meant that Julian knew everything while Lockwood knew only what Julian wanted him to know, and this was how the country had always been governed. He said, "Why was such a policy adopted?"

"Why? Because Julian was my chief of staff. That was always his job—to keep people from putting me in the wrong position."

"The position of saying no, or of preventing you from hearing inconvenient facts?"

"You got it." Lockwood went on, uninterested in such an obvious point. "So, getting back. After I asked Jack what was wrong with going on TV and telling the truth, he said, 'The truth works slowly, Mr. President. If you go on television, you'll be warning them, and you'll be too late.' "

" 'Them'?"

"The Eye of Gaza, Ibn Awad. I said, 'If I *don't* do it, they'll blow up the world, according to you.' Exact words."

Olmedo said, "*Are* these exact words?"

"Counselor, I'm maybe not the smartest guy that ever lived, but when I'm talking about something like this, I remember what I say. Okay if I go on?" Olmedo flicked a hand. Elaborately Lockwood bowed his thanks for permission to do what he was going to do anyway. "Now Julian began to talk. He thought I'd look real bad if I flew over there in *Air Force One* and my host blew up Tel Aviv or maybe New York City while we were having our tea party. Might even take me hostage. Then Philindros says, 'Ibn Awad is a manic-depressive. We know this because our doctors examined him. Right now he's in his manic cycle and that's why he wants to blow up the world, but when he's depressive he talks a lot about suicide. We think we can kill this crazy old man and make it look like suicide.' "

"Exact words?"

"No. Jack doesn't come right out with it like that. But close enough. I said—are you listening, both of you?—I said, '*There must be an alternative.*' Exact words. Jack said, 'Perhaps. It's up to you to decide.' I said, 'Kill a man? Assassinate somebody?' Exact words. Up to that moment the thought of assassination had never crossed my mind. I thought we'd send in the Marines or the Green Berets, find the bombs, arrest Ibn Awad in the name of mankind, and lock him up in his own private loony bin with a bunch of blondes and the best prayer rugs money could buy. But then Jack said something else to me, *psspsspss.* Whispering Jack, they ought to call him. You can't hear the son of a bitch if you're inside a shoebox with him, and just like the paper says, we were outdoors with the crickets singing, the Secret Service talking into their radios, and the floodlights buzzing."

"What did he say?"

"I didn't hear him. I was thinking about something else."

"You were thinking about something else, Mr. President? At a moment like that?"

Lockwood fixed Olmedo with a scornful eye. "That's right. I suddenly thought: If a bomb goes off in Israel, the Israelis will nuke everything and everybody in the Middle East. All the Arabs will launch in return. Then so will everybody else who's got a surplus Russian missile on a rocket made in China. This planet is going to be turned into a cinder."

"Those were your thoughts while Philindros was speaking?"

"I just got through telling you they were. I also thought, If Jack Philindros is so damn smart, why hasn't *he* thought of this?"

Olmedo said, "So you didn't hear Philindros ask if you instructed him to bring about the violent death of Ibn Awad?"

"No. Not a word of it. First I ever heard of that was when I read it in the newspapers yesterday morning."

"But it's on the tape."

"Then the tape is wrong."

"Mr. President, consider carefully. You heard every other syllable he uttered."

"That's because I had my ear pushed up against his mouth until he started talking about assassination. Then I walked away from him."

"Why?"

"I'll tell you again: *because I didn't want to hear what he was saying.* And I didn't hear it because I had other things to think about. That's my defense."

"But according to the tape you said, 'Yes.' "

Lockwood shrugged, vastly uninterested in this detail. "Prob'ly I did, but not in answer to that question," he said. "I don't know why I said it. I know it sounds implausible as hell, but the truth sometimes is. And by that time I was just trying to be polite—trying to get rid of him. I may not look it, but the truth is, I'm a sensitive son of a bitch. I didn't want to embarrass Jack; I'd just turned him down when he had his heart set on saving the world from nuclear holocaust. At least that's what I thought when I went to bed that night. However, the next thing I knew—the next *day,* Counselor—they were telling me, proud as punch, that the deed was done. They'd killed the poor old bastard."

"And when you learned of this, you didn't express surprise, didn't voice disapproval?"

"What was the point? It was over. I told Julian to keep Philindros out of my life from that point onward. I put the whole damn thing out of my mind and went on to something else."

"And *did* Julian keep Philindros out of your life?"

"Sure he did, until the assassination was about to come out four years later, just like I always knew it would. As soon as I got the word I called Jack in and reminded him I'd told him to do no such thing. You never saw such a look of surprise in your life. He said, 'No, sir, Mr. President, that's just not so.' And in these exact words he said, 'Julian made it plain it was my task to carry out your order without making small talk to you about it. It's not a pleasant thing to be made a party to murder. I detested receiving that order as much as you detested giving it. I detest the memory of it still.' Detested it? He *invented* it. Sanctimonious little shit."

Olmedo exhaled.

"Well," Lockwood said, "what do you think of *that* story?"

"I agree it's implausible, but if it's the truth we will defend it as the truth," Olmedo said, rising to his feet. "I think we'd better have Mr. McGraw look into this matter of the tape."

"Good idea."

"And with your permission, Mr. President, I'll go away now and let you get some sleep."

"Sleep?" Lockwood said. "No problem whatsoever, with this airtight alibi I've got."

VII

1

The peculiar thing about the impeachment situation, Horace Hubbard thought, was the way in which all parties were isolated from one another. He had not even seen Julian since their meeting with Busby at the Harbor, and the odd Washington protocol seemed to preclude Lockwood from having any sort of contact with any of the other players except through the news media, which seemed to function in America as a gigantic code room to which everyone had a key, though not necessarily a deciphering pad. Horace's only communication with the outside world was through the Shelleyan network, and of course that was of little or no use when it came to getting in touch with people like Alfonso Olmedo C.

Horace had no idea whether he was under investigation and might be charged with federal crimes at any moment or whether he was going to be called to testify. A lawyer might have been able to make inquiries for him, but Horace saw no point in paying someone a great deal of money to make phone calls to the wrong people. Only Lockwood, Olmedo, and Blackstone in his ivory tower knew what role, if any, Horace was going to play in the impeachment, and they were unlikely to confide in any attorney he might engage. The likeliest person to find out what was in store for him was Julian, and the fact that Julian had not communicated with his brother could only mean that even he could not find out the facts.

The suspense was hard on Rose MacKenzie. She was solitary by nature, but as the person in charge of the FIS's data banks, she had lived much of her life with the illusion that she knew almost everything that was worth knowing and could quite easily find out anything she happened not to know. Now she did not even know if she was going to be charged with a crime, or whether she was going to be dragged before the world on television and humiliated with questions she had sworn an oath never to answer. She was not a young woman. She was almost fifty, and the idea of going to prison terrified her. Living at the Harbor with Horace, she was disintegrating before his eyes: drinking too much, talking wildly about just vanishing, weeping continually, neglecting to eat, forgetting to bathe, making sexual demands that Horace had difficulty gratifying at his age, waking in the night and crying out, "Oh, God, jail! My *mother!*" She had always been untidy, but now she was turning the Harbor into a mare's nest—all the books in the wrong places, dirty glasses everywhere, clothes left anyhow. Horace could not keep ahead of it. The two of them had been intermittent lovers for many years, but they had never lived together. When he suggested a greater attention to neatness, Rose wandered into the woods and was gone for twenty hours before he found her huddled against the bole of an ancient sugar maple with an empty 1.75-liter bottle of Popov vodka at her feet. It was cold in the Berkshires in March; she caught pneumonia and went into the hospital.

While she recovered, Horace decided that he must do something to regain control of his own life and, if possible, to preserve Rose from the fate she seemed to be conjuring for herself. His idea from the beginning had been to provide information that would blow the situation open in an early stage, rendering it unnecessary to involve either Rose or Julian. He had always been willing to be the *osageyfo*, a title he had suggested to an able but ill-fated political-action asset in West Africa (not that there was any other kind of African political asset) more than half a lifetime before. The term, from the Efik, meant "he who bears the brunt."

Horace had information that no one else had, not even Julian or Philindros, and he saw no way out but to use it. It would have been foolhardy to phone Busby direct, so he called Five-Three, an international banker who was the first member of his Shelleyan cell, asking him to set up a rendezvous between Horace and Busby. That weekend, wearing a light but sufficient disguise and traveling under one of several false identities for which he had kept up the documentation, including even a pilot's license, Horace journeyed to the secret meeting with Busby. He was uncomfortable with the breach of discipline involved in using FIS documentation for private purposes, but given the choice between his friend and his country, he chose his friend. How strangely things turned out, Horace thought. All his life until now, he had done exactly the opposite as a matter of moral principle.

In a matter of hours he and Busby were sailing through the Grenadines in Busby's sloop, two lanky, well-kept, but almost elderly men, looking for humpback whales but talking about Horace's career in espionage, about which Busby knew little and was curious to know more. Although he had abominated the Outfit and all its works because these undermined the Definition and the Duty, Busby had always been puzzled by the fact that he had not been tapped for recruitment by the Outfit, as he had been tapped for membership in nearly everything else worth getting into at

Yale. A joiner by nature, he did not like the uncomfortable feeling that he might have missed out on belonging to something to which so many other good fellows belonged. Especially something that so clearly had been fun, scruples or no scruples. Not that he would have been any good at it. Unlike his old friend, who had never thought in terms of political virtue—in fact, Horace regarded the term as an oxymoron—Busby had always been an idealist. He had been impressed early in life by the intellectual harmony and moral symmetry of Karl Marx's ideas, which were so much like Shelley's in *Prometheus Unbound*. Rapturously Busby quoted: " 'Man, one harmonious Soul of many a soul, / Whose nature is its own divine controul . . .'

"That's where Marx got 'Workers of the world, unite! You have nothing to lose but your chains,' " he said. "What unforgettable stuff!"

Horace happened to know that Marx had stolen this famous phrase in *The Communist Manifesto* from Marat, but he did not bother to mention this. As the sloop sailed on before the wind, Busby expounded on his belief that the system envisaged by Marx had not worked because the Russians, who by an accident of history were the first to try to live by his maxims, were too primitive to understand them, too disorganized to put them into effect, and too clumsy to seduce even the skittish tart that was the West. "Ah, but if the Germans had had a Lenin in 1919 or the Americans had reelected Hoover in 1932, creating the objective conditions for revolution," he said, "who knows what the world might have been like today?"

Buzzer had always had the gift of enthusiasm; it was the hallmark of his character and had led him into many an unexpected result. Knowing what torrents of sophomoric philosophizing were coming next—he had been listening to his fellow Shelleyan expound on what he regarded as the inevitable revolution since undergraduate days—Horace abruptly cried, "Thar she blows!"

"Whales? Where away? How many?" demanded Busby, leaping to his feet.

"Off the port bow," Horace replied. "Three, I think. They sounded."

He put the helm over and let out the boom; the sloop heeled and reached for a line of surf a mile or two away.

"Careful, that's World's End Reef dead ahead," Busby said, scrambling forward. "But steer for it; the coral will turn them. We can anchor and put on snorkel gear and maybe swim with them. It's mind-boggling fun, Horace—the whales *like* us. God knows why."

Busby dashed below for flippers and masks. He was genuinely excited. Horace felt a certain contrition, because he had not really seen any whales. Not that Busby would ever know this. As the center who had passed the basketball to Busby for his famous last-second shot against Harvard almost half a century before, Horace knew that Buzzer had not been able to see the basket. That was why his nickname was such a byword—Buzzer's winning basket was almost the only shot he took that season and certainly the only one he made. He had always been too vain to wear glasses and claimed that he was allergic to contact lenses, and would no more be able to see these imaginary whales of Horace's than he had been able to make out the net from the centerline of the basketball court. Horace followed in the dinghy as Busby, a long, bleached creature trailing bubbles, struck out along the reef.

On a tiny sand island an hour later, Horace ate a chicken sandwich and drank a bottle of beer from the boat's picnic cooler while listening with a perfectly straight face to Busby's description of his pursuit of the whales. They had been right at the outer edge of vision, he said, but they had unmistakably been whales—three of them, a cow and two calves, swimming majestically through an iridescent screen of reef fishes.

"Baxter," Horace said, "I want to talk to you."

"What about?"

"About this situation in Washington."

"I'm all ears," said Busby.

Horace said, "The last time we met, up at the Harbor, you mentioned thinking about alternatives, and it occurred to me that your only alternatives have suddenly become pretty appalling ones."

"Meaning?"

"Mallory takes over the world if Lockwood goes down fighting."

"Too horrible to contemplate."

After a pause, Horace said, "Did Vice President Graves really die of natural causes?"

Busby was amused but startled by the question. "Good God, of course he did. What else? Cyanide in his ear? There was an autopsy. He had an embolism. Dead between one breath and the next, poor bastard."

"Getting back to the subject," Horace said, "let's say Lockwood admits he wasn't elected and leaves gracefully, but somehow Mallory cannot prove that he himself was elected."

"In that case you get Attenborough," Busby said.

"Can you live with that?"

"It's better than the alternative."

"Julian says Attenborough is a hopeless drunk."

"He is, in addition to now being an alleged rapist. The only thing in his favor is that anyone, drunk or sober, is better than Mallory. Because one way or another Lockwood is going to go down, you know."

"Is he? Julian says he may have enough votes in the Senate to avoid conviction."

"Julian's out of touch," Busby said. "Lockwood can't possibly survive now."

"Julian's not so sure. He says he can still get up off the canvas and amaze everybody."

"Julian's a loyal friend, but Lockwood's a convicted liar—an embarrassment to the party, to the Cause. He always was, of course, but there used to be Julian to do the thinking, to stick to the agenda, to keep everyone posted. Now there's no one—literally no one."

"All right. Suppose you're right. If Lockwood does go down, as you say, what happens then?"

Busby shrugged. "I've already said it. Attenborough becomes President and four years from now, if his liver holds out that long, we nominate a new face. If he doesn't live to the end of his term, he'll be succeeded by whomever he appoints and—important point—Congress approves as his Vice President."

"Interesting," Horace said again. He opened two more bottles of beer and handed one of them to Busby. "As you know, I'm a little concerned about Julian and my friend Rose in all this, and, most of all, about my young sister-in-law. Emily is upset, and has been since last fall. Lost a baby. Weeps continually. I feel responsible for that."

"Oh, the whole thing was your idea?"

"My doing. Therefore my responsibility. I thought I might be able to help through Lockwood's lawyer, but all that seems to have fallen apart, and I suppose I'm right in thinking that Attenborough is no great friend of ours?"

"He's no friend of Julian's, certainly. Or of yours, as a matter of fact. He feels that you two got Lockwood into this and—what really worries him—that the party may go down with him."

"No point in arguing about that now. But wouldn't it be better if the whole question of the election irregularities never came up?"

"Better for whom?"

"Better for the party. Better for the FIS. Much better for Rose."

"And for you, of course. But how can that happen?"

"My thought was, if Lockwood is convicted on the first article of impeachment, namely the Ibn Awad matter, then there would be no point in even voting on the others. He'd be out, and you'd go on from there. With Attenborough, for want of a better alternative."

"That was your thought, was it?"

"I'm sure it has occurred to others."

"Your point being?"

"Jack Philindros wasn't really asked the right questions about Ibn Awad in that hearing before the Committee of Managers."

"He wasn't? What *are* the right questions?"

Horace was searching for something in the cooler. He found it, a Ziploc plastic bag with a sheet of paper in it. "Here," he said. "I typed them out for you."

Busby frowned; as usual he'd brought no reading glasses with him. "Read them to me," he said.

Horace read out what he had written in a low and guarded voice. Straining to hear, Busby was amazed. "You mean the bombs were missing *for four years?*" he said. "You mean they weren't actually located *until last October*, while the presidential election was in progress?"

"That's right. And since the whole point of snuffing Ibn Awad was to get the bombs, this could be interpreted to mean that the operation accomplished nothing."

"The bombs could have gone off anytime."

"Yes, and they still could. Just ask Philindros where they were found and where they are now."

"*Where?*"

"Better you should be surprised."

Busby slowly shook his head in a combination of wonder and horror. "This is the smoking gun," he said. "It will finish Frosty. He might have got away with one lie, but not two."

"Too bad, but if the thing's to be done, maybe it should be done quickly."

"You're absolutely sure of your facts?"

"Oh, yes," Horace said. "It was me who found the damn things."

He took back the paper from Busby and set it on fire with a disposable cigarette lighter—a tool of the trade that he, a lifelong nonsmoker, always carried for such purposes. Busby was still registering amazement. Horace gave him a warm but quizzical smile. The trusty maxim applied: Knowing what Buzzer Busby wanted to do, he had made it possible for him to do it.

2

On Monday morning, as tradition dictated, all members of the House of Representatives, led by the Committee of Managers, walked in solemn procession from their own chamber across the length of the Capitol and knocked thunderously on the door of the Senate. They were admitted by the sergeant at arms. Speaking in a voice nearly as powerful as Attenborough's, Bob Laval addressed the president pro tempore: "Mr. President, the managers of the House of Representatives, by order of the House, are ready at the bar of the Senate, whenever it may please the Senate to hear them, to present articles of impeachment and in maintenance of the impeachment preferred against Bedford Forrest Lockwood, President of the United States, by the House of Representatives."

These had been the exact words spoken on March 4, 1868, by John A. Bingham, chairman of the Committee of Managers charged with prosecuting the impeachment of Andrew Johnson. It was a moment of solemnity and drama, something that had happened only once before in the history of the republic. The senators and representatives present were visibly moved by their own ceremonial behavior, by the sonorous voices, and by the majestic simplicity of the language.

As soon as the members of the House had delivered the articles of impeachment they withdrew and the Senate immediately voted to begin the trial eight days hence, on the following Tuesday. Senator Clark proposed that the Senate appoint a Committee on the Impeachment of Bedford Forrest Lockwood, President of the United States. This body would be composed of seven senators—the chairmen and ranking minority members of the Judiciary, Rules, and Government Operations committees, plus a chairman to be chosen by the whole Senate—and would recommend rules of procedure for the impeachment trial. This was the same number that had been appointed for the same purpose in the Johnson impeachment. The Senate approved, and on a motion from the floor, Clark himself was named chairman. This meant that the committee, like the Senate itself, was equally divided, with a member of Lockwood's party exercising the tie-breaking vote. The committee was instructed to deliver its report for the approval of the full Senate on the following Saturday morning. The Senate then adjourned.

Clark called an immediate meeting of the Committee on the Impeachment. He distributed copies of the rules adopted by the Senate in the Johnson case. All the members, having known for several days that they would be appointed to this committee, had been provided by their staffs with copious background materials on the Johnson trial. Clark eyed these with unconcealed disapproval; he had done a little research, too. "Before we get started," he said, "I want to quote James A. Garfield of Ohio, a future President of the United States who was a member of Congress in 1868. Quote: *This trial has developed, in the most remarkable manner, the insane love of speaking among public men.* Unquote. The way I see it, our job on this committee is to keep that from happening this time. We've got a week to do this job. Let's keep it simple and get it done."

Busby said, "Mr. Chairman, I support that sentiment completely. I'd like to suggest that we simply adopt the rules approved by the Senate for the Johnson trial, with one modification that will do more to ensure the speedy arrival at a just verdict than anything else this committee can do. Mr. Chairman—"

"We'll get to substance in a minute," Clark said. "Anyone have any objection to using the rules adopted by the Senate in 1868 for the Andrew Johnson trial and subsequently revised as a basis for the rules for this trial?"

Amzi Whipple said, "Fundamentally they're good Republican rules even if they are a hundred and thirty-three years old, Mr. Chairman. I've got one modification to propose when the time comes."

Clark said, "Anyone else?" There was no response. He said, "Let's start it off, then. Senator Busby?"

The others shifted uncomfortably in their chairs. As everyone on the committee knew, Busby's negotiating technique was simple: he simply kept saying the same thing over and over again, pretending to be deaf to all objections, until his colleagues were so bored, so frustrated, so eager to escape, that in the end they agreed to his demands merely to shut him up.

"As we all know, the Chief Justice will preside at this trial," Busby said. "The great problem in the Andrew Johnson trial was the ambiguity that surrounded the authority and powers of the Chief Justice. He was overruled after the fact by the Senate on points of law and procedure, he was deprived of the essential privilege of breaking a tie with his vote even though he was, under the Constitution, the presiding officer of the Senate during the trial of an impeached President. More than any other factor, these affronts to the dignity and constitutional authority of the Chief

Justice brought the Johnson trial, and the Senate itself, into disrepute. Friends, we can't let that happen again."

"Wait a minute," Amzi Whipple said. "What exactly are you proposing?"

"Two things."

"I thought you said one thing."

"They're the two parts of one thing."

Clark tapped on the table with a pen. "Propose them one at a time, Senator."

"I am proposing," Busby said, "that the Senate formally empower the Chief Justice to cast the deciding yea or nay in case of a tie vote, and that they accept his rulings on questions of law as if handed down by a judge presiding at a trial. That is, not overturn his ruling afterward by using the Senate as some kind of court of appeals to manipulate the law."

Whipple said, "You mean his rulings from the chair would not be subject to appeal even if erroneous?"

Busby gave Whipple a deferential nod. "I guess we could make provision for that, Senator—say, a three-fifths vote of the Senate to declare that a ruling should be called into question, and a majority to overturn."

"A majority to overturn? With the Senate divided evenly on party lines and the Chief Justice casting the tie-breaking vote? That's some provision, Senator. In the spirit of brevity to which we are all committed, I will say this to you, sir: Over my dead body."

The other two reactionaries said the same thing as Whipple in softer words. The senators from Busby's own party, neither of them a radical like himself, said nothing at all. This did not discourage him; overcoming reluctance was his specialty. He said, "What I'm proposing is simplicity itself: that the Senate formally empower the Chief Justice to cast the deciding yea or nay in case of a tie vote, and that the Senate accept his rulings on questions of law as if handed down by a judge presiding at a trial."

Clark said, "We heard you the first time. We'll take your suggestion under consideration, Senator."

"Of course you understand," Busby said. "It couldn't be simpler: that the Senate formally empower the Chief Justice to cast the deciding yea or nay in case of a tie vote, and that the Senate accept his rulings on questions of law as if handed down by a judge presiding at a trial."

"Exactly," Clark said.

"I'm glad you see my point," Busby said. "Let me sketch in my reasoning, if I may."

Whipple wrote the words *Shut him up!* on a slip of paper and slid it over the tabletop to Clark. Both men knew this was impossible. As Clark folded Whipple's note into smaller and smaller squares, Busby continued. "It makes sense," he said, "to formally empower the Chief Justice to cast the deciding yea or nay in case of a tie vote, and that the Senate accept his rulings on questions of law as if handed down by a judge presiding at a trial because the Senate is evenly divided for the first time in history, and this eventuality, insofar as it affects an impeachment proceeding, is covered by a clause in the Constitution."

Whipple said, "The Chief Justice is not a senator, Senator."

"Perfectly true," Busby replied, "but that's not the only reason. Now I'm not saying he should vote as a senator—no, sir, I'm not ready to say that. However, the Constitution says, 'The Vice President of the United States shall be the President of the Senate, but he shall have no vote unless they be evenly divided.' Only one paragraph later, the Constitution goes on to say, 'When the President of the United States is tried, the Chief Justice shall preside.' In other words, in this one clearly defined situation, the Chief Justice sits as President of the Senate. The Constitution has already told us that the Vice President 'shall have no vote unless they be evenly divided.' I would remind you that the Vice President is not a senator, either, Senator. He is a member of the executive branch, not even elected in his own right, but as the running mate of the President of the United States. Yet the Constitution likewise gives the Vice President a vote in the Senate in one clearly defined situation. He is not a senator, yet when the Senate is evenly divided he votes as a senator. That is his constitutional function, to preside over the Senate and break ties. So you can see how simple it is, how obvious it is, how clear is the intent of the Framers. Affirming this instruction from the Constitution is symbolic, that's all."

"Sweet Suzie in the morning," said Whipple, throwing up his hands.

"Symbolic in what way?" Clark asked. There was a stubborn light in his eyes. Busby had seen it there before when some compromise with the dead past, some creative approach to constitutional matters, was broached in his presence. Clark had made a career of putting the country ahead of everything—party, principle, progress, personal interest.

"It's a formula for Armageddon," Whipple said.

"I don't see how, if we believe what the Constitution says," Busby said. "The Chief Justice is not going to have a vote on guilt or innocence. How could he have? The issue of conviction or acquittal cannot be decided by breaking a tie. We all know that. A two-thirds majority is required to convict. If we're one short of that majority, I'm not proposing for a single minute that the Chief Justice should nudge the issue one way or the other. He can only vote in case of a tie on issues requiring a simple majority."

"Such as?"

"We don't know what may come up. Constitutional questions, questions of law. That is what a presiding officer is for, to rule on such questions. We need a way to decide unforeseen questions. The Constitution gave us a way. We have no right to ignore the Constitution. I'd go so far as to say that *we have no choice* but to take it literally."

"I don't doubt for a minute that you'd go even farther than that, Senator," Whipple said. "But damn few of the rest of us who ever went to law school would agree with you."

"Really?" Smiling his dazzling smile, Busby said, "Then behold the proud exception."

Whipple said, "Be serious. Doing what you suggest would bring the Chief Justice and the Senate into a death grip. The Senate is the maker of its own rules. No outsider has a place in this process. Why should the Chief Justice be empowered to decide questions that it is the constitutional duty of the Senate to decide?"

"The whole point of my proposal is to reassure the American people that this is not a put-up job, like the Andrew Johnson trial was, and not a whitewash, either."

"I wouldn't worry about the ability of the American people to see through us, if I were you," Whipple said.

Again Busby flashed his brilliant white smile. "If you were me, oh, yes, you'd worry," he said.

Clark said, "Let's move on."

Busby said, "First I just want to say one more word about this tie-breaker issue. Those who do not learn the lessons of history are likely to repeat its mistakes. Did any of you watch Patrick Graham this morning?"

Clark said, "Patrick Graham?" Busby was sitting right next to Clark, so he could see his face. Clark was watching him with that absence of expression, that deadness of regard, which meant he was completely out of patience and sympathy.

Nonetheless Busby plunged on. "Patrick's point," he said, "and I thought it was a good one, was that justice must not only be done, but must be *seen* to be done."

"Good point," Clark said. "But I think we had all grasped it even before Graham went public with it. Now we have to move on."

"I'm glad you agree it's a good point," Busby said. "That's why I keep saying it's the symbolism, not the substance, that counts in this issue. You see, Sam, fellows, what I'm proposing doesn't really give the Chief Justice any power to make history. That's because of the two-thirds requirement—"

Tonelessly, Clark said, "Senator . . ."

But Busby kept talking, making his vital point once more. Around the gleaming conference table, blurry faces turned away. Though he could not make out their features, he knew from experience that the other senators were avoiding his eyes and looking at each other with expressions of desperation—sure signs that they were almost ready to give in. All he had to do was make the point one more time, drive it home; they'd come around. He knew this was the case because he had made it happen so often in the past. He said, "What I'm suggesting is very simple, that we do what the Constitution clearly tells us to do and empower the Chief Justice to cast the deciding yea or nay in case of a tie vote, and that we accept his rulings on questions of law as if handed down by a judge presiding at—"

Amzi Whipple said, "Mr. Chairman, I move that this meeting be adjourned until one o'clock tomorrow afternoon."

Every other voice except Busby's said, "Second."

"Moved and seconded," Clark said, "and without objection this committee is adjourned until one o'clock tomorrow afternoon in this room."

The other senators rose to their feet and left wordlessly, without lingering—some of them, as Busby noticed, quite hurriedly. This was a good sign. Clark could hardly flee like the others since the meeting was taking place in his office. Instead, he headed for his bathroom, which was located in a narrow hallway between the conference room and the room where his desk was. Busby followed him.

"Buzzer," Clark said, "we're alone now, so I'm going to speak plainly."

"Sam, you always do. I admire that in you. You're my model in that regard."

"Buzzer, shut up and listen. We all understood what you said the first time you said it. Don't—*don't*—say it again, tomorrow or any other time. If you agree to that, the committee will vote on your proposal, we'll take it to the floor even if we have to do it as a minority report, and you can tell the whole Senate your reasons for wanting to place the fate of the nation in the hands of Archimedes Hammett. But this committee understands what you've told us. You don't have to tell us again."

"I hope so, Sam, because—"

Clark said, "Buzzer, listen to me. I not only understand what you're saying, I've also got a pretty good idea of what you're trying to make happen. Don't push it."

"I don't know what you mean by that, Sam," Busby said. "If you mean I support and admire and trust Archimedes Hammett, you're absolutely right."

"Nobody doubts your enthusiasm on that score, Senator. That's the problem."

Shocked, Busby said, "Sam, this is the Constitution we're talking about!"

"Is it?" Clark said.

"Darn right!" Busby said, drawing closer, chin out. What he wanted to say was: *If this were some political and moral tightrope walker of a Chief Justice instead of the courageous idealist we all know Hammett to be, you fellows wouldn't have a problem about this. You* fear *men of principle.* But he knew better than to deliver such home truths. Calling a hypocrite a hypocrite was a good way to lose everything. So what he actually said was "I'm not going to give up on this, Sam."

"I know that, we all do," Clark said. "All I'm asking you to do is shut up about it."

"And if I do, you'll help me get my rule to the floor?"

Clark nodded, and before Busby could utter another word, he turned on his heel and closed the bathroom door behind him.

This was unsenatorial behavior, most untypical of Sam Clark. Had he guessed or gotten wind of what Busby and Horace had discussed down in the Caribbean? No, that was impossible. Only a Shelleyan could have told him, and that simply could not happen.

Through the locked door, Busby could hear Clark urinating. This homely reminder that Sam Clark was only human seemed to be a sign sent to reassure him. He could win this one. He knew he could; the reactionaries were already on the run.

Back in his office, Busby made a call to a Shelleyan who relayed news of what he had done to Horace, and more important, to Archimedes Hammett. It would have been dangerous for Busby to discuss this matter directly with Horace, and improper for him to discuss it with the Chief Justice. On the other hand, he could hardly let his fellow Shelleyans read about it in the newspapers.

3

Late Friday night, after five days of intensive work made possible by Busby's nearly total silence during its deliberations, the Committee on the Impeachment agreed on the rules for Lockwood's trial. As was inevitable in the circumstances, the members deadlocked on party lines, three votes to three, on Busby's proposal to give the Chief Justice the power to break a tie vote and hand down irreversible rulings on questions of law. True to his word as always, Sam Clark broke the tie in Busby's favor, and the Busby Proposal, as it immediately came to be called, was sent to the floor of the Senate for debate and vote the following morning. Clark had acted as he did because he had been certain that it could not pass: Amzi Whipple's side of the Senate would vote against it in a body, and since they had exactly half the votes, the measure could not achieve a majority.

That same Friday night, on his way home after teaching the weekly Bible class for Senate pages, Senator Wilbur E. Garrett of Missouri, the leader of the evangelical wing of Mallory's party and an arch-detractor of Hammett's in any and all situations, was assaulted by a carjacker while sitting at the wheel of his brand-new Cadillac Eldorado at a stoplight at Reno Road and Yuma Street, Northwest. Incidents of this kind were increasingly common in the supposedly safe neighborhoods of upper-income Washington, so the attack on Garrett was mentioned only in passing by the media. It might not have been mentioned at all if Garrett's assailant had not chosen to wear a Franklin Mallory mask. The carjacker shattered the window on the driver's side with a hammer, smashed Garrett's left shoulder joint with a second hammer-blow, dragged his unconscious body from the car, and drove off. Because of the mask (for a fatal moment, the senator had thought that the face in the window actually belonged to his old friend Mallory), and because the assailant wore surgical gloves and a black athletic costume with a high turtleneck, Garrett was not able to tell the police whether he was white, black, yellow, or brown, young or old, short or tall. A woman who lived in a house across the street recorded the incident with a video camera, and the footage was shown on local television, though not on the networks, from which it was bumped by more sensational news. The woman with the camera was the only known witness to the crime. The police investigation was cursory. Carjackers were almost never caught, and the loss of a luxury car covered by insurance was not a crime that greatly interested the police.

The following morning, while the Busby Proposal was being debated and voted on the Senate floor, Wilbur E. Garrett was still under anesthetic after three hours of surgery to replace his shattered shoulder joint with an artificial one. This meant that Lockwood's party enjoyed a temporary one-vote majority, and the measure passed by a single vote after being amended to limit the Chief Justice's privilege to cast the tie-breaking vote to constitutional questions only. Because the term "constitutional question" was not defined, ambiguity persisted as to Hammett's actual powers, but Busby told Morgan Pike that he was satisfied with the outcome. "The authority of the Constitution has been reaffirmed," he said. "The symbolism is extremely important."

"Are you saying that the issue is merely symbolic?" Morgan Pike asked.

"In the great crises of American democracy," replied Busby, who was as pithy on camera as he was prolix *in camera*, "symbol *is* substance."

Minutes after this interview took place, Amzi Whipple caught up with Busby on the shuttle train between the Capitol and the Senate office buildings. "That was quite a triumph for your side," Whipple said.

"I wouldn't say that," Busby replied. "Everybody won."

"The American people you keep talking about may wonder just what they won when Archimedes Hammett casts his first tie-breaker."

Busby winked playfully and flung Whipple's own words back at him. "I wouldn't worry about the American people if I were you, Senator."

"I don't," Whipple said. "Because after this is all over, the man the American people elected President, Franklin Mallory, will move into the White House as our rightful chief executive."

Busby hesitated, then spoke his mind, but in a playful way that might be taken as more teasing. "In the words of that great American Amzi Whipple, 'Over my dead body.' No fascists in the White House."

"You actually think you can save Lockwood?"

"Who said anything about that? All I'm saying is, you ain't seen nothing yet."

"Then what *are* you and your faithful troops planning to do, Baxter—sober up Tucker Attenborough and make him President?"

Elated by his victory on the Senate floor, still in a state of self-congratulation after the ace he had just served to Morgan Pike, Busby gave Whipple a broad wink. "Good heavens, Amzi," he said. "Even you can't imagine we aren't thinking in terms of an alternative to *that*."

As soon as the words were out of his mouth Busby realized he had said too much. Evidently Whipple thought so, too, because his eyes, usually so fatherly and whimsical, suddenly became cold and suspicious. He started to ask another question, but before he could form the sentence, Busby leaped off the train and hurried toward the elevator.

4

That evening, in the library of Mallory's Kalorama house, Amzi Whipple said, "Something mighty funny is going on, Franklin. It looks like Busby and his crowd are trying to get rid of their own man."

"Why would they do that?"

"Beats me. But think about it. Just before the impeachment hearings begin in the House, they hang a rape charge on Tucker Attenborough, after leaking the Lockwood tape. Then, right on the eve of the session in which we're going to vote on that damn fool idea of Busby's to give that America-hating son of a bitch Hammett the power to break ties in the Senate and make law off the top of his head, Wilbur Garrett pulls up to a red light and gets hit on the clavicle with a hammer. Result: he can't vote, and consequently the tie Sam Clark was counting on to kill the worst idea anybody in the Senate ever had turns out to be a one-vote victory for the forces of darkness. And now Buzzer springs this one on me."

"That's quite a sequence of events, I agree," Mallory said. "But why did it surprise you that Buzzer Busby and the rest of the radicals don't want me to be President again?"

"It didn't surprise me, but that's not the point," Whipple replied. "Busby had just got through telling me in so many words that it was all over for Lockwood. We all know it is, but he had something up his sleeve. He couldn't say exactly what, wink-wink, but it was obvious he was busting his buttons." Whipple voiced these last three words in a parody of Busby's St. Grottlesex drawl.

"He was needling you?"

"Pissing on my shoe."

Mallory thought for a moment, then said, "If Buzzer really does have something up his sleeve, why would he tell you, of all people?"

"Because," Whipple replied, "Buzzer's not the brightest guy in the world. And you know him, Franklin—he's such a peacock he can't resist showing off."

"And that's all you've got to go on?"

"If you know Busby, not to mention Hammett and his Fifth Column, it's enough to make you wonder," Whipple said. "They want to get rid of Lockwood. That's phase one."

"Maybe so, but how does knocking off Lockwood serve their purposes? If he wasn't elected, I was."

"Since when did Buzzer's crowd give a tinker's damn about elections? They just stole one. If at first you don't succeed, try, try again. That bunch would rather burn Washington than let you back in the White House."

"Granted. But what other choice will they have if the Senate finds that the election was stolen?"

"I don't know, but I've got a funny feeling they're working on it," Whipple said. "Look up Hammett's words. He's been talking and writing about the Supreme Court as a mechanism to overthrow the elected government of the United States and seize absolute power for twenty-five years. I asked him about it in the confirmation hearings, quoted him chapter and verse from his own published statements, tried to pin him down. He just laughed it off, and Buzzer let him get away with it, but he meant every word he ever said on the subject. You know he did."

Mallory nodded absently. "Amzi, I respect your instincts. I thank you for this warning. But let's keep this idea to ourselves for a while."

"Don't worry," Whipple said. "I've been put through the holy inquisition before by those bastards. That's why I'm so damn suspicious. All I'm saying is, you should be, too." Groaning with arthritis, he stood up. "Got to go. Bitsy's having some Oklahoma people to supper tonight."

Mallory put an arm around the old man's shoulder and looked into his worried eyes. "Just hold those fifty votes in line, Amzi."

"You don't have to be concerned about that, Mr. President," Whipple said. "But that may be the only thing you don't have to worry about. These people are capable of anything. I *know* them, Franklin."

"I know you do," Mallory said.

5
———

On the opening day of the impeachment trial, a Tuesday, Attenborough sat in the best seat in the front row, flanked by the party leaders, whips, and committee chairmen—his last perquisite as Speaker. This was the first time he had been inside the Senate chamber for a long time, but he remembered everything about it, its somber hush, its front-parlor atmosphere of mahogany and plush, the senators loitering at their desks like bachelor uncles in their Sunday clothes. The familiar group of ferocious women glared at him from the visitors' gallery; he looked for Slim among them, but she was such a chameleon that he was not sure he would know her if he saw her.

In its first two hours the process unfolded at a ritual pace. The Senate adjourned its ordinary session and then reconvened itself as a court of impeachment. The roll was called and the sergeant at arms read out the proclamation of the trial. Then, as the Constitution provides, all one hundred members were sworn individually. The oath was administered in a trembling voice by Senator Otis W. Dyer of Rhode Island, the eighty-two-year-old president pro tempore of the Senate, who after the Speaker of the House was next in the line of succession to the presidency. Dyer was unable to stand because he had recently broken his hip, but every senator rose to his feet to take the oath, including the battered but gallant Wilbur E. Garrett. His upper body and left arm were encased in a cast over which it was impossible to wear a coat, so he wore the jacket of his suit draped over the uninjured shoulder like a dragoon's mess jacket.

At the end of these ceremonies the president pro tempore, assisted by two members of his staff, stepped down from the chair and Chief Justice Archimedes Hammett entered the chamber. He was accompanied by the senior associate justice of the Supreme Court, Bobby M. Poole, and escorted by a committee of three senators. Hammett wore his judicial robes and carried a tattered copy of the Bible in Greek—a gesture to the memory of his immigrant grandfather, as Patrick Graham, seated before a monitor several blocks away in a studio, explained in the funereal murmur he had adopted to describe these events. Without the slightest pause or hesitation, Hammett mounted the veined marble podium and took the chair reserved for the presiding officer. In a ringing voice, head thrown back, Hammett said, "Senators, I am here in obedience to the Constitution and in answer to your resolution for the purpose of presiding over the trial of the impeachment of the President of the United States, Bedford Forrest Lockwood. I am ready to take the oath."

Justice Poole administered the oath. Like the ones just taken by the senators, its language was the same as that repeated by Chief Justice Salmon P. Chase in the 1868 trial, the only difference being the substitution of Lockwood's name for that of Andrew Johnson: "I do solemnly swear that in all things appertaining to the trial of the impeachment of Bedford Forrest Lockwood, President of the United States, I will do impartial justice according to the Constitution and the laws; so help me God."

Hammett repeated the words in the same loud, firm voice as before, and marking himself as a person standing alone in this act as in all other things, he held the Greek Bible balanced on his left palm, with his right hand resting on top of the book. Sourly imagining the artful close-ups of sensitive hands and well-worn Bible that must at this moment be appearing on every television screen in America, Attenborough thought: He's like Napoleon crowning himself emperor in Notre Dame. Attenborough, who understood exactly what Hammett was doing, had to admire the skill with which he was doing it. It was like watching a Barrymore in the role of Chief Justice: if this was not the real thing, it ought to be. From his seat in the gallery, the Speaker looked directly at the podium, and when Hammett glanced upward as he finished the oath, the eyes of the two men met for an instant. The Chief Justice quickly looked away, a furtive movement—guiltily, by God.

Hammett rapped twice emphatically with the gavel, bringing the trial to order. "The sergeant at arms," he said, "will call the impeached."

The sergeant at arms threw open the doors of the Senate and called, "Bedford Forrest Lockwood, President of the United States, Bedford Forrest Lockwood, President of the United States, appear and answer the articles of impeachment exhibited against you by the House of Representatives of the United States."

There was no answer. Sam Clark said, "I understand that the President has retained counsel and they are now in the President's room adjoining this chamber. I move that the sergeant at arms invite them to enter and appear for the President."

Olmedo and Blackstone entered and presented a letter from Lockwood authorizing them to appear for him. Hammett invited them to take the chairs reserved for them at another table; the empty, more ornate chair reserved for Lockwood stood between them. Naturally the cameras lingered on this symbolic piece of furniture; Attenborough knew what the cameras were doing because he was surrounded by members of the House who, even though they were present at the living event, were watching the proceedings on tiny hand-held television sets and listening to it over earplugs.

By now more than three hours had passed without a recess and spectators and members of the press were beginning to drift in and out of the galleries. Of course senators were at liberty to leave for the same purposes, but none did so because none wished to be the first to be seen on network television slipping away to answer a call of nature at such a solemn moment.

Hammett pressed on. "The clerk will read the articles of impeachment," he said.

This done, Sam Clark rose to make a motion. "The Chief Justice,"

Hammett said, using the form of reference to himself that Salmon P. Chase had employed in the 1868 trial, "recognizes the senator from Massachusetts." Clark moved for a thirty-minute recess; Whipple seconded. Benevolently Hammett granted it, but when the senators filed out and the galleries emptied, he himself remained immobile in the chair. He was there when Attenborough left, in order to have a drink and a pill, and he was still there when the Speaker returned twenty-nine minutes later, as unmoving yet as charged with energy as a video image on PAUSE.

On the stroke of the half hour, with every seat in the galleries reoccupied, Hammett moved for the first time, striking the gavel to bring the Senate to order. "Mr. Olmedo," he said, "is the President of the United States ready to enter his answers to the articles of impeachment that have been brought against him by the honorable House of Representatives?"

"He is not, Mr. Chief Justice. May I approach the bench?"

"No, sir, you may not," Hammett said. "This is a constitutional proceeding touching upon the most fundamental questions, including the very legitimacy of our government. Such proceedings cannot be conducted in whispers. It is essential that they be conducted aloud and on the record in their entirety, without secrecy of any kind."

Amzi Whipple rose. "In their entirety? May I respectfully ask who decided that, Mr. Chief Justice?"

"It is a constitutional question. Therefore, the Chief Justice decided it, as authorized and mandated by the Senate under the rules adopted for this trial."

"Does this mean that the Senate itself cannot deliberate in secret?"

"That is a procedural question for the Senate, not a constitutional question, and therefore the Senate, not the Chief Justice, must decide it."

"I move for immediate consideration of this procedural question by the entire Senate."

Hammett said, "Senator, I respectfully remind you that the Senate may not conduct any other business when sitting as a court of impeachment. The Senate may adjourn the public trial, reconvene itself, and do as it likes, but while it sits under the Chief Justice as a court of impeachment, it may conduct no other business."

Whipple said, "What were those words, sir? Did I hear you say *under* the Chief Justice? The Senate, sir, does not fall beneath any person or body except the Constitution of the United States."

"Precisely, and in this case the Chief Justice is the designated agent of the Constitution," said Hammett. Once again his tone was friendly and reasonable, as though he were explaining the obvious to a rather slow student in a classroom.

"I move for immediate adjournment," said Whipple.

A chorus from the right side of the chamber seconded the motion.

"A motion has been made and seconded," said Hammett. "The clerk will call the roll."

Because of the need to maintain party discipline at all costs, the vote was evenly divided, just as Hammett knew it must be: the Establishment always responded to any threat to itself by acting according to its own brute nature. Casting his first tie-breaking vote, he decided the issue in favor of continuation. It was clear to all what this meant: Lockwood's party had voted against its own interests and Hammett had established his authority over the proceedings. The Cause had won the first round. From his desk, Busby smiled happily; the cameras registered this reaction along with the angry face of Amzi Whipple.

Ending the long moment of silence that followed his triumph, Hammett said, "Mr. Olmedo, you may proceed with the President's answer to the articles."

"Mr. Chief Justice," Olmedo said, "I ask for a thirty-day adjournment to give the President time to prepare his answer to these charges."

Hammett said, "The Chief Justice will entertain a motion on this question of procedure."

The vote resulted in another tie, broken by Hammett to deny the motion.

"The motion having been put to a vote by the Senate and denied," Hammett said, "I hereby order that the President of the United States, Bedford Forrest Lockwood, appear before the Senate at one o'clock in the afternoon on the Friday after next, ten days from today, to answer the articles of impeachment voted by the honorable House of Representatives. Let the record show that this ruling is made on the basis of a precedent established by the Senate. The Chief Justice is granting to President Lockwood the precise amount of time—ten days—granted to President Andrew Johnson by vote of the Senate in 1868. Do I hear a motion for adjournment?"

Olmedo was on his feet again. "Mr. Chief Justice, I am at a loss to understand your ruling in this matter," he said. "I ask that the date of the President's appearance be established by vote of the Senate, as provided by the rules."

"The Chief Justice will entertain a motion to that effect," Hammett said.

Once again Amzi Whipple offered the motion. Once again the Senate was evenly divided. Once again Hammett broke the tie to defeat the motion.

"The Sixth Amendment refers to 'a speedy and public trial,' Mr. Olmedo," Hammett said. "That is what the Chief Justice's ruling was designed to accomplish. Beyond that, the President has the right to what he demanded when he set this entire process in motion. For the record, I will quote his exact words: 'I ask that the Congress act on this supremely urgent and important matter with the least possible delay consistent with a just outcome.' Thirty days would clearly be an excessive delay."

Olmedo stood mute. Busby leaped to his feet and moved to adjourn. Hammett banged the gavel and strode from the chamber, leaving the senators still seated at their desks. Amzi Whipple sprang upright and charged across the floor to Sam Clark's desk.

"A breathtaking, a Solomonic, performance by Archimedes Hammett," Patrick Graham was saying into his microphone. "He is triumphantly the man in charge. The United States of America has found itself a Chief Justice worthy of the hour."

6

Like fingerprints, the vascular system of the face is unique and inalterable for each human being. The commercial potentialities of this anatomical characteristic were realized in the latter years of the twentieth century when Betac, a small private company just outside the Beltway, patented a simple, portable infrared scanner that was capable of detecting this pattern of blood vessels beneath the skin and transmitting it to a computer's memory. When the captured image was matched against the stored original, the result was historic: not merely positive identification but *absolute* identification was achieved for the first time in the annals of investigative science. Disguises, plastic surgery, the most hideous disfigurement by injury or disease, made no difference. The person in the memory bank could not possibly be anyone but himself or herself.

Horace Hubbard had traveled to the Caribbean on a false-genuine Canadian passport—false because Horace was not Kenneth Russell Holt, the businessman from Kanata, Ontario, whose name appeared on the passport, genuine because Holt (though unaware of Horace's existence) was a real person who had been in a coma for ten years as a result of injuries suffered in a highway crash. Horace had encountered no difficulties on the way down to Mustique. However, as he passed through passport control after landing at Miami airport on his return, he was identified by a scanner. He would have been astonished to know that his infrared image was on file because, for obvious reasons, FIS field officers had been exempted from facial mapping. However, knowing that he would never be able to monitor, much less follow, so elusive a subject as Horace with his own meager resources, McGraw had arranged with a friend in the U.S. Immigration and Naturalization Service for Horace's face to be mapped by a hidden infrared scanner when he had brought him back through JFK from Chile. This image was added to the terrorist watch list, and the computer at Miami had matched this stored image to Horace's bearded, bespectacled, and subtly darkened face in nanoseconds. Notice of the I.D., together with a rundown on Horace's incognito trip (commercial airliner from Miami to Barbados, then on to Mustique by self-piloted rented plane, whose flight path had been recorded on the black box installed with U.S. secret funds in all such planes as an anti-drug-smuggling measure), was immediately posted on an antiterrorist bulletin board to which McGraw still had access through the kindness of the same friend in the INS.

Immediately after receiving this information, McGraw scanned the open data bank for Mustique, and in running down the list of property owners on the island, he found the name of Baxter T. Busby. A further check showed that Busby had flown into Mustique in a chartered plane on the same day that Horace had arrived there. What was the connection? McGraw searched for more data. Working his way through the subjects' affiliations, looking for cross-matches, he found that Busby and Horace had played basketball on the same team at Yale and that both had been residents of the same undergraduate college, Calhoun. This explained how they knew each other. But what else might it explain?

It was almost dawn; even the most compulsive workaholics on the White House staff had gone home. As he did most nights, McGraw was working in a corner of the large, vacant West Wing office formerly occupied by Julian Hubbard. He had been looking through the computer log of Julian's phone calls from the White House. He didn't really expect to find much; Julian had spent most of his waking life on the telephone, making and receiving dozens of calls every day. Most were Washington numbers that appeared again and again.

Strictly routine. But McGraw had long ago learned to look for breaks in the routine. Working backward (last actions were usually the least typical ones), he asked the computer to search the logs for the last number Julian had called on the night he resigned and left the White House forever. The computer found and displayed the number. McGraw asked it to match it to a name and address. An instant later a name, Palmer St. Clair 3d of 1 Palmer Mews, Stamford, Connecticut, appeared on the screen. McGraw accessed *Who's Who in America* and looked up the entry for Palmer St.

Clair 3d. He, too, had gone to Yale. Yearbooks told McGraw that he too had resided in Calhoun College, graduating one year after Julian Hubbard and two years after Julian's good friend Archimedes Hammett. McGraw accessed St. Clair's Connecticut driver's license and copied the picture and Social Security number. The latter gave him access to St. Clair's credit card numbers. He asked the major credit data banks for a rundown of St. Clair's recent travel, and found that he had flown to Washington from La Guardia just a few days before, taking the seven A.M. plane to National Airport and returning to La Guardia on the ten o'clock shuttle. This had given him about one hour in Washington. McGraw found the record of the car St. Clair had rented, determined the mileage, twenty-four miles, and asked the computer to draw a radius based on this figure on a map of Washington and Virginia. This graphic suggested that St. Clair could have traveled to Mount Vernon, the Washington Cathedral, or the Capitol, assuming he hadn't gotten lost.

This was about as far as McGraw could go without outside help. He walked down the hall to the office of Norman Carlisle Blackstone and told him about Horace Hubbard's rendezvous with Busby.

Blackstone listened soberly, making notes. "If those two have been getting together, in secret or otherwise," he said, "it's most improper conduct."

"Yeah, completely out of character for a Hubbard," McGraw said. "There's one more datum, seemingly unrelated, but maybe it'll turn out to be a clue."

McGraw spoke the word "datum" deadpan, knowing that rigorous grammatical usage in all languages gave Blackstone pleasure. Grim and ashen from lack of sleep, the lawyer smiled in weary appreciation and said, "What datum is that, John?"

"Horace Hubbard and Baxter T. Busby played on the same basketball team at Yale."

"Ah, that would suggest a bond."

"Could be," McGraw said. "One datum sometimes leads to another."

"Is that what's happening in your investigation?"

"I think maybe that's what's beginning to happen. This particular datum got me thinking in a different direction."

Blackstone was suddenly alert. "Oh? What direction is that?"

"I'm not exactly sure," McGraw said, "but it looks like I'll have to visit New Haven."

7

As a general rule, McGraw did not believe in telephone taps, or "intercepts," as they were called by spies and others who did believe in them. Eavesdropping was a thief of time and money that almost never produced usable evidence. It stood to reason that no one who was engaged in espionage or other criminal activity on a professional basis was likely to say anything incriminating over the phone, and ordinarily McGraw was not interested in amateurs. At best, intercepts could be used to justify suspicions. But what was the point of doing that? There were no degrees of suspicion. If you had a suspect, you looked for hard evidence of his guilt. You looked for patterns. This was what McGraw believed in and what he lived by as an investigator: patterns.

In his quest for evidence that might help Olmedo save Lockwood, McGraw had no real suspect, but he did have a starting point: Palmer St. Clair 3d of Stamford, Connecticut, to whom Julian had placed his last call from his White House phone, and who had made that flying visit to Washington. With the help of a friend in the telephone company, McGraw put together a pattern based on St. Clair's incoming and outgoing telephone calls over the past five years. He discovered that a large number of calls had been placed to the number in Stamford from pay telephones in Washington or New Haven. Such calls were invariably followed, within sixty seconds, by a call from the telephone in Stamford to a third number. The most frequently called numbers belonged to Julian Hubbard and Archimedes Hammett. Within a minute or so after receiving a call from Palmer St. Clair 3d, the person called by St. Clair would dial another number, and then the person at *that* number would immediately make another call. And so on.

At the end of a night of work on the computer, McGraw had compiled a long list of interconnected numbers. He matched these numbers to names and matched the names to biographical files. It was now that the pattern emerged: every one of the numbers belonged to a graduate of Yale who held a position of influence in government, banking, business, law, academia, or some other learned profession or prestigious occupation.

They were of all ages from the twenties to the seventies; the oldest was the chairman of a private bank in Wall Street, the youngest a law student. Each member of the network was in touch with two other people, and those two were also in touch with two more. The entire network could be accessed in less than ten minutes.

McGraw had just compiled the first directory of the Shelley Society. He did not yet know its name or purposes. But he knew it existed and he knew the names, addresses, phone numbers, and thumbnail biographies of most of the people who belonged to it. It was organized exactly like the Eye of Gaza and every other terrorist network he had ever penetrated. An operation set up in this triangular fashion was, in theory, impenetrable because no one member could betray more than two other people. The theory was erroneous, however, because, as McGraw knew from experience, all you had to do to discover all its members was to identify one of them, persuade him to identify the next one, and keep going in either direction until you got to the end.

Not for a moment did McGraw think that these people were terrorists. But what *was* the purpose of the operation? What game were they playing? What unified them besides Yale? He had already established one interesting circumstance: Palmer St. Clair 3d's brief trip to Washington. Why would a partner in a large Manhattan brokerage house fly to Washington for an hour when the airline data bank showed that he had not visited the city even once in the preceding five years? McGraw accessed the news files for the days before and after St. Clair's trip to see if it might be connected to something in the news. He immediately struck pay dirt. Julian Hubbard's name popped up in Ross Macalaster's story about the Ibn Awad assassination, which had appeared in the papers the day after St. Clair's visit. This would have seemed mere coincidence apart from the fact that St. Clair had received a call from a pay phone in Washington the night before and had made only one outgoing call for the rest of the evening—to the airline to book his early-morning flight to Washington. McGraw checked the mileage on the rented car again, projecting it on the map against the locations of Macalaster's house, Julian Hubbard's house, and Hammett's apartment. All fell within the radius.

By now it was five o'clock in the morning. McGraw booked himself on a flight from National Airport to La Guardia, rented a car after landing, and arrived in front of a large, dramatically modern house in Stamford at a few minutes after seven. It was a rainy morning. With the defroster running to keep the windows clear, he ate a granola bar, drank a half-pint carton of skim milk, and read the tabloid he had bought at the airport. At 7:20 A.M. a tall, gawky WASP scarecrow, a man in his fifties, came out the front door wearing a sweat suit. Planting his foot on the doorjamb, he did a series of elaborate stretching exercises, then started off on his morning run, elbows and knees going every which way. McGraw recorded this activity with a video camera that stored the images on the disk in his computer.

8

Back in Washington a couple of hours later, McGraw drove straight from the airport to Macalaster's house. He did not know Macalaster, but he had been working with reporters all his life, and he knew that they were gossips at heart. They lived by trading information. He thought he had an item to trade that Macalaster would not be able to resist. It was still quite early in the morning. A sleepy-eyed Macalaster answered the doorbell, but when he saw a redheaded stranger standing on his doorstep wearing blue-on-blue polyester—navy blazer, powder-blue slacks, blue checked shirt, sky-blue tie, he nearly slammed the door in his face.

McGraw said, "Whoa!" and held up a hand with a vinyl White House security badge in it. He told Macalaster who he was and saw that he recognized the name. The journalist's face registered a mixture of wariness and curiosity.

"It's nice of you to come by so early, Mr. McGraw," he said. "But it may be a waste of your time. I can't discuss sources with you."

"I'd never dream of asking you to do that," McGraw said. "I know you fellows have rules. I just want your help on a small detail."

"What kind of a detail?"

"I want you to look at some pictures."

"What kind of pictures?"

McGraw had brought his computer to the door with him. He switched it on and punched up the video footage he had recorded in Stamford. Then he turned the computer around so that Macalaster could see the screen, on which Palmer St. Clair 3d was taking his morning run under the dripping maple trees. There were several close-ups, taken with the telephoto lens, of St. Clair's long-jawed, gin-ravaged society-page face. It was the same man who had collided with Macalaster in the parking lot and hooked the Ibn Awad tape to his coat.

"I have no idea who this man is," Macalaster said.

But McGraw saw recognition flickering in his eyes. "I believe you," he said. "But I'll tell you what. I'll give you this guy's name and address if you'll tell me how you happened to recognize him."

"What makes you think I recognize him?"

McGraw gave him a steady policeman's look. "Absolute confidentiality guaranteed," he said, instead of answering the question.

Macalaster stepped aside. "Come in, Mr. McGraw."

In the den, Macalaster said, "You were right. I do recognize that person."

"Okay," McGraw said. "Your move."

Macalaster told him what had happened in the parking lot, but nothing more than the details of the encounter itself. He protected Julian Hubbard; he protected everyone he had the slightest reason to protect. McGraw asked no further questions, but as he had anticipated, Macalaster's curiosity was an irresistible force. Without waiting to be asked, McGraw fed it by downloading his video of St. Clair onto a floppy disk and providing Macalaster with a printout of the biographical sketch he had compiled from *Who's Who in America* and other overt sources. He asked to see the fishhook, the plastic bag, the tape itself. Macalaster showed him these items. "Hey," McGraw said, examining the fly, "a Mickey Finn."

"A what?" Macalaster asked.

"That's the name of this fly."

"Are you a fly fisherman?"

"No, but I put one in jail once."

"For what?"

"He drowned his wife in ten inches of running water and tried to make it look like a fishing accident," McGraw said. "Is it all right with you if I take pictures of this stuff?"

"Go ahead. What else can you tell me about this man St. Clair?"

"So far, not much." McGraw was packing up his computer. "Looks like his hobbies are jogging, fly-fishing, and delivering stolen goods to strangers in parking lots three hundred miles from home. He went to Yale, class of '71. Did you go there?"

"No."

"Know anybody who did?"

"This town is full of people who went to Yale."

"That's funny, so is New York," said McGraw. He made as if to get up out of his chair, then subsided. "Look," he said, "I do know a little more. I don't mind telling you what it is, but I've gotta get something back."

Macalaster said, "What, for example?"

"Here's the deal," McGraw said. "I'll give you two names of people right here in Washington who knew this character at Yale if you'll let me make a copy of the tape."

"Why would you do that?" Macalaster said. "Everything on the tape was in the paper."

"Reading it isn't the same as listening to it."

Macalaster examined his visitor. The legs of McGraw's wrinkle-proof trousers had hiked up when he sat down. The meaty part of the left calf was marked by a vertical line of irregular roundish scars that resembled old-fashioned smallpox vaccinations. Macalaster, who had seen fresh punctures of this kind in Vietnam, recognized them as wounds inflicted by an automatic weapon.

"Yes or no?" McGraw asked.

Macalaster looked at McGraw's scars again. He said, "Okay."

McGraw held out his hand for the minitape, snapped it into a slot in the computer and typed in a command. The tape whirred at high speed as the computer copied it into its memory. He rewound it and handed it back to Macalaster.

"The names," McGraw said, "are Julian Hubbard, class of 1970, and Archimedes Hammett, class of 1969." He handed Macalaster a business card. "If you remember anything else you want to swap, tit for tat and strictly between the two of us, here's my number." He winked. "Just like on television."

After McGraw left, Macalaster looked at the evidence lying on the table. A tape cassette. In a Baggie. Hanging from a dry fly called a Mickey Finn. A wave of nausea rose in his throat. For the first time he perceived the smug, contemptuous joke contained in the method of delivery. The hook had been baited and he had swallowed it. Whoever had used him had known him well, and had known what he would do in response to the perfectly chosen lure.

9

"*Sinclair*," Julian Hubbard said, correcting Macalaster's outsider's pronunciation of the name St. Clair as two separate words. "Yes, I know a Palmer St. Clair. We were in the same college at Yale."

"Which college was that?"

"Calhoun. He was my junior by a year."

"Was Hammett in Calhoun College, too?" Macalaster asked.

"That's right, he was a year ahead of me. Just a moment, I think I see something interesting." He lifted the Zeiss binoculars to his eyes, focused them, and said, "Ah!" Handing the glasses over to Macalaster, he said,

"See that tall pine against the sky? Fourth branch from the top, left-hand side, right on the tip, a pine grosbeak."

Julian had suggested that they meet on Theodore Roosevelt Island, a wildlife preserve in the Potomac River; hardly anyone went there now because human life was not protected there, and as Macalaster had reason to know, the city itself was overrun with wild creatures. He looked through the Zeiss lenses but saw no bird.

"Wasn't that something?" Julian said.

"All I saw was the Kennedy Center," Macalaster said. He handed the binoculars back to Julian.

"Really? Bad luck; you may not see another pine grosbeak for a while." Julian lifted the glasses to his eyes again. "Why are you interested in Palmer St. Clair, of all people?" he asked.

"I came into contact with him," Macalaster said.

Julian focused the binoculars. "Did you now? How is he?"

"I don't know. It was a brief contact. He hooked the tape of you and Philindros and Lockwood plotting to murder Ibn Awad to my coat and disappeared."

Julian lowered the glasses and looked into Macalaster's face with a show of comic disbelief. "Palmer hooked *what* to your coat?"

"The tape, Julian. It was in a Baggie attached to a dry fly, a Mickey Finn."

Julian listened, unblinking. "A Mickey Finn?" he said. "Haven't seen anyone use that particular fly in years."

"Has Hammett? Or is he more a live-bait man?"

"To tell the truth, I don't think Archimedes knows one trout fly from another," Julian said. "Ross, what is it you're driving at?"

"I want to know what the hell you think you're doing."

"I'm watching birds," Julian said. He pointed at a large storklike bird that stood motionless at the edge of the water. "That's an American bittern down there. It's motionless because it thinks we're dinosaurs who can't see it if it doesn't move. It's the phantom of the American swamp. When it calls out in the marshes at twilight it sounds like a ghost splitting wood with one arm and pumping water with the other. Dull ax, squeaky pump. What do you think I have to do with Palmer St. Clair's hanging something to your coat with a Mickey Finn? Is he a friend of yours?"

"That was our only meeting. But he's a friend of yours. And Hammett's."

"Are you sure you've got the right Palmer St. Clair? The one I know is a harmless stockbroker, skinny as a rail, no meat on his bones at all, not the kind of fellow that goes around frightening innocent journalists."

Julian's equine face was open and amused. "Does that sound like the man?"

"This is the man," Macalaster said, handing Julian prints of some of McGraw's close-ups of St. Clair in his running togs.

Julian looked at the pictures, holding them out at the end of his arm and tilting his head backward to compensate for his long-sightedness. "That's Palmer all right," he said. "Looks like his house in Stamford in the background, too. Haven't been there in years, but it's all coming back. Have you been following him?"

"No, Lockwood's lawyers have."

"Not Blackstone?"

"An investigator who works for Alfonso Olmedo—McGraw is the name."

"Ah, yes, McGraw," Julian said. "Where did this strange encounter between you and Palmer St. Clair take place?"

"In a parking lot on Wisconsin Avenue. The man in the pictures was dressed as a runner. He bumped into me and knocked my glasses off."

"You broke your glasses?"

"No. The lenses are plastic."

"But they fell to the ground." Macalaster nodded. Julian said, "And when you looked up your assailant was gone?"

"Not quite. He was in the process of disappearing."

"How long were you face-to-face with him?"

"Seconds. When I got into the car I found the tape hooked to my jacket with a fishing fly."

"Which you immediately recognized as a Mickey Finn."

"No, McGraw told me its name."

"McGraw did? Remarkable fellow." Stooping slightly so as to be at the same eye level as Macalaster, Julian gazed into his face with the kindly interest of a nephew humoring a senile uncle. "When did this encounter in the parking lot happen? What time, what day?"

"About half an hour before I came to see you and you gave me the rest of the story."

"Odd you didn't mention it when it was fresh in your mind."

"I didn't want to burden you with it."

"I see. And now, because in my innocence I let you see my diary, you think I put Palmer St. Clair up to this cloak-and-dagger delivery of the purloined tape."

"Have I said that?" Macalaster was on the defensive.

"No, you've described what sounds like a fraternity initiation prank or something out of a bad movie. I can see why you didn't share this vignette of a journalist's life with your readers. Have you talked to anyone else about this?"

"No."

"You haven't been in touch with Hammett?"

"No."

"It's just as well. He wouldn't be amused."

"Does he know Palmer St. Clair?"

"Very possibly, given the incriminating nature of their mutual past as old Calhounians, but it's the sort óf question that wouldn't amuse him. It doesn't amuse me much, either, to be honest with you, Ross. Do you really think I went around bugging the President of the United States when I was the beneficiary of his trust? Obviously you've talked to McGraw about this so-called brush contact with Palmer St. Clair, if that's who it was."

Neither man was smiling pleasantly now. Macalaster said, "That's who it was, Julian."

"Remarkable that you'd be so sure when your glasses fell off and you only saw this fellow's face for seconds—Ah, look!"

The bittern had lurched into motion and was stumbling forward, flapping its enormous wings. After a few steps it took ponderous flight and rose above the trees. Flying over the river with its neck stretched out, it looked like a pterodactyl. Julian watched it out of sight in affectionate admiration. "Wonderful," he said. Turning back to Macalaster, he made a kindly face and said, "Are you going to write about this? Because if you do, the people who don't like you—for instance Patrick Graham, who has the idea that you stole his story—are going to be quite unkind about your ethics and methods."

"Gee, that's scary, Julian."

Julian said, "Forgive my frankness; I was just speaking as a friend."

Macalaster said, "How frankly do you think Palmer St. Clair would talk to me if I dropped in on him?"

"Oh, I don't think he would talk to a journalist at all," Julian said. "I'd certainly advise him not to. It always leads to misunderstanding."

"Is that what all this is, Julian? A misunderstanding?"

"That's my impression. Because you've never understood, Ross. When you write what you're told, you're *doing* what you're told and you take what you get. If I were you, I'd just let well enough alone."

Something in Macalaster's face must have touched Julian's sympathies because he suddenly smiled and put a comradely hand on his shoulder. He seemed even taller than usual because he stood a little above Macalaster on the pine-needle slope, antique binoculars poised in his uplifted hand as he awaited another sighting.

10

"Let me make sure I understand this," Lockwood said to Olmedo. "You want me to stand up in front of the United States Senate and say I'm the victim of a conspiracy of Whiffenpoofs?"

"No," Olmedo replied, unsmiling. "But if they've done what they appear to have done, we have reason to wonder what they're planning to do next."

"I told you that tape is bullshit."

"And I believe you, Mr. President," Olmedo said. "But the Senate is a jury like any other, and it's the jury that must believe you."

"They're not fools, Alfonso. They know me, and they know I didn't steal the election. They know I didn't know it was being stolen if it *was* stolen. What's more, I don't know to this day that it actually *was* stolen and neither does anybody else. All that the world knows about it is what the man I beat has told them, but even Mallory doesn't think I had anything to do with it."

Olmedo held up a hand, silently asking Lockwood for the impossible: patience. "Let me put a fundamental question," he said. "What do you want out of this process?"

Lockwood grimaced. "I'll make it real simple," he said. "I want my innocence established."

Olmedo nodded. "In other words, you want to use your appearance before the Senate to prove the negative—to establish that you yourself did not steal the election even if it was in fact stolen."

"Correct."

"Do you also want to keep the presidency?"

Lockwood's patience was exhausted. "Jesus Christ, Alfonso, that's the whole idea!" he shouted. "Do you think I'm putting myself through this ordeal in order to run away with my tail between my legs, so's I can go down in history as a piece of trash who stole a presidential election? You're damn right I want to keep the presidency."

Olmedo paused for a moment, his face as placid as Lockwood's was agitated. Then he said, "What makes you think you can do both?"

"Both what?"

"Establish your innocence and keep the presidency."

Through clenched teeth, Lockwood said, "Alfonso, what are you trying to tell me?"

"That you are in a position, sir, in which you must destroy yourself by telling the truth. You can only prove your innocence of election fraud by establishing that others committed that fraud without your knowledge and consent. But there's a catch: acquittal on such grounds would mean giving up the presidency, because to prove you aren't guilty you must admit that you were not elected."

Standing with his back to the fire, Lockwood did not reply for a long moment. The Lincoln sitting room was lit only by the flames and by a small night-light, so that the two men could barely see each other's faces. Finally Lockwood said, "What does that have to do with the damn tape?"

"Everything," Olmedo replied. "The purpose of leaking the Ibn Awad tape was not to impeach you as President, but to impeach you as a witness. Don't you see, Mr. President? Even if the FIS killed Ibn Awad behind your back, the tape suggests that you condoned the offense after it came to your knowledge by lying to the American people."

Lockwood held up a hand. "That's enough."

"Let me finish, please. You put your finger on the problem with your remark about the Whiffenpoofs. The same applies to your version of the conversation with Philindros and Julian Hubbard about Ibn Awad. Your enemies have put you in a position in which you cannot tell the truth without sounding like a liar or a madman. Mr. President, it's Hobson's choice. If you win, you lose."

Lockwood absorbed this, his battered face turning crimson. Suddenly he roared, "Mr. Olmedo, do you want to withdraw from this case?"

"No," Olmedo replied, "I want to win it. But I can't do so unless I know why the man you trusted most in the world and the man you appointed Chief Justice of the United States on his recommendation seem to be hell-bent on destroying you with the help of the chairman of the Senate Judiciary Committee. We must destroy their credibility if we are to save yours. That is the key."

Lockwood threw up his arms. "The key?" he said. "The *key* is that Julian and his brother are trying to save their Yankee asses, that Hammett has always been a little funny in the head, and that Buzzer Busby is a natural-born damn fool."

Olmedo drew closer and put a hand on Lockwood's forearm. He had not touched him since they shook hands on being introduced weeks before, and the gesture had a strong effect. "Mr. President," he said. "I urge you to consider the possibility that there is more to it than that."

"Alfonso, these are the people who supposedly stole the election to keep Franklin Mallory from being President. If I go down, Mallory takes over the country. The whole thing makes no sense. None. Not a particle."

"Not yet," Olmedo said. "Conspiracies seldom do, except to the conspirators."

Lockwood said, "What time is it?" He wore no watch, carried no money, remembered no names, feared no enemies—princely habits instilled by Julian Hubbard.

Olmedo said, "Two-twenty, and Carlisle Blackstone is waiting to see you."

Lockwood was not pleased. "What does he have for me?"

"A list of possible courses of action under the Constitution."

"What for? The only course of action I'm interested in is what I just told you."

"I understand," Olmedo said, "but your enemies may have other ideas. I think you should hear what he has to say."

"I haven't got the patience," Lockwood said. "If you ask Spats what time it is, he tells you how to build the damn watch."

"It might be wise to give him a few minutes, Mr. President."

"I can't make myself do it," Lockwood said. "What's wisdom got to do with anything?"

11

By now rumors of conspiracy, of something afoot within the Cause, made the whole town hum. This amused Baxter T. Busby. The simple fact, he said, was that everything that had happened to the Old Guard since Inauguration Day had happened as a consequence of its own falsity and corruption. True, Attenborough, Lockwood, and ultimately Mallory were being brought down by high-minded men and women who were able to put party loyalty aside and act on their convictions. Certainly everything Busby himself had done had been done in good faith and right out in the open. No hidden enemy could possibly have invented the dilemma the good old boys had contrived for themselves.

In the interim between sessions of the Senate trial, Busby explained all this to Slim Eve at a fund-raiser for the Cause at the spartan downtown headquarters of the Womonkind Coalition. They were by themselves in a corner of the room and they were getting along extremely well. In this severely radical milieu Slim wore dark colors, an ankle-length skirt, and perverse low-heeled shoes with laces, like the ones Busby's maiden aunts had worn in photographs taken of them as Red Cross nurses in France during the First World War. In spite of this costume, she was by far the best-looking woman in the room. Her sensitive face with its enormous deep-blue eyes was deathly pale, and she listened intently to every word he spoke.

"Not only did they do it to themselves, with no help from Reds under the bed or the Greens or radicals or feminists or subversives in the news media, but they earned it," he told her. "The whole affair is the fulfillment of the prophecy of Vietnam and Watergate."

In her throaty, Jean Arthurish voice, Slim said, "Maybe it was naïve to think that a corrupt system can produce virtuous leaders."

"Do you believe it never can?"

"What do you think? Look what happened to Vice President Williston Graves. You do know how he died?"

"An embolism, I heard."

"Incurred while sexually abusing a young lawyer on his staff."

Busby was wildly amused by this revelation. He put on a serious face. "A *lawyer? Willy?* I'm amazed."

"I don't see why," Slim said. "My point is, maybe they're all alike. The system makes them that way."

Slim was ready to turn back to the main topic, but Busby's curiosity was fully aroused. Graves was a famous quickie artist who had been hopping on secretaries and lady constituents in his office for years. Had Horace Hubbard, that sly dog, known something about this down in the Grenadines when he asked those questions about the cause of Graves's death? Busby had to be sure this story was true. He said, "Just a minute. How do you know this about Graves and the lawyer?"

"The victim belongs to the same feminist support group for rape victims as me. She told us."

"And she worked for Willy Graves? Strange bedfellows."

"She used to do worse than that; she worked her way through law school as a receptionist at a Morning After Clinic. But she saw the light."

"Thank goodness."

"Yes," Slim said, a trifle impatiently. "As I was saying, I admired Frosty Lockwood. I believed in him because I was told it was all right to do so. So did everyone else I knew, until a day or two ago. I can't help feeling that if Lockwood is destroyed, we lose something we may never be able to get back."

"The right to be naïve about the corrupt system?" Busby asked teasingly.

Slim detected a sexist, all-women-are-naïve undertone in this remark, and acknowledged it and ignored it with one tiny smile. "We put him in office because we thought he was one of us."

"And he betrayed your trust. But history moves in mysterious ways. Painful as this process has been, it may be all to the good. It opened everything up, ripped off the masks, gave the good people the chance to start over again clean. My advice is, Get out of bed in the morning and get to work. You can be damn sure Mallory will go to the mat on this one because he knows it means the end of him, too."

"Do you really believe that?"

"Don't you?"

"Intellectually I'm beginning to, I guess," Slim said. "Emotionally it's not so simple. What bothers me even more than the idea of Mallory taking power is the thought of Attenborough becoming President of the United States. Of course I have subjective reasons for feeling as I do. But is that possible?"

"Oh, yes," Busby said. "But tomorrow is another day."

"What's that supposed to mean?"

"I can't say more." Busby's air was mysterious, but in fact he had nothing more to say because he had not thought beyond Attenborough to the ultimate solution of the problem of the presidency. All he knew, really, was that this time, somehow, anyhow, the office had to be placed in the right hands, and he was not about to say *that* aloud.

"I won't ask you to say more," Slim said. "But you've given me an opportunity to tell you that I've been working on this problem."

"What problem is that?"

"The succession. That's why I wanted to talk to you." She looked around them, leaned closer, and said, "You did get the message over the Old Blue network?"

Busby betrayed nothing, but in fact he had come to this party on Shelleyan orders. Very early that morning he had received a call from the third Shelleyan in his cell—Horace Hubbard, of course, being the other. The call came from overseas on a hyperfrequency circuit. After the usual pleasantries concerning the object that Trelawny had snatched from the funeral pyre at Viareggio, Five-Three said, "A sky-lark tells me you've been invited to a reception at the Womonkind Coalition tonight."

"Good Lord, have I? I don't see how I can make it."

"It was hoped that you could turn up and have a private word with the guest of honor. She's more than just a victim of a beastly act." Five-Three meant this as a joke; his sensibilities had been formed in the Eisenhower era, and as a venture capitalist with a huge clientele among the primitive capitalists of the new Far East, he had no incentive to raise his consciousness. He continued: "It's said she's an interesting woman. Brilliant lawyer. From Yale Law School."

"This town is full of interesting women who are brilliant lawyers."

"Buzzer," said Five-Three in the tone of fatigue often adopted by those who knew Busby well, "I ask this in the name of the Poet."

"Ah, that's a horse of a different color," said Busby.

"I have something for you," Slim said.

She had backed herself into a corner and positioned Busby in front of her, with his back to the room. Now, concealing the gesture behind the screen of his body, she produced a computer diskette from the pocket of her skirt and pressed it into his hand. It was one of a new type, about the size of a matchbook cover. "It's all on this; I researched it, drafted it, and keyboarded it myself, and only one other person has knowledge of its existence."

"Who's that?"

"My principal."

Busby did not ask who her principal might be; he already knew it was a fellow Shelleyan.

"Considering what else is going on in your life, I wonder you could do it at all."

Slim touched his hand briefly and coolly. Busby felt a small thrill. It was not an uncomplicated reaction. This woman was not only beautiful, she was highly intelligent and maybe even a little crazy—everything that was attractive. No wonder Attenborough had gotten in over his head. Busby moved backward a step. Slim looked downward at the diskette—disapprovingly because Busby still held it openly on his upturned palm, and stepped toward him, closing the gap between them. "I hope you'll find what's on that interesting," she said. "The only other person I've discussed it with thinks that it may be the solution to everything."

"He does?" Busby said. "My goodness, whatever can it be?"

"A hidden wonder of the Constitution," Slim said. She covered the diskette with her own hand. "As I said, it's all on the diskette."

Slim took her hand away, but slowly. Busby looked downward at her long forefinger, which still rested ever so lightly upon the diskette, as if on a part of his body.

"That's a little vague," Busby said. "What if I don't quite understand the contents and need to discuss it?"

"Then you can call me," Slim said. "The number is on the diskette."

"Is it a work number?"

"It's a twenty-four-hour number," Slim replied. "Don't hesitate to use it. I'm perfectly familiar with all the details and with my principal's thinking."

"Then I may have to call you," Busby said.

"Fine."

Slim removed her fingertip from the diskette, as if breaking a psychic connection. "And now I think we'd better go and rejoin the crowd."

"I think so too," said Busby ruefully, stealthily slipping the diskette into his pocket.

Slim was smiling at him again, but only with her eyes. She had the air of a woman who had known exactly what to expect before she met him and had not been disappointed in the least by the reality. It was a look he recognized. He recognized the touch of her hand, too: back in the fifties Vassar girls, his wife among them, had cultivated the hand-on-your-hand-holding-the-cigarette-lighter trick, linked with the lifting of meaning-filled eyes, especially during senior spring, and nearly every member of his class had succumbed to this particular old one-two before finding out, to their lifelong cost, exactly what its consequences were.

"Good night, Ms. Eve," he said. "And thank you."

Next morning, very early, he had his secretary print out the contents of Slim's diskette in the extra-large type in which all his working papers came from the word processor. Reading, he gasped in astonishment and pleasure, then picked up the phone and dialed Slim's twenty-four-hour number. Though it was not yet seven, she answered unsleepily on the first ring. He blurted, "The Constitution actually *says* that?"

Slim said, "Yes. Didn't you look it up for yourself?"

"No time. Does it mean what it says?"

"It always means what it says. It's right there in black and white in Article Two, refined in the Twentieth Amendment, which shows serious intent not just by the Framers but by later generations of lawmakers."

"I tell you, this is a stroke of genius," Busby said. "I'm lost in admiration. Do you know what this can *mean?*"

"For Lockwood and Mallory, yes. But my principal believes it's a win-win situation for everyone else. A way out. A pragmatic, constitutional way out."

"And a new beginning." There was joy in Busby's voice. "Slim, you tell your principal that the Poet would be proud, capital *P*," he said. "He'll understand."

"I'll deliver the message."

"And you can tell him I take my hat off to the two of you. I was absolutely blind to this opportunity, and my guess is that everyone else in Washington is, too."

"Then I'm glad we were able to help," Slim said. "But remember, you have to lock both of them out before you can do this."

"Don't worry about that," Busby said. "It's the only way to save the party, and they all know that already."

"Then you're halfway home. The other half is getting the right person, a new face, into the game as savior of the situation. I hope you'll be thinking about this."

Busby didn't even have to think about it. "I already have," Busby said. "I know just the person for the job."

"Good," said Slim. "I'm so glad."

Whistling a tune, Busby locked the printout and the diskette in his desk drawer. He knew that Slim had just dealt him the last card in the winning hand. The pot contained the Constitution, the presidency, and the triumph of the Shelley Definition and the dawn of the Year Zed, and he was going to win it all—not for himself but for the Poet and for the Cause.

VIII

1

Vice President Williston Graves's funeral took place in the Washington Cathedral at nine-thirty on Friday morning, the day on which the Senate impeachment trial was scheduled to reconvene at one o'clock. By the time the crowd began to arrive, most insiders knew that Graves had expired while sitting in a swivel chair behind his desk with a buxom twenty-seven-year-old deputy vice presidential counsel straddling his lap. Graves, a warm-blooded but prudent man, was famous for the position. "They can't holler 'offsides' if they're on top" had been his motto.

The lawyer immediately called his wife and explained the situation. "Zip him up and comb his hair and wheel him up to the desk," Lydia Graves advised her. "Then fix your own hair, call the White House doctor, and keep your mouth shut." The young woman followed these instructions with considerable presence of mind, but blurted out the truth to Bud Booker of the Secret Service, who got to the scene moments before the White House medical team arrived and pointed out with the utmost tact that she was walking around with only one leg in her panty hose.

Now the image of Graves's last earthly moment hovered above the congregation like a hologram, bringing fleeting smiles to the lips of the many male friends, and some of the females, who had long known about his extramarital modus operandi. The circumstances in which the Lord had taken Graves home kindled affection for his memory in nearly everyone but his widow, who resented the timing and the absurdity of his departure. Like his final sexual partner, Lydia had been more than usually nice to Graves in his last days because, the way things were going for Lockwood, it seemed possible he might soon be President. She had been willing to settle for the title of First Lady as a reward for a lifetime of treating Willy's office playmates as invisible women. The lawyer had hoped for a White House job in return for her favors, one with a gender-neutral title and an office in the West Wing itself, not across the alley in the rococo limbo that was the Executive Office Building.

The funeral, attended by all Washington, would mark Lydia's last appearance at center stage, and she had designed it as the entr'acte in the constitutional crisis. Understanding the town she lived in, she knew that dead Vice Presidents seldom drew a crowd. Therefore she asked Lockwood to deliver the eulogy. He had not said no, but as the organ filled the nave with the first soaring notes of B. Cowan's Variations on "Onward Christian Soldiers," the question remained unanswered. The news media, the whole of Washington, wondered aloud if Lockwood, who had not emerged from the White House since Inauguration Day, would come out into the open at last. There were cameras everywhere.

From nine o'clock onward the cathedral filled up rapidly. Among the first to arrive was Attenborough, and as he waited for the service to begin, he sat all by himself at the far end of a row of chairs. No one offered to join him. Few of Graves's friends, nearly every one of them also an old friend of the Speaker's, so much as nodded to him as they made their way down the aisles. As these turncoats went by, Attenborough concentrated on the cathedral's famous and popular Space Window, set into the granite just above his head. He recalled from the dedication ceremony many years before that a piece of genuine lunar rock, enclosed in a capsule of nitrogen to protect it from the earth's atmosphere, was embedded in the stained glass. How long ago it seemed that Armstrong and Aldrin had landed in the Sea of Tranquillity, and yet how recent. The Apollo astronauts were about his age—old men. Were they all dead yet? Just about everybody else was.

Attenborough looked away. The organ played rueful music—classical stuff that Willy almost certainly would not have been able to recognize. The dense perfume of hothouse flowers filled the air. Down by the choir, propped up amid wreaths, baskets, and bouquets, the silvered urn containing Graves's ashes reflected sunbeams. Lydia had had him cremated as soon as the autopsy was complete, incinerating the entire corpse, Attenborough thought, in order to make sure of destroying the offending part. He made a mental note to tell Albert not to let anybody cremate him. "The body that is sown is perishable, but it is raised imperishable," First Corinthians, chapter the fifteenth, verse the forty-second. The fact that Attenborough had never got religion in his heart didn't necessarily mean that he didn't think there might be something to it, and if he was going to be resurrected on the Day of Glory and reign with the Lord for a thousand years, as the Book of Revelation promised, he wanted to keep his bones together in a good tight box.

By now it was 9:25. Everyone was seated. The vergers closed the doors; the organ emitted a final tremulous note. Awareness rippled through the nave from back to front as Lockwood, with Polly on his arm and his familiar homely, sad-eyed head sticking up above the phalanx of Secret Service agents, swept down the aisle to a seat in the front row.

Although Graves had been born and raised a Disciple of Christ, the Anglican service for the dead was read in a plummy voice by a clergyman wearing gorgeous medieval vestments. Then Lockwood rose, bent consolingly over the veiled widow for a moment, and mounted the steps leading to the lectern. He began to speak, without notes, in his own accent, which was as loud and American as the priest's had been discreet and mid-Atlantic. Towering over the audience, the President looked and sounded as Lincolnian as ever. He was an orator by nature, and he seemed happy to be speaking again and to be among people. Because of that, and because he had truly liked Graves, his eulogy was long and—because nearly all the lovable and interesting things about Willy were unsuitable for churchly utterance—boring. If Lockwood was in the least discomfited by the prospect of going on trial for his place in history in a couple of hours, he showed no sign of it. And that, as Attenborough understood, was the whole point of his showing up: What, me worry?

After the first five minutes of embroidered reminiscence—Lockwood reinvented Graves as he went along, making him singular and laughable, just as he had always done with everybody else he'd ever met—Attenborough stopped listening and concentrated instead on staying awake. This was difficult, even though he had taken an extra pill with the vodka he had drunk in the car on the way here, Albert watching him in the rearview mirror and shaking his head in disapproval. Attenborough was a student of the Constitution. He decided to keep his eyes open by remembering it, all of it, in his mind. Of course he knew it by heart, just as he knew at least two versions of the Bible and the Texas criminal and civil codes and most of the major Acts of Congress passed in the last thirty years. It came back to him in the exact same physical form in which he had first read it, in large clear type on the glossy, slightly yellowed pages of his ninth-grade civics book.

Just as Lockwood began hitting his stride, the Speaker reached the Twentieth Amendment. Because he was reading the text with the mind of the thirteen-year-old boy he had been when he memorized the Constitution, the sense of its language didn't come through, only the words and the meter, and though he tried to prevent it from happening and even reached into his ticket pocket for an extra pill, he felt himself falling into a profound sleep just as the lines about appointing an acting President appeared. In his mind, though not in reality, he sat bolt upright. The words of the amendment crackled through his mind like a spark leaping across a darkness, which was, of course, exactly what was happening inside his skull. Suddenly everything that had happened—everything— made sense to him, *frightened* him. *Gotta tell Sam.* That was Attenborough's last thought before he fell into a bottomless slumber.

Half an hour later, when he woke, he felt a pang of guilt. For the moment, that's all it was, a pang. He knew why he felt it: he had fallen asleep in the middle of remembering something, a cardinal sin. But what? Whatever it was, it was vital. He remembered being frightened, as if he had heard an oracular warning in a dream. But the circumstances, the reason for his fright, had flown out of his mind, and though he could still sense its overwhelming importance, he could not recapture it.

He opened his eyes. Willy's urn was gone; so were the widow and Lockwood. But he was not alone. He heard the hollow murmur of the departing crowd, the shuffle of feet over the stone floor, coughing. A pattern of light falling through a stained-glass window onto the back of his inert blue-veined hand reminded him of a tattoo. And because one thing memorized often triggered the recollection of another, he tried to remember what the Lord had told Moses to command the congregation of Israel about tattoos in . . . which book of the Pentateuch? He could not remember this, either.

All he could recall were words of warning shimmering on a page brightened by harsh Texas sunshine shining through a schoolhouse window in 1944. But he could not remember what the words said, or even the title of the work. He told himself, Relax, Tucker, it'll come back. But it didn't. Meanwhile, the mighty passed by, faces frozen, eyes averted. They might as well have given him a bell to ring and made him cry "Unclean, unclean." He'd known them all for years, but he couldn't put names to them. He felt the edge of panic.

Finally he was all alone. The silence was so deep that he thought he might still be asleep and dreaming. Were his eyes open? To answer the question he looked upward at the Space Window again—what were those astronauts' names?—and reflected once more that life was a hell of a lot shorter than he had expected it to be; it had been like one of those space voyages in the movies where they put you to sleep before you leave orbit and a robot with a sissy's voice wakes you up a century or two later and reminds you that you're still a kid but everyone you ever knew and loved on earth is long since dead and gone.

He still couldn't remember. "Damn!" he said in his frustration, at the top of his mighty voice. Or so he intended. But the echo that came back to him from the vault of the roof was tremulous, little more than a whisper. There was a numbness in his lip. When he lifted his right hand to touch it, he found that the hand was asleep; lip must be asleep, too, but how could that be? He felt deeply, deeply tired. He reached into his ticket pocket for a pill. Found it right away, popped it into his mouth: nothing wrong with the left hand. He looked up. Albert was standing over him with another of those fussbudget looks on his face. Must've got tired of waiting in the car and come looking for him.

Albert said, "You all right, Mr. Speaker?"

Attenborough nodded, waiting for the pill to kick in.

"Why you staring like that?" Albert asked.

"Just thinking, Albert," Attenborough replied. The words came out as a feeble croak. Albert's look of exasperation was replaced by one of alarm. Attenborough smiled, tried to stand up. Staggered, lost his balance; Albert had to catch him by the elbows to keep him from sliding under the pew.

"Shit!" Attenborough started to say, but stopped at the diphthong when he remembered where he was; Albert was a pious man.

Albert held the Speaker's biceps, the one on the good side of his body, in a grip like a blood-pressure cuff. With his other hand he was fumbling in his pocket for something. "We should call Henry on the telephone," Albert said. "Get you to the hospital."

"Not yet; got to stay with it," Attenborough said in the wheeze he now had as a voice. He could hardly keep his balance because his right leg was asleep, too. He knew it wasn't really asleep. He knew what was happening to him without talking to Henry, knew he had to keep this quiet, keep it away from the media. Everything depended on it; he knew that, too. In a while he'd remember why.

"Get me out of here, Albert," he said. He was damned if he'd die in church.

2

Albert drove Attenborough straight to Henry's office in the Watergate, but the Speaker refused to get out of the car. Henry came down the elevator to the underground garage and examined him in the backseat of his limousine, behind its one-way smoked windows.

"Is it a stroke?" Attenborough mumbled. The right side of his face drooped and his right arm and leg were still numb, though not so numb as they had been a while before.

"I don't think so," Henry said. "It's impossible to be sure without tests, but I think you've had a TIA."

"A what?"

"A transient ischemic attack. That means a certain area of your brain was deprived of blood for a short time."

"Why?"

"Arterial obstruction."

"You mean a blood clot?"

"Roughly speaking, yes. That's why you're experiencing these difficulties with your speech and your arm and leg. Is your memory affected?" Attenborough did not reply; this was not something he was prepared to admit and, besides, he was working hard to get it back. Henry eyed him and said, "What was your mother's maiden name?" Attenborough could not remember. Henry said, "How about your Social Security number?" Attenborough could do no more than shake his head helplessly. He found himself fighting tears. Henry said, "You should be in the hospital. You know that, don't you?"

"I remember your telling me that before," Attenborough said. "And I told you I can't do it. How long is this going to last?"

Henry did not like the question. "There's no way to predict. Could be as little as twelve hours, could be forty-eight. Or much longer."

"But sooner or later everything will come back including Mama's maiden name?"

"I can't say for sure, Mr. Speaker. You could also have a fatal stroke."

"I'll have to take my chances on that, Henry. Can you give me something to hurry it up? I need my brain in working order." He tried to wink but couldn't. "Maybe you could just kinda step back and kick me in the head, like we used to do to start the car."

This drew no smile. As Attenborough had noted on other occasions, Henry had no sense of humor whatsoever. They must have taken it out, like a malignancy, at Harvard; it happened all the time. "I can give you pills," Henry said. "But if you go on this way, Mr. Speaker, you won't need medication. You'll need an undertaker."

Attenborough smiled into Henry's earnest African face; he looked just like Albert at the same age. "Higbe," Attenborough said.

Henry was scribbling a prescription. He looked up. "What did you say?"

"Higbe. That was her name before she was married," Attenborough replied. "Mama was a Higbe."

"Good," Henry said. "Remembering that is a good sign. Keep it up."

"I'm working on it," Attenborough said.

3

The Speaker was worried about the cameras catching him dragging his leg as he took his seat in the Senate gallery, so he got himself a cane and made up a story about falling down in the bathtub. "Hit my head on the rim and busted up my mouth," he told Morgan Pike off-camera. Straining to understand his garbled speech, she looked at him strangely. "The Lord sure can pile it onto his servant when he's a mind to," Attenborough said. "I already had this damn malaria. Can't hardly talk, can't chew, can't walk." He winked at her, managing this time to open and close the lid in a slow-motion parody of lechery. "Only got about two more can'ts to go and I'll be completely harmless," he said.

Inside the bar of the Senate the chair reserved for Lockwood stood empty. After eulogizing Willy Graves, the President had retreated to Camp David, leaving his lawyers to appear for him. Chief Justice Hammett, grave and still, instructed the sergeant at arms to call the President to the floor. As before, the sergeant at arms threw open the doors and bellowed, "Bedford Forrest Lockwood, President of the United States, Bedford Forrest Lockwood, President of the United States, appear and answer the articles of impeachment exhibited against you by the House of Representatives of the United States." Once again there was no answer.

Hammett looked down from the podium at Olmedo and Blackstone, who were already seated at the defendant's table.

"Mr. Olmedo," he asked, "does the President of the United States intend to appear before the Senate for trial on the articles of impeachment exhibited by the House of Representatives?"

"Mr. Chief Justice," Olmedo answered, "my brother Mr. Blackstone and I are here as the President's counsel to enter appearance for him."

"Then he will not appear in person."

"Not at this time, Mr. Chief Justice."

"Is it possible he will present himself in person at some future time?"

"That is a matter for the President to decide according to circumstances, Mr. Chief Justice."

Olmedo spoke with a gravity that matched Hammett's, but he knew that all this was for the cameras. The Senate had been informed in advance that Lockwood would not appear in person. No one had supposed that he would be physically present, like a prisoner in the dock. However, Hammett's face took on a look of displeasure. On the rostrum before him, his folded hands rested on the Greek Bible he had brought with him again today; this worn volume was the only object on the polished desktop before him apart from the presiding officer's gavel. "Very well," he said at last. "Is the President prepared to present his reply to the articles of impeachment?"

"He is, sir."

Norman Carlisle Blackstone put on his pince-nez, and in a loud uninflected voice read out Lockwood's answers. To the surprise of many who knew Blackstone, these were brief, one-sentence replies. To the first article, the President denied that he had ordered the assassination of Ibn Awad or authorized the Foreign Intelligence Service to aid or abet it. "His denial on all points of this article is categorical," Blackstone read, "and any action that may have been taken by any officer of the United States contributing to the death of the said Ibn Awad was taken without the authorization or approval of the President."

This drew a gasp and a ripple of whispers from the galleries. These were small noises, but Hammett instantaneously gaveled them into silence. "If there is any further demonstration," he said, "the sergeant at arms will clear the galleries. Continue, Mr. Blackstone."

On the article relating to the theft of the election, Lockwood denied knowledge of fraud. "As he believed himself at the moment he took the presidential oath to be the duly elected President of the United States, and as he still believes himself to be such," Blackstone said, "he denies that he took the oath with mental reservations."

All this consumed no more than half an hour. "If the senators have no objection," Hammett said, "the answer of the President of the United States to the articles of impeachment will be filed." There was no objection from the quiescent Senate.

"Managers of the House of Representatives," Hammett said. "You will now proceed in support of the articles of impeachment."

Blackstone, who had been bent over his papers, hand to his pince-nez, looked up in astonishment. Olmedo rose smoothly to his feet.

"Mr. Chief Justice, we understood that the purpose of this session was to present the President's answers to the charges of impeachment. We have done that. But nothing was said about making opening arguments."

Though he indicated his surprise that Blackstone should interrupt him in this way, Hammett was gentle in his reply, and like all his moods, this one was perfectly attuned to the camera. "Mr. Olmedo, the question of proceeding with this trial with all deliberate speed was, I thought, discussed and decided at our last meeting. The Constitution mandates speedy action, the President himself has demanded a rapid resolution of this crisis, the need of the country to resolve the question of presidential legitimacy is paramount."

"Nevertheless we are surprised," Olmedo said. "May I ask for a vote of the Senate on this question?"

"You may, sir. Senators, do you desire to vote on the ruling of the Chief Justice on this matter?"

There was no reply from the floor. An impassive Hammett said, "The managers of the House will proceed with their presentation."

Bob Laval rose. His presentation of the evidence consumed the entire forty-five minutes allotted. Hammett turned to Olmedo. "Are you ready with your reply, sir?"

Rising, Olmedo looked upward at Hammett for the briefest of moments. There was no trace of expression on either man's face. Then he turned his back on the podium and addressed the Senate. "If it please this honorable Senate," he said, "the President's reply to the presentation of the managers of the House of Representative is brief. He will show that the articles of impeachment are without substance or merit, that he has faithfully executed the office of President of the United States, and that he has, to the best of his ability, executed his oath to preserve, protect, and defend the Constitution of the United States."

As Olmedo sat down, Hammett said, "Senators, the hour is early. I move that the Senate adjourn for thirty minutes and that it then reconvene and proceed to the examination of witnesses in regard to the first article of impeachment. Is there objection?"

Amzi Whipple rose. "There is, Mr. Chief Justice."

"Then the clerk will call the roll and the senators will vote on the motion."

The vote was tied on strict party lines like all the other ones before it, and as usual Hammett broke it in his own favor. The chamber emptied.

4

All afternoon, every time he raised his eyes to the gallery, Hammett had met the fixed stare of Tucker Attenborough, who sat directly in his line of sight like the diminutive mummy of some Yorick that had been exhumed from a peat bog, dressed in a suit and tie, and propped up in the front row as an absurdist comment on the trial. The Speaker seemed incapable of movement. His color was awful. Only his feverish eyes showed the spark of life. Never wavering, they bored into Hammett's eyes, glittering with an unnerving mixture of bitter accusation and Olympian amusement, as if the old man were already dead and knew the secrets of his enemies' hearts. Having grown up on his grandfather's stories of wronged Maniátes who came back from the next world as demons and succubi to avenge themselves in horrible ways on the living, Hammett half-believed that such a thing was possible.

"A message from Senator Clark, Mr. Chief Justice," said a female voice at Hammett's elbow. A matronly woman handed him a note in a barely legible scrawl he took to be Clark's; it was rare in this era of electronic mail to see another person's handwriting. It asked him to join Clark and the other members of his committee forthwith. Clark himself stood some distance away, watching while Hammett read the note. The Chief Justice looked up, nodded, rose briskly to his feet, and strode out of the chamber. He had the strong sensation of being followed by Attenborough's feverish eyes, but he did not look back.

The woman led him through rooms and corridors in what was evidently a shortcut to the back door of the Vice President's office, which the Senate had put at his disposal for the duration of the impeachment trial. He was offended by its opulence—the gilt, the silk, the waxed and burnished furniture and paneling, the deep carpet—and as much as possible he had avoided using it. As he approached the door, he heard Sam Clark and the other members of his committee guffawing inside. In the circumstances this was the last sound he had expected to hear, yet it did not surprise him; white males of the type who ran for the Senate were incurably frivolous, a self-perpetuating elite whose members ate too much, drank too much, told too many jokes. When he pushed open the door and entered the room in his black robe, they ceased laughing as if in response to a signal.

"We've just been caucusing," Clark said. Hammett gave him a saturnine scowl. Clark continued, "We all feel that these surprises from the chair are counterproductive—"

"Surprises?" Hammett said.

"Such as this latest one to proceed to the examination of witnesses without any sort of preliminary agreement to do so."

"How can there be a preliminary agreement between us? You are the judges in this case, Senators. I am the presiding officer. We must be independent of each other. This conversation is most improper. We should meet only in open court."

"By God, you are upright, aren't you?" Amzi Whipple said. "Just don't pull any more stunts like that one."

"The question was decided by the Senate," Hammett said. "The Chief Justice made a proposal. You yourself objected to it, Senator Whipple. I called for a vote as provided in Rule Twenty-four. The Senate voted according to party interest. I cast the deciding vote as provided by the rules."

"You're damn right we voted," Amzi Whipple said. "Had to. But you can't just spring these things on us that way."

"*What* way?" Hammett asked. He looked from one face to another in the circle of senators. "I'm sorry, Senators," he said. "But whatever point Senator Whipple is trying to make eludes me."

Throwing up his hands, Whipple said, "Sam, I yield. Maybe you can explain it."

Clark said, "Mr. Chief Justice, there are no witnesses present to be examined."

"Then you'd better summon some," Hammett said.

"On five minutes' notice?" Whipple bellowed. He advanced a step or two, ruddy and loud, then stumbled on the luxurious carpet. After catching his balance he pointed a finger at Hammett. A spark of static electricity flew across the space between them. Hammett recoiled. Whipple said, "Brimfire, by God!" All except Hammett laughed.

Clark's pocket telephone rang. He took it out, clicked on, listened, clicked off, and then turned back to the others. "That was Bob Laval," he said. "The House managers have found Jack Philindros driving around in his car and he's agreed to come in to testify. Laval is agreeable. But it will have to be pro forma and this will have to be the only witness of the day, Mr. Chief Justice. Nobody's ready. We just want you to understand that."

"I understand perfectly," Hammett said. "But I hope things will be better organized when the trial resumes on Monday afternoon."

"I think you can count on it," Clark said.

"Just remember, I must preside as the Constitution and the rules adopted for this trial provide."

"Jehoshaphat!" Whipple cried. He was seething.

"Forgive me, Senator," Hammett said, "but I was under the impression that you and your entire party voted for this motion. What's your problem?"

"My problem is that we were mousetrapped," Whipple said. "This makes a mockery of the Senate, of the whole damn process. And speaking for the opposition and in the spirit of that same Constitution and those same rules, I have this to say to you, Mr. Chief Justice: If there are any more of these procedural jack-in-the-boxes, there'll be no tie votes for you to break. The two parties will combine to deal with the situation by *changing* the rules and hanging your skinny ass out to dry on worldwide live TV. This is still the United States Senate. We can't have you making a mockery of it, sir."

Hammett gave the excited old man a look of cold contempt. "No comment, Senator," he said. "Senator Clark, my only objective is a swift resolution of the issue at hand."

"There's one hell of a difference between swiftness and indecent haste," Whipple said. "You and your confederate had better remember that."

"My confederate?" Hammett asked imperiously. "Who exactly would that be, Senator?"

Clark put a hand on Whipple's back. "We'll leave you now, Mr. Chief Justice," he said.

Hammett said, "Not until Senator Whipple answers my question."

"This meeting is adjourned," Clark said. "This is not the moment to work out these differences in detail."

"We'd better damn well find a moment," Whipple said. "And soon."

"All will be well by Monday, Amzi," Buster Baxby said.

Whipple glared at him with unconcealed revulsion. "I'm glad you think so, Senator," he said. "I'll see you all on the floor."

Clark watched him go, the others following him. "I think you realize that certain sensibilities have been engaged," he said to Hammett.

"Or something," Hammett said.

Clark sighed and left. Busby lingered. "What brought on *that* mood swing?" Hammett asked him.

Busby shrugged. The last indiscretion he would ever commit would be to mention the diskette Slim had delivered to him, but he thought that a bit of irony might not be out of place. "I think I may be the confederate Amzi had in mind," he said. "The old fellow thinks there's some sort of conspiracy going on between you and me."

"A *conspiracy*, Senator?" Hammett stared. "With you? I hardly know you."

"Nevertheless." Busby's handsome and still-boyish face crinkled in amusement, white teeth flashing through the fresh tan he had acquired on his sail through the Grenadines with Horace Hubbard.

"Paranoia, that's what we're seeing here," Hammett said. "Pure paranoia. I haven't even spoken to you, or anyone else, since this thing began. I don't want to talk to you now. If I withdrew any farther into judicial isolation I'd have to preside over this trial from the surface of the moon."

"I know that," Busby said. "So do they, even Whipple. You've been a model of probity."

"Then why are they so suspicious and unhappy?"

Busby's smile had not yet faded; he intensified it slightly. "Because you've gotten all the media coverage."

"I've done my best to avoid it. I can't control the media."

"They think you can."

"Is that part of the plot, too?"

"You bet. Look at it through their eyes. You seized the high ground from the first moment, and they can't admit the reality, which is that you're perceived as being above politics while they're perceived as being totally corrupted by it."

Hammett's lip twisted disdainfully. "Appearance is reality, except where their conspiracy theory is concerned. It's a contagion."

"Right," Busby said. "Anyway, I apologize for springing this witness thing on you."

"I assumed it was part of the conspiracy."

Busby put a finger to his lips. "Ssshhh! Not even in jest. But there was a good reason for doing what I did."

Squinting for a sign of encouragement before he went on, Busby stood quite close, a necessary practice on those occasions when he wished to study the face of the person he was talking to. Hammett did not utter a word or make a gesture, but something flickered beneath the aloof look on his face. This *was* a conspiracy, and both men knew it.

Moving even closer, Busby began to whisper, a warm stream of breath that smelled of the fresh California fruit he had had for lunch. "Can you hear me?" he asked. Hammett nodded, turning his head aside. "As you know, the rules provide for senators to write down questions for a witness—"

/ 409

"But any such question must be put to the witness by the presiding officer," Hammett said. "Rule Nineteen."

"That's the one." Busby grinned. "I see you're on top of things as usual," he said. "Here's my question for Jack Philindros—actually, several questions. It will be handed to you by the clerk, along with others, no doubt. I hope you'll ask it first."

"For what purpose?"

"In the name of the Poet."

He handed Hammett a sheet of legal-size paper folded in quarters. The Chief Justice opened it and speed-read it. A chill ran up his spine but he showed nothing of this to Busby. Instead he nodded so briefly that the human eye, Busby's myopic ones anyway, could scarcely register the movement. "It shall be done," he said.

A bell rang.

"Wouldn't he enjoy all this?" Busby said.

"Who?"

Busby grinned wickedly, as Shelley might have done, like an eternal boy. "The Poet," he said. The questions he had just handed to Hammett were based on what Horace had told him during the picnic in the Grenadines, and he felt that it was going to be a bombshell. He smiled happily at the thought as he hurried back to the chamber.

5

On the appointed minute, Hammett struck his gavel and the trial reconvened. As he hammered, he threw a glance at the gallery. Attenborough was still there, the same staring jester effigy. Philindros was already seated at the witness table. He, too, was as unnatural as a manikin. Hammett had never before seen him in the flesh, but he had always been interested in him because of his Greek name, and now he studied him carefully. He was a dark-haired, dark-eyed man with olive skin and a straight Hellenic nose that descended from joined black eyebrows. The clothes he wore were dark and inconspicuous yet vague in their origins, like himself. The object of his behavior, unsurprisingly in a spymaster, seemed to be concealment—concealment of his true personality, concealment of the contents of his mind, concealment, even, of his real voice. Hammett assumed he must have another, more audible one in addition to the undertone in which he was testifying. Maybe, Hammett thought, he spoke in a natural pitch only when torturing an enemy agent. There was something tribal about Philindros, something primal, something deeply crafty and unpredictable, that Hammett found himself admiring. He could imagine this man's ancestors plotting revenge, whispering against their enemies in some ruined house. He was contained, Spartan. Just possibly he was a Maniáte like Hammett himself. For the second time that afternoon the Chief Justice longed vaguely for Gika Mavromikháli; given a single genealogical clue, the old man would have been able to deduce the entire list of martyrs, heroes, and enemies that constituted Philindros's ancestry.

While Philindros testified, the silence in the chamber was absolute. Even Attenborough had closed his glittering eyes and put on the headphones of a pocket video receiver in order to concentrate on his words. The Senate stenographers had switched from the chamber's sound system to headsets attached to the more sensitive television feed in order to record his words. Hammett did not strain to hear; he already knew what this man was going to say. The Chief Justice felt a great sense of tranquillity. The exchange with Clark and Whipple in that obscenely ornate room backstage (dying empires build coffins for their useless leaders) had told him something important. They had surrendered; he was in control. He could make things happen. He could write the ending of this drama. He was not in the least surprised that this should be so. He had always known that the Establishment would collapse one day under the weight of its own corruption and hypocrisy, and that the fall would be sudden and complete when at last it came. This was the fate of empires and the law of history. But he was surprised that it had happened so quickly, so logically, and that there had been so little resistance.

In the witness chair, Philindros sat without gesture or motion, lips moving soundlessly as he whispered his account of his fateful conversation with Lockwood into the microphones; air could not carry the sound of his voice, only electrons could. This was the first time the world had heard the details of the Ibn Awad assassination plot from the lips of a participant. Even amplified by the latest digital technology, the horrifying truth was barely audible. In the gallery, Attenborough briefly opened his eyes. But instead of fixing Hammett with another beady stare he gazed into space. On his podium, the Chief Justice enjoyed perfect privacy; even the cameramen were fascinated by Philindros.

Bob Laval finished his direct examination of the witness. This had been little more than a recapitulation of his earlier testimony before the House Committee of Managers. Steady as a rock, Philindros sipped water from a paper cup. Olmedo was in the act of rising, a yellow tablet in his hand, waiting for Hammett to invite him to cross-examine.

Instead Hammett said, "It's getting late. If the Senate pleases, the Chief Justice will suggest that the examination of this witness continue on Monday at half past noon as provided by Rule Twelve. President Lockwood's counsel will have an opportunity to cross-examine at that time. Is that agreeable, Senators?"

There was no objection. Amzi Whipple rose, presumably to move for adjournment, but Hammett ignored him. "Before entertaining a motion for adjournment," he said, "I have a written question for the witness from the senator from California. As provided by Rule Nineteen, I will put the question. Will you indulge me, Senator?"

Whipple stood mutely in place, uplifted hand frozen in midair.

Hammett folded his own hands on the Greek Bible and fixed his attention on the witness. "The question concerns the nuclear devices purportedly in the possession of Ibn Awad at the time of his death," Hammett said. The Senate stirred. Philindros waited. Camera lights glowed. The Chief Justice unfolded the paper. "Actually, I see it is a series of questions concerning the two ten-kiloton nuclear devices to which you have referred in your testimony today and previously," he said. "I will read the first question. Would you agree, Mr. Director, that the existence of those devices constituted the best proof of Ibn Awad's intentions to hand them over to terrorists?"

Philindros cleared his throat. "Yes."

"And was that intention the rationale for the assassination order?"

"Yes."

"No question in your mind on either of those points?"

"No question, Mr. Chief Justice."

Hammett absorbed these answers, then went on. "And is it your opinion that gaining possession of those two bombs and thereby preventing their falling into the wrong hands was an important objective of the mission?"

"Yes, sir."

"Thank you. Now, sir, I will ask you this: After Ibn Awad had been eliminated as ordered, did you in fact locate the two ten-kiloton nuclear devices and disable them?"

Philindros sipped water from a paper cup. "We located them, yes," he said.

"Can you describe them?"

"The devices were described by experts on the scene as two plutonium compression bombs of the Nagasaki type, each about the size of a Pullman suitcase. Except for their portability, the weapons were quite primitive, technically speaking."

"Where did you locate them?"

"In a cave in a remote area of the desert."

"When?"

Philindros hesitated. Then he said, "On October fifteenth of last year."

For the first time Hammett raised his voice. "*Four months ago*, Mr. Director?" he said. "Is it your testimony that it took the FIS four years after the death of Ibn Awad to locate those devices, which are capable of destroying New York City and killing several million people?"

Philindros still held the water cup in his hand. He looked at it thoughtfully as if restraining himself from crushing it, then set it down on the gleaming tabletop. "It took that long to locate them, yes. More precisely, three years seven months, Mr. Chief Justice."

Hammett said, "Thank you. And for that entire period of time their whereabouts were unknown to anyone in the United States government?"

"That is correct."

"When you found the devices after four years, did you disable them?"

"An attempt was made to do so."

"And did this attempt succeed?"

Philindros took a deep breath, audible over the loudspeakers, before replying. "No," he said. "It did not. The devices were booby-trapped. Our technicians withdrew from the cave when this was discovered."

"Why was that, Mr. Director?"

"The booby traps were extremely ingenious."

"It is your statement that there was more than one booby trap?"

"Yes, several on each bomb. They were set up in such a way that disarming one activated another. We believed that the risk of detonation was unacceptably high. The bombs were dirty because they were primitive. An explosion would have released radiation—gamma rays, radioactive particulate matter, all the other debris associated with fission bombs—into the earth's atmosphere in amounts roughly equivalent to that released by the Hiroshima and Nagasaki bombs combined."

"Even though the bombs were in a cave?"

"The mouth of the cave was open. Weaponry experts believed that the cave would act as a chimney or mortar tube, if you will, concentrating the radioactive dust of the explosion into a fast-rising column which would enter the upper atmosphere and be carried around the globe on the jet stream, eventually falling to earth and contaminating the food chain. Also, the site would have been rendered highly dangerous almost indefinitely."

"How long is 'almost indefinitely'?"

"Plutonium," Philindros whispered, "has a radioactive half-life of eighty-three million years."

"I see," said Hammett. "So what action did you take to deal with this problem, Mr. Director?"

"We are still studying the problem."

"The bombs have not been disarmed?"

"No, Mr. Chief Justice, they have not. We haven't disturbed them again."

"You mean the bombs are still where you found them four months ago, still not disarmed?"

"That's correct."

"And the danger of an accidental explosion is undiminished?"

"So long as the bombs are undisturbed, the risk of accidental detonation is small."

"But not nonexistent?"

"No."

"Why did you not seal the cave and detonate the bombs inside it?"

"Two reasons, sir. First, the cave is not deep enough to contain an explosion of that magnitude. Second, the vibration set up by the heavy earthmoving equipment required to seal the mouth of the cave might set them off. One of the booby traps is sensitive to vibration. If you move either bomb, it goes off and could conceivably detonate the other sympathetically."

"I see," Hammett said. "What else might set them off, Mr. Director? A wandering shepherd? Terrorists?"

Philindros refused to rise to this sarcasm. "Those risks are small," he said evenly, "inasmuch as only we know the location of the cave and it is under constant guard."

"Are you telling the United States Senate and the American people that there is nothing to worry about?"

"No, because that is not the fact. The chief risk is from earthquake. The cave lies quite close to the fault line between the Arabian and Eurasian plates."

"How close is 'quite close,' Mr. Director?"

"On the order of ten miles."

Hammett put down the list of questions. "I must ask you this, Mr. Director," he said. "Is it your testimony that you reported all these facts to President Lockwood?"

"No, it is not," Philindros said. "I have never discussed the matter with the President."

"Why not, sir?"

"He has refused to see me."

"Did you report your findings to anyone in authority?"

"I reported the incident to the person in the White House designated as my liaison with the President."

This person, as everyone in the Senate chamber knew, had to be Julian Hubbard, but Hammett did not ask Philindros to identify him by name. He said, "And what was the reaction of this person who was the liaison between you and President Lockwood?"

"He instructed me to restrict knowledge of the existence of the bombs to those who already knew about them."

"Did that list include the President himself?"

"I don't know if he ever was told."

"Why would he not be told, Mr. Director?"

"I can't speculate on that, Mr. Chief Justice."

"But at the time you and he discussed the matter, the presidential election was less than two weeks away."

"Yes."

A few senators stirred; a noise, more like a murmur of fear than the buzz of curiosity, ran through the gallery. Hammett struck a ringing blow with his gavel. The flutter subsided. He said, "Mr. Director, did you realize that the facts you have just related might, if they had become public knowledge, have jeopardized the President's chances of reelection in what was already an extremely close contest?"

"I recognized that as a possibility," Philindros answered. "Yes."

"And did you think that was why the President's man ordered you to keep this matter secret?"

"I don't know what was in his mind."

"But you followed orders, as you had done in the case of the assassination four years before, and concealed what you knew from the Congress of the United States and the American people."

"Until now, when the question was finally put to me, I treated it as I would treat any other sensitive classified matter."

"Well, Mr. Director, you seem to have protected the secret," Hammett said. "But I'm sure the American people are grateful for your candor under oath today."

The Chief Justice nodded his head in silent thought, several slow, deliberate nods, as if giving his mind time to absorb and program the bizarre data that had just been put into it. By now the hush in the chamber was absolute; not even the media were stirring. At last Hammett said, "One final question." He paused again, as if reluctant to put the question that duty required him to ask, then went on. "Isn't it a fact, Mr. Director, that the failure to recover the bombs meant that the assassination of Ibn Awad accomplished absolutely nothing?"

Philindros did not reply. Hammett said, "The witness will answer the question."

Philindros cleared his throat. "I am not," he said, "competent to make that judgment."

"I wonder who is, Mr. Director," said Hammett. He averted his eyes, a seemingly involuntary gesture of deep weariness and shock that was captured by all the cameras present. "Senators, I have no further questions. Is there a motion from the floor?"

Sam Clark moved for adjournment until Monday at half past noon. This time there was unanimous consent.

Hammett struck the gavel, picked up his Greek Bible, and leaving Philindros motionless in his chair and the senators at their desks, strode from the chamber, all cameras tracking his thoughtful and somber figure.

Outside the chamber, the news media awaited Baxter Busby. Morgan Pike, looking herself again, held her pink microphone to his lips. "Senator, what prompted you to submit that particular question?"

Busby was somber, reluctant to answer. "I thought it should be asked."

"Did you know the answer before you asked the question?"

"It would be improper for me to say any more about an evidentiary matter while this impeachment is before the Senate. But I will say this. The United States of America has been vouchsafed a superb Chief Justice in an hour of great constitutional peril."

Morgan, frowning, listened over her earpiece to a question from Patrick Graham. "Do you think Archimedes Hammett has the makings of a President?"

"You mean President of the United States?"

"Yes."

"My goodness, that's a thought," Busby said, as though the same thought had never occurred to him. Who, he wondered, had been putting ideas in Patrick Graham's head? Or was it a case of great minds running in the same channel? "I'd love to comment," he said. "But, Morgan, to do so would be a disservice to our country, to our President, who is on trial here, and to Chief Justice Hammett. The whole country knows that this fine American is the man of the hour. Let's just leave it at that."

6

It had been a long session. After the adjournment, in the men's room reserved for the press, queues of journalists formed at every urinal. Macalaster, who had remained to watch the Senate floor empty, was among the last to arrive. At the end of the shortest queue stood Montague Love, dancing in place. Though he had phoned Love two or three times while he was convalescing, Macalaster had not seen him in the flesh since he had left him lying unconscious in the men's room of the Library of Congress on Inauguration Day. Evidently Love's insurance claims had been satisfactorily settled because he was wearing a spotless new British-tan Burberry trench coat instead of his old chocolate-brown fly-front Kmart raincoat with the zip-in acrylic fleece liner. Nothing else about him had changed: While he waited his turn at the urinal, sucking in breath through clenched teeth, he was absorbed by the voluminous notes he had made on his wad of newsprint.

Macalaster tapped him on the shoulder. "Monty, how are you?"

Love regarded Macalaster without interest. "So-so," he replied. "Did you get Philindros's exact words on the booby traps?"

"I think so."

"Can I see it while we wait? I've got to call in my copy."

Macalaster tapped the over-the-shoulder bag that held his computer. "It's all in the computer's memory. I'll access it for you after I pee." They moved forward a step. Macalaster said, "How's the head?"

Love looked mournful. "Aches all the time," he replied. "Double vision, grinding noises inside the skull. Aspirin does nothing for it. Fracture your skull, there's bound to be aftereffects. Like temporary amnesia. Couldn't remember a thing about what happened for weeks afterward."

"What about now?"

"It's coming back."

"All of it?"

"Who knows? I may never remember parts of it, they say. Another little aftereffect."

"Does it come back bit by bit or all at once?"

"In flashes," Love said. He was in distress. "*Let's move it up there!* Funny, I could remember things in the past, way back when I was a kid—faces from the third grade, my teacher's name, the picture on my cereal bowl, which was a dinosaur. Stuff I hadn't thought of in years. Just couldn't remember anything between the time I sat down on the crapper and woke up in the emergency room."

"Monty, tell me," Macalaster said. "What exactly do you remember now?"

"What difference does it make?" Love waved a hand in dismissal. It was his turn at the urinal. Groaning in relief, he used it. Then, leaving Macalaster's question unanswered, he hurried toward the door.

Macalaster called after him, "Monty, wait a minute."

"It's okay, I don't need that stuff about the booby traps," Love said over his shoulder. "I just thought of a way to write around it."

The man next in line behind Macalaster, an aging wire-service reporter who had a chronic hangover and an adversarial relationship with everybody, said, "Take it out and aim it or get out of line, hotshot." Macalaster left the line and ran after Monty Love, who was already through the door, limping with astonishing rapidity on his built-up shoe through the milling crowd of journalists who had come from all over the world to cover the Senate trial.

Macalaster caught up with him as he reached the bank of telephones reserved for the press and found them all in use. Because of his lowly status, Love did not rate a phone of his own, but he had to call his radio stations in time for the six o'clock news. "Shit," he said, whirling around in desperation. "Gotta find a phone." Macalaster pulled his own cellular phone out of his pocket and offered it to Love. It was the same one with which he had called 911 on the day Love was assaulted. "Use mine," he said.

"Thanks," Love replied. His mind was fixed on what he was going to do next: utter five sentences in his weedy Nebraska voice into a conference hookup to seventeen 500-watt AM stations scattered across five states between the Platte and the Arkansas rivers. On Macalaster's bill. At no cost to himself or his clients.

Love reached for the phone with unconcealed glee. Macalaster held it above his head. "Talk to me, Monty," he said. "What do you remember?"

As his hand closed on empty air, Love made an angry noise in his throat. "Come on, Ross," he said. "What is this, for Christ's sake, recess time in the fifth grade? I've only got ten minutes to file my copy."

"Tell me."

"*Then* will you give me the phone?"

"It's a promise," Macalaster said.

Love looked around. He lowered his voice. "Okay, ready?" he said. "I remember the hands coming under the door. I saw them because I was looking down at my shoe, this one." He pointed at his orthopedic oxford. "It was untied. And then here come the hands under the door, and as soon as I saw them I thought, Who's screwing around? I thought it was a joke. That was my last thought before the guy grabbed my ankles and pulled me off the stool and I went down. The next thing I knew, I heard my skull crack. *Heard my own skull fracture.* That's the last thing I remember. Now can I have the phone?"

"That's it?" Macalaster said.

"Yeah."

"All of it?"

"Give me the phone."

"You're leaving something out," Macalaster said. "I see it in your eyes."

"You do? No wonder you're rich and famous," Love said. "Okay. I left out one detail the shrink says is a fantasy, a denial mechanism. Something I don't really remember, according to him."

"Tell me, Monty."

"The guy's fingernails were painted."

Macalaster seized the lapel of Love's trench coat. "*Whose* fingernails were painted?"

"Which ones do you think?" Love said, worried about his Burberry. "The mugger's."

"Describe the hands."

"I told you. This character had bright-red fingernails."

Macalaster said, "A shrink told you this was a fantasy? What shrink?"

"The police shrink," Love replied. "That's how I finally remembered. They called me in and hypnotized me. They made a video of the whole session. On it, I look and sound like I'm awake, but I'm not."

"But they didn't believe what you remembered?"

"They believed everything but the bit about the nail polish," Love said. "I don't blame 'em. It makes no sense. Now can I have the phone?"

Macalaster tossed him the instrument. He himself was remembering something: the assassin coming out of the men's room, smelling of strong foreign cologne, hurriedly putting on leather gloves: a flash of carmine.

As soon as Love was finished, Macalaster snatched the phone out of his hand. The working day had ended for the federal bureaucracy, so he went outside where he could be alone and called the detective in charge of the Susan Grant investigation.

Macalaster said, "I just talked to Montague Love."

The voice on the phone was flat, bored. "And?"

"He told me what he remembered under hypnosis. The part about the painted fingernails impressed me deeply."

The detective said, "It did? Why is that, Mr. Macalaster?"

"Because I think I saw them too."

"Really? You didn't tell me that before."

"I didn't remember it before."

"I see. But now you do."

"I'm not absolutely sure that I do. The assassin was putting on gloves in a hurry when we bumped into each other. I think I saw a flash of what could have been nail polish."

"You think it could have been nail polish." The question was put in a tired and elaborately toneless voice.

"That's right," Macalaster said.

"Okay," the detective said. "Why didn't you remember that before?"

"I, too, bumped my head that day when I fell down in the snow. Remember?"

"I remember."

"I thought you should know what I just told you because your psychiatrist told Monty it was a fantasy, a denial mechanism. But maybe it was no fantasy. Maybe the assassin did have painted fingernails."

The line went silent. Macalaster said, "I sense that you have a problem with what I'm telling you."

"You could say that, friend," the detective said. "Put yourself in my position. I'm asking myself, why would a famous reporter like yourself, trained to observe every detail, trained to remember, why would that individual look at a *man*—a member of the male sex—with painted fingernails and remember everything about him except that one rather striking piece of evidence?"

"I don't know. Maybe it was the bump on the head. Or what happened afterward. But it's a fact."

"Facts are good, I like facts," the detective said. "Why don't you describe the assailant again for me? I'm talking about what you actually saw that day, not what you just rediscovered in your subconscious mind."

Macalaster refused to be provoked. He said, "Okay, male in his late twenties, early thirties. Maybe Middle Eastern. Olive complexion, large dark eyes, heavy dark eyebrows, below average height, slender, medium-long black hair with a purple scalp, wearing sunglasses on a snowy day and a dark-colored topcoat with an astrakhan collar."

" 'Slender,' you say?"

"Yes."

"Slender in the sense of appearing to be physically weak?"

"No, but not husky. Wiry, walked slightly sideways, the way some homosexuals do."

"Effeminate?" the detective said. "That's another new detail. Maybe that explains the nail polish."

"I haven't heard the word 'effeminate' spoken aloud for fifteen years," Macalaster said.

"Excuse me. Will you accept 'androgynous'?"

"Yes."

"In that case I'll accept your description. Would you say it was possible that this person, under that topcoat with the Persian lamb collar, was muscular, stronger than your first impression suggested?"

"Must have been, to do what he did to Monty Love and Susan Grant and get away from the entire federal and local law-enforcement apparatus when it was on full alert for the inauguration. But no, I didn't get the impression I was looking at a muscular person."

"Then maybe you weren't looking at the right person. Because the assassin was a bodybuilder."

"How do you know that?"

"You understand this is an internal matter and we are totally off the record?"

"If that's how you want it. But why are you telling me?"

"To put your mind at rest. This is a closely held detail. The assassin took a leak and forgot to flush the toilet in his apartment before he went out on Inauguration Day. His urine contained heavy concentrations of anabolic steroids. But there was no nail polish anywhere to be seen."

"Anabolic steroids?" Macalaster said. "You're rejecting what I tell you on the basis of urine you found in a slum toilet that anybody could have wandered into and used?"

"You're questioning appearances," the detective said. "That's good. But I don't want you to do that for us anymore. Thank you for calling, but if this office needs to talk to you again, you will be notified."

"Don't worry," Macalaster said into the dead and humming line. While on the phone he had been walking blindly around the east plaza of the Capitol, concentrating on the conversation, and as he disconnected he realized that he was standing only a few feet from the spot where Susan Grant had been killed. He stared at the stones as if, like film, they had captured pictures of the event.

"Pictures," he said aloud to himself. Then he punched in the number for Mallory's computer. He had not spoken to Mallory for days, and remembering their last heated conversation, he wasn't sure that the computer would put him through after it recognized his voice. But it did, and when Mallory came on the line, Macalaster told him what Monty Love had told him and what the detective had subsequently said.

"The police don't think this is significant?" Mallory said.

"The man in charge scoffed."

"But you think it's important?"

"Yes, that's why I'm calling. For help."

"What kind of help?"

"I'd like to see the pictures taken by your people that day."

For a long moment after this Mallory was so still that Macalaster thought that he had put down the phone. But he was still on the line. "Come over now," he said. "Lucy and Wiggins will show you whatever you want to see. Then we'll talk."

7

Lucy had never before looked at the pictures of the attack on Susan Grant. The analysis had been handled by others who had not actually been present at the murder, as she had been. Her job had been to keep Grant safe, and because she had failed so terribly she had never been able to bear the thought of watching her die again. Lucy had admired Grant—loved her, really. She had wanted to be like her, a woman who respected no boundaries, who had no anxieties.

Not that she had actually seen Susan die. Like Wiggins, like everyone else on the scene, she had been blinded by the smoke grenade, convulsed by the CS gas—and, most intense memory of all, paralyzed by the horror of knowing what was happening and being prevented by the natural responses of her own body to the gas from doing anything to stop it. It was the worst thing that had ever happened to her. The idea of seeing it happen again, maybe seeing herself floundering helplessly over the ground, blinded and vomiting, was almost unbearable. Especially since she would be doing so in the company of Macalaster—a journalist, a stranger, a scavenger, someone who had no right to invade the reality and sorrow of the experience. She let Wiggins do the talking.

"What exactly are we looking for, Mr. Macalaster?" he asked. The three of them were alone in a soundless, frigid computer room in the basement of the Norman manor house.

"A physical detail," Macalaster replied. "It could be important in identifying the assassin."

"*Identifying* him?"

"Possibly," Macalaster said.

"Whatever you're looking for may not be visible on-screen," Wiggins said. "The scene was very confused. There was smoke, snow was falling. The network cameras got very little because the cameramen were overcome."

"I remember all that. And I've seen the network footage. That's why I called Mallory and asked to see your pictures. You must have had your own cameras operating."

Even though he had been ordered by Mallory to show Macalaster everything, Wiggins responded to this suggestion with silence. Of course their own cameras had been operating: eight remote units disguised as traffic signs, as bicycle headlamps, as almost any everyday object, all controlled from a mobile communications center. Every moment of every public appearance Mallory made was videotaped; every syllable he and others uttered was recorded. But that was sensitive information. Even to reveal the existence of these techniques compromised Mallory's safety by opening a chink in the protective system.

"*Did* you have cameras going that day?" Macalaster asked. Wiggins did not reply. Macalaster said, "Look, I understand how you feel. But I'm not here as a reporter."

Lucy, who did not believe anything any journalist said or wrote, did not believe this for a moment, but she had been ordered to show him anything he wanted to see, so she sat down at a terminal. "It will simplify matters if you tell us exactly what to look for," she said.

She was proper, withdrawn, sober. Macalaster saw little sign of her usual brisk condescension. He told her what he was looking for. Lucy nodded matter-of-factly and sent a command to the computer. Huge back-projected screens, divided into four windows each, filled with flowing imagery: establishing shots of the Capitol and the scene of the news conference, network cameras and microphones and other media gear being set up, Mallory and Susan walking through the falling snow along Constitution Avenue, hundreds of freeze-frames of individual faces in the crowd. Macalaster had never seen anything like it. This was visual gluttony, like watching a photographed dream of the event that was far more vivid than the event itself.

Lucy sent the computer another command. The screens went black and the assassin appeared simultaneously in all eight windows, a spectral figure in white with a gas mask for a snout, rising from the snow, holding a smoking canister about the size of a beer can in either hand. Lucy touched another control and the figure moved in extreme slow motion, caftan flowing gracefully. Dreamily the killer tossed the canisters, shoveling the one in the right hand into the crowd and expertly spiraling the one in the left hand like a forward pass above the heads of Mallory and Grant. In other windows the intent faces of Mallory and Grant and various journalists appeared; they had not yet seen the figure in the caftan. Dreamily the assassin caught a pistol that swung from a lanyard and dreamily lifted it. At this moment, both canisters exploded, filling the screens with a shower of sparks and then with lazy dense smoke. Journalists fell writhing to the ground as if struck down by an invisible force. A portly network cameraman went down, taking his camera with him; this was, Macalaster realized, the origin of the dizzy accidental shot of dome and sky that became the signature network image of the event. A security agent in a skirt whom Macalaster recognized as Lucy floundered over the snow toward the flash of the assassin's pistol, vomiting convulsively, unable even to draw her weapon.

Grant's face, so fine and intelligent, filled a window all its own. She was not yet affected by the gas; less than a second had elapsed in real time; evidently the CS fumes had not yet reached the place where she and Mallory stood, several paces downwind from the knot of reporters. Gowned and masked, feet planted in the snow, body leaning forward into the rock-steady weapon, the assassin continued to raise the pistol. Grant, arms outspread, eyes fixed on the killer, leaped in front of Mallory. Colors and shapes were blurred and softened by the falling snow. With shocking suddenness, a long jet of blood and brain tissue ejaculated in slow motion from the back of Grant's skull, and as it met the resistance of the air, was transformed into wavering tendrils as if the victim were underwater. A second, much less concentrated jet exploded outward from what remained of the cranium. Four more rounds, so evenly spaced in time as to have been fired by an automaton, emerged from Grant's body, which was still upright though she was already dead. Like the others, these bullets were trailed by streamers of blood and tissue. They struck Mallory in the chest, staining his bulletproof coat with gore.

"The hands," Macalaster said. "Can you move in close on the hands?" Lucy worked the controls, and the multiple images broke up and rearranged themselves until nothing remained but close-ups of the assassin's hands, encased in surgical gloves, holding the weapon. "Go in close on the fingertips," Macalaster said. "As tight as you can."

The windows filled with freeze-frames of the assassin's fingertips. Inside the transparent gloves the nails were painted bright red. "There it is," Macalaster said.

"There's more," Lucy said. Her face was wet with tears but she sent more commands to the computer. Wiggins said, "Did you notice something?"

Lucy nodded and went on working. All the elements she had isolated in all the windows combined into a single large image of the assassin, caftan and gas mask and pistol, moving jerkily across the large screen. This image resolved itself into a birdcage of lines, the three-dimensional outline of the figure. A small window opened in the upper right-hand corner for the display of data. Lucy let it scroll, line after line of solutions indicating height, weight, age, and other probable characteristics of the assassin until it came to the one she apparently expected to see. She froze this line.

"Good God," Macalaster said.

On-screen the assassin's image turned this way and that. Lucy froze it, too, as it disappeared into the pall of smoke with the murder weapon in its hand.

"This is a woman," she said.

8

Half an hour after the Senate trial adjourned, just before twilight, a weather front moved through the Catoctin Mountains of Maryland, dumping rain and fog onto Camp David. Lockwood, dressed for the outdoors in a battered black slouch hat and U.S. Navy oilskins, stood on a promontory overlooking a panorama of forested hills, listening to the noise of a helicopter that hovered above the squall. A strong west wind bent the rain-soaked trees and dispersed the fog. Moments later the low-lying sun broke through and a big green U.S. Marine Corps chopper came down through the clouds in a burst of rotor noises.

The weather was clearing rapidly now and the rain-drenched broken upland, miles and miles of sunshot woods, opened up before Lockwood. The view did not interest him. He kept his eyes on the helicopter. He had come up here at noon to escape the media and because Camp David was the only spot in America where he could be certain of privacy, but he did not like this place and never had. Its Appalachian vistas reminded him of the mountain hollows of eastern Kentucky and everything that went with them: mushrat stew, chilblains, shame, anger, penniless trips into town, and his father taking off his hat to a fat man with a cigar who was humiliating him before giving him a job digging coal at twenty-five cents an hour, his father smiling for the sake of his family at the insults and saying yessir, Mr. Pettigrew, yes*sir*.

Lockwood the President dealt with these memories as he dealt with most things, by making jokes. "Welcome to Hillbilly Heaven," he said to Alfonso Olmedo C. as the lawyer appeared on the path in the company of a Secret Service agent.

Olmedo had come direct from the floor of the Senate and was in no mood for banter. He said, "How much do you know, Mr. President?" It was still raining lightly, and Olmedo also wore a Camp David–issue bright-orange slicker with USN stenciled on the back and the presidential seal on the chest. Inside the hood, his face was anxious and resentful.

"About what?" Lockwood said.

"About the trial. Did you watch any of it?"

"No," Lockwood said. "Why would I do that?"

"You've had no word at all?"

"I just said I didn't. Spit it out, Alfonso."

"There was another bombshell," Olmedo said. "Literally." He summarized Philindros's testimony.

"Okay," Lockwood said. "So that's out in the open."

Olmedo said, "Are the facts as Philindros stated them?"

"As far as he went," Lockwood replied with an impatient gesture. "Hammett must have jumped out of his goddamn skin when they began talking about radioactive fallout. The ultimate harmful additive."

"Mr. President, please."

"Sorry. But we can deal with this. What was I supposed to do—go public and start an Easter egg hunt, with every terrorist in the world in on the game? The winner gets to blow up New York?"

"I agree. But this is another blow to your credibility, Mr. President, another dangerous secret exposed. It's systematic, day in and day out, and it's devastating to your case, sir."

"Looks that way," Lockwood said. "But there's time on the clock and we haven't had the ball yet." Beneath the brim of his slouch hat, a look of shrewdness came into his eyes. "Have I got it right—Hammett asked all the questions and Busby fed 'em to him?"

"That's correct."

"Well," Lockwood said. "It looks like you had a point about the Whiffenpoofs."

The Secret Service agent who had led Olmedo to this spot stood just out of earshot on the path. Lockwood gestured him nearer. "Get Jeannie on the line," he said. The agent punched a single key on the scrambler telephone he took from his pocket, listened until there was an answer, handed the instrument to Lockwood, and stepped back out of earshot again.

"Jeannie," he said, "Get hold of Tucker and Sam and say I want to see them up here for supper tonight." He turned to Olmedo. "How's the crowd around the White House?"

"It's a siege."

Lockwood nodded; he had guessed as much. Into the phone, he said, "Soon as it's dark have the unmarked helicopter pick 'em up at Andrews or someplace where there's no damn press. And don't talk to secretaries or assistants. Talk to Sam and Tucker only. Or Ablert. Nobody else."

He handed the phone back to the agent. The sun had disappeared again and a misty rain had begun to fall. Olmedo's hair was beaded with moisture. He shivered. "Mr. President, we must talk," he said.

"Not now," Lockwood said. "We'll wait for Sam and Tucker. We've got to wrap this sucker up right quick. Go on inside and dry off. I'm going for a walk. Got some thinking to do."

9

As the helicopter flying out of Andrews Air Force Base in the last light of day crossed the Anacostia River on its way to Camp David, Attenborough looked down on a burning slum house, red tongues of flame inside a maelstrom of smoke, a black woman screaming soundlessly in the street with arms outstretched toward the flames, no cop or fireman or neighbor to help her or rescue whoever was burning to death within. The next house in the row caught fire and all of a sudden, looking into the raging flames, he remembered one of his father's sermons about how little it took to go to Hell. *"A tattoo is enough, one forbidden stain on the flesh is all you need to burn forever!"* The old man took his text from one of the many screwy commands Yahweh on his mountaintop had ordered Moses to pass on to the incredulous congregation of Israel huddled in the desert below: "You shall not make any cuttings in your flesh on account of the dead or tattoo any marks upon you: I am the LORD." Book of Leviticus, chapter the nineteenth, verse the twenty-eighth.

Recalling this, he remembered his place in his ninth-grade civics book and, in his mind, turned to the glossy page on which he had been reading the Constitution when he had his blood clot. *"Section 1, terms of the President and Vice President. Section 2, Congress shall meet at least once a year, beginning on the third day of January. Section 3, qualification of the President and Vice President . . ."*

The words shimmered on the sun-dazzled page. Attenborough cried, "Sweet Jesus!" Then he fell into a violent fit of coughing.

Sam Clark, sitting beside him, jumped at the outcry. "Tucker, what's the matter?"

"I just figured it out," Attenborough said.

"Figured what out?"

"The whole damn thing," Attenborough said, gasping for breath and waving away any further questions. "Leave me be, Sam. Got to think. I just hope that big dumb son of a bitch we're going to see will listen." He closed his eyes for the remainder of the trip, as if asleep—or, as Clark feared when he gazed at his old friend's corpselike profile, comatose.

In the main cabin at Camp David, Lockwood stood with his back to the fire, listening to something Olmedo was saying to him. He still wore his old clothes, and he held a drink in his hand. Norman Carlisle Blackstone stood off to one side, looking oppressed and worried.

"Howdy, Mr. President," Attenborough croaked.

"What's the matter with your voice?" Lockwood said.

"Frog in my throat," Attenborough said, stepping forward into the light.

Lockwood had not seen him up close for weeks, not even on television since he had given up watching the news. "Jesus, Tucker," he said. "What have you been doing to yourself?"

"Malaria's worse," Attenborough said.

"You been to a doctor?"

"Got a good one—Albert's boy Henry."

Lockwood stared in shock and disbelief but asked no more questions. With a jerk of his head in the direction of Olmedo and Blackstone, he said, "Tucker, Sam, you both know these fellows. I need your advice. Alfonso here thinks somebody's out to nail my hide to the barn door and I've already stepped on the trap. He says the only way I can be cleared is stand up and admit the ele .on was stolen. What do you say to that, Mr. Speaker?"

Coughing again, Attenborough deferred to Clark with a weak wave of the hand. Clark said, "If you do that, you cease to be President."

"That's what Alfonso told me," Lockwood said. "Tucker?"

Attenborough mopped his streaming eyes with a handkerchief. "As a lawyer," he said, "I'd have to say there's no way to do otherwise on the basis of the evidence."

Lockwood gave him a mirthless grin. "What would you say as the next man in line to be President of the United States?" he asked.

Attenborough's eyes blazed. He said, "I'd say, Wake up!" He took a step toward the towering Lockwood, pointed a trembling finger, and started to say more. Clark interrupted. "Hold it," he said. "We can't talk about the impeachment. It's wrong. I'm one of your judges, Mr. President. I *won't* talk about it."

"All right, let's stick to politics," Lockwood said. "This is a party matter or it's nothing. As head of the party, I ask you this: How many votes am I going to have in the Senate on judgment day, Samuel?"

"It's too early to count," Clark replied. "The other party will hang together no matter what happens. On our side, I don't know. After adjournment today I counted at least six who'll jump ship if one more lie comes out."

"Does that include Busby?"

"Yes, but they're *all* radicals. If that's all you lost today, you've got a base of forty-four."

"So I can lose ten more and still win?"

"Technically, yes. Thirty-four is all you need to survive—if all you want to do is survive."

"First things first," Lockwood said. "What about this Hammett, the terrorists' friend? Alfonso thinks he's a bad guy."

Clark's eyes moved to Olmedo for a moment, then back to Lockwood. "Thanks to his friend Busby he's got the power to break ties and decide what the Constitution means."

"*Can* he do harm?"

"It may be a little late for either one of us to be asking that question, Mr. President. But he's a smart guy, just like Julian said."

"Best-laid plans of mice and men," said Lockwood with a tight-lipped smile. "Worst-case scenario: I lose. What would happen next? Does the House make Franklin President?" His head swiveled on his long neck. "Tucker?"

"Under the Constitution, if nobody has a majority of the electoral votes, the House elects a President from among the three top candidates," Attenborough replied. "But in a case where one of the three top candidates, namely you, has already been declared President by the Senate, which has subsequently reversed itself by declaring the election null and void, I don't think the House can elect anybody."

Lockwood turned to Blackstone. "Is that right, Spats?"

"It's a sound argument, based on the Twelfth Amendment," Blackstone said.

"All right, then what?" Lockwood said. "Do I invoke the Twenty-fifth Amendment and make Tucker President?"

"Only a legally elected President or Vice President can do that," Attenborough said, "and from the moment you admit the election was stolen and the Senate votes to declare it null and void, you won't be President anymore."

"At that point *nobody* would be President," Clark said. "Is that what you're saying, Tucker?"

Attenborough said, "That's right."

"How do you figure that?" Lockwood said.

"It came to me in a vision," Attenborough replied.

"You're talking about chaos," Lockwood said.

"No, sir," Attenborough said. "The Constitution does not provide for chaos. Article Two, as refined in the Twentieth Amendment, provides for just such a situation. I quote: 'Congress may by law provide for the case wherein neither a President-elect nor a Vice President–elect shall have qualified, declaring who shall then act as President, or the manner in which one who is to act shall be selected, and such person shall act accordingly until a President or Vice President shall have qualified.' "

"I thought Congress had already passed a law of succession," Lockwood said.

"That's right, and amended it four times, plus adopting the Twenty-fifth Amendment to the Constitution," Attenborough said. "And Congress can amend it again anytime it wants to."

"Why the hell should it? The whole thing's cut-and-dried: If there's no President or Vice President, the Speaker of the House becomes President, then the president pro tempore of the Senate, then the Secretary of State, and right on down the cabinet."

Attenborough held up a hand. "The existing law rests on the assumption that everybody in the line of succession is fit to serve," he said. "But this time you've got a moral degenerate, me, first in line, and Otis Dyer, who's so senile he can't tell time anymore, right behind me."

"And behind you two, the whole damn cabinet."

"What cabinet? If you weren't elected, you had no legal power to appoint anybody to anything."

Lockwood glared. "Tucker, what you're saying is nothing but one of your bullshit intellectual exercises. Get to the point."

"Glad to," Attenborough said. "The point is, if the election was stolen, this is a unique situation not envisaged by Congress when it passed the law of succession. What they're going to say is, 'All bets are off, and the only thing we can do is go to the Constitution—back to basics, get us a real President.' "

"The Supreme Court will never let them get away with it," Lockwood said.

"No?" Attenborough said. "Remember who the Chief Justice is and who his friends are. Frosty, wake up and listen to what I'm telling you."

"Jesus," Lockwood said.

Clark said, "What's the time limit for qualifying a President or Vice President to take the place of the acting President?"

"There is none in the Constitution," Attenborough said. "What's more, nothing specific is said about holding an election in a case like this, so the country could go on for quite a while without voting on the matter."

"But who the hell would they make acting President?" Lockwood said.

"The answer is, anybody but Franklin Mallory," Attenborough said. "But you've got to admit it's a historic combination of circumstances."

"Spats," Lockwood said. "Is what he's saying right?"

"In terms of his hypothesis, it's certainly plausible," Blackstone said. "This is the alternative I've been trying to tell you about, Mr. President. It's a time bomb in the Constitution."

A long moment passed as the five men, standing in the firelight, looked at one another. At last Lockwood said, "I spent twenty-two years in the Senate and six in the House. I just don't believe Congress would let itself be stampeded into something like you're talking about, Tucker."

"You don't?" Attenborough said. "Then you must have slept through the last three weeks."

Blackstone said, "May I make an observation?"

Lockwood ignored him. Clark said, "Go ahead, Carlisle."

Blackstone said, "You're describing a conspiracy of lunatics."

Attenborough said, "Maybe I am, but that doesn't necessarily mean I'm the one that's crazy."

Lockwood was shaking his head. "I guess I'm just the dumbest son of a bitch in the room," he said, "but I've got just one question: Why would they do this?"

"Why would who do what?" Attenborough asked.

"Busby and his crowd. The radicals. Julian, for Christ's sake, who was like a son to me. Why would they take me down this way? Why would they use the Constitution to overthrow the government?"

"Well," Attenborough said, "you've got to remember what they were trying to do in the first place, when they stole the election."

"Elect me, that's what they were trying to do," Lockwood said.

"No, sorry, that wasn't the idea," Attenborough said. "They would've done what they did for Fred the Chimp." He spoke the next words in something resembling his old mighty voice. *The objective was to prevent Franklin Mallory from being President.* That's still the objective, because he was their worst nightmare come true the first time he got himself elected,

and if he gets in for the second time, just imagine what he's going to do
to them after what they tried to do to him."

Clark was the first to speak. He said, "Tucker, you're asking us to think
the unthinkable."

Though he knew it was an illusion, Attenborough had never felt more
alive than at this moment, or more in command of the powerful brain he'd
been born with. He said, "Hell, Sam, that's what got us all this far. We
might as well go home with the girl we brung to the dance."

10

When Lucy and Wiggins reported their findings on the gender of Susan
Grant's assassin to Mallory, his first thought was for Zarah Christopher.
"It was a woman who was following Zarah around," he said. "Where is
she now?"

"At home," Lucy replied, "in the upstairs study, reading a book."

"You're sure?"

Lucy stole a glance at Macalaster. Talking about these matters in the
presence of a journalist was a breach of procedure and it bothered her
greatly. But she answered because she had to. "We just checked, Mr.
President, not more than ten minutes ago."

"Why check if you're not concerned?"

"It was a routine event, sir."

Lucy did not describe the means by which she had pinpointed Zarah's
whereabouts inside her own house. Not only was Macalaster present, but
it was a fundamental principle of the craft of security that the person being
protected should not know exactly what methods were being used to keep
him from harm lest he give them away by drawing attention to them. But
immediately after that first dinner party, as soon as Mallory had started
to call on Zarah in an unpredictable way, Wiggins and Lucy had set up
a routine watch for his own protection. They simply piggy-backed existing
systems, installed in the house by Outfit technicians years before when it
was occupied by the O.G. Random camera sweeps activated by sensors
detected any movement or unusual infrared signatures within the house
walls. The computer recognized the radar and sonar signatures of Zarah's
image even in the dark—along with Mallory's, of course.

"Good, I'm glad you have an eye on her," Mallory said. "But I meant
the other woman. The jogger you were so concerned about."

"No sign of her in the neighborhood since that last encounter with Zarah on the street," Lucy said. "Of course we know who she is now."

"Thanks to Zarah."

Lucy did not acknowledge this remark, even though it came from Mallory. She said, "We've done a preliminary assessment."

Macalaster realized that they must be talking about Slim or Sturdi. He asked which. Surprised but reluctant—Lucy really did not like sharing information with this man—she told him.

Mallory gave Lucy a hard and searching look. "What exactly is your assessment of this woman?"

Wiggins answered. "We're still looking at her, Mr. President," he said. "Once we learned her name it was a simple matter to run down her whole biographical record. Nothing out of the ordinary except that she's a world-class athlete—just missed making the Olympic heptathlon team in her last year at Berkeley. Menstrual cramps on the day of the trial."

Macalaster, seated in the twin of Mallory's leather wingback library chair, had been listening intently to this report. He said, "Where did she go to law school?"

"Yale, full tuition grant and stipend," said Lucy.

"What does the computer have to say about her relationship with Archimedes Hammett?"

"Relationship?" Lucy said. "She took a course with him at Yale. But that's all. This subject has had no relationships with men. None, ever. She's a lesbian who came out while she was still in high school."

"No kidding," Macalaster said.

Mallory waved a hand and Lucy and Wiggins left the room. To Macalaster he said, "I have a question. Knowing that the killer was a woman, what do we know that's important?"

"Well," Macalaster said, "we've stopped looking at the wrong half of the human race for the person responsible."

"Will that make it any easier to find the right person?"

"It ought to make it more likely. But I think we need help."

"Help?" Mallory said. "What kind of help?"

"I'll be frank," Macalaster replied. "Your people are too close to the situation; they feel responsible and hurt. You need someone who can come to it cold and see things for what they are."

"Like you?"

"I'm the worst of the lot because I have a theory I want to prove. The cops are right about that."

"So far your theory seems to be holding up."

"Luck. If I hadn't run into Monty Love I would never have picked up on this detail."

It was growing late; the weather had changed. Rain sluiced through the floodlights in diagonal sheets and beat against the bulletproof windows at Mallory's back. He was no longer upset, but he was restive. "So what do you advise?" he asked.

Macalaster told him about John L. S. McGraw. He was not surprised to learn that Mallory knew all about him already. He said, "I agree that he'd be good, but he works for Lockwood."

"Not Lockwood, Olmedo. And he'd be working with me, not for you."

"That's a thin cover story."

"Yes, but sometimes it's worth taking a chance."

All this time Mallory had been holding a book in his lap; he seemed to read in the way other Presidents talked on the telephone to an endless queue of half-strangers, as a way of escaping back into humanity. While he considered Macalaster's idea he drummed his fingers on the binding of the book, a rare sign of nerves in Mallory. At last he said, "Will McGraw do this?"

"I think he will."

"Can he keep it to himself?"

"You mean can he keep it from Lockwood?"

"He can tell Lockwood anything he wants. I mean keep it from the media, the bureaucracy." He paused. "The Patrick Grahams of this world felt Susan deserved to die, you know."

Macalaster took a deep breath. "I know," he said. "But McGraw is just a cop."

"All right, talk to him. He can have anything we have."

When Mallory called Lucy and Wiggins in the control room and gave them the necessary orders, Lucy turned to Wiggins with devastation in her eyes and said, "Oh, no."

11

Bundled up in the Gore-Tex Eddie Bauer parka he had bought for his trip to Chile, McGraw awaited Macalaster at an indestructible vinyl picnic table on the banks of Bull Run. The day was windy and gray; they were alone except for groups of schoolchildren trudging along the trails of Manassas National Battlefield Park.

McGraw offered Macalaster take-out coffee in a disposable thermos cup from Dunkin' Donuts. "Okay, I'm listening," he said.

Macalaster related what Monty Love had told him, what he himself thought he remembered, and what the pictures of the assassination showed.

"You're sure it was a woman?" McGraw said.

"Yes. Or at least the computer says so. Does that interest you?"

"Girl terrorists are one of my main things," McGraw said. "I think maybe I was shot by one once."

Macalaster said, "Then you'll have a look at the pictures?"

"They're Mallory's pictures, I'm working for Lockwood right now. Why me?"

"Because you'll be looking at the images with a detached mind. You might see something the rest of us missed."

McGraw snorted. "Don't be too sure about the detached mind," he said. "But now I'm curious, so okay." He sat in silence for a moment, then held out his hand for Macalaster's empty coffee cup. Macalaster handed it over, then handed him a leaf from his notebook with Lucy and Wiggins's secure phone number written on it. "You're sure this will be all right with Olmedo?" he asked.

"That's not your problem," McGraw said. "Believe me, he'll know what I know."

It was raining harder. McGraw was already wearing an Irish tweed cap that matched his parka, but he covered his head with the hood and pulled the drawstring tight. "You should wear a hat," he said. "On a cold day you can lose fifty percent of your body heat through your scalp."

12

When McGraw got Lucy on the telephone just after sunrise the next morning she said, "We've been expecting your call. Where are you?"

"In the White House."

"Good. It's oh-six-eighteen. Go for a walk. At oh-six-twenty-five, make a call to the weather number. Keep listening to the forecast and keep walking."

At 6:31, having homed in on the unique transmission code of McGraw's pocket telephone with the special equipment in the charcoal-gray van they were using that day, Lucy and Wiggins glided up to the curb beside him. He was walking along a quiet stretch of New York Avenue a few blocks west of the White House. The back door slid open. The person inside fit Lucy's description as furnished by Macalaster: Italian girl, strong teeth, big old-country nose, abundant dark hair tied up behind, wonderful body, no perfume, wedding ring, and nestled beneath her designer jacket, an airweight 6mm all-vinyl machine pistol in a quick-draw shoulder holster. As McGraw got in, Lucy leaned forward, shook hands firmly, and looked him straight in the eye while he carried out his visual inspection. The combination of womanliness and desexed professional manner tickled him. His eyes crinkled. She said, "You are amused, Mr. McGraw."

He said, "Just thinking how nicely all this lives up to expectations."

The van was equipped with one-way windows and insulated with some sort of soundproofing material that seemed to capture every syllable in midair, cleanse it of static and ambiguity, and deposit it gently onto the eardrum. The interior was a sort of miniaturized conference room with aromatic leather swivel chairs, a table, telephones, and other outer-edge-of-the-envelope equipment. A heat-sensitive keyboard computer was set flush into the tabletop, like a chessboard in a games table.

"We thought it would be more convenient to work in the car," Lucy said, sliding the door shut. Locks clicked. "And more secure, of course."

"Fine by me," McGraw said.

Wiggins, up front, drove across the Memorial Bridge and then followed labyrinthine roads through Arlington National Cemetery before passing through the gates of Fort Myer and parking in the nearly empty lot of the post chapel. Then he moved into the front passenger seat, ran it back on its track with a whine of servomotor, and swiveled to face McGraw. He too shook hands. No names were exchanged. The two of them called him Mr. McGraw, very respectfully, as though they were even younger than they looked, and he honored their professional discretion by calling them nothing at all.

Lucy handed him a pair of opaque blinders that resembled a snorkeling mask. She said, "It will look to you like the images are suspended in air, about six feet in front of your eyes. Put them on." He did so, adjusted the focus, and saw a three-dimensional, natural-color, life-size image of a football player, the great Jim "Freeze-Frame" Cerruti of the Steelers, making an acrobatic catch at the goal line. McGraw could read the trademark on the pigskin and count the individual whiskers on Cerruti's unshaven chin.

"That was a test shot, okay?" Lucy said.

"As long as they weren't playing the Gi'nts it was," McGraw replied. "Is this what they call virtual reality?"

"The media used to call it that," Lucy said. She manipulated the mouse, turning the image upside down, bringing it closer, then farther away, zooming in on various body parts, and finally walking around it by instructing the software to deduce and paint the figure from all angles of sight on the basis of the front view. "All right, here we go," she said. "If you want to see anything twice, or from a different angle, or enhanced in some fashion, say so."

She ran the footage of the assassination. The images were much more disturbing in this form than they had been yesterday on the screen. Lucy could not bear to look at them, and after a moment she closed her eyes inside the blinders. She had spent a terrible night filled with specters, trying to think instead of feel. The discovery that the assassin was female had set her off on a chain of suspicion. Every link had something to do with Zarah. Lucy had never trusted her. Wiggins refused to go along with her suspicions; Mallory had put Zarah beyond suspicion, and as far as Wiggins was concerned, that was that. "You have no rational basis for feeling the way you do," he told her over and over.

But that was precisely the problem: rationality would not do the job. Zarah was a blank file. Backgrounding her was like checking out an invader from space: you had no idea where to begin. Was she what she seemed to be, or was there a cunning extraterrestrial reptile hidden beneath that glowing skin, that golden hair? Did an alien brain brood behind those preternaturally intelligent eyes? Did this intruder speak so many human languages because no human being could possibly understand her own strange vernacular? Did she know so many of the arcane facts in which Mallory delighted because she had been prepared for a secret mission by some agency that had somehow mapped the contents of his memory?

Lucy had not felt such hostility and suspicion toward another member of her gender since junior high school. Before such terminology was banished from American English, her emotions would have been described as woman's intuition or girlish jealousy. Though he was not so foolhardy as to say so, this was what Wiggins thought they were. Lucy realized this and regarded his refusal to treat Zarah as a suspect as the best reason to respect her own intuition. She had made up her mind in the night to access all the many stored images of Zarah and subject them to the same analysis as the images of the assassin. If she found what she thought she might find, she might even go a little further. She'd have to break ♂ ↔ ♀ rules and do it alone or trick Wiggins into it; he'd never go along willingly.

Lucy's eyes were still shut. She realized the projection session was over when McGraw said, "Amazing. Is there any way you can get the computer to make a stab, like an IndentiKit picture, at how this female looks without the gas mask?"

Lucy opened her eyes and saw the final image, the birdcage representation of the killer, hanging in space. "No, what you see is as far as the software can take us," she said. "There's not enough data for a facial reconstruction. Would you like to see the footage again, or any part of it?"

"Maybe later, parts of it," McGraw said. "Have you got any suspects?"

Lucy realized that this gave her the opening she had been looking for: she had found a way to break Zarah down into her component parts and discover what made her tick. They still had their blinders on, so she was able to say what she said next without meeting Wiggins's eyes or revealing what was in her own. She said, "Not exactly. But I'd like you to help me look at some footage of another woman, as a controlled comparison, and to show you what this system can do. We have some new software from Universal Energy that classifies behavior by breaking down body language and vocal factors and analyzing them against a pattern-weighted experiential-derived data base."

"No fooling?" McGraw said. "You mean like the twitchy hijacker tics they used to look for in airports?"

"That's the origin of the system, but this is a lot more sophisticated."

"What does it tell you?"

Lucy organized her reply. McGraw observed that she was tense, impatient, distraught, and that her eyes were swollen from a lot of recent crying. This kid must be getting her period, he thought. Wiggins intervened. "It gives you a numerical score of how honest a person is, based on the spontaneity of gesture and speech, and so on."

"Just like Grandma used to do," McGraw said. "Let's have a look."

Because of the Sturdi situation, which had been so time-consuming, Lucy had never before had the leisure to capture the many stored images of Zarah into a single file for analysis. She did this now, using only images and voice samples collected while Zarah was interacting with Mallory. At the speed at which this system handled data, it did not take long for the result to pop up. Zarah's score was in the ninetieth percentile. This meant that she ranked in the top ten percent of all subjects ever tested for the unconscious signs of honest, spontaneous, unfeigned behavior.

The number amazed Lucy. She had never before seen such a high score, and she fought against the impulse to regard it as another reason to be suspicious of Zarah: it was hardly human. Had she, Lucy, made some sort of input error? She ran the data again in a slightly different sequence and came up with the same result within three decimal places—in Zarah's favor.

After the appearance of Sturdi, and especially after Zarah began to take those interminable walks around the city, the surveillance had moved outdoors. The product of these operations was much less fragmentary; the cameras and microphones had been running all the time. As a control factor, Lucy searched the files for pictures and voiceprints of Zarah interacting with others: the agents who had approached her on the street, casual contacts with strangers while on her rambles through the city, and finally the telling encounter with Sturdi. But in no case did Zarah's integrity index ever fall below the ninetieth percentile; in the encounter with Sturdi, when she was angry, it registered in the ninety-ninth.

McGraw's voice said, "What's the passing mark?"

"The sixtieth percentile is considered average," Lucy replied.

"Looks like this chick made the honor roll," McGraw said. Lucy made no reply. He said, "Do me a favor, will you? Test the other female."

"The other one?" Lucy said.

"The stalker," McGraw explained.

"Good idea," Wiggins said. "Maybe the system is susceptible to gorgeous blondes."

"That's entirely possible if the program was written by a certain type of man," Lucy said tartly.

She ran the Sturdi tapes again from start to finish, forward, backward, and inside out. As images and fragments of speech flashed in random sequence, she thought she saw something. It was subtle, way out on the far edge of perception. She wasn't quite sure what it was.

Apparently McGraw saw something too. He asked to view certain frames again, some of them two or three times and from a number of different perspectives. Finally he said, "Before you score this dame, run the parts we looked at twice one more time in slo-mo, will you?"

Lucy projected the footage again, this time concentrating closely on Zarah instead of Sturdi. She did not see—or, more accurately, *feel*—whatever it was she thought she had perceived the last time. This was disappointing but not conclusive. Except that they never got tired or bored or cranky, computers were a lot like people because they were programmed by people, and sometimes they missed or misunderstood the obvious, just as human witnesses did.

"Let's see the scores," Wiggins said.

They popped up. Lucy was stunned. Sturdi's numbers were all in the fortieth percentile, and even lower than that when she was eyeball-to-eyeball with Zarah.

"Maybe I see something," McGraw said. "Way back, there's one where she's kneeling beside her bike." Lucy brought the image up: Sturdi outside the Kennedy Center wearing her yellow goggles and biking outfit, looking upward at the car as it rolled past.

"There's another one, a shot of her eyes when she's talking to the blonde. Can you take off the goggles?" McGraw asked.

"That was the only day she didn't wear them," Lucy said.

"Nice wig, too," McGraw said.

Lucy combined the two images and the goggles vanished as pixels were rearranged and Sturdi's large haunted eyes appeared in her head.

"Now make her bald," McGraw said.

"*Bald?*"

"Can you do it?"

An instant later an egg-bald Sturdi knelt before them. "Now move her down so we're standing about ten feet above her," McGraw said. Lucy hesitated, not quite understanding what he wanted. "Like she was in an elevator shaft," he said. "On top of a jammed car."

The computer generated an image of an elevator shaft from the data stored in its nearly infinite memory. The result was extremely naturalistic; McGraw could almost smell the grease on the cables and feel the chill seeping from the concrete walls of the shaft. In a moment, in weak light that filtered through the open elevator door in which McGraw and Lucy and Wiggins "stood," he knew that he would shortly see muzzle flashes, sparklers in the void, stars, blackness, just as he had done the time the bald unisex terrorist with the big wild eyes had shot him.

McGraw said, "Can you save that last part?"

"Sure," Lucy said. "Do you see something?"

"Maybe. She reminds me of a suspect we never caught up with."

"Enough for positive I.D.?"

"No. I've got a personal stake, so I could be seeing things."

Outside the van the parking lot had filled up with the cars of a funeral procession. An honor guard of soldiers in dress blues and white gloves carried a flag-draped coffin into the chapel.

McGraw's phone rang. He took it out of his pocket, listened and said, "Okay, I'm on my way." He put the instrument back into his pocket. "Gotta go," he said. "But I'd like to work with you on this."

Wiggins smiled with unfeigned pleasure. "Excellent, Mr. McGraw. When can you start?"

"Tonight, seven-forty sharp, Fair Oaks Cinemas parking lot. Is that okay? I gotta go out of town for a few hours, but there's one step further I'd like to take this."

"Fine. What can we do to prepare?"

"Just bring these same pictures and software," McGraw said. He handed his blinders to Lucy. "Very impressive equipment. Can you guys drop me at the Metro?"

13

Attenborough had spent the night at Camp David, and shortly after dawn he joined Lockwood and his lawyers for a stand-up breakfast in front of the fireplace in the presidential lodge. He found the President watching the morning shows on the huge video screen that descended from the ceiling.

"Thought you gave up TV," Attenborough said.

"I just took it up again," Lockwood said. "Look, they're fulfilling your prophecy."

The equipment was antiquated, the images fuzzy, but the message was plain. *Newsdawn with Patrick Graham* devoted a full hour to a discussion of the presidential succession, cutting away only for five-minute news summaries. The other networks covered the issue at lesser length, but on every show pundits discussed the frightening prospects in the line of presidential succession: an accused rapist and a senile party hack. Mallory's name was not even mentioned.

Hammett's face with its brooding eyes filled the screen.

"There's the candidate," Attenborough said.

"*Him?*" Lockwood cried. "He don't even know why the Lord hung a pecker between his legs. How the hell can he be President?"

"I told you how last night," Attenborough said. "The Twentieth Amendment."

"You didn't say anything about Hammett."

"No, but it fits. The radicals are going to go for a messiah—somebody who couldn't get himself elected in a million years, somebody who's above politics."

"'Above politics'?" Lockwood said. "That's rich. Go on with the thought."

"Think about it," Attenborough said. "Hammett has no party affiliation. He just *stands* for something, a disinterested patriot. Tune in tomorrow; I prophesy that's what they'll be saying. And he's also got a big constitutional advantage."

"Like he's already Chief Justice."

"That's right. It's got to be somebody who's already in the government."

"Already in the government?" Lockwood said. "Where's that written?"

"In Article Two," Attenborough said. "Which says that in case there is neither a President nor a Vice President, Congress has the power of 'declaring what officer shall then act as President, and such officer shall act accordingly, until the disability be removed, or a President be elected.' That's the wording: 'what *officer.*' Nothing in the Twentieth Amendment supersedes that requirement. Any lawyer worth his salt would argue that the Founding Fathers clearly intended and anticipated that someone already holding office under the Constitution should become acting President, not somebody from outside the government."

Lockwood said, "Do you buy that, Spats?"

"You could certainly make the argument that there is no real question of the Framers' intent based solely on the language they used," Blackstone replied.

"Right," Lockwood said. "And when was the last time the judiciary took the Founding Fathers at their word?"

Nobody answered. A roaring log fire burned on the hearth, sending sparks up the chimney and the sour odor of wood smoke into the room. Rain drummed on the roof and pelted the windowpanes. The damp bothered Lockwood; he stood so close to the flames in his thick outdoor clothes that the others smelled scorched wool.

Oblivious, Lockwood said, "Got to get control of this thing. Any ideas?"

"Only one thing left for you *to* do," Attenborough said. "Get out. But do it on your own terms."

Lockwood made a noise and an angry gesture. He had almost no patience left.

"And do it today," Attenborough said, "before you bleed to death in the media."

"Today?" Lockwood said. "What in hell are you talking about?"

"Frosty, you've got no choice. You're dying the death of a thousand cuts. All anybody in the Senate wants to do now is save the party."

"By lynching the head of the party?"

"That's what it's come down to. Hanging you is the key to everything now. They want you out. They want the presidency vacant so they can fill it with a man on horseback."

"They've got to get sixty-seven votes in the Senate to do that."

"Suppose they don't?" Attenborough said. "Suppose you do hold on to your thirty-four votes? It'll be all over anyway. They'll never let up on you; the country will go right down the tubes. But you can still do it your way while you've got the powers to do it."

"How? Appoint Franklin Vice President and resign like he wants me to? That would be a great move for the party."

"Congress would never approve Franklin, not in a million years."

"That leaves you."

"That's right. I'm preapproved."

"That's not all you are. For God's sake, Tucker, look at what's happened to you. You're a rapist in the eyes of the media. You'd be a ten-minute President."

"Maybe less," Attenborough said. "That's the whole point. Let me talk to Franklin."

"About what?"

"Working things out."

"What things?"

"If I tell you that, they'll impeach *me*. Frosty, you've got to trust me on this."

"Sure I will," Lockwood said. "Look where trust has got me already."

Attenborough shrugged. "I can't argue with that, but I'm no Whiffenpoof. This is for the country, Frosty."

"Damn right. But if I show a sign of weakness, they could change the rules and convict me on the first article tomorrow."

"That's exactly what I've been saying. It's going to be one hell of a temptation to our folks in the Senate to figure if they get you on Ibn Awad they won't ever have to vote on the other article and admit the election was stolen. And then the Constitution will hit the fan."

"According to this theory of yours."

"It's no theory, Frosty. These people are going to *do* it. They're going to seize power like this was some damn banana republic. There's just no other explanation for everything that's happening."

"That's nothing but suspicion. You never did trust the liberals, Tucker."

"What the hell do you think I am and you are and have been all our lives?" Attenborough said. "I'm not talking about liberals."

The lawyers had been silent through all this. Now Blackstone cleared his throat and said, "Excuse me, Mr. President. But as a matter of fact we have a little more than suspicion to go on."

"We do?" Lockwood said. "What have we got?"

Blackstone said, "We have enough facts to gain a little time. Untrack the process. Create a diversion, raise a doubt."

Lockwood glowered. "You're talking about the Whiffenpoof plot, am I right?"

"I'm referring to Mr. McGraw's discoveries. About eyewitness testimony."

"If you mean Macalaster, forget it. The Senate will never subpoena a journalist."

"If he's a voluntary witness, the Senate will have no choice but to hear him on the record. There is another potential witness. McGraw knows where he is and he can bring him in on a subpoena. This testimony would be devastating to your enemies."

"Who the hell is going to believe a surprise witness?" Lockwood said. "They'll just say we're desperate and crazy. Do you know how hard it is to prove conspiracy?"

"Yes, sir, I do," Blackstone said. "From long experience. So does Alfonso. But this is not a legal process. It's a political process."

"Congratulations, Spats. You're beginning to see the light."

Attenborough said, "Wait a minute. What's this all about?"

Blackstone's eyes were locked with the President's. "May I brief the Speaker and ask his opinion?"

Lockwood expelled an angry breath. He gave a curt nod. "Go ahead."

Attenborough listened to Blackstone's methodical description of the evidence McGraw had developed. When the lawyer was finished the Speaker said, "The Hubbard boys, Hammett, and Busby are all in on this thing, plus all the rest of the ones he found out about? What's the name of this secret outfit?"

"We don't know that yet."

"But you've got a material witness."

"Yes."

"Then call him. All you have to do is put him under oath and ask the question. Do it. Get a subpoena from Sam and Amzi—they can issue it on behalf of the committee—and drag that sorry son of a bitch up in front of the Senate. Today. Macalaster, too. He may be a writer, but he's an American. And he's a poor boy, too."

"A poor boy?" Lockwood said. "What the hell's that got to do with it?"

Attenborough said, "Good God A'mighty, Mr. President. Don't you see what this is? It's the rich boys against the poor boys. That's what it's come down to. You and me and the rest of us nobodies from nowhere are all on one side and all these people who talk like the Duke of Ding Dong's touchhole relations are lined up on the other. The American people are going to understand *that* when they see it on television, media or no damn media, and so will the U.S. Senate."

Olmedo spoke up for the first time. "The Speaker is right, Mr. President."

"He'd better be," Lockwood said.

Olmedo looked up at the towering President, who seemed even taller than usual because he was standing on the raised hearth. "I ask your approval to act on McGraw's information and the Speaker's advice," Olmedo said. "Your only hope, sir, is to go on the attack."

"What forlorn hope is that, Counselor?"

"To save your place in history."

"Noble words," Lockwood said. In silence he looked from one man to the other. At last he said, "All right. Go ahead."

"With how much of it?" Attenborough said.

"Alfonso's part," Lockwood said. "As for you, Tucker, do your duty as you see it. I can't stop you from doing whatever you want to do, talking to anybody you want to talk to."

"Including Franklin?"

"Just keep your hand on your wallet." With that Lockwood left the room.

It was then that Blackstone picked up the secure telephone and called McGraw in the ♂ ↔ ♀ van.

14

Hammett glanced upward to the gallery reserved for members of the House, expecting to meet Attenborough's intense and glassy regard, but to his relief the chair reserved for the Speaker stood empty. As he settled himself on the podium, squaring his tattered Greek Bible before him on the desk and composing himself for his role as the serene and impartial arbiter of the nation's fate (Patrick Graham's magisterial phrase of the day on *Newsdawn*), he looked down into the Senate chamber upon the senators, all one hundred of them attentively waiting for him to take his seat before they did so themselves, as if he were the headmaster and they were so many overage schoolboys in coats and ties at undersize school desks. The House managers and Lockwood's lawyers had taken their seats inside the bar. The snouts of the cameras scented the atmosphere. Philindros sat at the witness table, a man filled to the brim with secrets.

All of these people were gazing at Hammett, and after the revelations he had wrenched from Philindros the day before, there was a subtle difference in the way they did so. They had all seen the morning shows, and they had all understood that this mysterious outsider might somehow be in the process of being chosen by destiny for some higher role. He sensed this. He also felt that the inexplicably absent Attenborough would have found some way to ridicule this idea, if only by the sardonic display of his own ruined person. And so he was glad that the Speaker, who obviously had been trying to distract him by playing some sort of clumsy mind game with him these past days, was not present.

No hint of these secret and elaborate thoughts showed in Hammett's demeanor. He sat down and struck the gavel. Before speaking his first words, however, he took a deep breath and held it for the count of five, an anchorman's trick Graham had confided to him years before with the explanation that for reasons nobody understood, the television camera registered inhalation as thoughtfulness.

"Mr. Olmedo," the Chief Justice said, "do you wish to proceed at this time with the cross-examination of Mr. Philindros?"

"In a moment, Mr. Chief Justice," Olmedo said. "But first my brother Blackstone and I will wish to call two expert witnesses whose names have been disclosed to the Committee on the Impeachment and also to the House managers."

Hammett did not like Olmedo's habit of using the archaic term "brother" to refer to a legal colleague. It was verbal dandyism; besides, as a matter of political usage, the word no longer belonged to people like Olmedo and Blackstone. He took another deep breath, counted to five, and answered. "You wish to swear and question these defense witnesses before the House managers have completed their case?"

"We believe this is the logical moment to do so, and that it will speed the process," Olmedo replied.

Hammett was not pleased with this turn of events—he sensed a court-room trick—but he knew that he must grant Olmedo's request unless the Senate by some miracle decided the issue by a vote. He said, "Senators, there is nothing in the rules that precludes this innovation. Have you any objection?" The entire membership of the Senate sat solemn and silent. Even Amzi Whipple was passive, clearly willing to let whatever Olmedo had in mind come to pass.

"Very well," Hammett said. "There being no objection from the floor you may proceed, Mr. Olmedo. Please step down for the moment, Mr. Philindros."

Olmedo lifted a hand, ruby cuff link flashing. "Before he does so, Mr. Chief Justice, may I ask the Director a single question?"

"You may, Mr. Olmedo."

Olmedo said, "Mr. Philindros, will you kindly read aloud, in your nor-mal voice, the passage from the tape recording of your conversation with the President that I now hand to you?"

Philindros read aloud, or what was aloud for him: " 'I must have a clear, spoken order. Do you instruct me, Mr. President, to use the assets of the Foreign Intelligence Service to bring about the violent death of Ibn Awad, and to gain possession of the two nuclear devices now in his possession?' "

"Thank you, Mr. Director, that is all. Mr. Chief Justice, if it please the Senate, we will now move on to the other witnesses. Then we will recall Mr. Philindros."

"Very well," Hammett said. "The clerk will call the witnesses. Mr. Philindros, you remain under oath, and you may remain in the chamber."

It was Blackstone, not Olmedo, who handled these witnesses. He did so with remarkable brevity. Before calling them to the stand he entered two exhibits into evidence. The first was the copy made by McGraw of the tape Macalaster had been given by Palmer St. Clair 3d, together with a transcript of its contents. The second consisted of two technical analyses of this tape—one by the National Security Agency (NSA), the other by a team of three experts from the private sector, one each from the Massachusetts Institute of Technology, Caltech, and Bell Laboratories.

Blackstone called one expert from the NSA and one from the private-sector team and asked both the same two questions: (1) Was the tape a complete copy of the original? and (2) Had any portion of it been enhanced by electronic means?

In each case the answer was the same: Portions of the original appeared to be missing from the copy and the volume level had been augmented in certain portions of the tape.

"Augmented in what way?" Blackstone asked.

"One of the three male voices recorded was very faint in the original," said the expert from the Caltech-MIT-Bell Labs group. "It was brought up to the same approximate level as the others when it was rerecorded."

"Which voice?" Blackstone asked.

"The voice we designated Speaker Two. No names were put to the three voices on the tape and we were not asked to identify them through comparative analysis."

"Have you heard the voice of this so-called Speaker Two in the course of these proceedings?"

"With the unaided ear, yes, I believe so."

The witness, Professor Suzanne Eques-Kane of Caltech, was a precise woman, a fellow spirit to Blackstone. "On that subjective and admittedly unscientific basis," Blackstone said, "can you put a name to the person you have identified in your report as Speaker Two?"

"My opinion, based on zero technical analysis, is that Speaker Two and the witness identified as Mr. Philindros are the same person."

"Then the tape was altered to make Mr. Philindros's voice louder?"

"To make the voice of Speaker Two more clearly audible, yes."

"No further questions. I will not consume the Senate's time by asking these witnesses to describe the technical methods by which they reached their conclusion," Blackstone said. "These are fully described in their separate reports, which agree in all the relevant particulars."

Hammett turned benevolently to Bob Laval. "Your witness, Mr. Manager Laval."

Laval rose. "Is it possible, Professor Eques-Kane, to reconstitute these missing sections?" he asked.

"In the absence of the original, which was most likely a diskette rather than a tape, no," replied the expert. "The portions in question never formed a part of this copy. Whoever recorded it simply snipped them."

"How many parts were snipped?"

"Seven."

"Is it possible to estimate the length of the gaps?"

"They are not gaps. Portions were snipped—edited—out to create the effect of an uninterrupted and complete recording. But the answer is no."

"But you are quite certain that seven passages were removed?"

"Oh, yes. The technical analysis left no doubt about that."

Philindros returned to the witness table and Olmedo took over the cross-examination. "Mr. Director," he said, "I have only a few questions to ask you on behalf of the President of the United States. My first question is in the nature of a clarification. Yesterday the Chief Justice asked you if, quote, it took the FIS four years after the death of Ibn Awad to locate those devices, which are capable of destroying New York City and killing several million people, end quote. Do you remember that?"

"Yes, Mr. Olmedo."

"And you replied, quote, It took that long to locate them, yes, end quote. I will ask you this question, Mr. Director: Was it the FIS that located the nuclear devices?"

"Strictly speaking, no. They were found by a former FIS officer, acting independently."

"Will you state his name?"

"If instructed to do so, Mr. Olmedo. It is not customary to disclose the identity of American intelligence officers in open sessions of the Congress."

Hammett said, "Is the name relevant to the President's defense, Mr. Olmedo?" Olmedo replied, "It is, Mr. Chief Justice." Hammett said, "Very well. The witness is so instructed."

"The devices were discovered by Horace Hubbard."

Olmedo said, "That is the same Horace Hubbard whose name is mentioned in connection with the alleged irregularities in the tabulation of votes in New York, Michigan, and California elections of last November?"

"Yes."

"And he was an officer of the FIS?"

"For many years, yes. But he retired before these events took place."

"Did Horace Hubbard report his discovery of the bombs to you soon after it was made?"

"No. He told his brother, Julian Hubbard, the chief of staff in the White House, and Julian Hubbard told me."

"Why did he not report to you directly?"

"There was no reason for him to do so. He no longer worked for FIS."

"Thank you, Mr. Director," Olmedo said. "That clarifies the point for the record. Now let us turn to another aspect of your testimony. You have attested that the words published in Mr. Ross Macalaster's syndicated newspaper column and purporting to have been transcribed from a tape recording of that conversation are accurate to the best of your memory and belief. Is that correct?"

"Yes, sir."

"The President has submitted into evidence a tape recording, which I will call the Macalaster tape, that purports to be a copy of the one used by Mr. Macalaster as the basis of his writings. A copy was made available to you. Have you listened to it?"

"Yes."

"You listened to the whole tape?"

"Yes."

"Is it a complete transcription of the conversation?"

Philindros coughed. "It appears that it is not."

"Is that a reference to the expert testimony the Senate has just heard?"

"Yes."

"I will ask you for your own opinion. Do you agree with the experts' statement that parts of the conversation are missing? In short, words that were spoken on that night at Live Oaks by you and by President Lockwood, and perhaps by Mr. Julian Hubbard, have been omitted from the Macalaster tape? Is that the fact?"

Philindros took a sip of water. "I am relying on memory. But it seems so to me."

"Can you recall the unrecorded words?"

"Not verbatim."

"As best you can, then," Olmedo said. "I will ask you this: Did the President suggest to you that he personally fly over to see Ibn Awad in the hope of persuading him not to pass the weapons on to the Eye of Gaza?"

"Yes," Philindros said.

"And how did you reply to that?"

"I advised against it for security reasons."

"Why?"

"Ibn Awad was mentally unstable and unpredictable. I thought it possible the President would be taken hostage."

"Did President Lockwood also suggest making a public statement, a broadcast to the world, revealing all that the United States government knew about the plot?"

"He did."

"And what was your advice in regard to that idea?"

"I thought it might provoke an action to explode the devices ahead of schedule, before we could do anything to prevent it."

"By the phrase 'before we could do anything about it' I take it you mean 'before we could kill Ibn Awad.'"

"Neutralize him," Philindros said. "Gain control of the nuclear weapons. Prevent the loss of life that would have been involved in the explosion of nuclear bombs in a population center."

"Did the President want to neutralize Ibn Awad as you recommended?"

"I don't know what was in the President's mind. I made no recommendation on the issue. He was presented with a set of options supported by the best available intelligence. Assassination was the option he chose."

"He made this choice spontaneously?"

"'Spontaneously'? It was a presidential decision. I can't characterize the mood of his decision, Mr. Olmedo. Nor did I presume to read the President's mind at the time. It was his choice to make. He made it on the basis of the best information and analysis available."

"Forgive me for pressing this point," Olmedo said. "But with what degree of volition did he make this choice?"

"With the degree of volition necessary, since he did in fact make the decision," Philindros replied. "I don't understand your point, Mr. Olmedo. By law only the President could make the choice, and he made it."

"Let us try to clarify the point together, Mr. Director. I will give you three words that might describe the way in which the President made the choice you say he made, and ask you to choose the one that best describes the visible signs of his behavior as best you remember them."

Hammett interrupted, his voice seeming loud in contrast to Philindros's parched undertone. "Really, Mr. Olmedo," he said. "Word games? You are leading the witness in a most extraordinary way even by the tolerant standards of this proceeding."

"It is no game and I do have a purpose, Mr. Chief Justice. This is a vital element of the President's case."

Hammett looked dubious, but he said, "Very well. Continue."

Olmedo said, "First word, Mr. Director. To the best of your recollection of his facial expression, his body language, his tone of voice—"

"We were outside," Philindros said. "It was night. It was difficult to see his face."

"I understand. Nevertheless, would you say that the President was enthusiastic?"

"I would not use that word."

"Was he resigned?"

"I cannot say."

"Was he reluctant?"

"Yes. Clearly."

"So reluctant that he would not give the order until you asked him to do so?"

"Mr. Olmedo, I repeat: I was not privy to his thoughts."

"But you did demand that he give you, as you have testified and as the tape records, 'a clear, spoken order'?"

"I had to ask him that, yes."

"You *had* to ask him. Why?"

"Because only he could say yes or no to an operation of this gravity."

"So you put the question to him because he would not come right out with it. Is that what happened?"

"I say again, I put the question."

Olmedo said, "I ask you this, Mr. Director: *In how loud a voice?*"

After two days of testimony by the barely audible Philindros, the question was electrifying. The Senate stirred, the gallery murmured. Hammett struck a blow with his gavel.

Philindros said, "The President answered my question in the affirmative, Mr. Olmedo. That suggested to me that he had heard and understood it."

"Did it really?" Olmedo said. "How did you know? Did he look you in the eye and give the order?" Philindros did not reply. Olmedo said, "Yes or no, if you please, sir."

"He did not look me in the eye."

"He did not look you in the eye. Was the President even facing you when you asked the question?"

"No. He had turned his back a moment before."

"Remaining where he had been in relation to yourself? That is to say, he did not step away from you?"

"He stepped away."

"How far away?"

"Two or three steps."

"Did you follow him?"

"No."

"Did you raise your voice?"

"No."

"So you spoke to him in your normal voice, the one we are hearing now, and asked what may, with no exaggeration, be called the fatal question, out of doors, at night, when lips cannot be read nor facial expressions detected, over a distance of about three paces. Is that your testimony?"

"Yes."

"And the President replied from this distance with his back still turned?"

"Yes."

"You heard what he said?"

"Yes. Perfectly."

"You did not repeat your question?"

"No. He had already answered it."

Olmedo paused. "And you were absolutely confident that he had heard and understood your question?"

Philindros's whole career had been based on discovering truths and reporting them to those legally entitled to know them. In this case, as Laval had pointed out in regard to his own less august committee, the Senate was backed by the unlimited authority of the Constitution in its right to know everything. Philindros lifted his head slightly and replied, "No, I was not absolutely confident that he had heard me."

"There was a doubt in your mind?"

"Yes."

"Then why did you not ask the question again?"

Philindros did not reply.

Olmedo said, "I can see that this is difficult for you, Mr. Director. Let us suppose he had not answered. Suppose he had said neither yes nor no. What then?"

"Then there would have been no authority to proceed."

"Not even on the basis of silent assent?"

Philindros reacted strongly to this question. Hammett saw it, the cameras saw it, the Senate saw it. "No."

Olmedo said, "*Especially* not on that basis, Mr. Director? Is that what you are saying? If you cannot be sure what was in President Lockwood's mind, you certainly know what was in your own. And isn't it true, sir, that Presidents in the past have authorized, even ordered, intelligence services of the United States to carry out assassinations with a wink of the eye and a nod of the head, and then gotten themselves off the hook and put the blame on that same intelligence service when things went awry and the deed became shameful public knowledge?"

"Yes," Philindros replied. "That has happened in the past."

"How often?"

"Every time the White House ever ordered an operation of this kind."

" 'Every time,' you say. Mr. Director, was it not your intention to protect the FIS against such a contingency and to make sure that no such thing happened on this occasion?"

Philindros replied, "That was in my mind."

"And isn't that why you didn't ask that fatal question a second time— because you already had it on record, had it on tape, in fact? You had what you wanted, you had all you needed, the means to protect the FIS and make sure the blame fell where it belonged, on the President of the United States, if the truth ever came out?"

Hammett said, "Mr. Olmedo, you are taking great liberties."

"Great issues are at stake, Mr. Chief Justice," Olmedo said. "Will the witness reply to the question?"

"Very well, answer the question, Mr. Director," Hammett said. "But a little more decorum, if you please, Counselor."

Again Philindros cleared his throat. "That is correct as far as it goes, Mr. Olmedo."

"Even if you weren't absolutely sure he had in fact ordered you to do what you did, that is, take the life of a foreign head of state."

"I had reason to believe that I was doing what the President wanted done."

Olmedo drew back his head. "Did you indeed?" he said. "Please tell the Senate why you held that belief."

"The plan had been discussed in advance with the President's chief of staff—"

"That would be Mr. Julian Hubbard?"

"Yes. He assured me that the President's approval was a formality. After the conversation I asked him to confirm the President's decision. He did so."

"Was all of that recorded on tape or chip as well?"

Philindros paused to take a breath. "I have no reason to think that it was not," he said.

"I see," Olmedo said. "But let us forget Mr. Julian Hubbard for the moment and turn back to the President himself. What did Bedford Forrest Lockwood himself say to you about the assassination of Ibn Awad after the deed was done? Did he say, 'Good work, Jack!'?"

"No."

"Or did he say something like 'In the name of God, what have you done?' And banish you from his presence for the rest of his term?"

"Is that a question?" Philindros asked.

"Is that your answer, Mr. Director?"

Hammett said, "I think that's quite enough, Mr. Olmedo."

"You do, Mr. Chief Justice?" Olmedo said. "You do, sir? Then I will risk your displeasure by asking the witness one more question. Mr. Director, is it true, as you have testified, that President Lockwood refused to see you ever again after you had done what you say you had reason to believe he wanted done—namely, cold-blooded murder. Is that true, sir?"

"We had no further personal contact after the Ibn Awad operation until last October," Philindros said.

"Thank you, Mr. Director," Olmedo said. "I have no further questions for this witness at this time."

Hammett looked up at the gallery for the first time since the cross-examination began. Attenborough was back, gruesome and watchful, his skin the color of a shrunken head.

15

Palmer St. Clair 3d was a man of regular habits. Every day after his morning run he shaved and showered and, while watching the last segment of *Newsdawn with Patrick Graham*, drank a healthshake made from a secret formula containing yogurt, bran, honey, and wheat germ. On this particular morning, the show was especially engaging because its primary subject, Archimedes Hammett, had given St. Clair the recipe for the shake, and of course it was always pleasant to see a Shelleyan getting on in the world. Graham was an Old Blue too, though not of the sort St. Clair would have been likely to know in college days.

As soon as *Newsdawn* broke for its final commercial, St. Clair got dressed, drove to the railroad station, and took the train into Manhattan. He liked to get to the station a little early so as to position himself on the platform to get aboard first and claim the front window seat, which had a little more leg room than the ones behind it. While waiting on the platform he always read the book, movie, theater, and music reviews in *The Wall Street Journal*, but never ventured into the swamp of right-wing biases that was its opinions page. On the train he studied the rest of the

Journal, marking articles for his secretary to clip and file, and started on the news pages of *The New York Times,* leaving its mind-stretching editorials, with whose judgments he seldom disagreed, for reading on the subway ride from Grand Central Station to Wall Street. St. Clair never talked to anybody on the journey into the city. In fact he never *looked* at anybody in any public conveyance or public place, but this was such an ingrained habit that he was not really aware of it himself.

This being true, he did not notice John L. S. McGraw standing close beside him on the station platform, or following him into the train, or taking the seat beside him. Nor did he hear McGraw speaking to him in a broad New York accent until the man got his attention by poking him sharply in the arm with a rigid forefinger. St. Clair wheeled and saw a perfect stranger with a battered, freckled Irish mug. He was dressed all in brown—cinnamon "tweed" jacket, tan trousers, terra-cotta shirt, autumn-leaf necktie. The poke in the arm had been so painful that St. Clair half-expected to see a gun in the fellow's hand, but instead he was holding out his hairy hand, offering to shake. He spoke a common name—his own, St. Clair supposed, but he did not catch it. Obviously he was some sort of nut. St. Clair stared at him in distaste.

The man smiled. Crooked teeth. With the usual mispronunciation he said, "Are you Palmer St. Clair the thoid?" St. Clair did not respond. He thrust his *Journal* under his arm and reached for the briefcase at his feet. The man bent over when St. Clair did, choreographing the movement so that their faces were only inches apart. "Don't go just yet," McGraw said. He was holding a calling card in his hand, close to St. Clair's reading glasses. Scrawled across the back in Greek letters was the Shelleyan bona fides, Ναμε οφ τηε ποετ. "In the name of the Poet?" This character? This was impossible; it was somebody's idea of a practical joke.

Still bent over, St. Clair gave McGraw a frozen stare. "I am astonished," he said.

"No," McGraw replied. "You are surprised. Palmer, I want you to get off the train with me at the next stop."

"You do?" St. Clair said. "I don't know who put you up to this, but I don't think it's funny. And the only thing I'm going to do for you if you don't get away from me *now* is have you arrested and taken off this train for a psychiatric examination."

"Fine, we can all use a little professional help. Palmer, there's a federal agent right outside the door on the platform between this car and the next one, and another one at the other end."

The train was beginning to brake as it approached the station. McGraw said, "I have something else for you." He handed St. Clair a subpoena to appear that afternoon at twelve-thirty to testify before the United States Senate in the trial of President Bedford Forrest Lockwood for high crimes and misdemeanors.

"Testify? In the impeachment trial?" St. Clair said. "I'm not going anywhere with you."

The train pulled into the station. The door at the end of the car slid open and a large black man stood in it, swaying with the motion of the train. He wore a large, shiny badge pinned to the breast pocket of his wrinkled blue blazer. The blazer was unbuttoned and St. Clair could see a holstered revolver beneath it.

"Who are you?" St. Clair said to McGraw. "You don't even have credentials."

"No," McGraw said. He pointed at the man with the badge. "But he does. And he has the power of arrest. Please follow me, Palmer."

"I want to call my lawyer."

"We've done that for you, Palmer. He'll be waiting for you in Washington."

The train stopped. The conductor called out the station. St. Clair had never even noticed that there was such a place as this on the line between Stamford and Manhattan. He looked over his shoulder, thinking to escape that way. But another massive person wearing a badge on his coat appeared beside their seat. This one was Hispanic. St. Clair felt that he had been stricken by paralysis. McGraw handed him his briefcase.

He said, "This is where we get off, Palmer."

St. Clair glared at him. "Why do you keep calling me by my Christian name?"

"Sorry. This is where we get off, Mr. St. Clair."

"It's *Sinclair*," Palmer St. Clair said.

"I'll remember that, Palmer," McGraw said. "After you."

"No. Absolutely not."

"Okay, let's go, Palmer," said the large black agent in a loud voice. St. Clair looked up at him. The fellow must once have been an offensive lineman; he was enormous. "Move it," the agent said.

Move it. Up and down the car, people were staring. Some of them knew St. Clair even if he did not know them. He rose to his feet section by section, like a stick figure coming dazedly to life in an animated cartoon, and followed McGraw off the train.

16

In the library of the Norman manor house, Mallory listened as Atten-borough repeated everything he had already told Lockwood. "You may be onto something, Tucker," Mallory said, "but surely you don't really think they'd try to get away with anything as brazen as this?"

"Why not, when the alternative is you?" Attenborough said.

"But *Hammett?*"

"That's exactly what Lockwood said. Same sneer, same tone of voice. Both wrong." Attenborough had one of his coughing fits, wheezing and gasping for breath.

Mallory reached over and touched him. "Tucker, do you need help?"

"No," Attenborough gasped. "But the country does." He recovered. "Franklin, I'm telling you," he said, wiping his eyes. "This is the joker in the constitutional deck. Those loonies have never been able to get them-selves elected, but now they've finally found a man who's stupid enough to try and take over the United States of America."

"You sound like Amzi."

"Amzi makes a lot of sense on certain subjects."

"Suppose, for the sake of argument, that they actually got away with this," Mallory said. "There'd have to be an election sometime, and as you just got through telling me, people like Hammett can't win elections in this country. He'd be out on his ear the day the polls opened and closed."

"That may not be something they're worried about," Attenborough said. "We may be talking about this country having an acting President for Life. All he'd have to do if Congress declared an election is put on his black robe and strike down the legislation in the Supreme Court."

Mallory said, "You're saying that somebody could be Chief Justice and acting President at the same time?"

"No reason why not," Attenborough said. "This is a constitutional issue, and nothing in the Constitution says otherwise. It's right there, plain as day. What Article Two says happens in a case like this is as follows: Congress shall declare, quote, what officer shall then act as Presi-dent, and such officer shall act accordingly, until the disability be removed, or a President be elected. Unquote. Doesn't say a damn thing there or elsewhere about resigning the office already held while serving as acting President."

Mallory shook his head with what he realized was a kind of twisted delight in Attenborough's crafty reading of human nature and the Constitution. "That's quite a stretch even for your byzantine mind, Tucker," he said. "No one can hold two federal offices of profit or trust at the same time."

"Don't underestimate their revolutionary creativity in these extraordinary circumstances," Attenborough said. "Study it out. Watch the tube. If you think I'm wrong by this time tomorrow, good luck to you. Otherwise, call me."

"And?"

"And I'll tell you what I've got in mind."

Mallory was nodding again. "Does that by any chance include the possibility of your succeeding to a vacant presidency?"

"You sound more like Lockwood every minute. The answer is not for long. But don't jump to any conclusions. The longest way around is sometimes the shortest way home."

" 'Trust me.' Is that the message?"

"You've done it before, Franklin. Now I've got to get back to town in time to watch the burlycue. You've got Albert's number?"

"Yes."

Attenborough struggled to his feet, fought for balance, shook hands. His touch was cold; the upper lip that he drew back in a smile was filmed with sweat. "Albert or me," he said. "Nobody else."

"I'll call either way."

"I know you will. There's one more thing I want to say. I know damn well you're the rightful President of the United States and so does Frosty. That's why he's let this whole thing get out of hand the way he has. He knows he's in the wrong and he can't stand the thought. Whatever they say on TV, Lockwood's an honest man. That's the starting point."

Mallory saw more signs of Attenborough's desperate physical condition. A pulse beat in the Speaker's temple; his eyes, always before filled with humor and intelligence, had been deadened by whatever was happening to his body. Mallory said, "Tucker, are you telling me you want to make me President?"

"What I want or anybody else wants doesn't come into it," Attenborough replied. "The people have already given you the job."

17

Mallory's call came while Zarah was watching Olmedo's cross-examination of Philindros on television. Mostly the camera ignored them and lingered on Hammett, as if the real truth was to be found not in the testimony itself but in his reactions to it. Television did for Hammett what El Greco had done for the inmates of the Spanish asylum who were his models for portraits of the saints—transformed the signs of madness into the aura of sanctity.

As this thought passed through Zarah's mind, Mallory's disembodied voice spoke into her ear. "I need to talk to you," he said. "Can you come out to Great Falls?"

"I'd rather not," she said.

"I know that. But this is about that woman who was following you. And related matters. There are things you must be told, a question I must ask you."

Zarah had never been to the Norman manor house. She said, "I don't know the way."

"I'll send a car," Mallory said.

"No, thanks."

"But you will come?"

"All right," Zarah said. "But no limousine. I'll just follow the leader."

Two ♂ ↔ ♀ cars, a point vehicle and a chase vehicle, had shadowed Zarah since her encounter with Sturdi. On the way to Great Falls she drove at high speed, weaving in and out of traffic, driving the lead car ahead of her and shaking the chase car, so that the teams assigned to cover her almost lost her on the parkway and had to call for backup. In her mind's eye she saw Lockwood, Julian, Hammett, Philindros, Attenborough, Macalaster, the temptress Slim of the dinner party and the woebegone Slim of the subsequent video passion play. Emily Hubbard in tears. Sturdi in her outlandish blond wig on the closed-circuit of the O.G.'s security video. Mallory on Inauguration Day. How could these figures she saw on television be the same men and women she had encountered as living persons? How could this Punch and Judy show that was American political life go on endlessly as it did?

Every resident of Washington seemed to be plugged into a single brain that provided everyone with the same thoughts and sensations. She thought: They were right, those primitives in darkest Africa and Polynesia and the Amazonian rain forest who believed in the early days of photography that the camera was a device for stealing souls. A century later, flesh is the dream. Only the image is real, only the image endures; all this picture-taking by the media is a harvest of souls. The purpose of life is to await the camera, to keep in shape for it in case it ever comes. Out of celebrity, immortality. Should the universe collapse and then be re-created out of nothing, the image will still be present in the nothingness. When new galaxies form, when intelligence arises again, when technology is reinvented, the images will be recaptured and become visible again: tight shots of immortal beings who have escaped the bonds of flesh and mind, who have no memory of them, who merely *are*. Dear God, she thought, what am I doing here among the living dead?

Zarah parked the car in the drive and went inside. The house was strange to her; when its fantastic nature registered on her senses at last, it was like a continuation of her earlier train of thought. This place was like a hologram, an image designed for an image to live in: if you knocked on the door your fist would go right through it, passing between the electrons you had mistaken for oak. What could its history be? What Hearst or Mussolini had commissioned this wonder? Mallory could not have built it.

Or maybe he could have. He awaited Zarah in the library, a much grander room than the ones in his city houses, three stories high, galleried for access to the thousands of volumes on its shelves. Handsome face glowing with pleasure, Mallory rose to greet her. They had not seen each other for days. He was dressed as usual in a tweed jacket and corduroys and his white hair was slightly tousled. He must have just come in from outdoors, because, she realized, he smelled of the open air in a musty room where nothing else did. Of course he had been reading and he held a book in his hand, the place marked with a forefinger. Before speaking to Zarah he touched a control that turned off all his electronics systems. The computer screen at his elbow, the television screens behind him faded to points of light, then went to black; the telephone emitted a single piercing, impossible-to-ignore note that notified the user that it was now inert. It was his version of privacy. Zarah burst into laughter.

"What?" Mallory asked with a puzzled smile.

"Nothing," Zarah said. "I've been having strange thoughts all day."

"You're not the only one. Sit down. Your friend Attenborough was just here. I want you to hear what he had to tell me, and then tell me what you think." He told her. Then he said, "What would you do about this?"

"If I were me or if I were you?"

"If you were me. I think I may already know the other answer."

"All right," she said. "If I were you and thought what you think, I would assume that what Attenborough suspects to be true *is* true. Then I'd investigate to test the assumption, and lastly, if it turned out actually to be true, I'd do what I could to prevent the whole thing from happening."

"But can I make that assumption?" Mallory asked. "Remember, Attenborough is next in line for the presidency himself."

"Why would he want it?"

"I don't think he does. But he's suffered a lot recently from people like these. He has plenty of reason to be paranoid."

"Has he been subject to paranoid fantasies in the past?"

"Not in my presence."

"Is he a truthful man?"

"Truthfulness is his stock-in-trade," Mallory replied. "I've never known him to lie about anything except his malaria."

"And what are the people he suspects famous for?"

"For lying about everything. But virtuous lies are mother's milk to political extremists. Denial of reality is the basis of their existence."

"So you've said before. It's also the definition of insanity."

Mallory blinked. "That should be in *Bartlett's Familiar Quotations*," he said. "You've observed Hammett. Could he be part of something like this?"

Zarah said, "I think he's mad and bad and listening to voices. You can see it in his eyes from the first moment, hear it in every word he says."

"You saw all that in the time you spent with him?"

"Anyone would."

Mallory smiled very faintly. "Not quite anyone," he said. "What makes him the way he is, do you think?"

"I don't know, but what difference does it make?" Zarah answered with an impatient shrug. "Has anyone ever figured out Hitler's motivations? Did Stalin slaughter thirty million Russians, or fifty million or whatever the real number was, because he was a homicidal maniac or because he was a Georgian patriot and wanted to bury as many Russians as possible so that the odds wouldn't be so great against his homeland in future invasions by the Muscovite army? Where madmen are concerned, actions count; motives are meaningless."

Mallory absorbed her words, then turned his back and went to the mullioned window, apparently lost in thought. Finally he said, "You're quite right."

"About what?"

"All of it."

"Don't be too sure," Zarah said. "I don't understand this country or these people. I've never been so confused in my life."

She joined him at the window and looked out. In the mellow light of afternoon, ♂ ↔ ♀ teams roamed about dressed as gardeners, workmen, runners, tennis players, even a few as presidential assistants-in-waiting in suits or dresses. The grounds were planted to resemble a French park, with fountains, formal flower beds, graveled walks, hedges and mazes and avenues of pollarded trees. Zarah felt that the architect's intention had been to mimic beauty rather than to create something that was beautiful in its own right. But that was the controlling intention in this world of illusions. Suddenly she understood something about this estate and therefore about Mallory. The whole place had been designed by its original owner as a shrine to the camera cult, but Mallory had transformed it into a fortress to keep the camera out.

Mallory stirred at her side, almost imperceptibly as was his way. "There's something else," he said. "Something quite important has been discovered about the person who murdered Susan. It's thought you may be able to help."

"Help? How?"

"By looking at pictures."

"Of what?"

"Of the assassin."

"On that day?"

"And maybe afterward. It's felt that you may recognize this person."

Felt by whom? Zarah wondered, but did not ask. She said, "All right. Why not?"

18

St. Clair's lawyer, Jasper Trout, great-great-grandson of two of the founders of the austere downtown firm of Trout Jasper Timberlake Biolley & Noel, was not a criminal lawyer. But most of his clients were financiers, a line of work that bred felons at a steady and predictable rate, and he knew what to advise a man who suddenly found himself caught up in the toils of the criminal justice system. In an anteroom of the Senate chamber he said, "All I can tell you, Palmer, is what they're offering: complete immunity from subsequent prosecution in any court in the land on the basis of anything you say here that may tend to incriminate you."

St. Clair said, "*Incriminate* me?"

"It means that if you tell them everything you know, you walk, no matter what you've been up to."

"What am I supposed to have been up to?"

"That was not disclosed to me."

"I thought they had to tell a man's lawyer everything."

"These people don't. The United States Senate isn't a court of law, it's a force of nature. They seem to think you are an accessory to a felony. If you have reason to think they may be right, take the deal."

"That's preposterous."

"Then go in there and tell them so. But if you conceal or cover up a material fact from the government, you'll be liable to be charged with a felony under Section 1001 of the U.S. Criminal Code. Same result if you make a false statement. Also you'll be under oath. Perjury is not covered by the agreement."

"Do I *have* to appear? Don't they have to give me time to prepare a defense?"

"Yes, you have to appear. That's a federal subpoena lying on the table. No, they don't have to give you anything. You're not a defendant, you're a witness—for the moment."

For the moment? St. Clair gaped in disbelief; panic flooded into his face. This reaction was not altogether displeasing to Trout. He had never liked St. Clair—not at Lawrenceville, not at Princeton-Yale games, not at dances when their respective future first wives were debutantes, not on the golf course, not out in the garden in East Hampton with Trout's disheveled third wife on a ginny summer night in 1992. Not now. He waited with a look of fraternal concern and sympathy for St. Clair's answer.

St. Clair said, "Will you be in there with me?"

"Afraid not," Trout replied. "Witnesses are not allowed to bring their lawyers with them. Anyway, the thing is cut-and-dried. Either you talk or you don't. It's your decision, depending on what material fact you think they think you'll be trying to cover up."

"I can't begin to imagine."

Trout smiled urbanely. "In that case you'd better let me tell them you accept their terms," he said.

St. Clair thought, then nodded resentfully. "This is outrageous," he said. "They abducted me off the train and flew me down here on a military plane, Jasper. Bucket seats. Lowlife thugs with guns and badges. Is this the United States of America?"

"Oh, yes, Palmer," Trout replied. "I'm afraid it always has been. What shall I tell them?"

"What choice do I have? Obviously I'm in the hands of the Gestapo."

Minutes after this, St. Clair found himself swearing on a Bible to tell the truth, the whole truth, and nothing but the truth. He did so quite stylishly, with head uplifted. Of course it was a comfort to look up at the podium and see Hammett sitting there, though he little resembled the awkward drudge of undergraduate days, and then to look outward into the chamber and see Buzzer Busby, older than himself but well known to him. There were other men he knew among the senators—not Shelleyans like Hammett and Busby, of course, but he knew them and they knew him. He had never been in the Senate chamber before. It was smaller and cozier than he had expected. He found it surprisingly pleasant—lulling, even. No wonder they called it a club; it had the same subdued atmosphere as, say, the Knickerbocker, the same sense that everyone who belonged here knew exactly what everyone else was talking about at all times.

St. Clair had never seen Alfonso Olmedo C. before. Of course he knew who he was from the newspapers, and this was the difference between Olmedo and, say, Busby: one knew the Busbys of this world but only knew *about* the Olmedos. The man's suit looked as if it had been tailored in Havana for a drug baron. He wore an extraordinary tie that seemed to have been snipped from a bad abstract painting, and when he waved his hands, as he did more or less continually, masses of gold flashed and precious jewels twinkled. Smiling in amusement, St. Clair thought, He looks like someone who used to be married to Esther Williams. Olmedo seemed to divine St. Clair's line of thought. He did not exactly smile back, but the line of his mouth changed and he nodded almost imperceptibly. Then he asked St. Clair to state his name and address. St. Clair did so, taking pains to pronounce the surname slowly and distinctly, in the same confident voice as before. Good name, good address.

Olmedo said, "Did you graduate from a university, Mr. St. Clair?" Clearly he was a quick study; he pronounced the name right on the first try.

"Yes, sir," St. Clair replied. "I graduated from Yale University, class of 1971."

"Do you recognize any other alumni of Yale here in this chamber, Mr. St. Clair?"

"Several, yes, the Chief Justice among them."

"Did you know the Chief Justice personally at Yale?"

"Yes, I did. We were in the same residential college."

"That would be Calhoun College?"

"That's correct. He was two years senior to me."

"And in undergraduate days in Calhoun College at Yale University did you also know Mr. Julian Hubbard, the former chief of staff to President Lockwood?"

What was this, an interview for the alumni newsletter? St. Clair said, "As a matter of fact I did know Julian Hubbard. He was *one* year my senior." He looked upward at Hammett and detected an answering flicker of puzzlement in his stern and guarded face.

Olmedo was saying, "I will ask you this, Mr. St. Clair: Have you kept in touch with Chief Justice Hammett and with Mr. Julian Hubbard on a regular basis in the years since graduation?"

"We chat from time to time."

"On the telephone?"

Curiouser and curiouser. But this could not possibly be leading where it seemed to be leading. St. Clair was feeling quite relaxed. "Usually on the telephone, yes. We live in different towns."

"And you also keep in touch with certain other alumni by long-distance telephone?"

"Yes, of course."

"I will read you a list of names, Mr. St. Clair. Will you be so kind as to answer yes if you have been in telephone contact with the person named at any time in the last six months, either personally or by requesting a third party to pass a message. Please answer no if you have not."

Abruptly, even a little roughly, Hammett intervened. " 'A list of names,' Mr. Olmedo? What is this? May the Chief Justice see it?"

"Of course you may, Mr. Chief Justice. I was on the point of asking that it be entered into evidence." Olmedo handed the list to a clerk, who took it to Hammett, who studied it for a long moment. When he looked up he said, "Let the record show that there are forty-seven names on the list. Does that accord with your count, Mr. Olmedo?"

"Yes, Mr. Chief Justice."

"Good," Hammett said. "Because if we are going to have a list of names I think it is important to establish at the outset exactly how many names are on it and stick to that number."

An appreciative giggle ran through the press and visitors' galleries, where many recognized that the Chief Justice's remark was a devastating reference to the infamous "list of Communists in the State Department" that had been the Ur-document of the late Senator Joseph R. McCarthy's notorious Communist witch-hunt in the 1950s.

Hammett gaveled them into silence. "If there is any further display, the sergeant at arms will clear the galleries," he said. "Mr. Olmedo, what purpose do you hope to serve by reading these names aloud?"

"I have stated the purpose in my last question to the witness, Mr. Chief Justice."

"Its usefulness remains murky to me, and I imagine to the Senate as well."

"I hope to make the purpose crystal-clear in a matter of minutes, Mr. Chief Justice."

"There is a potential for embarrassment in this to a great many distinguished Americans who have no conceivable connection to this proceeding. The Chief Justice cannot permit this."

Olmedo said, "Mr. Chief Justice, I don't see how you can prevent it under the rules. This testimony is vital to the President's case."

"Every innovation you put forward seems to be vital to the President's case, Mr. Olmedo. You may not read this list aloud in this chamber. Nor may you release it to the news media or disclose it outside this chamber under the penalties for contempt."

"May I enter it into evidence?"

"Under seal, yes. Proceed."

"With great respect, Mr. Chief Justice, this ruling does not appear to be consistent with your earlier ruling that every word uttered in the proceeding must be public."

"The distinction is evident. Do not quibble with me, sir. Proceed." For the first time in the whole course of the trial, there was emotion in Hammett's voice and in the expression on his face. The cameras cut away from him and panned to the many sympathetic faces in the gallery. Hammett's supporters understood that he was defending an American principle, that he was preventing injustice and slander; they were proud of him.

Olmedo seemed unperturbed, even pleased by the ruling. "Very well, Mr. Chief Justice," he said. "The names on the list have been declared sacrosanct and so they will remain. I will proceed in another way. Mr. St. Clair, were you a passenger on Universal Airlines Flight 3215, leaving La Guardia at seven o'clock on the morning of March eleventh of this year, arriving at Washington National Airport at seven fifty-nine?"

The question was like a blow to St. Clair's stomach. It knocked the wind out of him. How could anyone possibly know this fact? He waited for Hammett to rescue him again. Nothing happened. Olmedo said, "Shall I repeat the question, sir?"

"I'm afraid I don't recall," St. Clair said.

"I see. How many times have you flown from La Guardia to Washington in the last year?"

"I don't recall."

"How many times have you been in Washington in your life?"

"Really, I have not kept track."

"Once, twice, a hundred times?"

"Three or four times."

"So it is not a routine event for you to visit Washington?"

"No."

"Thank you, Mr. St. Clair, but we might have arrived at that answer with less difficulty, don't you think?"

"Yes or no?" St. Clair said. "Yes, I certainly do think so."

Olmedo's smooth and friendly voice grew less so. "Mr. St. Clair, it is getting late. We have no wish to detain you longer than necessary. You have agreed and subsequently sworn to tell the whole truth here. Once you begin, time will fly. Please answer the original question."

Hammett said, "What was the point of that badgering remark, Mr. Olmedo?"

"To encourage, Mr. Chief Justice. Will you instruct the witness to answer?"

In a kindly voice Hammett said, "Answer as best you can, Mr. St. Clair."

St. Clair felt absurdly grateful for this tiny sign of sympathy from the Chief Justice. Maybe everything was going to be all right after all. He said, "Yes, I suppose I was on that plane. I did come down here about that date."

"We are not dealing in approximations, Mr. St. Clair," Olmedo said. "On that date and no other, on that plane and no other, sir. I have here a passenger list showing your name and that flight, that time, that date."

A passenger list? Blood drained from St. Clair's face. This *was* the Gestapo at work. They *had* been spying on him. But he remained outwardly calm, jaunty. He said, "In that case I will consider the time and date as established."

"With the indulgence of the Senate, I will try to get us to the point a little more quickly from now on," Olmedo said. "On the day before you flew down to Washington, at eight forty-three in the evening, you received a call from a person whose name I have written on this piece of paper. Is that correct? Let the record show I am handing the paper to the witness."

St. Clair put on his reading glasses and glanced at the paper. Again he blanched, or thought that he felt himself doing so. The name was that of Five-Three, the senior man in the Horace Hubbard—Baxter Busby cell of the Shelley Society. And Five-Three *had* been the Shelleyan who called that night.

"Is that correct, Mr. St. Clair? Yes or no."

"Yes."

"And in that call did he ask you to perform a service, and if so, what was the service?"

"He asked me to go to Washington the following morning."

"On that particular flight, on that particular day?"

"Yes."

"For what purpose?"

"He asked me to wait on the corner of Wisconsin Avenue and Newark Street at a certain time, I believe eight-twenty in the morning, where I would be contacted."

"Contacted by whom?"

"He did not say."

"Did he ask you to dress in any particular way?"

"He asked me to wear running togs. Harvard sweats."

"Do you usually wear Harvard sweats?"

"No, I bought some fake ones at the airport."

"You saw nothing odd about this request?"

"Yes, of course I did. But I thought it was funny."

" 'Funny' as in 'comical'?"

"Right. I assumed it must be some sort of prank."

"In the nature of a fraternity prank?"

"Something like that."

"Did you carry out the caller's instructions?"

"Yes, to the letter." St. Clair was growing more and more uncomfortable. From his seat at the witness table he could see about half the senators. Many of them were battling faint smiles or shooting amused glances at one another. The story *was* ridiculous, he knew that, but after all—

Olmedo said, "And did anything occur at eight-twenty on the corner of Wisconsin Avenue and Newark Street?"

"Yes," St. Clair replied. "I was given a package."

"By whom?"

"I don't know. It was a delivery person, somebody on a bicycle."

"This person was also wearing Harvard sweats?"

"No. Bicycling clothes. Big yellow goggles."

"Male or female?"

"I didn't notice. The person came and went in a moment."

"How large was the package?"

"It was an ordinary manila envelope, nine by twelve inches or whatever."

"You opened it?"

"Yes."

"What was inside?"

St. Clair really had thought he would have been rescued by Hammett before now. He paused in hopes of an interruption, which did not come—paused rather too long, he realized too late. By his hesitation he had made himself look as if he had something to hide. He spoke up bravely: "The envelope contained a picture of a man, a plastic bag with one of those little tapes for a tape recorder inside it, and a sheet of instructions."

"Instructing you to do what?"

"To go to a bodybuilding place called ye gods on Wisconsin Avenue, wait outside until the man in the picture came out, then bump into him as if by accident and hook the plastic bag with the tape inside it on his coat."

"*Hook* the plastic bag on his coat, Mr. St. Clair? Hook it by what means?"

"It had a string on it, a piece of fish line, I think, with a fishing fly at the other end."

"And did you do as you were instructed and hook the plastic bag onto the man's coat with the fishhook attached to the length of fish line?"

"Yes."

"Then what did you do?"

"I apologized to the fellow for bumping into him and ran on."

"You got a good look at him?"

"Good enough to know I had the right man, based on the photograph."

"Did you know the man in the photograph, the one you hooked the plastic bag to?"

"Know him personally? No."

"Did you recognize him?"

"No."

Olmedo said, "I will hand you a photograph, Mr. St. Clair, and ask you if this is a picture of the man in question?"

St. Clair put on his reading glasses again and examined the photograph. "It very well could be him," he said. "It was a brief encounter."

"But a memorable one, I should think."

Hammett said, "*Mister* Olmedo—"

Olmedo kept right on talking; he had a much stronger voice than Hammett. "Can you be more definite? Is this the man?"

"Yes. I believe so. To the best of my recollect—"

"Thank you. Let the photograph be entered into evidence and let the record show that the witness has identified the man on whom he hooked the plastic bag with the tape recording inside it as Mr. Ross Macalaster, the syndicated newspaper columnist."

Diligent newspaper reader that he was, St. Clair suddenly understood what this meant. He was overwhelmed. As on the train, his painfully thin limbs drew up and then collapsed in an acting-class rendition of fright, realization, denial, and despair. He shot a glance at Hammett, who was stony-faced. Was no one going to object, intervene, stand up for what was right, put an end to this humiliation? He glanced around the chamber. There were no smiles to be seen now.

"I am coming to the end, Mr. St. Clair," Olmedo said in a tone of sympathy. "Please bear with me. After you had done what you came to do, what did you do next?"

"I went back to the airport, changed clothes, flew to La Guardia, and went to work."

"No. Before that. In Washington."

"I made a telephone call."

"To whom, Mr. St. Clair?"

St. Clair hesitated. "Am I permitted to say?"

"Is the name one of the forty-seven on the list?"

"Yes."

"Then it is a material fact in this impeachment trial and concealing it from the Senate would be unlawful. Please answer the question."

Hammett sat impassively on the podium.

"The person I called was Julian Hubbard," St. Clair said.

"Why?"

"It was part of the instructions."

"And what did you say to Julian Hubbard in that phone call?"

"I said, 'I just delivered the Mickey Finn.' "

"That's all?"

"Yes."

"What did he say to you?"

"He said nothing, just hung up the phone."

"Did you try again?"

"No. I only had one quarter with me."

"You didn't have a cellular phone on your person?"

"Yes, but the instructions said not to use it under any circumstances."

"I see," Olmedo said. "Mr. St. Clair, what is the meaning of that phrase, 'I just delivered the Mickey Finn'?"

"I have no idea," St. Clair said. "It was written down on the instruction sheet."

"So naturally you uttered it without thought or hesitation," Olmedo said. "You must trust your friends."

"I have never had any reason not to."

"I see. Are you a fly fisherman, Mr. St. Clair?"

"No," St. Clair said, hardly noting the question.

"I come now to the question that must be in many minds in this chamber. Why did you do this bizarre and inexplicable thing?"

"Because I . . . Frankly, I don't know that I can explain in terms that would be understood by an outsider."

"But you must try, sir, because we outsiders must also try to understand," Olmedo said. "I will ask you this: Was it because you *do* trust your special friends? And when you were asked by a friend in that telephone call to come down to Washington, meet a total stranger on a bicycle on a street corner, hook a plastic bag onto another total stranger"—Hammett stirred on the bench; Olmedo raised his voice—"did you do all this because you were asked to do it 'in the name of the Poet'?"

St. Clair's heart leaped in his chest. He knew that he must not look at Hammett or at Busby, knew that they could not help him, knew that his whole life turned on the answer to this question that he could not possibly answer. He thought, My God, if these fascists know enough to know *this*, what else do they know? "Yes," he replied in a voice that trembled ever so slightly, "that was the reason."

Olmedo nodded encouragingly as if he were some sort of priest who could grant absolution. He said, "Is that phrase, 'in the name of the Poet,' a password or code word or recognition signal used by the members of some sort of secret or fraternal organization to which you belong?"

St. Clair crossed his spindly legs. "Yes, it is."

"Of whom exactly forty-seven members, no fewer and no more, are listed on the paper the Chief Justice has sealed to keep it from the eyes of outsiders?"

"Yes."

"Will you tell this honorable Senate the name of that organization?" St. Clair could not get the words out. Olmedo said, "Shall I ask the Chief Justice to remind you, sir, that the oath you have just taken here supersedes all other oaths whatsoever?"

St. Clair looked at Hammett, who gave him no sign. "The name of the organization," St. Clair said, "is the Shelley Society."

"Named for the English poet Percy Bysshe Shelley, who lived from 1792 to 1822, was drowned while sailing in a storm off Leghorn, and was cremated on the beach at Viareggio by his friend Edward John Trelawny?"

St. Clair's face twitched; he could not control it. *They knew everything!* "Yes."

Olmedo saw St. Clair's panic, wondered what caused it. "Mr. St. Clair," he said, "I will ask you this: Is Mr. Julian Hubbard a member of the Shelley Society? Yes or no."

"Yes."

"Is his half brother, Mr. Horace Hubbard, also a member of that organization?"

"Yes."

"Do you, at this moment, see any other members present besides yourself, sir?"

"Yes."

"Will you name them?"

St. Clair could not understand why Hammett was letting this go on. He had told Olmedo not to do this, yet he persisted in doing it. Everything was being twisted and made to look sinister. The reputations, the lives, of all Shelleyans were in Palmer St. Clair's keeping. There was only one thing to do.

"It is not what you suggest," he said. "And I'm sorry, I cannot name names."

"Then I will put another name to you and you will answer yes or no, if you please."

Hammett gaveled repeatedly. "Mr. Olmedo, this is not an inquisition. You are out of order."

Olmedo said, "One more question, if the Senate please, sir. Mr. St. Clair, is Chief Justice Hammett a member of the Shelley Society?"

"I will not say," St. Clair said.

"That is your choice, sir, and I will not insist," Olmedo replied. "But as one man to another I want to ask you a final question. What on earth did you think you were doing with that plastic bag and that fishing fly and that tape recording?"

Palmer St. Clair 3d blinked. He looked up. He saw the cameras. He remembered that all this—every fidget, every word—had been going out over the air to tens of millions of television sets, that his privacy had been destroyed, that he had been made to look like what he certainly was not, never had been, and what no person of his breeding, background, and schooling ever could be: a fool. He answered Olmedo's question with the absolute unvarnished truth: "I thought it was a game," he said. "A harmless joke."

Olmedo scrutinized him with deep commiseration. "If it is any comfort to you, Mr. St. Clair," he said, "no reasonable person could look at you at this moment and believe otherwise. I have no further questions, but I do have a request."

"Make it, Mr. Olmedo," Hammett said.

"I ask that the Chief Justice recuse himself from this trial on grounds that he has an undisclosed and irreconcilable personal interest in its outcome, and that a mistrial be declared by the Senate in this impeachment."

Hammett looked down on Olmedo with eyes in which fury mixed with the contemptuous light of fulfilled expectations, as if he had known all along that something like this was bound to happen. "Your request is not in order," he said.

The words were hardly out of his mouth before Busby was on his feet, moving for adjournment.

19

In his NYPD days McGraw had questioned a famous movie star whose terrorist boyfriend had crawled out of her bed one morning and blown up a subway train. Radiant on screen, the actress was just another anxious, thin, sad, hungover, halfway pretty blonde in real life. Zarah Christopher was the other side of the coin, a woman who was more beguiling to the naked eye than to the camera. In the video footage McGraw had seen she looked attractive enough; in the flesh she was a disturbing presence. She joined McGraw and Lucy and Wiggins in the $\male \leftrightarrow \female$ van in the parking lot at Fair Oaks Cinemas. Macalaster was there, too, and McGraw saw that he was taken with this young woman. So was Wiggins. Lucy was less glad to see her.

McGraw said, "Why is the lovely young lady here?"

"President Mallory's orders," Lucy replied.

"They know each other?"

"They are good friends."

Her voice was tight, her eyes veiled, all cheek and lip muscles under strict control. No doubt Franklin Mallory felt the same about Zarah as the other members of his gender present in this van. No wonder Lucy wasn't a fan.

Lucy handed Zarah her blinders and explained how to use them. Then she said, "How much has President Mallory told you?"

"Only that some sort of discovery has been made about the terrorist who murdered Susan Grant," Zarah replied, "and it's thought that I might be able to help somehow."

Lucy reacted coldly. "Why do you say it was a terrorist?"

"It's the word that came into my mind when I saw the murder on television," Zarah replied. "Do you prefer another term?"

Lucy said, "We'll soon know the right word, I think." She handed out the rest of the blinders. She was slightly flushed, there was a trace of acetone on her breath, her voice quivered slightly. Something girly going on here, McGraw thought. He raised his hand. "Forgive me for asking, kids," he said, "but speaking of the bad guys, what if somebody decides to drop a CS grenade through the window of this van while we've all got these blinders on?"

Lucy gave him a resentful look, but Wiggins understood that McGraw's question was not a serious inquiry but a means of changing the subject. "We're covered by two other teams outside the van," he said, "the one that brought Miss Christopher and the one that brought Mr. Macalaster. Besides, it's an hour till the first movie is over; nothing's moving."

"That's a relief," McGraw said. "So what are we going to see?"

"For starters the same footage as before," Lucy said.

"The exact same stuff?" McGraw asked.

"A somewhat edited version," Lucy replied. "But essentially the same, yes."

The footage they watched omitted the pictures taken inside Zarah's house and the behavioral analyses of Zarah and Sturdi. Everything else was there, including the horrifying footage of the assassination. When the blinders came off, Lucy's gaze was fixed on Zarah.

Zarah said, "You're very thorough."

"You mean the surveillance on you and the Eve woman?" Wiggins asked.

"Among other things, yes."

"Now that you've seen exactly what happened to Susan, you'll understand why we ran the surveillance," Lucy said.

Zarah did not reply to this. "What exactly will this program do besides project these images?" she asked.

Wiggins said, "The system has a number of additional analytical functions based on the comparison of images. Lucy is the expert."

Zarah turned to her. "It will analyze physique, sort out habitual movements and gestures, penetrate disguises, make identifications?"

"Exactly," Lucy said. "It's called Logarithmic Impersonation Entropy— LIE for short."

Zarah said, "Then I'd like to suggest that you compare the images of the assassin to the images of me." She looked straight at Lucy, who blushed slightly.

"That's hardly necessary," Wiggins said.

"I'm interested," Zarah said. "Aren't you, Lucy?"

"Why not?" Lucy replied. "It's a start."

They put their blinders back on. Images of Zarah and the assassin appeared side by side, were broken down limb by limb, gesture by gesture, movement by movement. Reduced as before to the form of a birdcage graph, every single image of both women was analyzed in this way, dismembered heads, arms, and legs moving back and forth from one figure to the other. Finally the system put the original images of the two females back together, stood them side by side, turned them in space like manikins on turntables, and flashed the result: LIE = 0.257.

"Meaning what?" McGraw said.

Lucy replied, "The scale is one to ten. Five is a possible impersonation, seven is suspicious, ten is Bingo—absolute confirmation that the two images analyzed belong to one and the same person. Zero, of course, is the opposite of ten. If my arithmetic is right, in this particular case the system says there is less than one chance in two thousand that Zarah and the assassin are the same individual."

"What a relief," Wiggins said.

Zarah said, "Try Sturdi."

Lucy was still resisting this line of analysis; she resisted anything Zarah suggested, McGraw thought. She said, "Did you observe something that makes you think the result will be different?"

"Maybe," Zarah said. "Didn't you?"

Suddenly Lucy looked taken aback, then pensive. The fact was that she *had* felt there was something there the first time she looked at the footage—something indefinable and way out on the edge of perception. But she had been concentrating on Zarah and now the system had just told her she was wrong. "Okay, why not?" she said again. "Here we go."

In moments, the system produced its result: LIE = 7.387. No one commented.

"It's not conclusive," Lucy said at last. "But it is a very high factor of probability."

"Ask it why it's not absolutely sure," Zarah said.

Lucy did so. The system replied, BODY WEIGHT DIFFERENTIAL BETWEEN KILLER & SUSPECT APPROXIMATELY 9.0 KILOGRAMS. MUSCULATURE DIFFERENTIAL 3.78%. GESTURE INDEX INDETERMINATE.

"You said you had all her records as an athlete," Macalaster said. "Can you access those?"

"Just a minute," Lucy said.

Almost instantaneously a series of charts popped up, graphs of Sturdi's body weight over a ten-year period as kept by her high school and college track coaches. Just before and after major competitions in the heptathlon her weight had gone up or down by a factor that ranged from five to nine kilograms.

Macalaster said, "Can you check her performance statistics in practice a month before and after each competition against her times and distances in the competitions themselves?"

The numbers came up; the differences were significantly better in competition than in practice, especially in the events requiring strength, such as the shot put and javelin throw, one-hundred-meter hurdles, and high jump. Her times in the two-hundred- and eight-hundred-meter races also improved, but less dramatically.

"Looks like she either dogs it in practice or she's a real clutch hitter," McGraw said.

"That's one explanation," Macalaster said. "But there's another, more likely one."

"You want to tell us what?" McGraw said.

"Not yet," Macalaster said. "Was it really menstrual cramps that kept her off the Olympic team? Can that be checked?"

"That's not in the data base," Lucy said.

Wiggins said, "What do you think, Lucy? You've always gotten a lot of exercise."

Lucy had gone to college on a track scholarship. Her periods had always been irregular and were even more so now, owing to the regimen of strenuous exercise that was part of her job. Running five miles five days a week and mountain-biking ten miles on the other two, lifting weights every other day, working out with the martial arts trainer and swimming fifty laps once a week, not to mention passing the grueling run-bike-swim-shoot test once a month, all had the effect of turning off the cycle. So did the minute-by-minute ruthless suppression of womanly mannerisms, traits, and instincts that went with doing a man's job. As McGraw had sensed, her body was trying to be a woman's body right now and causing her problems.

Lucy said, "It's possible, but not too likely." She searched the data bank. "But the answer to your question isn't in the system, Ross." She had never called Macalaster by his first name before, and he felt oddly flattered.

McGraw said, "Lemme make a call. I've got a friend." He punched in the number from memory, got through almost immediately, asked the question, waited for a minute, listened to the answer, and said, "Thanks, pal, that's a big help."

McGraw turned to the others. "She was canned from the team because anabolic steroids showed up in her urine sample," he said.

"Just like they found anabolic steroids in the urine in the assassin's toilet," Macalaster said.

"Wait a minute," Lucy said. "Don't forget she'd have to lose nine kilos in one month. That's the interval between the assassination and the period when this subject began following Zarah."

"Have you ever used steroids?" Macalaster asked.

Lucy was offended by the question. "No. They make you crazy."

"According to my trainer at ye gods, thirty days is all it takes to put the muscles on and take them off again," Macalaster said. "Check it out."

"I'll take your word for it," Lucy said. "What do we do now?"

"Good question," McGraw said. "What we've got here is a hypothesis, not proof that will stand up in court. Would you write this in your column, Ross?"

"No," Macalaster said. "But we can't just let it go. This maniac killed a woman for no reason at all."

Zarah said, "Wait. Don't assume there was no reason at all."

"What reason could there be?"

"I don't know," Zarah said. "Does the system recognize that people who live together acquire each other's gestures?"

"I'll ask it," Lucy said.

The answer was yes. Zarah said, "Do you have the video pictures of the carjacker who attacked Senator Garrett with a hammer and stole his car?"

Lucy scanned the data bank and found the home video taken by the neighbor who witnessed the assault. The system compared the carjacker's body language with that of the assassin and flashed a LIE of 8.988.

"The hammer-blow was struck with the left hand," Zarah said. "Ask the system which hand Sturdi used to throw the javelin and put the shot."

Lucy checked. "The right hand," she said. "Why?"

"Because the assassin is left-handed," Zarah replied.

"She *is?*"

Lucy brought up the pictures again. Zarah was right: the killer was a left-handed shooter, and had also thrown the smoke grenade, the one that spiraled like a forward pass, with the left hand.

"That's using the old eyeballs, Zarah," McGraw said. "We all missed it."

"So did the damn system," Lucy said. "And that's supposed to be impossible."

IX

1

Olmedo's cross-examination of Philindros and, even more, his interrogation of Palmer St. Clair 3d, who had stood up to his inquisitor with such bravery, was described by most opinion makers as a brief but foredoomed attempt to return to the nightmare of the witch-hunt long after every rational person in America had realized that there were no such things as witches. Nothing was said about the names St. Clair had confirmed—after all, the Hubbard brothers had already been named in the case, so what was the harm?—but he won admiration and praise for his sturdy refusal to slander Chief Justice Archimedes Hammett.

The counterattack in the news media came mainly in the form of ridicule. On *Newsdawn with Patrick Graham* the president of Yale University said quite truthfully that he had never heard of the Shelley Society and could not locate anyone at Yale, past or present, who had, but in his capacity as a teacher of English literature he could confirm that Percy Bysshe Shelley had been a thoroughly dangerous character who had been an open supporter of the American and French revolutions and wanted to rid the world of kings—in fact, of all tyrants. St. Clair, who made an excellent impression on camera with his bony face and meager flesh, appeared on all six segments of *Newsdawn*, with Graham himself handling the interviews, an honor usually reserved for the durably famous. As Graham put it, St. Clair looked "a bit scorched but quite debonair, everything considered." Simply and modestly St. Clair said, "All I did was what anyone who hates fascism would have done." Graham did not blink at the implication that this term applied to Lockwood, for whom the media's adjective of choice until a few days before had been "Lincolnian."

Asked by Graham what exactly the Shelley Society was and what it did, St. Clair smiled sheepishly and replied, "It's a little embarrassing, actually. We call each other up and recite poetry."

Graham said, "Inflammatory poetry?"

"Oh, yes," St. Clair replied, "*The Mask of Anarchy, Ode to Liberty*, the lot."

Graham made a sober face. "I can understand why you've kept all this a deep dark secret," he said. "Now, as a Yale man on whom the shadow of suspicion has inevitably fallen, I will read you a name: Patrick Graham. Is he a member of the Shelley Society? Answer yes or no." Behind the cameras the unseen studio crew guffawed, a rare occurrence.

St. Clair said, "No."

Graham gave the camera his trademark glower of gruff confidentiality. "I don't know whether to believe this dangerous radical or not," he said.

Insiders knew that all this was on the surface. In its bowels the Cause seethed with righteous anger and fierce apprehension. Tens of thousands of telephone calls, faxes, and E-mail messages warning of the imminent rebirth of McCarthyism poured into the offices of senators, congressmen, and media personalities. Nearly all of these messages expressed support for Hammett and outrage that his integrity had been so shamefully dragged into question. Overnight the drama changed, among radicals, at any rate, from a process that would decide the fate of a President to a moral struggle between the Goliath that was the Establishment and Hammett's David— "armed only with the Constitution," as Patrick Graham put it.

Outside the Senate Conference Room, where the Committee on the Impeachment was locked in a closed meeting until the small hours of the morning, Baxter Busby told Morgan Pike that he himself had already received more than five thousand messages of concern from the American people. "They are running ninety-nine to one in favor of Chief Justice Hammett," he said. "And, Morgan, a lot of those concerned Americans are mentioning Archimedes Hammett as a possible President. They like what they see up there on that high place of judgment—a man of learning and integrity and courage who's absolutely untainted by political ambition."

Morgan Pike said, "So you now regard the Chief Justice as a possible future President? Even in the near future?"

Busby said, "History has a way of matching the man with the hour, especially in this fortunate land of ours, Morgan. But the rule I live by is One thing at a time. And now I have to go in to this meeting and reason with my colleagues." He hurried through the great gleaming doors of the Senate Conference Room.

Morgan Pike signed off, "More later. Back to you, Patrick."

To his attentive viewers, Graham looked very, very thoughtful. "*Much* more, Morgan," he said, "and sooner rather than later, if this reporter is any judge of things past and things to come."

These developments did not surprise Hammett. He understood them for what they were, a predictable, programmed, Skinnerian response by an organism to a stimulus. The organism was the Cause. The stimulus was

Olmedo's charge that there was something false about Hammett. This implied that the secular religion which was the Cause must also somehow be false and deceptive. All but a few of those messages of concern to the Senate and much of the commentary in the news media had come from people who held radical beliefs with evangelical passion and would spring ferociously to their defense at the slightest sign that they were being questioned. Hammett knew their minds: Correctness was virtue; belief was personal validity; doctrine was truth. All else was evil. Hammett was the defender of the faith. Destiny had placed him inside the camp of the enemy in what many in the Cause were beginning to see—Graham again: he had superb writers—as "the Yorktown of the second American Revolution," an engagement on which the whole future of truth and justice turned.

All this Hammett explained, in slightly different terminology, to Sturdi and Slim, who had brought him dinner in a thermos bag. Since the beginning of the trial he had been living in his chambers at the Supreme Court, an impenetrable fortress, seeing no one, speaking to no one, knowing nothing of what anyone had done or was planning to do. He had not seen or heard from Julian since his confirmation. Busby had told him nothing. Slim and Sturdi told him nothing about the Attenborough case or anything else that might be discoverable by the media or the Senate. His telephone life, formerly so consuming, had come to a stop; every day, dozens of calls from journalists, members of the Apparatus, and Capitol Hill went unanswered. All this was by design: Hammett always worked best from hiding, and where this situation was concerned he had more reason to conceal his role, to quarantine himself from any possible contamination, than ever before in his life. No Shelleyan had called him in weeks. Owing to Julian's decision, taken weeks before at the Harbor in the meeting with Busby and Horace, to isolate him from the actual management of this crisis, Hammett knew nothing of Julian's plans or projects. He'd had no warning at all that his cell-fellow Palmer St. Clair 3d was going to drop out of the sky and be questioned about the Shelley Society, no inkling that St. Clair had done what he had done in regard to Macalaster and the Lockwood tape. In fact he was amazed that Julian, or whoever it was who had managed this particular operation, had even thought of St. Clair or that St. Clair had been able to carry out the mission with such efficiency. Was it possible that Horace, the spy of spies, had trained him?

With Slim to his left as always to accommodate her left-handedness, Sturdi to his right, Hammett ate his supper (two kinds of squash, garlic, dried figs and prunes and unsalted farmer's cheese in a sweet sauce over brown rice, with boiled spring water to drink), while watching a video recording of the day's proceedings in the Senate. Although he had perfect hearing, his television set was equipped with a closed-caption function. What he saw on the muted screen confirmed his inner version of what had happened that day. A magisterial Hammett made a silent ruling, solemn and composed. His remark about the List of Names scrolled across the bottom of the screen. The camera panned to the choleric visage of Amzi Whipple on the floor of the Senate, then to the ravaged face of Attenborough in the gallery, then to Olmedo's silent-movie Latin-lover countenance. Finally, turning to the visitors' gallery, it showed the identical knowing half-smiles on the faces of the people of the Cause. In the Skinnerian sense, these men and women were reinforced by every word, every ruling, every gesture Hammett made. Each of them was touched by the sound of Hammett's words in exactly the same part of his psychology, and all reacted as one.

This was not mere chance, either. Hammett had seen what could happen, what advantages could accrue, as soon as Olmedo went into his act, and as soon as poor terrified St. Clair had been dragged into the dock, the Chief Justice *had* given the signal: *The List of Names.* He had made an instantly recognizable reference and that was what had activated the organism. That was the stimulus that set off the whole reaction, projecting into every good person's mind the famous black-and-white television image of unshaven, uncouth, unspeakable Joe McCarthy, while in the background the quavering voice of reason asked, "Have you no decency, sir? At long last, have you no decency?" Hammett was pleased with himself; he had triggered it all with subliminals. It did not begin with Skinner or even Pavlov. His grandfather Gika Mavromikháli, lying in wait on the Mesa Mani for a hidden enemy to show himself, had willed his target to urinate, and when he did so after hours of absorbing Gika's irresistible thoughts, the old fighter aimed his rifle by sense of smell and killed him. Ah, Grandfather, Hammett thought.

The recording came to the part in which St. Clair was describing his encounter with the bicyclist. Hammett had finished his plate. Sturdi's was untouched; she crouched in her chair beside him as if she meant to spring into the monitor and grapple with Olmedo in its green electronic depths as with a shark. Hammett said, "That wasn't you, I hope?"

Sturdi turned a pale, frowning face toward him. "What wasn't me?"

"The androgynous messenger in yellow goggles on the bike. It wasn't you."

"What a question."

"It wasn't an accusation," Hammett said, "it was a pleasantry. Lighten up, Sturdevant. You seem tense, disturbed."

In jest he always called her by the name she had used before she changed it to Eve, and since it was Hammett, Sturdi did not mind. "Who wouldn't be disturbed with all that's happening?" she said. "Aren't you?"

"All this is just the Establishment behaving according to its nature," Hammett said. "What bothers you in particular?"

"This Shelley Society business."

"Because you didn't know it existed?" He smiled. "Or if it actually does exist?"

"How *should* I know? I have no need to know. But somebody did need to know in order to do what was done today. All those details. If it does exist, they penetrated it. How?"

"Sounds like they tapped telephones."

"But they had to know which phones to tap. How could they possibly know whom to tap if only the members know who they are?"

"Treason, obviously."

"I agree," Sturdi said. "Do you remember your concerns about a certain relative of the Hubbard brothers?"

"Ah, the ubiquitous, all-seeing Lady Zed," Hammett said. "The Valkyrie. What about her?"

"Maybe you were right. Maybe she did hear something from someone in the family and pass it on to Lockwood in one of those secret meetings she had with him. Her father must have been a member of the Shelley Society."

"Her father went to Harvard," Hammett said. "The Harvards don't have any secrets."

This was the sort of detail Hammett loved to know and reveal. After his enormous success today, he was in one of his playful, almost giddy moods. Sturdi did not like his mood; it disturbed her when his sense of humor ran away with him like this. It wasn't the real him; he was like a *man* at such moments. She shot a glance at Slim. Coming to her aid, Slim said, "The O.G. bequeathed Zarah Christopher his house. Surely *he* must have been a member."

Hammett happened to know that the O.G. had been in the same cell as the Hubbards' father and Paul Christopher's father. Hammett raised his eyebrows as if intrigued by Slim's suggestion but kept this information to himself. He was not prepared to admit even to Slim and Sturdi that he knew anything about the Shelley Society. He knew that they would admire him for this. He also knew that withholding information from Sturdi acted as a stimulus to her. Some of her most remarkable behavior had been a response to this. When she needed managing, he would *not* tell her something. She would respond with resentment. He would then reinforce her desire to be trusted with an irrelevant scrap of data that made her even more curious. Thereupon she would go out and do something she supposed he wanted her to do (she did not always read his wishes accurately), and then he would reward her, temporarily, with the confidence she craved.

Both Hammett and Sturdi enjoyed the game; Slim did not like it at all because it reduced her control over Sturdi. Now, knowing that Slim understood what was going on and did not approve, Hammett fed Sturdi the irrelevancy. "She's everywhere, I agree," he said.

"Who's everywhere?" Sturdi said carelessly, but an excited light began to kindle in her wild Romany eyes. She looked more than ever like a Gypsy tonight, dark and full of the lore of the caravan. As always in his presence, she was wearing a bandanna instead of one of her innumerable wigs; he was allergic to wigs, disgusted by the idea of dead hair decorating the head of a living person.

"Lady Zed is everywhere, on both sides of Armageddon," he replied. "Sowing doubt and disharmony. It's amazing. I asked Julian why she was shacking up with Mallory when he's trying to put her whole family in jail. He had no reply."

"The WASPs invariably choose family over principle even though they pretend to do the opposite."

"There's more to it than that. Julian holds her in some kind of ancestral awe. Hubbards and Christophers have been marrying each other for a couple of centuries. Julian told me so. He says the saying in their family is 'The Christophers screwed the Hubbards smart.' "

"Charming," Slim said. "Sturdi, help me with the dishes."

Hammett was enjoying himself, the last thing he had expected to be doing when he got up that morning. He held up a hand, freezing the women in place. He said, "I said to Julian, Suppose they're making little Mallorys and putting them in the deep freeze? Imagine a child of Mallory and that Valkyrie being gestated a thousand years from now, when the species has evolved beyond suspicion and greed and learned perfect trust. With that combination of regressive genes the little fiend would take over the world in a matter of hours." There was no truth in this story: Hammett was in a teasing mode. The light went out in Sturdi's eyes; she gritted her teeth. He saw that his joke had disturbed her. She had no sense of humor, none at all; in that respect as in so many others she was a foot soldier of the Cause par excellence. Slim put a hand on her arm before she could blurt out whatever was on her mind; Hammett was slow to forgive outbursts.

"The dishes," Slim said calmly, "and then home. We all have to get up early in the morning."

As Sturdi stuffed sterile plastic plates and glasses into a bag, Slim compressed her lips, looked at Hammett, and shook her head in a parody of disapproval. Most of the time the two women merged in Hammett's mind into a single female; it was only at moments like this that he saw how different they were: Sturdi slow-witted, muscular, and swarthy; Slim quick-minded, fair, and lithe—and the stronger of the two in every way.

Hammett did his best to smooth things over. "It was all in fun, Sturdevant," he said. She ignored him. He said, "Let's play famous sayings. I'll start. 'Everyone should have some fun every day. A day without fun is a day wasted.' Who said that?"

Sturdi sulked. Slim said, "I have no idea."

Hammett said, "Give up? It was Dwight D. Eisenhower. At a presidential press conference in 1957, one of his famous jabberwockies. Ike would turn over in his grave if he knew how obediently the news media have followed his advice."

Even though none of the three actually remembered Eisenhower, they knew that the mention of his name was always good for a chuckle in the right company. Slim smiled; Sturdi relaxed.

2

At Camp David, Lockwood hurled the morning press summary into the fireplace. "I told you it would backfire, damnit!" he said. Pages caught fire, giving off an acrid chemical odor. A few fluttered up the chimney on the draft. Blackstone watched them go, unsure that he could conceal his true feelings if he shifted his gaze and met the red feral glare in Lockwood's eyes. The President said, "Where the hell is Olmedo? I want to talk to him before he does something like this again."

"He'll be here soon."

"Why isn't he here now?"

"He's meeting with Senators Clark and Whipple to discuss today's proceedings," Blackstone said.

"At seven o'clock in the morning?"

"The schedule is tight, Mr. President. The defense case on the first article of impeachment commences today, assuming that the trial continues."

"It'll continue, all right." Lockwood uttered a hollow laugh. "Empty exercise though it is after yesterday." Then, with a sudden crafty stare, "Why the hell wouldn't it continue?"

"As you will recall, Olmedo made a motion for a mistrial."

"Showboating. Don't mean a thing. Nobody but a senator can make a motion on the floor of the Senate."

"That's what is being discussed. Procedure. The next step."

"The next step is to subpoena that damn tape Jack Philindros made, the unexpurgated version, and get it on record that I never told him to kill that old man or any of the rest of it."

Blackstone, perfectly controlled, said, "With respect, Mr. President, that's the worst thing we could do. We don't know what's on that tape, if it exists, and besides, it's valueless as corroboration in light of the experts' reports on the Macalaster tape and Olmedo's cross-examination of Philindros."

" 'Valueless'? How can it be valueless if it's got the truth on it?"

"We have shown that tapes can be altered. After this, no tape recording can be accepted without question as evidence in this trial. That was our objective."

Lockwood reared back and made his windmill gesture signifying that he had just been driven beyond the limits of human endurance. "Then you cut me off at the ankles, Spats. Jesus!"

"Not at all, Mr. President," Blackstone said. "We, more accurately Alfonso Olmedo, laid the basis for a resolution of this case on the terms you laid down—your exoneration of blame for the high crimes and misdemeanors named in the articles of impeachment."

" 'Exoneration of *blame*'? What about guilt?"

"You see the distinction, sir. These things happened, but you did not participate. That has always been the thrust of our defense."

"I thought the idea was to put the blame on the Hubbard boys."

"That's the next step. First we established that certain things happened. Now we will demonstrate that they happened not only without your knowledge but against your wishes, even by treachery."

"And you figure Julian and Horace will go right along with that?"

"They will have no other choice. We've got the goods on them and their accomplices. I can't put it more simply than that."

"*I* can," Lockwood said. "You'll knock off two spear-carriers and wound a few others. What the hell does that accomplish? I am the responsible officer of the government."

"Yes," Blackstone said. "But it is our hope that making the case for perfidy by your trusted aides will restore the sympathy and the affection of the nation to you and preserve an honorable place for you in history. As I understood it, that was the objective you laid down."

"Damn right it was. But it's not what I'm willing to settle for and Alfonso knows that. Who told you that you could stipulate that the damn election was stolen?"

Despite the earliness of the hour, Blackstone was dressed in his usual waxworks style: glossy pumps, pin-striped three-piece suit with only the top button of the four-button coat fastened, stiff collar, flowing cravat, pearl stickpin, gold watch chain with Phi Beta Kappa key slung across his middle. There were no clocks in this room, another omission designed by Julian as an aid to presidential relaxation. Blackstone took out his antique chiming watch.

"We don't plan to stipulate anything, Mr. President," he said. "But the fact that fraud took place will be established. There is nothing we can do to prevent that. However, it is entirely possible that the Senate will, in fact, find it convenient to declare a mistrial."

The sound of a helicopter engine came to their ears. Blackstone nodded in satisfaction and put his watch back into his waistcoat pocket.

Lockwood said, "Is that Alfonso?"

"I believe so, Mr. President," Blackstone said. "The Speaker and the Majority Leader may come with him."

"What for?"

"Your attorney believes, and I agree, that the moment has come to discuss an arrangement that will be satisfactory to all sides, Mr. President."

"What about 'what's best for the country'?" Lockwood said. "That's the usual line at a moment like this."

This time Blackstone met his eyes. "That is your area of competence, Mr. President," he said.

Lockwood looked down on him, all exasperation spent. "You want me to cop a plea," he said. "Is that what your partner and the rest of 'em are coming up here to advise me to do?"

"Essentially, yes," Blackstone replied. "But I beg of you, sir." He paused. "Whatever it is that they have come to tell you, listen."

3

Lockwood took this advice, and as he heard what Sam Clark had to tell him he grew calmer and calmer, changing before Blackstone's eyes from the petulant, profane client he had just been dealing with into something resembling the presidential, indeed Lincolnian, figure Blackstone had believed him to be before coming to work for him. Lockwood's vocabulary did not change, just his tone and demeanor.

Clark and the other members of the Senate Committee on the Impeachment had been up most of the night listening to a filibuster by Senator Busby. "What Tucker said was going to happen is starting to happen," Clark said. "What Busby wants to do is end it today, go right to a vote on the question of the charges of election fraud."

"How?" Lockwood said. "The trial isn't over."

"I'm not talking about the trial," Clark said. "Busby wants to do this during the regular morning session of the Senate. He says the country can't stand another moment's delay; this crisis is tearing it apart."

"So he's going to start a second circus in the media?"

"Let me continue, Mr. President," said Clark. "What he plans to do is introduce a resolution vacating Congress's certification of the election results. If it is adopted, the election will be null and void. In my opinion it will pass the Senate if it gets to the floor. Mallory's party will have to vote for it right down the line. Busby and some of his friends will join them."

"Then it goes over to the House. Tucker?"

"It'll pass," Attenborough said.

"And the moment it does, I stop being President," Lockwood said. "Is that it?"

"Not exactly," Attenborough said. "Like Sam said yesterday, what happens is that the United States of America ceases to have a President."

"That's the objective," Clark said. "Busby kept talking about a constitutional solution."

"Exact words?" Lockwood said.

"He kept repeating them. 'A pragmatic, constitutional way out. A new beginning in honor.' "

"Did he say what he meant by that?"

"He didn't have to. He's been working the phones to the media talking on background about how history is matching the man with the hour in the person of the Chief Justice."

"Did anyone press him?"

"Amzi did. He said, 'Senator, when you say all these admiring things about the ingenuity of the Founding Fathers, you wouldn't happen to be talking about the nonqualification provisions of Article Two and the Twentieth Amendment, would you?' Busby just went on repeating himself as if he hadn't even heard the question."

"Amzi let it go at that?"

Clark said, "I think Amzi figured he already had his answer. If the plan works, there'll be no other way to go."

Lockwood said, "There's something else. How healthy are you, Tucker?"

"Not healthy enough to worry about," Attenborough said. "But that'll work out. Let Sam finish."

Clark said, "That was my next point. The Twenty-fifth Amendment never looked like a worse solution. They've set the whole thing up. First they did what they did to Tucker, with the idea of making him unthinkable as your successor. Nobody can imagine Otis running the country, fine old gentleman that he is. Busby's next step will be to concede how right the media have been about this terrible dilemma, wrap himself in the flag, and cry, 'There's only one way to save America! Change the law!' "

"This doesn't sound much better for Franklin than it does for me or old Tucker here," Lockwood said. "What's Amzi really going to do?"

"I don't think he knows yet," Clark replied. "He's suspicious as hell. But if the validity of the election comes to a vote, his party has got to vote to invalidate. Otherwise they give up the ghost."

"What you all are saying is that they're so damn smart they've got us coming and going, fifteen ways from Sunday."

"Not quite yet they haven't," Attenborough said. "Not as long as you're the legal, sworn-in President. And for the moment that's exactly what you are, no matter what happened in New York, Michigan, and California."

Lockwood said, "You've got a plan."

"I do," Attenborough said.

"Shoot," Lockwood said.

"I'll tell you what you need to know but I'll be damned if I'll conspire," Attenborough said. "All you need to know is this: If you want to save the country, you've got to resign. Probably today. It's the only way."

"And make Franklin President?"

"No. At least not right away."

"You think Franklin will buy that?"

Attenborough sighed. "I hope he will," he said. "I think he will."

"What makes you so hopeful, knowing Franklin?"

"Same reason you'll give it up, same reason I will."

"You don't have it yet."

"Good point," Attenborough said. "But let that dog lie. Franklin may be worth a couple of billion now, but he grew up just like you and me and Sam, poor as Job's off ox on a hardscrabble farm in a place the Lord forgot. In his mind and gonads he's a poor boy and he'll never be anything else. He knows what it means when things go wrong and the well runs dry and there's no way out."

"That's all you're going to tell me?"

"For now. I'm going to talk to Franklin. Then I'm going to talk to you again. Then I'm going to talk to one other person who's the key to the whole thing. I'll call you when I'm done. Then you can decide if you want to come along with the rest of us."

Lockwood examined Attenborough. The Speaker was having one of his coughing fits, yellow eyes staring, limbs jerking. Lockwood felt a tug at his heart. Poor little cuss looked like somebody had skinned him, tanned the hide, and then sewed him back up in it. He looked like he wanted to get the hell out of that poisoned body of his and was just barely resisting the temptation. Lockwood thought this but did not shout it out, one of the rare times in his life when he had resisted this particular temptation.

"All right, Tucker," the President said, when the Speaker's coughing subsided. "You do what you've got to do. When you've done it, call me up here. I'm not going anywhere. Not right now, anyhow."

4
___

When Sam Clark returned to his office he received a telephone call on his private line, the one he always answered himself. It was from Associate Justice Bobby M. Poole of the Supreme Court, a nice but remote man with whom he rarely spoke beyond routine social pleasantries because Poole was a deep-dyed conservative and Clark was not.

Poole's hesitant North Carolina voice said, "Your Committee on the Impeachment, Senator, is that, quote, the committee to receive evidence and take testimony, end quote, described in Rule Eleven of *The Conduct of Impeachment Trials in the Senate?*"

Clark said, "Yes, Mr. Justice Poole, it is."

"Then I may have something for you. But first I must ask you for a clarification so as not to risk wasting your time."

"Go right ahead, sir."

Poole said, "In Mr. Olmedo's cross-examination of the witness St. Clair yesterday, I was struck by a reference to a Mickey Finn, followed by a somewhat obscure reference to fly fishing. May I take it that the Mickey Finn referred to was a fishing fly?"

"If I remember the supporting evidence correctly, yes, I believe so," Clark said.

"The Mickey Finn is a most unusual fly that went out of general use more than forty years ago, then made a comeback. As you may not know, I tie my own flies."

"I did know that, sir. I'm a fisherman too."

"Then we must go out together some weekend. I own two miles of an excellent private stream, stocked with brookies, only two hours away in Pennsylvania."

"I'd enjoy that."

"I tie flies here in my chambers while pondering cases that come before the Court," Poole said. "My objective is to tie every fly ever known to fishermen, and thanks to the Court's busy calendar I have finished a good many. I keep them on the credenza behind my desk, mounted in a row of albums rather like old-fashioned snapshot books except that the pages are faced with velvet with little windows in them just big enough for a fly. My wife makes these pages and mounts the specimens in alphabetical order, marked underneath with the earliest known date of use. Each has a beautifully written label. Calligraphy is one of Mrs. Poole's hobbies."

"Very nice. And handy too, in case you want to look at them."

"Exactly. One of the flies I tied was the Mickey Finn. Now we come to the point of this call. After watching that cross-examination I got down my M-to-Z volume for streamers. As you undoubtedly know, the Mickey Finn is not a dry fly but a streamer. That particular fly was missing from its place between the Marabou Muddler and the Muddler Minnow. It had been torn out of the album. Roughly." He said no more.

Clark said, "I see."

"As I said," Poole said, "it is not a common fly. The album it was in is part of the streamer collection."

"I've never seen one myself."

"The dominant color is yellow with admixtures of red and white," Poole said.

"I don't suppose there's ever been too much worry about petty theft in the Supreme Court."

"No," Poole said. "But I have now taken the precaution of locking my albums in the safe in case you'd ever like to have a look at them. I have also impounded the surveillance camera tapes for a certain period of time, should your committee wish to examine them."

"Thank you for your call, sir. I may need to get back to you."

"Please don't hesitate to do so, Mr. Majority Leader," Poole said.

5

Inside the parked ♂ ↔ ♀ van, Lucy ran down the data base on Sturdi. It was extensive, even exhaustive. As in Lockwood's earlier case, Sturdi's athleticism had made everything possible for her: she was a working-class girl from Houston who would never have become the first member of her family to go to college if she had not been able to run faster and jump higher than most boys. She had attached herself early in her campus life to the belief system of the people who befriended her at Berkeley, and she collaborated eagerly thereafter in the process of transforming herself from an individual into a type.

"The point is, she *is* a type," Lucy said. "And types are predictable."

"You're right," Zarah said. "But remember, the computer can tell us who Sturdi knows, what Sturdi knows or ought to know, what the combination of traits and experience that make up Sturdi ought to produce. That may reinforce our suspicions. But it won't tell us who the assassin is. The assassin, and only the assassin, can give us that information."

Lucy frowned in bewilderment. Why did Zarah keep turning them away from the obvious conclusions? What was her purpose? Suspicion of Zarah welled up in her again. She said, "So where do you suggest we go from here, Zarah?"

"Let's look at what we've got on the assassin," Zarah said.

"What point is there in watching Susan die again?" Lucy said. She was sickened by the prospect.

"Not those pictures," McGraw said. "The police data from the crime scene."

Lucy shrugged. At almost the same instant, the expression on her face changed, as if she had suddenly remembered something. "You're going to have to excuse me for a minute," she said. "I need some privacy." She handed the control to Wiggins.

With a look of female understanding, Zarah said, "Do you want me to go with you?"

Lucy said, "No. Absolutely not. I don't need to be here while you search. I'm already familiar with all the files." She switched off the interior lights so that no one could see into the van as she got out of it, slid back the door, and stepped out.

"All right," Wiggins said. "There's not much, just what was found in the killer's room." He projected images of the interior of the room: the religious graffiti on the walls in Arabic and English, the newspaper clippings pasted onto the Sheetrock, which apparently had been punched out by angry fists, the diary entries, the shabby prayer rug and well-thumbed Koran left behind. Printed data scrolled before their eyes: interviews with witnesses, inventories of the scene, forensic reports. "The only thing not mentioned here is Ross's tidbit about the anabolic steroids in the urine," Wiggins said. "We weren't told about that."

"It seems to be significant," Macalaster said.

"No question," Wiggins said. "That's why the cops kept it quiet."

The diaries came up again, the ill-formed handwriting transcribed into type. Wiggins highlighted passages of special interest. "Presents self as father of frozen embryos about to be shipped into outer space as slave labor," he said.

Zarah said, "This person was obsessed with frozen embryos."

Wiggins nodded, but without agreeing. "That is the surface indication," he said. "But we've been unsure how genuine it is."

"How do you mean?" Zarah asked.

"Well, it's crazy stuff," Wiggins replied. "Almost a little *too* crazy."

McGraw said, "Excuse me, but let me tell you there's no such thing as too crazy."

"Agreed," Wiggins said. Zarah was watching him intently, waiting for him to explain. He said, "The history of assassins has been that they construct a narrative history of their own psychosis. The elements are always essentially the same—news clippings about the target, pictures of the target *as* a target with bull's-eyes drawn over the face, prophetic writings on the wall, a diary that tells all."

"What the assassin is doing is making a case for the rectitude of his act," Macalaster said.

"Exactly, but that's easy to fake," Wiggins said. "Granted, a real psychopath would follow the pattern. But so would a calculating killer who wanted to be *taken* for a psychopath."

"So you think this whole body of evidence was faked to throw investigators off the trail by fulfilling their preconceptions?"

"We don't know that, but we haven't dismissed the possibility."

"Why?"

"For one thing the physical evidence provided absolutely no clue to the killer's real identity," Wiggins said. "Not a fingerprint was found, not a handprint, not a fingernail clipping, no semen or fecal smear in the bed. Only that urine in the john, a strange oversight. It has seemed to us that the person who did this was highly intelligent, highly organized, following a detailed plan. All the diary entries and the graffiti, for example, seem to have been written with the left hand by a right-handed person."

"Are you sure about that?" Zarah asked.

"Oops, a left-handed person using the right hand; sorry," Wiggins said. "The fact remains that this was no dumbbell."

"You don't have to be stupid to be crazy," McGraw said. "But I agree it's a little funny. Something else is funny: This assassin was highly trained. A lot of rehearsal went into that hit. Terrorists are slobs. They don't usually have that kind of discipline outside of the movies."

"That's right," Wiggins said. "But let me finish my thought about the nature of the evidence. First, the so-called obsession. The idea that the frozen embryos of minority persons are going to be shipped to the moons of Jupiter and used as slave labor in mines that don't even exist is just too delusional, too far out. Anyone who was going to kill Mallory would kill him for what he is, not for what he might do as Emperor of the Dark Side in some science-fiction scenario out of *Counterculture Comics*. At least that's been our working hypothesis."

Zarah said, "It's your thesis that the assassin did not really believe what the diary says was the reason for the killing?"

"That's right. It was an elaborate lie from start to finish. Also, of course, it was a nice potential insanity defense if the assassin got caught. Which was a high order of probability, considering the time and place and the presence of worldwide television, not to mention several hundred cops and agents." Wiggins paused. "Including my wife and myself."

Wiggins's phone rang. "Speaking of which, she's back," he said, switching off the lights and opening the door. When the lights came back on, they saw a change in Lucy. She was shaken, pale. Clearly she had been thinking a terrible thought.

Zarah said, "Lucy, we were discussing the assassin's obsession with frozen embryos. Wiggins doesn't think it's significant."

"I didn't say that," Wiggins said, his eyes fixed anxiously on Lucy's stricken face. "What I wanted to convey was the thought that it was not a reason to kill Mallory, even for a psychopath."

Zarah said, "But it wasn't Mallory who was killed. It was Susan Grant."

"We have worked on the assumption that this outcome was happenstance," Wiggins said, "that Mallory was the primary target and shooting Susan was a mistake."

"Oh?" Zarah said. "Why, when the assassin made no other mistakes of any kind?"

Lucy took several deep breaths, recovered her composure, and broke in. "Two reasons," she said. "First, as we have all seen for ourselves, Susan stepped between Mallory and the assassin and took the bullets for him. And second—"

Lucy broke off. Her eyes filled with tears. She looked desperately at Wiggins and her hand flew to her mouth.

Gently he said, "And second *what*, Lucy?"

Lucy said, "We thought that killing Susan could change nothing."

McGraw said, "But?"

Lucy said, "But it could. Susan was pregnant."

Macalaster said, "Wait a minute! That didn't show up in the autopsy, did it?"

"No," Lucy said. "It wouldn't. She was only eight days pregnant. She'd taken the test, and she was going to go down to the Morning After Clinic that afternoon after the speech, to have the embryo recovered."

McGraw said, "And frozen?"

"That's right. It was the last day it could be done. She asked me to go with her—just me alone. Not as a security person, but as a woman who had been through it herself."

Zarah said, "You mean she made an appointment? In her own name?"

"I made it for her. It was a secret. She was going to tell Mallory after he got the presidency back, then be reimplanted. She had to do it soon. Susan was thirty-seven, a little older than me. We talked about doing it together; Wiggins and I have a child in amniosis. Susan knew that; she and I talked about doing twins."

" 'Doing twins'?" Zarah asked.

"The embryo can be divided in the lab before implantation," Lucy explained. "It's not a complicated procedure. You get identical twins."

McGraw said, "How many days before her death was the appointment made?"

"Seven," Lucy said. "She took the test the morning after unprotected intercourse. There's a home test kit. One drop of blood on a patch and you know."

"And the killer rented the room six days before Susan was killed?" McGraw said. "One day after you called the Morning After Clinic. Is that right?"

"That's right," Wiggins said.

McGraw said, "Do you know who you talked to at the clinic?"

"It's got to be in the computer," Lucy said. "My God, Wiggins. Where has my mind been?"

Wiggins looked long into his wife's desolated eyes. He said, "I wonder if you folks would mind leaving Lucy and me alone for a few minutes."

Zarah, Macalaster, and McGraw went outside the van into the parking lot: firefly luminescence of sodium lights, smell of suburban greenery, metallic chill given off by hundreds of parked cars. Macalaster said, "Something has to be done about this."

"That may not be so easy," McGraw said. "What we've got here, if we've got anything at all, is one hundred percent circumstantial. No D.A. would move on it. The killer would have to try to do the same thing again and get caught. You'd have to grab this maniac in the act."

"Set something up?" Macalaster said.

"It's been known to happen," McGraw replied.

Zarah had been staring at the van, her thoughts obviously with the other women inside it, one dead, the other alive. "Maybe it would be easier than you think," she said. "After all, we now know what activates the maniac, don't we? It's frozen embryos—but not transplanting them as slaves to the moons of Jupiter. It's the idea of a woman conceiving a child of Mallory's right here on earth."

There was a silence. "Makes sense to me," McGraw said at last. "But it's one hell of a risk."

6

The op-ed pages of the leading Washington, New York, and Los Angeles newspapers carried articles by elder statesmen of Lockwood's party questioning the capability of Attenborough, an accused rapist, to exert moral authority if he succeeded to the presidency. All three writers also mentioned, with delicacy but with concern, the advanced age and fragile health of Otis Dyer, citing the president pro tempore's tendency to call his colleagues by the names of senators long departed. He habitually addressed Baxter Busby as "Senator Fulbright" and Amzi Whipple as "Ev," apparently confusing him with an earlier archconservative Minority Leader, Everett Dirksen of Illinois.

It was Dyer who was presiding over the Senate when Busby rose in the regular morning session to move for the repeal of the Senate's certification of the results of the presidential election. Busby also spoke of moral authority. "No President can govern without it," he said to the nearly empty chamber and to the cameras. "Some will say that the alternatives to the present crisis are too frightening to contemplate. To those pessimists I respond, 'Remember the Constitution of the United States of America.' This is a government of laws, not men, and that great document will be a guide to us even in this darkest hour of American democracy." At this a number of Malloryite senators rose and walked out of the chamber. Busby took this as an excellent sign that his argument was having the desired effect.

When at last he finished, Otis Dyer, upright and alert in the chair, briskly recognized Senator Wilbur E. Garrett, to whom many other senators had yielded their time. Garrett, a loquacious man by nature, held the floor, retelling homilies from the lives of the Founding Fathers, until the Senate adjourned two hours later and reconstituted itself as a court of impeachment. This maneuver kept Busby's motion from coming to a vote, or even being seconded. During the trial, of course, neither Busby's motion nor any other regular business of the Senate could be conducted.

Mallory watched the broadcast of Busby's speech while talking to O. N. Laster of Universal Energy on the telephone. "Franklin," Laster said from Chile, "I thought you'd want to know that Patrick Graham is going to break a story on the evening news saying that Tucker Attenborough is dying from cirrhosis of the liver."

"Is the story true?" Mallory asked.

"No question. He's got no more than a couple of weeks to live. One of our subsidiaries runs the hospital whose staff Graham suborned to get his story, so I was able to check. It's also true that Otis Dyer is terminally gaga. Not a reassuring picture, Franklin."

Neither man paused to express pious sentiments. Though both liked Attenborough, he had done this to himself. Mallory said, "What other unpleasant truths do you have for me this morning, Oz?"

"Busby has talked to at least fifteen other senators about vacating the election and finding a constitutional way around the line of succession."

"By way of the Twentieth Amendment."

"I see you're on top of things. The media's no longer even mentioning your name in connection with the presidency. The radicals are burning up the phone lines and mobbing the cloakrooms lobbying for what they're calling 'the constitutional deliverance.' They intend to throw out the election, burn the ballots, and appoint Archimedes M. Hammett President of the United States."

"Does this outcome seem in any way implausible to you?"

"You must be joking," Laster said. "They stole the election. Getting caught was a little setback, but if the original plan didn't work, why wouldn't they steal the presidency? Franklin, you finally see what's happening, don't you?"

"Yes," Mallory said. "A coup d'état, exactly as you predicted. But it hasn't happened yet."

"No, but the night is young. You'd better move your ass, because Lockwood sure as hell can't handle this unless he's ready to order the Air Force to nuke the Supreme Court."

"I don't think they'd carry out the mission."

"Alas and alack. Franklin, *act!*"

Mallory disconnected and put through a call to Albert Tyler.

On hearing Mallory's voice, Albert said, "Thank you for calling back. The Speaker said to tell you he thinks you two should go for a short ride in your airplane. Right away. Things happening."

It was ten-thirty in the morning. Mallory said, "Can you get him to the Baltimore airport by noon, straight up? A young couple will meet you in front of the general aviation terminal. You'll be able to drive right to the plane."

"He'll be there," Albert said. "My car, dark-green '99 Buick, bad dent from a red car in the right front fender."

"The young couple will be—"

Albert interrupted again. "Can't miss your boys and girls," he said.

7

In the Gulfstream, as it climbed steeply through thirty thousand feet above Chesapeake Bay, Attenborough said, "I saw Frosty this morning up at Camp David."

"How's he holding up?" Mallory asked.

"All right. He understands that he's got to go."

"But not on my terms," Mallory said.

"If you mean concede the election four months after the fact and after he's let himself be sworn in, no. But he wants to do what's right."

"Which is?"

"Invoke the Twenty-fifth Amendment."

"That has been suggested to him before."

"Yes, sir, I know that. But there's a time to keep and a time to cast away. Book of Ecclesiastes, chapter the third, verse the sixth."

Mallory said, "Who keeps and who casts away?"

"Everybody does a little of both," Attenborough said. "You spent a few years on the Hill and you've been watching this freak show on the TV, so you know just as well as I do that Congress in its present state of uproar is about as likely to name you Vice President so's you can become President through the back door as to levitate the Capitol dome by burning chicken feathers and whistling 'Dixie.' "

Attenborough coughed, waving a hand for patience. Albert Tyler, who had come aboard with him, holding him upright as he labored up the gangway, now came down the aisle of the Gulfstream and offered him what looked like a half-full glass of spring water. Attenborough drained it and said, "Got any pills?" Albert said, "Not time for one yet, Mr. Speaker." He went back to the rear seat and looked out the window. Mallory had thought that the two men, who had been inseparable ever since he'd known them, were about the same age, but now Albert looked twenty years younger.

The Speaker went on with his thought. "I think we've got till sundown to settle this thing, Franklin," he said. "That slick New York lawyer of Frosty's may slow 'em up a little bit in the trial, but what we've got to work with is the rest of today. No more. Do you agree with me on that?"

"Yes, more or less," Mallory said. "Let's get down to it, Tucker."

After his drink, Attenborough looked better, breathed more easily, sounded more like himself. He said, "The key is control of the Senate. Whoever has the majority calls the tune. Do you agree with that?"

"Yes."

"That's your down payment," Attenborough said.

Mallory said, "What is?"

"The Senate. This is the way it'll go. Lockwood resigns. I become President and immediately—in my first public statement—nominate a Vice President the Congress has to approve. *Has* to. Not you, for reasons already stated. One of their own, like Jerry Ford was the last time the radicals tried to take over the world. Time before that, with Andrew Johnson, it was the radicals again. Three different situations, three different parties, three different centuries. Same sorry hate-filled bunch who think they're smarter than the people every time. Remember that."

"I'm keenly aware of it, Tucker. Who are we talking about for Vice President?"

"Sam Clark."

"No," Mallory said. "Amzi Whipple."

Attenborough said, "I can see you've been thinking about this. But hear me out. Your way won't work; it's too obvious and the radicals would go ape. Sam is from Massachusetts, just like you. The governor up there is a member of your party. He'll appoint a good soldier to the vacancy; he might even discuss it with you beforehand as head of the party. The Senate will reorganize immediately with Amzi as Majority Leader, and Sam will be approved in a day."

"Both houses?"

"Yes. I'm owed more favors by the membership of the House than there's cactus in Texas, and all I'm going to ask is just this one last thing in return."

"All this is going to happen in one day?" Mallory said. "Nobody can make Congress move that fast."

"They'll have an incentive," Attenborough said. "You know what Frosty said to me? He said, 'If you get my job you'll be a ten-minute President.' He was right, because what I'll do as soon as Sam's approved is invoke the Twenty-fifth Amendment and hand it over to him."

"Invoke it on what grounds?"

"That I've just about finished drinking myself to death and need a few more days to wind up the job."

"Is that the case, Tucker?"

"Look at me," Attenborough said tersely. "You want a note from my doctor?"

"I'm sorry to hear it."

"So was I. Always thought it was malaria," Attenborough said. "But I never wanted to be President anyway. So as soon as Sam's sworn in as Vice President—by Albert, by God; he's a justice of the peace—I will do what the Twenty-fifth Amendment requires, i.e., quote, transmit to the president pro tempore of the Senate and the Speaker of the House of Representatives my written declaration that I am unable to discharge the duty and powers of my office, unquote. At that point Sam becomes acting President. Not President, Franklin, *acting* President."

"Meaning?"

"Meaning you're next. He's just temporary, filling in until things get straightened out. The minute Frosty gives up the ghost the impeachment trial ends, leaving the issues unresolved."

"Who investigates the fraud and certifies the true outcome?"

"The election authorities of New York, Michigan, and California, just like the Constitution provides," Attenborough said. "If you'd asked me in the first place, I would have told you this is not, repeat *not*, a federal matter, and if you control the Senate you can make sure it doesn't become one. The three states in which fraud has been alleged will reexamine the totals and establish the true results from the computer memories. Their electors will then cast their ballots for real, only this time they'll be your electors, fairly chosen by the voters. The president of the Senate, presumably Wilbur E. Garrett, opens the ballots before the Senate and House as provided in the Twelfth Amendment. Sam steps down as acting President as provided in the Twenty-fifth Amendment and you take the oath."

"As administered by Chief Justice Hammett?" Mallory said.

"Albert would be better. Be good for your image."

"Agreed, on the point about Albert only."

"That's progress," Attenborough said. "The whole thing should take about a month. You'll be President by the Fourth of July. How do you like it?"

"It's worthy of you, Tucker," Mallory replied. "What happens to the investigation of the items in the articles of impeachment?"

"The Department of Justice will still be in existence and the attorney general will be working for you. Prosecute them rich boys and make sure you get a judge who'll send 'em to the right federal prison—the real article, not some summer camp—where they can have lots of firsthand contact with the suffering masses they so nobly did this for. What's your answer?"

Mallory took a deep breath. "You've asked me to trust you, Tucker. And you're right, I know I can."

"Not just me. Sam. He's the collateral."

"Has he agreed to all this? He'll be making a big sacrifice, giving up the Senate and his party's control of it in order to be President for a few weeks."

"He'll make it," Attenborough said. "It's for the country."

Mallory said, "Sam doesn't worry me. But others are involved, Tucker, including the Senate as it's presently constituted."

"I don't blame you for being nervous, but you and I know that at any given moment the Senate is composed of eighty-five honorable men and fifteen who think they are in spite of all the evidence to the contrary. Give 'em a chance and they'll behave like the Founding Fathers always told 'em to."

"Lockwood?"

"Same thing in spades. His only sin is, he's a babe in the woods—always has been, even if he did just find out about it. All he wants is to be found innocent of any wrongdoing, and he will be because he is. He knows that. But I have to take him something from you."

"What?"

"I've got to be able to tell him that you're going to leave him alone on this Ibn Awad thing after you get back in."

"I've already told him I'll do that."

"Then you won't mind my telling him again."

"No."

Attenborough's old sly look came back for an instant. "After he's cleared on the election thing and that's announced, it might be nice if you appointed him to something, soon as a little time goes by."

Mallory elongated the Speaker's name: "Tuuuuuckerrrr!"

Attenborough looked surprised. "Don't get me wrong," he said. "What I'm talking about is maybe ambassador to Japan. He'd have to eat raw fish day in and day out and listen to 'em whine about unfair trade practices for two, maybe three years."

"It's a thought," Mallory said. "As to the rest of it, all right. If it's Sam, it's a deal."

"Got to be Sam," Attenborough said. "Otherwise where the hell would the country be if I'm wrong about how all this is going to work out?"

Mallory said, "There's a loose end. Hammett."

"One thing at a time," Attenborough said. "Want to shake on it?"

Mallory extended his hand. Attenborough's fingers lay lifeless on his palm, as if the blood had already stopped flowing through the old man's body.

Mallory was overcome by sympathy. He said, "Tucker, I'm sorry to see you go."

"Been here long enough," Attenborough replied, and just in case Mallory might think he was talking about earth instead of the airplane, he added: "Tell the pilot to land this thing, will you? Don't want to miss the Hubbard Brothers Show."

8

Sometime during the rainy night following Philindros's testimony Rose MacKenzie got out of bed and went outside wearing nothing but the old T-shirt in which she slept. Horace found her in the Hubbard burial ground at five in the morning, lying on Paul Christopher's grave with another empty vodka bottle beside her. There was frost on the grass. She was in a state of hypothermia, lips blue, skin clammy, pulse almost indiscernible. Horace carried her down to the car, wrapped her in blankets, turned the heater on high, and drove at perilous speed to the hospital in Pittsfield.

The emergency room doctor told him that Rose had relapsed into pneumonia. "If she comes out of it, and there's no guarantee, you might consider institutional care—Austin-Riggs, maybe," the young man said, looking Horace over and seeing old money.

"Excellent suggestion, Doctor, thank you," Horace replied. Psychiatric care at Austin-Riggs cost thousands a week. Neither he nor Rose had drawn a paycheck for months, and though Horace owned paintings and other objects that could be converted into cash, they had no ready money, and both knew that if the Harbor did not exist they would probably be living in a cardboard box on the sidewalks of New York.

Horace remained with Rose, sitting beside her bed all night and on into the morning. She was unconscious. The other women in the four-bed room watched a series of agony shows on the television monitor that hung from the ceiling. Having lived in Islamic and Buddhist and Confucian countries for most of his nearly seventy years, Horace had had little exposure to daytime television, or any other kind of television, for that matter, and had never imagined that people would go before the cameras and confess the sorts of things he was now hearing them say. Spies and terrorists he had interrogated over the years would have stood up under torture unto death before confessing to the bizarre sexual acts a weeping female on the screen was now describing with evident pleasure and relief.

Horace was about to rise and leave when the interview ended and another guest was introduced. When he heard the announcer say that this would be Ms. Slim Eve, ecolawyer, the recent victim of sexual abuse by the Speaker of the House of Representatives, he waited out of idle curiosity to see what she looked like. He did not already know because, as a matter of house rules, there were no television sets at the Harbor. After the commercial, Slim entered to cheers and tumultuous applause. To his great surprise, Horace recognized her at once as someone he had known in a former life, as spies call long-ago operations. To be certain that there was no mistake he sat down and watched the entire interview. Slim was older, her hair was shorter, and her vowels were more elongated, but the lavender eyes, the glorious legs, and the gestures were unmistakably the same.

Rose remained motionless and mute, her eyes closed. Horace put a hand on her feverish cheek, warning her first that he was going to do so in case she was awake, and then placed his lips close to her ear. "My dear," he said, "I'm going to have to leave you for a day or two. Mind the doctors. I'll call as soon as I have news."

He then drove to the Harbor, packed a bag, loaded it into the car, and went for a walk in the woods. About half a mile from the house, in a grove of maples, he knelt, turned over a rock, reached into a natural chamber in the ledge that lay just below the spongy surface, and extracted what appeared to be another, smaller stone. He put on his reading glasses, examined this object until he found the mark he was looking for, then inserted the blade of a penknife, twisted, and opened it up. He took two tiny Lucite boxes, smaller than ring boxes, out of the compartment within, slipped them into the pocket of his jacket, and then carefully put the fake stone back together and returned it to its hiding place. Then he went down the hill, got into his car, and drove to the bus station in Great Barrington. Taking the express bus to New York, a pleasant ride on country highways, and then changing to the Metroliner, he could be in Washington in time for dinner.

9

On his long bus ride Horace was visited by many thoughts of Rose Mac-Kenzie, and of Emily Hubbard. He did not think that he could bear to stay in the same house with another distraught female, so he checked into a club that had a reciprocal arrangement with his own club in New York. It had a few cheap, penitential rooms on the top floor, just down the hall from the private dining rooms, and as he came out the door after unpacking his bag, he ran into the last man he expected or wanted to see, Baxter T. Busby. Horace stood still in the doorway and kept quiet, thinking Busby might not make out his face as he rushed by, but Horace was unmistakable, even to a man who was too vain to wear glasses.

"Horace!" Busby hissed, placing a palm on Horace's chest. "Back inside, quick."

Horace backpedaled into his tiny room and Busby followed him in. "I've been wanting to talk to you for days," he said. "But after that fool St. Clair went on the tube I didn't think it wise."

"Quite right," Horace said. "This is not wise, either, Baxter. I'm likely to be the next witness."

"That may not be necessary," Busby said in a loud whisper. "Have you been watching the tube?"

"Not religiously," Horace said.

"You should, for your own sake. Thanks to you, the Year Zed is about to dawn."

"Thanks to me?" Horace frowned. " 'The Year Zed'?" What on earth was that? Owing to his long sojourns abroad and the spymaster's daily burden of keeping real secrets on which agents' lives depended, his recollection of Shelleyan code words was shaky. He did not reveal this because he knew that any such lapse was inconceivable to Busby, who had gone on whispering in his breathless way. "It was you who made it possible, first with that dope about the lost bombs—didn't our man handle that beautifully?" Busby hissed. "And then that incredible stroke of genius about the you-know."

"About the *what?*" Horace asked in a normal voice.

"Ssshhh," Busby said. "The Twentieth Amendment."

"The Year Zed and the Twentieth Amendment," Horace said. "You lost me going round the turn, Baxter."

"Horace, you sly fox, you're denying everything. I might have known."

Voices went by in the hallway. "That's my dinner group," Busby said. "It's time to tell a few key people what to expect before I make the final move. But, Horace, that last thing you sent me by hand of messenger really was a stroke of genius."

"What messenger?" Horace said.

Busby beamed in conspiratorial joy. Suddenly Horace remembered what the Year Zed was. He said, "Baxter, I think you'd better tell me exactly what it is you're talking about."

Busby told him, in detail, still in a whisper.

When he was through, Horace said, "You're going to make Archimedes Hammett President of the United States, and you think I'm the author of the operation?"

"Well, aren't you?" Busby asked, smiling up at him, an aging version of the nearsighted rich kid who, half a century before, had attached himself to the teenaged Horace at Yale and hung on like a limpet ever since.

"No," Horace said. "I'm not."

Busby grinned anew. Horace thought he might give him the elbow. Busby said, "You mean to say you don't know a thing about the lovely Ms. Slim Eve."

"I didn't say that. However—"

"Ah ha! And now I suppose you're going to say you didn't know about the diskette she slipped to me at that party or the master plan that was on it? Or that Five-Three didn't call from China on your behalf and set up the whole delightful encounter?"

"Baxter, listen to me. Whatever you may think, none of this has anything in the world to do with me."

"Of course it hasn't," Busby said. "I never for a moment thought it did. But if you happen *not* to see Julian, be sure *not* to tell him that that last ticktock he talked about up at the Harbor is almost upon us."

Busby squeezed Horace's arm, looked into the blur that was his face, the noble face of Bucephalus himself, according to brilliant old Booth Conroy, who had taught them "Greeks and Cheeks," as his required sophomore course in classical literature and art was called. "Got to go," he said. "Can't afford to arouse so much as a whisper of suspicion. But go on, be as modest as you want to be. The Poet would be proud of you."

"He'd be even prouder of you, Baxter," Horace said. "But please do not go one step further with whatever you're up to until you hear from me again."

He looked alarmed; Busby mistook this for pleased embarrassment. "Too late," he said. "The thing has taken on a life of its own. That's the beauty of it."

"You've got it wrong, Baxter," Horace said, looking at Busby in what was the closest thing to horror he had ever felt in a long life filled with treasonous persons and dark deeds. "All this is, God help us, is the law of unintended results."

He went downstairs to the telephone cabin and called John L. S. McGraw on the number Mcgraw had given him on the way back from Chile. McGraw recognized his voice at once.

"Let's get together soon," Horace said.

"Buffalo bridge, nine tonight," McGraw said.

"Sorry, tied up tonight on a family matter," Horace said. "Tomorrow morning?"

McGraw did not quibble. "Make it six-thirty A.M. then."

"Fine."

Horace hung up. Dumbarton Bridge over Rock Creek Parkway, famous for its guardian bisons with their prominent testicles, was so convenient to Embassy Row, was such a picturesque place for a clandestine meeting, was so hard to bug because of the racket made by the traffic passing beneath it, that it would resemble a spies' reunion by the dawn's early light. No matter, thought Horace; not at this stage of the game.

10

When Horace reached Emily on the Georgetown number she told him that Julian had retreated to Camp Panchaea. Horace knew the place well; he had gone there as a boy, when it had been the woodland retreat of a defunct men's club, the Society of Euhemerus, to which his father and grandfather had belonged. It was named for the mythical island where, according to the Greek poet Euhemerus, the gods had resided before ascending Mount Olympus.

Horace said, "Can you drive me out there, Emily? I don't have a car."

"Rent one," Emily said. Her voice was lifeless and uninterested; a lot was wrong between her and Julian—a lot was wrong between her and Horace, for that matter.

"I'd rather not, really."

"All right, where are you?"

"I'll come to you. Kennedy Center garage, Level C elevators, in twenty minutes?"

"That costs ten dollars, even if you only stay a minute," Emily said.

"I'll spring for the parking fee," Horace said, smiling in spite of the situation. Emily was as tight as paper on the wall, just the girl Julian needed, because he was like their father, with no head for money whatsoever.

She was waiting for him in her battered Fiat beyond the glass doors when he stepped off the escalator and onto the parking apron. Before Horace could find the seat belt and buckle up, she put the car in gear and peeled out of the garage and onto Rock Creek Parkway, scattering oncoming vehicles and fishtailing the rear end with a screech of tires.

She drove across the Theodore Roosevelt Bridge and down I-66 in silence. Horace did not try to make her talk; he had some thinking to do. From time to time he checked their backs. There was no pursuit; as he had anticipated, Emily was of no interest to anyone, the unemployable, uninvitable wife of a has-been in her little old car. After an hour or so she turned off the interstate onto a two-lane blacktop running straight through a swamp that grew nearly to the edge of the pavement. Tree trunks flashed by, and deeper in the underbrush Horace could see moonlight glimmering on stagnant water. A pickup truck hurtled by, lights blinking and horn blaring, then another making the same frantic signals.

"Emily," Horace said, "the headlights." Emily had driven all the way from Washington without them. "Whoopsie," she said, her first word of the trip, and switched them on. The car had a European instrument panel. Now that it was lit, Horace saw that they were moving at 130 kilometers an hour—80 miles an hour. Emily fumbled in her purse and put on a pair of glasses with large round lenses. Horace smiled again: his sister-in-law was almost as myopic as Busby, though infinitely smarter.

After a while Emily screeched to a stop, backed up, and turned into the woods on a logging road that was nothing more than a pair of ruts worn into the slippery clay. Transfixed by the headlights, a deer ran crazily toward the car and grazed it with its antlers. Emily switched off the lights and continued by moonlight. Other antlered animals, moose and elk, moved through patches of fog. Smaller creatures scurried across the track and peered down from the trees. Emily slammed on the brakes and nearly skidded on the slick clay into a large, shaggy beast that blocked the road.

Horace said, "A woodlands bison?"

Emily said, "I wouldn't be a bit surprised."

The animal refused to move when Emily sounded the horn and flashed the lights, staring at the machine out of dull rolling eyes, snorting, and finally dropping a huge steaming pancake of dung onto the track. Emily backed up again and drove around, bouncing among the trees. Under the terms of the will of the O.G.'s rich Euhemerian uncle Snowden, Camp Panchaea and the five-thousand-acre private forest that surrounded it had been turned into a wildlife preserve dedicated to rediscovering and restoring original American species. Julian was still chairman of the board of the tax-exempt foundation that ran the place, the last honor and stipend he retained.

Finally the Fiat emerged into a clearing where tumbledown log cabins loomed in the predawn darkness along the near shore of a glassy lake. Inside the largest of these buildings, Julian waited. A log fire burned in a stone fireplace. Hissing gasoline lanterns gave off a poisonous smell. Dust lay over everything. The walls were hung with male souvenirs—paintings and pinups from the Gibson girl to Marilyn Monroe; school and college pennants and antique footballs, basketballs, and baseball bats on which teams had written their names; tarnished silver trophy cups on shelves; group pictures of young American males in athletic and military uniforms; captured flags and insignia cut from the wings of enemy airplanes; spiked helmets, Lugers, samurai swords. These items had been brought here by Euhemerians, long since dead, who used to come here to hunt, fish, and swim naked in the chilly spring-fed lake ("Lake Shrivel," in club parlance), and in general be boys together again.

Emily handed them jelly glasses filled with red wine. "This is all I could find," she said. "I'm going upstairs." She flourished a book at them and vanished.

In undertones Horace and Julian talked about their women for a moment—health and sanity bulletins. "Emily has fallen into a silence," Julian said.

"I noticed that; Rose has been affected in the opposite way," Horace said. He told Julian what had happened the night before.

"Will she be all right?" Julian asked.

"She'll probably get over the pneumonia, but she has a bad case of shame and remorse," Horace replied.

"Well," said Julian, "taking the consequences is no great fun. What brings you here?"

"I have two things to discuss with you, actually," Horace said. "The original thing, which has to do with your friend Hammett's lady friend, and another thing I found out after I got here."

Julian looked mildly interested, his lifelong usual expression. He was a stranger to laughter and enthusiasm, Horace's greatest friends. Horace did not know why. The two brothers, years apart in age, raised by different mothers, living at great distances inside different systems, hardly knew each other.

"All right," Julian said. "Worst first?"

"Not much to choose between them, I'm afraid," Horace said. He told Julian what Busby had said to him in the club.

For once, Julian's face showed a great deal of expression as he listened. "And Busby thinks that this was your idea?" he asked.

Horace replied, "That's what he said, and he's too simple-minded to make it up. Apparently the call came over the Shelleyan network, but I assure you it wasn't instigated by me."

Julian said, "I should hope not."

Horace said, "Julian, you must tell me the truth about this. Was it you?"

"No," said Julian, "Certainly not." He was amazed by the question. "What is Busby thinking of?"

"That's the first thing," Horace said. "The second is what I came down here to tell you. That young woman Speaker Attenborough is supposed to have raped or whatever?"

"Slim Eve," Julian said. "Hammett's handmaiden. What about her?"

"I saw her on television and recognized her from an operation we ran fifteen years ago to penetrate the Eye of Gaza."

"She was one of yours?"

"The other side. All of the Eye's operations were suicide missions, as you know from your experience in the presidential campaign. Before they sent a man out, they'd have him breed his replacement—father a child on a female believer. Not many Arab girls were keen on this arrangement, so the Eye tended to recruit blue-eyed romantics—Germans, Brits, Scandinavians, even the odd American, if you'll forgive the pun. This woman Slim was one of the brood mares."

Julian, back nearly to normal, absorbed this without visible reaction. "You're absolutely certain about this?"

"I'm relying on memory, but yes. She was recruited in college, brought to one of their camps in Libya for terrorist training, then selected as a mother of the jihad. That was the drill: guns and bombs as foreplay, then the idyll in the sands and the planting of the seed of a future terrorist."

Julian winced, not at the substance of the story but at Horace's tone of ridicule. "What happened to her kid?"

"The usual thing. She gave it up to the Eye of Gaza as soon as it was born and they put it in storage for future activation. That was the drill. By then, of course, the father had blown himself up for the Cause."

Julian said, "That was a long time ago, of course. I mean the business with the baby."

"Yes, she was about twenty-two then," Horace said, "so by now the kid must be almost ready for detonation himself. But the fact remains that she is a trained terrorist who has an emotional stake in the Eye of Gaza from which she is never likely to recover." Horace looked into the fire for a moment, then back into his brother's wary eyes. "Julian, I know you've already answered this question, but before I take the steps I think I must take before the sun goes down again, I want to be absolutely sure that none of this thing that Busby is doing has anything whatever to do in any way with anyone who's related to me."

"It's nothing to do with me, if that's the question. I can't speak for our only other living relation."

"Zarah? I had thoughts about her coming out here this evening."

"Why?"

"This is where she and her Berber friends trained for Patchen's last operation."

"Against whom?"

"The Eye of Gaza," Horace said. "She walked right in on them with David, afraid of nothing, shades of her old man and her grandmother, and damn near rid the world of them all. Paul himself was in on it, most reluctantly."

Julian said, "Wait a minute. Are you telling me that Zarah was part of the Outfit or FIS?"

"No, never; she went in on this with the O.G. and Patchen for reasons of her own. The team, Paul specifically, captured the head of the Eye, Hassan Abdallah, but the whole operation took place on French territory and there were dead people lying around, so they had to hand him over to the French. They gave him to the Syrians in order to get some of their people out of captivity. Hassan killed Patchen, of course, and Zarah suffered a bit before she got out. More than a bit. They pumped her full of dope, stripped her, chained her to a bed, and queued up on her."

"She was raped?"

"Ganged, the survivors told the French. The drug they used induces deep amnesia when administered in massive doses, so of course she had no memory of what happened until some genius from the Outfit used hypnosis to debrief her. By then she had turned up pregnant. Miscarried, thank God. Wouldn't abort it, a Christopher to the marrow."

"She was lucky a baby was all she took away from the experience."

"Maybe it wasn't all," Horace said. "One of the corpses the French autopsied was HIV positive."

Julian gasped. "She has the disease?"

"Not so far, and this happened in the early nineties. But you can turn up with it years and years afterward, depending on which mutation of the virus is at work. She may never be sure."

Julian's face was contorted by the shock of hearing what Horace had just told him. "I had no idea," he said, "None."

"Let's hope nobody else does, either," Horace replied. "Hassan Abdallah and his friends are not a let-bygones-be-bygones crowd." He drank the rough wine in his jelly glass at a swallow, made a face, and changed the subject. "But back to my question. If not you, then who is aiding and abetting Busby in this harebrained plan?"

"I don't know. I had no idea he was even onto anything like this. When we talked to Busby up in the Berkshires I thought what we all had in mind was a new Vice President with the right point of view, maybe even Buzzer himself, God help me, who could take over from Lockwood and pick up the pieces."

"I'm glad to hear that, because your friend Hammett is as crazy as a bedbug and that woman he hangs out with is an enemy of mankind," Horace said.

"That's harsh."

"Truth sometimes is. Hammett didn't just defend those bloody bastards in the courts. He wants them to win." Julian said nothing. Horace said, "But golly, the irony."

Julian gave him a comprehending look; "golly" had been the favorite exclamation of the O.G., from whom Horace had learned so much. What was coming next?

Horace uttered a mordant chuckle. "You do see the ultimate irony, don't you, Julian? If Busby succeeds, what we'll get for killing Ibn Awad to save the world is Ibn Awad's double as President of the United States."

11

In the computer's main memory Lucy found the phone call to the Morning After Clinic she had made three months before on Susan Grant's behalf. After that it was a simple matter to identify and check out the woman to whom she had talked about Grant's appointment and do a rundown on her outgoing calls. The first one she placed, twenty-one seconds after disconnecting from Lucy, went to a cellular telephone in the Connecticut area. The phone was registered to the Hartford offices of Eve & Eve, Attorneys at Law, who had represented the woman at the MAC clinic in her divorce from a husband who had battered and then deserted her. The records showed that the woman, a nurse-midwife from Hartford, had gotten her job on the recommendation of a member of her support group at the Womonkind Coalition. She still worked in the same job, at the same extension.

McGraw said, "One more bean for the Bingo card."

"More than that," Zarah said. "It gives us a way to take the initiative."

"To do what?" McGraw said.

"Bring the assassin into the open."

"Oh? How would you do that on the basis of this particular bean?"

"I'd do the obvious," Zarah said. "Lucy makes another call to the MAC clinic and keeps calling until she gets the same woman as before on the line. Then she makes an appointment in my name and, to make sure she understands, tells them Mallory is the father."

"Then what?"

"Then I show up for the appointment."

Wiggins said, "And the assassin will be there waiting for you. And we'll be waiting for the assassin."

"Wait a minute," McGraw said. "Zarah, I know you've had some experience with types like these, and I know Lucy and Wiggins and their friends are good at what they do and that they'll cover you. But they were covering Susan Grant, too."

"They didn't know what to expect then," Zarah said. "They weren't in control of the situation."

"No, but maybe they thought they were. This is dangerous. These are

/ 514

world-class nutcases but they're not stupid. The killer always controls the situation. This one will come at it entirely differently the second time around."

Wiggins liked Zarah's line of reasoning. "But they have to act within the limits of the situation we create," he said. "First of all, they must act within a rigid time frame: the embryo must be recovered seven days after the call to the clinic, no more, no less."

"So they've got seven days to hit her with a rifle on one of her lonely walks."

"So she makes the appointment and then vanishes until the day of the appointment," Wiggins said. "The only place she can be at the appointed hour is in front of the MAC clinic. And we'll be there, too."

"Just like in the movies," McGraw said. "But suppose there's a demonstration in front of the clinic and the assassin is one of the demonstrators and hits Zarah with a KGB surplus poison dart shot from an umbrella tip? Suppose this character is *inside* the clinic dressed like a doctor and flushes the embryo with cyanide? Or makes an appointment for the same day and uses a knife in the waiting room? This is not sound procedure."

Lucy had listened in silence to this conversation, eyes never leaving Zarah's face as she and the others spoke. Now she said, "They'd expect us. Our coverage of Zarah has been blown. Thanks to Zarah."

"If the assassin is psychotic, none of that matters," Zarah said. "We have to isolate this person."

McGraw said, "One on one, you and her?"

"Exactly," Zarah said. "But on our own ground. I have an idea." She described it.

When she was done McGraw said, "It could work. It could also get you killed. Why should the killer believe you really are pregnant?"

"Because the killer will want to believe it. As Lucy said, this person is a type—the type who sees what it wants to see," Zarah said. "We'll see if your woman calls Eve & Eve again. If she does, the killer will take the next step and so can we. Make the call, Lucy."

Something like a smile of comprehension came and went in Lucy's eyes as she listened to these words of Zarah's. With a brighter smile she said, "Fine." She dialed the number through the computer, and while she waited for the call to go through, she watched Zarah with a cold and knowing expression, female on female.

She made the appointment, identifying Zarah by name. "You should know," she said, "that former President Mallory will be taking a close personal interest in this particular recovery. All details should be held in the strictest confidence."

Forty seconds later the computer detected a call from the MAC clinic to

Eve & Eve's cellular number, registered in the 203 area code, Connecticut, but answered in the 202 area, Washington, D.C.

"So far, so good," said Lucy. "Amazing, how Zarah can see into the future."

"Now we hang around and wait," McGraw said.

"Not for long, I imagine," Zarah said.

12

In the palmy days of U.S. intelligence, agents who were incompetent enough or unlucky enough to be captured by the opposition were under standing orders to hold out under torture or the threat of it long enough to convince their interrogators that they would rather die than talk, and then abandon bravado and spill their guts. It was thought that this scenario would play well because it confirmed the idea so firmly held by many at home and abroad that Americans are soft, weak, selfish, afraid of pain, and believe in nothing. As long as headquarters knew everything the captive knew, nothing was lost by timely confession because even the briefest show of defiance gave the people back home time to hide the best silverware before the burglars arrived. The problem with this theory was that captured spies are usually questioned by counterspies who are unlikely to believe them even when they are telling the truth.

Horace Hubbard told Alfonso Olmedo all this in the living room of Blackstone's town house in Bethesda, Maryland, where McGraw had delivered him after their meeting on the Buffalo bridge.

"Meaning what?" Olmedo said. "That you're trying to avoid torture or hide the best silverware?"

"Meaning that I think my best chance of being believed is to be questioned by you. Your knack for pulling the truth out of people whether they want to tell it or not is the bona fides a fellow like me needs."

"I don't quite follow you."

"Let me explain," Horace said. "My cousin Paul Christopher crash-landed inside Red China during the Cold War and was thrown into prison. His sentence was, I quote, Death with twenty years' suspension of the execution at solitary hard labor with observation of the result. It meant he had twenty years to rehabilitate himself as a good Maoist and also that his captors could execute him at any moment they decided he wasn't sincere, or was beyond rehabilitation, or for any other reason. Or shoot him at the end of twenty years no matter what he did."

"I remember the case," Olmedo said. "But he did get out in the end, didn't he?"

"Yes, because, in the end, the Chinese believed him."

"Your situation is not very similar."

"Maybe not in every particular, but let me make my point," Horace said. "It took the Chinese ten years to believe the poor guy when, having told them everything else he knew, he refused under the daily threat of execution to admit that he had spied on China, because he never had. Scrupulously honest man, my cousin Paul; got him into all kinds of trouble all his life. The Chinese had never before encountered a prisoner who would not oblige them by making a false confession. At last they decided he was not hopelessly recalcitrant but a man of principle, so they commuted his sentence. But it was a close thing."

Olmedo said, "Instructive anecdote. But you realize that I can make this case without you."

"Oh, yes. But not without leaving Lockwood's innocence, which is total, in some doubt. You can't exonerate Lockwood without knowing how and why I did what I did. I don't see how you can get at the whole truth without me."

"You know the whole truth?"

"Only the missing parts," Horace said. "I have in my possession a memory chip on which the entire election-night computer operation is recorded. That is to say, an inventory of every vote that was diverted in New York, Michigan, and California, and the record of what candidate it really belongs to."

Olmedo said, "How can I know that this record is authentic?"

"You will find that it exactly corroborates the Mallory file, which is obviously based on an intercept by O. N. Laster's boys and girls. Besides, according to Rose, a computer never forgets, even when lobotomized. Somewhere in its brain all these data are sleeping. The chip will wake them up." Horace lifted his eyebrows, which were grayer now than Olmedo remembered their having been only a few weeks before. "The Prince Charming chip," he said, taking it out of his pocket in its little Lucite case and holding it up for Olmedo to see.

Olmedo said, "Do you also happen to have in your pocket a copy of the recording of the entire conversation between Lockwood and Philindros?"

"You know I do. You listened to it in New York."

"Only parts of it, I think. How did you get it?"

"Jack Philindros wasn't wearing anything as old-fashioned as a tape recorder. The conversation went through his tie clip and was transmitted through a relay to the satellite, then beamed back to earth and recorded at headquarters. Among other places, including my listening post in Beirut."

Olmedo said, "Refresh my memory. Does the complete recording corroborate Lockwood's version of what was said and not said?"

"From what I deduce from your questions to Philindros," Horace replied, "I would say yes, very likely it does."

"Why are you approaching me now?"

"Because you did not come to me. And because the situation has changed in ways that I'm confident you will discover while questioning me before the Senate."

"There must be a reason beyond that. You'll go to prison."

"Not such a frightening prospect when a nursing home is the alternative. Besides, Mr. Olmedo, I have engaged in criminal activity on my country's behalf all my life, and but for the grace of God I might have been locked up years ago under far worse conditions—like poor Paul Christopher."

"Why didn't that happen?"

"Because always before I stuck to the principles of tradecraft. I have been in the business of altering reality, but never before did I make the mistake of altering reality for personal reasons. It was a far, far greater mistake than I ever imagined it could be, and at my age I had no excuse for making it. I don't know if you can understand what I'm saying."

"I'm trying. Are you coming forward because you wish to make amends?"

"Something of that nature," Horace said. "Are we on?"

"In my opinion you'll make an interesting witness," Olmedo said. "I must leave you now. The trial recommences at twelve-thirty. My colleague Mr. Blackstone will join you in a moment. Please speak as frankly to him as you have spoken to me, because I will be using what you tell him as the basis of my questions to you in three hours' time."

"Excellent."

Olmedo held out his hand. "May I have the memory chips now?"

Horace handed them over to him in their tiny transparent containers. "A pleasure," he said. "And if I were you, I'd make copies."

13

Horace gave Blackstone enough information to provide the basis for at least a week of testimony. After hearing the essentials—as Blackstone defined essentials—in an anteroom of the Senate chamber, Olmedo told Horace that he would confine himself to the heart of the matter. "It may be a rough passage," he said.

"Fire away," Horace replied. "Just bear in mind what I told you about my cousin."

Olmedo's opening question was "Mr. Hubbard, you have just sworn to tell the truth, the whole truth, and nothing but the truth. Do you intend to do so?"

Horace said, "I do so intend, Mr. Olmedo."

"You are a professional intelligence operative, Mr. Hubbard, and have been all your adult life. Is that correct?"

"Yes."

"There is a widespread belief that spies are to their targets what heartless seducers are to women. They lie as a matter of technique to get what they want. Would you regard that as a fair perception of the reality?"

Horace answered this provocative question as if sensing in it the possibility of a pleasant chat. "A reasonable man must answer yes to that question," he said. "Although it has always been maintained that there is a difference between lying for your country and just plain lying. Also, good spies do it in the name of something rarer than a lady's virtue."

"Which is?"

"The truth."

"Which makes men free?"

"That is the motto of American intelligence. The reality, as a late director of my former organization once remarked, is that it only makes them angry."

At this point Patrick Graham, chuckling in spite of himself, defined Horace to the television audience as "an irresistible scoundrel." The camera captured Olmedo's scarcely veiled amusement.

Hammett intervened from the bench, saying, "Mr. Hubbard, have your rights been explained to you?"

"I understand them fully, Mr. Chief Justice."

"Are you represented by counsel?"

"I am not represented by counsel, sir, nor do I wish to be."

"You understand that you have no immunity here, and that anything you say in this proceeding may subsequently be used against you in criminal or civil proceedings in a court of law, and that you have the right to remain silent and the right to counsel at the expense of the United States?"

"Yes, thank you, Mr. Chief Justice, I understand all of that," Horace said in his civil, nerveless manner. With a charming smile he said to Olmedo, "I shall go where you lead me, sir."

Olmedo said, "Mr. Hubbard, during your career as an intelligence officer you achieved the highest possible civil service rank, were decorated for your secret achievements on six different occasions, and were the principal officer of the Foreign Intelligence Service in the Middle East at the time of Ibn Awad's death. All correct?"

"Yes."

"And did there come a time, almost exactly four years ago today, when you were ordered to carry out an operation to assassinate Ibn Awad?"

"Yes."

"By whom?"

"By the DFI—that is to say the Director of Foreign Intelligence—in a coded cable for my eyes only."

"By the DFI you mean Mr. Philindros?"

"Jack Philindros held the office at that time, yes. As he still does."

Olmedo said, "You were not ordered to assassinate Ibn Awad by the President of the United States himself?"

"No."

"Are you personally acquainted with President Lockwood?"

"Yes, but only on a casual social basis."

"Have you ever met the President in an official capacity?"

"No, only in a social setting."

"Did you discuss the aforesaid order to assassinate Ibn Awad with President Lockwood in any sort of social setting before carrying it out?"

"No."

"Your half brother, Julian Hubbard, was at that time chief of staff to President Lockwood. Did you discuss the director's order with your half brother before you carried it out?"

"No."

"Did you, in fact, carry it out?"

"Yes."

"With your own hand?"

"No. I activated a nonwitting asset."

"Please define that term."

"He didn't know what I really was or who I really worked for."

"You are referring to Ibn Awad's son Prince Talil?"

For the first time Horace blinked. Several times. As Patrick Graham had reported on *Newsdawn* only that morning, Horace had been fond of Prince Talil, whom he had known since early childhood. He said, "That is correct."

"Did you discuss the assassination with President Lockwood after the event?"

"No."

"Did you discuss it with your half brother?"

"Yes. Last August. At length."

"What was his reaction?"

"He was greatly surprised and dismayed that I had been assigned to carry out the operation."

"Did he express a reason for his surprise and dismay?"

"He seemed to regard it as an attempt by the DFI to place him and also the President under some sort of constraint."

"What sort of constraint?"

"It was my impression that Julian felt that Philindros involved me in the belief that my involvement somehow made it less likely that the White House would blame the FIS if the matter became public."

"Did this suspicion seem reasonable to you?"

"Frankly, no. I explained to Julian that I was the responsible officer in the field. When the order came to me, I did not stop to consider who my half brother was or whom he worked for. I simply carried it out."

"Even though it was a warrant for the death of a foreign chief of state?"

"Yes."

"Even though it did not bear the President's own signature, even though you did not hear the order in the President's own voice?"

Horace looked at Olmedo with polite curiosity: what an odd question. He said, "Mr. Olmedo, the answer is yes."

Olmedo said, "Thank you." He handed a small Lucite box and an inch-thick stack of computer paper to the clerk. "If the Senate pleases, this memory chip and printout of its contents is entered as evidence."

"What is it, Mr. Olmedo?" Hammett asked, holding out his hand to the clerk.

"It is a recording of a certain conversation and a transcription of that conversation, Mr. Chief Justice." As Hammett flipped through the pages of the printout, Olmedo turned back to Horace. "Now, Mr. Hubbard, I will ask you an important question," he said. "Have you reason to believe, based on any hard evidence now in your possession or formerly in your possession, that President Lockwood actually ordered, in his own words, in his own voice, of his own volition, the assassination of Ibn Awad?"

"On the contrary, I know that he never did so."

The galleries stirred. Hammett gaveled. He said, "You *know?*"

"Absolutely, Mr. Chief Justice. He never gave any such order. It's quite clear from the original recording of the conversation, which I deduce has just been entered into evidence by Mr. Olmedo, that President Lockwood didn't hear a word Jack Philindros said to him in that regard that night at Live Oaks."

"Then why," Hammett asked, "did President Lockwood say yes in answer to Philindros's question?"

Horace shrugged, an elegant gesture that drew attention to the rather shabby condition of the fine old suit that he wore. "My impression is that he was just being polite. Didn't hear the question, didn't want to embarrass Jack. You can ask my brother Julian his opinion—he was actually there—but I think you'll find that's what happened."

Olmedo said, "May I interrupt, Mr. Chief Justice? Mr. Hubbard, you knew all this at the time?"

"No. I was in the field when my people copied it off the satellite. And then I didn't listen to the chip for a long time afterward."

"Why not?"

"Among other reasons, I did not want to know what was on it."

"Will you tell the Senate why?"

"Because the thing was done. It had produced consequences, including the beheading of Prince Talil, that were dispiriting."

"You had regrets?"

"Of course I did. But the enemy was armed and constituted a danger to my fellow countrymen, whom I had taken a solemn oath to defend, and I was at the end of the chain of command."

Thoughtfully, as if struck by the logic of what he had just heard, Olmedo nodded. "You take oaths very seriously, Mr. Hubbard. Is that a fair statement?"

"Taking them seriously is the whole point of oaths, I should have thought," Horace said. "Yes, I take them seriously."

"More seriously than anything else whatsoever?"

"No. There are limits."

"What limits?"

"Only one, really, and it is universally acknowledged. Conscience."

"So you would not obey an oath it if meant violating your conscience?"

"In principle I would not."

" 'In principle.' Then there are exceptions when some higher duty intervenes?"

"Yes."

"Is that why you stole the presidential election, Mr. Hubbard?"

Hammett said, "Hold on, Mr. Olmedo. The Senate is not considering the articles of impeachment dealing with that question at this time."

"It is inextricably bound up with all the other questions before the Senate in this trial, Mr. Chief Justice."

Horace said, "Excuse me. I don't mind answering."

Hammett said, "The Chief Justice appreciates that, sir. But that is not the issue."

Horace looked up at Hammett and said, "If I may, Mr. Chief Justice, I would like to point out that I was no longer bound by my oath when I stole the election. I had resigned from the Foreign Intelligence Service—resigned, not retired—and was no longer bound by any obligation to the government. Nor was I in its pay in any way, shape, or form."

Olmedo said, "Then you admit that you stole the election?"

"Yes," Horace said, "but I was acting as a private citizen. I caused votes to be diverted by computer in New York, Michigan, and California from other candidates to President Lockwood."

"As a *concerned* citizen, Mr. Hubbard?"

"Well put," said Horace.

"About what were you concerned?"

"About the possibility that the investigation of the assassination of Ibn Awad promised by Mr. Mallory would result in the destruction of the American intelligence service."

"And in harm to President Lockwood?" Olmedo asked.

"I didn't care two figs about President Lockwood. In the past I had seen American intelligence dragged through the mud before to save a President's anatomy. The reason was always the weakness of the President. This was more of the same, in spades."

"You wanted to perpetuate in office a President whom you regarded as weak?"

"Better that than the alternative, given the circumstances and the stakes."

"I see," Olmedo said. "We will leave it at that for the moment."

Hammett stirred restlessly on the bench but did not intervene.

Olmedo said, "Mr. Hubbard, I must ask you this. As a concerned citizen, did you discuss the theft of the election in any way, shape, or form with President Lockwood?"

Horace said, "No. Certainly not."

"Why not?"

"Because I knew President Lockwood would never countenance my acting as I did or accept a counterfeit outcome if he knew about it."

"So you did what you have described doing without the knowledge of President Lockwood, without the authorization of President Lockwood, knowing that it was an act that he would never approve or authorize personally or through others?"

"Precisely," Horace said.

"As a matter of conscience?"

Hammett said, "Counselor, stop right there. You are prosecuting this witness. Mr. Hubbard, you understand the import of what you are saying under oath and its probable consequences to yourself?"

"Yes," Horace said. "Absolutely."

Olmedo said, "May I proceed along this line, Mr. Chief Justice?"

"You may not," Hammett said. From his place on the left side of the chamber Busby caught Hammett's eye. He avoided it sternly. All his instincts told him that Horace's testimony had lasted long enough.

To Olmedo he said, "Stick to that which is relevant to the article of impeachment under consideration, Counselor."

"Mr. Chief Justice, I am in the process of demonstrating the total innocence of an impeached President. I am most reluctant to leave this hanging in air."

"Counsel, the way you're going about it is not a proper exercise in terms of the witness's constitutional rights."

In visible surprise, Olmedo said, "May I respectfully ask in what way it is improper? The witness has volunteered a profoundly important admission. Why should I not pursue it?"

"It is a question of who is pursuing whom. The witness is leading counsel." He turned a disinterested glance on Horace. "Mr. Hubbard, you will have an opportunity of answering what I am sure will be a great many questions in regard to the testimony you have just given. But you are hereby ordered to volunteer nothing more on the subject and to answer no further questions about it until the Chief Justice orders you to do so. Is that clear?"

"Absolutely, Mr. Chief Justice," Horace said.

Hammett said, "Mr. Olmedo, kindly change the subject."

"Very well, Mr. Chief Justice," Olmedo said. "Mr. Hubbard, it seems we must go back to where we came from." Horace smiled at him in an encouraging and friendly fashion and waited for the next question as if he knew in advance exactly what it would be and could not wait to supply the answer.

Olmedo said, "Let us return, Mr. Hubbard, to the question of oaths. Yesterday a witness, Mr. St. Clair, testified before the Senate that you are a member of a secret society called the Shelley Society. Was that a true and accurate statement?"

"Yes."

"And it is a secret society that requires the taking of a solemn oath?"

Horace nodded his head in amusement. "Very secret, very solemn. Worse than the Illuminati. Until yesterday I didn't know that any outsider even suspected that it existed."

"What is its purpose?"

"Very high-minded. One swears to try to imagine what it is like to be poor and downtrodden, and to work for the elimination of differences in wealth. When the millennium, called the Year Zed, comes and truth and beauty rule the world, all men will be equal in all ways. And happy too, of course."

"Is there an estimated date on which this is going to happen?"

"No."

"Do Shelleyans sign over their inheritances to the poor in the meantime?"

Horace smiled. "No. The vow of poverty is indefinitely postponed. These are twenty-year-old boys, Mr. Olmedo."

"But they remain Shelleyans for life, and one of the ways they do good in the world for the rest of their lives is to help one another out when asked to do so?"

"It goes a bit beyond that," Horace said. "If asked a favor by a fellow Shelleyan in the name of the Poet—that's the wording—one is theoretically not free to refuse."

"No matter what is asked?"

"That's right. Of course not everyone takes that requirement as seriously as Palmer St. Clair."

"Is a request made in the name of the Poet always verbal?"

"Not always. Sometimes it's written out in Greek letters. It's still in English, of course, just written in the Greek alphabet—what the British called the Greek cypher when they used it to baffle the natives during the Indian Mutiny."

"Thank you for the explanation," Olmedo said. "I will ask you this. Who recruited you for intelligence work?"

"The man who was then director of the American intelligence service."

"Was he a member of the Shelley Society?"

"Yes."

"How did you meet him?"

"I knew him from childhood. He was a friend of my father's who frequently came to our house."

"Was your father a member of the Shelley Society?"

"Yes."

"And your half brother is a member?"

"Yes."

"How many members are elected every year?"

"Just one is tapped in each class, in the spring of junior year."

"Who does the tapping?"

"The Shelleyan in the next class above you."

"Then you tap the chosen man in the class below you?"

"With the advice of your senior, yes. That's right."

"Who tapped you, Mr. Hubbard?"

Horace paused, a mere heartbeat. "Baxter Busby," he replied.

"To clarify," Olmedo said, "you are referring to Senator Baxter T. Busby of California?"

"That's correct. Right over there."

"And you and Baxter T. Busby have stayed in close touch with each other ever since?"

"As close as possible. I have lived abroad, mostly."

"You met at reunions of the Shelley Society?"

"There are none. In theory, even the members aren't supposed to know who else belongs, apart from the man who taps you and the man you tap. Of course it becomes obvious enough as the years go by."

"Then the members are divided, in effect, into cells of three and know only each other as fellow Shelleyans?"

"That's the premise, yes. Most cells fall short of the ideal."

"I see," Olmedo said. "Do you know whom your half brother tapped when it came his time to tap somebody in the class below him?"

"I believe it was Palmer St. Clair, but that's hearsay."

"And who tapped Julian?"

Hammett said, "More hearsay, sir? You are skating on thin ice in regard to that list of names, Mr. Olmedo. Is there some point to these questions?"

"We are coming to it, Mr. Chief Justice. If I may proceed."

"You may, but with due regard to relevance and earlier warnings about that list of names, Mr. Olmedo. And we will have no more hearsay, sir."

"As you wish, Mr. Chief Justice," Olmedo said. "Mr. Hubbard, I will ask you this: Did you travel to the island of Mustique in the Caribbean Sea on March the fifth last, and there meet a member of the Shelley Society in secret, and did you make that journey under a false name, using a false passport, and wearing a disguise? And if so, for what purpose?"

"Enough," Hammett said, gaveling. "Enough, enough. The witness is instructed not to answer the question, if it can be described as a question instead of a grab bag. *Disguises,* sir? *False passports? Secret meetings?* Mr. Olmedo, where is your decency, sir, what is your purpose? You are recklessly endangering this witness and exhibiting outrageous contempt for this honorable Senate."

"If you believe that is so, I am sorry, Mr. Chief Justice," Olmedo said. "And if avoiding the perils of answering truthfully under oath is the criterion, I will put the question elsewhere. Article One, Section Six, of the Constitution provides that a senator may not be questioned in any other place for any words spoken on the floor of the Senate. With that in mind, I ask that the Senate call Senator Baxter T. Busby of California as a witness for the President of the United States."

Hammett said, "That is not in order."

Olmedo radiated calm. "Mr. Chief Justice, if it please the Senate, it is entirely in order. Rule Eighteen of *The Conduct of Impeachment Trials in the Senate* states, quote, If a Senator is called as a witness, he shall be sworn, and give his testimony standing in his place, end quote. The question I wish to put to Senator Busby is material to the matter in hand."

Hammett said, "That is quite enough, Mr. Olmedo. The Chief Justice will not permit you to use the rules of the Senate and the Constitution of the United States of America to make a mockery of this most solemn process by attempting to subject members of the Senate to inquisitorial questioning for having belonged to a college fraternity."

Olmedo said, "On behalf of the President of the United States, bearing in mind my earlier request for a mistrial, I ask for a vote of the Senate on this question."

"Mr. Chief Justice! Mr. Chief Justice!" Amzi Whipple was on his feet. "I move that the Senate instruct the Committee on the Impeachment to consider the question of a mistrial in closed session, and that the Senate adjourn so that it may do so without further delay."

"Second," said Sam Clark.

Looking into the solemn, determined faces on the Senate floor, Hammett realized that this was not a motion that would end in a tie vote. He struck the gavel. "Without objection, so ordered," he said.

14

Looking down on Hammett from the gallery Attenborough thought, The scoundrel's methods are wicked, and he makes up evil schemes to destroy the poor with lies, Book of Isaiah, chapter the thirty-second, verse the seventh. After the adjournment all the spectators except the Speaker had cleared out in a hurry, but he had a reason for staying where he was for a while. Albert reached Attenborough while some of the senators, including Clark and Whipple, were still on the floor and Hammett remained on the podium.

Attenborough said, "Just stand in front of me for a minute so's the cameras can't see me, Albert, and hand me the little telephone." The Speaker punched out Sam Clark's number and down on the floor the Majority Leader took his phone out of his pocket and answered.

"Sam, the President is going to resign within the hour," Attenborough said. "I'm asking you to be my Vice President and hold yourself in readiness to become acting President under the Twenty-fifth Amendment within forty-eight hours."

After a silence Clark said, "Tucker, let this cup pass."

"Can't," Attenborough said. "Two more days is about all I can last and you're the only one can get approved in the time available."

"What about Mallory?"

"He agrees. He knows you'll do the right thing by him and the people who voted for him. Sam, it don't make a dime's worth of difference who's President for the next four years. Right from the start the only important thing has been to save the party because the country can't go on like it always has without it."

"All right," Clark said. "What now?"

"Start saving the party," Attenborough said. "Go into that committee meeting and smoke those bastards out. I'm going to call the President now."

All this took no more than a minute. Despite the serenity Hammett radiated, his legs felt weak because in the wake of Horace's testimony he remembered Gika's most important lesson: a Maniáte trusts no one. There was a plot against him; he had known it instinctively ever since the séance at Macalaster's when Zarah Christopher had played her Ouija-board mind games with him. He waited a moment longer on the bench for the strength to come back into his limbs. For the benefit of the cameras he inhaled deeply and lifted his eyes as if asking for guidance from above. Actually he was looking for Attenborough but what he saw was a black man in a dark suit standing in front of the Speaker's usual front-row seat.

The man moved aside. Hammett saw Attenborough hand him a cellular telephone and take his arm, pulling himself to his feet. He seemed barely able to manage this; Hammett assumed he was drunk. For once the Speaker was staring not at Hammett but at Sam Clark, who was looking up at him. Their eyes met and Hammett saw that he had been wrong about the Speaker's condition. Attenborough was not drunk. He was triumphant.

The Speaker nodded once, dismissively, then limped up the aisle on the black man's arm. Hammett looked at Clark again. The Majority Leader's eyes—pale suspicion-filled riffraff eyes, just like Attenborough's—bored into Hammett's for an instant. Then he turned his back, put an arm around Amzi Whipple's shoulders, and whispered something into his ear. Ominous signs.

15

In the meeting of the Committee on the Impeachment, Amzi Whipple said, "This won't take long. Senator Clark, my party will not object to a unanimous consent agreement in order to debate a motion for a mistrial in this impeachment."

"May I have a word about first principles here?" Busby said.

"Not now," Sam Clark replied. "But you can make whatever statement you want when you are called as a witness, sworn, and examined by the President's counsel."

"That's exactly what I wanted to talk about," Busby said. "I will gladly testify about every aspect of my own life and record until the cows come home, but I won't consent to a witch-hunt involving blameless Americans, and that's what that unscrupulous shyster Olmedo is stampeding us into here."

Clark said, "Senator, as chairman of this committee I won't consent to your using the term 'witch-hunt' in connection with a constitutional procedure of the United States Senate. Furthermore, Senator, if you choose not to join in a unanimous-consent agreement, the Senate will adjourn the trial, go into regular session, and I personally will move for your censure by the entire Senate, as well as for an investigation by a Select Committee into the questions raised about the ethics and behavior of the Chief Justice and yourself in this trial."

Busby stared at Clark in disbelief. He was saying these things in the presence of the entire committee—Sam Clark, who never embarrassed a colleague by word or deed, even in private. Busby said, "Censure me on what grounds?"

Clark said, "On grounds that you and Chief Justice Hammett are engaged in a conspiracy to thwart the will of the American people and to pervert the Constitution in order to give them a President they did not elect and would never elect in a million years."

"That's laughable."

"Then we'll have a merry session," Clark said. "Will you vote with your party on unanimous consent?"

Busby said, "What exactly do you hope to accomplish by that?"

"The short answer is, adopt new rules that will let the Senate run this trial. The Senate. Not the Chief Justice. Not the media."

"Who will preside?"

"The Chief Justice will preside as provided by the Constitution. If he is called as a material witness, as I think probable, he will be sworn and will testify from the place where he sits."

"You're talking about a circus, Senator. That word 'circus' is a censored version of what I really mean. You'll never get away with this."

Clark said, "Maybe not. But I'm going to suspend this meeting of the committee for fifteen minutes while you consider your decision, Senator, and confer with anyone you wish."

The other members were mute. Busby was sure he could bring these people around if they would only listen to him. He said, "Sam, Amzi, gentlemen, let us reason together."

Clark said, "Fifteen minutes, Senator. Meeting adjourned."

16

Feeling his way along back passages of the Capitol, Busby reached the Vice President's office unobserved. He had to knock loudly, then even more loudly, at the back door in order to get in. After an inexplicable delay it was unlocked and opened by Hammett himself, still in his black robe. The Chief Justice was not pleased to see Busby. While still on the bench, after seeing the triumph and hatred in the eyes of Attenborough and Clark, he had realized that the prophecy made by Manal Macalaster's Ouija board, the promise that Five-Five would betray Six-Nine, had come true today on the floor of the United States Senate before a worldwide television audience. Horace *had* betrayed him, though he knew it was no prophecy spoken out of "darkness" by an angry spirit called Susan—it was the culmination of a plot that had Zarah Christopher at its center. How she had managed this he did not know; but he was as certain as anyone could be that she had done so.

"I don't know why you're here, Senator," he said. "But please go away. We should not meet or have any contact of any kind."

"This will only take a moment," Busby said.

"This is not the moment," Hammett replied, but Busby did not hear him. He was already talking at full throttle, a phenomenon Hammett had not previously observed, and despite the Chief Justice's protests he advanced into the room, driving Hammett before him with a fusillade of words.

"There's no time to waste," Busby said. "This is the last ticktock."

Hammett said, "The last *what?*"

"The moment we friends of the Poet, friends of the Cause, have been waiting for and working for ever since the beginning, Six-Nine."

" 'Six-Nine'?" Hammett said. "After what is being said out there by that turncoat Hubbard and that imbecile St. Clair, you burst in here and address me as Six-Nine? Are you out of your mind?"

"I've never experienced a saner moment," Busby said. "Nor a happier one. Don't you understand? This is the first day of the Year Zed. Don't you see the opportunity here? We're in control. If they come after us, they'll destroy themselves, thanks to your brilliant work in there exposing their true motives. The media think this is a witch-hunt, the last desperate gasp of the old order, and they're right.''

"And that's all it takes to make you happy?" Hammett said. "Media massages? They're trying to impeach me and disgrace you. Don't *you* see what's developing?"

"They'll never get away with it. Olmedo is a flashy courtroom operator, all right. But he's no politician. I haven't told you—*nobody* has told you because it has been imperative that you be left out of this, imperative that the situation develop without your knowledge so that you would be clean as a hound's tooth in every way."

Another man than Hammett might have laughed on hearing these words. Left out of it? The situation develop without his knowledge? He was the author of the situation! He had invented it! Busby, the fatuous ass, was his pawn! He had made everything happen—everything. Busby was right about one thing: Hammett was as clean as a hound's tooth. He had managed the whole thing so beautifully, had been such an invisible man, that nobody could possibly prove that he had anything to do with the outcome.

Hammett struggled to control the expression on his face. "I see I've taken you by surprise," Busby said. "Sorry about that, but the time has come to reveal to you that there *is* a plan and you are the vital human element in it. And when I tell you the details, as now I must tell you because you must consent to play the role assigned to you before we can go a step further, you will see why we have proceeded as we have."

" 'We'?" Hammett said. "Who exactly is 'we'?"

"No names," Busby said. "Not even"—he paused for a meaningful split second—"class numerals."

He then described the plan, repeating the important passages to drive their significance home. Hammett did not seem to be at all surprised by what he was hearing. Of course Busby could not read Hammett's reaction too well because the Chief Justice retreated as the senator explained things to him, walking backward and keeping just beyond the short limit of Busby's vision. Finally, however, Hammett backed into a wall and Busby pinned him there, momentarily spreading his arms in good-humored parody of the windmill guard he used to be.

"Now, Mr. Chief Justice," he said, "I must ask you. Will you accept the office of acting President of the United States if Congress in its wisdom selects you for that office under the Constitution?"

"Senator," Hammett said, "how can that possibly happen with the suggestion of conspiracy already hanging over both our heads? The minute you suggest it, the Old Guard will say it proves the charge."

"Let them. The media are on our side, and I have reason to think it will happen precisely *because of* the attacks on the two of us, especially the vicious onslaught against you. When I go back into that committee meeting down the hall, I will be asked if I will participate in throwing you to the wolves. I will refuse, indignantly. This will be on television moments after it happens. Sam Clark and Amzi Whipple will adjourn the trial and call the Senate into session. They will introduce a motion of censure against me. I will rise to answer, and when I do, I will describe their shameful plot to seize the presidency for themselves and then will again move—this time successfully—that the election be set aside as defective and null and void. I will then introduce a resolution to set aside the corrupt order of succession, and nominating you as the first acting President of the United States under the appropriate provisions of Article Two and the Twentieth Amendment of the Constitution."

Hammett did not say no to this. Instead he asked, "Will you have the votes?"

"We've had them every time we needed them so far. We will have the media. The media will give us the people. The people will give us the party, and with it, the votes. They will demand a new beginning. Congress will understand that Mallory is the only other alternative. By the time it comes to a vote, we—or rather, Archimedes Hammett—will have the votes. Will you accept if called?"

Hammett said, "Whose idea was this plan?"

Busby said, "Quite simply, he is a friend of the Poet." This was a magnificent moment in history; Busby felt this strongly. He said again, "Will you serve if you are called, Mr. Chief Justice?"

Hammett, who had excellent eyesight, read every thought and sentiment that moved across Busby's face. He had never seen a clearer example of an organism behaving in response to long-term systematic conditioning. To strengthen the behavior, he offered a precisely measured portion of positive reinforcement. "It would be improper for me to acknowledge that this question was even asked," he said.

"Wonderful! That's all I need to know," Busby said. "And now I must go." He grinned down at Hammett, who was about to become the shortest U.S. President since James Madison. Of course the man they were keeping out of the presidency was Attenborough, who was shorter than any of them. Busby did not have time to share this amusing thought. "Now I must go," Busby said, "but first, I've got to *go*, if I may." Hammett's back was against the wall beside the lavatory door. With schoolboy gaiety—Hammett was *so* solemn—Busby faked left, stepped right, reached past him, twisted the door handle, and flung it open.

The light was already on. Slim Eve, who had brought Hammett his lunch and was hiding in the lavatory in order to avoid being seen by Busby, stood just inside the door. She wore a miniskirt: beautiful legs. She had been eavesdropping, of course, and the smile of deep-seated pleasure and amusement on her face was just beginning to change into one of surprise and consternation.

"Oops! Sorry! Wrong door!" cried Busby, slamming it shut. He hurried across the spongy carpet, then slipped out the back door without another word.

Of course he had not recognized Slim. During their previous meeting at the Womonkind Coalition, the innermost lair of the Anti-Sex League, he had not glimpsed the memorable legs that had just been revealed to him, and her startled face had been a blur to him. All he perceived when he opened the door was an indistinct human form with feminine attributes— Hammett's secretary probably, or one of his law clerks, trapped in there by Busby's unannounced arrival and discreetly keeping out of sight till he went away. He wondered what, if anything, she had overheard. It didn't matter, not anymore. He had his answer from Hammett; the die was cast. He looked at the big numerals on his wristwatch: his chat with Hammett must have taken longer than he thought. Sam and Amzi would be furious. But it was all in a good cause.

As Busby strode purposefully toward the Senate Conference Room he did not see Tucker Attenborough in the midst of a knot of men and women, obviously security people of some kind, emerging from the unmarked door of the seldom-used President's Room just down the corridor. Even if, in his hurry, he had spotted the little man, he would not have been interested enough to say hello. The Speaker was yesterday's news.

17

When Busby reentered the Senate Conference Room he found it empty except for Sam Clark. Sensing victory, Busby grinned happily and said, "Sam, sorry to be late, but I'm glad we're alone, if only for a moment, because I'm sure we can iron all this out and avoid the embarrassment of a really messy brouhaha if you'll just hear me out before the others come back. What I'm going to propose will put everything to rights, Sam, providing a pragmatic, constitutional way out of this impasse. A new beginning in honor. I call it 'the constitutional deliverance.' Let me explain it to you briefly before the rest of the committee comes back—"

Clark said, "Buzzer, they won't be coming back. Where have you been?"

"Fixing the last nail," Busby said. "Now, first, about this idea of Amzi's to declare a mistrial. That's clearly a Malloryite trap. Don't think I'm afraid to testify. I welcome it, but—"

"You won't have to testify," Clark said. "Buzzer, listen to me." Busby opened his mouth. Clark said, "*Listen.* The mistrial is a dead issue. The trial is over."

Busby halted in midbreath. "Over? How can it be over?"

"Lockwood has resigned," Clark said. "Tucker Attenborough was just sworn in as President of the United States."

Busby gasped. "Tucker Attenborough?" he said. "They can't do that! This can't happen in America."

"On the contrary," Clark said. "It's just about the only place on earth where it *can* happen. Now I have to call on the President."

"I thought you just said he resigned."

"I was referring to President Attenborough."

"*President* Attenborough?" Busby said. "You call that drunken dwarf the President?"

"As of ten minutes ago, when he was sworn in by Albert Tyler in the President's Room with the leadership of both houses of Congress as witnesses, that's what he is."

Busby was staggered by the audacity of this maneuver by the Old Guard. "But how could something like this happen just like that, with no warning, out of the blue?"

"Because we have a Constitution which delivers us from evil," Clark replied. "Sorry you missed the ceremony, but nobody knew where you were and we couldn't wait for you."

18

Lockwood's farewell to the nation was brief and to the point. In an all-networks broadcast from Camp David, in the time segment immediately preceding the evening news, he announced his withdrawal from the presidency.

"On the basis of evidence and testimony before the United States Senate today, and its careful verification and analysis by my counsel and myself, it is now clear to me that I was not elected President of the United States last November. Furthermore, the American people now know beyond a reasonable doubt that the irregularities that took place, including the secret commission of a homicide of a foreign head of state that set off the sad chain of events in which our country has been entangled, were none of my doing. However, I was the responsible officer of the government at the time that these matters occurred, and even though they were concealed from me, I must and do accept full responsibility and offer a most heartfelt apology for the actions of persons in whom I mistakenly placed the sacred trust bestowed on me by the American people. I also ask the forgiveness of the Great Judge for failing to do that which I ought to have done to prevent these sorrowful events from happening at all. The Senate in its wisdom will, in due course, make known its judgment on the questions before it, and I am content, as a former man of the Senate, to abide by its judgment. I myself asked that the Congress discover the truth, and as I confidently expected, Congress has done so. Now that we are in possession of that truth, we must live by it. I cannot remain longer in an office which the people did not give to me, and therefore I hereby withdraw from it under the terms of the Twenty-fifth Amendment to the Constitution of the United States. The Speaker of the House, the Honorable R. Tucker Attenborough, Jr., has succeeded me as President, and in my last appeal to you, my fellow Americans, I ask you to give him your support, your prayers, and, yes, your trust. He is one of the most stouthearted and truthful men I have ever known, and as history will record, he is a great American patriot. I am going back with my beloved wife to the place where we came from. My last service to you—this search for the truth which has set things right with our democracy, preserved our Constitution, and renewed our freedom as a people—is the one over all the others in a long public life that I hope the Lord will let me be remembered for.

"And now I say goodbye. God bless the American people. God save the Constitution. God preserve America and the noble dream that made it."

Because Lockwood was Lockwood, there was a tear in his eye. He wiped it away as the camera lights went out, and stepped into the next room, away from the stunned television crew. After closing the door behind him he picked up the phone, on which Tucker Attenborough was waiting on an open line. "Tucker?" he said. "Don't die before you get rid of that son of a bitch I was damn fool enough to make Chief Justice of the United States."

Lockwood departed immediately by helicopter. As the tilted blurry improbable machine, emblematic of so many ambiguous American endings, rose into the night, it was silhouetted for an instant against the fourth full moon since Inauguration Day.

19

Just after midnight on the night of Lockwood's resignation, Macalaster parked his Jaguar next to McGraw's rented Ford in the unlighted back lot of the fish market on Maine Avenue. With Macalaster beside him in the front seat, McGraw drove slowly by the row house five or six blocks away where Slim and Sturdi had been living rent-free as guests of a sympathizer who wished to do something to ease the financial and other burdens imposed on Slim by her legal battle against Attenborough. "That's it," McGraw said to Macalaster. "Number 507, pink door, black iron fence, Volvo with Connecticut plates parked in front, light on upstairs. Got it?"

Macalaster nodded.

McGraw said, "Don't try to be Spencer Tracy in there. Play yourself. That's the part you've been rehearsing for all your life."

"To wild applause," Macalaster said. He did not like the feeling of behaving like an agent provocateur or the prospect of carrying out the mission under journalistic cover, but he agreed that he was the only one who could possibly do what he was about to do: bait the hook.

McGraw swung the wheel. "What I'm going to do is turn the corner here, drive two blocks, turn another corner, and let you out," he said. This neighborhood was risky at night, though not remotely so dangerous as some others not far away to the east and north. Here the streets were empty of pedestrians except for the occasional flitting shadow at the edge of an amber puddle of street light. McGraw switched off the lights and pulled into a dark parking place. "Okay, you're up," he said. "Walk like you know where you're going, don't look back, and when you get there, knock on the door and say the sooth. Then go back to your car and go straight to the destination. Everyone else will already be out in the woods, you'll be a hundred percent on your own, but it can't be any other way."

"Understood."

McGraw said, "Remember, the whole idea is to get them to follow you. Forget you're in a Jaguar. If you get yourself arrested or lose your tail, everything goes up the flue."

Macalaster got out and walked briskly down the middle of the street, a routine precaution advised by the police and all newspaper and magazine articles on urban survival.

After the adjournment sine die of the impeachment trial that afternoon—that is to say, its end—Hammett had vanished. The media watch on the Supreme Court and the one on his apartment building on Pennsylvania Avenue reported no sightings there. Not even Patrick Graham could reach the Chief Justice on the telephone.

However, Macalaster was where he was because ♂ ↔ ♀ teams had followed Sturdi to the borrowed house near the Federal Center Metro station when interest in her was high. They had also placed a tracer bug on the Volvo—a pinhead of radioactive matter disguised as a speck of tar whose emissions could be read from a considerable distance with the right equipment but was undetectable by ordinary counterbugging measures unless you happened to have a Geiger counter with you. Today, on Wiggins's orders, other ♂ ↔ ♀ teams had followed the Volvo home from the Capitol and reported that Hammett had emerged from it and entered the house. At half past midnight Macalaster rang the doorbell.

Slim answered the door. "Sorry," she said coldly. "This is not convenient."

Macalaster said, "I have something important to tell him."

"He's not seeing anybody. Goodbye." The look Slim gave him was one of concentrated suspicion, hostility, and disgust—as if he were a Neanderthal who had suddenly popped up in the middle of a Cro-Magnon religious rite.

He smiled brightly and said, "You've never really liked me since I killed the deer, have you?" Slim started to slam the door. Macalaster put his foot in it and took out his telephone. "If he doesn't want to see me, one of his oldest friends," he said, "how do you think he'd like to have a media encampment out front?" He punched six digits into the phone. "One more digit and he's got it."

The look of primal animosity on Slim's face intensified. But she said, "Follow me. But I promise you, he's not in the mood for this."

In the living room, Hammett was watching television, the late-night roundtable shows, four of them on-screen in individual windows, switching the sound on and off in random sequence. All four windows were filled with shots of the Speaker, who was now the President, or with the faces of men and women who were talking about him as obsessively as, only hours before, they had been talking about Hammett. They had already stopped talking about Lockwood and Mallory. Of Attenborough's accession Patrick Graham, looking somewhat stunned, said, "It was surely the most *surreptitious* taking of the presidential oath in history, administered by the President's longtime valet, who turns out, lo and behold, to be a justice of the peace. The ceremony, such as it was, took place in privacy, in the presence of a few old cronies. There was no television, no visual record of any kind to give the occasion legitimacy, except a black-and-white still photograph by a man who takes pictures of weddings. And he hasn't been seen since. No one knows where he is."

Hammett had changed back into the never-soiled work clothes that had been his trademark before he became Chief Justice. Sturdi sat in another chair, her head wrapped in a proletarian bandanna, and when she saw Macalaster follow Slim into the room, her eyes snapped angrily and she cried out, "Shit!"

Slim said, "Mr. Chief Justice, it's Ross Macalaster." Hammett jumped slightly when his attention was broken but otherwise showed no surprise. He said, "Ross. Of course it's you. So how do you like your friend Attenborough now?"

"I've always liked him," Macalaster said. He chose his next words carefully for maximum effect on Sturdi. "A fine American." With a cry of wordless disgust, Sturdi leaped to her feet and rushed out of the room.

Hammett said, "I guess she didn't think that was funny."

Macalaster said, "Really? She has no idea how unfunny it's going to get."

Hammett said, "What's that supposed to mean?"

"I picked up a funny story today," Macalaster said. "It's all about you and the two Eves." Slim was standing close behind Macalaster, and he could feel her alertness level rise.

Hammett switched off the television. He said, "What story is that?"

"Well, my source tells me that Lockwood's legal team has identified the Mickey Finn St. Clair used to hang that tape on me."

"The fishing fly, you mean."

"Right. They think it belongs to Associate Justice Bobby M. Poole."

Hammett said, "Poole hung the tape on you?"

"No. A Mickey Finn was stolen from his collection of hand-tied flies in his chambers at the Supreme Court."

"Stolen? Who says so?"

"Poole reported it stolen. Lockwood's people asked the FBI crime lab to examine the one I had."

"You handed it over?"

"They subpoenaed it."

"And you didn't resist? I thought you were a journalist."

"I am. That's why I'm so curious. The crime lab says that this particular Mickey Finn was made from materials that correspond exactly to the ones used by Justice Poole. He ties his flies in alphabetical order, so the cuts he made in the materials used in the one before and the one after match exactly under the microscope."

Hammett said, "I'm impressed. That's your big story for the day?"

"That, and the fact that the two Eves are the prime suspects."

"What two Eves?"

"Your two Eves."

Hammett stared. "You're joking."

"No. This is serious. The Eves had access to Poole's collection; the logs show them as the only outsiders who came in and out of the building late at night. Also there are tapes from the security cameras of one of them going in and out of Poole's chambers in the night."

"Which one?"

"I don't have that detail. But I think this may break quite soon."

"Break?" Hammett said. "Who's the reporter going to be, Franz Kafka? No journalist in this town would break that story. Not even you, Ross. We've been through too much together."

"True. I couldn't write it as is."

Sturdi came back into the room wearing a short black mannish wig. It was slightly askew. Into Macalaster's mind's eye came the computer-generated image of Sturdi with shaved head, and he realized that she always covered her head with a bandanna or one of her wigs because she was bald. How had Lucy's computer missed this detail? How had he? Her bold gaze seemed to challenge Macalaster to say what he was thinking. He looked away and realized why he had never noticed her baldness: he had always avoided looking at her.

Hammett said, "Sturdi, did you happen to hear what this guy was telling us?"

"I heard," Sturdi said.

Hammett shook his head in disbelief. "They'll stop at nothing," he said. "This is so obvious. First they pull my college fraternity out of the hat and make it sound like Smersh, now it's a fishing fly that has a sinister meaning. What next?"

Hammett and the two unsmiling women were examining Macalaster. "If you think that's bizarre," Macalaster said, "wait till you hear the Zarah Christopher theory."

"The Valkyrie strikes again." Hammett snorted and rolled his eyes. "I can't wait."

"Well, she thinks that Sturdi has been following her."

"*What?*" Hammett said. His lip curled in disgust.

"Not just following her, but wearing disguises," Macalaster said.

"Good grief," said Hammett. "More disguises."

Macalaster said, "Mallory's security people got on the case because Zarah's so close to him. They took a lot of pictures of this alleged activity."

"You've seen these pictures?"

"Yes. According to computer comparisons, it could be Sturdi. But that isn't where it ends. Zarah has much more serious suspicions."

"Like what?"

"I don't know yet, but I'm going to find out tonight. Something to do with Susan Grant. She's extremely upset. I'm going out to talk to her—Zarah, that is—when I leave here. But before I went I wanted you to know you may have a problem."

Sturdi said, "Where is this psychotic liar? I'm filing suit in the morning."

"For what?" Macalaster said. "Violation of your right to stalk Mallory's girlfriend?"

Hammett said, "That's not funny."

"Nothing's funny anymore—haven't you noticed?" Macalaster said. "Are you going to be here for a while? I'd like to chat with you after I've spoken to Zarah."

"You mean you're working on this as a story?"

"Working on stories is what I do for a living."

"I remember," Hammett said. "The question is, do you remember what you owe me?"

"Sure, leprosy," Macalaster said.

"Plus riches and fame." Hammett was being circumspect about whatever was between him and Macalaster. Slim and Sturdi realized this and became even more watchful of Macalaster.

Macalaster said, "Dr. Faustus thanks you. Do you want to get together or not?"

"When will you be back?"

Macalaster looked at his watch. "It's a long drive to where she is."

Hammett said, "Where's that?"

"I can't tell you that. Zarah made me swear not to. But it's a long way. I won't get back in town until morning. Then I have to write."

"How long a way? North, south, east, west?" Hammett was asking all the questions; as was their habit, the Eves were as mute in his presence as obedient wives in a religious commune.

"You're not going to get it out of me," Macalaster said. "She's in hiding. She thinks Sturdi is a real threat. I think pretty soon, after she's done whatever she's going to do, she's going to vanish back into the Mountains of the Moon or wherever she came from."

"And what exactly is she going to do?" asked Hammett.

"That's what I'm on my way to find out," Macalaster said. He was surprised at how well he was doing this; it was like being in a movie, just remembering to be debonair, and that he was not responsible for the dialogue. He looked at his watch again. "It's one o'clock. I've got to get started. My car is parked in the fish market."

"You're planning to walk through this neighborhood at this hour?" Slim said.

"I don't think I'm likely to find a taxi."

"Come on," she said with sudden friendliness. "I'll drive you to your car."

Macalaster grinned at her again. "You want me to live?"

"I just don't want you to die in this neighborhood," she replied. "I'd be too likely a suspect." Suddenly she smiled at him, and the glum, overexercised ideological harpy who had met him at the door became the giddy *Cosmopolitan* girl of the Attenborough dinner party. She really was a knockout.

They went out to the Volvo together. Slim drove in silence to the parking lot and let Macalaster out. During the short ride he was conscious of her body, as if it were emitting energy along some weird emotional spectrum that he could not quite tune in to. Macalaster had never regarded Slim as a sex object, but now he was aroused. As he fought against this, he suddenly realized why: he used to feel the same alternating waves of hatred and sexual invitation coming from Brook. He said, "Thanks," and got out of the Volvo.

Slim got out too and walked around the Jaguar as he unlocked it. As he opened the door she rapped sharply on the trunk and said, "This car is disgusting."

Slim's face had reverted to its normal expression of barely contained rejection and disgust. But she was right about the Jaguar.

Without looking back he headed down the freeway and across the Potomac, watching the speedometer carefully, the car fretting under the restraint he was imposing upon it. Since its collision with the whitetail buck on Foxhall Road, Macalaster had had the vague feeling that the Jaguar had gone loco. It seemed possible to him that it might suddenly spook like a horse and swerve to the left or right and hurtle suicidally off the road.

20

Before going out to meet the assassin, Zarah refused the weapons offered to her by Wiggins and Lucy—a pistol, an aerosol canister of red-pepper spray, an umbrella made of bulletproof cloth that fired tranquilizer darts from the ferrule—but accepted a protective vest that stopped all known bullets up to 12mm. Inasmuch as the assassin, like all gunmen who had been trained on KGB principles, always got close and aimed for the head, Zarah did not think this would be of much use, but she took it for the sake of unit morale.

Lucy handed her a small glass object about the size of a walnut. "This thing is called MɪɴɪNovA, as in exploding star," she said. "It's attached to a ring. Slip it over your finger, hold it in your hand at all times, and when the moment comes, press the bulb back into the ring—see?" Zarah nodded. Lucy said, "Close your eyes." She pressed the switch and the MɪɴɪNovA went off with a blinding flash of light that dazzled Zarah even through her closed eyelids. McGraw, who had been entertained by the impressive array of $\male \leftrightarrow \female$ weaponry, said, "Neat. Just like Jimmy Stewart in *Rear Window*."

After this they went over the plan, detail by detail, one last time. The women would play the most dangerous roles.

The two of them discussed each contingency, each move, each signal, calmly and intelligently, with no outward display of emotion, but the air was charged with Lucy's doubts.

Wiggins showed his worry. "You'll have to be flawless, both of you," he said. "I'd feel better about this if we had time for a rehearsal. If we had backup."

"I've been rehearsing it monthly for years," Lucy said, "and you're my backup. All Zarah has to do is smile and set off the flash at the right moment."

"At *exactly* the right moment," Wiggins said.

"I don't know how that could be rehearsed," Zarah said. "It's going to be a matter of instinct."

"That's why I've loved this whole idea from the start," McGraw said with heavy irony. "Instinct makes the world go around."

Zarah gave him a smile. Lucy did not acknowledge his words or the thought behind it in any way. For days now he had been watching Lucy watching Zarah, and he knew that Lucy had not been able to overcome her instinct. She still thought something was wrong about Zarah, that she was not to be trusted, not to be believed.

Lucy and Wiggins had to get into position before dark, so they left first. There were no goodbyes.

"See you there," Zarah said.

"No, you won't," Lucy said. "But I'll see the light. But remember, I won't be able to hear or see a thing before that, and you won't be able to see a thing after it goes off."

Zarah smiled. "Then I guess we'll be at each other's mercy," she said.

After Lucy and Wiggins had left, McGraw said, "Tell me something, Zarah. Do you sense a problem with your partner?"

"Lucy? She doesn't trust me; she may even think I'm leading them into a trap."

"That doesn't make you uncomfortable?"

"No, it doesn't matter," Zarah said. "She doesn't have to trust me. All she has to do is see the light."

"And follow her instincts."

"No," Zarah said. "Her training."

21

Zarah's destination was Camp Panchaea. Although she knew the way and asked her not to do so, Emily insisted on driving her out for what she believed would be a reunion with Julian. "The way things are going for the Hubbards we may never have a chance to talk again," she said. They started out at three o'clock in the morning, and Emily talked without stopping all the way to their destination.

Dawn was only a few minutes off when they arrived. It was a cloudless night with stars overhead and a spherical moon reflecting in the lake. A single long, slow ripple moved across its limpid surface. There were no waterfowl in sight. They sat in the car and Emily talked about her lost baby. Zarah looked long at the ripple before getting out of the car, then paid no more attention to it.

"Well, so much for the past," Emily said. "I'll wake Julian up and tell him you're here. I brought breakfast in that cooler." She pointed at a blue thermos bag in the back of the car.

"Tell him not to hurry," Zarah said. "I'd like to take a little walk before the sun comes up."

"A *walk?*" Emily said. "There are wild animals in these woods."

"Lions?"

"Cougars, anyway, and wolves—native American species. The Euhemerians don't admit they've turned wolves loose but they have, with chips implanted under their skin. Something electrical is buried around the perimeter of their territory. If they cross a certain line they get a shock. I'll come with you."

"No, go inside, Emily, if you don't mind," Zarah said. "I have memories of this place. I'd like to be alone for a moment."

"All right." The memories could only be of Paul Christopher. Nobody but descendants of Euhemerians ever came to Camp Panchaea.

Zarah was already well down a path leading into the trees. Because she knew the place so well, having scouted every foot of it—every trail through the woods, every place to swim ashore from the lake, every shooting stand—she followed a carefully chosen route. It was exactly as she remembered it; every step she took was planned. She came to a shooting range. The targets, relics of club shoots, were whimsical: original Disney characters, Mickey and Donald and Pluto, with bull's-eyes drawn on their comical potbellies. Not a cougar or wolf was to be seen. Zarah did not look out for danger; she sauntered unconcernedly on.

She reached the shore of the lake. The eastern horizon was growing brighter, the moon dimmer. A frieze of cattails was etched black against the sky. Zarah turned around and looked into the woods toward the place where the sun would rise minutes from now. The lake was utterly calm, without a ripple or even the ghost of one remaining. It lay in a cup of land, so that the wind seldom disturbed it.

Behind her in the clearing by the cabins, almost half a mile away now, she heard Julian's voice calling her name. She ignored him and walked on. A moment later, as if a door had been opened a crack, a shaft of sunlight flashed out of the east onto the water. Songbirds awoke by the hundreds, murmuring. This sleepy tumult increased as the light grew brighter.

Zarah turned around and saw exactly what she had expected to see, a figure in a hooded white caftan standing among the trees about sixty feet away, luminous in the forest gloom with the sun rising behind it, an Ingmar Bergman composition: Death as the Bride. In a loud, cheery voice Zarah called out, "Good *morning!*" Julian, nearer now but still not in sight, called out an answer.

The figure waved with its right hand and, also as expected, started to walk toward Zarah. She held her ground and waved back. The other advanced with long strides, smiling inside the hood of the caftan as if in happy recognition of a friend. When within ten feet the assassin stopped, planted her feet, and threw her weight forward, raising her left hand, in which she held a 9mm pistol exactly like the one that had killed Susan Grant. It was a smooth, much-practiced movement, and as on Inauguration Day, the technique was flawless. She was still smiling in the most friendly way imaginable. Zarah smiled back. Then, a fraction of a second before the gun stopped rising, she set off the MiniNova she held in her upraised hand. In its brilliant flash she saw that the assassin's large blue eyes were fixed as if hypnotized on an imaginary spot in the center of her forehead.

Half an hour earlier, Lucy had swum across the lake underwater, her snorkel tube creating the beautiful ripple Zarah had seen from the clearing. Now Lucy saw the brilliant flash through the lake's surface and rose to her knees out of the shallows in which she had been lying. She knelt in the water just behind Zarah and a little to the left of her. There was no time for Zarah to move out of the way or dive for cover, nor was that necessary. Lucy had a clear view of the target, and she recognized it immediately for what it was. Though dazzled by the MiniNova, the assassin also saw Lucy, or perceived movement or felt it, and turned toward the threat this represented.

Lucy had practiced this drill dozens of times, the swim, the wait, the flash, the shoot. Training eliminated the need for thought—even, as Zarah had foreseen, for intuition. Holding her 6mm all-vinyl ♂ ↔ ♀–issue machine pistol in both hands at the end of rigidly outthrust arms, Lucy fired a burst of twelve mercury-weighted, vinyl-tipped, soft copper rounds into the heart and lungs of the person who had killed Susan Grant. The first round killed the target; the woman grunted just once, then spun completely around and fell face downward.

After entering the thorax, each tiny bullet, only .23 inch in diameter on exiting the muzzle of Lucy's pistol, expanded to the size and approximate shape of a Delicious apple, destroying all tissue around it but remaining safely inside the target instead of exiting like a Parabellum round and striking some innocent bystander.

There was practically no noise. The birds rose from the trees as if they were the nerves of a single invisible creature, then settled back onto the branches. A moment later the full orb of the sun appeared and in unison they burst into full-throated song.

Julian arrived in time to see the bullets strike and the target fall. "No! No!" he cried—mistakenly thinking, as he said later, that the assassin had struck again, and that the figure lying on the ground was Zarah. Wiggins rose from the lake in his wetsuit and covered Julian with his own unfired pistol. Zarah said, "It's all right. It's just my cousin." Wild-eyed, just up from sleep, Julian stared at Wiggins's gun, which was still pointing at the bridge of his nose, then stared down at the corpse. It held a large black pistol in its hand.

He said, "For God's sake, what is this?"

Julian began to tremble: he had never before witnessed a death by violence, not even in Vietnam, because he had flown so far above the war.

Lucy kicked away the assassin's weapon. Then she turned the body over with her foot, sliding toe and arch beneath the armpit and heaving the weight with a smooth, almost balletic movement. Because there were no exit wounds, there was no blood on the snowy caftan apart from the twelve red dots where the bullets had entered the body.

With her pistol pointed at the corpse's head, Lucy folded back the hood of the caftan. A shining cascade of hair spilled out onto the damp soil. The face was quite beautiful in its wide-eyed astonishment. Slim wore no mask this time, and to Zarah she looked very much as she had when she was enticing Attenborough, like an actress summoning up a former self to make the character she was playing believable.

Voices called. McGraw appeared, followed by a ♂ ↔ ♀ team, who supported a stunned and silent Sturdi between them. She had lost whatever head covering she had been wearing, and her polished scalp shone in the strengthening light. She stared at Zarah out of eyes in which there was no expression of any kind.

McGraw knelt by the dead assassin. Slim's left hand, encased in a transparent surgical glove, was thrown across her bodice, five vermilion fingertips among the tiny bloodstains on the cloth. "A lefty?" he asked. Lucy nodded.

"How did you know?" he said to Zarah, who had gone to stand beside Julian.

"She asked to change places with me at a dinner party once so she could have elbowroom," Zarah replied. "Even though I'm left-handed myself."

"So I noticed," Lucy said.

22

In the next morning's newspapers, Ross Macalaster broke his story identifying Slim Eve as the person who had assassinated Susan Grant, and her law partner, Sturdi Eve, as the accomplice who had led investigators down a false path by renting the hideout apartment and leaving a trail of fabricated evidence therein. Sturdi was also charged with the assault on Montague Love and the theft of his press badge and with complicity in the hammer attack carried out by Slim on Senator Wilbur E. Garrett. Macalaster had written as he went along, so the article was long and detailed, taking up the entire lead column on page one and two full pages inside. Because the story was really about Hammett, Macalaster broke a journalistic taboo and identified him as the original source of the story that launched his ambiguous journalistic career by shattering the presidency of the unfortunate man who had been defeated eight years before by Franklin Mallory.

Though he was in seclusion, Hammett was reached by Patrick Graham for comment about Macalaster's revelations. He said, "I am unable to comment. The constitutional cycle is not yet complete, and as Chief Justice I must hold myself aloof from this fever of slander, allegation, and political maneuver." To his audience Graham said, "I think what the Chief Justice is saying in his restrained and dignified way is that the good fight is still being fought." But even Graham was subdued. More in moral fatigue than in insinuation, he reported, as the last word in the last segment of that day's edition of *Newsdawn*, that Casey Isaacs, Ross Macalaster's literary agent in New York, had announced plans to auction the book rights to his client's story, and that he had already received a floor bid of two million dollars from a publisher.

The Senate and House convened at noon. No motion was offered placing Hammett's name in consideration for the presidency. By one o'clock the Senate had approved Sam Clark's nomination for the vice presidency by ninety-six votes to two, with Clark abstaining and Senator Busby of California absent and not voting. The House did not vote until four in the afternoon and the result was less overwhelming, with more than one hundred die-hard radical votes against the nomination, but effective work by the probable next Speaker, Bob Laval of Louisiana, and by other staunch allies of President Attenborough carried the day.

At five P.M. Sam Clark was sworn in as Vice President at Camp David, where Attenborough had taken up temporary residence in one of the smaller cottages. The witnesses included the leadership of both houses of Congress and the Joint Chiefs of Staff in full uniform and ribbons—"an ominous bit of symbolism," Graham mused. The oath of office was administered by Albert Tyler—"an opaque bit of symbolism," said Graham.

By six P.M. the governor of Massachusetts had appointed a former governor who was a member of Mallory's party to Clark's vacant seat, and the Senate immediately reorganized itself with Amzi Whipple as Majority Leader. Bob Laval was elected Speaker of the House half an hour later, ending a day of decisive action rarely matched in the peacetime history of the legislative branch.

While the House was voting, Attenborough talked to Alfonso Olmedo C. and Norman Carlisle Blackstone.

"Mr. Olmedo, you're one hell of a lawyer," he said. "So are you, Carlisle."

"So are you, Mr. President."

Attenborough went on as if Olmedo's words had not been spoken. He said, "The country will thank the two of you for this when the history of it comes out. Did Lockwood?"

"In his way," Olmedo said. "His farewell speech was thanks enough."

"Nothing in the world wrong with Lockwood's way," Attenborough said. "Heart of oak; head, too. Well, you got him what he wanted—the chance to do right. And he did it, may he have his just reward."

Olmedo said, "My work is done, Mr. President—"

Attenborough said, "Not yet. In your opinion—yours too, Carlisle—can Archimedes Hammett be successfully prosecuted for any crime?"

Olmedo hesitated, then inclined his head to Blackstone. "Carlisle?"

After a moment of thought Blackstone said, "Possibly. There's a great deal beneath the surface there. He thinks he's covered his tracks, but that's impossible."

"You think he can be linked to a felony?"

"Almost certainly. He was the puppet master."

"Meaning what?"

"Meaning he knew what was going to happen from the start because he *made* it happen. In terms of circumstantial evidence, we've got the goods on him. But that might not be enough. That woman Eve will never testify against him, and Hammett being Hammett, the more incontrovertible the proof, the more he'll cry 'frame-up' and the more his tribe will beat the drums to drown out the evidence."

Attenborough wore a look of grim determination. "That's how the believers do it, all right," he said. "Alfonso?"

Olmedo said, "I agree with my colleague in every particular. But, Mr. President, if I may say so, this is a one-question case. What could possibly be gained from such a prosecution that would justify the damage it would do to a nation that is already so battered and bruised?"

"Not a damn thing," Attenborough replied. "Thank you, gentlemen. It's been a pleasure working with you."

Olmedo looked at the little wizened President with deep affection and deeper concern. He had never seen a sicker man conscious, upright, and talking, let alone making jokes.

At eight P.M. Attenborough went on television and told the American people that because he was unable to discharge the duties of the presidency for reasons of health, he had notified the president pro tempore of the Senate and the Speaker of the House that he was handing over the powers of the presidency to Vice President Clark, as provided in the Twenty-fifth Amendment to the Constitution.

After speaking these words he paused and looked long into the camera with the same intensity with which he had gazed down at Hammett from the gallery—as if he were already beyond the grave and were examining a human heart from the vantage point of a being who now knows everything. "There's one more thing," he said. "As my final act as President of the United States, I have affixed my signature and seal to a full and unconditional pardon to Archimedes Mavromikháli Hammett for any criminal offenses whatsoever that he may have committed since being appointed Chief Justice of the United States. Regarding any possible impeachable offenses, that is a matter between Mr. Hammett and the Congress of the United States. As *Federalist* Paper Number 65 tells us, far better than I could ever say it, the Founding Fathers granted the power of impeachment to Congress because 'the involutions and varieties of vice are too many and too artful to be anticipated by positive law.' "

In his studio Patrick Graham gasped audibly. "The old fox," he said, "the old redneck. He has beheaded the Cause."

Graham was far too professional to repeat this insight or anything like it on-camera or into a live microphone after he recovered from the stunning blow Attenborough, with the last ounce of his political strength and savvy, had delivered to him and everything he cared about.

23

On their last day together Mallory and Zarah Christopher walked to a hilltop above Great Falls. They paused beneath a spreading oak on a spot that commanded a view of the Norman manor house. In the distance the Potomac, tumultuous with rain that had fallen on the Appalachians, ran through its narrow defile. Horace had gone to prison that day. It was not yet known what would happen to Julian or Rose MacKenzie. They talked about Attenborough's long coma; Lucy's decision to have her twins; the charges filed in New York against Sturdi for acts of terrorism including the attempted murder, years before, of a police officer, John L. S. McGraw; Hammett's resignation as Chief Justice and his billion-dollar lawsuit against Mallory for invasion of Sturdi's privacy; Macalaster's giving up journalism to write his book.

Zarah said, "I want to say this to you, Franklin. I wish your child had been saved."

"So do I," Mallory said. "How I wish you'd stay. It's very hard to accept that there's no chance of having the child I've waited for all my life."

"I thought you knew that already," Zarah said.

"Not in quite the impossible way I do at this moment. I've never thanked you. What you did, seeing the truth, seeing the obvious, walking into the woods that way and . . . willing your death not to happen." He paused. "I just wish you didn't want so badly to be"—he searched for the word—"apart."

"It runs in the family," said Zarah. "Goodbye."

Just the word, not the smallest gesture. She simply left. Watching her walk down the hill, so singular and uncaptured, he fell into a reverie, wishing for a child in which they both could go on living. He had often thought of such a thing before, and he lost himself in the idea of it. In his mind he actually saw the child holding its mother's hand. This was not an image, not a reality. It was something else—a memory he would never have. When he looked again the real Zarah was gone, as if he had fallen into a tiny sleep after an act of conception and given her the fleeting moment of solitude that was all she needed to become a memory.

EPILOGUE

Just as Dr. Chin had predicted, Attenborough's heart kept on beating for a long time after his other vital organs stopped working one by one. The Speaker died on the first day of summer and was buried on Dead Horse Mountain, as far away from his father's grave as possible in the little windburned cemetery that overlooked the desert below. While he was still able to do so, he had dictated and signed strict instructions about how the thing was to be done: the best aluminum casket money could buy, no flowers, no prayers, no clergymen, no eulogy, no politicians except those who had held the office of President of the United States or that of Speaker of the House of Representatives. No media. No women. No hymns. American music was all right, but no bugle calls. Albert Tyler, his sole heir and executor, carried out his wishes to the letter.

The new Speaker, Bob Laval, was out of the country and no former Speaker was able to attend, but Mallory, Lockwood, and Sam Clark were there. The only other mourner was Albert. A sergeant from the U.S. Marine Corps Band sang Attenborough's favorite songs: "The Cowboy's Lament," "Army Blue," and "America the Beautiful." The sergeant's unaccompanied baritone lent a sentimental timbre to these innocent works about the sorrows and joys of American manhood. As the last note faded there was a faraway look in Albert's eye and a tear in Lockwood's. Sam Clark lifted his hand as in a toast and said, "Absent friends." Mallory silently nodded.

Lockwood said, "Sad day, Albert." It was the first time since the day they had met in Attenborough's office three decades earlier that Lockwood had not called him Ablert. Albert had never mentioned this before, but now he said, "I see you've lost your speech impediment, Mr. President." Peering into the open grave, Lockwood said, "That's not all I've lost lately. I guess we're not allowed to say any words?" Albert said, "No, but there's nothing says you can't stand here and think for a while."

It was late afternoon but still hot here on the fringe of the Chihuahua desert. A wind filled with powdery grit blew from the west. To the south, through the haze, they could make out the blistered humps of the Chisos

Mountains where the Rio Grande made its Big Bend. Sam Clark said, "Which way is Terlingua from here?" Albert pointed toward the river, to the right of the mountains. There was nothing to be seen between the graveyard and the ghost town except a windmill with only one unbroken blade remaining. Lockwood said, "We all remember Terlingua and the blushing bride." Albert's eyes were fixed on the windmill. "True story," he said. Clark said, "They were all true stories." Albert said, "That's right, Mr. President. But he didn't necessarily tell every story he knew."

Two old men, Mexicans, each holding a hat in one hand and a shovel in the other, stood fifty yards away by a fence made of twisted mesquite branches. Mallory said, "Albert, I've always wondered. How did you and Tucker get together in the first place?" Albert nodded toward Terlingua. "It was right by that windmill down there, year the two of us was eleven," he said. "We ought to each of us throw in some dirt on top of the box, gentlemen, and get out of here and let those boys over there cover the Speaker up before dark." Each of them scooped up a handful of dust and threw it in. It really was dust, all the moisture and weight long since bleached and blown out of it, and instead of falling onto the coffin it rose playfully back up out of the grave as if propelled by a breath. "Better go," Albert said.

They walked by twos down to the cars, Lockwood and Clark first, Mallory and Albert following. There was one limousine for each President plus the hearse Albert had come in, all the way from El Paso, with the casket. The Secret Service and the $\male \leftrightarrow \female$ teams were farther down and farther up the hill and flying around in helicopters overhead. Mallory said, "We may not see each other again soon, Albert, and I really would be interested in knowing how you and the Speaker got together, if you don't mind saying." Albert said, "I don't mind. But wait a minute." They stopped where they were and watched Lockwood walking on toward his limousine, talking earnestly to Clark. Mallory was President now and they were both in private life, and they looked diminished.

When Lockwood was out of earshot Albert said, "My father and I came through here in the summer of '46, headed for Mexico, traveling at night. He'd had a little trouble in Abilene over my mama. He was a gambling man just back from the war. Had a '29 Packard with a squeaky right rear wheel. The wheel fell off about five miles from Terlingua. It was Saturday night and a bunch of drunks came along in a pickup truck, jumped out, and beat up on him because he had a watch in his pocket and some rings on his hands. They put a rope on him and pulled him along behind the pickup for a ways, me running along behind, keeping out of sight like he told me to. Got to that windmill down there. They tied my daddy up with some rusty old bobwire they found lying around and threw him in the water tank, then drove off. He was unconscious and bleeding. I couldn't wake him up or get him out, so I held his head above water till morning. Right after sunrise this kid just about my age but a whole lot smaller in size came down to water some real skinny horses. I told him my problem and he climbed up to help me out, but my father was dead. We talked it over. He said, 'What do you want to do?' There was no going back to Abilene. I said, 'I want to go on to Mexico.' He said, 'They'll never let you across the river; look what they done to him. You say you've got a Packard automobile parked up the road?' I said, 'My father does.' Tucker said, 'In my opinion you just inherited it. You've got to have someplace to live till you're old enough to travel. Will you authorize me to negotiate?' Those were his words; he talked like that even then, loudest voice ever heard, got it from his old man, who was a preacher. I authorized him. The long and short of it is, his father took the car. In return he hauled my daddy out of the tank, buried him, and prayed over him, first and last nigger he'd ever done that for, he kept telling me, and I lived with the Attenborough family till I grew up. The Reverend would give me less on my plate than everybody else but Tucker would slip me food off his; eating never was one of his pleasures."

Mallory said, "Thank you, Albert. Now I understand."

"You're the first one I ever told that to," Albert said. "Years later I asked Tucker how he ever thought his father, who was a real son of a bitch, mean to the bone like runts can sometimes be, would take in a colored boy in a place where they'd just drowned his father for being colored. He said, 'The key to the deal was, the Reverend Dick T. Attenborough was a believer, the first of many in my life, and for believers the whole idea is to do good if you're going to get something out of it, going to Heaven and the life everlasting being the original examples. Do the trick right and you get the dog biscuit. My father's reward for the meritorious act of taking you in was a '29 Packard that got him to his tent meetings in style. Plus points with the Almighty and all the work you did free of charge on what he called the ranch for the next ten years.' "

"What happened to the men who did that to your father?" Mallory asked.

"Nothing. What they did wasn't unusual for the time. Everybody knew them. They were rich boys by West Texas standards, ranchers' sons, pillars of the community, just out drinking and raising a little hell on a Saturday night."

Lockwood had been eyeing Albert and Mallory as they talked. Now he walked back up the path to meet them. "Well, boys," he said when they came together, "do you suppose he's looking down on us?"

"Up," Albert said.

Lockwood laughed and put an arm around Albert's shoulders. "That list of mourners Tucker drew up," he said. "You know, at first glance it looks snobbish—Presidents only. But I just realized that the only ones on it are us four poor boys."

"That was on his mind a lot when he talked about what happened to all you Presidents at the end there," Albert said. "The Speaker always said the Lord must love rich boys because he made so many of the sorry dumb left-footed sons of bitches. His own words, gentlemen, not Scripture. Best friend the poor man ever had in this country."

"Amen," said Lockwood.

Shelley's Heart is a work of the imagination in which no resemblance is intended to anyone who ever lived or anything that ever happened. Outside the realm of fiction, on the other hand, I have tried to respect the historical record. Concerning the life, thought, writings, and posthumous influence of Percy Bysshe Shelley I have invented nothing except, presumably, the Shelley Society. The verbatim transcripts, press reports, and other records of the impeachment proceedings of the House of Representatives and the Senate against Andrew Johnson in 1868 and Richard M. Nixon in 1973 provided factual background for fictitious situations designed to be somewhat less unbelievable than the reality. Anthony L. Harvey provided expert advice on Senate rules and procedures. For material about Maniáte folkways I am particularly indebted to the classic *Travels in the Morea* by William Martin Leake (London, 1805). The techniques used to recover and preserve human embryos in the Mallory Foundation's Morning After Clinics were modeled on well-established veterinary procedures described by George E. Seidel, Jr., in "Superovulation and Embryo Transfer in Cattle" (*Science*, Vol. 211, 23 January 1981) and elsewhere, but the idea that these methods might be applied with equal success to human beings originated in conversations with my brother Miles, an animal scientist. Although this novel is set in the near future, all of the technology described therein exists in the here and now; the computer program used by the San Francisco Giants to transform video images of batters and pitchers into graphic representations of body parts and physical movements, for example, is not so very different from the system employed by Wiggins and Lucy to establish the identity of Susan Grant's assassin. In medical matters I have benefited, as in previous novels, from the technical advice of Bruce M. Cowan, M.D., who is in no way responsible for the un-Hippocratic way in which I have afflicted, medicated, and, in the case of the recovered embryos, deep-frozen my characters. Readers of *The Better Angels*, published in 1979, will recognize that some of the characters in this story are dealing with the consequences of acts described in the earlier work. Though I have striven to avoid inconsistencies between the two books, I will not be surprised if it is discovered that they do not match in every detail. In fiction as in life, people do not always reveal the whole truth about themselves on first encounter, and the novel, like the Congress of the United States, makes its own rules, by which it abides at its own convenience. *De nil omnia fiunt.*

C. McC.

CHARLES McCARRY established an international reputation as a novelist with the publication of his worldwide bestseller, *The Tears of Autumn*. He is the author of twelve other critically acclaimed novels *(The Miernik Dossier, The Secret Lovers, The Better Angels, The Last Supper, The Bride of the Wilderness, Second Sight, Shelley's Heart, Old Boys, Christopher's Ghosts, Lucky Bastard, Ark,* and *The Shanghai Factor)* that have been translated into more than twenty languages. His nine non-fiction books include *Citizen Nader,* the authoritative first biography of Ralph Nader. He is the former Editor at Large of *National Geographic* and has contributed dozens of articles, short stories and poems to leading national magazines. His op-ed pieces and other essays have appeared in *The New York Times, The Wall Street Journal* and *The Washington Post*. During the 1950s and 1960s, McCarry served for a decade under deep cover as a CIA operations officer in Europe, Africa and Asia.

The Novels of **CHARLES McCARRY**

THE MIERNIK DOSSIER
978-1-58567-942-3, $14.95 pb

THE TEARS OF AUTUMN
978-1-58567-890-7, $15.95 pb

THE SECRET LOVERS
978-1-4683-0108-3, $15.95 pb

THE BETTER ANGELS
978-1-59020-155-8, $15.95 pb

THE LAST SUPPER
978-1-59020-014-8, $15.95 pb

SECOND SIGHT
978-1-59020-150-3, $15.95 pb

SHELLEY'S HEART
978-1-59020-475-7, $16.00 pb

OLD BOYS
978-1-58567-545-6, $26.95 hc

CHRISTOPHER'S GHOSTS
978-1-59020-113-8, $13.95 pb

"The best writer of intelligence and political novels in the world."
—*The Boston Globe*

"McCarry is the best modern writer on the subject of intrigue—
by the breadth of Alan Furst, by the fathom of Eric Ambler, by
any measure."
—P.J. O'Rourke

also available as e-books

OVERLOOK DUCKWORTH
New York • London
www.overlookpress.com
www.ducknet.co.uk